I0787966

Legions

Quest Academy

Book 5

Brian J. Nordon

CONTENTS

<u>DEDICATION</u>

I'd like to dedicate this one to the Legion Publishers and their incredible team. There are so many unsung heroes that help bring this series to the market, and I would like to give a special thank you to them.

Many of you will be familiar with Jez Cajiao, who gave me my start with publishing Quest Academy, but this wouldn't be in your hands without Chrissy, Michelle, Faith, Dantas and Rashed. Formatting, developmental edits, line editing, continuity and the beautiful artwork you see on each cover. If you saw an advertisement for this series, then that was probably Geneva and Kristen.

Then we have the beta readers to catch all the hiccups that occur throughout the process. It's an incredible team, and while I'm the one in the writing chair, their improvements make the series the success that it is today.

Finally, to you that's reading the acknowledgements instead of the book. I hope you enjoy reading it as much as I loved writing it. Thanks for continuing on this journey with me.

CHAPTER 1: ARRIVAL

Sal leaned against one of the walls on the Credit floor. He was waiting for Fabi to join him before they dropped their luggage off at the new dorms. She was talking with the valet about student parking, and Sal was surprised to find out that Saviors were guaranteed a parking space as one of the many perks that came with the title.

Vanessa wasn't at any of the desks, nor was Greg. It was an entirely different roster of staff, which made Sal reconsider his plan of putting in an order of silver. He had a good chunk of Q-Cred in his account balance, so he wanted to stock up on precious materials to build out the rest of his battle gear. The Mythic blight jackal was phenomenal in pretty much every category, but the fact that he needed to keep its core a secret was definitely an issue. He had spent the remainder of his break working on gear for his parents and friends, which made him feel good, but he still needed to take care of himself.

Sal crossed his arms as he thought about the Arkwright. It was back in the Argento Auction House, and despite his hopes, there was no way for him to utilize it with Arsenal while he was at Quest Academy. Yes, he could send it blueprints and have it work on Crafting, but there was no method for him to send the completed goods to his subspace. That realization had thankfully arrived before he left home, and he was able to stock up Arsenal with a whole range of materials that the Arkwright had synthesized and refined. He'd have plenty of materials to work with, but he was missing silver.

"Sorry for the wait." Fabi arrived with an awkward laugh. "I have to go through the same song and dance every time I park here. They take one look at the car and assume I'm lying about being in the Savior class." She glanced around the Credit floor as she joined him. "Kinda expected you to be neck-deep in negotiations when I came back."

Sal shook his head. "Nah. The staff I usually deal with aren't here. I'll request a price list from Vanessa later, but all I'm really missing for the next build is silver."

Fabi nodded in understanding. "Well, since you were waiting for me so patiently, what do you say about getting some coffees from Alex? My treat."

Sal perked up, grinning. "You might need to do the ordering because I'm pretty sure he won't sell me anything. We have a deal that I haven't exactly delivered on."

With a wave of her hand, Fabi dismissed the thought. "Well, you've got a couple of days before the semester starts up for real…you could always do it now? No matter how complex the build is, I'm sure it'll only take you a few hours."

"The concept I came up with for Alex was actually the inspiration behind the Arkwright…which took more than a few hours." Sal chuckled awkwardly. "I don't think this thing needs to be nearly as ambitious, but it could end up spiraling in that direction."

Fabi didn't even falter as she looked at him seriously. "Okay, talk to me while we head to the workshop. What exactly was the deal?" She tapped a button on the wall to call the elevator to the Credit floor. Her gaze was on Sal the entire time.

Sal hesitated slightly. "Just as a small disclaimer, I really overcomplicated this for no reason." He smiled before continuing. "I was trying to create a solution for Gallant. He was on my team for the tower trial and the excursion, and he wasn't able to control his power. I was trying to find a method to increase his innate mastery, and it turned out that Alex was able to make an elixir for it."

"He tried to fleece you for all your Q-Cred?" Fabi guessed dryly.

Sal nodded. "Yeah, and a part of me wondered if I could use Alex's ability and just automate the creation of elixirs. A combination of Alchemize, Refine, and Growth. I already have access to the weaves for Alex and Anderson Royce, and I can get Refine from the simulation orb."

Fabi frowned as the elevator doors opened. Before stepping through, she looked at Sal in confusion. "Alchemize and Refine are self-explanatory, but how does Growth factor into the build?"

"I was going to make a sort of enclosure where I could artificially grow the ingredients that Alex uses. Use essence to fuel Growth, which would start producing a steady supply that I could either use or resell." Sal walked through the doors and turned around to face Fabi, who eventually joined him.

"Interesting," Fabi responded with a nod of understanding. "What was the blocker in your build?"

"Time, mostly," Sal admitted as the transparent doors closed in front of him. "There were a few dozen commission requests that came in before the excursion and the tower that I never got around to doing, mostly from the faculty who knew I was Myth. I guess I just subconsciously added Alex's request to that list."

Fabi chuckled as she placed her hands on her hips. "Sounds like you've never starved for Q-Cred..." She gave him a thoughtful look for a few seconds. "I'm not saying you should be frantically closing out all the requests, but it would probably alleviate some of your worries if you worked on some of the backlog. Reject the ones that don't appeal to you, and just blitz through the ones that could be done quickly."

"Probably a good idea," Sal agreed, sighing. "I don't like the idea of letting people down. I'll get around to them eventually. I just didn't have the time."

"You have it now, though." Fabi smiled brightly. "Think of it this way. If you get that project done for Alex, you'll pretty much create a Q-Cred generator. Arkwright can earn you money back in Silver Sanctuary, and that elixir machine can make you Q-Cred while you're here."

Sal couldn't help but smile at her infectious positivity. "Don't suppose you'd like to help me out with it? I'm pretty sure there's going to be a lot of essence programming involved." Being honest with himself, Sal had no idea whether there was going to be essence programming involved, and he wasn't fond of the thought of spending his last couple of days of freedom sitting with the painful coding exercises.

"You know, you're going to have to learn eventually." Fabi laughed as she pointed at him accusingly. "And without that super-tracker of yours. You can't just have it dictate the logic to you all the time—you need to understand it."

Grimacing ever so slightly, Sal offered a shrug. "Is it a bad thing that I'm more focused on the outcome than the process? The tracker did a good job with MythOS, but it took forever."

Fabi sighed as the elevator came to a stop on the workshop floor. "Seriously, you're able to spend hours at a time working on fine-tuning your Crafting. Essence programming is pretty much the same thing, and it's seriously addictive once you get the hang of it. You'll see countless ways that crafted items can be improved with it."

"Like your Macclemark?" Sal ventured, wondering whether that was what she was talking about. It had only been Uncommon to Rare grade in terms of build quality, but it had functionality and output that was closer to an Epic grade. It was a nightmare to properly Appraise without context.

"Exactly." Fabi smiled as she exited the elevator. "That's one of the many reasons essence programmers are obsessed with drones. Artificial behaviors that can be programmed into a device…there are so many possibilities that come with that. I'll obviously be there to help you out when you don't understand something, but I'm not going to just do it for you."

Her passion was obvious, and Sal finally understood why both she and Upgrade were drawing up blueprints for drones. Initially, he had thought of it as a fun project idea. But after seeing Jackal in action, he was convinced that they could be an absolute game changer on the battlefield.

Sal caught sight of Alex within just a few steps into the workshop. The place wasn't nearly as deserted as Sal had expected, with many of the workbenches occupied with first- and second-year students. Upgrade was nowhere in sight, but Alex and Forge were casually chatting at his makeshift market stall at the edge of the room.

Glancing at Fabi, Sal explained the rest of the context before they approached. He wanted their stories to match. "By the way, I told Alex that I was going to try to get the Argento Auction House to source the materials for his elixirs. Thought I'd be able to hit two birds with one stone, and sell him ingredients while also making the elixirs. He gave me a load of small pieces that I intended to use to get the elixir machine started."

Fabi nodded in understanding as she walked over to Alex, her radiant smile catching his attention immediately.

"Oh, to what do I owe the pleasure?" Alex asked smoothly as he pulled a foam cup from a stack. "Guessing you need your fix after the break?" He grinned knowingly as he shook the cup in his hand. It only took a few seconds before he registered that Sal was a step behind Fabi. His expression darkened ever so slightly. "And you brought the charlatan."

Fabi frowned as she looked between Alex and Sal. "A charlatan? What is he talking about?" She feigned ignorance as she glanced at Sal for context, before turning her attention back to Alex. "Did something happen?"

Alex let out the most melodramatic of sighs as he started to prepare a coffee. "Young Argento is holding some valuable goods hostage, and then disappeared for the break without giving me even a sliver of reassurance that our deal was being worked on." He grimaced as though it actually pained him to speak. "And he sends that viper from the Credit floor to get his fix of the Grand Design and

Kaizen." Alex used his free hand to point at Sal accusingly. "And don't deny it—I know for a fact she got those for you."

Fabi frowned as she looked at Sal. "Is this why you made that deal with my father? For the ingredients?" She played the role of confused friend impeccably.

"The what now?" Alex tore his attention away from Sal. "Your father?"

Fabi nodded. "Maccles Materials. He specializes in alchemical ingredients from portals, dungeons, and towers. We're a humble enough outfit, but now that Lawrence Baron is working with my father and the Argento Auction House, there's not a single material we can't source." She smiled innocently as she looked at Sal. "I never really understood why he was going to such lengths to create those relationships, but I guess I get it now."

Alex's face blanched in an expression of pure horror as he looked between Fabi and Sal. "Lawrence Baron? You actually spoke with him?"

"Yep," Sal responded with an innocent smile. "He attended one of the auctions we held over the break, and was very interested in working with our partnership." He gestured at himself and then at Fabi.

Alex wordlessly picked up a second empty cup and continued to prepare the coffees. "Ah, is that so?" He nodded before a sly grin twisted his lips. "Well, it's a good thing that I never doubted our deal, isn't it?"

"You just called me a charlatan," Sal answered flatly.

Alex shrugged it off. "Nicknames are exclusively for friends. It's not like I called you a cheating bastard, is it?" He continued to smile as he poured out two fresh coffees. "Now, when it comes to timelines…when should I expect this new partnership to open the doors? I have projects on hold until I can source new stock, and time is very much money."

Sal opened his mouth to give a vague sort of timeline, but Fabi beat him to it.

"A couple of weeks at most." She was firm in her response. "We just need to do a little bit of finessing with the guild paperwork, and sort out our logistics a bit. Sal is impatient to get it done, but I'm the one slowing him down on it. I want to make sure it's done perfectly."

Sal wanted to stare at her in shock, but kept his outward emotions muted. She had simultaneously saved his skin with a masterful lie, and then indentured him a half second later. Did she really think that they'd be able to make an Arkwright equivalent elixir device, in two weeks?

Alex let out a sigh of relief. "Excellent. And just to show my sincerity…and my trust…I'm going to accept some contracts with that timeline in mind." His smile was almost wicked. "So, if you don't come up with the goods in two weeks, then I'll be financially fucked with zero recourse… No pressure."

"Isn't that a little excessive?" Sal asked awkwardly. "Surely you don't need to put yourself into that sort of situation?" He had no idea why Alex would risk financial ruin for something like this. All Sal had offered was a new supplier of goods, so there shouldn't be such high stakes for a simple transaction. Was Alex putting down parameters so Sal couldn't fob him off?

The Alchemist passed over the two coffees, all while staring at Sal. That wicked smile hadn't so much as budged since he lay down the ultimatum.

When the cup was in Sal's hand, Alex finally spoke. "You've got two weeks, Charlatan." He glanced at Fabi and his smile became much friendlier. "I'll add the coffees to your tab."

CHAPTER 2: GUIDE

"Two weeks," Sal repeated to himself in disbelief, glancing over at Fabi to ensure she realized what she had just done. "I designed that elixir device in a haze, and when Upgrade saw it, she put me into Resilience sessions with Sergeant Head. I don't have much faith in the blueprint, so I'll have to start from scratch."

He was working through all the details in his head and tried to figure out how he was going to even approach the build. Would he need to talk to Anderson Royce to get his permission to use the ability? He wanted to create a method that benefited him in some way, rather than just taking his weave and using it.

Fabi gave Sal a sideways look as they walked through the lobby of the dormitory tower. "You're overthinking this. Bring everything back to the basics. You've already constructed the Arkwright, which is a far more ambitious build. Two weeks with the Mythcrafter ability should be more than enough time to get things right, and I can assist you from the sidelines."

Sal grimaced as he pressed the button to the elevator. "I just don't know where to start. I was initially thinking of it as a sort of greenhouse-type enclosure, but the space requirement for something like that would end up being quite big. It's not exactly something I'd be able to keep a secret, and I don't even know what's going to happen with the workshop upgrades." He let out a resigned sigh and shrugged. "I kinda hoped that we'd be given a special space for the guild, and I could make the device there."

Fabi tapped Sal on the shoulder and walked away from the elevator doors. "Those elevators don't lead to your floor." She gestured at a sleek black door that was on the other side of the foyer. It was an area that Sal hadn't really noticed before. "You need to take this one."

Sal frowned as he followed her, catching sight of the vendor stalls spread out on the marble floor. He was reminded of the first time he purchased coffees for Kane and Hannah. That thought alone was enough to give him a pang of regret. He hadn't made any effort to clear the air with Hannah, and he hadn't checked in on Kane since that day. Sal wasn't even sure Kane had made it through to this semester.

"Come on, you're going to want to see your new dorm. I've got a feeling it's going to solve your space problem," Fabi said with a lighthearted laugh as she led the way to the black door. Her Q-Card was already in hand.

Sal returned a halfhearted smile. He had begun to realize that he wasn't able to help everyone, but he felt bad when he thought about how happy and chipper Kane had been when they first met. The last time they had interacted was during Administration Class, where Kane had been using crutches to walk around. With healing being readily available at Quest Academy, he couldn't help but wonder why he had opted to avoid it.

Fabi tapped the terminal at the side of the black door, and it seamlessly glided to the left, revealing a ridiculously opulent interior. Full-length mirrors on both sides, which operated like screens, relayed information on the current student rankings. There were small updates and announcements, with calendars of the upcoming outings with the guilds, scheduled scavenger runs and even dungeon schedules. News reports were coming through as a live feed, with reports about the changes in the Hunter Bureau rankings alongside the exploits of its members. It was an incredibly condensed snapshot of everything worth knowing at Quest Academy and beyond.

"What do you think?" Fabi stepped into the elevator and gestured at the walls. "They had to find a way to keep us entertained on the journey to the upper floors, and I think they did a great job." She laughed as she pointed at Sal's name on top of the first-year leaderboard. "There you are."

Sal didn't answer her immediately, as he started to read through the different articles. He wasn't looking for anything in particular, but was instead more taken in by the fact that there were so many changes coming through at any one time. A part of him assumed that the Hunter Bureau gala was the occasion where the rankings changed, but according to the screens, they were constantly moving. Just a single dungeon clear was enough to elevate names up a few places in the rankings. It was a ridiculously competitive landscape, and Sal wondered how far he'd be able to climb in the second semester.

"I'll take the silence as approval." Fabi laughed as she pressed her finger against one of the screens and dragged it upward. "You're able to interact with them, too. Just like the Arkwright, you can search for things. It's quite useful when you're planning outings, but it pales in comparison to the setup in the war room."

Sal blinked in surprise; not sure he heard her correctly. "War room? What's that?"

Fabi pointed upward. "It's one of the shared spaces in the private dormitories. We've got a communal workshop, a stocked canteen, and a strategy center. Most people just call it the war room, though. It's a Controller's wet dream, with so much intelligence gathered for the students to use. You'll understand when you see it."

Sal wasn't sure how to process all of that. "Wait, the private workshop is actually communal? So, I'll have to Craft in front of other people?" He wasn't exactly shy when it came to Crafting, but he had thought it would be a similar sort of setup to his original dorm, where he had a private room for himself.

"Yes and no." Fabi laughed as she shook her head. "Each of the rooms are on the top floor, and all of them have a dedicated workspace that opens up to a communal area. Think of it like a series of interconnected rooms, so you can work on your own stuff in private, or you can open the door and join the others." Her expression softened as she continued. "It was pretty lonely last semester because there weren't too many third-year Crafters who could afford the penthouse upgrade, so I'm hopeful that it'll be a little livelier this term."

"If all the Saviors are going to be on the top floor, then Blathnaid will likely be there a lot. I wonder if I could convince Barry to give Crafting a try…even though I think that would probably end in disaster." Sal chuckled at the thought, but had to admit that Barry would be able to bring blueprints to life with his Illusion ability.

Fabi snapped her fingers. "Also, there's a sparring room. It's usually quite busy there, since most of the penthouse residents are Offense types. Sakura keeps them in check, though, so don't be worried if you want to use the place." She seemed to think about it for a few seconds before laughing. "Although, you should probably wait until Sakura is actually there. I'm positive they'd try pulling you into a fight to see how you got the top Savior spot in first-year."

"Never going there. Got it." Sal laughed. "The strategy center does sound really interesting, though. Do people just use it for research or something?"

Fabi tilted her hand back and forth. "You can research demons there, like weak points, habitats…pretty much all the coursework and case studies that students have done for Harlan's classes. They've got a whole library's worth of tactical information and operational reports, from the first portal opening all the way to the current day. It's actually really interesting just reading about the war from different perspectives."

Sal nodded in understanding. "That does sound pretty useful. I'll need to check it out."

Fabi chuckled as she shook her head. "You're going to be obsessed with the simulator. You plug in a few different Hero combinations into a combat scenario, allocate behaviors and see what it comes out with. It's seriously addictive, especially when you put yourself into it and see how you'd fare in historical battles. Like, the one I'd always recommend is the first portal opening. It's good for the ego, because you're always going to be the strongest Hero in that scenario."

"How many combat scenarios does it have?" Sal asked out of curiosity. She was completely right about him wanting to try it out. It sounded fantastic, and he genuinely wanted to know what sort of dream team he'd be able to come up with from his friend group.

"Tens of thousands. But they have a token system, so you can only run a set number of simulations for free. It's seriously worth it, though." Fabi sighed. "I'd say I've actually paid my yearly rent on that damned simulator, so it evens out with the free stuff."

Just as Sal was going to ask about the cost, the black door slid open to reveal a lobby that looked like it belonged in a top-tier guild. A domed glass ceiling bathed the entire space in sunlight, only obscured by a metal frame that was laced like a spider's web. Each strand held a pane of glass in place. It was positively mesmerizing, and the almost reflective marble shone on the floor. The most impressive part that caught Sal's gaze were the walls that reached about thirty feet into the air.

Countless live portraits of Heroes adorned the walls, accompanied by a series of statistics. Sal's eyes latched onto the one directly in front of the elevator's entrance, and was mesmerized by the winking face of Eclipse, who he had seen at the gala. Rather than it being a static image of her, Eclipse moved on the screen with what had to be a signature battle pose. Wisps of essence wove around her fingertips as she raised her hand, before offering another wink to the viewer.

"Awesome, aren't they?" Fabi laughed as she pointed farther down the wall. "You should see Upgrade's. It's one of the best—it's at the entrance of the workshop."

Sal quickly glanced through the text and saw that Eclipse had been a student at Quest Academy. It highlighted the different classes she had excelled in, and went on to celebrate the creation of her guild. It even had an inspiring quote, followed by a few pieces of advice. One in particular caught his eye.

Healers are treated like they're invisible until they're needed. You deserve to be seen.

"Quite profound," Sal said awkwardly as he pointed at the quote. "Are all of them like this?"

Fabi glanced at the quote before she snorted. "Nah, they're on a rotation. That's one of the tame ones. She has another quote that pretty much tells Healers to diagnose problems rather than offering solutions. Essentially giving them a way to put a price on their services. She was pretty cutthroat by all reports, but her synergy is unbelievable when you put her into the simulations."

Sal laughed as he was reminded of Rochelle. They both had the Transference ability, and he wondered whether Rochelle would someday become the next Eclipse. He looked along the wall and saw close to a dozen portraits that were mirrored on the other side of the lobby. There were no duplicates. "How many of them are there?"

Fabi tilted her head slightly. "Hard to know. It really depends on how many of the rooms are occupied. They have these screens for each occupant and some notable alumni. You'll get to make your own, and you can customize it with different gear sets to see how it improves your stats. It's the same profile that they use for the simulator."

She laughed at his stupefied expression. "I was the same when I first saw all of this. I'm positive they make it as impressive as possible so you'll never want to go back to the basic dorms."

"Starting to get that idea, too," Sal agreed as he shook his head in wonder. "I highly doubt I'll be able to strike a pose like these guys." He looked at the different portraits with a smile before he realized something. "Wait…you said there's one of Upgrade?"

Fabi chuckled as she pointed at a corridor. "Yep, and it's totally worth it. Wait until you see her scowl." She indicated that he should follow, as she excitedly set off with a bounce in her step.

Sal followed her, laughing, not sure why they were rushing through the corridor. He barely had time to appreciate any of the Hero portraits as he passed, but a few of them looked familiar from the gala, in the split second he was afforded to see them.

"And voilà," Fabi declared as she came to a stop in front of a singular portrait that was mounted onto a black screen.

From the elevator before and the few panels he had seen between portraits, Sal was certain that it was a door. He took a second to appreciate the portrait, before a laugh escaped his lips.

Live in such a way that people will remember you. Don't just be a name on a damned placard, because you are so much more than that. Try your best, and if everything goes to shit, you can always come back to Quest Academy to teach.

"This is incredible," Sal breathed as he read Upgrade's quote. Her picture was one of her sitting at a workbench with one hand propping up her face, like she was bored. A guilty smile appeared on her face, before disappearing. It was similar to Eclipse's wink, in that you had to watch for a while to see it.

Sal couldn't help but wonder why they had decided on Upgrade for one of the portraits. She was pretty incredible, but wouldn't Doc Ameye have been a better choice for Crafting? Or even Forge? Were they exclusively picking people who had attended Quest Academy?

Fabi pointed at the base of the screen. "Finishing in the ninetieth rank back then as a Support is absolutely ridiculous. If you think Quest Academy is combat-oriented now, it was apparently a hellscape back then. Crafting wasn't even a full module, and was just a few workshops with Forge."

Sal stared at the area Fabi indicated and his jaw gradually dropped.

Support Hero: Upgrade
Student Name: G. Ziemele
Quest Academy Final Rank: 90th
Hunter Bureau Rising Star Award (Shared)
President's Award for Academic Excellence

"Shared?" Sal repeated the word that caught his attention. "Like, someone else got the rising star award at the same time as her?" He couldn't help but be surprised that Upgrade had been a recipient of actual awards, especially with how she spoke about the Hunter Bureau.

Fabi just nodded with a knowing smile. "You already know who it is, too." She pointed at another portrait that seemed to face off against Upgrade's, like some sort of playful irony.

Sal turned to see the familiar visage of Vanessa, standing with a single hand on her hip, checking her nails on her other hand. Every few moments, she'd glance up, grinning.

Controller Hero: Diva
Student Name: V. Blake
Quest Academy Final Rank: 1st
Hunter Bureau Rising Star Award (Shared)
President's Award for Combat Excellence

"Her Hero name is Diva?" Sal repeated as he looked at the records on the screen. "I didn't know her family name was Blake, either." He had assumed she had been a powerhouse, but to be the top ranked at Quest Academy?

Fabi sighed as she stared at the portrait, shaking her head. "Such a waste for her to give up on being a Hero. Her profile in the simulator is disgustingly powerful, but nobody really knows why she retired to work on the Credit floor. Guess the calculations don't always get it right."

Sal glanced over at Fabi with an awkward smile. "It's a long story, but she had her reasons. She got fucked over by the guild that scouted her, and she's been waiting for an opportunity to get back into the field."

Fabi looked surprised at the new information, but she didn't latch onto it. Instead, she shot Sal a smile. "You're going to try to smooth talk her into joining your guild?"

Sal laughed awkwardly as he offered Fabi a noncommittal shrug. "Eh, she was one of the first people to talk to me about setting up a guild. She was very clear about wanting a place on the team."

Fabi's mouth opened and then closed without making a sound. She looked at Sal carefully, as though trying to determine whether he was lying to her. "That's a joke, right?" She turned on the spot, away from the portraits, to give Sal her full attention. "Is Vanessa actually joining your guild?"

"You're making it sound like it's a really big deal." Sal chuckled as he gave her a nod. "I'm serious, and it's not a joke. She wanted to be business partners originally, but I told her that I'd be doing it with my family and Quest Academy, instead."

Fabi tilted her head to one side. "Sakura, Gallant, and…Vanessa?" She just shook her head in disbelief. "If you get Upgrade to work with you, the roster is going to be absolutely insane."

Sal pointed at her. "Don't go thinking that I'm letting you off the hook. I'll need you there if I want to make a dream team."

"As if." Fabi snorted as she pointed down the corridor. "We could literally go to the simulator right now, and you'll see how much of a disaster that team composition would be. You'll need a few Healers and Defense people to even it out a bit."

Sal glanced over his shoulder. "Should we head there? It sounds pretty damn cool, if I'm honest."

Fabi shook her head as she gestured at Upgrade's portrait. "Nope. You've only got two weeks to make that elixir thing. If I let you anywhere near that simulator, we'd lose you for a month."

"You're making it sound even cooler now," Sal argued as he looked at Upgrade's portrait with a resigned expression on his face. "When we finish up this thing, will you show me the simulator?"

Fabi shook her head, huffing out an exasperated sigh. "Seriously, your priorities are a mess…but yes, I'll show you the simulator when we're done. Deal?"

Sal nodded in agreement. "Deal."

CHAPTER 3: WORKSHOP

"So, which one would you like?" Fabi smiled, as she gestured at all the empty workstations. "You can pretty much have your pick. I think we're the only people to arrive at Quest Academy a day early."

Sal took a few steps forward and marveled at the size of the workshop. It wasn't the open-plan setting he was accustomed to, but rather a collection of glass cubes, each one equipped with a workbench and a multi-tool. There were two floors of cubes, all of which were fused together with metal railings and walkways painted white.

"I'll be honest, it's not what I was expecting." Sal looked at the staircase warily. "Won't the sun hit these and make them unbearably hot?"

"Nah, they're all air-conditioned…and you'll notice that all the modular workspaces have access to the central hub. Come on, I'll show you." Fabi walked underneath one of the glass enclosures, pointing straight ahead. "Rather than having duplicates of the same machines, they put in a few state-of-the-art ones and created a ticket system, so you'll have to wait for your turn to use them."

Sal nodded in understanding as he tried to take everything in. The entire glass enclosure seemed like an unnecessary design choice, as all it really did was allow for everyone to see one another at any one time. Sal guessed he'd be distracted by even the slightest movement from across the workshop.

"Oh, and the walls frost over when you're working on something secret. You can adjust the settings in whichever pod you use, but it's nice watching the sunrise in the mornings, so I typically leave them transparent." Fabi smiled as she finally arrived at the central hub. "You're going to love this."

Sal chuckled as he shook his head. "It'll take quite a bit to impress me after the Arkwright…but go on."

Fabi winked at Sal before she waved her Q-Card in front of the glass wall. An audible click echoed out before a part of the glass wall slid off to the right, revealing a large communal area that was stacked with boxes.

"What am I looking at?" Sal asked for more clarification. "Because it looks like a storage area?"

Fabi nodded, the grin not leaving her face. "Yeah, it's a storage and delivery area." She pointed at the far end of the corridor that led to the edge of the penthouse floor. "The Credit floor will deliver items up here, and leave them here in the hub, or in your workshop. You can put an order through on your tablet and it'll be down here within hours."

Sal stared at the area Fabi pointed to for a few seconds. "Is there a workspace near the delivery area?"

"Trust me, you don't want it. It gets windy when the doors open, and no matter what conditioning they have in place, it's a really disruptive breeze," Fabi warned him as she shook her head. "I can show you the ones that get the best sunlight. It'll make you feel like you're back in your workshop at home."

Sal thought about it for a few seconds before he shook his head. "I think I'll take the windy one." He laughed when he saw Fabi's shocked expression. "I mean, don't get me wrong. The sunlight sounds lovely, but I'm thinking about Jackal."

"The drone?" Fabi looked down the corridor. It took a few moments for realization to hit her, and she practically whirled around in disbelief. "You're not seriously considering letting the drone out at the loading bay?! We're like eighty floors up, and the wind would likely throw it to the other side of the city!"

Sal shrugged as he walked in the direction of the loading bay. "I'm sure Jackal can learn how to navigate the strong winds. I kinda want to see how far Jackal can travel without running out of power. This should be a good enough method, no?" He looked at Fabi to see whether she agreed with him.

Fabi let out an exasperated sigh. "You can't test a Mythic grade like that! What if it runs out of power halfway across the city? Are you just going to leave it there, or leave class to go and find it?" Her expression was a mix of disbelief and concern as she shook her head. "Seriously, take it to a dungeon and send it off in one direction… There's no point in taking an unnecessary risk with altitude and people seeing it."

"Jackal is able to learn, though." Sal gestured at his bare left arm. "I can keep a track of the power levels with my visor, too. Surely there's some sort of protocol we can set up that it will return whenever it's at risk of running out of power?"

Fabi stared at Sal as though he had two heads. "Giving a drone a set of protocols isn't the same as learning, Sal. It can only fulfill the tasks set out in the programming. I don't mean this in a condescending way, but there's no way that you were able to create a learning module in a drone, even if it is Mythic grade."

Sal pulled out his visor and clipped it over his eye. "Okay, let's get to the bottom of this." He twisted his left arm to summon the blight jackal. It wasn't a necessary movement, but he found that it reduced the amount of fabric being crumpled if he did it before summoning. "Rather than me looking around for ages, put this on and have a look at the programming," Sal stated as he plucked off the visor and handed it to Fabi.

Fabi took it from him and pulled her hair to one side so she could look at it properly. With only a minor bit of readjusting, she got the visor secured over her right eye. That same eye narrowed as she looked at the arm for a few moments. "Okay, I'm looking at it now…give me a few minutes."

"Take your time." Sal flexed the metal fingers of the gauntlet. He wanted to continue testing Jackal, soon. There were just so many things he needed to do before that could be a reality. With the increased capacity of the visor, the new gates he had unlocked, and the increases for both Skill Master and Mythcrafter, Sal was genuinely curious how the build would go for the elixir machine.

Two weeks was a good amount of time, and if he could finally put that single project out of his head, it would give him a lot more peace of mind. There were still a few commissions he needed to get around to, but Sal guessed he could probably outsource them to the Arkwright and just get them delivered in from the Argento Auction House. The elixir machine was a different feeling because it was something he had agreed to do, rather than a commission that was thrown at him.

"Salvatore," Fabi started, breaking Sal out of his reverie.

"Yeah?" he answered tentatively, not sure why she sounded so worried.

"You gave Nexus permission to sync across all your devices?" Fabi asked, which caught Sal by surprise.

"Yeah, it synced up with my tablet, the visor, and Arkwright. A few other things, too," Sal answered earnestly, not sure where she was going with this.

Fabi nodded slowly before continuing. "Well, the good news…is that it absolutely is a learning module. I know it is, because I designed it." She took off the visor and handed it back to Sal, grimacing. "Looks like Cypher has used pretty much every piece of information available to it. I can't be certain but when I showed you the Macclemark designs on my tablet, I've got a feeling that your visor might have looked through a lot more than just those pages."

Sal's stomach lurched at the implication. "You think it went through all your designs?" He was horrified by the thought, and had assumed that Cypher had added in the missing pieces of information. By the sounds of it, his visor had just stolen the information needed rather than calculating it. "I'm so incredibly sorry, Fabi."

"Don't be." Fabi smiled as she shook her head. "I went through the files to see how it was constructed, and to be honest, it's collated far more than my research papers. There are whole sections which were determined from forum posts, and other parts that were plucked from timestamped sections of my videos on the Credit Store. There's even some software contributed by the Mythcrafter algorithm. It's genuinely extraordinary."

"Still, though, I'm really sorry that it happened." Sal was sincere in his apology. He didn't want to steal her hard work, even if it had resulted in the creation of the blight jackal.

Fabi smiled as she gave him a playful nudge on the shoulder. "Don't worry. You can totally make it up to me when you help me build my drone. By the sounds of it, your visor has managed to skip all the difficult calculations to reach the finish line. It's kind of a relief to see that my theories were actually able to work in practice!"

She laughed as she offered him a shrug. "But I'm sure there are still a few areas that can be improved. There are a few basic protocols at the moment, and without the right shaping, you'll probably just have access to those three focus areas—learning, harvesting, and recharging."

Sal just stared at her. "Wait…you're saying that Jackal can be improved?"

Fabi grinned as she nodded slowly. "And I think we've just found the perfect carrot for you to learn essence programming. If you learn it properly, you'll be able to look at countless files and figure out what's wrong. Diagnosing issues can be super fun, and then patching in fixes…and seeing them work? It's the best feeling ever."

"But specifically…what way would it improve Jackal?" Sal pressed, trying to figure out what possible way there was for the little murder-robot to be better.

"The learning module is currently defaulted to a proficiency-based system called Adaptive Behaviors," Fabi began, smiling. "What that means, is that Jackal will focus on learning how to do a set number of tasks in the most efficient manner possible. Having a system like that will cause it to eventually plateau when it finds the optimal strategy… But, if you were to have a set of protocols where it is learning new behaviors, that's when the fun really starts. Honestly, the capacity of this thing is enormous."

Sal just stared at her. "Okay, repeat that, but this time like I'm five years old."

Fabi snapped her fingers and pointed directly upward. "Let's go to my workspace, and I'll show you. It's easier to visualize with Interface." With a knowing chuckle, she set off toward one of the nearby stairwells, pulling at the railing as though it gave her momentum, and launching up the first few steps, which she took two at a time. "You're going to love this."

"You've said that a few times now." Sal laughed as he followed her. "I'm starting to think you don't really know what I love and don't."

"This time, I'm positive you'll love it. Trust me." Fabi reached the top of the stairs and walked along the pathway leading to one of the glass cubicles.

By the time Sal caught up with her, the door was already open and she stood there triumphantly, as though it had somehow been a race. "This is your workspace?" he ventured, not sure whether it was another communal area.

"Yeah, this is where I do the vast majority of my essence programming. I'll show you." She tapped at her workbench, causing all the glass walls to frost over and become a brilliant white. "The thing that really puts newbies off essence programming is the code. When you combine it with Interface, it becomes far more user-friendly and inviting."

As Fabi spoke, the largest wall started to load with an image at its center. It was a circular form, like a snake chasing down its own tail in a spiral, but never quite reaching it. After a few rotations of futility, it vanished to reveal an elaborate dashboard of statistics, figures, and menu screens. Just from a cursory glance, Sal saw dozens of customizable options, with profiles loaded for the Macclemark sets.

"I'll probably regret this, but can you get Nexus to synchronize with this screen?" Fabi asked with an awkward laugh. "It'll be easier for me to show you the modules that are loaded into Jackal."

"Are you sure it's a good idea?" Sal asked to make sure she was okay with it. He wasn't fond of the idea of stealing even more of her work, even if it was accidental.

"Yeah, I'm a little curious myself how it will adapt to it." Fabi gestured at Sal's visor. "Just know that once you see this, you're going to fall in love with essence programming. You better be prepared."

Sal couldn't help but laugh. "You're also underestimating how painful it was creating MythOS. There are very few things that would be able to help me forget that torture."

"Wanna bet?" Fabi asked with a sly grin.

Sal stared at her for a few seconds as he readied his visor. "You seem too confident, so I'm going to decline the bet. Give me a second to give Nexus permissions."

Fabi waited patiently, and when the prompt appeared on the screen to share information, she accepted it with a swipe of her Q-Card. "Okay, so…now I need a few seconds to create a new profile for Jackal."

Sal watched as she tapped at a series of menus to create a profile. There were a whole range of permissions that she had to manually allocate, and then some limitations on what information would be shared with Nexus. It seemed like all his concerns around taking over her system were unfounded, and it was a genuine relief.

"That should do it." Fabi smiled as she turned back to look at Sal. "Share the blight jackal profile. You should get a request straight to your visor, which you can just accept."

Sal saw the prompt appear in front of his right eye, just as she spoke. He accepted it, and was immediately met with a loading screen on his visor. It was the same one he had seen on the massive screen.

"Since I don't have the same computational power as Cypher, you're going to have to wait a little for the results." Fabi gave an almost apologetic shrug as she pulled over a stool to sit down in front of the screen. "Sure you don't want to take the bet?"

"Positive," Sal answered as the profile finally materialized onto the screen. Whatever he had been expecting, this was far from it.

Blight Jackal
Recognized Module Categories
- Strategy (4)
- Navigation (1)
- Adaptive Behaviors (3)
- Countermeasures (5)
- Recharge Efficiency (1)

"So, what do you think?" Fabi asked with a smug grin, already knowing the answer.

Sal just stared at the screen in pure fascination. "So…all of these modules are things that can be improved with essence programming?"

Fabi nodded. "And so much more. Wait until you get to the point where you're uploading custom strategy modules to Jackal. That's when it'll really scare the shit out of you."

"That good?" Sal asked in confusion. He had Appraised Jackal a few days ago, and there was so much information missing on the report Fabi seemed so proud of. The growth aspect for one, where Jackal could take materials from Arsenal for upgrade or repair. There was nothing about the Subsume ability, that allowed him to claim the abilities of slain opponents. Sal guessed that Fabi would need to see Jackal in action before she understood just how much potential it really had.

"You've got no idea," Fabi responded confidently. "But…all of that will come after you enroll in the essence programming course. I've only got one semester left at Quest Academy, so you better be a fast learner."

CHAPTER 4: LEARNING

You have successfully been enrolled in the Essence Programming Foundational Course.

Sal stared at the words on his tablet, letting out an involuntary sigh. Despite Fabi's protests, he decided to start with the foundational course rather than beginner. If he was going to learn how to do essence programming, he wanted to do it the right way.

"How are those drawings coming along?" Fabi asked without turning around from the large, window-like screen. She was copying sets of code from a folder on the left, and placing it on the right-most screen. It looked like a janky mess of text with all sorts of functions and logic, but she seemed to read it effortlessly.

Sal quietly placed the tablet back on the workbench he was borrowing from Fabi. He picked up the stylus and looked down at the blank sheet of paper. "Great, actually. Just ideating some improvements."

"I heard that you were unresponsive when you were in a flow state." She turned around to grin at Sal. "Trust me, the essence programming course is going to be fine. You picked foundational, so it's going to be the most basic stuff that you probably already saw in my tutorials." She gestured at the page in front of him. "So, just throw yourself into some Crafting and put it out of your head."

"Yes, boss," Sal answered, smiling as he clipped on his visor. Perfect formed in his mind, and he activated it with ease. There wouldn't be any Kakushin this time around, but he wasn't looking for any real breakthroughs. It was just going to be an ambitious coffee machine that could make elixirs.

As Fabi got back to her programming, Sal focused his attention on the task at hand. He brought the stylus up to create a three-dimensional box. It was just a sketch of sorts, but he wanted to get the concept down to see whether Mythcrafter could read his intentions and offer some corrections. When the lines came together, he created a set of shelves within the box, similar to the conveyor belt system that he had used for the Arkwright.

Next, he built out the coffee machine concept. His visor had Alchemize already mapped out from his first semester at Quest Academy. He had taken the liberty of inspecting Alex's weave. Anderson Royce's weave, on the other hand, wasn't something he was familiar with. But he was pretty sure that the Growth ability that he had imbued into the rock fort during the excursion would be suitable. Considering it was just the ideation stage, there wasn't really any issue with trying to use it for this purpose.

Perfect helped him create perfect lines for the enclosure that would act like a compact greenhouse, attached to the back of the coffee machine. Rather than a bean grinder, it would be closer to the size of an actual vending machine. Sal was careful not to fall into scope creep, lest he end up with another enormous machine like the Arkwright.

The coffee machine blueprint was quite simple, as Sal had not only Appraised the coffee machine he had at home, he had also saved it to his visor. It was more like tracing an existing machine onto the page, with his Perfect ability saving him a lot of headache, with pinpoint accuracy for each and every internal mechanism.

Refine was going to be an ability that he needed to look up, or get Grant to send over to him. With just Growth and Alchemize, he should have enough to create elixirs…and coffee. Getting them up to a potent level could be an upgrade for another time.

"Wow, I guess you really do go into the zone," Fabi remarked from right beside him, causing Sal to jump in shock at the sudden noise.

"Whoa! How long have you been standing there?" he exclaimed as he almost dropped the stylus. Rather than falling back to the page, the stylus danced around his fingertips in an almost mesmerizing pattern. It was the muscle memory of the trick he had performed as a test on the effects of Perfect.

Fabi shrugged. "A few minutes; but I have to say, your blueprints are far cleaner than I was expecting. I should have realized since all the ones back at your workshop were immaculate." She leaned in closer to get a better look at the design. "It's a cute little design, too. Looks like it would be super compact."

Sal's heartbeat finally calmed down as he followed Fabi's gaze to the design he was working on. It still had a lot of detail that needed to be added, but it was thankfully enough for Mythcrafter to latch onto. His ability practically thrummed in the background, as if begging to activate and highlight all the problems in the blueprint.

"Thanks. I still have a lot to do. How is your essence programming project going?" Sal glanced up at the massive wall of text in front of him. "It looks…complicated."

Fabi waved it away like it was no big deal. "Just taking a break. Lots of the groundwork is done, but I won't know how to customize it until I know what you're dealing with over here. Do you want a payment system integrated into the build?"

Sal looked at her blankly for a few moments. "A payment system? You can build something like that?"

Fabi nodded. "It's like one of the main things you'll learn in the foundation course. Probably an end of semester project. When I was in that class, I had to make a mock-up payment solution, but it's mostly just security protocols like verification of identity, funds, and stuff like that." She continued to look at him expectantly. "So, are you going to be selling the concoctions this thing makes? I assumed yes, but you seem to give everything away for free, so I thought I'd ask."

"Definitely charging for it." Sal laughed as he marveled at the wall of text. It was wild to think that a collection of words and symbols was able to translate into something as practical as a payment system. "Will it be a lot of work?"

Fabi shook her head. "Nope. Like I said…I already built it a few years ago, so it's just about incorporating it into the build. We can add all sorts of other functions, too. You'll be able to see records of transactions, and see what products are the most popular. All of this is really basic."

"What's an example of advanced, then?" Sal asked in wonder. "Like, what sort of stuff could you put in that would be a challenge?"

Fabi looked over at the interface on the wall and frowned. "What would be a challenge?" She asked herself the question almost out of curiosity, and pondered over it for a few moments. Then, she blinked and a wide smile crossed her face.

"I could try to make a simulator of sorts. Something that could run a series of ingredient combinations, similar to how the Arkwright does its research. It would need a lot of ingredient cataloguing, and it might result in a lot of ruined goods, but if the enclosure is reproducing them…trial and error isn't that expensive!"

Sal smiled as he gestured at the wall. "So, are you going to start working on that? Or are there other things I can answer for you?"

Fabi turned to look at him, an eyebrow raised. "Oh, are you trying to get rid of me already?" She laughed as she moved away from the workbench with a wave of her hand. "Okay, I'll let you get back to your ideation and drawing. I'll finish up the payments part, and then we'll tackle the simulator."

"Sounds good," Sal agreed as he focused his attention back on the blueprint. "I'll get to work on making this feasible."

"Looked pretty good to me already," Fabi shot back as she moved over to the wall.

Sal smiled as he looked at the blueprint with Mythcrafter activated. What caught him by surprise was how easily it adapted to his sketch. In the past, there had been countless changes that needed to be made, but this time it was quite straightforward. Was it because he was only focusing on Growth and Alchemize for the build? Maybe it was because he was making a greenhouse enclosure and a coffee machine he'd already analyzed? Either way, he was happy with the support of the ability, and got back to drawing.

As the evening came and moved on, Sal found himself consistently working on minor improvements to the design. His intention had been to draw out a few different ideas to find the one that would be the best fit. Unfortunately, he was still very much working on the first concept. By his estimates, there would need to be a massive amount of essence storage in the machine. Powering Growth was a huge ask, and for it to work, he'd need to practically make the entire enclosure out of refined cores.

Sal played with the idea of trying to recreate the Capacitor ability that he had put on the Mythic grade, but the moment he put it down on the page, the build shattered like it had been severely compromised. That had been a tough one, as it would have solved most of his problems. A part of him wondered whether he could just charge people in cores, rather than in Q-Cred. He could just throw on an evolutionary rune and hope for the best.

With a grin on his face, Sal wanted to fail fast and just remove the temptation. He designed an evolutionary rune that incorporated the entirety of the enclosure and the actual machine. Holding his breath for a few seconds, he waited for Mythcrafter to dissolve in front of his eyes…but it didn't happen. The elixir machine was able to hold an evolutionary rune? Sal wasn't exactly sure how to process that. Growth and Evolution seemed to be a little close to each other, so wouldn't it cause a conflict between the two?

"Fabi…" Sal started as he looked up at her, across the room. He waited for her to turn around before he continued. "Hypothetically, if we incorporated a payment system that traded cores for elixirs, and the elixir machine had an evolutionary rune… Do you think that the additional cores would end up getting used for Growth, or would they all be used for evolution?"

Fabi just smiled as she pointed at the wall behind her. "You're adding evolution? Then I guess it depends on what it is you're looking for? I can program it to do whatever we want. If you want a certain percentage of accumulated essence going toward evolution, or going toward Growth, I can make that a part of the programming." Her smile was wide as she locked eyes with Sal. "And adding in multiple payment types is smart. It's better knowing now rather than later, as I won't have to double up on too much work."

Sal let out a relieved sigh. "Okay, that's good. I was worried I went a little overboard there. I'll start figuring out what materials would work best with the design, but my guess is that it won't take too kindly to the stuff I took from the dungeon."

"Keep me in the loop. It all sounds really interesting." Fabi turned back toward the wall. Then, just as though a thought popped into her head, she looked around at him. "We can totally do a few dungeon runs, too. It could be a good opportunity to get some new materials, and I'd get to see Jackal in action!"

"Sorry…" Sal said with a resigned shake of his head. "Someone threw me under the bus and gave me only two weeks to get this project finished. I don't think we'll have time for any dungeons."

Fabi put her hand on her hip and gave Sal a level stare. "Nice try. But I'm sure you're dying to show Upgrade, too. We could just kidnap her for a few hours and go run a dungeon. It'll be good to get some points for your Trainee Guild before the semester even starts."

"You really think Upgrade would want to run a dungeon with us?" Sal scoffed at the notion. "She'd probably have to be torn away from the workshop."

Fabi nodded emphatically. "She loves running dungeons. We did them all the time when there were materials we needed for projects. Seriously, I could message her and see what she's up to this evening?"

Sal looked at the drawing, frowning. "Okay, but only after I finish this and know what sort of materials we actually need. Deal?"

"Deal." Fabi grinned. "And I'll have your payment method long finished by then."

Sal smiled. "Great. Then you'll have plenty of time to get started on the simulator?"

Fabi laughed as she waved him away, moving back to her walls of text.

With a twirl of the stylus in his hand, Sal got back to work. He was excited to see Upgrade, and wanted to see her reaction when he gave her the present he made for her.

CHAPTER 5: MISTAKE

Fabi stared at the design in disbelief. "Is that a tree?" She pointed at the roots supporting the base of the enclosure on the drawing.

Sal had his arms crossed as he nodded quietly. "It was a fuck-up."

"How do you mess up like this? It looks like a tree." Fabi laughed as she twisted the page so she could look at it from a different angle. "I mean, were you unconsciously drawing a tree?"

Sal's gaze flickered down to the page, and he could only offer a resigned sigh. He had screwed up by misremembering the ability of the tower he had constructed during the excursion. As far as he had been concerned, it was the same ability as Anderson Royce's. He would have bet money that it was the Growth ability…but it wasn't. It was the Rooted ability that gave a similar growth-like effect. When he made corrections with that ability as a key basis for the design, it resulted in the enclosure gaining branches and roots.

"It still looks cool, though," Fabi insisted as she twisted the page back to him. "Other than the fact that you need to plant it. Are you going to need soil from the dungeons or something?"

Sal shook his head. "It's an absolute mess. Rooted and an evolutionary rune should be in direct conflict as they pretty much do the same thing. If I was going to make something like this, I'd need to pretty much carve the elixir machine into a tree, and have the ingredients growing on the branches."

"And? What's the problem with that?" Fabi asked, genuinely curious. "You're a Mythcrafter, right? Why don't you just keep going…see where the inspiration takes you?"

Sal stared at her in disbelief. "Don't you think it's a waste of time? I could find the Growth ability from Anderson Royce, or the simulation orb. I think they were setting one up in my room, so I could go there and check it out."

Fabi shrugged as though it wasn't any of her business. She slid off the work-bench and moved back to her wall. "I'm just saying that it's a fun concept and I'm curious to know how it would work out if you saw it through to the end."

"Even if the build didn't break with Mythcrafter, it's far from optimal. It could end up growing into a massive botanic garden if left to its own devices. And where would you even store something like that? Nothing would grow inside Arsenal, so that option is out." Sal explained his reasoning as he waved his hand over the design. "Then there's the issue with the roots, which will limit it to ground level more than likely. I just don't think this is the way."

Fabi nodded from the other side of the room. "That makes total sense. Proba-bly best to restart with the actual ability you want in there." She gave him an encouraging smile and a thumbs-up gesture before she turned back to her own screens.

Sal sat there for a few moments, wondering how much time he had wasted by using the wrong ability in the design. It was likely more than an hour, and it stung just that little bit more that he had made the mistake in front of Fabi, even if she didn't seem fazed by it. He continued to stare at the design before shaking his head and getting to his feet, grimacing.

"Sorry, Fabi…but this is it for me today." He gave her an apologetic smile as he stretched his back. "I want to check out my room and get a better idea of what I'm dealing with. It'll be better once I have the right weave for the design."

Fabi blinked in surprise, and glanced at the time on her screen. "Ah, shit… I didn't realize how long we were at this. Guess I suck at giving guided tours. I pretty much just took you straight here instead of the actual dorm you'll be staying in." She smiled apologetically as she gestured at the door leading out to the walkway. "You'll be happy to know that you're far closer to your room than you think."

"How so?" Sal followed her, rotating his slightly cramped wrist.

Fabi pointed at a collection of black doors along the walls. They were spaced out almost indiscriminately, as though the distances between them were at random. "Those lead to the Savior dorms, or more specifically, the Crafting Savior dorms." Her finger angled over to the far left. "That's mine there. You can try your Q-Card on the others, and whichever one opens, that'll be yours."

"I'll give you bonus points as a tour guide, since you technically brought me here," Sal said with a tired smile. "Sorry I'm not better company today. I'm annoyed with the design stuff."

Fabi shook her head. "Don't apologize. We all have those days. I'll be a raging cow in here from time to time, but it won't be anything for you to worry about." She glanced at the other cubicles before smiling at Sal. "But maybe put in a little more thought into which workspace you want. If it's just going to be a few of us, it doesn't make sense to have us on the opposite sides of such a massive space."

"I'll think about it," Sal promised as he moved around the railing to find the best path to the black doors. It was only when he rounded the corner that he saw the sunset in all its glory. The enormous glass wall that curved upward into a dome looked almost otherworldly, with the entirety of the workshop being bathed in a warm and comforting light.

"Beautiful, isn't it?" Fabi walked past him to reach the stairs. "Took me almost a year to get used to it."

"I'll give it the attention it deserves another evening." Sal followed her. "I'll feel a lot better once I have this thing over and done with."

Fabi paused on the stairs and looked at Sal. "Why aren't you excited by this? Isn't it something you wanted to build in the first place?"

It might have started that way, but ever since the creation of the Perfect ability, Sal realized he didn't need the elixir machine. It was originally a plan to help Gallant, which came from a sense of obligation. That obligation had transferred over to Alex the moment Sal accepted the ingredients from him. Coupled with the timeline that had been imposed on him, it felt more like a chore hanging over him when the slate should have been wiped clear.

"I didn't think I'd have to worry about something like this going into the second semester. It's kinda killed my excitement, but I'm sure it'll be fine," Sal answered before giving her a smile. "Once I get it finished with, then I'll have a fresh start."

Fabi frowned slightly. "If it's not making you excited, change it into something that will. You'll always get better results from your Crafting when your heart is in it." She raised a hand to stop him from responding. "And I know I'm being preachy, I'm sorry about that. I went through a lot of stuff over the last few years, and I know this feeling well. You don't need to listen to my advice, but I'd feel like I was being a shitty senior if I didn't at least try to warn you."

"I appreciate that, really," Sal answered truthfully. "I'm just not feeling it at the moment. I'll work around with the weaves for a bit and then get back to the design. I'm sure something will spark my interest along the way."

Fabi tilted her head. "Or…you could spend the first few days reconnecting with your friends. They should arrive tomorrow, so you could hang out with them and clear your head a bit. You've gone from some insane Crafting over the break, straight into an old project. It's probably for the best if you cut yourself some slack and rest up a bit."

"Maybe." Sal shrugged. "I might just need to get some sleep, or an early night."

Fabi nodded as she resumed her descent down the stairs. She gestured at the nearest black door and stepped back for Sal to try it with his Q-Card.

Sal obliged by waving it near the terminal, but nothing happened.

"Second time lucky." Fabi smiled as she pointed at the next one farther down. "Guess we're not going to be neighbors." The first one he tried had been the one closest to her own door.

Sal tried the next one and was inwardly grateful when the door slid open. He couldn't tell where the bad mood was coming from, but he didn't want to take it out on Fabi. All he was looking forward to was getting himself a shower and resting up for the evening. No matter how nice or fancy the dorm was, he could appreciate it tomorrow.

At least, that was his intention.

"What do you think?" Fabi grinned as she leaned against the doorframe. "They really didn't spare much expense, did they?"

Sal was practically speechless. He had seen the pictures on his tablet from the rooms that cost a few thousand Q-Cred a month, but this was superior to those in every conceivable way. He had his own staircase, a kitchen, a living room…library and separate workshop? He was able to see everything due to the open-plan design, but also because of the glass walls that acted as partitions between the spaces. With just a glance, he could see the bookcases lined with manuals, the simulation orb whirring in anticipation of a new project, and most interestingly, he could see his bed.

It was absolutely massive, with purple pillows and duvet, all lined with a silver trim. Sal wondered whether they were all the same, or whether they had customized it for his Silver cohort and Support class designation? Either way, he loved it. The color scheme could be seen in every single room. It was what Sal would have envisioned a high-ranking Hunter to have as an apartment, and he couldn't believe he was going to be living there for the next semester.

"You'll more than likely have a workbench up there, beside that machine. Is that the simulation orb, by the way?" Fabi turned her helpful information into a question at the end as curiosity seemingly got the better of her. "How does it even work?"

"I'll show you tomorrow." Sal smiled as he gave it only a cursory glance. Any doubts he had about his evening were vanquished at the sight of the massive bed. He was absolutely certain that it would be claiming him in the next few minutes. "I think I'm just going to have a shower and get some sleep."

Fabi laughed as she moved off the doorframe to stand upright. "I forgot you had a hangover this morning. I guess I can't blame you. I'd have done the same. Will I come knocking to find you, or will I see you in the private workshop?"

Sal glanced over his shoulder in surprise. "You want to meet up tomorrow?"

Fabi shrugged as though it were no big deal. "You said it yourself that you want to get this project over and done with. I just guessed you'd want to get an early start on it. We can put it off until you catch up with your friends and pick your classes? Most of the essence programming is already done, but I'll need to customize it to whatever the project ends up requiring."

"I think I'll spend tomorrow catching up with people. Maybe a more in-depth tour of the dorms, to see things like the strategy place with the simulator, and the fighting place," Sal said as he read her facial expression. He didn't want her to feel like he was blowing her off. Nothing on her face gave him even a hint that it was the case; on the contrary, she looked almost relieved.

"That's good. I was worried you'd be up all night working on something." Fabi chuckled. "But if you're actually getting some sleep and meeting up with friends, then I'll wait until you're ready to tackle the project again." Before she moved away to go toward her own room, she pointed a finger at Sal. "And don't go thinking you're off the hook when it comes to the dungeon runs. I'll message Upgrade and let her know that tonight doesn't suit, but we'll go together soon, deal?"

"Deal."

Sal barely said the word before Fabi tapped the terminal with a smile, giving him a playful wink as the door closed in front of her, leaving Sal in his room by himself.

He stood there for a few seconds, a little shocked by the abrupt goodbye. He turned to look at the massive space around him and finally started to relax. As much as he wanted to get to the workshop with the simulation orb, it could wait until tomorrow.

CHAPTER 6: BEARINGS

Bleary-eyed, Sal pulled the bedsheets to the side and wondered whether he had managed to get a few hours of sleep. The sun was setting when he had left the workshop with Fabi, and now it was pitch-black outside. He sent an inquisitive hand into the mass of purple pillows, feeling for his tablet.

"What time is it?" Sal groaned as he tried to get his bearings. What didn't help was the entire wall of glass in front of him illuminating with the intensity of the sun, relaying the time in digits designed to be seen from a neighboring skyscraper.

"Ugh, why do you exist?" He clawed at his eyes to stop the sudden pain. "Dim. Less light?" He barked the commands, but none seemed to really work.

"Off!" Sal finally tried, which seemed to do the trick. The screen flickered momentarily before shutting off. Any ability Sal had to discern his surroundings had vanished after the advent of light, but he nonetheless got to his feet and fumbled around the room, looking for a terminal or some form of light switch. No matter what he found, it would be better than the sun that was installed into his wall.

After a few toe-stubbing moments, Sal bounced off the glass walls with an accompanying grumble until he managed to flop onto the couch. That's where he stayed for a few minutes until he got his bearings. Propping himself up against the cushions, Sal squinted in the darkness. "Lights?"

The entire apartment illuminated at his word, and bathed Sal in a far gentler glow. Clearly the display in his room hadn't got the memo, but Sal was relieved that he wasn't at risk of going blind. It was four in the morning, and it meant he had managed to get close to eight hours of sleep.

Sal had briefly explored the apartment the night before, but he was far less fatigued now and could finally appreciate just how incredible his new dorm truly was. As much as he loved the aesthetic of the auction house, the apartment was more like a corporate and modern approach. There were no rustic accents, or hints of history around the different rooms. It was like a blank canvas for Sal to leave his mark, and customize it to his own liking. Various empty frames were on the walls, with menus asking which types of pictures he'd like loaded onto them.

There was even one of those portraits that Upgrade, Eclipse, and Vanessa had. He had heard from Fabi that he'd be able to customize his own variant, but it was ridiculously low on his list of priorities. When it asked him to assume a pose, he immediately canceled it and backed away from the wall it was mounted to. It was a little unnerving that there was a camera in his wall, but it thankfully only faced a wall leading out of the room to the main hallways and the elevators.

The workshop had been an area he wanted to see, but he wasn't going to repeat the process of the auction house or the workshop when he was in his first semester. There was a lot of Crafting to be done, and he was excited to get stuck into projects like the Valkyrie wings, and to a much lesser extent, the elixir machine. But his goal this semester wasn't to hide away in a workshop. He was a part of the Saviors class now, and he had promised himself that he would become a better combatant.

With that thought in mind, Sal moved to his bedroom, where he had unceremoniously dumped most of the clothes he had been wearing the day before. Rifling through them, he plucked out the visor and secured it over his eye. It being on the floor was a testament to how tired he had been, even though he hadn't realized it at the workshop with Fabi. His plans for a shower had gone out the window the moment he sat on the bed to test its firmness.

Sal smiled as he picked up his clothes and threw them into a laundry basket in the joined en suite. Gorgeous marble floors twinkled invitingly, but the true beauty was the free-standing bath in the center of the room. Sal had never really been a bath person, but he looked forward to giving it a try. But that would have to come later.

With his visor on, Sal opened the closet and was surprised to see a collection of Savior class uniforms. He was inwardly grateful that they weren't even remotely similar to the grey blobs they had been forced to wear at the start of the first semester. The outfit for the Saviors was jet black, with purple-accented shoulders. The stitching was faintly visible, but the visor picked it up clearly as he moved around it to have a look. It was also purple, with the pockets in that same velvety color.

"Not bad," Sal muttered as he counted the rows of outfits. There were five in total, and although they looked very nice, there wasn't anything special about them. No durability enhancements or anything of the sort. They were just high-quality fabric, with no essence infusions at all. Taking one of the outfits from the closet, Sal tried it on. He knew he probably should have a shower first, but all he was going to be doing for the next few hours was reading.

After a few moments of indecision, Sal sighed and threw his visor onto the bed and brought the new outfit into the bathroom with him. Even if he wasn't going to be doing much, he still wanted to feel clean. Maybe he inherited that trait from his mother? It wasn't really worth thinking about.

Sal was not prepared for the power of the shower. Nor was he prepared for the dozen directions the water hit him from. It wasn't just a waterfall shower like his old dorm, but it was accompanied by a series of jets that shot water at him from every angle. A menu allowed him to increase and decrease the intensity, and Sal laughed at how extravagant and pointless the whole thing was.

He couldn't help but admit that he did feel a lot better after it. The uniform was also a worryingly good fit. Despite him sending over the measurements for himself, it still felt a little wrong that they got it so perfect. The last thing he did in the room was pick up the visor and secure it over his eye.

"Okay, let's get started." Sal padded toward the couch. He wanted to get a look at the manuals his father had gifted him for the Silverson Arts, but hadn't had a chance until now. Rather than just sitting in a workshop, working on weaves or Crafting, Sal wanted to see what the manuals had to offer.

That wasn't to say that he was going to take the difficult approach. Ever since the moment he sat with Rochelle in the canteen and used Analysis on her drawings, he realized that the visor would be able to process text and create potential solutions for him. If there was a way for him to utilize the ridiculous processing power of Judgment and Cypher, then it would be an incredible advantage.

Sal sat cross-legged on the couch and willed the manual to be summoned from Arsenal. What actually happened was Arsenal opening in the center of his living room, a pearlescent door of white waiting for him almost invitingly. Sal frowned as he got to his feet and moved into the space; he walked straight past his luggage that hadn't moved an inch from where he stored it. The boxes that contained a few pieces of gear and presents were all in the same location, too.

The manual he was looking for was neatly stacked on top of the boxes, and Sal plucked it from its perch, smiling. He didn't waste any time in getting back to the couch, where he plopped back onto the cushions and dismissed the Arsenal. It folded in upon itself until there was no sign of it having ever existed.

"Let's see…" Sal opened the manual to the first page.

If we fail to adapt, we will die.

Silverson Arts Foundation Manual, 14th Edition

Written by P. Silver & A. Silver, Strategic Division of the Silverson Group.

Sal smiled at seeing his father as the author of the book. His eyes lingered on the page for a few moments, looking at the quote and wondering when it was written. The fact that there were thirteen previous iterations of the manual was a promising sign that there would be a lot of learning material in them.

Sal went through each page, deliberately reading them himself and ignoring his visor, who was far faster than him. He would use the analytics and insights later. This wasn't going to be an exercise where he offloaded all the task to his gear, because his father wrote the book. He was going to read it carefully.

What genuinely surprised Sal was how easy it was to read. Maybe it was because he grew up with a close relationship to his father, but he could hear his dad's voice in his head with every word. It was a pragmatic tone that stated the facts, but there were little tidbits of humor thrown in every now and again. The first few chapters spoke about the various stances and came with illustrations on how to best move in them. Rather than immediately moving on to attacks, it focused on footwork and highlighted the importance of mobility.

The next chapters also had nothing to do with offensive measures, but rather around controlling fear. If you couldn't move your body because you were paralyzed by fear, then you'd never be able to use the Silverson Arts. Sal couldn't help but feel annoyed at how valuable the insights would have been for himself growing up, but he pushed those thoughts to one side. His parents had made a decision, albeit a poor one, and he had forgiven them for that fact.

If he had been raised with these sorts of teachings, there was no way he would have been as terrified of demons. Of course, the words on the page were one thing, and the reality was a completely different beast altogether. That said, Sal could read all the excerpts of named combatants within the Silverson Group overcoming the odds that were stacked against them. Normal people, empowered with an adaptive combat style, were able to take down the demons.

Sal completely lost himself in the text. He was about halfway through the eighteenth chapter when he had to sit up and massage his neck. Adjusting himself on the couch so he could get more comfortable, Sal restarted the chapter on recognizing attacks of opportunity. There was so much content that his head was practically swimming, but it was incredibly engaging to see how it all evolved from one form to the next: the resilience of the mind, the stability of the stance, the fluidity of the form, and the technique being blended together to execute a powerful skill.

Just from reading it, Sal could tell that the few sessions he had with his father had covered the basics to an incredible degree. He couldn't help but wonder how much more he would have improved if he had started years earlier. The best time for him to start would have been when he was a child, but the second-best time to start was right now. Sure, he had a few techniques memorized, but the more Sal read, the more convinced he was that the Silverson Arts were made for him.

Sal didn't even notice the sun rising, as he continued reading. The section on kicking was especially in-depth, and Sal guessed it was his father's specialty. What had started as Sal reading meticulously had turned into him reading for fun. He was genuinely enjoying himself as he got to know more of his father's techniques.

Reading about something and putting it into practice were two completely different things. Even with Perfect, he'd need to find a way to simulate the exact movements before he could put them into practice. There were no two ways about it, considering his father's own words in the manual stated it clearly…

Understanding. Practice. Repetition. Refinement.

You need to make these arts a second nature.

You need to adapt to your environment instinctively and without thought.

When the Silverson Arts are as instinctive as breathing, you can then build upon them.

Sal couldn't help but smile as he read everything in his father's voice. There were no useless embellishments or claims of the combatant taking on legendary opponents. Everything was rooted in practicality and common sense. Each of the diagrams showed a gradual buildup of movement ranges, and tests to know when it was safe to move onto the next stage. Some were as simple as holding a stance for a period of time without discomfort, while others were around endurance and stamina. Mobility was a massive component of the Silverson Arts, and Sal had already started to wonder whether that would be his downfall. Having flexibility was integral to the success of the style, and Sal's exercises weren't going to cut it.

At the end of the manual, Sal was almost sad to see it was finished. He had enjoyed the read, and was eager to read whatever the next edition was. The only thing that stopped him from sending a message to his father to ask for it was the last line on the final page.

Only those who can showcase their mastery of these foundations will be given the next manual.

Those who can master the foundations likely won't need the next manual.

You have all the tools you need to become a dependable ally and formidable opponent.

Sal sat back against the couch and closed the manual with a relieved smile. It had absolutely been worth it to go through the whole thing. So many little details in the book mirrored the teachings he received directly from his father. Yet, there were hundreds of more exercises and practices in there that he hadn't even heard of. Sal was certain that it would take a person years to really benefit from the teachings, but not if that person had the Perfect ability.

"You've been patient enough. Go through the Analysis," Sal said as he gave the visor permission to analyze all the text he had just read. With Cypher and Judgment working on it, he assumed that he'd be able to get some good insights into how he could rapidly improve his progress with the Silverson Arts.

Analyzing Silverson Arts: Foundation Manual...

Sal felt a draw of essence being pulled from his center by the visor. There was no longer a revolver working as an essence battery, but that was fine. It was mostly a method to help the visor evolve; but now that the gun was gone and it was out of range of the Arkwright, Sal was the only source of power it could tap into. He had more than enough in reserve to let it run the required simulations.

"Simulations." Sal repeated the last thought aloud, frowning. He wondered whether he'd be able to utilize Barry's Illusion ability with the Silverson Arts manual. His control of the ability wasn't the best, and he still had a hell of a lot to learn with it, but it might end up making his training a little easier to follow?

Analysis Complete

Calculating Progress Report of Silverson Arts...

Sal hadn't been wearing the visor during his training with his father. Nor had he worn it when he went through the dungeon runs. It would be a little ridiculous if the visor was somehow able to estimate his capability and mastery without having any proof of his progress.

Insufficient Data

"Well, that answers that one." Sal chuckled as he got to his feet and stretched his arms over his head. He wanted to know how his skills compared to what the manual expected of him. It would be an excellent measure of how much work he needed to put in to master the foundations.

With the smile not leaving his face, Sal went to find his shoes. Fabi had said there was a sparring area in the dorms, and Sal figured that some early-morning practice would be the perfect start to the day.

CHAPTER 7: FACTOR

When Sal left the dorm, he realized he didn't really know where the other rooms were. Fabi's guided tour and detour into the crafting areas, left a lot to be desired, and he wasn't exactly sure how to navigate to the sparring area. Still, it was early morning and most students would be arriving at Quest Academy today. He and Fabi had just managed to get there a day early.

Wandering the corridors, Sal looked at each of the Hero portraits, but didn't wait around to inspect them in detail. There were a lot of strong people who were alumni from Quest Academy, but he didn't recognize a lot of the names. The pictures looked cool, though.

When he rounded the corner to where the elevators were, he saw a group of four people carrying luggage. Rather, it was one woman…and three identical men carrying the other bags. Like, perfectly identical. But all of them seemed to be ridiculously haggard in appearance: mops of brown hair, bags under their eyes and quite gangly in physique. The woman, on the other hand, looked unapproachable. The sort of aura that just told you it would be a mistake to strike up a conversation.

"Morning!" Sal announced from his side of the hallway. He didn't want to accidentally sneak up on them as he walked in their direction.

With an incomprehensible speed, two of the identical male bodies were sucked into the third, who turned in alarm. His haggard appearance instantly faded, as though he were suddenly revitalized. The cases the two clones had been carrying fell to the floor, which earned a disappointed sigh from the girl with golden curls.

"Seth…" Her tone was low, and wasn't one of disapproval, but rather one of resignation.

The guy did a double take between Sal and the woman, before he grimaced and apologized to his partner. "Sorry, I got spooked." He then turned in Sal's direction and just gave him a curt nod. "Morning."

Sal couldn't believe what he had just witnessed. He had heard from Alastair that there was a student who could clone himself, but he hadn't anticipated him to be in the Savior class. By all accounts from the Tactics professor, the clone guy was lazy as hell and didn't apply himself. So how did he manage to become a Savior?

Rather than bringing the clones back out, Seth packed the bags near the doorway of the elevator and looked at the girl, frowning. "You go on ahead, Mica. I'll do a few trips back and forth."

Mica looked at Sal for a moment, her expression unreadable. "He's already seen your ability. Don't hurt yourself by trying to do everything alone." Her words were aimed at Seth, who lifted one of the cases and smiled.

"It'll be fine," Seth muttered as he cast an apologetic glance in Sal's direction. "Sorry if that scared you. You caught me a little off guard. Didn't think anyone would be up this early."

Mica lifted two enormous cases of luggage by herself and gave Sal another glance before heading off in the direction of her dorm.

Seth watched her leave with an almost pained sigh as he lifted a much smaller case. It seemed too much for him, and he struggled to get a grip on the sides of it. Despite the hardship, he looked borderline angry at his own inability, and eventually managed to cup it in his arms.

It was only because Sal had his visor on that he could see what the issue was.

Name	Seth McDuffee
Alias	Factor
Class	Controller
Profession	Current: Student, Quest Academy
Rank (Hero)	Quest Academy: First-Year Rank | 30 Guild Association: No Affiliations Hunter Bureau: Current Rank | 24,032
Accreditations	Challenge Crests: 3 Completed Master Classes: 1 Completed Advancements: 0 Licenses Acquired: 0
Ability	Skill Name: Clone | Rating: 16 Skill Category: Replication, Energy Manipulation Skill Mastery: 84% (16.8%) Skill Efficiency: 52% (10.4%) Progress to Next Rating: 71% Evolutionary Capability: No Potential Cap: 25 Natural Synergy: Concept | Cultivate | Adapt
Essence	Essence Type: All Essence Gates: 180 Essence Absorption Rate: 58% (290%) Essence Control: 92% (460%) Essence Refinement: 81% (405%) Essence Calibration: 100% (500%)
Wealth	Q-Credit: 2,540

Sal frowned when he saw the details. Seth, or Factor as his alias showed, was apparently able to make up to four clones of himself. It looked like a double-edged sword, though, because he had a multiplicative effect for essence generation when the clones were active…but his actual skill efficiency and mastery were reduced to a fifth of the overall capability.

"You're one of the first-year Saviors?" Sal inquired as he moved closer to where Seth was staring at the suitcases. "Need a hand carrying them? I was going in that direction, too."

Seth gave Sal a tight smile before shaking his head. "Nah. I appreciate it, though. Need to pull my own weight, or Mica will leave me in the dust."

"You're sure?" Sal asked again, not sure whether it was just pride speaking. "Because it's really no issue."

Seth straightened his back and gave Sal a much warmer smile. "Very sure. You're Salvatore, right? It's good to meet you. Professor Maxwell told me you helped him out massively last semester."

Sal moved over and offered his hand. "That's me, and you're Seth McDuffee? The Clone expert?" After seeing the stats, Sal knew that Seth was far from being considered an expert in any field, but it was just a nice way to open the introduction.

Seth blinked in surprise as he accepted the handshake. "The number-one Savior knows my name and my ability. Can't say that was on today's bingo card."

"Professor Maxwell told me about you, too." Sal smiled. "I take it you're one of the new Savior class?"

"Yeah, was dragged into the rankings kicking and screaming by my girlfriend." Seth pointed down the empty hallway, where Mica had gone. "There's zero chance of me being here without her, if I'm honest."

Just as Sal was about to respond, the elevator chimed, followed by the doors opening to reveal another arrival. It wasn't anyone he had interacted with before, but he recognized the face from the videos in the amphitheater.

"Factor." The new arrival stepped over the cases that blocked the exit of the elevator. He was lean with toned muscle, wearing a loose T-shirt and jeans. His hair was cut short and his expression was calculating.

"Spectre," Seth replied with a tight expression. "Safe travels?"

Spectre nodded as he turned to look at Sal, his expression becoming much more friendly. "You must be Salvatore? I'm Chris Spectre, the one right behind you in the rankings." There was no offered hand. It wasn't an introduction, but rather a statement.

"Nice to meet you." Sal made no effort to offer his hand. "I hope you'll excuse us. I was just helping Seth with his luggage." Sal was able to read the visible discomfort between the two new arrivals, and decided that he'd much rather interact with Seth if he had to make the choice. Despite his insistence on not wanting help, Sal could see that he wanted any opportunity to get away from Spectre.

"Three of us will have it done in no time." Spectre grinned as he lifted two cases by himself with ease. His gaze fell on Seth expectantly, as if daring him to protest.

Seth sighed as he looked at the remaining cases, but Sal got there before him, picking up both.

"You're going to need to use your Q-Card for the room, so you'll need your hands," Sal added with a smile, as though it might lessen the blow to Seth's pride. The visor detected Seth's frustration every time he tried picking up the cases. That frustration was borderline anger whenever he looked at Spectre.

"Lead the way." Spectre tossed the luggage up a foot in the air and spun it on his finger before twisting and catching it. "Are you and Mica staying in the same room?"

Sal caught the flash of annoyance cross Seth's face. He would have missed it, if it weren't for the visor. There was clearly some history between the two people, and Sal wasn't exactly sure why he stuck around to witness it. If he was going to be spending the next number of semesters with these people, he determined it would be a good idea to be friendly with them. It was just tough to know whether Spectre was an asshole, or whether it was his typical dynamic with Seth.

Seth led the way, with both Sal and Spectre following him with the bags. "I think it's down this way. We requested rooms beside each other, but I've got no idea if that request went through."

"What did you guys think of the elevator, by the way? All the news reports and ranking information?" Sal ventured into the topic, hoping it would alleviate some of the tension. It could very well have been the case that Spectre was similar to Barry, and just liked to poke fun. But something about how Seth was reacting made Sal unsure.

"Hmm?" Spectre turned to look at Sal, eyebrow raised. "The elevator? Can't say I was paying too much attention. I was catching up on some Crafting tutorial videos."

"Oh, you're a Crafter?" Sal had never seen Chris Spectre in the workshop, or in any of the classes. Was he Crafting in his own dorm room like Sal had tried, or was it something else?

Spectre practically scoffed at the notion and shook his head. "Nah, not really for me. I just do it to gain proficiency in my ability. If I keep doing the same things, I'll end up plateauing." He chuckled, as though the very thought were ridiculous. "It's common knowledge that I pick up techniques pretty fast, and it's just a project I'm working on."

"What sort of project requires you to learn about Crafting?" Sal asked in a little more guarded fashion. He wasn't certain, but it felt like Chris Spectre was looking down on the profession.

Spectre looked at him as though it were obvious. "If you know how something is built, you know how it can be destroyed. I'm the best Offense class out of all the first-years, and I gotta keep my skills sharp."

"Don't take it to heart." Seth spoke from in front of them. "He looks for weaknesses in absolutely everything. That's just his personality."

Spectre's grin grew wider. "Well, I'm not sure if that was meant as a compliment…but it's natural to push your ability to its limits. Helps that I'm pretty competitive. I'd likely not be trying nearly as much if I came first out of the Savior class."

Sal felt a pang of dread. "Wait, are you learning about Crafting because I got the top spot?" There was no way the man would be that focused on dethroning him, just a single day into the new semester.

"It's nothing personal." Spectre laughed as he shrugged. "It's just a fact of the place. If you want the best offers from the guilds and the bureau, you need to be the very best…and that's what I'm aiming for."

Seth stopped at one of the black screen doors and gave them a tight smile. "This is me, here. Thanks for the help."

Both Sal and Spectre placed the luggage down on the ground. From just the few minutes of conversation, Sal was pretty sure that he didn't want to spend much time around Chris Spectre. Seth seemed like a nice enough guy, but was somewhat reserved.

"Hope you get settled in." Sal excused himself, pointing farther down the corridor. "I'm just on my way to the sparring room, so I'll see you around."

"There's a sparring room?" Spectre asked in surprise. "Lead the way!" He laughed as he gestured with both hands for Sal to be his guide.

Sal nodded, the smile not leaving his face. "I'm going to be doing my own thing, so I'm not actively going to be sparring."

Spectre's expression shifted to one of disappointment. "Lame. Well, hit me up if you're ever in the mood to duke it out. I want to see how my skills compare to yours." And with that, he started walking back in the direction of the elevators. "See ya in class."

Sal watched him leave, not really sure how he managed to dislike the guy in such a short period of time.

"Be careful around that guy. He's not someone you want paying attention to you," Seth muttered as he glanced at Sal. "You probably knew that already, though."

Sal sighed as he looked at the empty corridor where Spectre had left. "Yeah, pretty obvious vibe." Forcing a smile to his face, Sal gestured at the other end of the corridor. "Training awaits. See you around."

Seth just nodded as he opened his door and started to move the luggage. It was only for a moment, but Sal was able to glimpse into the room. Yellow accents representing his Controller class were the first thing Sal noticed, but the size and scope of the room was also radically different from his own. Sure, it was nicer, but it was nowhere near as big or luxurious as Sal's room.

It made Sal realize that the inequality existed so people like Chris Spectre would be motivated to climb up the rankings. He hadn't really anticipated that he'd need to defend his rank, but Sal was starting to appreciate that an invisible target was likely circling over his head.

After leaving Seth, Sal returned to his search for the sparring room. He wanted to get a handle on his Silverson Arts, and meeting Spectre only managed to increase that desire in his mind. Perfect was a better version of Adapt, and if Chris Spectre wanted to learn how to take down a Crafter, Sal would be ready to disappoint him.

CHAPTER 8: SPARRING

Confirm Identity…
Name: Salvatore Argento
Rank: 1st, First Year
Class: Support

Sal tapped Accept on the door of the sparring room. He had been prompted the moment he had presented his Q-Card. There were questions about whether he was alone and whether he wanted his visit to be registered against his profile. Sal didn't see any harm with it, so after he accepted the prompts, he was finally awarded with the door opening for him.

When it finally slid to one side, Sal was greeted by an impossible amount of equipment packed against every available wall. There was an essence cube at the center of the room, identical to the one that Rust had showed them in the first semester. It looked like the area that was used for sparring without essence, or at least a protected area that would stop essence attacks from damaging the equipment.

Sal's gaze landed on each of the machines around the room and was surprised to see models of leechers, prowlers, voiders, and hulkers. The hulkers and prowlers were operated by tracks on the ground, while the voiders and leechers were attached to both the walls and ceiling, all connected by a series of non-invasive cables. It only took a glance to figure out that it was a way to simulate battle against the various types of demons, with all their movements dictated by their actual real-life movement profiles.

Beyond the demon simulation area, there was an area dedicated to weights training, with a lot of exercise equipment Sal didn't even recognize. He could tell from the visor that they were expensive, and it looked like there was a whole automated setup for increasing difficulty levels. A few fridges rested against the wall, with untouched rows of pre-made drinks in labeled containers. After that, there were a few stationary targets that were rooted to the ground. There were humanoid shapes, as well as demonic variants. They were probably the ones that Sal needed.

As he walked in that direction, he looked over to the other side of the room and saw a wide-open space with targets lined up against the wall. Which likely would have been perfect for when he had his revolver, but was no use to him now. Up high, on the next floor, a series of platforms levitated in the air, and a whole host of targets separated them in midair. It looked like a simulation for aerial combat, and Sal genuinely wondered whether there was anyone other than Barry who could manage to finish it.

Sal was quite impressed with the setup. When Fabi had told him there was a sparring room, he had envisioned an open area that was completely empty. This was far beyond his expectations and looked like it had almost everything he could need to refine his combat skills. With that thought firmly in mind, Sal moved over to the stationary targets. He'd be able to work his way up to the moving ones later.

Getting into the stance that his father taught him, Sal let the visor know that he was going to start the Silverson Arts. He wanted to see what sort of proficiency he had, compared to the analysis of the manual.

With Perfect embraced and active in his body, Sal started to slowly go through the forms. He first went with the raise of the leg, the angling of the hips, counter-balance and then extension of the leg. It was just a simple exercise without even unleashing the kick it was designed for.

Silverson Stance
Form: Perfect (100%)
Practice: 1/20

Sal stared at the words that appeared on the visor. The manual had preached about the importance of practice and repetition…but was the visor seriously going to ask him to do these forms a hundred times? Rather than restarting from the beginning, Sal continued the form until he was able to prepare the Silverson Sweep.

Silverson Sweep
Form: Perfect (99%)
Practice: 1/20

"You've got to be kidding me," Sal breathed as he got back into the standing position. Each of those movements only counted as one singular practice? It wasn't nearly as bad as it could have been. If he had been told to do it a thousand times to get the technique right, then it would have been much worse.

Sal tried to figure out what was going on with the ratings, and why he was being asked to perform practice routines by the visor. As far as he was concerned, he was going to be showcasing what he knew to find out how far he needed to go…but instead it was teaching him from the outset.

It took a few different queries through the visor and sifting through useless information he wasn't interested in before he found what he was looking for.

Assessment Grades: Rank (Proficiency)
Cadet 1 (60%)
- 1,000 repetitions with course correction
- Cadet 2 will be unlocked at 70% Proficiency

Cadet 2 (70%)
- 800 repetitions with course correction
- Cadet 3 will be unlocked at 80% Proficiency

Cadet 3 (80%)
- 600 repetitions with course correction
- Cadet 4 will be unlocked at 90% Proficiency

Cadet 4 (90%)
- 100 repetitions with course correction
- Cadet 5 will be unlocked at 100% Proficiency

Cadet 5 (100%)
- o   20 repetitions, no course correction required
- o   Sequences will be unlocked after completion of prerequisite repetitions

"Oh," Sal said. Suddenly, the twenty practice sessions didn't really feel like that big of a deal when he compared it to the previous ranks. If he didn't have Perfect, then he'd be in for at least two and a half thousand practice forms.

Sal stared forward, not looking at anything in particular, as a horrifying realization took hold. He had only done a single form and kick. There was an entire catalogue of martial arts…

Looking at the progress tracker, a growing sense of dread welled up from within. There was no way that his fear was true; it would be insanity.

Progress Report on Silverson Arts: Foundation Course
In-Progress:
- o   Cadet 5 Forms: 1 (0.2%)
To Be Completed
- o   Cadet 1 Forms: 2,499 (0.04%)

"So, without Perfect…" Sal did the calculation in his head, not relying on the visor for this one. It was already ridiculously depressing. "It would be two and a half million repetitions to master the foundational course of the Silverson Arts?"

Sal grimaced as he lifted his leg back up. "But with Perfect…that number is closer to fifty thousand." Even saying the words out loud felt like it was an impossible mountain. Perfect would allow him to shave off some of the extra work required, but he had no idea that there would still be so much to do. It was just a foundational course, yet it required so much investment of time and effort.

The only thing that made him firm in his resolve was the fact that his parents had both endured the training without the help of a visor. They likely practiced it to death, during an active war where they saw combat regularly. Just that thought was enough to make Sal pause. Fifty thousand was a big number, but it was actually just a series of bite-sized chunks that he could manage piece by piece. Right now, he was being asked to repeat the form twenty times…and then he'd do it again. And again…and as much as it was required.

As great as that inner resolve was, Sal played around with the idea of getting that Moonsilver Monocle back so he could numb himself to the process. It was a fun thought, but he needed to actively learn the Silverson Arts if he wanted to put it into proper practice. The hope was that the training and repetition would create muscle memory that would allow him to react automatically on the battlefield to whatever situation that arose. Sal just wasn't sure the foundational course was going to be enough to do that, and whether fifty thousand repetitions was going to be a waste of his time to just get to the starting line of proficiency.

Pushing those thoughts to one side, Sal decided he'd at least cover the basics that he had learned with his father. Twenty of each, with Perfect active, wouldn't be too bad of a way to start things off. He gave himself the arbitrary goal of achieving two percent overall with the time he had available. That would be close to two hundred exercises at Cadet 5.

Even though each movement was fluid and honed to perfection, it took about ten iterations before Sal's body naturally started to loosen up. The movements were smooth and graceful as he closed the distance to the stationary target of a leecher. With a slow and precise kick, Sal brought his right foot around in a beautiful arc to tap against its rubber body. Holding himself in that pose, Sal brought his right foot back down and lowered his torso to prepare for the Silverson Sweep. If he was able to find a way to stack the exercises he knew, then a single practice session could give him proficiency across a number of forms, stances, and techniques.

Sal's master plan came up short as the distance between himself and the stationary target didn't change. It wasn't like his mother or father was dancing around the sparring floor with him, making him close the distance to launch an attack, or to evade. He had to reposition himself before each and every sequence, and it broke him out of his flow state.

With a sigh during the break between sequences, Sal glanced over to the area that had the moving targets. He had initially talked himself out of it when he first saw it, and had chosen to go for a more gradual exercise…but now that he saw the limitations of the stationary targets, he wanted to try it out.

Less than a minute later, Sal was in front of the moving targets and at the small terminal that controlled them. He was able to select the "demons" that he'd be fighting, and he picked the voider, leecher, and prowlers. There was no way he was going to add hulkers to the mix. He put it at the beginner stage because he didn't want it to disrupt his flow. As long as there were multiple moving targets, he'd need to adapt to their movements.

That had been a mistake.

The demons barely moved, and Sal found himself running toward them rather than getting swarmed. Added to that, when he hit something with a punch or a kick, it ended up putting the "demon" as a stationary target for close to five minutes. By the time he had hit all of them, he received a notification that he had completed the beginner course. There had been zero challenge, and Sal ended up getting a little annoyed.

When he made his way back to the terminal, Sal picked the adaptive setting that would try to change the difficulty based on his performance. When he stood in the starting area, that was illuminated under his feet, he watched the "demons" and waited for them to move.

A leecher descended from a cable above. Sal didn't even hesitate as he brought his leg up to smack it out of the air. It was just a simple attack, a singular kick…and it was apparently enough for the terminal to calculate that Sal was far more capable than his Crafter profile had indicated.

Two voiders snapped up from the floor and came in to suppress Sal's movements from both sides. A Silverson Sweep managed to hit both of them in one swift movement. All the "demons" were coming to him, and Sal was delighted that he barely needed to move from the starting area. Another leecher was repelled with a punch, then another three in quick succession. A prowler launched from outside of his peripheral vision, using the blind spot created from a voider attack, but the Silverson Sweep managed to catch it on the recovery rotation.

Sal laughed as he continued fighting against the onslaught of demons. It was a strangely euphoric moment of feeling both competent and capable. Each and every attack connected, and he wasn't running out of stamina, either. His foot ached a little from the repeated kicks, but the adrenaline coursing through his body made him numb to anything that wasn't a constant barrage of attacks.

Being honest with himself, he knew that the training wasn't anything remotely close to accurate. There was no way that the demons would just bump into him and retreat in an actual dungeon. Yet, for what Sal needed at that moment, it was perfect. He was able to seamlessly transition through all the movements his father had shown him, and the visor was definitely happy with the progress.

Recalculating Sequences...

Sal kept at it for what seemed like most of the day, but in reality, it was close to an hour. In the midst of battle, even simulated, his adrenaline was pumping and he was kicking and punching within seconds. Those became minutes, and the entirety of the fight, nonstop for close to an hour, was both mentally and physically taxing. It was only when he came up for air, by stepping back from the apparatus, that he was able to catch his breath.

That was when he felt the incessant vibrations coming from his tablet. He wondered whether this was going to be a message from Divinity, asking what he had just done. Surely the Silverson Arts wasn't going to skew the future in another unexpected manner?

Barry Francis: What the hell are you doing?

"Wait...what?" Sal stared at the words on the screen. Not the message, but rather the sender.

CHAPTER 9: RATINGS

Sal decided that taking one of the towels from the sparring room rack wouldn't be a massive deal, and he draped it across his shoulders as he walked into the simulation room. Barry had instructed him with a barrage of messages that he needed to come as soon as he could. It sounded urgent, and Sal was just looking forward to seeing him.

When the doors opened, Sal was a little disappointed to see Chris Spectre sitting at the end of a large table that had been partitioned into separate workspaces. A pair of headphones were cupped on his ears as he gave Sal a passing nod to acknowledge his entrance. In front of him were a series of illusionary characters sparring against each other in an empty arena. Their movements were currently paused mid-fight, and Spectre seemed to be reversing the flow of battle and watching it play out slowly.

"Ignore him." Barry appeared in front of Sal, a wide grin on his face. "We've got so much more to talk about. What were you just doing?"

"Sparring, mostly." Sal gestured at the door. "It's just down the hall. We've got a whole range of equipment. There's even an aerial course that I think you'd be great at."

Barry waved his hand like Sal wasn't answering the question. "I've been here for pretty much the entire night, poring over team strategies and dynamics. Your stats suddenly shot up, and I couldn't figure out what happened."

"My stats?" Sal asked in confusion. "Like, what? Combat stats?" He had used his profile to enter the room, but he hadn't anticipated that it would be grading him while he was there. Curiosity got the better of him.

Barry beckoned for him to follow him, and that was when Sal saw the collection of empty coffee cups scattered around Barry's workstation. It was a terminal just like Chris Spectre was operating, but there were no visual representations on the board.

"You have to pay extra for the recordings, and I don't really care about them for the moment," Barry explained as he pulled a seat toward the station for Sal to take a seat. "This is where the real value lies." He gestured at the screen, before reaching behind it and pulling it upward so that Sal could get a better look at it.

Barry blinked a few times before tapping on a few menus, clearing out previous tabs to reduce the clutter on the screen. "These are the important ones." He smiled as he looked at Sal expectantly.

Salvatore Argento
Combat Rating: 61
- Martial Techniques: +4
  - Demonic Pattern Simulation
  - Adaptive Grade: Novice
- Demons Defeated: +27
  - Hulkers (+12)
  - Voiders (+8)

- - Prowlers (+5)
  - Leechers (+2)
- o Registered Weapon: +30
  - - Tower Trial - Scarlet Moon Revolver (Upper Rare)
    - Excursion Trial - Scarlet Moon Revolver (Rare)
    - Cohort Tournament - Voracious Rapier (Rare)
- o Registered Ability: +0
  - - Standard Replication Ability

"Pretty cool, isn't it?" Barry pointed at the rating. "This is what changed when you were sparring. You went up a whole four points, which has massive effects across the board."

Sal felt like Barry was going to continue even if he didn't say a word. Rather than asking a stupid question, he thought it best to just wait for Barry to finish with the explanation. The only thing that was really going through Sal's mind was that he had gained more points from the Silverson Arts than from every leecher he had ever killed. It was a sobering thought, that something that had plagued his dreams for months was worth so little in the scoring chart.

The other part that was a little more entertaining was the fact that the registered weapons were completely wrong. The Scarlet Moon Revolver had been gifted to the Arkwright to help in research and development, and if half of his entire combat rating was determined by equipment, then it was likely a very inaccurate number. He wondered how Barry would react if he knew about the Mythic-grade attack drone.

Barry seemingly didn't care about Sal's hesitation, or he was caught up in the moment. He brought up a second screen with a set of familiar names.

"You're able to use the raw processing power of this place to pretty much run simulations on team compositions. You can assemble a dream team of sorts, and see how they perform against other teams." Barry pointed at Divinity's combat score. "There are also synergies that are put into the calculations, but it's not always accurate. Like, we get a bonus because we did the cohort tournament together, but we don't get a bonus if Divinity is on our team."

Sal frowned at that. "I'm pretty sure that every team should get a bonus when they have Divinity on their team." It just made sense. She could see the future and would be able to give them the best strategies for victory.

"Oh, they absolutely give her a ridiculous rating for her ability. It's like a plus twenty or something stupid like that. I got hit with a plus five because it's deemed an evasion-focused ability," Barry muttered, as though the rating system had personally offended him.

Sal looked at the screens, and finally realized that the countless tabs that Barry had opened were all for different combinations. "What are you trying to achieve…that would keep you up all night?"

Barry shrugged. "I don't know anything about half of the Savior class, and I don't like going into a situation blind. I want to know everything about them with the resources we have, rather than pestering Divinity for a reading. If we end up being told to pick teams or something like that, I want to know the best combinations as soon as possible."

"And any interesting insights?" Sal asked out of curiosity. "Or surprises?"

Barry leaned back and quietly pointed in the direction of Chris Spectre. "He's the second-best Offense in Quest Academy, if you just go by the statistics."

Sal paused at that as he glanced over at Spectre. "Not the first? He's second in the rankings, after me. Wouldn't that make him the top Offense class?"

Barry shook his head. "Not according to the data. He's not a team player, which sounds hilarious coming from me, I know." He grinned before he continued. "But when it comes to team composition, he's actually a subtraction to most of the cohesion scores. The highest combat rating out of all the Savior class is a girl called Mica, and she's way down in the Savior rankings. That said, I think those figures will change when the Body Manipulators stop lying to themselves about being Controllers."

"You think they'll change?" Sal asked in disbelief. "And not the Supports who are moonlighting as Controllers?" He gave him a pointed look, but Barry shook his head as though it were obvious.

"I'm telling you now, Darren Lenihan and Kyndra Scott will be in the Offense class before the end of the semester. When you're being assessed as rabble, it's better to stand out as a leader. But when you're surrounded by the top students in the entire academy…it's better to stick to your strengths."

Barry said it with such certainty that Sal had to do a double take.

"Don't suppose you think Erika will switch from being a Controller?" Sal laughed at how alien the thought was. He couldn't for the life of him imagine Erika Clifton relinquishing control.

"She'd make a very good Offense, but probably not realistic," Barry agreed as he brought up a few more tabs. "You should stick with Rochelle, by the way. She's a good combination match for whatever team you end up going with."

"And who else have you been pairing me up with?" Sal smiled as he leaned in to get a better look.

Barry sighed as he shook his head, as though it genuinely pained him. "I was desperately hoping that Erika would be the best Controller for your team, but she didn't make the cut. Divinity is a really good choice, but not the most optimal."

"Let me guess, you're the best fit?" Sal asked, as though he were truly shocked by the revelation, going so far as to cover his mouth with his palm.

"Second-best, actually." Barry grinned. "That girl with the super knotted weave you spotted at the gala, Maxine Volta. She's the best match for your team, with me a very close second."

"Oh," Sal said in actual surprise. "I wasn't expecting that one."

"And Michael Rogan, with the crazy shadow binding stuff. He's an excellent fit for whatever team I'm on, and is, once again, the second-best fit for your team. That Mica girl is the best Offense you can go with." Barry paused as he looked at the screen for a few seconds. "Oh, and yeah…Defense is the same for literally every team. If you get Derek Norman, you are top of the charts."

"He's that good?" Sal leaned in to get a better look at the stats.

"Nope, he's the only one we have information on. There was a single Defense in the entire fifteen who were announced before the break. Hopefully the next batch has more variety. Otherwise, you might have to talk to your ex-girlfriend or make a defensive robot or something." Barry smiled at the joke, but faltered a bit when he caught Sal's expression.

Sal had been putting off the talk with Hannah since the blow-up before the excursion. Even with the context from Divinity that she would push herself to get into the Saviors, he didn't want there to be any animosity between them. Her words had really stung, and even though she had been brainwashed by a rogue Controller, it had just been easier to leave things as they were. She hadn't come to him, and he hadn't gone to her.

Wester Templeton's Influence ability had sown doubt into her, rather than outright control. Which meant that all the words Hannah had said to him were a version of her own thoughts, but twisted into a verbal attack. That was the part that stopped him from reaching out.

"It was just a joke, man. You don't need to worry about it," Barry insisted as he leaned back in his chair. "There'll be plenty more Defense people coming in, and we don't even know if we'll need to make teams. As long as there's no bullshit race, or letting the weakest people pick their groups…we'll be golden."

Sal nodded and tried to put Barry's mind at ease. "It might be easier to make the robot."

"That's what I'm talking about." Barry grinned as he gestured at Sal's combat rating. "And you just know they won't register it as a weapon and you'll get zero additional points."

Sal smiled at the joke and looked at the screen. "How is Hannah's compatibility, by the way?"

Barry looked at him in surprise. "You mean…for your team? If there's a selection, you could probably get Derek since you ranked top out of everyone. Statistically, he's a powerhouse."

"Yeah, for my team. Let's say that I go with Rochelle, and we leave the Offense and Controller spaces blank for now. Actually, no…put Divinity on the team. And then for Offense, either Michael Rogan or you."

Barry blinked as his back straightened. He turned to look at Sal with a playful smile on his face. "Seriously trying to dethrone me as a Controller? I've had a yellow bedspread for like three minutes, and you want to make me sit in a red room?"

"Humor me," Sal suggested. "Make sure that the Vengeful Vambraces are counted as a weapon. You can input it as an Epic grade, and it'll probably give you a score."

Barry sighed as he tapped in the composition. "I'm trying it with me first, just so we can show you how terrible an idea this is. I'm not made for Offense work. They have to run in and put their lives on the line, which is very much against everything I believe in."

Combat Rating: 335/600
Team Composition
- o   Salvatore Argento - Support: 61
- o   Barry Francis - Offense: 57
- o   Divinity Khan - Controller: 74
- o   Hannah Unruh - Defense: 60

      o   Rochelle de Verdon - Healer: 83

"That's with the Vengeful Vambraces?" Sal asked, just to clarify. He wouldn't have imagined that Barry would be the lowest of the roster, and he didn't even know whether the overall score was a good one.

"Yeah, the top score possible is a hundred and twenty," Barry remarked dryly. "And I'm in the bottom half of that, which is definitely a kick to the ego…but what can you do? I like that they don't put in useless things like the Challenge crests or our rank as Saviors."

Sal nodded as he listened to Barry. "And what's the highest composition you've seen? Like, out of the full six hundred?"

Barry smiled as he moved to another tab. "Thought you might ask that."

Combat Rating: 402/600
Team Composition
      o   Blathnaid Clean - Support: 64
      o   Mica Egan - Offense: 99
      o   Divinity Khan - Controller: 74
      o   Derek Norman - Defense: 82
      o   Rochelle de Verdon - Healer: 83

"It's kind of wild that Rochelle has one of the highest scores out of anyone I've seen so far," Sal breathed as he pointed at her name.

Barry looked at him as though he were an idiot. "Yeah, what are the chances? It's not like she has a Legendary-grade coat that kills anything that moves."

"Ah." A wide smile appeared on Sal's face. "Good to know that we can absolutely break these rankings with equipment, though."

"Should I prepare myself to see you skyrocket past the one-hundred mark?" Barry asked genuinely as he turned to face Sal.

Sal shook his head, the smile not leaving his face. "Nah, I've started a bit of a project with the sparring, so it'll be slow and gradual increases, if anything."

Barry's eyes narrowed. "And what about on the equipment front? I don't see you wearing your usual outfit."

Sal clapped him on the back as he got to his feet. "That's still a work in progress, but you'll be the first to know." He gestured at the screens in front of Barry. "This was cool. I'll ask you how to operate it all when I get a bit of downtime."

"You've got somewhere else to be?" Barry raised an eyebrow. "Let me guess, the workshop?"

Sal nodded, laughing. "Yeah, I've got something I want to give to Upgrade, and I don't want to wait until I see her in class." He looked over at Chris Spectre, who was still concentrating deeply on the simulation in front of him. Sal turned to look at Barry thoughtfully. "Did you hear from Divinity, about when she's getting in?"

Barry nodded. "Yeah, she's training some martial art thing in her room. If you check your messages, you'll see we've been invited to a lunch with her tomorrow.

My best guess is she's going to tell us what kind of shit-show this semester is going to be."

CHAPTER 10: GROWTH

Sal had intended to go straight down to the workshop, but after catching a whiff of himself in the corridor, he quickly changed that plan. A shower and new uniform later, Sal found himself in the sleek black elevator on the way down to the lobby. The news reports and rankings hadn't changed in the day since he had seen them, but he couldn't help but stare at them with a wide smile on his face. It genuinely felt incredibly sophisticated and visually impressive. Even the small touches of the portraits on the wall were incredible, and Sal started to wonder whether he could implement something like that back in the auction house.

He didn't know exactly how he'd do it, but it would be great to have the Appraisal information highlighted on similar screens so people could see all the stats. It might eat into his father's showmanship, but it would certainly reduce a lot of the stress on the sales staff.

Sal turned to look at the other panels and was greeted by a schedule for upcoming scavenger runs. He reached out his left hand and pressed the screen, wondering whether it was interactive. To his equal surprise and delight, he was prompted with a registration menu for the next scavenger run. It wasn't like he needed any materials, but he had enjoyed the previous one with Blathnaid and Darren. He guessed that the elevator would arrive at the lobby any second, so he made the quick decision to sign himself up for the next one, which would be happening in a week.

It would be a good opportunity to use Jackal; having a drone navigate to all the difficult areas and harvesting items would be ideal. If it increased his rank within the Scav Network, that would just be a bonus. He also wanted to check out what they had at the market stalls at the end of the runs.

Just as his application of interest was registered, the doors opened to reveal the lobby. Sal smiled as he walked through and made his way across the gleaming marble floors. A few students were moving back and forth with luggage, and he felt truly grateful that he had access to Arsenal. Although he'd only had it for a few days, he could tell that it was going to be a massive advantage for storing materials and useful items.

Sal crossed the garden path and looked over at the empty amphitheater in the center of all the Quest Academy towers. A few people were seated in the stands, catching up after the break, but nothing really of interest. Sal didn't recognize any of the faces, and it was harder to determine which students were from which year of study. Everyone wore casual clothes or the black uniforms. There wasn't a grey blob in sight.

His journey to the workshop was uneventful, and Sal was grateful for how empty the hallways had been. There wasn't even a line for the elevator up to the right floor, which was a definite bonus. When he rounded on the final stretch of the journey, he smiled at the sight of the workshop's double doors. He probably should have sent Upgrade a message to see whether she was actually in the workshop, but he guessed that she would be. It was her last day of peace before the students were officially back, and he assumed she'd be at her desk, working on personal projects, or last-minute course materials.

When he opened the doors, he was surprised to see a welcome sight. Sitting at one of the benches, dressed in black with purple shoulders, was the answer to one of Sal's biggest problems.

Anderson Royce glanced up at the new entrant and gave a friendly wave. "Welcome back, Sal."

All thoughts of seeking out Upgrade were put to one side as Sal smiled and approached the first-year. "Good to see you, Anders. How was the break?"

Anders shrugged as he crossed his arms and leaned on them, sighing. "Guessing the same as yours. Did your parents put you to work the moment you got back, or am I just the unlucky one?"

"Ha. Exact same, but I was happy to work on a few auctions. You only realize how much you miss it when you're away from it." Sal laughed as he pulled up a stool to sit beside Anders. "I actually wanted to ask you a favor, by the way, so it's a good thing I bumped into you."

"Oh?" Anders turned to face Sal, a curious expression on his face. "How can I be of service to the shining star of the first-years?" Although the words could have come across as cutting, the warm smile on Anders's face showed that it was clearly said in jest.

"You know the way I'm a Replicator? I do a lot of work with Skill Weaves." Sal gestured at Anderson's chest. "And there's a project I'm working on that requires the Growth weave."

"That's…unexpected," Anders answered with an awkward laugh. "What do you need it for? And I'm not really sure what to do to help. Do I need to tell you about it or something?"

Sal gestured at his eyes. "I can read it just by looking at you, but I didn't want to copy and replicate it without asking for permission." He looked at Anders to see whether there was any change in his expression. When it was clear that all Anders felt was curious, Sal continued. "I'm working on a project that will let me grow Alchemy materials."

His smile became grim as he shook his head slowly. "Ah, you're not the first to have that idea…but I can tell you from personal experience that you're in for a rough time. Rather than just bludgeoning the seeds with essence, you need to create entirely new strains for them to grow into. It'll be a ridiculous amount of learning and research, and won't be worth the time and effort for what you'll end up with."

"But it's possible?" Sal asked, just to clarify that he was understanding it properly.

Anders nodded. "Possible, yes. It's just that it'll be an inferior product to whatever you're trying to make. Then there's a whole range of issues when it comes to actually making the strains. It's like Crafting. You need a good blueprint for all the stages of what you're trying to make…but, when you nail them down, then you can do it much faster." He smiled sheepishly. "I've been trained on the ingredients our restaurant uses since I was a kid, so I can make pretty much any vegetable you'd ever want, but nothing alchemical, I'm afraid."

Sal was surprised to find out how complex the Growth ability was, and he thanked himself silently for talking to Anderson before trying to just utilize it. He was pretty confident that his visor would be able to calculate the necessary strains with the Cypher ability, but he would need to check to be sure. When it came to a huge amount of essence, his Capacitor ability had a monstrous amount of essence in reserve, so that would be fine, too.

"Okay, that's perfect." Sal clapped his hands together, surprising Anderson. "How would you feel about helping me with this project? I'll give you some of the royalties if it works out how I hope."

"Royalties?" Anderson repeated in confusion. "Just for letting you look at my weave? That seems a bit unfair, Sal."

Sal smiled as he shook his head. "Well, what about if you helped me a little more? I don't have the plan completely worked out yet, but I think you could end up being a great help. It might involve you pushing the limits of your ability, though."

"I don't want to give you the wrong idea, Sal," Anderson stated with his hands up. "I would be happy to help in whatever way I can, but I need to manage expectations. I don't have any of the research about alchemical strains, and then there's the cost involved of actually getting the seeds or saplings of whatever you're looking to grow."

"Okay, that's good enough for now." Sal got to his feet. "I wanted your permission to use the Growth ability, but if what you're telling me is true, then I think there's an opportunity for us to help each other. If I got you the ingredients and the fully researched strains, how confident would you be?"

Anderson thought about it for a few seconds, going so far as to look off to one side as though he were trying to calculate something in his head. When his gaze landed back on Sal, he shook his head slightly. "I don't think my weave is strong enough to handle anything that didn't originate on this side of a portal. Infused vegetation is viable, but the alchemical stuff that's popular is far more advanced than what I can handle right now."

"You've tried before?" Sal asked out of curiosity, wondering how Anderson could be so certain of the limitations of his ability.

"Of course. Was one of the first things I tried to do when I enrolled... I got the idea from the Administration lecture, but it ended up as a bust," Anders admitted with a guilty smile. "Would have been a fantastic earner, though. I can't blame you for having the same idea."

Sal smiled in return. "And...hypothetically...if your ability was to grow stronger, do you think that would change things?"

This time there was no hesitation as Anderson nodded. "Absolutely. The fact that I can trace out the first percentage points of strains tells me that it's designed to do the full thing; it just doesn't have the potency or essence reserves to get the job done."

"Okay, leave it with me," Sal said. "I'll keep you in the loop with any developments, but I appreciate all the insights you've given me."

"Don't you need to look at the weave?" Anderson asked in confusion as he tapped at his own chest.

"Already done." Sal smiled as he clapped Anders on the shoulder. "And I meant what I said about the royalties. If I make any sort of income with this project, you'll be getting a cut. It would be impossible without your ability, after all."

Anderson scoffed at that as he shook his head. "Just don't blame me if it all falls apart, okay?"

"Deal," Sal agreed as he kept a mental note of Anderson's weave. There were a lot of knots in there, so he was confident that there were far more advancements to be made without worrying about a weave evolution. He'd need to double-check it with the simulation orb, but Sal was confident that Anderson Royce's ability was the solution to the elixir machine. If he could properly commercialize it, then he'd be able to help Anderson financially, too. It was a win-win situation.

"See you later, I guess?" Anders laughed as he waved at Sal. "No idea if we're going to be in the same classes with you being a Savior now. But hopefully I'll see you down here."

Sal nodded in agreement. "I'm sure we'll be in a few classes together. Did you see Upgrade anywhere, by the way?"

Anders nodded as he pointed over to the far side of the room. "She was chatting with Alex and Forge a little while ago…probably at her bench."

"Thanks, Anders!" Sal finally departed from the workbench with a wave. He turned his attention back to where Upgrade was last seen, and got to thinking about how he was going to work on the Growth weave. He barely got a single step into his planning when Upgrade suddenly appeared ahead.

Upgrade looked directly at Sal, and a wide smile crossed her face. Rather than approaching him, she turned on her heel and walked toward a stairwell at the other side of the workshop. Lifting a hand, she beckoned him to follow her.

Sal obliged, not sure what she was doing. When she pushed through the door, he broke into a semi-jog to catch the door before it closed. He had been completely right in thinking that it was a stairwell. Upgrade's footsteps could be heard going upward, as well as the sound of her chuckling.

"Is there a reason we're playing tag?" Sal called up the stairwell as he followed her, taking two steps at a time.

"It's worth it," Upgrade called down, laughing. "Well, it will be…eventually. So, hurry up!"

Sal smiled as he chased up the stairs, wondering where she was leading him, until he finally crested the landing to see a door held open for him. With a deep exhalation, Sal moved to the opened door and walked through, not sure what to expect.

"It looks like shit right now, but the workshop upgrades are well under way," Upgrade said proudly as she cast her hand across the massive open space. A series of white tarps covered various sets of machinery, and there were partitions being created that mimicked the private booths they had in the original workshop. "What do you think? It's a little rough, but I'm sure you can see the potential of it!"

Sal couldn't help but smile as he made eye contact with Upgrade. "It's good to see you again."

"Come on, at least say something about the room." Upgrade groaned as she gestured at it with a wave of her hand. "I helped a lot with all of this, and it's going to be ready in a few weeks. Just need to do some finishing touches and we'll be ready to move in."

Sal sighed as he took in the sight of the very much in-progress workshop. He didn't really get to see what was under those tarps, but he was hopeful it was some good equipment. "It looks really good, Upgrade."

"See? That wasn't so hard." Upgrade laughed. "Thank you for the genuine and unprompted compliment. I very much appreciate it."

Sal grinned as he crossed his arms. "So, do you want the present I got for you now, or later?"

Upgrade blinked in surprise as she looked at Sal in confusion. "Why did you get me a present?"

"Because you've helped me so much, and I wanted to do something nice for you," Sal answered truthfully. "So…do you want it now?"

"Aren't you worried that I'll hate it?" Upgrade teased as she looked at him pointedly. "It's a tough job to buy for someone you barely know." Her expression softened. "But I do appreciate the sentiment. I'm not even sure I'm allowed to accept gifts from students. Could be considered a bribe, I guess?"

Sal grinned. "I already know you'll like it because I cheated." He watched Upgrade, to see whether she'd figure it out, but when he received a suspicious look, he filled in the blanks. "Divinity looked into the future for your reaction, and we kinda narrowed down the best gift from that."

"That's absolutely cheating!" Upgrade burst out laughing as she took a step closer. "I don't see a massive box or anything, so I'm guessing it's something small. Is it a tracker, or did you think of an amulet with an essence core?" She looked at Sal carefully, as though trying to get the information out of his silence. "Ooooh, is it something conceptual…like a blueprint for me to unknot my weaves?"

Sal still hadn't said a word, and Upgrade continued. "This is the worst. Just put me out of my misery and tell me…otherwise, I'll guess something and get super attached to the idea."

"Okay, but prepare yourself," Sal warned as he lifted his hands into the maestro position. The tablet in his pocket was registered to the Nexus ability, so he didn't need his visor for this one. The Mythical blight jackal was able to be summoned with a hand gesture, and he picked the one that Upgrade mocked him relentlessly over.

Upgrade's smile grew wider. "It better not be a dance or something. I'd actually kill you." Her laugh died as the Mythical blight jackal appeared on Sal's left arm.

"Just to manage expectations…this isn't your present," Sal warned as he twisted his left palm, pulling a large box from the Arsenal subspace. When it materialized in his palms, Sal placed it down on the ground and repeated the process until another two boxes joined the first. Lastly, he flicked his wrist and summoned a long tube of rolled paper that was tied up at the center.

Upgrade didn't even notice the blueprint or the boxes because her eyes were locked onto the Mythical blight jackal. Even without knowing about the drone component, she was in awe of the sleek design. "It's gorgeous, Sal. You've managed to create an advanced subspace? What material combination did you use?"

Sal cleared his throat as he lifted the blueprint tube and handed it to Upgrade. "Rather than me explaining what this one does…why don't you make your own? All the materials you need are in these boxes, and I'll handle the essence part at the very end to get it over the line."

Upgrade was clearly caught off guard by everything, but an awkward smile appeared on her face. "I'll have you know that I made that Legendary-grade coat with Blathnaid. I'm not completely useless."

Sal launched Jackal from his arm and was happy to see that the little drone hovered above the ground, each of the abyssal steel tentacles weaving in the air as the blight core bathed the surroundings in an eerie green light.

Upgrade's hands started to shake as she looked from Sal's shoulder to where Jackal was suspended in midair. "You made…a leecher drone?" It was a double take as she moved her attention almost unwillingly back to his shoulder. "And it lives in your arm?"

Sal smiled as he once again offered Upgrade the blueprint. "Yes, and this is how you make it."

Upgrade's mouth hung open as she accepted the blueprint. "This is a joke, right?"

Sal shook his head. "No, which is why I said I'd do the essence part at the end of your build. I managed to make it in a day, but you'll probably be a bit faster than me."

"Why would I need your essence? I can handle that part myself." Upgrade breathed as she looked at Jackal from every angle possible, without getting too close to it. She was like a moth to a flame, constantly pulling her hand back every time she grew curious enough to reach out.

Sal smiled broadly. "You kinda need Mythcrafter essence for a Mythic grade…"

CHAPTER 11: GIFT

Upgrade sat on the ground, cross-legged with a confounded expression on her face. In front of her, laid out on the floor, was the blueprint that Sal had gifted her. Beside her, on both sides, were the opened boxes containing the materials he had brought for her. She kept moving her attention from the blueprint to the materials in a haze of confusion, as though there were a mental checklist in her head competing with the fact that it wasn't some elaborate joke.

Every so often, she would glance up at Jackal, who hovered beside Sal's seated form, innocently bobbing up and down while the abyssal steel tentacles weaved in an almost hypnotic rotation at its base.

This went on for a while, as Sal had been hushed the last two times he tried to initiate a conversation with her. She had gone completely white at the mention of the Mythic grade, and rather than talk it out or react like he had expected…she had defaulted to problem-solving mode and started to look through the blueprint to see whether Sal was lying to her.

There hadn't been much progress, and Upgrade looked like she was fast approaching her breaking point as she traced her fingernail across the details on the blueprint. Her gaze snapped up to stare at his arm, and a triumphant smile appeared on her face.

"There's no way that you made a Mythic grade with venomstone! It's an Epic-grade material, and I can see it listed right here," Upgrade declared with one finger on the blueprint and another pointing directly at Sal's arm. Her victorious grin showed how much she had enjoyed the whole investigation. "So, fess up…and tell me what grade it actually is."

Sal simply smiled as he got to his feet and moved over to one of the remaining boxes of materials. Popping the lid, he reached down and withdrew a glowing blue stone that was bigger than his clenched fist. "This is a Legendary-grade material. Venomstone is a part of the design so you can have the Assimilation ability."

Upgrade stared at the stone in Sal's hand. "What is that?" She looked almost scared by the prospect that all of this was real. "Why do you have Legendary materials? You shouldn't be able to Refine things to that level… You haven't even been taught how to synthesize things, or shown the known recipes." Her voice had a tremor to it, as though she were trying to convince herself rather than Sal. "There's a limit to what the Arkwright can do, too. It was struggling to make Epic-grade pieces at the party…so I know it didn't come from that."

Sal couldn't help but laugh at how strange the scene was. Upgrade was one of the most confident people he knew, and she was in a pretty rough state. He had thought she'd be excited or in disbelief over the Mythic grade…but he didn't expect her to literally have a nervous breakdown.

"Okay, are you ready for an explanation? I'm allowed to talk this time, right?" Sal smiled, eyebrow raised. He was sure she'd end up jumping to conclusions the moment he started to talk.

Upgrade just stared at him from the floor. "I can't even make sense of half of this blueprint. It's all conceptually possible, but I've never heard of abilities like Assimilation or these other three. What is a void seeker?"

Sal raised both of his hands in a calming gesture, as though it would somehow stop the barrage of questions coming from Upgrade. It seemed to work as she finally relented with a groan and waved at him to continue.

"The Arkwright was able to handle a lot of the material synthesis. I created new materials from the leecher cores…which led to the discovery of venomstone." Sal hesitated slightly. He wasn't going to lie to Upgrade because she had his back and kept his secrets. "It also led to the creation of a blight core." He held his breath and watched her reaction carefully.

"Am I supposed to know what that is?" Upgrade blinked at him. "I know that venomstone is rare as hell, though. Is blight core something better than that?"

That caught Sal off guard. He had been certain that Upgrade would have known about how dangerous the blight core was, or the subterfuge surrounding it. Having spoken to his father about it, he was being very cautious about who he told about it. Upgrade not knowing about it was a little disconcerting, because it made him feel like it actually was a well-kept secret.

"Can you promise to keep that part a secret?" Sal asked in a serious tone. "My father spoke to me about how dangerous the blight core is, and that people have died over the discovery of the last one. It has a really insane ability, which you'll come to appreciate with the venomstone."

"Of course," Upgrade responded, nodding slowly as she read his earnest expression. "But…if yours was made with that blight core thing, what is that blue stone?"

Sal breathed a sigh of relief as he held it up for her to get a closer look. "I synthesized all the voider cores in the same way as the leecher cores. It led to the creation of this." He held out his hand to pass the blue stone over to her. "It's called the void seeker, according to the Arkwright. I double-checked with my father, and there's no danger surrounding this one."

"So, you're saying you changed the design so I wouldn't be in danger?" Upgrade asked with a thoughtful expression. A smile crossed her lips as she took the blue stone from him. "Or did you just want me to be the guinea pig for a new build that might not even work?"

"It'll work," Sal said with absolute certainty. "I've run so many simulations with my visor, and this build works much better for you than it does for me. I was originally going to make something for my right arm, but when I saw the details…I decided that this would be a much better present for you."

Upgrade blinked in surprise. "What was the original present? Not that I'm ungrateful for the opportunity to have the second-ever Mythic grade in existence." She laughed at the very thought, then quickly added, "I don't think there's anything that I would have preferred more than this. It's my two favorite things— new technology and drones!"

Sal smiled as he offered a shrug. "I haven't finished it, so don't get your hopes up." When he had asked Divinity for a reading in the future, he realized that the best present for Upgrade was going to be a method for her to unknot her weave.

He had started with a simulation from Cypher about how he could gradually unknot her ability and help guide her to the Evolve ability. Divinity had said that Upgrade would be overjoyed with that, and Sal had only changed his mind after seeing the options on the void seeker material. There was no reason he couldn't fix her ability in the future, especially when he got the all clear from Quest to unknot weaves.

Upgrade stared at Sal for a few seconds before she shook her head with a rueful smile. "You need to stop putting everyone else in front of yourself. I think you're the only man who would commission a Legendary-grade coat and then hand it over to another student without even trying it on…"

She waved at the boxes around her. "I don't deserve any of this, Salvatore. It's an incredibly thoughtful and well-intentioned gift, but I don't think I can accept this." Her smile was bright as she glanced down at the blueprint. "I'm just delighted to see your progress, and I'll be cheering you on from the sidelines as you go toe-to-toe with Doc Ameye in the future."

Sal nodded, his smile wide. "I thought you'd say that." He pointed at the boxes. "This is a bribe for you to join my guild as a mentor."

Upgrade stared at him for a few moments. "Okay, I'm in."

"I thought you'd say that. You can accept the gift now?" He laughed as he pretended to pull one of the boxes away. "Or should I just put it back in the subspace?"

Upgrade laughed as she lunged forward to wrap both arms around the box. "I absolutely accept the bribe. Count me in as your mentor…but just be warned I do have to keep up the classes at Quest Academy."

"I wouldn't have it any other way," Sal agreed as he sat back down. "So, now that we've gotten over the moral quandary of you accepting the gift, what do you think of Jackal?" He gestured at the floating drone that Upgrade had been stealing glances at the entire time.

"It's honestly beautiful," Upgrade admitted as she sat back and crossed her arms. "I can see that it's abyssal steel…and I don't even want to know how much that cost you. Hell, all the materials on this blueprint are enough to buy a few buildings in a Reclaimed Zone."

"All sourced ethically from dungeons." Sal smiled. "Fabi helped a lot for the initial stuff, and I got a few good deals from her father, too. Most of it came from a dungeon I ran with my parents, though."

"What?" Upgrade snapped out of whatever reverie she was in as she looked at Sal in surprise. "Your parents? The Auctioneers…went into a dungeon for you?"

"With me," Sal corrected with a laugh. "In between sparring and teaching me some cool martial arts."

Upgrade stared at Sal, her stupefied expression mirroring the reaction to the Mythic grade. "I'm missing so much context, that I don't even know where to start. Abyssal steel isn't common in a leecher or prowler dungeon. You'd have to be fighting off scuttlers, at the bare minimum."

Sal pointed at Jackal, grinning. "Oh, I should mention… Jackal killed its first scuttler a week or so ago. Pretty cool, right?"

Upgrade's head tilted, her eyes not leaving Sal's face. "You made…a combat drone?"

"Well, yeah. What did you think it was?" Sal scoffed, as though it were obvious. "It cleared through an entire dungeon pretty much by itself, and harvests all the materials and puts them into my subspace. It's still learning, though. It only has a few countermeasures loaded, but Fabi thinks that we'll be able to improve its modules in the future."

Upgrade just stared at Sal, not saying a word. It was like a fuse had sparked in her head and she was in standby mode. It took a short while before she could even formulate a question, and it looked like it was a herculean task at that.

"Adaptive Behavior," Upgrade practically whispered to herself as she closed her eyes. "You put Adaptive Behavior on a combat drone?"

Sal wasn't sure whether he had somehow screwed up, but Upgrade's next words put him at ease.

"You're a first-year…who's never attended an essence programming lesson…and you've created a drone, with the Adaptive Behavior module?" Upgrade spoke in a quiet voice as she looked at Sal with a lost expression on her face. "At least tell me that MythOS was able to do the heavy lifting for you on that one? That would soothe my ego a little at least."

"I could have used MythOS?" Sal asked with a hint of annoyance and surprise. He hadn't even considered using it to help program the drone's behaviors. Well, if he was being honest with himself, Jackal came to life fully functional, and it wasn't really like he had done much on the programming side of things. The visor had handled everything where that was concerned, and it was only when Fabi brought up the modules that Sal noticed there were ways to improve it.

There wasn't anything wrong with Jackal, but if it could be improved further, Sal wanted to do whatever was in his power to get it there.

Upgrade sighed. "Ahh, that's reassuring. At least you're still doing things the impractical way… I feel better now." Her laugh was lighthearted as she shook her head. "I'm not poking fun. I hope you'll let me take a look at the essence programming at some point? I'm sure it has a basic framework from the drone dock, since this is absolutely Fabi's design." She pointed at the drone dock segment on the shoulder of the blueprint. "She's like you in the fact that she overcomplicates everything, too."

"Let you have a look at it?" Sal grinned as he gestured at all the boxes. "The gift of a Mythic-grade drone is absolutely a bribe…but it's also a great method to have you make the optimal modules for your drone, that I can steal for Jackal."

Upgrade blinked in surprise before she started to chuckle. "I feel like there's a lesson in here I could be teaching you…but I'm just going to agree." Her shoulders slumped as she gestured at everything around her. "Even though we still need to build it, this is by far the most incredible gift I've ever received. Thank you, Sal."

"Bribe," Sal corrected her with a warm smile. "And you're welcome."

CHAPTER 12: BRIBE

"I have so much coursework materials to write up tonight," Upgrade complained as she carried two of the boxes into one of the private workrooms. "But all I want to do is get started on this!" She groaned as she slid the boxes in her arms onto the table.

"It looks different without the simulation orb. Much spacier," Sal remarked as he jutted his chin over to where the terminal had been a few months ago. "I had guessed this place would go back to the second-years."

Upgrade snorted dismissively as she turned to look at Sal. "They can work on the benches outside." An almost conspiratorial grin crossed her face. "You know, I'm actually kind of relieved… I thought you'd spend all your time in your fancy penthouse workshop with Fabi, instead of slumming it down here with me."

"Hey, maybe I'll just come down to do the finishing essence parts?" Sal teased as he placed the last box and blueprint down on the table. For some reason, Upgrade didn't want him to use Arsenal to transport the materials. Almost like she was scared that they wouldn't come back.

"Come on, you'd miss it down here…and you know it. Those glass cubes are the worst architectural design I've seen in years, and are ridiculously impractical." Upgrade gestured around the cramped private room. "Whereas we have everything you'd want here. No natural light, a door that locks, and a student body that knows better than to knock!"

"Not the most convincing argument." Sal laughed as he sat on the edge of the table. "You could always come up to the private workshop and hang out with us?"

Upgrade waved her hand at him like he was being ridiculous. "And see my own face on those stupid portraits every single time? No thank you." She laughed it off before continuing. "In all honesty, though…the real reason is because it feels far too much like favoritism. If you have lecturers spending nearly all their time up there with a couple of students, the ones down here will have no guidance."

Sal just stared at her for a few seconds. "You know that you literally lived in this workshop with me for the entire first semester, right? I'm pretty sure that every student thinks Forge is our Crafting lecturer."

"Come on, I needed to make sure that the Mythcrafter didn't blow himself up. I think I did a pretty good job of helping you survive," Upgrade insisted as she started to unpack the boxes excitedly.

"You dragged me into a dungeon." Sal corrected her, smiling.

Upgrade tilted her head to the side, wincing. "Which I thought was what you needed at the time…" She glanced up at him with an awkward smile. "It's not like I put you up against a hulker and asked you to punch it to death." Upgrade gave him a playful wink as she continued to lift out all the materials.

Sal chuckled as he watched Upgrade. "I did need it, to be honest. I think it's crazy how far I've come in the last few months; from being terrified of demons, to now learning close-combat martial arts to fight against them. It's kind of wild."

Upgrade looked up abruptly. "That's what I wanted to ask you about!" She tore her attention away from the materials to look at Sal carefully. "It's close combat? What brought this on? Did the gun break or something?"

Sal winced ever so slightly at the mention of the revolver. "I may have sacrificed the revolver to the Arkwright. It needed it for a uniform build I was working on…and let's just say you shouldn't randomly combine blueprints for research purposes."

"But it was such a good weapon!" Upgrade complained in an almost mournful voice. "Like, it had the evolutionary rune and scarlet screen in the barrel. Why did the Arkwright need to eat it?"

Sal grimaced as he offered her a shrug. "It was doing a viability build and needed to break the revolver down. I made a Macclemark suit with the Dominion ability, the weave I created here ages ago. Well, it worked off essence signatures and I was registering the Legendary equivalents of the revolver and its rifle variant."

Upgrade blinked in surprise. "Wait…you're saying that by giving the Arkwright the revolver, it was able to create a summonable essence signature of a rifle?"

Rather than explaining it to her, Sal summoned the Mythic blight jackal arm and opened up Arsenal. "Give me a second." He hopped off the table and walked into the pearly white subspace that had opened up in the center of the room.

The table screeched as Upgrade caught the corner of it. She had moved so fast to the entrance of Arsenal that she nearly took out the table and everything on it. Her face was a mixture of astonishment and horror.

"Is this…a subspace?" she breathed as she immediately recognized how big Arsenal's interior was. "This is insanity, Sal. You could store an entire guild's worth of loot in here!"

"Probably why it's called Arsenal. It's a higher form of Pocket," Sal called over his shoulder as he moved a few boxes around within the white room. It only took him a few moments to find what he was looking for. Rather than taking it out of the metal container it was locked in, Sal lifted the entire thing and brought it out of Arsenal. With a flick of his wrist, the subspace closed, leaving no trace that it had ever existed.

Upgrade did a double and triple take, looking between where Arsenal had just been and to Sal. She stared at him for a few seconds before bolting back to the table and unfurling the blueprint like a woman on a mission. She scanned it for a few seconds before looking up in delight. "THIS HAS ARSENAL!"

"Guessing that's one of the abilities you didn't recognize?" Sal laughed as he opened the container to bring out the failed Mythmark suit. It was the combination of the Ultimate Argento set, Scarlet Strategist set, and the Vendetta Macclemark set, courtesy of the Arkwright and his own lack of parameters. "This is what I was talking about." Sal handed it over to Upgrade, who was still beaming at the prospect of having her own Arsenal.

"And it'll be the same sort of dimensions?" Upgrade asked excitedly as she ignored the offered piece of fabric. It was abundantly clear that all she could think about was Arsenal.

Sal decided it was a good time to reiterate how valuable the drone was when coupled with Arsenal. "Your drone will be able to store items in Arsenal. Like, it'll pick it up from the battlefield and it'll be immediately sent to the subspace."

Despite the fact that he had already told her this, the context of seeing Arsenal and Jackal finally made her realize the potential. It was absolutely worth it, with Upgrade's eyes going wide.

Sal smiled as he offered her the fabric again. "And this is what I sacrificed the revolver for. It's called Strategist's Dominion. The essence signatures are hard-coded into it, and the essence programming is apparently a shit-show."

Upgrade took the garment from him and looked at it with a raised eyebrow. She turned it over in her hands a few times, bringing it up closer to her face to get a better look at it. This went on for a few minutes before she nodded in satisfaction. "Build quality is excellent…and the upgrading path is a little complex but possible." She smiled as she looked up at Sal. "Want me to fix it up for you? I'll need to take it to the lab to see what's going on with the essence programming stuff, but it shouldn't be impossible."

"Fabi made it sound like the amount of work involved would be a nightmare to get it functioning properly," Sal said, to manage expectations.

"I'll be the judge of that." Upgrade smiled. "It's not often I get to show off my skills, and it's a good excuse to keep them sharp. Leave it with me, and I'll let you know the results when I get around to it."

"After the Mythic grade?" Sal laughed.

"After the Mythic grade," Upgrade agreed as she looked at the blueprint fondly. "There won't be a single bit of work done on course materials this evening. I'm half tempted to just launch into it now and pull an all-nighter."

"It would be pretty irresponsible for me to do that on the night before semester two starts." Sal sighed dramatically. "But I guess I could make an exception."

"Ha…no." Upgrade dismissed him with a wave. "I'm not sharing any of the fun assembly stuff with you. You can go and get some beauty sleep while I play with this. I'll call you for the essence components, or whatever parts I think will need a Mythcrafter."

"You're sure?" Sal asked, a little surprised that she didn't want to work together on it.

"Positive." Upgrade smiled brightly. "Oh, and if you need any coffees from Alex, let me know. He's been a little irate lately."

Sal snapped his fingers. He had completely forgotten about his earlier interaction with Anderson Royce. He did have plans for the evening, and it involved the Growth ability and the simulation orb. He moved toward the door and looked back at Upgrade. "Just get some sleep. I don't want my introduction to essence programming tomorrow to be a disaster because you're half-asleep."

Upgrade smiled as she glanced in his direction. "Really glad you signed up for it, by the way. You'll breeze through the foundation stuff, but hopefully there will be some stuff in there that's useful."

"Looking forward to it." Sal returned the smile. "I'll see you tomorrow."

"If I call in sick, you'll know why." Upgrade laughed as she waved him off. "Thanks again for the greatest bribe of all time."

Sal chuckled as he left the private meeting room, making sure to close the door behind him. The place was practically empty, and it was still the afternoon. It took him a few seconds to register that there was still so much of the day left. Having woken up to read the Silverson Arts, then put it into practice, then meeting with Barry, Anderson, and then Upgrade…it felt like it should have been nighttime.

Shrugging off the confusion, Sal headed in the direction of the Savior dorms. He didn't want to push himself to the extreme by going back to the sparring. His body needed a bit of time to recover and he didn't want to risk any injuries. He was going to eventually go back to Craft with Fabi, but that wouldn't be useful until he had the Growth ability figured out.

The simulation orb was the only logical thing that he could work on next, and Sal was excited to get back into the flow of things with it. Sal had initially thought he was dreading working on the elixir machine because it felt like a chore of his own design, but after talking to Anderson Royce, Sal regained a desire to see the project succeed.

Creating a new revenue stream was great, but he was more excited at the prospect of seeing Anderson Royce's face when the royalties started to come in. If he was able to fix up Anders's weave, he might be more inclined to help Sal out in the future; and having someone who could create alchemical goods would be an incredible advantage for his guild.

Sal smiled as he started to ideate on the build for the elixir machine. Even the screw-up from the day before wasn't actually a bad idea. If they had a dedicated botanic garden in the guild, then they would have a massive amount of produce.

"Money would be literally growing on trees." Sal chuckled to himself as he moved through the double doors of the workshop.

CHAPTER 13: GENESIS

Even though Sal was determined to get back to his room, he ended up stopping by the canteen on the Savior floor. It didn't have nearly as much range or options as the main canteen, but there were some pre-packaged meals that looked quite decent. He wasn't sure whether Quest Academy just assumed that the Saviors had expensive tastes, but there were a lot of options he had never really paid any attention to before.

Sal took a little longer than he expected, trying to find something that had meat without all the salads. He ended up having to go for a sandwich option, and just to be on the safe side, he brought two of them with him.

After leaving, Sal noticed that there were more than a few people walking through the hallways of the Savior floor. He guessed that everyone else was still arriving and making the repeat trips for their luggage. Thinking back on it, his stuff had been brought to the room on the day of enrollment…so did they stop offering that for returning students?

Putting it out of his head, he got back to his apartment and made his way up the stairs to the simulation orb. He brought the sandwiches with him and placed them to one side of the terminal. Looking around at the machine, he was relieved to see that it was already powered on and waiting. He had been curious how he'd start it up, but it looked like he didn't need to.

The sandwiches were forgotten the moment Sal's hands touched the weave cables. He had the image of Anderson Royce's weave burned into his head, and he wanted to replicate it as soon as possible. It was an interesting shape for sure, and Sal was curious how it would look without all the knots. In the center was a sort of nucleus that was wound so tight that it looked like it would collapse in on itself if left alone. Sal threaded the weave cable through the small spaces and started to lace it in the pattern he had seen in Anderson.

"Let's see…" Sal breathed as he hastily created the surrounding loop. To put it simply, it was like a tight-knit ball of string in the center, and a singular speedway-like thread that looped in a massive arc around the outside, before plunging into the center of the weave. Sal knew from his previous experience that the outside loop's curvature was designed to speed up the essence. It told him that Anderson likely was able to do bursts of power rather than prolonged sessions with the ability.

A green light emanated around the room, surprising Sal for a moment before a wide smile crossed his face. He had almost forgotten about that particular signifier for success. Rather than waiting around for a report on an ability he already knew about, Sal got started on the second weave with a different amount of thread. He looked at Anderson's weave for a few seconds before getting stuck in the refinement process. That tiny clump of weave needed to be expanded outward to give it more breathing room. There were so many inefficiencies where the threading had interlaced outside of the actual pattern.

Sal couldn't explain how he knew that, but he could just tell that there were many redundancies within the design. It was as if a child had tried to duplicate the work of an artist. Sal could see what the original was supposed to look like, and could identify every single mistake where the weave didn't conform to the correct path.

A smile tugged at Sal's lips as he pulled the clustered thread outward to give it more space. He unraveled a nasty-looking strain where two threads had wound around each other. In that moment, Sal's instincts told him that something was wrong. He pulled his hands back slowly and looked at the weave. This hadn't happened before, as his instincts and everything he had learned usually pointed him in the right direction. It was clearly two threads of a pattern that needed to be unwound.

Sal stared at it for a few more seconds before a sigh escaped him. It was definitely time for a sandwich, and then he'd come back to the weave to see what caused his sudden uncertainty.

The food items in question had turned out to be mediocre at best, and Sal desperately wished he had gone to the main canteen. Flatbread was the key culprit in that thought process. It was his first time trying it, and he wasn't really a fan considering all the moisture in his mouth had evaporated upon trying it.

That said, it gave him enough time to mull over everything and Sal returned to the simulation orb with his tracker equipped. Rather than trying to determine what went wrong, he could see whether Cypher or Judgment had the same reaction.

Sal recreated the scene as he carefully watched with the tracker. He began to interlace the weaves together, wrapping them in a stretched rotation so he could unravel them later. That was when a peculiar thing happened.

His visor signified that the lacing of the threads…was a good thing? The essence load didn't change between the weaves, but the speed of transfer actually increased. Sal had experimented in the past with creating loop patterns for the same effect, trying to artificially create a faster flow of essence. Yet, this way looked like a far more compact method in which essence could transfer faster.

What didn't make sense was how this was an increased efficiency in the eyes of the visor, but all his previous weaves were marked as perfect at a hundred percent. How could there be an additional efficiency that he wasn't aware of?

Sal pulled apart the second sandwich and plucked the meat from inside. It was beef, and a far cry from the beautiful steaks he loved at the main canteen. He chewed on the tough meat as he stared at the weave for a few minutes, wondering how he was going to proceed. All he needed from the machine was the Growth ability, and he had all the tools necessary to bring it to fruition. Yet, he was curious whether there was merit behind this new method…or whether it even was a new method.

Sal decided he'd just finish up the weave in his normal manner, and then see whether there was an improvement that could be made with the interlinking method. Was that what he was going to call it? He could do the ravel method? That sounded better. It was going to be called the *Ravel method*.

With that thought in mind, Sal completed the Growth weave with his normal method. The green flash signified that it was a success, and then, before accepting the victory, Sal went in and started applying the Ravel method. The visor was watching each and every lace, and it turned out that it was only effective on certain strands of essence thread. Sal was also proud of himself because his innate understanding of Skill Master was actually faster than the computational power of his visor. It really helped him understand why Quest was adamant about him learning to use his power without the visor's assistance.

If Sal was to take a guess—and there was actually no need to, because the visor already did the calculation—he would have said that less than ten percent of the overall weave was able to take the new method. The visor chimed in with the actual figure of eleven percent. Yet, Sal was able to see how much more effective it was just from simulating the flow of essence through the entire thing. The nucleus had been extended out into an almost circular mesh of intricate patterns, with the formerly looping ring of essence being condensed down into a raveled chain that encased the nucleus.

Sal tweaked the Growth weave to the point that he was happy with it. When the ends met, Sal took a step back and looked over to the terminal for validation. He was rewarded a few seconds later with a flash of green light.

[Skill Registration: Successful]
[Weave Stability: 100%]
[Category: Invention, Energy Manipulation]
[Name: Genesis]
[Grade: 32]
[Description: Allows user to use refined essence to shape and transform organic matter into its highest possible form.]

Sal stared at the description on the terminal before a humorless chuckle escaped his lips. A part of him had assumed he'd be rusty after a few months, but this was a little ridiculous. His first weave had come out as something incredible. Yet, as surprising as it was, there was another surprise in store for him.

[4 compatible users found]
[Closest Synchro Rate: 97%]

"Four?" Sal was curious who could have managed to get that high for a completely new ability. He genuinely hoped that one of them was going to be Anderson Royce. He tapped the screen to see the profiles that matched the new Genesis ability.

[97% Synchro Rate: Fabrizia Maccles]
[90% Synchro Rate: Elina Lux]
[82% Synchro Rate: Anderson Royce]
[71% Synchro Rate: Jenni Stravos]

Sal let out a sigh of relief as he saw Anderson's name near the bottom of the list. The fact that his synchro rate was so high was great. It meant that he'd be able to get the Genesis ability if he was ever eligible for an implant. That wasn't the key priority, though. Sal now had a weave that could work for the elixir machine. Genesis looked to be the final evolution of the Growth ability, so it would give him more options. It would take a little bit of effort, but he'd now be able to factor Genesis into his designs with Mythcrafter.

Fabi being top of the list made a lot of sense. She had the most number of gates, and a few lifetimes' worth of essence accumulated. She topped most of the essence categories with near perfect scores, so it was only natural that she'd have a high synchro rate with essence-intense weaves. Elina Lux was a new name for him. He recognized her as a Healer class in the Saviors class, but that was all he really knew about her. Jenni Stravos was like a mini version of Prestige, with the same Catalyst ability.

All that mattered was that Anderson was suited to the new Genesis ability. Sal was now able to move on to the next part of the puzzle. Refine.

He was curious about this one as it had a lot of crossover with his own abilities. He wanted to know how good the weave could be when he started playing around with it. That, and the fact that Grant and Quest would be giving him Q-Cred for every new registered and improved ability. He had likely made a few hundred Q-Cred by finding four suitable candidates for Genesis.

Sal wondered whether Quest Academy would end up sponsoring Skill Implants for people who could take on incredible abilities. If he made a really good Healing ability, then maybe the person who could use it would just be given it?

Sal glanced out the massive wall of windows and saw that the sun was still quite high in the sky. He had time, and it was once again a surprise. Was this the power of getting up early after a lot of sleep? No matter how much he promised himself that it wouldn't become a habit, he was only a single all-nighter from falling back into his husk-like state.

It didn't take him long to load in the profile for the Refine weave. He double-checked that he had the right one, because he had absolutely learned his lesson from the time he used Interpolate incorrectly. It had resulted in the Perfect ability, but it also made the simulation orb unusable while it processed the results.

"What are we dealing with..." Sal turned to see one of the strands of cable rise and twist into the pattern for Refine. It was ridiculously complex, and according to the terminal, it was only at grade six.

Smiling to himself, Sal took off the visor and put it down on the table. He wanted to keep improving his instincts with Skill Master, and he could always just use the visor later to verify the work and make some tweaks if it was necessary. He lifted his arms and traced his fingers along the thread to figure out how everything flowed.

Rather than jumping straight into fixing it, he wanted to understand it a little more. There had to be some differentiators for the distinct schools of essence, and the grades. The question was whether Sal would be able to identify them and understand them to the point that he could create weaves without relying on the database of other skills.

He stood there for about ten minutes, just tracing his fingers along the weave and looking at all the different aspects. There were no anomalies that jumped out at him, and although there were sections where he could implement the Ravel method, there was nothing in him that felt it was necessary. He'd be doing it for the sake of doing it.

Sal sighed as he started to work on the weaves. His fingers massaged the threads to conform to the shape he wanted. Nothing revolutionary, just working out the various knots and giving the actual weave itself space to grow. It was very straightforward, almost to the point that Sal was bored with it. Was it because he had just come off the back of making Genesis that he was looking for something a little more interesting?

[Skill Registration: Successful]
[Weave Stability: 100%]
[Category: Invention, Energy Manipulation]
[Name: Refine]
[Grade: 12]

Sal crossed his arms as the green light flashed overhead. He couldn't feasibly rely on a weak Refine ability to match up with Genesis. It would be ridiculously imbalanced. Sal wondered whether he was being snobbish in the pursuit of higher numbers. There was nothing wrong with a low-grade number, and he knew that.

The other aspect was that he could do the same thing he had done with the visor and revolver: design it at a really high level, and then pull back the scope to a more basic state and add an evolutionary rune. Sal thought about it for a while, but wasn't sure how he wanted to proceed.

Picking up his visor, he clipped it over his eye and gave the weave another look. There was no improvement suggestion, which he had already expected. It meant that there was a higher version of Refine that he needed to research or find.

Research "Refine" Ability?

It was a prompt from Cypher. Sal's gaze narrowed on the text that appeared when he kept staring at the weave in front of him. He really didn't have anything to lose. "Yeah, go for it." He accepted the request and let it get to work.

Just as he was about to go downstairs, Sal had a thought. What was the point of just giving Cypher a singular task of a much bigger problem? Nexus connected the Arkwright to the visor, so it had access to MythOS. Although there had been some questionable design choices, they were mostly attributed to negligence on Sal's part. He could give it a wider authorization on what to research.

Sal pulled out his tablet and navigated to the blueprints he had been working on yesterday. He guessed that it would be able to pull the information from it.

Before he gave the instruction, Sal paused and tilted his head to one side. "Would that work?" he asked himself as he activated Mythcrafter. Rather than getting Cypher to look at a drawing, why couldn't he just show it the blueprint as he worked on it with Mythcrafter? The visor had access to both MythOS, Nexus, and even Mythcrafter essence when it was constructed. Maybe it would be able to properly interpret what he was looking for.

Sal started to visualize the elixir machine with Genesis, Refine, and Alchemize. That last one had already been stored in the visor, so it was recalled with ease. To Sal's surprise, the visor flickered a few times as separate windows of information kept appearing in front of him. One had a suitability assessment on the three weaves being used together. Another had started to formulate the build, while another researched the Refine ability.

It was only when the tenth window appeared that Sal felt a chunk of his essence get pulled into the visor. It wasn't a huge amount, but it was still noticeable.

When the fifteenth window appeared in Sal's view, a plethora of conclusions flashed in front of his eye before three more windows appeared to handle the new theories. New windows of information appeared faster than the old ones disappeared. It was a terrifyingly fast multiplicative effect, and Sal barely managed to read through a fifth of it before it would disappear.

When he was on the thirtieth page, Sal realized that he might have made a mistake. Just as he was contemplating canceling the instruction, the windows fell away to reveal Mythcrafter…or a version of it. He had activated the ability so he could manually shift around the design to find something that could work, but the visor had a lot of conclusions to implement first.

Sal watched in fascination as the blueprint for the elixir machine was sketched out with the Mythcrafter ability. The strands being shown weren't the same as the threads he had just worked with. Sal could tell that there was going to be a lot of time before the Mythcrafter design came to fruition, and rather than just being a passenger along for the ride, he went back to the simulation orb to recreate the new weave pattern.

He was intentional as he moved and although there were some choices he wouldn't have personally made, it was still quite serviceable. Sal had to concentrate on keeping Mythcrafter going, along with the pull of essence from his visor…while still operating Skill Master. It was a lot, but he actually found himself smiling at the increased difficulty.

Maybe it was because the build was complex, but Mythcrafter was barely a tenth of the way done with the full design when Sal finished the new thread. It didn't really look like Genesis, Refine, or Alchemize when he looked at it on the screen…but now that he stood in front of it, he could see the Ravel method all over it.

The nucleus was still there, albeit in a much more condensed and intricate pattern. It looked like it now housed far more complexity than before. Five separate rings surrounded the interwoven ball of thread, and all of them looked to be swinging on an invisible axis where they would never touch during rotations. Sal couldn't help but visualize them as a thinner thread than the simulation orb had equipped. He wasn't sure whether that was just his own design brain, or whether Skill Master was telling him that the threads needed to be thinned out.

What he did know for certain was that there was nobody in Quest Academy who would be able to handle a weave of this magnitude. Visually, it was far more complex than anything Sal had encountered before. He continued to tweak the threads as much as he could make sense of, but it was pretty complete as it was.

Sal glanced over his shoulder, waiting for the green light…but it didn't arrive. He waited a few minutes, but there was nothing. Something was off.

Usually, the processing time took a while, but this was the longest he had waited for a light. With Mythcrafter still working with the visor, Sal decided he'd go down and wait on the couch. He'd be able to see the flash of the simulation orb when it happened, and he guessed it wouldn't take too long before he saw either a red or green flash.

It took five more hours before the green light filled the room.

CHAPTER 14: SIMULATION

Sal didn't exactly notice the green light when it happened. He was so absorbed into the Mythcrafter project for the elixir machine that he only caught the tail end of the flash in confusion.

It was a very interesting method of ideation, because although he had assumed Mythcrafter was on autopilot during his work on the weaves, it actually wasn't the case. It was showing him visuals through the visor of what changes he could potentially make to the blueprint. The last number of hours on the couch had been dedicated to trial and error as he dismissed each window individually, testing the theories of Cypher through Mythcrafter.

The success rate was actually not that amazing, but it was fun. Sal got to see why certain build ideas were dismissed, and it was like a learning opportunity. Logically, the suggestions made sense, and although they matched structurally, they were impractical. A key example was the scale of the project that required a garden the size of a small building, partitioning the different plant groups.

The next would have increased elixir production time by days, but kept the build compact. That was a tough one to decide on, because Sal liked how small the build was. It was smaller than the coffee machine they had at home…and the reason it was so small was that it would grow a single alchemical ingredient at a time, in painfully slow stages, to match the essence replenishment of the tiny core that powered it.

Another that was very interesting allowed the user to provide the essence required for the elixir. It would screw up his payment plan, though, and could potentially lead to students suffering from the dregs if it pulled too much from them. He realized through each of these scenarios that there were downsides to all those builds.

Every time he accepted a condition and tested it in the build, it would create additional windows of suggestions based on the new information. It created a cycle of Sal reviewing the build, accepting a new condition, and then half of the already completed research being dismissed and recalculated. It was fun because it hadn't resulted in the Mythcrafter build breaking, not even once. The success rate, which he had thought was low, was because of how many suggestions had to be scrapped.

Sal was enjoying himself quite a bit, so when the green flash happened upstairs, he decided that it could wait awhile. The weave combination that he was using as a basis for the build was the same as the one upstairs with the simulation orb. All he'd learn from going up was what it was called. As for what it could do, the Mythcrafter build was telling him that it could do exactly what he designed it for: taking alchemical ingredients, infusing them with essence to reproduce them, turning them into elixirs with Alchemize and finally using Refine on the result to create something great.

Curiosity did finally win out during a particularly disappointing build suggestion. Sal got to his feet, groaning. His legs had previously felt fine, but now they were like lead. He didn't need to dedicate a single second to figure out why. The

Silverson Arts had taken a toll on him, but the muscle ache wasn't painful…just inconvenient when the simulation orb was upstairs.

With measured steps and a grimace, Sal made his way toward the terminal. He still moved through the suggestion windows on his visor, and he could feel his essence being pulled again. He was now below half of his total reserve, which was a testament to how much power Cypher needed to run the calculations. He could have used the Mythic blight jackal arm to take the brunt of the essence draw, but it wasn't worth the effort considering he'd probably have recuperated most of it the next day.

When Sal crested the top of the stairs, he walked haggardly over to the terminal, sighing.

[Skill Registration: Successful]
[Synchronization: GateMeshError]
[Weave Stability: GateMeshError]
[Category: Invention, Energy Manipulation]
[Name: Contact Administrator]
[Grade: Contact Administrator]
[Description: Contact Administrator]

Sal stared at the words for a few seconds. It certainly managed to wake him up a bit. He didn't even know how to contact Grant in situations like this, nor did he really know what the problem was. Sal had already combined a few weaves before to create new ones, so this shouldn't have been that big of a deal. Was it because he used the Ravel method? It had worked for Genesis, and that was fine. Maybe it was because Cypher had ideated the pattern rather than him?

Taking out his tablet, Sal glanced at it for a few seconds but didn't see any scary messages or anything like that. There was one from Barry with a new composition that he seemed pretty proud of, which Sal rewarded with a thumbs-up icon.

Every time he did something like this, Divinity would send him a message. Yet there was nothing happening. Did that mean it wasn't something revolutionary?

Sal stared at the machine for a few more seconds before he shrugged it off. If Divinity wasn't panicking, then there wasn't anything to panic about. He smiled at the thought that he was using Divinity's freak-outs as a metric for how much he was changing the future.

He paused as he went back downstairs. Rather than just going back to the couch and going through the different Mythcraft designs, Sal decided he'd be the one to send the first message.

Salvatore: Hey, did you get settled in okay? I hear we're meeting for lunch tomorrow.

It wasn't crazily late in the evening, but it took Divinity a few minutes to get back to him. In that time, Sal had hobbled over to his bed. He threw himself onto the mattress and distracted himself by returning to the various windows that Mythcrafter was experimenting with. It was hard to tell whether the result would be made better because of this approach, but Sal was enjoying the activity. If he learned a few things in the process, then it was even better.

Divinity: Just trying that Style martial art manual. It's really difficult, but I'm enjoying it!

Divinity: Please thank your dad again for me. I can already see how it'll help me in the long-term.

Salvatore: You mean you checked the future, or you're just confident it's a good choice?

Divinity: Both. I can see how great it will become, and it's already showing me how to utilize space better. You should really try the sparring room. They've got a crazy setup in here.

He wondered whether Divinity was going to get a higher score than him. She had incredible prowess already when it came to martial arts, but this time she was learning a completely new set of forms, stances, and techniques. He didn't know how long it would take for her to gain mastery of it. Sal was also quite happy to see that she wasn't being stubborn about looking into the future. She had insisted on learning essence control the hard way, but with Style, she was apparently using her powers to speed up the process.

Sal was doing the exact same with the Perfect ability. He was shaving the training down to a fraction of what it should have been.

Salvatore: I was there earlier, and it was great. Did you try the aerial stuff with the platforms?

Divinity: Nah, I'll wait until I can grow a pair of wings.

Salvatore: Probably a good idea. Anyways, just wanted to check in. I'll see you tomorrow.

Divinity: You don't want to ask about the simulation orb error?

That was a surprise. Sal's heart rate quickened at the sudden question from Divinity. Experience had told him that whenever Divinity referenced something he did… it usually had wild results.

Salvatore: Ahh, I thought that not hearing from you was a good sign that nothing bad happened.

Divinity: Nothing to worry about. Apparently, you made a weave made for objects, not people. Grant won't understand it for a few months, so don't go wasting time or energy looking into it. :)

That was a massive relief to Sal. He had wondered whether he had somehow created an entirely new realm of Skill Weaves… but it just turned out to be his innate capability with Mythcrafter and Skill Master. Being able to Craft with specific ability outcomes was something he had discovered with Hannah in his first few days at Quest Academy.

Salvatore: Thank you! I was wondering what happened.

Divinity: See you tomorrow, if I'm able to move my body after this training…

Salvatore: Trust me, I know exactly what you're talking about.

Sal put his tablet on the pillow beside him and stared at the ceiling. Well, he was looking at the blueprints that were projected in front of him that only his eyes could see. His visor seemed to notice he was giving his full attention, because there were more than a dozen new variations waiting for review.

With a chuckle, Sal started to go through them. He paid special attention to the little improvements and the minor concessions he'd need to make when accepting or denying them. It was a wild approach to design that he had never bothered with before. Was it the difference between instinct and process? Sure, a lot of his designs had come to fruition with minimal issues…but he wondered whether there was an advantage to pouring so much time into the design process.

If it managed to go on for a few more days, it would officially overtake the Arkwright in terms of design planning. That was something Sal really didn't want to take on this early into the second semester. If he could find a good solution that matched all his needs, then it would be enough. This thing didn't need to be fancy or something groundbreaking like the Arkwright. It just needed to earn him money, and provide elixirs.

He lay there on the bed for a few hours until he reached the last of the windows. It wasn't a relief to get to the end, but it was satisfying. When he looked at the fully simulated blueprint, Sal was able to see each and every choice he had made clearly. There were very few parts that had been magicked into existence by Mythcrafter reading his intentions. Sal activated the Perfect ability and reviewed the blueprint carefully to see whether there were any tweaks or refinements that could bring it a step further.

There wasn't a single one. With a broad smile crossing his face, Sal saved the blueprint with his visor that had been tracking every single detail of the build. He would need a lot of materials to make it, that was for sure. A compact glasshouse made with plates of essence. Soil sourced directly from a dungeon, and a coffee machine he needed to build from scratch. He caught himself in the lie; it was an elixir machine, but it would definitely be able to make coffees. That was for certain.

Sal didn't bother getting out of bed as he took off his trousers and jacket. He threw them to the side of the bed and pulled the covers over his body. He'd be off to sleep soon, and would be ready for the first day of class. That said, he still had plenty of time to work out a few last details with the visor equipped. First, he asked it for a breakdown of materials and to cross-reference what was available in Arsenal.

When that list appeared, Sal took a chance by asking another question aloud. "Can you do a price estimate on the materials from the Credit Store?"

To Sal's surprise, his tablet illuminated from the pillow beside him. It navigated to the Credit Store and their price list, and a half second later, his visor started doing the work he had assigned it. Each of the materials were listed, with their price in a secondary column. Some pieces were missing, but Cypher estimated that they could be created by combining certain lower-tier materials. The same scenario happened when it came to the glass enclosure. Some of Sal's previous material synthesis results had been listed as viable options. Specifically, the shadow glass he had made from obsidian shards.

Sal guessed that it would make the machine look incredibly sleek, and he was excited for it. He could always get his father to send a shipment over from the Arkwright if he really needed some made.

All those thoughts and more kept Sal's mind busy for the next hour, as he planned the build in meticulous fashion. There was no more guesswork involved, and he had a stable design that looked perfect. It was when he was questioning his visor about the differences of soil in dungeons, and the risk of creating leechers, that he finally fell asleep.

CHAPTER 15: ESPRESSO

Any fears that Sal had regarding the separation of Saviors and first-years had been completely unfounded. It was only when Anthony had sat on one side of him, with Jack on the other, that Sal let out a sigh of relief. First and foremost was that Anthony had stuck it out for the second semester.

"All we're missing is Barry, and we've got the dream team back together," Blathnaid said from the row of seats behind them, surprising him in the best possible way.

"Blathnaid!" Sal practically declared with a laugh. "What do you think of the rooms? I didn't see you over the last few days."

"Arrived late last night…but yeah, they're pretty damn amazing." Her eyes practically sparkled as she looked at Anthony and Jack. "You guys need to come up and hang out with us. There's so much space in the workshop, and I've already checked that I can take guests up, so there should be no issue."

Anthony looked like he was about to decline, but Jack beat him to it with the most enthusiastic agreement ever witnessed. He practically hopped out of his chair and turned to face Blathnaid.

"Seriously?" Jack glanced at Sal to see whether it was true, or whether Blathnaid was playing with him.

Sal just nodded with a smile. "Yeah, it's massive and there's practically nobody in the Crafting spaces. Would be amazing to have you guys up there. I've been Crafting solo for ages, so having some company would be great."

Anthony still looked a little conflicted. It was clear from his expression that he didn't want to be in the way. He distracted himself by pulling out a folio of drawings, which he kept in front of him, but the first page caught Sal's attention.

"Can I see that, Anthony?" Sal pointed at the first one on the pile.

A sheepish smile flickered across Anthony's features before he offered a slight shrug. Sliding out the top page from his folio, he double-checked it before passing it over to Sal. "It's just a concept, but nothing special."

Jack grinned as he leaned over Sal's shoulder to get a look. "No runes? Anthony… you're killing me here." He pretended to be disappointed. "I'll have to find another way to help out."

Blathnaid half stood so she could see it over Sal's shoulder. "That's special," she corrected Anthony as she pointed at it. "Because I could easily follow that as a pattern."

"Blueprint," Sal amended with a smile.

Blathnaid let out a pained groan as she sat back down. Then, as she was seated, she thought better of it and got to her feet. Her hand gripped Anthony's shoulder and gave it a friendly squeeze. "Seriously though, Barry's the bullshitter… that's a proper design you have there."

Anthony waved off the compliment but couldn't keep the smile off his face. "I just thought if I could make something basic, I would be able to use my ability on it to supercharge it." He gave an almost guilty glance at Sal. "I didn't want to keep your Voracious Rapier forever."

Sal blinked. It wasn't like he had forgotten about it, but it was a Rare-grade sword that could send out arcs of essence as attacks. That, combined with Absolute Counter, was the perfect weapon for someone who didn't want to work in close quarters. If it had been of help to Anthony for the tower trial, then it was in the right hands.

"Someone tried to scout him as an Offense class." Jack grinned as he pointed at Anthony, while looking at Sal in disbelief. "Can you believe it?"

Blathnaid leaned forward again with the same grin. "I recall someone being considered a Controller? Or did I hear that wrong?"

This time it was Jack who got all awkward, which elicited a laugh from Anthony. He followed up with a nudge to Sal's elbow. "Mister Runes was invited to a master class with Nemesis. She couldn't understand why he was pretending to be a Support."

"I swear, everyone is becoming a Controller." Sal sighed as he thought of Divinity and Barry. His conversation with Barry had been about the opposite, with him sure that the Body Manipulators would switch to Offense. It led him to wonder what style of combat Jack would have his team doing. He had only ever seen Ioseph using runes as a Defense class. Could they really work as a Controller?

Before he could ask any follow-up questions, Upgrade dragged herself, almost reluctantly, to the podium at the front of the room. In her shaking hand was a coffee, no doubt brewed by Alex. Despite her haggard appearance and energy, there was a bright, genuine smile on her face. Rather than addressing the class, she turned to one side and tapped the lectern. A visual appeared on the massive screens behind her, for the entire class to see.

(EssPro) Essence Programming: Foundational Course

"EssPro." Sal tested the word by saying it aloud. It sounded like *espresso*. Anything that sounded like coffee was good in his books. Although he knew that wouldn't last.

Upgrade looked at the room with a weary sigh, her smile not wavering in the slightest. "Welcome to the foundational course for essence programming. I'll be your host for the day, and I need to start with a disclaimer that many of you will understand."

She pressed both of her hands to the sides of the podium, gripping it as though it were the only thing keeping her upright. Her eyes were filled with mirth as she glanced around the room slowly. "I was Crafting all night." She laughed guiltily and any tension that was in the room evaporated. Pointing at herself, she shook her head. "Seriously, I'm supposed to be setting a good example, and I was up playing with it until just a few minutes ago."

"What are you making?" Blathnaid asked as she raised a hand.

Sal had to do a double take. The quiet and normally shy Blathnaid had just spoken up in a classroom of more than forty people. Was it because she was familiar with Upgrade from all their time working together, or was it a confidence earned in the excursion and tower runs?

Upgrade grinned as she snapped her fingers and pointed at Blathnaid. "I don't want to hype it up too much, but..." She pretended to think about it for a few moments before coming to a decision.

"It's the second-greatest invention of all time," Upgrade continued with an almost teasing air of mystery. The best part was, she didn't look like she was joking. It led to her getting peppered with questions from almost everyone in the room.

Holding up her hands, she shook her head. "Unfortunately, I can't go into too much detail… It's a difficult build, and if I manage to make it happen, it'll be the second time it's ever been done. Just know that I'll be showing it off constantly if it works out. If it doesn't, we're all going to pledge to never bring it up. Deal?"

That relaxed the crowd, and had more than half of the group smiling and chattering to one another about what it could potentially be. Even Jack leaned in to ask whether either Blathnaid or Sal had any clue what was going on.

Blathnaid just shrugged. "If Upgrade's the second to do it, it means she's taking on Doc Ameye…or Sal's been busy during the break."

Anthony's eyes widened as he looked at Sal in disbelief. He knew about the Mythcrafter stuff because Barry had told him, but apparently the context of Sal being able to Craft at a higher level than Upgrade was new information.

Sal put up his hands placatingly. "Hey, I'd be a pretty shit guildmaster if I didn't help my new members." He nodded in the direction of Upgrade, making the implication crystal clear. It was him who made the first Mythic, and Upgrade would be making the second.

Blathnaid's face scrunched as she tried to think of something that had never been created before. With the context of Sal being able to do it, and then Upgrade, it was only a few seconds before the color drained from her face.

Sal thankfully caught her attention before she said what had just occurred to her. He put a finger to his lips and gave her a desperate look to keep it to herself.

It was a war of emotions, but eventually Blathnaid let out a hoarse whisper, as though stifling the excitement had actually hurt her throat. "You made something more than Legendary grade?"

"I'm afraid I can only discuss that with guild members," Sal teased before giving her a slight nod. Upgrade was bound to tell her, and when they went into dungeons together in the future, or on scavenger runs, she'd see Jackal.

"Fuck." Blathnaid slumped back in her chair, laughing. She glanced at Jack's stupefied expression and offered him a shrug. "So much for catching up."

While they had all been talking, Upgrade had successfully calmed the crowd of students. Minor deflections and a few laughs had really eased them after the break. When everything eventually quietened down, she pointed at the screens. "Rather than me asking you all what you think essence programming is, I'll give you the basic rundown. When you have that understanding, then we can move onto brainstorming how it can be applied to what we've learned about Crafting in the first semester."

What is Essence Programming?

The words appeared on the screen, and Upgrade moved around the podium to look at the students. "I don't want to give you useless analogies…yet, so I'll instead use hard examples. You all know the barriers that keep out the demons?"

Everyone nodded.

"Barrier is an ability." Upgrade gestured out the windows, to the walls of blue in the distance. "What is the difference between a Red Barrier and a Blue Barrier?"

Everyone paused. It wasn't a difficult question, but everyone suspected that it was a trap. A tentative hand moved upward, and Sal looked over to see Anderson Royce offering himself as the target for humiliation.

"They're different colors?" Anderson said in the most uncertain voice that Sal had ever heard.

Upgrade's face lit up as she clapped her hands together. "Perfect marks!" She laughed as she looked around the rest of the room. "Now…let's build on that. If those Barriers are the same ability, why are they different colors?"

"Oh," Sal said suddenly, eyes wide. He had never thought of that before.

The question itself had been rhetorical, and Upgrade launched into her explanation. "Essence programming allows you to customize the behaviors of an ability. Those Barriers are able to differentiate between demons and humans, which allows us to move freely between them, but not the demons. If a Red Barrier breaks, all of its protocols kick in, and the surrounding area will get a massive boost of protection. Guilds get notifications, Blue Barriers will turn red, and the air lock will automatically adjust itself to ensure there are no outbreaks."

Upgrade looked around the room with a smile. "But that's a more complicated example. I just wanted to use something you're all very familiar with. Let's look at another example."

Duration
Range
Potency
Cost

The words appeared on the screen, and Upgrade pointed at them. "These are some of the basic principles to understand essence programming. It's not exhaustive, but it's a good start. Let's say that we have a piece of equipment. Give me an example." She pointed at Anthony.

"Voracious Rapier!" he blurted, before apparently realizing that Upgrade likely didn't know anything about the weapon. Anthony shifted and tried to correct himself by saying something like *sword*, but Upgrade had already clapped her hands.

"For everyone who isn't familiar. The Voracious Rapier is a sword with Absolute Counter and Arc Strike. You've likely seen how Rust can fend off any attack? Well, this sword can do the same. Arc Strike is a very good example, though. So, let's break it down."

Anthony calmed down when Upgrade listed out the stats of the weapon. He rifled through the pages of his folio and hastily took notes. Sal wondered why he didn't use his tablet, but it looked like Anthony had his own chaotic process.

Upgrade gestured at the four keywords on the screen. "Arc Strike sends out a wave of essence in a slash-like attack. Let's work our way up from the bottom. How much essence will an Arc Strike cost? Is it being drawn from internal or external essence? Potency. How powerful is the attack? Is it strong enough to take down a hulker, or will it fizzle out against a leecher? Range. How far can you fire an Arc Strike? Does it go too far and lose all its potency? Because that's Duration. How long will it keep its potency and range?"

Anthony looked like he was in heaven. He actually laughed as he took notes, and it would have been unnerving if it wasn't so infectious. Before he even had the final note taken, his hand was in the air.

Upgrade looked at him curiously, as though she was worried she hadn't explained it properly. She pointed at him. "Go on."

"What if you programmed a cap on Absolute Counter? Would you be able to make Arc Strike more powerful by allocating resources to it, from the abilities you don't want to use?" He then held his breath as though the answer was a matter of life and death.

Sal couldn't understand why Anthony was so passionate about this particular aspect, but he found himself curious to know the answer. It seemed unlikely, though. From his own understanding, Abilities were hard-coded into equipment, and there wouldn't really be any way to lock them to the benefit of other abilities. In Sal's mind, the most effective method would be not to Craft the equipment with those abilities in the first place.

Upgrade stared at Anthony before a wide smile pulled at her lips. "Excellent question." She walked over to the podium and raised her hand over the console to move to the next slide. "I have to ask, though…" She looked at Anthony in amusement. "Do you have a Foresight ability?" When she clicked the next slide, the entire class was still left in the dark.

Everyone except Anthony.

CHAPTER 16: NATURAL

"Let's imagine for a moment," Upgrade continued as she pointed at the slide in front of her, "that this is the Voracious Rapier we were just talking about."

Reflective Armor (Ability: Reflect)
- Duration (25%)
- Range (25%)
- Potency (25%)
- Cost (25%)

Upgrade tapped something on the console, until another slide appeared beside the first.

Defensive Armor (Ability: Harden)
- Duration (60%)
- Range (0%)
- Potency (30%)
- Cost (10%)

"Okay, ignore the numbers to the side for a second." Upgrade laughed as she glanced over at Anthony. "I expected a few of you to pick it up quick, but this is a very pleasant surprise." She pointed at the first slide to the left, that showed the Reflective Armor. "To answer Anthony's question, I need to explain to everyone what the question was. So, like I said, this is the Voracious Rapier we're looking at."

Upgrade looked like she was enjoying herself. Fatigued, but smiling. "Let's assume that Reflect is Arc Strike. Harden is Absolute Counter. Both of these abilities are in the same piece of equipment, but Anthony is asking if we could reduce all those numbers to zero for Absolute Counter, to give Arc Strike twice as many resources." Upgrade smiled at Anthony. "And the answer is yes. It absolutely can."

Anthony didn't catch the smile because he was neck-deep in his notes. He was like a man possessed. Sal wondered whether that was how he appeared when he had been frantic in the workshop. Casting a curious glance back at Blathnaid, she seemed to read his mind and gave him an almost worried shake of her head.

Upgrade didn't seem bothered by Anthony's enthusiasm. It had seemingly brought her closer to the beginner course of essence programming rather than the foundational course. That very thought seemed to occur to her as she paused and looked at the group. "Is this stuff too high level, or are you getting the gist of it?"

A few people had questions, like what the numbers meant, and whether the Harden ability could work with just ten percent allocated to it.

"Wonderful question." Upgrade laughed as she practically danced back to the screens. "That example with Harden, which is only at ten percent, could be due to a few factors. Maybe you have a strong essence core embedded into the design? Maybe it works on your own essence supply, and you've got loads to spare.

Maybe the ability doesn't need a huge supply, or maybe you're looking for precise control? There are so many variables!"

Another asked what the optimal range was for each, which just fueled Upgrade even more. "That is part of the fun. You can do all sorts of tests to see what works best! There are ways to even change the nature of the ability itself, just from essence programming. I'd love to go into more detail, but this is just the foundation course, and we have to move onto the part where you all leave."

"What?" one person asked aloud, not sure he heard correctly.

Upgrade smiled as she tapped the screen to show a script of nonsensical terms. "This is what essence programming actually looks like. We could sit here all day and talk about the wonderful ways that it could be executed…but the harsh reality is that you'll need to learn the logic that makes it possible. There are training programs that you can play with that will make it far easier, but you should understand how they work."

With a steady breath, Upgrade continued. "Now for the analogies! You all experienced the maze during the tower trial. Let me use it as an example here." Upgrade's smile turned cautious, as though she were worried that half the room would leave at the sight of the programming language on screen.

"Essence programming is like creating a maze. Every turn is purposeful. You can take the short route or the long route, and depending on the complexity, you can add more and more details. Yet, the more elaborate the maze, the less space you have to build. You'll make compromises, and the other routes will be dead ends. Only by getting to the end will you have made a route. When you program, you need to respect that initial route you made, because if you break it, you break everything. You can add to it over time, and create branches to new exits…but the space available to you will reduce, and you'll have pockets of dead space."

The next slide showed five straight lines. Upgrade pointed at the bottom of them. "This is the entrance to the maze. You walk straight, and you get to the exit. It's reflected in parallel with the others. You'll notice that by going straight, each of the routes are equal and would be around twenty-five percent of capacity. Does that make sense?"

A few people frowned, but the majority nodded. It was an unexpected analogy, but all of them had been in the maze. Sal wondered what sort of examples she gave before the first-years were expected to wage war on a tower.

Upgrade went on to show them a few more slides of how the routes became more elaborate, without cutting off the others. She even had percentages to showcase how much more there was of one route than the other. At the very end, she explained why she was using this particular analogy.

"One of the foundational principles of essence programming is that there are finite resources. You need to understand that you'll make compromises. Grades of abilities, grades of equipment, grades of materials… all of them matter, and they're so far removed from the essence programming side. Sometimes you'll have to work on a piece of gear with no potential. You'll have to undo someone's broken routes or branches. You'll need to recreate a new path throughout all of that, and all that work is before you can then start adding your own refinements. You could make a full career out of fixing other people's mistakes."

Upgrade lifted a single finger in the air. "But where's the fun in that? In this foundational course, we're going to be covering the basics of essence programming. The language, terms, logic… everything you'll need to start making your own stories. But to give you a teaser of what you can someday aspire toward? Here's a bit of test footage, when I was working on a tricky build."

A video appeared on screen of Upgrade wearing a black suit that looked scarily familiar. Sal had seen Fabi wearing it, and the red lightning covering the arms and face were identical. In the scene, Upgrade smiled for the camera and directed it toward a target in a training area. No. There were several targets. With a hand raised lazily, she stretched out her fingers and…shot lightning out in several directions. Each one smashed through the center of a target.

A round of applause echoed through the room as the students tried to parse the video for context and how it related to essence programming. Sal knew exactly what it was, though. It was the Vendetta Macclemark that he had given to Upgrade to fix. When Fabi had used it, there was only a single bolt of lightning…so how had she turned it into several?

"This is a piece of equipment that I'm fixing up for a *student*." She emphasized that last word, and it had an incredible effect. "I was able to take the Ravage ability, and reprogram it. Combining things like Potency and Range will make things like this possible. Imagine it was done with a Healing ability!" The example was certainly enough for the group's imagination to run wild. It was clear that Upgrade was trying to balance the hardship of essence programming with the incredible feats that it was capable of.

Sal, on the other hand, was just amazed that Upgrade had been working on the Mythmark in the middle of the night. He was sure she would have been focused on her Mythic grade…so why was she working on fixing it?

Jack's hand went up, and Upgrade pointed at him to continue.

"Couldn't you just supplement the available…maze space, with runes?" His expression wasn't confusion, but curiosity.

Upgrade shook her head. "I'm not a runes specialist by any measure, but I should probably explain the differences. Essence programming is fluid, and allows you to customize the abilities on a piece of gear. Those hard-coded abilities are called essence signatures. Runes are independent of abilities, but complementary. None of the essence programming principles will carry over to runes. If you try customizing a rune with what you learn in this class, it will break. They're more similar to the hard-coded essence signatures."

"Is that so?" Jack smiled as he nodded at Upgrade.

Upgrade's gaze narrowed for a moment before a smile tugged at her lips. "Let me add a caveat." She gave him all her attention for a few seconds. "I'm unable to find the bridge between runes and essence programming…but I'd be very interested to meet someone who can. Are you up for the task, Mr. Allen?"

Jack's eyes widened at the mention of his surname. It was evident from the shock on his face that he expected to be an unknown entity. His voice wasn't as confident as before, but he gave her a curt nod. "I'll try my best."

"That's more than good enough." Upgrade smiled brightly. "I've seen some of the runes you've made, and I can't make sense of half of them. I hope you'll be taking Nemesis up on that master class offer. She's an incredible Hero."

"I am," Jack said, this time in a more confident tone. He shifted in his seat and leaned forward, as though he were paying even more attention.

Sal couldn't help but smile at the changes happening around him. Any worries he had about Anthony and Jack being left behind had evaporated. It looked like he'd have a few friends in the Essence Programming class, which would be ideal for any projects they had to do together. That said, he expected the crushing reality was going to happen at any moment.

Upgrade smiled as she moved to the next slide. "You've probably already figured out my teaching approach for this class. Show you something cool, an easy concept, get you excited…and then right back to the hard stuff."

Sal sank into his seat as he saw all the symbols that had haunted him for two weeks straight. Symbols wasn't exactly the right term: there were brackets, spacings that made no sense, line indentations, colored text and punctuation that seemed designed to confuse. It was what he had transcribed with his visor back home, when he was making MythOS.

Jack had sat back, and from the sound of her chair, so had Blathnaid. Anthony was the only person in their row to crane forward to get a better look.

Upgrade seemed conflicted. She could see that Anthony was raring to ask a million questions, but the rest of the class looked intimidated. With a nod, almost to herself, she pointed at the screen and started to explain everything, piece by piece. There were two screens. One held the strange script, while the other broke it all down into somewhat understandable pieces.

Sal could only marvel at how Fabi and Upgrade did this, and found it fun. He tried to keep up, and found himself as one of the last ten percent nodding at the explanations. Without the visor, he wasn't a model student, and using it here would have given him an unfair advantage. He wanted to learn this, so he could improve his Crafting. The silver lining seemed to be that Anthony was an essence programming savant. He was completing the code through a series of mumbles, and was predicting Upgrade's words.

Sal recalled how Anthony had expressed an interest in having a tracker. It was something about listening to the Bastion frequencies, which Sal had tried to conceptualize with a Crafting ability but failed. But something about seeing how Anthony was in his element made Sal reconsider. How unstoppable of a force would he be if he had the right tools?

Two hours of class went by. Sal felt them both. It wasn't like the Crafting classes with Upgrade that just flew past. It was, instead, filled with anxiety and tedium. Anxiety from not understanding things as fast as others, and tedium when everything became ridiculously technical. For a foundation-level class, it packed a lot of information into it, and Sal couldn't understand how Fabi thought he'd be fine in the higher level. She clearly overestimated his natural affinity for essence programming.

That said, Sal had taken notes and he had understood all the concepts that Upgrade presented…but it didn't feel natural. There were no fireworks in his brain about what was possible with the information, just a series of building blocks that would never finish a puzzle. He unfortunately needed a lot more, and every new thing presented left him feeling even more ignorant than before.

All it took was a glance to Anthony to see the stark difference in capability. He was *creating* scripts. Different from what Upgrade had shown. Sal continued to look at the page, until he made a decision.

Anthony was getting a visor.

CHAPTER 17: IDEATION

"You still look shell-shocked." Jack laughed as they made their way into the canteen. He had taken a break from peppering Anthony with questions about the essence programming lesson they had just left.

Sal gave him a half-smile. It was frustrating that he had fallen behind the others. There was a lot of studying in his future if he wanted to look at the scripts and understand them. Right now, he could barely differentiate between the functions without confusing himself. Upgrade had done her best to give them the information piece by piece, and there were course materials that would go into painful detail for everything they had covered. Apparently, the first lesson had been just a light introduction…and that thought was sobering.

"He'll pick it up in no time. It's Salvatore," Anthony said without a shred of hesitation. "He'll create something amazing and get fast-tracked to the next class."

Sal blinked in surprise as he looked at Anthony. They had moved into the line, and Sal was excited for his upcoming steak, but what Anthony said had caught him off guard. "You're joking, right?"

This time it was Anthony's turn to look confused. "No? It's really straightforward. If you're able to Craft things like the Voracious Rapier, I can't imagine this stuff is going to be much of a challenge. It's just circuitry and logic."

"Tell you what, if I can't figure this stuff out by the end of the semester…I might just hire you into the guild as our essence programming specialist." Sal chuckled as he thought about it. "I've got no idea if Fabi will actually join, and Upgrade will be there as more of an administrator, I think."

Anthony shook his head as though the thought was ridiculous. "You're going to pick it up. If you don't, I'll help you. No need to talk about guild stuff. I'd be happy to help."

That caught Sal off guard. On one hand, he was loving the new side of Anthony that was quietly confident. But on the other, he wondered whether it was just a case of early-stage competence. They had gone to a single lecture with Upgrade, and Anthony asked the right questions, picked up the logic pretty quickly, and started experimenting. Most had failed, but Upgrade was delighted with his train of thought.

There was no guarantee that Anthony was going to be great at essence programming, but he was the top of the class as it stood. Nobody was even close to him.

Rather than dwelling on it, Sal laughed it off. "I'll hit you up for help if I'm not getting it. I appreciate it, Anthony."

"Are we sitting with Barry and Divinity?" Jack asked suddenly as he pointed across the canteen to where Barry was waving lazily.

"Ah, I said I'd have lunch with them. You guys are more than welcome to join," Sal suggested as he looked around them, making a point to glance at Blathnaid, who was a few steps behind them.

Blathnaid smiled in response.

Anthony seemed a little awkward as he eyed Barry at the far table, and Jack appeared to be excited. He turned to Sal and nudged him. "Think we can find out from Divinity if I end up combining essence programming and runes? It would save a shit ton of time."

Sal shook his head. "That's up to you. Rather than giving her something vague that would take forever to find out, ask her specific questions. That'll help her home in on what you're looking for."

"Do you know how everyone's ability works?" Anthony looked between Sal and where Divinity sat.

Sal was about to laugh and say no, but he thought about the question. When it came to weaves, he knew a good bit about Divinity's, but that was because he had used it and had her guidance. As a Replicator, it was a fair question…and definitely not worth laughing about. Turning to look at Anthony, Sal smiled. "Only the ones I've managed to copy. I usually need a person to tell me how they work, though, since it doesn't come to me naturally."

"That's a shame." Anthony scratched the back of his head. "You could have made a killing with telling people how their abilities work for a bit of Q-Cred."

"I'm pretty sure they know how they work." Sal couldn't suppress the laugh this time. "They got to the second semester, so they obviously know what they're doing. Besides, Lombardi would be out of a job if I ended up doing that."

Anthony shook his head from side to side. "Knowing is only half the battle, though. There are loads of people who have been warned off using their powers because they're unstable. Some got a good bit of control with Skill Registration, but there are others who refuse to use their powers because of the side effects."

"Like who?" Sal asked, genuinely curious as they moved up the line. He wasn't sure what angle Anthony was taking with this.

Anthony looked a little uncomfortable, and quickly changed the topic… to an adjacent topic. "If you could treat essence programming like Skill Weaves, wouldn't that be possible for you? You're a Replicator… before the other thing." It was like he had just sidestepped the last question and continued the conversation from a different branch.

Sal looked at him strangely. It didn't make any sense. Essence programming was specifically for equipment with abilities. Was he talking about re-programming Skill Weaves?

Sensing the confusion, Anthony added more clarification. "That Defense class, Hannah. You made her gauntlets, didn't you?"

Sal nodded, still not understanding where this was going. They were quickly approaching the top of the line, but his hunger could wait. He wanted to know what Anthony was thinking.

"Her ability is Barrier, but it changed completely because of those gauntlets. You were able to make something that fundamentally changed how her ability works. She can create custom barriers when she points her fingers like a gun, and she said she could never do that before." Anthony looked at Sal, and was getting increasingly worried. "You didn't do that with essence programming? I thought you were just being modest or something."

Jack looked between Anthony and Sal in confusion. "Wait, is that true? The equipment is tied to the user's ability, and the equipment is customizable. Wouldn't that make the ability customizable?"

Sal just stared off into space, not sure how to process that information. He didn't understand enough about essence programming to refute it. He hadn't understood how Mythcrafter worked when he made those gauntlets. All he remembered was taking a piece of Hannah's essence and planting it into the gauntlets.

Twisting his neck, Sal looked at the floor as countless thoughts went through his head. He had taken essence from Hannah, and placed it into the gloves. At some point, he had assumed that the only way to recreate an ability was to match up the right materials, like Upgrade had taught him.

"So, if you made something with their ability and you Appraised it," Anthony continued, "you'd be able to tell them everything about how their ability can be used. The guys with no essence reserves would be able to use the item instead."

Sal nodded to himself as he went through the information in his head. He was on autopilot, so much so that he didn't argue when they gave him a side dish of salad with his steak. Jack had thankfully picked up a coffee for him and they went over toward the table where Barry and Divinity were seated. He was still going through the memory of Hannah's gauntlet. It *had* been different. Was it because her ability had a physical manifestation? She was able to create something in front of her, which was what he took. Would that work for people who couldn't manifest their essence? It wasn't likely he could take an explosion from midair for Jenni Stravos.

"Did essence programming break you that much?" Barry laughed as he cupped his chin, elbow resting against the table's surface. Despite his goading, he looked the worst of anyone at the table. If Upgrade had looked fatigued, Barry was a picture of walking death. Dark rings were under his eyes, and he twitched slightly, like his body was ninety-five percent coffee.

"Nope, he's just had his mind blown by Anthony." Divinity smiled at Anthony. "Was it from seeing how good you are at EssPro?"

Anthony glanced awkwardly around the table. The poor man seemed allergic to praise, and he just shook his head before pointing at Jack, as though this were his fault.

Jack held his hands up immediately. "All Anthony, I'm afraid."

Barry glanced at Divinity for context he knew he wouldn't get. With an audible groan, he looked at Anthony. "This isn't the Bastion thing again, is it? The frequencies?"

Anthony looked a little hurt by the comment, but shook his head. "No, it was just a question about how Sal can combine Replication and essence programming. I thought he was already doing it, but I guess I was wrong."

Sal blinked as he focused on the steak in front of him. He had gone through so many profiles in his head, that he had lost count. He couldn't think of many people who could make physical manifestations with their essence. The ones who could, weren't solid. Unless you counted the likes of Anderson and Alex, who infused their essence into something to make it better?

"Oh," Sal whispered almost to himself. That single thought was enough to derail him completely.

Maybe it was his face, but the dawning of that single thought was enough for Divinity to curse and put down her utensils. Sal barely registered that her eyes were white.

"What did he change now?" Barry laughed before he grinned at Anthony. "Well done. I think you accidentally just changed the future...*AND* made her curse."

Anthony looked horrified by the prospect. He clearly had no idea what had just happened, and he wasn't sure who he was supposed to apologize to.

Blathnaid appeared and tapped him on the shoulder, smiling.

"Don't worry about it. Sal does this all the time. You probably just brought him to a conclusion a little faster than usual." Blathnaid chuckled as she sat down with a strange fish-something casserole. Rather than digging in, she waited, looking between Sal and Divinity, as though something interesting was about to happen.

"Man, is this what we've been missing? This is wild," Jack quipped as he looked at Barry for confirmation. "You just say random things to Sal, and then the future changes?"

"Pretty much," Barry agreed as he massaged his eyes with both hands. "Divinity tends to follow his future more than others, so she's pretty much a master of finding out what ripples he's causing."

"Aren't we all changing the future, though?" Anthony asked in confusion. "Thousands of permutations, choices, free will... even this conversation. When she says something, it'll change because we didn't know that information before?" He frowned at the implication.

"Don't go down that route," Barry advised as he pulled his hands away. "I spent a whole week trying to do the same thing, and it's bleak. Just makes you more confused."

"Wait... what the hell?" Divinity laughed as she incredulously looked at Sal, her eyes no longer white. "I expected a doomsday scenario with the look you just had!"

"What was it?" Blathnaid asked the question everyone wanted to know. Divinity's vibe had relaxed most of them, but they were still curious.

Divinity playfully threw her napkin at Sal's face, which he didn't catch.

He smiled awkwardly, knowing he'd been found out.

Divinity turned to everyone else, the smile on her face at risk of turning into a laugh. "He's just figured out how to make a better coffee machine."

Anthony's shoulders slumped, as though he was waiting for something far more dramatic. "Ah, well...that sounds pretty good, I guess."

Divinity just shook her head. "You don't understand. His first idea was going to revolutionize the elixir market."

Anthony's jaw dropped as he looked at Sal with wide eyes. Jack's hand paused as he lifted the soup spoon to his mouth. He stared at Divinity as the soup dribbled back into the bowl, splashing his black uniform in the process. Blathnaid started to crack up, and Barry just gave his trademark grin.

Sal looked at Divinity as a laugh escaped his own lips. It was just a concept in his head, a method to create the machine in a different way. He was scrapping everything Mythcrafter had presented him with, because he felt like this way would work better.

Divinity couldn't help but let out a giggle. "And now he's only gone and made it better…a *lot* better."

CHAPTER 18: BREATHE

Sal barely listened to anything that happened in Professor Lombardi's Skill class. It wasn't because he wasn't interested in the subject matter, but rather that he couldn't think of anything other than the elixir machine project. It was a shame, too, because he had so much he had wanted to ask the professor. The gates that had been a requirement for the first semester had increased again, and Sal guessed that he'd need to ask Divinity or Barry for context around that.

The few snippets he did manage to pick up had been interesting. Rather than a class dedicated to meditation, they had gone through the practicalities of utilizing weaves. It wasn't anywhere near the depth he had personally explored with the simulation orb, and a few of the statements regarding the internal weaves… were incorrect. But Sal didn't feel like it was his place to correct the teacher. It wasn't intentionally misleading, but it still had him conflicted.

Barry seemed to be almost as bored as Sal, and it took a few minutes for Sal to realize that he had actually fallen asleep. The first time he snored, Sal gave him a quick jab with his elbow. Barry had snapped awake and gave Sal a momentary glare before realizing the context of what happened.

"Did anyone notice?" Barry rubbed his eyes wearily. When his hands came down, his gaze darted between the rows of students. No hidden observers, apparently, as he settled back into his chair with his eyes closed. "Wake me again if something interesting happens. I want to get some sleep before Quest's announcement later."

"Not very Savior-like of you," Sal teased as he mimicked Barry's posture in the chair. "Were you seriously in that war room all night, or was it something else keeping you awake?"

Barry shrugged without opening his eyes. "I've been working on the team tactics. It's nothing worth talking about yet, but it's pretty decent so far. I can even run simulations on composition, and it adds a cohesion bonus to the stats. When that happened, it resulted in another all-nighter."

Letting out a sigh, Sal looked at Barry appraisingly. There was no need for him to be locked up in the war room for days, just to run simulations for something that might not even happen. Cohesion bonus did sound interesting. Was it like he had said before, where he got a points bonus when he was teamed up with Sal, but not when he was with Divinity? Did the simulation assume they would naturally learn how to work with each other?

Sal glanced at Lombardi at the front of the room. Things had felt a little off when Lombardi caught sight of him entering the room. Sure, the guy knew that he was in the Doom Society, and he knew about the Mythcrafter thing. But the look of astonishment, mixed with uncertainty… there was only one logical conclusion there, and it was the massive amount of gates Sal had unlocked at the gala. Lombardi had accurately guessed that Sal used a Body Manipulator to unlock his gates in the first semester, but it was apparent that he had zero idea how Sal was able to not only triple his available gates, but to activate most of them.

Because of that, Lombardi's gaze constantly flitted to where Sal was seated. Maybe it was because of that, that Barry hadn't been noticed. Despite being clearly asleep beside him. Lucky bastard.

Sal tried to do one of those grimace-smiles every time Lombardi looked over, and when that got a bit awkward, he looked at the screens to see whether he could parse some of the context about what was happening. There were still students who needed to hit all sixty gates. When that happened, Lombardi promised to teach them all a method on gathering atmospheric essence into their essence gates. It was an adapted form of meditation, and he explained that it was vital for people needing to replenish their essence reserves between battles.

When it became clear that Lombardi wasn't going to be teaching that today, Sal checked out once again to consider the elixir machine. The original concept had been excellent, and the designs from Mythcrafter and Cypher were flawless. But... the stupid idea he had in the canteen had been verified by Divinity. He couldn't help but wonder about how much of a difference there would be.

With his tablet open in front of him, Sal started to mock up a plan of action. He'd need to raid the Credit floor for a shit ton of supplies, but he could afford it. The Argento Auction House would need to send him a shipment or two of materials, and that was worth the wait. If he had his Arkwright spinning up refined materials, that would make everything easier. *Much* easier.

Drawing things out with a stylus, Sal sketched out his plan. Everything before had been about convenience. Since he had made the Arkwright, Sal had focused on having one machine doing the work of three. That approach had been adopted and used for the elixir device...and although it worked, it wasn't the most effective.

Sal's new plan was to create three separate entities, and make them completely independent of one another. He'd create an enclosure to grow the ingredients using Genesis. He'd then create a distillation chamber thing for the Alchemize ability, and finally, he'd create an area that used Refine. It was going to be an assembly line approach rather than trying to get all three of them in one. Using a single ability on a single device would allow it a lot more room for growth, which was why all of them would be working with evolutionary runes.

When the Scarlet Strategist's Visor had combined the lesser abilities into a single, stronger version, Sal realized that he needed the same sort of outcome for the elixir machine. Rather than having three abilities competing with one another in a single device, he wanted to give each ability a proper runway to grow into something more incredible. If he combined that with the best materials possible, then the runway would get even longer. The only issue was the space.

Divinity was a few rows away and he didn't want to message her during class. She'd probably get annoyed with him if it wasn't important. Instead, he ideated on where he could put the machine... or rather, three machines. The new workshop seemed like the smartest decision, but it wasn't exactly the most secure place. How would they feel if he took over an entire wall for one single machine? What would stop students from just plucking the ingredients from the enclosure when he wasn't there?

It would probably be safer for him to create it in his room, or in the Saviors workshop… but that would severely limit the amount of people who would be able to purchase elixirs. Yeah, the Savior class had Q-Cred, but it wasn't about them. He wanted the products to be available to everyone.

Sal thought about it for a few seconds, wondering whether he was overlooking something important. There was plenty of space in his workshop at home…

"The guild!" Sal said suddenly, thankfully with the sense to keep his voice low. It was enough to rouse Barry, who gave him his second glare of death.

"What about it?" Barry sat up properly, seemingly aware that he wasn't going to get much sleep while Sal was buzzing on a new concept.

"I'm thinking of a place I can use for the elixir machine. The guild headquarters seems like the best idea, but it's back in Silver Sanctuary." Sal's excitement kinda died off when he thought about it. If he were to build it there, then they wouldn't be able to sell anything to Quest Academy. "But it probably would be taxed or something if we tried producing out there and sending it here."

Barry shrugged, as though it didn't really need much consideration. "Yeah? Well, make the machine here and sign a contract that it's on loan from your guild. They'll send it back when you graduate. Done."

Sal just stared at Barry for a few seconds. "When did you start learning about contracts?"

Barry propped the side of his face up on his palm and gave Sal a level look. "When I decided to be a very rich Hero. What's your excuse? You were raised in an auction house."

Sal smiled as he considered that. "Think I just got a little excited with the idea for the build, that I wasn't thinking rationally. It could earn a lot of money, this idea." He looked at Barry, meaningfully.

Barry groaned as he sat up straight. "Okay… let's say it makes a lot of money. What do you need from me?"

"I need help with visualizing the space. If I draw it, can you make an illusion in the space so I can plan it out better?" Sal asked, curious whether he was asking too much of his friend.

Barry snorted as he slid back in his chair. "Yeah, that's easy. I thought you were going to ask me to make an illusion of you for the next week so you can hide in the workshop."

Sal's grin grew wider. "Would you have done that for me?"

"Probably. It would have been decent training for me." Barry shrugged as he looked around the room. "Man, this place is bleak. Half of us have already maxed out our gates, and we're being held back like it's some sort of punishment. Guess it's true when they say that society moves at the pace of the slowest member." He frowned as he continued to look around the room. "I'd say we could probably skip the next lecture and see if everything's good by the third."

Sal was conflicted. He didn't like the idea of anyone being left behind, but at the same time, he was a little frustrated that there wasn't anything for them to do in this class. If it was Crafting class, he'd have been able to race ahead with his own designs, but with Skill, there was a clear bottleneck that he needed Lombardi's guidance to pass.

"If it's just the meditation to gather essence, I'll probably skip that one too," Barry muttered almost to himself. "Come back for the good stuff, like how to get more gates after you hit the cap."

"Why would you skip the gathering one? That's what I'm looking forward to the most." Sal laughed at how dismissive Barry was of the concept.

Barry, on the other hand, looked surprised. "Wait… you can't do it? But your essence control is really high?" There was no getting rid of the haggard appearance, but the flicker of shock had given Barry the smallest sliver of vitality.

Sal spread his hands. "I'm not some genius like you with no knots in my weave. Did you learn it from someone?" Of course Barry, of all people, would have found a way to do it. It made sense with how much he used his ability. What was surprising was how convinced he was that Sal already knew how to do it.

"No." Barry shook his head. "You know when you got Vanessa to activate your gates? That's accepting essence from someone. Rather than having someone send their essence into your system, imagine that the entire world is a body of essence and just pull from it. Meditation just lets you see it if you really concentrate."

Sal opened his mouth to explain that he didn't know how to do that, but Barry was already pivoting to a different approach.

"You know the way you can tap into essence cores? It was like the first lesson we did here. You were able to send out some essence to make the connection, and then pull it into yourself?" He looked at Sal to see whether he was following.

Sal nodded as he recalled how easy it was for him to do that. Was it the same with essence absorption?

Barry stared at Sal, as though he had just explained everything in excruciating detail, but when he didn't get a response, he broke it down.

"Imagine the empty air in front of you is an essence core that you need to connect to. Atmospheric essence is everywhere, and you can pull it in from every part of your body. Rather than just a finger touching a core, you can have your entire body acting like a magnet for essence." Barry explained it slowly, so he wouldn't have to repeat himself. "The best method I've come across is through breathing. You pull essence in with each breath, and let it settle within you."

Sal gave the breathing approach a go. It made more sense to start off small with absorbing atmospheric essence through his hands, but Barry's conviction that he'd be able to do it was reassuring. It was quite odd that in a space of a day, Anthony, Jack, and Barry had been fully convinced that he was capable of so much more than reality. With a tentative glance at Barry to see whether he was doing it right, Sal started his attempt at the breathing method.

If he was wearing his visor, he might have been able to track the atmospheric essence in his surroundings. Sal didn't want to use that as a crutch, and tried his best to replicate the sensation of drawing essence into him from a core. With the first inhalation, there was nothing… not even a trace amount of essence.

Sal didn't lose focus, though, as he kept trying to find that connection with an essence source. He didn't try any visualizations, but just tried to capture the slightest hint of essence in his surroundings. Each deep breath ended up calming him and it was easier to stay in a meditative state. On the twentieth inhalation, Sal felt a twinge of essence. Barely a trickle, but it was there. On the next inhalation, that amount doubled.

Barry remained quiet the entire time. All the noises in the classroom faded away from Sal as he kept his focus and moved one step at a time. None of the sensations in his body were important. All desires for Crafting were forgotten. Breathing was everything.

On the fiftieth breath, a steady stream of essence flowed through his body. It was small, but gradual. The most important part of it was how deliberate it was. He knew how he had gotten there, and the small sensations in his body were telling him how to do it again. It was the choice of continuing with the progress, or stopping to see whether he could recreate it at this level.

The answer was easy. Sal continued to breathe.

CHAPTER 19: FORTIFICATION

"Welcome back, Mr. Argento."

Startled, Sal jerked forward, or at least would have… if Professor Lombardi wasn't gripping his shoulder and keeping him in place. It took a few moments of blinking before Sal realized where he was, and what was going on. His breathing exercise had gone a little too well, to the point that he lost all sense of his surroundings.

When the sound of Lombardi's voice had come through, so had the laughter of the entire class around him. Had he made a scene or something? Was he snoring like Barry, or was it something worse?

"Just to catch you up on what's happening." Professor Lombardi let go of Sal's shoulder and used the same hand to gesture at the class. "I was just explaining the dangers of meditation when you're not in a safe environment. We called your name, more than a little loudly… quite a few times! Thank you for being an excellent example for the class."

Sal swallowed as he glanced to his left. Barry sat upright, looking wide-awake and incredibly innocent. It was impossible to tell whether he was maintaining an illusion, or whether Barry was just committed to making him look worse.

Offering a weak smile, Sal bowed his head slightly. "Sorry about that, Professor."

Lombardi tilted his head as he crossed his arms. "Since we started with you as an example, I think it's only fair that we continue to use you until the end of the lesson." His voice became louder as he looked around at the other students in the class. "Mr. Argento here is top of the class right now. Perhaps that's why he feels like there's nothing to learn in this class. He's managed to activate over a hundred and twenty gates. I know of all the methods that students use with Body Manipulators… but splitting gates is practically unfathomable for a first-year."

Lombardi didn't sound annoyed, or even surprised. He was calmly looking at Sal, as though all of this was within his own expectations. That vibe contradicted with everything he had just said. Had someone told him about what happened at the gala? Did Prestige report on his new gates or was Lombardi just guessing from when Sal walked into the class? Either way, Sal was annoyed at himself for giving Lombardi the opportunity to focus on him.

"So, you were working on an absorption technique," Lombardi stated. It wasn't a question. "As I was telling the class, it's a very dangerous method of meditation because you can get lost within yourself and lose all senses. You're very vulnerable in that state. Where did you learn it?"

Considering Barry was acting like the model student, Sal was more than happy to throw him into the line of fire. With a jutting thumb, Sal pointed at him without any hesitation. "He taught me how to do it."

Lombardi frowned as he looked at Barry, who nodded calmly, as though something profound had just been said. With a single finger, Lombardi pointed at Barry's forehead and slowly moved his finger toward Barry. "You've got to be kidding me," he muttered to himself as his finger went straight through the illusion of Barry's forehead. "Illusions while he's asleep?"

The class erupted in laughter, and Lombardi couldn't help but smile himself. It was the unexpectedness of the whole thing, before he seemed to remember he was teaching a class.

"You don't lose grades for not turning up to my class," Lombardi said in exasperation as he looked around the room. "That goes for all of you. If you've opened all your gates, you can skip the first set of classes. We'll be teaching meditation techniques and essence absorption in a month. I want everyone to be on the same page, so that you all have the opportunity to learn from one another. Some of you will excel and race past your peers, but you still can contribute to their success by working together."

Lombardi's attention came back to Sal. "I understand that you've surpassed the group in terms of gates, but I would rather you paid attention when you're in my class. As a Replicator, you stand to learn the most from this module."

Sal frowned as Lombardi turned and moved back toward his podium at the front of the class. Maybe it was because of the laughter, or the eyes that were still watching him. A part of him felt like he had invited this sort of outcome, but something about how Lombardi had shamed him for not paying attention… it didn't sit right with Sal.

"What would you suggest I focus on?" Sal asked to the retreating Lombardi. It sounded arrogant, even as he thought about it, but there wasn't really much point of him being in this class. If all they did was activate gates, and work on essence gathering, he already had both of those achieved. Neither had been taught to him by Lombardi.

Sal thought about the start of class. Lombardi hadn't said anything about skills being a part of evolutionary families, how they could evolve, or how knots were formed. Everything he had been teaching them assumed the formation and development of skills was down to fate. Okay, it wasn't that extreme, but it wasn't far off.

Lombardi raised an eyebrow as he looked back at Sal. "You can either learn the materials I give the class, or you don't attend. It's that simple. If you're here, you focus on the discussions and coursework."

Forcing a smile to his face, Sal gave a polite nod and let the class resume. If the requirement for finishing the class with a top grade was just unlocking the rest of the natural gates, then Sal was already done. The first semester required thirty gates to pass the class; if it was sixty this time, then he'd have it beaten three times over.

Lombardi went back to the lecture, and tried to calm things down. A few people still looked over in Sal and Barry's direction, likely wondering whether Barry was asleep or whether he had just left an illusion in his place. The attention they garnered wasn't lost on Lombardi, who let out a dramatic sigh.

"It wouldn't be right if I was to punish you for excelling at the subject. Accomplishing mastery over the breathing meditative technique is no easy feat, Mr. Argento," Lombardi started as he looked in Sal's direction. "The fact that Mr. Francis was the one to teach you makes me feel like I'm failing as an educator. But, if you two have achieved so much, I think it would be good for us all to collectively learn from your methods. Would you care to share how you've managed to unlock so many gates?"

Sal was a little taken aback by the sudden change in tempo. He had been certain that Lombardi was getting aggravated with him, but just a half second later, he was relaxed and curious. It wasn't a hard question, but he wasn't sure how wise it was to tell the truth.

"I maxed out my gates with Kaizen elixirs," Sal started, which caused a few murmurs to break through the crowd. He could see Whisper Ding frowning, as though it were her first time hearing about the product. Same with Nova.

"And then?" Lombardi pushed for an answer.

"I went to the Hunter Bureau gala." Sal gestured at his chest. "There was a bit of a situation with a student getting a Skill Implant, and there was a lot of Invention essence in the air," Sal continued, finding the exact location that Prestige's cane had pressed against him. "And then Prestige split all sixty of my gates to give me capacity for two hundred and forty."

Lombardi crossed his arms, a frown deepening his brow. "You then blitzed your entire system with more Kaizen?" It was clear there was a massive dosage of disapproval. A lecture on caution was incoming.

Sal didn't care for it, so he added a little more context. "Rochelle created an essence calibration method with her Transference ability. I created a tracker that would calculate the best version of it for myself, then I reconfigured my gates and it resulted in something called essence fortification."

"Fuck off," Lombardi said in utter disbelief, before realizing that he had just blurted it out in front of an entire classroom. He blinked in surprise before lifting his hands in apology. "Ah, I'm sorry for the word choice. That's just… incredibly difficult to believe. Essence fortification isn't as simple as you've made it sound. I'm not trying to discredit you, or make a fool of you. I just need you to understand what it is, and you'll see how unlikely it is."

Sal was more than happy to get a better understanding of it, even if it was going to be explained from a humoring stance.

"Essence fortification is only possible through meticulous amounts of refinement and control. You're essentially creating a stable reserve of refined essence that can naturally replenish itself. Fortification is when you teach a collection of gates how to spin up refined essence, to the point that they produce it without command. It drastically reduces the time needed to activate abilities that require refined essence." Lombardi had started in a lecturing voice, but it had devolved into a sort of emphatic reasoning. Like he was desperately trying to convince Sal that he had somehow got the terminology wrong.

Looking at Lombardi, and knowing that he wanted him to say that it was some form of mistake, made it that much more fun to double down. Sal kept the smile on his face, but this time it wasn't forced. "It's a twenty-five percent fortification, by the way. The calibration wasn't…pleasant. But I felt incredible afterward."

"Is that a lot?" Whisper asked, her eyes glued to Lombardi.

"It's impossible." Lombardi barely hesitated as he looked at Sal disapprovingly. "Ten percent is already incredible, and is usually only ever achieved by

Healers. They use it to speed up their Healing capabilities, but I've never heard of a Replicator doing it."

"So, you're saying that Salvatore is lying?" Lucia was next in the line of questioning, but her words sounded a lot more like a threat than anything else.

Lombardi sighed as he shook his head. "No, I'm not saying that. I've never seen a first-year walk into the second semester with a hundred and eighty active gates. The very notion that he learned a breathing technique *after* he attained essence fortification is frankly ridiculous." He looked over at Sal. "Breathing techniques are the main method of building up toward essence fortification. What do you say to that?"

Sal shrugged. "I already told you how I did it. I'm good at making things, and I needed to get stronger. So, I made something that would help me get stronger. You don't have to believe me if you don't want to." He hadn't intended on it sounding dismissive, yet that's exactly how it was delivered.

"Next class," Lombardi smiled as he gestured at the podium, "I'll bring along someone to verify your essence fortification, how does that sound? We'll all owe you an apology if it turns out to be true. But… if it turns out to be false, I'll be docking you marks for disrupting class time."

Sal laughed and was about to snap back that he didn't care whether he was docked marks. He didn't want an apology at this point; he just didn't want to be doubted. It felt a little ridiculous that he was being penalized for learning, or for answering a question that Lombardi asked. Before he got his chance, Divinity piped up from a few rows behind him.

"It's all true. He has essence fortification. Coach comes in and verifies it next week, and you apologize to Sal." She spoke in a tone that was telling Lombardi to drop the topic.

"How do you know Coach?" Lombardi started the question, but when his gaze fell on Divinity, he realized what had happened. He held her gaze for a few moments before exhaling loudly. "Ah, thank you, Miss Khan. Be that as it may—"

"He gets annoyed with you because you pulled him away from his Skill research when he's so close to a breakthrough," Divinity continued in a stern voice, as though telling Lombardi to let go of his argument. It was a strange reversal of roles.

The room went quiet. It was a standoff between Lombardi and Divinity. It had successfully defused the tension and ire directed at Sal, but it had been replaced with another pairing.

A flickering to Sal's side caught his attention. He turned to see Barry's illusion gone, and the haggard reality was back with a groan. He stretched his arms and glanced at his tablet. "Just in time." He smiled at Sal, who was looking at him in bewilderment.

A bell chimed outside the door, signaling the end of class. It ended with Lombardi staring at Divinity for a few more seconds before he nodded in defeat.

"No demonstrations of the essence fortification are necessary, Mr. Argento. Let's chalk this down to me poking some fun in poor taste. You've achieved an extraordinary amount of growth, and if Miss Khan is to be believed, you've far exceeded what I'll be able to teach you in this class. You're welcome to sit in class with us, but there's no requirement for you to attend for the remainder of the semester. Advanced Skill, or a master class with Coach would be the next stage of development for you." Lombardi smiled warmly as he gestured at the door.

"As for the rest of you. The expectations for this semester have been set. You will need to unlock all sixty of your gates to pass. Top grades will be allocated to those who can replenish all sixty cores in the space of two hours through meditation." Lombardi pointed at the board that displayed the requirements.

"Doesn't Sal have to do the replenishing thing?" Whisper asked in confusion as she looked over at Sal. "To pass, I mean."

Lombardi shook his head with a grin tugging at his lips. "No. I just watched Mr. Argento replenish seventy-two of his gates with a very difficult meditation method. He's more than passed."

CHAPTER 20: STRONGEST

"Oh, so he caught me sleeping?" Barry scratched at the back of his head. A smile was still on his face as he shrugged it off, like it was no big deal. "Shame he didn't say I could skip out of the class, too."

"Were you not awake for that part? He said that you wouldn't need to turn up if you already had all your gates unlocked. They're not going to be doing essence gathering stuff until next month or something," Sal responded as they navigated toward the canteen.

After the class had concluded, Sal wanted to speak with Lombardi to clear the air. He hadn't been a fan of how the professor had picked on him in the class, but he didn't want there to be any animosity, either. Unfortunately, before he could get a chance, he was swamped with students asking him how he had managed to unlock so many gates, how much did Kaizen cost, and could he show them the breathing technique?

Whisper came over just to congratulate him on it. He had expected some animosity, but there was none to be found. She was all smiles and congratulations. The same was true for Nova, who had jokingly told him that she was going to double the number of gates he had, and that he should watch out.

A few people had huddled together to talk about him, not to him. Those groups had a few glares and looks of confusion, but Sal didn't care. He had just secured himself a top grade in a class, and opened up a good amount of free time in the second semester. The real question was what he was going to do instead of Skill class. It almost made the days of vomiting and agony worth it. Almost.

Divinity appeared at their side and pointed at an upward angle that led through one of the large corridor windows. "I'll be going up to the top floor to get some food. Will I save you guys seats at the amphitheater, later?"

"Please," Barry responded as he followed her hand. "I guess I could get some more simulations in before we hear from Quest. The food isn't that bad, either."

Sal glanced in Divinity's direction. "Thanks for speaking up in class, by the way. I'm pretty sure it would have turned into a drawn-out back-and-forth if you hadn't." He smiled appreciatively before exhaling slowly. "I was getting annoyed with how he singled me out."

"Oh, I know." Divinity laughed. "It's good that it happened, though, because this way you'll get to meet Coach. If you can get a master class with him, it'll be way better for you than what Lombardi's teaching."

"That good?" Sal asked in an amused tone. "Because if he starts talking about weaves in the same way as Lombardi, it'll be a very useless master class."

Divinity shrugged, as though she didn't know the answer. "I'm trying my best not to meddle, but that one was important. Coach worked with Grant on building out the database for the simulation orb. You can check with Upgrade—he's the real deal."

Sal blinked in surprise. "Any idea what his ability is?" He was prepared for a spoiler in this instance. If Coach was helpful to Grant with the simulation orb, then there was a good chance he was a Replicator. His Hero name even sounded like someone who helped others with weaves. Would he have the same sort of ability as Skill Master?

Divinity's grin grew wide. She didn't say anything as she switched her attention to Barry. "How are the simulations going? Make friends with anyone?"

Sal absolutely read into that smile. It meant that it was a really interesting ability, or it was something funny. Either way, he was excited to find out what it was. Maybe it was something like Refine, which would be the perfect missing piece of the elixir machine. He already had a weave for it on the database, but if there was a higher form of it in a person, that would be amazing. That said, he already got lucky with Alex and Anders having two of the three weaves he needed; it would be almost unfair if the third one just landed into his lap.

Barry smiled as he shook his head. "I really can't tell if you're genuinely asking or trying to twist the knife? Chris Spectre and Erika Clifton are the only two people who sit in that room. You can imagine that the conversations are riveting. Spectre is a prick, and Erika seems to still be licking her wounds from the break."

"Did something happen to her?" Sal asked out of curiosity.

Barry raised an eyebrow. "She's the mind-reader, not me." He laughed before offering a shrug. "I don't know… it's like a quiet intensity; like she's trying to work out a problem. I'm pretty sure I know what it is, too."

Both Sal and Divinity continued to stare at Barry. They weren't going to give him the satisfaction of asking for an explanation. After a few short seconds of silence, Barry eventually caved.

"Her cohesion score is completely fucked," Barry said, as though it were the most obvious thing in the world. "You'd think that her being able to control her team like puppets would make the score really high… but when she's in the Controller position, her entire team loses a massive number of points. I ran a few simulations with her in position, and with the exception of your team that cleared the tower trials and excursion, she's mid-pack at best."

Divinity laughed. "Well, I'm sure she's already on her way to Quest's office to complain about the programming of it. Surely it's wrong, and Erika is right."

"That's the thing, though," Barry said excitedly. "The data doesn't lie. Erika without her powers is far more compelling as a Controller. The tower score was far higher than the excursion one, and if you put her into an Offense class position, her score skyrockets."

Divinity didn't look convinced. A frown creased her brow as she folded her arms. "Have you considered that she's warping your memories to make you underestimate her?"

Barry barked a laugh as he put his hands up in front of him. "Oh, come on. I haven't been staring into her eyes and inviting her in. You saw me in class, looking all chipper and happy. I usually keep a layered illusion equipped so she wouldn't be able to actually see me."

"Does that even work?" Sal asked in confusion. "I have some pieces of gear that can block out Psionic attacks, so you could just wear one of them?"

"No need." Barry waved his hand dismissively. "Honestly, I know she's a bitch, but there'd be nothing to gain from rooting around in my skull. Besides, I've studied expressions and body language all my life to make better illusions, so I can tell when someone is hyper-fixated on something. Erika is giving all the telltale signs that she's reaching a breaking point."

"All the more reason to have something that protects you!" Divinity insisted a little more harshly than she might have intended. She blinked, catching herself before sighing and shaking her head. "I mean, it's not like you're broadcasting that you're scared of her by wearing it. If that's what you're worried about?"

"Nope, it's nothing like that." Barry smiled as he glanced at Sal, as if to see whether he was on Divinity's side for this one. "Let's just go and get some food, and then we can talk about this, yeah?" He gestured around the corridor as if to prove his point.

Divinity bit her lip and looked at Barry carefully. "Just don't be cocky about all of this. She's still a threat, especially after what she did to Sal during the excursion. You know what rogue Controllers are like. They went after Alastair, Hannah, and Quest. I'm not saying she's Bastion, but she's still dangerous."

Barry sighed as he nodded at Divinity. "Okay, I promise I'll be careful. I'll even take that gear from Sal. Can we drop the topic now?" His tone was pained, like he was far too exhausted for this conversation. Barry glanced at Sal. "Or do you want to double down on how scary she is?"

Sal turned his head and lifted some of his coarse black hair, revealing a small clip. "I've been wearing mine since the break. I made something that shouldn't be public knowledge and needs to be kept secret."

Barry just stared at Sal. "And when were you going to tell me?"

Sal grinned at the sudden shift in energy levels. Barry looked wide-awake now. "That depends. When do you want to run some dungeons with me?"

Barry did a quick glance at Divinity, checking her expression, as though trying to see whether he was being messed with. When there was nothing for him to read on her face, he frowned. "Tomorrow?"

"Can I come?" Divinity asked with a raised hand, like she was in line to be selected for a team.

"Yes," Sal agreed, smiling. "You already know what it is, though… you saw it yourself."

"It's different when it's in a vision. I want to see it for real." Divinity looked to be genuinely excited by the prospect of seeing Jackal in action. "Leecher dungeon, I guess?"

"Prowler or voider would be better," Sal said as he thought of the better materials he could get. "I'll see if I can book something when I'm in the fancy elevator next. I've already signed up to do a scavenger run. You guys are more than welcome to join me for that if you want. It's a good way to get some extra funds, materials, and even Challenge crests."

Sal explained what the scavenger runs were like, and told them about his first time with Darren and Blathnaid in the last semester. As he spoke, they made their way toward the Savior dorms. There was time to kill before they were brought to the amphitheater. Barry was deeply invested when he heard about the hidden caches of loot. Divinity was more interested in the memorabilia that could be found.

By the time they got out of the elevator, Sal had signed both of them up for the same scavenger run. Thankfully, their Savior status gave them priority for joining, despite not having any previous experience.

"I love those portraits," Barry remarked as he eyed Eclipse's battle pose. "Have you registered yours yet?" He looked between Sal and Divinity, asking them both at the same time.

"Absolutely not." Divinity scoffed as she barely gave the portrait a passing glance. "I tried one, and it looked awful, so I deleted it."

Sal shook his head. "Nope, I haven't even looked at it. Did you?"

"Eighteen battle poses uploaded already. Ten of them are with made-up illusions that make me look badass. I tried to emulate Sigils's style from when he was at the gala, and I have another one with Trickster's arm draped around my shoulder. I've been having a lot of fun with it, to be honest." Barry chuckled as he moved in the direction of their small canteen area. "You should absolutely put one in. Register some of your gear so you can get an update of your points in the simulations."

"You seem a little obsessed with that thing," Divinity said, her tone a mix of worry and confusion.

Barry shrugged. "Knowledge is power. We've been given tasks in the past about analyzing one another's strengths and weaknesses. There's no way that they're not going to do that again. I want to know everything about the other Saviors if we're going to be making teams again."

Divinity was about to say something, but then stopped herself. Barry didn't take notice as he walked ahead of them, but Sal shot her a questioning look. Divinity shook her head as though it were nothing.

"And here we are," Barry remarked as he opened the doors of the small canteen. His eyes seemed to light up as he caught sight of another Savior seated with a collection of packed lunches in front of them.

Sal recognized her as Seth's girlfriend. She looked to be deep in thought as she read through each of the packages.

Barry turned to look at Sal as he flung his hand in the direction of Mica. "She's the strongest Savior out of everyone I've looked at."

Mica glanced up from the sandwiches and salads in confusion. Her brow lowered slightly as she assessed each of them in rapid succession. "It's Mica, and I'm not the strongest Savior."

Barry hesitated as he looked from Sal and Divinity to Mica. "I've been running the simulations, and according to it, you're the highest rated Offense in Quest Academy."

Mica sighed as she pushed two of the sandwiches away, and pulled one of them closer. She then pulled two salads in her direction before getting to her feet.

Sal watched as she picked up the unselected meals and replaced them back in the refrigeration tray. It wasn't like she was actively ignoring them, or that she was being rude. She just didn't look bothered by the conversation. Barry could have chosen a better method for introduction, but it was Divinity who came through in the end.

"Who do you believe to be the strongest?" Divinity smiled as she walked forward with an extended hand. "I'm Divinity Khan, it's nice to meet you."

"Mica Egan." Mica responded with a smile that lit up her entire face. Piercing blue eyes bore into Divinity for a few seconds, as though weighing up the question. After a moment, she let go of Divinity's hand and moved back to her seat. "Strength is subjective. If you want adaptability, then Chris Spectre is the best. If you want the best strategy, then it's Erika Clifton. If you want fastest, you get Maxine Volta. You get the idea?"

Divinity nodded as though transfixed. Sal couldn't blame her; Mica was not the standard Offense class who ran in and broke things.

Mica looked past Divinity to where Barry stood. "The best subversion tactics, Barry Francis. The best gear, Salvatore Argento." Her gaze went back to Divinity, focusing on her like she was the only one in existence. "And if you want to have the best chance of a perfect outcome, Divinity Khan."

Barry sat down at the far end of the table and smiled in Mica's direction. "Excellent analysis. Can I ask what you think you're best at?"

Mica returned the smile. "That's a better question." She laughed in an unexpectedly gentle and melodic note. "I'm the best at killing everything."

CHAPTER 21: PREDATOR

Sal was underwhelmed with the food options available, and ended up having a chicken salad. Rochelle would have been proud of him for eating vegetables, but that fact alone wasn't worth it. Stabbing his fork through the greenery, he distracted himself by listening to the conversation between Mica and Divinity.

"It's going to be our first scavenger run, so I'm a little excited," Divinity explained, smiling brightly. "Sal was telling us about the one he went on in the first semester, and it sounded like a lot of fun."

Maybe it was the infectious nature of Divinity's positivity, but Mica was nodding along with her. It had been quite the bombshell when she proclaimed she was the greatest at killing, but something about the quiet intensity she gave off told Sal it wasn't a lie.

Mica took a few moments to finish her food before weighing in. "Are you going on any other outings? I've been dragging Seth on a few of them, but it's going to be a while before he's able to take care of himself. There's a Paradox one that's very Controller-focused." She left the thought in the air, as though weighing up whether she should continue the line of thought.

Barry caught the apprehension immediately. "Divinity and I could go on that one. Is Seth a Controller?" He had been unusually energetic since they started talking to Mica. Any casual observer would put it down to infatuation, but Barry's interest was more likely aimed at her statistical capabilities.

Mica nodded, smiling. "I'd feel a lot better if he was able to go on outings with competent people. His abilities are getting stronger, but it's just not fast enough."

"He managed to get into the Savior class, though?" Divinity countered. It was no mean feat to get to the top of the leaderboards, and it was nigh-impossible to fail upward that successfully.

"I dragged him up the ranks, kicking and screaming throughout the first semester," Mica corrected with a musical laugh. "I ran so many dungeons with him, that our points were impossible to ignore. It helped that we had the same team for the excursion and the tower."

Barry's brow furrowed. "It can't be that simple, though. Gallant would have gotten into the Saviors class with just dungeon clearances." He glanced up at Mica and momentarily panicked, bringing his hands up. "I mean, I'm not calling you a liar…it's just hard to believe."

Mica held Barry's gaze for a few moments. "I have four confirmed commander kills. Ranked in the top thousand in the Hunter Bureau, and getting actively scouted by close to forty guilds. In addition to that, I'm a Platinum token holder with the Reclamation guilds worth talking to."

"For context," Sal said to Barry, "I'm only a Silver token holder with the Reavers Guild for Appraisal." He just wanted to make it clear how impressive a Platinum token was. Being honest, he didn't know they went above Gold. The benefits being thrown at Mica must have been insane.

"Villa is fun." Mica aimed a smile at Sal. "If it wasn't for Fierce, I'd likely have considered them as an actual contender. Bringing a guild up from Tier 2 to Tier 1 would be a lot of fun, I think."

Divinity blinked as she glanced between Sal and Mica. "What about bringing a guild up from Tier 10?"

"A Trainee Guild?" Mica scoffed as she looked at Divinity in disbelief. "No way. They wouldn't be able to afford me. Even if they did have the budget, it would be a shit-show for a few years. Not enough ranking to secure delving rights, no budget for multiple teams, and you'd end up having to deal with shitty advisors who aren't good enough to bring their own guilds to Tier 1."

Mica seemed like she desperately wanted Divinity to understand how ridiculous the statement had been. There was no mocking expression, just emphatic resolve. "The established guilds are the right call, even if you have to play the politics of them. They have programs in place to help fast-track you to officer positions. If you get your own strike team as an Offense, you're practically guaranteed all the best spoils."

She turned to look at Sal, as though it was aimed at him. "Materials for the best gear are earmarked by the strike teams. They get the majority of the proceeds from selling the loot, but the best guilds will have an internal Crafting Department. I heard you're starting a guild, but you should give it up and just join one of the Tier 1's. You'll never manage to get the stuff you'll need to Craft, and you'll likely bankrupt yourself trying."

Sal shrugged. It wasn't his plan to try to convince Mica to join his guild. He had no idea what her weave was, or whether her stats were the real deal. One point in her favor was that she didn't look down on the Supports and seemed to understand the value of internal Crafting departments. At the end of the day, Anna Sakura was going to be joining. If Gallant ended up retaining enough sanity to be useful to the guild, then that would give them two excellent Offense class prospects straightaway. Then Barry as a Controller, Rochelle as a Healer, with himself and Blathnaid as Supports. Hell, if he could get Hannah on his side, that would give them the perfect roster. O'Brien could shift between roles, so they'd have plenty of people to rotate through the teams.

"Don't worry, we'll be fine," Sal said confidently and smiled at Mica. "I don't blame you for not wanting to join an unknown entity. If you have the best chances at a top-ranked guild, you should absolutely go for it."

Mica looked a little surprised until a smile crept onto her features. "How are you so sure that you'll manage to get through the early stages? Climbing tiers as a Support guild is going to be expensive…and getting members is going to be even harder."

"I've got a lot of administrative work to do for us to get started, but after that, it'll be smooth sailing, I'm sure," Sal replied, laughing as he glanced at Divinity. "Otherwise, I'd be hearing about how screwed I am."

Divinity gave him a playful glare as she tapped the table. "It's true, though. A lot of the visions for the future have the guild doing well. But it's no reason to be complacent." She aimed that last part at Sal before smiling at Mica. "I was just curious what you'd say."

Mica rested her chin on her palm as she looked between Divinity and Sal for a few moments. "I won't be making any decisions for a few more semesters…so, how about you show me what you've got for the next couple of years and then you can ask me again."

"There'll be a waiting list." Barry laughed. "I can guarantee you that much."

Mica's eyes widened as she glanced at Barry. "I understand you're trying to hype up your friend, but don't you think that's a little excessive?"

Barry shrugged, as though it wasn't a big deal. "Where would you rank yourself against Anna Sakura?"

Mica looked to be caught a little off guard, but she considered the question, frowning. "I don't see how that has anything to do with it…but she's incredible. Her ability to nullify essence takes away pretty much all my strengths; coupled with her having the master classes in Assassination…she'd win. Pretty much every time."

With a solemn nod, Barry pursed his lips. "Well, she's already joined his guild. I wonder what she knows that you don't." He smiled warmly at Mica before getting to his feet, turning his attention back toward Sal and Divinity. "I've got a few more simulations to run. Might try the guild roster to see how it crushes the competition. Really curious how Gallant works with Sakura and O'Brien."

Mica's jaw dropped as she stared at Barry in horror. "Wait. Gallant is joining?" She took a few seconds to register the other parts of the sentence. "Sakura and O'Brien, too?" Her expression was completely different, and for the first time since they had interacted with her, she actually looked lost.

"Didn't you hear?" Barry asked in feigned confusion. He was about to say something else, but Sal interjected.

"Don't listen to him," Sal said to Mica in a warm tone, and smiled as he waved Barry away. "I've got a lot of work to do to get the guild deserving of the roster we've lined up. Right now, there's nothing I could offer you to sweeten the deal…and, being perfectly honest, I've got no idea if you'd be a fit for us."

Mica blinked in surprise. "Did I just get rejected from applying?"

Laughing and shaking his head, Sal put up his hands defensively. "Again, there's no application process right now. It's just been a few people I've wanted to work with, and I need to get things set up before I can talk more confidently about recruitment."

"I'm telling you, Sal. She's a good bet. Her stats are incredible," Barry insisted as he gestured at her emphatically. "You'll be kicking yourself when you see her fight."

Sal sighed and gave Barry a pointed look. "Leave it alone for now. We're in no position to compete against the Tier 1's."

"Bullshit," Barry muttered as he sat down. His meaning was abundantly clear. If Sal made something for Mica, then he'd be able to secure her as an asset for the guild. It was how he managed to get Sakura, and to a lesser extent, even Gallant.

It still wasn't clear whether Gallant was going to end up joining the guild, or whether Sal even wanted him. The tower exercise had been a bit of an eye-opener to how Gallant could be a real liability. But, he was still the former Super Rookie, and if he got his abilities back, there was a good chance he'd be an incredible addition to the guild.

"How did you get Sakura?" Mica leaned forward, her piercing blue eyes locked onto Sal.

"Gave her some gear," Sal replied, not really wanting to go into too much detail. This whole situation was foisted on him by Barry, and he wasn't really prepared to get into a drawn-out negotiation. He knew next to nothing about Mica, and negotiating from a place of ignorance would just spell disaster.

Barry looked at Sal strangely. As if asking why he was purposefully sabotaging the conversation. It looked like he was dead set on not allowing the golden goose to go to another guild. He let out an exasperated sigh and turned in his chair to look at Mica. "It had evolutionary runes, so it would grow alongside the wearer. He's given me Epic-grade Vengeful Vambraces that give me a lot more firepower. Divinity got an Epic-grade crown that amplifies her abilities; it also has an evolutionary rune. Upgrade is likely joining, too. One of those useless advisors. She made a Legendary-grade coat with Blathnaid, who is also joining the guild."

"Rochelle's coat," Mica stated simply. It wasn't a question, as she was clearly aware of it. Her gaze narrowed as she looked at Sal. "A Replicator who uses Appraisal… Are you using your family's money at Quest Academy to secure these things?"

"Nope. I replicated a Crafting ability," Sal answered, smiling. "If you'd like, we can take Barry out of here and we can stop the two-way interrogation?"

Mica shook her head. "No need. I like this. So, you're able to Craft up to what grade? Where is your money coming from if you started at the same time as everyone else?"

"Ah, I think you need to answer a few things about yourself first. Since we're not negotiating here, and just getting to know each other… shouldn't you tell us something about your ability?" Sal countered as he looked at her carefully, wondering which way she'd react.

"Mimicry category," Mica answered instantly, her gaze unflinching. "Although some might call it closer to Body Manipulation or Replication."

Sal had a thousand questions. He hadn't seen many Mimicry abilities with the simulation orb, and was curious how they worked. As far as he was aware, they allowed the person to take on aspects of animals. So how did it get confused with Replication?

Mica smiled as she saw the gears working in Sal's head. "I'll tell you more, but what grade can you Craft?"

"I've made Legendary," Sal answered without glancing at either Divinity or Barry. They knew better than to tell a stranger about Mythcrafter. Well, Divinity would know better.

It was definitely impressive enough to get a reaction from Mica. She sat back in her chair, her eyes not leaving Sal. A wide smile crossed her face. "Okay…that's pretty damn good. But you'll still need some pretty high-end materials to make stuff. You've been selling stuff in the family auction?"

"I made a Legendary sniper rifle for the Reavers Guild. You can ask Vanessa on the Credit floor about it," Sal responded, still trying to figure out why she was fixated on the money aspect.

Mica nodded. "So, you didn't make an outfit called the Wraith Walker? There's one of the Saviors who claimed to get a suit of gear that was made at Quest Academy, but it pretty much popped out of nowhere and nobody is taking credit for it. She skyrocketed up the ranks so much that I needed to shift up a few gears to keep my place. Seth barely scraped through because of her."

Keeping a poker face was difficult. Sal had made it during the break, and they auctioned it off to a guy who had taken it for his daughter. Sal had completely put it out of his mind, but now it was coming back to bite him in the ass. As far as he was concerned, he had made it, and sold it outside the academy. All wrongdoing was on the part of the father and daughter. If it contributed to her becoming a Savior, then that was likely going to be a problem.

"Got it." Mica laughed. "So, that was you. It's impressive enough to bring someone decidedly average up to the top spots..." She looked like she was deep in thought, and Sal left her to it.

While Mica was left to mull over what she was hearing, Sal gave Barry a pointed look. He offered a guilty shrug, but there was no remorse on his face. As if to say, *I'd do it again.*

They continued to eat their meals, with Sal fishing through the salad to find the pieces of chicken that were hiding. It took Mica a few more moments to rejoin the conversation. She was clearly introspective, which was yet another point against her being a typical Offense class.

"It was nice meeting you all. I've got a lot to think about, but hopefully we can team up in the future and get to know each other better," Mica said finally as she got to her feet.

"Would you mind telling me what your ability is?" Sal asked suddenly. "I've been trying to figure out what sort of Mimicry ability could be confused with Replication."

Mica smiled as she threw out the trash and placed her empty plate in the stack of trays. "It's called Predator. I'm able to mimic the physiology of the strongest demon I kill."

Sal's jaw dropped. He hadn't heard of anything like that before. Mimicry that was designed to take on the aspects of demons? It didn't answer his original question, and Mica seemed happy to explain.

"How is it like Replication? Well, in addition to the physiological improvements, I also mimic the essence structure of my strongest kill. I permanently get whatever abilities they had, only replacing them when I kill something stronger." Mica seemed to be enjoying herself, and it might have been because she caught sight of Barry.

His normal air of composure was gone. Barry's face paled as he looked at Mica in an entirely new light. "Wait, you said you killed a commander variant..."

Mica grinned as she got to the door. "See you guys around."

CHAPTER 22: REMORSE

Sal walked straight into his dorm and made a beeline toward the simulation orb, stopping only to put on his visor. He had agreed to meet up with Barry and Divinity in the amphitheater, and Divinity countered with an offer to knock on his door when it was time to go. Apparently, she knew he was going to go into a flow state and didn't want him missing Quest's announcements for the start of the semester.

All he could think about was the Predator ability and what it looked like as a weave. The moment he heard about what Mica could do, he compared it to the Subsume ability. Where Subsume was the clear victor over a long time period, with incremental gains to his base stats, the Predator ability skipped all of that progress and just overwrote everything when a stronger opponent was killed.

Subsume would allow him to take the abilities of his defeated opponents, but there was nothing about taking on the physiology of the opponent. Predator seemed to be an evolution of another weave, or it was just a ridiculously powerful base ability. Sal was excited to find out more about it and get into the weave research. He tapped the dashboard of the database and input the title of Mica's ability, and wondered whether it would be one of the registered abilities.

The simulation orb pulsated as it booted up, but Sal ignored it as he stared at the terminal screen. It was loading, and the wait was painful. While he stood around for it to get its act together, he turned to the simulation orb and unraveled the weave he had previously made for the Genesis ability. It was already saved in his tracker, so he wouldn't need it again.

Glancing back to the terminal, he was rewarded with a blank text bar. His previous query had vanished. With a groan, he carefully re-typed *Predator*. Just one instance of using the wrong ability had made him cautious. It started searching through the database, and thankfully emerged with a description that pretty much matched Mica's explanation. It was grade nineteen, which was a nice surprise, and the only registered Hero with it was Michaela Egan. There were no other synchro rates, which was interesting.

With a smile appearing on his face, Sal turned to the cables as they formed a version of the Predator ability. Maybe it was the equivalent of Subsume, but for people, rather than equipment? Sal walked around the simulated weave with a curious expression, trying to look for any sort of natural progression. If he could figure out how it was made, he'd be able to deconstruct it and possibly discover a few more abilities in the process.

First, though, he needed to fix it up. The weave itself was in great condition, with little to no knots visible. If he had seen this a few months ago, he likely would have assumed that it was as good as it was ever going to be, but now he had the visor and a lot more experience. His Ravel method was going to come in handy to create a more efficient essence flow.

"We can think about it later," Sal muttered to himself, as he was reminded that the announcement was happening in just a couple of hours. He couldn't afford to zone out.

Pulling at the weaves, Sal started to optimize it as best he could. It was likely his imagination, but the way the weave darted up and down in jagged triangles made him think of a set of fangs. It was the first weave appearance that actually looked like the ability it represented. It barely got a smile out of him as he smoothed out the harsh edges. Having sharp angles in the weave would cut off essence flow and reduce efficiency, so he curved each of them with the Ravel method at the bottom. It was instinct rather than science. If he could somehow manage to speed up the essence circulation through the weave at the base of the curve, it would likely provide more output.

The tracker didn't seem to agree with him. It hadn't identified it as a solution, and kept trying to calculate with new parameters. It was an excellent reminder that he shouldn't use the tracker until he was done with the weave itself. The simulation orb was the same, and would have been flashing red constantly until he was finished with the weave. Neither machine had any patience for the process in between weaves.

Sal was enjoying himself as he created tighter sets of weaves. He had no idea whether removing the triangles would screw things up, but he guessed that it would be some form of improvement. There was no new weave being added to it, so all he could hope for was a higher grade. Then again, Growth had turned into Genesis with the additional raveling, so maybe Predator would have a similar outcome?

More than a few times, he needed to pull apart a weave cluster to get into the interior. It slowed things down, but he didn't want to just assume that it was efficient because it was compact. His instincts turned out to be correct, because each of his improvements seemed to have a knock-on effect that screwed up another part of the weave. Sal continued to meticulously break it down and rebuild it from scratch.

Normally, a weave would only take him a few minutes to fix up, but something about this one kept him on his toes. Where all the previous weaves had felt static, this one was almost reactive. There was so much thread involved, and he wondered how many gates Mica had managed to open to even fuel this thing. That thought made him curious whether he should have conducted this on the torso machine instead of just the cables, but it was too late to restart. He was all-in on this process, and he wanted to see it through to completion.

A knocking at his door broke him out of his flow, and Sal scowled as he glanced down the stairs. There was no way that it was time for the announcement. Just to be sure, he pulled off his visor and took his tablet out of his pocket. He'd only been working for an hour, so there was still time. Going down the stairs, he wondered whether it was a delivery or something… or whether Barry was coming with a simulation update. Neither of them had sent him a message, though. Knocking at his door would have been the last resort. Would it have been Mica? Did she suddenly decide she wanted to join his guild?

None of his theories made any sense, so Sal was confused when he opened the door to reveal the last person he would have expected.

"Hey, Sal. Can we talk?" Hannah asked with an uneasy smile. Her blonde hair had been shaved on one side, giving her a warrior-like look. She was dressed in their standard uniform with blue shoulders, denoting her role as Defense class.

Her hands were at her sides, with fists clenching and unclenching. It wasn't in a threatening manner, but rather an action of trepidation.

"Yeah… come on in," Sal answered, still a little shocked at her sudden appearance. He stood to one side and gestured into the room.

Hannah made her way inside and stood awkwardly in front of the couch. She waited for Sal to come back into the room. "Very nice place. Looks like you've got a decent workshop, too."

"I'm sorry I didn't talk to you since… you know." Sal gestured for her to take a seat on the couch.

"Since I was a raging bitch?" Hannah answered for him as she plopped onto the couch, sighing. "I came to apologize. Before we start working in the same classes, I wanted to clear the air and make sure things are okay with us."

"I don't think there is an us." Sal interlocked his fingers in front of him. He looked at Hannah carefully. "I know you were under mind control, but the things you said were your real feelings, weren't they?"

Hannah paused before speaking. She sat up properly and took a steadying breath, tilting her head to one side and grimacing. "Yes. They were my feelings." She glanced at Sal for a second before finding a spot across the room to stare at instead. "That mind control ability made all my fears a reality, and I lashed out… mostly from insecurities about myself. I was so sure you were somehow undermining or using me. That you didn't respect me. Little things like you getting me coffee had turned into you pitying me. I cannot stand being pitied! It was a vicious cycle of fear, uncertainty, and doubt."

When Sal didn't respond, she continued. "They were my real feelings, but… they were wrong." She took another breath and looked at Sal, smiling. "I expected the worst after everything happened. Even after my mind cleared up, the remnants of the damage were still there. I was convinced that the rumors would start up… that Hannah is a psycho ex, or she broke Sal's heart, or something that made me the villain, and you the sympathetic victim. I accused you of some horrible shit, calling you a cheater and saying you'd never be a Hero. You had every reason to tear me down."

She leaned back against the couch and rubbed her hands over her face. "But none of that happened. Not a single word from anyone. And Divinity, who I'm pretty sure I accused of trying to steal you from me, asked me to be on her team?" Hannah's voice cracked a little as her pitch went higher. Her fists clenched again as she shook her head. "And then, the one I accuse of not taking Quest Academy seriously… the one I said would only ever stand behind Heroes and never among them… fucking punches a hulker to death!"

Hannah laughed as she wiped a tear from her eye. "That reel was awesome. You were incredible, and I was screaming in that crowd louder than anyone when you got the top Savior spot. I came here to apologize to you, for everything that happened. Victoria said you'd need some time, and that I should talk to you when my head was in the right space."

Sal felt guilty for feeling relieved. Hannah was crying in his room and apologizing to him, and he had left her to wallow in that guilt for the last few months. He could have put her mind at ease a long time ago, but she was forced to be the mature one who came to him.

"I came here to give you these back." Hannah pulled the Barrier gauntlets from her hands and placed them on the couch cushion beside her. "You made them for me, and I used them to get into the Saviors. Yet another point of me being a selfish bitch, when I wouldn't have managed it without your help."

"I'm sorry," Sal finally said as he looked at her. "I should have spoken to you after it all happened. I could blame the excursion or the tower, but really… I just didn't want more conflict. I didn't want to make you feel worse, and I selfishly didn't want to feel more pain." It was easier to admit than he thought it would be. Sal didn't want to make Hannah feel bad, but he felt like she deserved honesty.

"Also, I won't take them back." Sal gestured at the gauntlets. "I made them for you, and it was the first time I ever used Mythcrafter. You were the first person I ever told about it; before I truly realized it needed to be a secret. You could have told everyone that I cheated my way to an amazing ability, and hell, I could have been kidnapped or locked up by one of the guilds because of it."

He smiled as he looked at Hannah. "They're yours, so please don't ever try to give them back. If you want them upgraded, that'll be different, and I'll accept Q-Cred or materials."

Hannah looked at the gloves and was about to speak when Sal interrupted her.

"Put them back on, or I won't accept your apology. You're one of the top Defense classes, and if I'm ever building a team, I'll want to know you can keep me safe," Sal said resolutely with a gentle smile.

"You'd have me on your team?" Hannah asked in surprise. "Even after everything?"

Sal laughed as he thought about it. "That depends. Would you let a few attacks through so I'd learn a lesson the hard way?"

Hannah's face drained of color at the mere thought of letting that happen. "Who the fuck would do something like that?! Nothing would get near you if I was your Defense."

"Who indeed." Sal chuckled as he shook his head. "So… what way would you like to do this? Do we pretend nothing happened, and try to be friends again?"

Hannah shook her head, smiling wistfully. "No, I don't think either of us would be able to manage that one. You said it yourself, we don't know anything about each other. We met up, we fucked and said goodbyes… and repeated. We're going to have to start over a little differently this time."

Sal winced as he was reminded of his retort back then. "Not my finest choice of words."

Hannah laughed as she extended her hand. "I'm Hannah Unruh. I grew up on the Darwin Cruises, and was brought to Quest Academy on a scholarship. I'm the only one in my family who has an ability, and I want to be someone they can be proud of. Those gauntlets were the first present I ever received in my life, so I'm happy you're letting me keep them."

Sal's jaw dropped as he looked at Hannah in disbelief. "No way…"

"This is the part where you take my hand." Hannah pointed at her outstretched right hand with her left. "It's apparently a big deal with Auctioneers."

Sal was completely lost for words. Hannah grew up on the Darwin Cruises? Everything about how she commented on his spending, to the fears of being pitied… it all suddenly clicked into place. Who better for Bastion to target than someone who likely resented the Hunter Bureau? All these revelations came through like a rapid current, and Sal had no idea where to even start with processing all of it.

Sal accepted the handshake. "It's… a genuine pleasure to meet you, Hannah."

CHAPTER 23: RESTART

The weave was completely forgotten as Sal walked out of the dorms with Hannah. He sent off a quick message to Barry and Divinity that he'd meet them at the amphitheater. He was still fumbling around their current conversation, because he had a thousand plus questions about the Darwin Cruises, but he didn't want to make her feel uncomfortable, either.

"You don't have to worry so much." Hannah chuckled. "There are typically two types of reaction, disgust from the elitist types who don't think I deserve to be here, or the awkward, well-intentioned ones who don't want to offend me. I'm proficient in dealing with both."

Sal scratched at the back of his head. "Sorry. It's just so new to me… I had no idea. I've been learning so much about weaves, and I was sure that they originated from parents."

"Not in this instance." Hannah smiled. "Neither of them had powers, and they wanted to protect me from the rest of the ship we were on. It was called the *Odyssey*, not that it went on many epic voyages. The few people who showed potential had the weight of the world placed on their shoulders… like, expectations that they'd become an incredible Hero, and never forget their roots. My parents just wanted me to be happy." Her voice was filled with warmth as she spoke about them. "I probably would have been a lot stronger with my ability had I been trained by Heroes growing up, but I wouldn't change a thing."

Sal couldn't help but resonate with those words. He had his own revelations with his parents about their Heroics back in the day. He wouldn't have wished for a different upbringing, but it was hard not to wonder how he'd have turned out if they had been completely honest with him from the start.

"Over the break, I learned that my parents were actually far stronger than they let on," Sal admitted. "They were trying to protect me, and give me a normal life, rather than training me to be the next Gallant."

"Parents are like that, though. I'd probably do the same if I ever have kids." Hannah shrugged. "Like, I guess the dream would be to end the war before even considering a family?"

"That would be nice. I wonder if we'll see it in our lifetimes." Sal paused when he saw Hannah's amused expression. "What? Did I say something stupid?"

Hannah shook her head, but the smile didn't leave her face. "No, it's just that Divinity focuses on you, and she's probably one of the most powerful diviners in existence. I'm pretty sure our best chance at ending the war will involve you…so maybe it *will* be in our lifetime."

Sal shrugged off the presumption and went back to the Darwin Cruises. "One of the prizes from the tower was to go on an outing with the Harmony Guild to the Darwin Cruises. Which ship would be the best one to visit?"

Hannah's expression brightened as she looked at Sal in surprise. "Harmony is the absolute best! They've done sooo much for us over the years, and meeting Marcus was one of the reasons I decided I wanted to come to Quest Academy. Did you get to meet him? You can't miss his yellow eyes!"

"I met him, but he was really interested in Rochelle. She was the Healer on our team," Sal explained. "I hadn't really given it much thought, because… well, I've not given anything much thought in the last while. I seem to be bouncing from project to project these days. I'm setting up a guild, learning martial arts, and I've got a long list of Crafting projects; as well as a whole project with Quest surrounding the Skill Implants. It's pretty damn exhausting."

"Honestly, I'm not surprised." Hannah laughed as she poked Sal playfully in the side. "You'd be miserable if you didn't have something exciting to work on. So, out of that list, which are you most interested in doing?"

Sal frowned as he thought about it. The weaves project wasn't anything particularly exciting. It was a good Q-Cred earner, but that was just a means to an end. When he discovered the ideal weave for himself, it would likely dull his enthusiasm for the overall process. The elixir machine had a lot of potential, but he already had a ridiculous number of gates activated, so there weren't really any elixirs he was excited about. That might change when he got some recipes from Alex in the future, but for now, it wasn't top of his list.

"I'm looking forward to properly starting up the guild. There are a good few strong people already in the roster, and when it's all confirmed and set up… I think it'll be a lot of fun to see how quickly we can go up the ranks," Sal admitted with an almost guilty smile. "Like, I've never considered myself competitive, but there's something about having an entire progression track in front of you, and knowing that by reaching thresholds, or getting prerequisites, you can ascend higher. It's pretty damn fun to think about."

"I'm guessing you've got Ioseph Bitterwater in there as your resident Defense class?" Hannah stared straight ahead. "Maybe Dominic Walters?"

Sal laughed at the concept. He was immediately reminded of Ioseph wanting to piss in the water purifier. Dominic, on the other hand, didn't conjure any positive memories. Sal had heard the eulogy at the gala for Dominic's father, Aegis. He had fallen in the ranks pretty severely in the first semester, and Sal genuinely hoped he was doing okay.

"Well, if you ever find yourself needing someone for pick-up dungeons, just let me know. I'd be happy to lend a few fingers." She imitated the pistols with her gauntleted fingers. "I mean, if it's not weird."

"I'll keep that in mind." Sal wasn't sure he wanted to immediately ask Hannah to join his guild. She was a great Defense and one of the best out of the first-years. It would be stupid for him to overlook her, especially as she was offering. But the important thing to him was that she was doing it for the right reasons, and not out of guilt or feeling like she owed it to him. Rather than dwelling on it, or falling down a rabbit hole, Sal changed the subject.

"So… Divinity left out a lot of details. How much fun was it doing the excursion and tower with Melanie? Did she go full necromancer?" Sal laughed, wondering what sort of reaction he'd get.

Hannah closed her eyes and raised her head to the ceiling with a pained sigh. "Whatever Divinity told you, it was a thousand times worse…"

They both made their way to the amphitheater and secured their seats well before other students started to arrive. Sal listened to all the hilarious stories about how Melanie had grown fond of her reanimated prowler, so much so that she gave it a name. Apparently, it made the creature stronger, and they were able to clear a lot of the tower with it. The funniest stories were from the excursion where Melanie kept having conversations with spirits, and would randomly start screaming. Hannah did an excellent job of recounting each instance, almost like they were burned into her memory.

"Do you see Kane much these days?" Sal looked around the amphitheater, as though he'd suddenly appear out of nowhere.

"He was struggling a lot before the break." Hannah shook her head. "I wasn't really in much of a state to help him out when he was at his worst, and then we went on the excursion and pretty much straight into the tower. He stopped responding to messages, and I wouldn't be surprised if he left after the first semester."

"Fuck," Sal breathed as he looked down at his own hands. "I had seen him with crutches and wondered why he hadn't just gotten healed at the infirmary. Like, they pretty much heal everyone."

"His ability has this strange sort of effect. He tried explaining it to me, but I wasn't really getting it. It's like a dissipation of essence. To prove it, he literally shattered my barrier with just his palm. Apparently, whenever essence tries to enter his system, it gets completely disrupted." Hannah shrugged helplessly. "I offered him some Q-Cred, but he refused out of principle. I think Quest went easy on him because he couldn't actually heal, but he'll probably have to repeat some of the tests next year when he's fit for them."

Sal frowned as he tried to recall Kane's name in the database. He wasn't sure whether it was the same one. "Is his family name Brigadir?"

Hannah blinked in surprise. "Yeah, that's him. I didn't think you knew that."

"I came across his weave. It's a part of the Replication project for Quest… and I think it was called Resonance. I wonder if Sakura could nullify his ability long enough that he could be healed properly?" Sal thought about it, even though he was far too late to make any difference for the results of the first semester.

"You could always do that thing you did in the stairwell. Cutting off his ability completely." Hannah chuckled.

Sal froze as he looked at her in surprise. "You saw that?"

"Of course. I was having a full breakdown, but I could still hear Divinity's voice asking you to use your power to cut off his. It was pretty terrifying, learning you could do something like that… and I added it to my spiral of fear. I kept apologizing, thinking you were going to take away mine too."

Hannah gave Sal a guilty smile before winking at him. "But I wasn't really in my right mind, so maybe I'm misremembering things."

"I'd never do that to you," Sal reassured her as he looked at her carefully. "And, yeah…probably best that we say you misremembered that part."

"Done." Hannah gestured at Barry and Divinity walking up the steps. "So, how are you feeling about restarting the friendship? If it's too soon, we can just be friendly acquaintances." It was clear from her face that she was hoping for the first option.

Sal smiled as he playfully nudged her with his shoulder. "I'm really happy you knocked on my door today. It's a little wild to think that I've learned more about you today than… you know."

"I've enjoyed it, too." Hannah smiled as she stood up to make space for Divinity and Barry.

"Where are you going?" Sal asked in confusion as he pointed at the seat she just vacated. "We're not going to be secret friends. Sit down."

Hannah rolled her eyes as she sat back down beside him. "I don't know… I thought you'd want to talk to them in private before we hung out again."

"No need. And by the way, if you do actually want to join the guild, I'd happily consider you," Sal added in a quiet voice. "I'll just ask you to wait until I have a guild that your family would be proud of you joining."

Hannah stared at Sal for a few seconds before she nodded slowly, a warm smile tugging at her lips. "I'll hold you to that."

Barry was the first to arrive, and he sat down with a pained groan beside Sal. "Please, for the love of all that is holy… please tell me you asked her to join the guild. We seriously need a Defense class."

Divinity rolled her eyes as she sat beside Hannah. "Ignore him. He's been playing with the simulator too much. Oh, I like the new haircut!" She turned to get a better look at the shaved side.

Barry leaned forward and looked down the aisle at Divinity. "Hannah or Derek Norman, that's all I'm asking. If he picks one, then we've got an unstoppable combination. Just get Mica onboard, and we could probably take on a Tier 6 guild right out of the gate. Tier 5 at a push."

Hannah stared at Barry in disbelief. "A Trainee Guild beating a Tier 5…don't you think that's a little unrealistic?"

Barry just gaped at Hannah before turning to Sal. "Please, Sal…get her locked in before she learns how good she is!"

CHAPTER 24: ANNOUNCEMENT

Quest waited for the last of the students to take their seats in the amphitheater. He stood at the podium, with the holographic screens switched off to start. It was hard to see his facial expression clearly, but he looked to be in good spirits from body language alone.

Sal glanced at Barry to his right. "Any predictions for what we're going to hear about?"

"Likely going to be the new Saviors list." He frowned as he thought about it a little more. "Hopefully a heads-up on whatever bullshit activity we need to complete by the end of the semester. It'll probably be a real tower. What do you think?"

Sal shrugged as he looked in the direction of the podium. "I don't know, other than what Divinity had said about the new weave project... I don't really know what to expect. Maybe a guide to some of the new classes?"

Welcome back! I am very pleased to announce that of the thousand students who joined us in the first semester, we have one of the highest retention rates on record. Only a hundred and fifty-three students have elected to leave Quest Academy, and we wish them all the best in their future endeavors.

"That's still too many," Sal muttered almost to himself, but Barry nodded in agreement beside him. When they had first arrived, the norm had been closer to a quarter of all students dropping out. Reducing that number by a hundred was no mean feat.

"When you consider we did the excursion and the tower, I'm surprised it wasn't more than that," Barry said under his breath. "Especially after getting that crash course on all the demon types from Harlan."

I'd like to personally thank those of you who reconsidered after meeting with me. I'd like to explain to the rest of you what I said in those conversations. Quest Academy's first semester was unconventional, and relied on the assistance of the Hunter Bureau to get you all up to a suitable starting line. We exposed you to the realities of the war, and prepared you in a series of exercises that mimic what our Heroes do on a daily basis.

Now, we're taking a step forward in the academic side of your studies. You will no longer be required to take the War Zone module with Sinclair, Rust, and Lars. Each of you will need to make up those credits by taking on alternative modules, and signing up for intermediate courses or master classes. Our hope is that you've learned alongside your peers on what is necessary in our war efforts. Your experiences on the battlefront will inform your research and creations, and help keep you safe in times of emergency.

The release of tension in the entire crowd was visible, with countless students slumping into their chairs in relief. Excited chatter broke out in a few groups, and it was hard to blame them. Each of them had gone through an ordeal unlike any other student at Quest Academy. They had the baptism of fire with Chatfield, and now they were free to actually lean into their strengths.

Sal finally understood why so many students had elected to remain at Quest Academy: they wouldn't be asked to fight anymore. The ones who had left likely took a few licenses from the evaluations and went straight into working for the private corporations and guilds. Sal just wished that there had been more transparency around the whole thing. Maybe so many students wouldn't have had to leave if their skills were fostered properly from the beginning.

Hannah frowned as she leaned forward in her seat. Both of her elbows rested on her knees as she cupped her chin with both palms. "Kinda shitty of them to do a bait and switch like that."

"My thoughts exactly," Sal muttered as he folded his arms.

You've already completed some of your classes. The window for selecting new modules will be open for the next couple of weeks. You can try out different ones, sitting in to see if they're what you want to enroll in. There will be less competition for places this time around, because there are quite a number of students advancing into the intermediate and advanced classes.

Those of you who achieved high scores within your respective modules will be eligible to move into the next level of difficulty. You will all receive a report card later this evening, and it will tell you what you're eligible for.

Many of the courses will be class specific, but exceptions can be made for those of you who are unsure of your class. It's normal for there to be some switching around at this stage, especially for Supports to try their hand at something new, so please pay special attention to the suggestions of your lecturers.

Your report cards will have their recommendations of class changes, as well as a list of modules they believe would be beneficial to your development. Ultimately, the decision will be yours, so don't feel pressured to accept their advice.

"Okay, that's pretty cool." Barry looked at Sal. "Think they'll put me in the Assassination master class straight out of the gate?"

"I doubt they'll be suggesting master classes for the second semester. You'll probably be put into Tactics or Analysis, I'd say," Sal answered truthfully. He couldn't help but be curious about the recommendations that he'd see in his own report card. Would they tell him to become a Controller class instead of a Support?

To our growing list of Saviors, you will be allowed to take on specialist modules that are designed for your success. Although they will be open to the rest of the students, Saviors will have first priority in securing seats. There will also be some individual training in the form of master classes that have been offered by Heroes and guilds that have seen your exploits over the first semester. You'll have a summary of all the invitations that you've received in the report card.

Just to ensure that we don't end up having a mutiny, I'm delighted to announce that a few students who aren't in the Saviors class have been invited on an individual basis to take part in some master classes.

"That's Jack." Sal grinned as he looked at Barry. "Nemesis from the gala wanted him to do a master class."

Barry smiled as he shook his head. "Quest said a few. Who knows, maybe Trickster will change her mind and recognize my brilliance?"

"As if you'd tell us." Sal laughed as he focused back on Quest. "I'm genuinely curious what they'll put in the report card. It would be pretty funny if they told me to avoid essence programming, in favor of something else."

"Nah, you'll be in Advanced Crafting, or they'll make up some bullshit weave class or something just for you," Barry said with a straight face. He wasn't joking.

Before Sal could respond, Quest's voice flooded the amphitheater again.

I know that each of these announcements have usually been co-chaired with Captain Chatfield. You don't need to worry about any big changes to the curriculum this time around. Many of the corrective exercises were brought in to realign Quest Academy with the expectations of the Hunter Bureau. We've managed to achieve that balance, and as a result, we're going to be catching you all up on the academics that were sacrificed in the first semester.

Rather than using an end-of-year event to determine your grades, we're going to work toward it with incremental gains. We want to see continuous development from all of you, and the prize at the end of the semester will be your eligibility to join an organized raid with the Hunter Bureau. That will be taking place in your third semester. For those of you who fail to meet the requirements, or decide to not take part, there will be other areas for you to contribute.

The relaxed atmosphere that was earned from War Zone no longer being mandatory had been completely destroyed by the announcement of the raid. Very few people in the crowd expected it, and it very much caught them by surprise. It took a few minutes for Quest to calm them down. The fact that it was over a semester away, and that it wasn't a compulsory activity, should have been enough, but he was inundated with questions from the crowd.

After a short break of him telling them to keep their questions until the end, Quest finally managed to get them under control and started to explain the next part of the announcements.

The leaderboard for the Saviors will change, too. But rather than losing your spot as a Savior, you will move down the priority list for receiving a Skill Implant. Due to unforeseen circumstances during the break, we've had to put a hold on the Skill Implanting process, but we're confident in our ability to offer the implants by the end of this semester. Top performers will have their chances a little earlier, so don't become complacent in the meantime.

Depending on performance, and the continued investment from the Hunter Bureau, we may be able to extend the roster of Saviors even further throughout this semester. We've already reflected this change in the second-years. When our list is finalized, we'll be announcing all the new additions to you like we did with the first group. There are still some places left to fill, so keep working hard.

"Mica made it sound like the list was already finalized," Barry muttered in confusion. "How many are they trying to take in, fifty?"

Sal didn't know the answer either, but he didn't really care. If there were more Saviors, then there would be more people in the shared classes. It would probably be better if they had to make teams. "Maybe they're low on Defense types or something? There were only a couple in the first batch."

"You saying I didn't get in with merit?" Hannah joked beside him, pretending to be hurt by the comment. "I won't complain, though. I'll take whatever benefits they throw at me."

Divinity leaned forward and looked down the aisle. "Some of the Heroes have picked out people for private tuition, and they're demanding they be added to the Savior class." She shrugged it off, like it was just a natural thing. "Apparently, they're waiving payment in some cases so it can happen."

Hannah blinked in surprise. "Wait, so… isn't that like they're training them up for their own guilds? Isn't that a bit unfair?"

Barry nodded. "It's no different than the Bastion trying to give students an advantage to win their trust. If Heroes are able to come in and start demanding changes to the merit system, or throwing money around to get their favorites into the top spot, I can't see it ending well."

"They need the funding," Divinity answered lamely, clearly not picking a side of what was right or wrong. "But if it makes better Heroes, then I guess it's a net positive?"

Sal agreed with her. "If the people being selected are like Jack, then I've got no issue with it. It still kinda undermines the whole competition part of selection, though."

"Easy to say when you're in the top spot," Barry goaded him, grinning. "As far as I'm concerned, as long as we're not getting penalized for their opportunity, I'm good with it."

Lastly, I'd like to highlight something very important. You've all successfully completed your first semester, which means the training wheels are now off. Guilds will now be able to approach you directly. They have a process that they need to follow, and will need to highlight to you which areas of development they would like you to focus on. These requests will come with stipulations where they will part-fund the modules, supply you with equipment, and attempt to foster good relations with you.

Although we'll do everything in our power to ensure that there are no unfavorable expectations or deals coming through the guilds, some will slip through the net. Please feel free to consult our faculty members with any concerns you may have from the guilds reaching out to you. None of you will be able to sign on with them until you've graduated, but letters of intention are honored, so they'll have the right of first refusal if you take their support.

Quest smiled as he looked over at Sal's group in the crowd. It was a little strange to Sal that he knew exactly where to look to find him.

The exception to this will be the Trainee Guilds that are created within Quest Academy. All students can participate in a Trainee Guild that has been approved by the Hunter Bureau and United Guilds Association. We actually have one that has just been approved, led by our top-ranked Savior from the first-years.

Sal felt every gaze turn to his direction. It had been a while since he was the center of attention, and he certainly didn't miss it. With a smile that was more like a grimace, he nodded in Quest's direction, hoping that he'd turn the attention away quickly. Thankfully, the headmaster did just that.

Now, before we wrap up, I wanted to reiterate that the report cards are merely a suggestion based on your performance to date. You don't need to adhere to our recommendations. The guilds that have expressed interest will also be in those reports, and you'll be able to make your decisions on which modules you'd like to enroll in.

Skill class will remain as a mandatory module, as we need each of you to maximize your natural essence gates before you can be considered for a Skill Implant. Continue to work hard, focus on your studies, and forge your own path. From this point onward, you have full control of the type of Hero you want to become.

Welcome to the second semester of Quest Academy!

CHAPTER 25: REPORT

To say that it took forever for the report card to come through was an understatement. Divinity and Barry had already received theirs and had sent over messages with the surprise modules that appeared on their cards. Trickster had apparently been swayed enough by Barry at the gala, and now he was doing a master class with her. What wasn't great was how much gloating they'd have to endure considering he was the only person selected for the master class.

Divinity had been a little less enthusiastic, but that was to be expected. There was no way she hadn't looked at the future a thousand times to ensure nothing was left to chance. One of the surprises that she hadn't been expecting was a bursary offer from the Argento Auction House. Sal didn't have any context for what that meant, but he assumed it was something nice that his parents did for her.

As time moved on, Sal continuously refreshed his tablet, waiting for it to load up his report card. He was too anxious to do anything else. Rather than sitting together, they decided to go to their respective dorms. Sal had told himself he'd work on the Predator weave, but he couldn't focus. He was too curious about the different modules, as well as what way the faculty voted. Would they suggest that he become a Controller?

Sal didn't care if they did; he wasn't going to be switching. He stood up for the dozenth time and paced around the room, his gaze never straying too far from the tablet. After a few seconds of indecision, he decided that he might as well be productive in a non-cerebral way. There was no way he'd be able to work on weaves or Crafting, but he'd be able to do some kicks. He sighed to himself and tried to get into a somewhat focused psyche.

With his visor equipped, Sal loaded up the progress tracker for the Silverson Arts. He kept Perfect active and went through the repetitions of each kick. It was infinitely easier when he wasn't fighting against the simulated opponents, and it allowed him to move slower without worrying about the distancing. To Sal's surprise, it ended up being quite calming and after a few kicks, he started to lose the pent-up nerves.

Each of the forms only required twenty perfect performances, and Sal was flying through them. The visor showed the diagrams and movements from the manual, and Sal went into autopilot. It took him about ten minutes to get into a flow state, and even though there were no actual opponents in the living area of his dorm, he managed to make it fun.

It was an incremental process of visualizing enemies in the room. The lack of impact required precise movement control, where Sal had to stop his foot from following through attack patterns. Otherwise, they wouldn't register on the visor as progress. Each movement became more deliberate and vicious. The slow movements started to speed up, and Sal sequenced a set of moves together that naturally flowed with each other: stance, sweep, recovery, and then an uppercut. It was just basic forms that came together, giving him a short respite after the uppercut.

Recalculating Sequences...

The visor had rewarded him with some progress, and he needed to switch to a different set of forms. The suggestions were a little more fun, but much more exhausting. Sal almost laughed as he saw the diagram and ended up moving his couch to be tight against the windowed wall, just so he wouldn't damage anything with a flying kick. Yes, a flying kick. That's what the visor had suggested as the natural progression.

Sal tried it stationary, but it wasn't going to work. Evidenced by the fact that he nearly twisted his ankle by falling to the ground. Apparently, the kick needed momentum to strike the opponent, so he had to figure out the timing of his breathing, the amount of force he used to launch into the air, and then the angle of his legs. For it to work properly, the kick seemingly required his right leg to be fully extended, with his left angled to support it, the left foot resting on his inner thigh. Sal attempted it three or four times, and it became better as Perfect read his intentions and tried to course correct. The only issue was how little time he had in the air to get it right.

On the eighteenth try, Sal grinned as everything clicked into place. It was just a single maneuver, but it was tricky and he wanted to execute it perfectly. By the twenty-first, he was gaining even more air-time. The twenty-sixth attempt felt like the momentum behind his kick was something to be reckoned with. His timing had become almost second nature, and by the thirtieth attempt, he had finally registered a perfect flying kick on the visor.

Rather than celebrating and leaving it at that, Sal continued to perform the kick perfectly, again and again, until the visor registered it as complete. Sal dropped to his knees with a goofy smile as the words appeared in front of his eye. It was the most difficult body movement he had attempted so far, and he was delighted with the results. There was something addictive about the feeling. To put it in a more primal way, he felt like he could now kick a hulker in the head! It was a terrible idea, but the fact that it was possible was hilarious.

With that complete, Sal got back to his feet. His heart was still racing, despite Perfect's attempts at regulating it. He had so much adrenaline, and he wanted to keep going, just to experience a little more progress. Time kinda drifted away from him as he went through a series of jabs with his arms raised to protect his face. Silverson Arts did include quite a number of hand movements, and Sal was perfecting them as he caught his breath.

When he recovered and his legs felt like they could move a little more, he incorporated the kicks into the sequence. The visor kept up with his movements and every single one was attributed against his progress target. The numbers going up were addictive, and Sal found himself obsessing over getting to the next full percentage number. There was no way he was going to leave things at four point seven percent, when he could just as easily get to five percent.

In between sets, Sal went to get some water from the kitchen. He didn't even consider the report card as he went through the different sequences, analyzing his own performance and wondering how he could improve with the next set. The only thing that managed to break him out of his flow state was the sunrise appearing in the distance, through the windows.

"What the…" Sal breathed as he looked at the morning light. "There's no way." He moved to the tablet and navigated to the messages from Barry and Divinity. The last one from him had been sent at nine twenty in the evening… and now the sun was rising? Sal couldn't believe it. All-nighters in the workshop were normal, but martial arts training?

Sal navigated the visor away from the sequence of training and looked at the overall progress, but was immediately confronted with confusion. The visor had seemingly gone rogue during his training, resulting in yet another calibration.

[Updated] Silverson Arts Framework
[Updated] Synchronization for Salvatore Argento
[Updated] Progression Tracking
[Removed] Rank Designations
[Removed] Technique, Stance, Sequence Redundancies
[Removed] Iteration Matrix
Profile: Salvatore Argento
Silverson Arts Suitability: Perfect
Silverson Arts Mastery: 6.1%
Streamlined Course Breakdown:
- Stances: 36
  - Neutral, Grounded, Offensive, Evasive, Adaptive
- Techniques: 1,124
  - Strikes, Evasion, Counters, Grapples, Blocks, Weaponry, Special
- Sequences: 578
  - Offensive, Defensive, Evasion, Locking, Takedown, Overload, Counter, Deception, Weaponry, Speed
Preferred Stance: Offensive
Preferred Techniques: Strikes, Special
Preferred Sequences: Offensive, Takedown

It seemed like his first stint in the sparring arena hadn't given the visor enough information to calculate his overall progress. And while it made some sort of sense, it also was very frustrating. He had been working under a clear set of guidelines, but now everything had been reformatted and switched around. It gave him more insights into the actual martial arts, and he recognized a lot of the terms from the manual his father gave him. The silver lining was that he no longer had two thousand and five hundred things to learn. Seven hundred or so items had been shaved off the list.

Sal wanted to sort through it all to see where his progress actually was, but he was content with the six percent. His first time using the visor for tracking had earned him close to two percent, and he had effectively doubled that effort this time around…in a lot more time, with a lot more iteration. It wasn't a victory by any means, but he was happy with his flying jump kick.

"Report card," Sal muttered to himself as he pulled off the visor and slumped onto the couch. Reaching over toward his tablet, he realized it was out of range. Moving the couch had put too much distance between him and the coffee table. With the grace of a dying cat, Sal hooked the leg of the table with his foot and pulled it toward him. There was no way he was getting off the couch anytime soon. Eventually, after a lot of leg cramping and physical protests from his body, he was able to get his tablet.

His report card was waiting for him, sent seven hours ago. With a guilty grimace, he tapped into it to have a look.

Name	Salvatore Argento
Alias Options	Myth (Mythcrafter) Maestro (Skill Master) Greed (Account over 15,000 Q-Cred)
Current Class	Support (7 Votes)
Suggested Class	Controller (4 Votes) Offense (2 Votes) Healer (0 Votes) Defense (0 Votes)
Standard Modules (0/3)	Skills (Advanced: Lombardi) War Zone (Intermediate: Rust) War Zone (Advanced: Chatfield) Crafting (Advanced: Upgrade) Administration (Advanced: Jez) Demonic Behavior & Analysis (Intermediate: Geist)
Special Modules (0/3)	Essence Management (Savior Exclusive) Specialized Combat (Savior Exclusive) Leadership Training (Savior Exclusive) Excursions Training (Savior Exclusive) Dungeon Delving (Savior Exclusive) Essence Programming (Crafting Exclusive) Ethical Crafting (Crafting Exclusive) Guild Mastery (Administration Exclusive)
Master Class Modules (0/2)	Skills (Master class: Coach) System (Master class: Quest) Tactics (Master class: Maxwell) Crafting (Master class: Forge) Administration (Master class: Jez)
Guild Interest	**Tier 1** Arc Guild

- Bursary: 2,500 Q-Cred Property Fund
- Remain as Support Class
- Take the Administration Module
- Cannot accept assistance from Hunter Bureau
- Cannot accept assistance from Syndicate

Ameye Locomotive

- Bursary: Specialist Care Packages
- Remain as Support Class
- Take the Essence Programming Module
- Care packages will include blueprints of machinery, equipment and weaponry, as well as a surplus of exotic materials
- Until all items are proved to be successfully constructed, Salvatore Argento cannot participate in a Portal Expedition

Cirque

- Bursary: 1,000 Q-Cred
- Change to Controller Class
- Remain in Savior Class
- Remain in Top 10 at Quest Academy

Paradox

- Bursary: 750 Q-Cred toward Combat Equipment
- Remain in Savior Class
- Take the War Zone: Intermediate Module
- Monthly Dungeon Clearances: 10

Syndicate

- Bursary: 2,000 Q-Cred
- Remain in Savior Class
- Take the Analysis: Intermediate Module
- Submit Scouting Reports on Classmates

Tier 2

The Reavers

- Bursary: 3,000 Q-Cred Monthly, Platinum Token
- Guild Partnership Program: Reavers will protect Salvatore's Trainee Guild
- Villa as Trainee Guild Advisor
- 5 Epic-Grade (With Evolutionary Runes) pieces of equipment to be made for the Reavers throughout semester (Price negotiable)
- 50 Appraisals completed for the Reavers throughout semester (Price negotiable)

	The Invention • Bursary: 500 Q-Cred, Blueprint Challenges • Remain in Savior Class • Remain as Support Class • Each successfully solved or improved Blueprint will result in a bonus payment to student
External Interest	Argento Auction House • Bursary: Material Care Packages • Remain at Quest Academy Lawrence Baron • Bursary: Material Care Packages • Remain at Quest Academy Hunter Bureau • Bursary: 5,000 Q-Cred per Month • Personal Training with Robert Locke • Reject all other Guild Bursaries • Remain in the Savior Class

"Awesome," Sal breathed as he kept looking through the various bursaries. Doc Ameye was going to gift him materials and blueprints for not going through a portal? That just sounded like free money to Sal, and he was more than happy to take the Crafter up on the offer. The Hunter Bureau would require him to reject everyone else, so that was a flat no. The Syndicate wanted him to spy on classmates, and Eric from the Arc Guild didn't want him working with the Syndicate. Two birds with one stone. Sal mentally crossed out the Hunter Bureau and Syndicate.

"Someone's desperate…" Sal smiled as he read the offer from the Reavers Guild. Villa must have threatened the life of the guildmaster to get the deal over the line. It was a lot of benefits, and he'd surely be able to do the commissions and Appraisals. It was absolutely worth it for so much Q-Cred coming in. "Is there a limit to how many I can take?" Sal asked himself, as though the tablet would have an answer.

Between Lawrence Baron, the Argento Auction House…which was likely just his father giving him materials that the Arkwright made… and Doc Ameye, he'd have a trove of materials coming through on a monthly basis. It would be amazing for Crafting, and he wouldn't even need to spend anything on the Credit floor. Cirque wanted him to become a Controller, so that was a no. It was nice to see that the top votes from the faculty were that he remain a Support class.

Sal tore his gaze up from the bottom of the report card. When he saw the Alias options, he actually snorted in laughter. "Greed and Maestro? Think we'll stick to Myth." It felt weird that they'd suggest a few Hero names based on his accomplishments, but it did make him wonder what Greed would turn into if he accumulated a lot more Q-Cred in the coming months. If all went well with the elixir machine, he'd be ridiculously wealthy.

The happiness coursing through him wilted when he read through the module list. Although it was great that he was being invited to master classes, the number of modules wasn't feasible. He had to select eight out of the entire list? Hadn't he already enrolled into the Crafting and Tactics ones? Would he be able to switch those out?

Sal continued to stare at the list for a few more seconds before he let the tablet slide out of his hand. Looking at the ceiling, he willed himself to get to his feet so he could have a shower and get some sleep. Unfortunately, his body decided it wasn't interested in complying.

With a final groan, Sal closed his eyes and sank into the couch. The last of his strength was used in bringing both legs up to the cushions. He'd figure out what modules he'd take tomorrow.

CHAPTER 26: CHOICES

"Do you think they'd let me switch my dorm colors to purple?" Divinity turned around on the spot in Sal's dorm, marveling at the layout and design. "This is so much better than yellow. I love it!"

Sal smiled as he gestured at the couch, which he had returned to its original position earlier that afternoon. "You'd know better than me, but I guess it wouldn't hurt to ask?"

Divinity laughed as she sat down. "Nah, I'll keep it for now. I kinda expected us to get a different color scheme because we're Saviors, but I'll happily settle for the better dorms." She perked up as though suddenly remembering something. "Oh, and can you give me the contact details for your parents, please? I want to thank them for the bursary."

"Of course," Sal answered. "But do you mind me asking, what sort of bursary did they go for? Were there any stipulations?" He was genuinely curious whether she got a material package like he did, or whether it was just flat Q-Cred. Either way, he was delighted that his parents had included her.

Divinity's smile grew wider. "It's awesome. It's Q-Cred rewards for whenever I achieve points of mastery within Style, that martial art that your dad gave me. I've been throwing myself into it, and it's ridiculously fun!"

"I learned a flying jump kick last night. It's a part of the Silverson Arts, but the visor has been screwing with me a bit. I had a whole progression track listed out, but it changed itself yesterday in the name of optimization." Sal sighed as he pointed at the visor on the table. "I'm sure that it's still pointing me in the right direction, though."

"Whoa! That sounds pretty cool. Can you show me?" Divinity asked excitedly as she patted the cushions with both hands.

"Wait until we go to a dungeon. I want to try it out on a leecher." Sal smiled. "It's a lot of flying limbs, and the amount of space in here isn't really ideal."

Divinity nodded in agreement. "We're still doing the scavenger run this week-end, right?"

"Yeah, and I'm looking forward to it. I've just got a few things I need to do before then." Sal pointed at the tablet. "Like figure out the modules, which is where you come in."

Divinity tapped the screen as she leaned closer to it. "Oh…you have some good ones here. What sort of help are you looking for? You know that you can defer the ones that you don't want to take now? You can take them next semester—they're not time limited."

"Okay, that's exactly why I asked for your help. I didn't know that," Sal admitted, laughing as he sat down beside Divinity. "So, I previously enrolled in the Tactics master class, and then Upgrade's suggestion for Advanced Crafting… does that mean I'm locked into them?"

Divinity shook her head. "Nope, they're not highlighted on the report card, so it's pretty much a blank slate. You've been accepted into those, which means you can just do them at a later date. If you were invited, like with the Tactics one, you don't have to pay Q-Cred for it. You'd have to pay for Administration and Skill as master classes."

"And I can only choose eight in total?" Sal muttered as he looked through the list again. "It's a shame, because so many of them look good."

Divinity laughed as she shook her head again. "Nope, you can take as many as you like, but that's the number they recommend. Some of the master classes are only going to be a few weeks, or a few months. They're not entire modules, but could require you to be offsite for a period of time. Wait, you've got a master class from Quest?" She looked at him in shock. "I've never heard of this one."

"That's what I mean." Sal sighed as he explained his thoughts. "It's good that I can take more than recommended, but I don't want to set myself up for failure. I definitely want to do the master class with Coach, which means I won't really need to do the class with Lombardi. I'm leaning toward doing the Advanced War Zone class with Chatfield, then maybe taking Upgrade's Advanced Crafting."

"What about Administration?" Divinity looked at it. "Would you take that instead of Harlan's class?"

"I'm thinking if I do the master class with Jez, I wouldn't really need the advanced one," Sal suggested as he mentally crossed it off his list. "So, of the standard modules, I'd be doing Advanced War Zone, Advanced Crafting, and Intermediate Demonic Behavior and Analysis. How does that sound?"

Divinity bit her lip as she looked at the list. "They're good choices, but are you sure you want to do War Zone with Chatfield? It's going to be a lot more fighting, and you've already done your part in the tower. There'd be no shame if you focused on the more administrative modules, especially as a Support class."

"Are you and Barry doing War Zone?" Sal asked out of curiosity.

Divinity nodded. "Yeah, it's a prerequisite for getting into the Assassination module. Barry is doing it too, because he needs Assassination to get into the Advanced Stealth and Deception modules."

Sal blinked in surprise. "How come you know about the prerequisites? I didn't see that in the report card."

"They're listed as exclusives on the list. You've got Essence Programming and Ethical Crafting because you're eligible for Advanced Crafting. You'd have gotten them even if you just went from basic to intermediate, though," Divinity explained as she pointed at the different modules on the list. "Guild Mastery is only there because you've done well in Administration. If you do Advanced Administration, you'll get loads of modules like Asset Management and Heroism as a Business. The Savior ones are exclusives, too."

"Gotcha." Sal nodded as he scanned through the modules. "I'm thinking that I don't need Essence Management considering I've gone through the calibration thing with the visor. Specialized Combat likely won't compare to the Silverson Arts, so I'll avoid that one, too." He glanced at Divinity to see whether she had any thoughts to the contrary, but she just smiled and nodded in agreement.

"Leadership feels like it's probably a Controller-specific one. If I'm doing Guild Mastery, then I won't really need to double up with Leadership. If it turns out to be good, I can just pick it up next semester," Sal continued as he mentally checked it off the list. "Excursions... sounds like a lot of time investment. I wouldn't mind doing more camping trips, but I don't think that it's the best choice.

I am leaning more toward Dungeon Delving, though. If I can clear them with Jackal, then it could be a relatively easy way to build up guild rank and get a high class grade."

Divinity nodded. "You've already started Essence Programming, so that's a definite one. What about Ethical Crafting?"

Sal hesitated slightly as he looked at it. "I feel like it's a mindset rather than a worthwhile class. If it was a choice of taking it or a master class, I'd pick the master class."

"Nope," Divinity argued as she pointed at it again. "This is one where you're pretty much given a set of tasks to complete based on current issues. I'm trying not to lead you astray or push you into any specific modules, but this one would give you a lot of opportunities to help people. I'm pretty sure you'd end up enjoying the challenge of it."

"I'm glad I asked for your help. I'll take it." Sal laughed as he tapped it on the screen to highlight it with the others. "So, the big question is, which of the master classes are worth my time?"

"I'd drop the Tactics one," Divinity said with an awkward smile. "Professor Maxwell is a great guy, but to call it a master class is a little generous. You can pretty much sidestep Tactics as a prerequisite and go straight into Strategic Warfare next semester. All you need is War Zone and Demonic Behavior and Analysis."

"Strategic Warfare?" Sal repeated slowly. "What's that?"

Divinity's eyes lit up. "Raid preparation. They pretty much give you real-world threats that need to be taken down, and let you plan out the best counterattacks. Understanding how to fight in War Zone, and knowing the Demonic Behaviors are the perfect match for it. If you only do Tactics, you'll get to take the Strategic Warfare class, but won't be able to advance in it beyond intermediate."

"That does sound pretty cool… shame it's not offered until next semester." Sal sighed as he looked at the list. "But it makes me feel better about dropping Tactics for now."

Divinity shook her head. "Ah, you're thinking about this the wrong way. In one semester, you were able to get into Advanced Crafting. You got to the final floor of the tower and got a pass into the Advanced War Zone module. See where I'm going with this?"

Sal frowned as he looked at the list. "You think it's possible to get into Strategic Warfare before the end of the semester?"

"I know it's possible." Divinity grinned. "All we need to do is blitz the War Zone class, which is going to be a set list of dungeons and towers that need to be cleared. If we put together a good team and run through it, then we'll get top marks from Chatfield." She raised her other hand. "Demonic Behavior and Analysis will be easy, too. It's pretty much just memorizing their patterns and habitats. As long as we do all the coursework, we can fly through it. Then it's just turning up to lectures to listen to Harlan for the other pieces of context. They want us to succeed, not trap us in a drawn-out process."

Sal smiled as he thought about it. "Okay then…what other modules could be blitzed?" He was wondering whether it was as simple as Divinity made it sound.

If he could theoretically clear the Dungeon Delving module with just Jackal, then it would be amazing.

"You can ask Fabi or Sakura, but it's common for students in the higher years to tear through the modules. I was talking to O'Brien at the gala and he takes a minimum of ten modules per semester, because it adds up for the prerequisites, and unlocks more advanced courses. Advanced War Zone is not the same as Advanced Strategic Warfare. One will have you competent on the battlefield, while the other would have you as a competent raid leader," Divinity said excitedly as she pointed at the tablet on the table.

"Okay, so…Ethical Crafting you could probably finish in a week. That elixir machine probably counts as the final project, but Upgrade might push you to do something else. Dungeon Delving is a set number of dungeons, and reports being written up about them. Your master class with Coach might even be a few days. He'll likely just tell you what you need to do to get Skill Master and Mythcrafter leveled up." Divinity walked through them fast.

"Wait," Sal said in disbelief. "A few days? How does that even count as a master class? He's able to just take a look at me and determine what I need to do to increase my weaves?"

Divinity stared at Sal. "I imagine if you were doing a Skill master class—it would be a few minutes of you adjusting their weave to something better. Coach is no different. He's able to determine what sort of work you need to put in to advance your weave."

"It sounds like he has a really interesting ability. I thought it was something along the lines of building proficiencies and techniques. When I was looking for a solution for Gallant, Quest had suggested bringing in Coach." Sal explained his thoughts aloud. "Since he never came around, I guess he was busy."

Divinity's smile tightened ever so slightly. "He was the one responsible for Gallant's weave evolution…so he's not the most popular person these days. I doubt he'd want to show his face much around Quest Academy." She tilted her head to one side. "Especially now that Prestige has been floating around. I can't imagine he'd feel safe around her."

"And he's doing a master class?" Sal repeated with a shake of his head. "I highly doubt that he's doing it out of the goodness of his heart or wanting to see the next generation do well."

"Very unlikely." Divinity smiled. "He's likely trying to find a way to restore his image. It's impossible to know the full story. Did Gallant actually take Coach's advice, or did he blaze his own trail and screw everything up? Did Coach accidentally break Gallant's weave? There are too many unknowns, to be honest, but he's definitely going to do your master class. It might be an offsite thing."

"Still… that does sound like a pretty good contender for the Skill Implant. Being able to determine how a weave can grow is likely a great match for Skill Master." Sal shrugged. "Doing the master class with him could be worth it just for that."

"So, what are you thinking? Are you going to do more than eight, or are you going to play it safe?" Divinity's eyes practically sparkled as she looked at Sal expectantly. "Time is going to be one of the biggest drawbacks, but you only need to get top marks in a few of the classes to stay competitive."

Sal smiled as he picked up the tablet and finished highlighting the different modules. "Going to go with these eleven. Hopefully you're right about the master class with Coach only taking a few days. Three Crafting modules, four if you count Essence Programming. What do you think?" Sal showed Divinity the tablet with the ones he was selecting.

Standard Modules (3/3)	<ul><li>War Zone (Advanced: Chatfield)</li><li>Crafting (Advanced: Upgrade)</li><li>Demonic Behavior & Analysis (Intermediate: Geist)</li></ul>
Special Modules (4/3)	<ul><li>Dungeon Delving (Savior Exclusive)</li><li>Essence Programming (Crafting Exclusive)</li><li>Ethical Crafting (Crafting Exclusive)</li><li>Guild Mastery (Administration Exclusive)</li></ul>
Master Class Modules (4/2)	<ul><li>Skills (Master class: Coach)</li><li>System (Master class: Quest)</li><li>Crafting (Master class: Forge)</li><li>Administration (Master class: Jez)</li></ul>

Divinity nodded, grinning. "If it makes you feel better, I've taken fourteen and Barry has thirteen. If you can clear a few of them before the end of the month, you'll have a much higher chance of getting into Strategic Warfare. I haven't looked into the future with this assortment, but I'm guessing there'll be a few more exclusive modules you'll be able to pick up."

"I do feel better. I'll finalize these and see what comes of it. Do you think I should pick up a couple more of the Savior exclusive ones? I feel like only taking one is a little stupid." Sal laughed awkwardly as he pointed to Dungeon Delving.

"Nope. You're good with what you have. The new Savior ones don't really have clear progression paths like the other subjects. War Zone is vital in your list because it's combining Survival, Combat, and Field… which means that you're getting three times the prerequisites for the more advanced modules," Divinity explained with a shake of her head. "Just focus on that list and you'll do amazing, I'm sure."

Sal submitted the options and reclined back on the couch. "That's one less thing to worry about. Any plans for the rest of the day?"

Divinity smiled as she got to her feet and smoothed out the creases of her black uniform. "I was thinking of hitting the sparring room. Want to team up for the simulator fight?"

Of all the things Sal would have considered, fighting was the last on the list. His body was in bits from the night before, and his muscles were not happy with the repeated flying kicks. Sure, Perfect was suppressing a lot of the pain, and his body was naturally repairing itself at optimal speed, but was he really going to throw himself into training so quickly? He looked at Divinity's bright smile and sighed.

"Lead the way."

CHAPTER 27: DISTRACTIONS

Sal wasn't sure exactly why, but fighting against the simulation machine was excellent for his progress tracker. Probably the impact against something solid and not having to exhaust himself with fine-motor controls. But whatever it was, the visor was having a blast. Just a few hours of training with Divinity had been ridiculously productive, with his percentage climbing all the way to nine percent overall. What was made even better was the shout of excitement and surprise from Divinity when he had launched a perfect flying jump kick at one of the fake leechers.

Their training had devolved from that point, as Divinity wanted to see all the other cool moves. It was a little discouraging at how quickly Divinity picked up the flying jump kick. She didn't have access to Perfect, and she had only seen him doing it… yet after four or so attempts, she glided through the air like it was second nature. Sal was happy for her, though, because she seemed to be genuinely enjoying herself.

By the end of the exercise, Sal was truly spent and didn't want to move his body at all. He was sure they had just built up some cohesion score by working together, and Sal had to admit they were a pretty good team. Where he was able to attack with power and range, Divinity was lithe and fast. Death by a thousand cuts really was the perfect description of her fighting style.

Divinity went off to get some food, but made him promise that they'd do sparring like that again soon. Sal had readily agreed because he was surprised at how much he enjoyed himself. Training his body and Silverson Arts at the same time was starting to become a little addictive. He told himself that it was because he could see a numerical value going up, but honestly, it was seeing his growing capability.

When he got back to his room, he had enough strength to take a shower. The jets on the walls and ceiling battered his body more than anything the simulation had thrown at him, but at least it felt refreshing. He stayed in the shower for a while and collected his thoughts.

He needed to keep up the training of the Silverson Arts. That was a nonnegotiable that would help him improve his fighting skills. He now had a collection of new modules where he'd need to attend lectures and work on projects. With Crafting being four of them, Sal was confident that he'd fly through those. If those Crafting sessions could double up and allow him to make more gear, that would be even better. Doc Ameye's bursary would give him new blueprints to work with, as well as the Invention's blueprint challenges. With the Mythic blight jackal on his left arm, and Upgrade working on the Strategist's Dominion, he only really needed to work on a Healing apparatus.

Yes, his father had asked him to make something… and Sal had half-assed the project, because it wasn't really a priority. But now? Now he was borderline whimpering in a shower because he'd abused his body two days in a row with martial arts. If he could create a Healing device that eliminated fatigue and repaired his muscles, then he'd be able to progress even faster. The face mask wasn't a bad idea, but he didn't have the right abilities to make it work the way he wanted.

Transference was good, but he needed something like Regenerate or Heal. The one he had made for his father wasn't durable enough for what he needed, because it was created almost exclusively from cores and Kaizen. What if he altered the face mask design to have a canister that would give him a health elixir whenever he needed it?

Sal turned off the shower and reached for a towel. He was frowning as he thought through the concept for a Healing mask. It didn't feel like it would be that difficult of a build, but he wanted something that would last a long time. Evolutionary runes made the most amount of sense.

While drying himself off, Sal looked in the mirror and paused. He was no stranger to the abdominal muscles that appeared in the last semester…but the definition of his biceps, triceps, and pectorals was a definite change. Was it because he had just come from training or was it the result of his Strength stat going up via Jackal? Sal humored himself with a few flexes of his arms, and was instantly hit with karma as his muscles protested against the movements. He might have looked nice, but his body was in no state to massage his ego.

Finishing off the drying, Sal moved to the closet and picked out the last of the black uniforms. He'd need to do some Restoration or at least figure out where the washer and dryer were in the apartment. There was apparently a communal one somewhere, but he hadn't a clue where that was. Restoration was far easier.

When he was dressed, Sal made the arduous journey up the stairs after retrieving his tracker, wincing with every step. He finally came to the simulation orb and saw the half-prepared Predator weave still suspended.

"Okay… where were we?" Sal breathed as he leaned his palms against the sides of the terminal screen. "We get the Predator weave done first, and then we move on to a Healing weave." He spoke to himself, as though it might muster up some long-lost reserve of energy. It didn't.

Tilting his head to look at the weave, Sal tried to remember where he was on it. After a few seconds of looking at the different lines, Sal broke apart sections of it with the intention of rebuilding it back up. The tracker had caught up with his work and was highlighting the inefficiencies with the weave, but Sal ignored them as he worked through instinct. There were so many areas he could make improvements, and he wanted to trust himself first before applying the logic from Cypher.

When Sal got to the central mass of the weave, he finally felt like he was back in action. He deconstructed it and then reconstructed it for the familiarity, before making the tweaks that could improve it. The sharp triangles that he had smoothed out the other day were looking good, but he was curious why they had formed that way in the first place. What would happen if he were to create more of those fang-like sections? Sal put the thought out of his head for a second and completed the weave with the curving and Ravel method.

It took a few seconds for the green light to fill the room, and Sal wasn't interested in the success. He wanted the description.

[Skill Registration: Successful]
[Weave Stability: 100%]
[Category: Mimicry, Body Manipulation]

[Name: Predator]

[Grade: 25]

[Description: Allows user to permanently claim the capabilities of a defeated entity by consuming its core. Physical- and Essence-based attributes will be enhanced to the level of the defeated entity.]

Sal moved over to the terminal to re-read that first sentence of the description. There was no way that it was this simple… Would Mica be able to consume the blight core and gain a higher benefit? There had to be a catch somewhere that made it impossible, but the description said that it just needed to be a core. Would an artificial one work?

Biting his lip, Sal moved back to the threads and started to experiment. The profile was saved for the latest version of Predator, but he wanted to know whether there was a way to improve it beyond its current realm. What he was aiming for were the fangs that he had previously curved out of the weave. This time, he was curious what would happen if he was to add more of them. Make them even more vicious.

It shouldn't have taken long, and Sal likely should have stuck with one idea… but the Ravel method fit perfectly as a sort of compression tool. It would push the essence to those jagged points. His thought process was that the curving would allow for a more natural flow of essence. The jagged points would typically be a blocker, or would slow down the current… but the Ravel method would speed it up. At least, that's what he thought.

When the fangs were done, Sal used excess thread to create more of them. It was stylistic and it was overkill, but it still felt right. There was no imbalance, and Sal tracked that new thread throughout the weave to reinforce the primary design of Predator. By the end of it, Sal determined that he wouldn't even be angry if it didn't work… because it looked positively badass.

Suspended in front of him was the maw of what looked like a dragon. The fangs were razor-sharp, or at least would be if the thread had allowed a severe angle, but… with a bit of imagination, it was fierce. Sal smiled as he completed the last of it with a laugh, turning to wait for the red light. A few moments passed and the red light didn't arrive, but neither did the green.

Using his tracker, Sal inspected the weave to see whether Cypher had any insights for him, but there were none. As far as Cypher was concerned, this wasn't the Predator weave. It was something else, and it was seemingly perfect.

Sal loitered around the terminal, waiting for the conclusion before he started to look up Healing weaves. It gave him time to think about the Predator ability and what was potentially possible with a high-tier core. If there was such a massive clamor for the blight core when it was first discovered, then maybe it had nothing to do with the Subsume ability. Maybe it was just being consumed by someone with the Predator ability, and naturally granting them the Subsume ability.

If Robert Locke had the Predator ability, would that explain his insane powers at the tower trial? With pretty much a snap of his fingers, he had wiped out entire floors of demons. If he really did have Subsume as an internal ability, it likely would have added countless stats to his attributes.

Sal winced as he thought about it. The immediate flaw was that low-level demons didn't cause Subsume to activate. He had only gotten small amounts of stats when Jackal was roaming around the place. The other issue was that the blight core didn't naturally come from a demon, which meant that the Predator ability might not accept it.

Just as he was mulling over the pros and cons of the Predator ability, a green light washed over the simulation orb, startling Sal.

[Skill Registration: Successful]
[Weave Stability: 100%]
[Category: Mimicry, Body Manipulation]
[Name: Sovereign]
[Grade: 40]
[Description: Allows user to permanently claim the capabilities of defeated entities by consuming their core. Subsequent cores consumed, of each species, will progress the user toward their pinnacle states.]

Sal stared at the description and could only shake his head. There were zero synchronization targets for this one, because not even Mica was fit to handle an ability like Sovereign. It was quite literally the most powerful ability he had ever seen the description of. Endless growth from consuming cores of the same species? He had no idea what the pinnacle state was, but guessed it was the end of the evolutionary tree. Would it mean that killing commander variants constantly would result in a power level of the greatest commander? The fact that it had said states, rather than state, made Sal question whether Sovereign allowed the user to have multiple ability trees. Would the user be able to concurrently hold onto the pinnacle state for leecher and prowler?

A fun thought appeared in Sal's head as he glanced at his own shoulder. He wondered what materials would be needed to make something with the Sovereign ability. The playful side of him was curious whether a drone would be able to use it. Sending a drone into a Red Zone indefinitely and waiting for it to get stronger by consuming cores? It was an amusing concept, but was unlikely. Powering that sort of ability would be one hell of an undertaking… unless it had Capacitor.

Sal frowned as he thought about it a little more. There was a good chance that this ideation was going to lead to the big drone that Divinity had referenced back at his workshop. His intuition alone was telling him that the scale of the project would be massive.

What if it also had the Upgrade ability, or at the very least, Repair? Wouldn't that give it a lot more survivability out in the wild? If Capacitor took care of essence, and Repair could keep it fixed up with materials from Arsenal… wouldn't that work? Sal thought about it a little more and frowned. Jackal was able to recharge and repair itself using Arsenal. There was no Repair ability listed, though. So maybe he didn't need to specifically add it to the build?

Sal closed his eyes and took a breath. When he opened them, he'd work on the weave for Healing… and then, he'd focus on what he needed to do for the upcoming modules. If he was being good, he'd even spend some time working on the elixir machine. He didn't need to add another project to the pile. Even if it sounded absolutely incredible. He had his own drone, and it was amazing. Sal didn't need to make another one with Sovereign.

When his eyes opened, he could see the purple reflection of his irises in the terminal glass. Mythcrafter was active, and Sal was already ideating on what type of drone the Sovereign would be.

"Why am I like this?" Sal muttered as he started to construct the blueprint.

CHAPTER 28: SOVEREIGN

"Fabi!" Sal called out enthusiastically as he entered the Saviors workshop. He had a tube of parchment rolled underneath his arm and a wide grin on his face. After countless hours of agonizing over the best path to take, Sal had discovered the perfect solution.

"Sal?" Fabi leaned against the railing of the second-floor cubicles. "What brings you here? I haven't seen you in a few days and thought you slipped into a coma or something." Her hair was tied back and her sleeves were rolled up, but the most surprising addition to her wardrobe was a glass eye-patch.

"You made a tracker?" Sal asked excitedly as he took the steps two at a time to get up to where she stood in confusion. He didn't care that his body was screaming at him. It was a necessary sacrifice.

"Yeah, and a few other things. I'm still waiting on the promised scarlet screen from Doc Ameye, but this thing is pretty good," Fabi admitted almost guiltily before her face broke into a smile. "I was going to call you when it was all done, but I still think you'll be pleasantly surprised." Her gaze moved to the parchment and her right eyebrow shot up. "Here to do some Crafting?"

"No, actually. I've got a million things I'm supposed to be doing, and I wondered if it would be possible to outsource some of it." Sal chuckled as he presented the parchment to her. "Can you give me a quote on how much it would cost to build?"

Fabi slowly unfurled the parchment and nearly dropped the second blueprint. "There's two of them?" she said almost to herself as she jutted her chin in the direction of her cubicle. "Let's have a look in here. I've been feeding my tracker blueprints for the last few days, so this will be some good practice."

"Perfect, thank you," Sal agreed as he followed her.

"I didn't say I'd work on them, I'm just curious what sort of project you'd bring me that you wouldn't work on yourself." Fabi laughed as she placed one of the blueprints down on her desk. The second one she unfurled properly and had a look at it in her hands. "A face mask?"

Sal nodded. "Yeah, I thought about back when you made that void needle at the auction house. You just needed a blueprint and you were able to instantly manifest the weapon. I was wondering if you could try that again, but with something like this."

"A spear and a face mask are very different," Fabi said in a tone like she was trying to manage his expectations. But rather than just dismissing the thought, she looked at the blueprint carefully. "But Figment is a continual surprise, so who knows?"

Sal watched as Fabi's eye-patch turned blue with a series of white squiggles darting across the surface. It looked like it was using Analysis on the blueprint. He could tell with just a glance that it was a high-level Epic grade. Sal was delighted for her, as it would allow her to channel her Figment power that much more efficiently.

"Okay…but why are you asking me to do this?" Fabi frowned as she looked up from the blueprint. "This is well within your capabilities, and it shouldn't take you all that long to make it."

Sal shrugged as he gestured at the other blueprint on the desk. "My father wanted me to work on the face mask as a Healing apparatus. My eyes get hurt from using Mythcrafter and he's worried that I'll start going blind because my body isn't strong enough to handle it yet. But, I brought that other design as an incentive. Two birds with one stone."

Fabi paused when Sal started to talk about his eyes. She looked at him intently for a few seconds before letting out a sigh. "Okay, I can give it a try, but I'll be charging a premium for these materials. You sure you don't want to do it yourself? It would be far cheaper." She smiled and tilted her head. "But it would be pretty great to get more practice in. I've been pushing myself to try more elaborate crafts in the last while."

"Yeah?" Sal looked around to see whether there were any big changes since he had last been in her office. Other than a few more drawings on the workbench, there wasn't really anything of note.

"Look toward the loading bay." Fabi grinned as she unfurled the second blueprint. "Man, I can tell which of these you're more passionate abou—" Her words died off as she looked at the design concept for the Sovereign drone. Her jaw practically dropped as she looked between Sal and the design. "This is borderline impossible!"

Sal put his hands up. "Okay, so I thought you might say that, but I'd be very happy to help with whatever parts you need me for. I can get the cores cut into plates to make Capacitor, and I can pretty much simulate the effects of Sovereign and Arsenal with Mythcrafter. Now that I've seen the weave, I can pretty much make it for the drone."

"I don't even know what Sovereign is!" Fabi laughed as she cleared a space on her desk to lay the parchment out flat. "Okay… what am I looking at here? Is this even stable?" Her eye-patch kept flashing red, to the point that she had to pull it off. "Guess my tracker is useless for this one. Which tells me this thing is higher than Epic grade?"

Sal smiled at her as he waited for her to come to a different conclusion.

Fabi stared at Sal when she got no answer from him. "Wait… no."

Sal eventually broke, laughing. "No, don't worry. It's Legendary grade, with an evolutionary rune to get it up to Mythic grade at some point in the future. I tried conceptualizing a way for it to be a lower grade that could have more evolutionary stages, but the problem is the Sovereign ability. It's pushing the build to the highest tiers. I can source a lot of the materials, but I don't have a drone assembly dock that could deal with this… and I'd end up spending close to a month working on it."

"But a month is nothing when you could be making a soon-to-be Mythic-grade drone, Sal." Fabi laughed, as though he missed the whole point. "Aren't you excited by this? Why are you bringing it to me, of all people? I wouldn't be able to make something like this!"

"Have you ever tried?" Sal asked the question he had been curious about. "Your ability grade is far higher than mine, so I'd say you could probably do it with the right materials and blueprint."

Fabi stared at him as though he had slapped her. "Can I... borrow your visor for a second?"

Sal didn't hesitate as he handed it over to her. "If you want, I can give you the blueprint of the visor. You can use my visor while building it with your ability."

"I need to learn how to use it without a visor, though," Fabi muttered as she studied the blueprint again, but this time with a visor that could process the information. "Okay, this doesn't seem impossible." She sighed, shaking her head. "I can't believe I just said that..."

Sal smiled as he looked out at the loading bay as Fabi had instructed earlier. He could see the same containers with materials, which were all stacked neatly to the sides of the room. The reason was clearly to make space for the behemoth that proudly stood in the center of the room. It was a janky mess of contraptions fused together, and looked like some form of torture device with multiple mechanical arms poised to work on whatever lay within. Each arm had several joints, and the hands? Sal was going to call them hands—the hands were adorned with multi-tools. Lasers, cutters, pincers... it looked positively menacing. Also, it was easily the size of Fabi's car.

As Sal started to Appraise it, he found that there was a Deduction ability at the very least. The monstrosity of parts was apparently Rare grade, which was a big step up from the simulation orb that was Uncommon grade. When he imagined a drone dock, this was not what came to mind.

"Are you trying to go with an Von Neumann approach?" Fabi asked suddenly as she looked up from the blueprint. "You're giving it the ability to upgrade itself, but that could potentially become an issue with the evolutionary rune. Is this thing designed to self-replicate or just sustain itself forever?"

Sal gave her his best blank smile. "I've got no idea who that is, but yeah... the concept was to have it sustaining itself in a Red Zone. Capacitor would allow it to recharge itself constantly with accumulated cores, and Arsenal's materials could be used to either repair or upgrade itself. I've not really worked out the details, but Jackal is able to restore itself when it's docked, by using the materials in Arsenal. It was called a growth focus when I Appraised it."

Fabi just stared at him in disbelief. "Did you change Jackal's modules? There was nothing like that when we looked at it on the screen." She pointed at the blank wall that she used for essence programming.

Sal shook his head and gave her an awkward smile. "No, it was always there. According to the appraisal, Jackal can learn, develop, and grow. You seemed confident that the Adaptive Behavior thing could be improved, so I just went with your judgment."

Fabi tilted her head slightly as she thought about it. "Okay, for future reference... push back when you think I'm wrong. I'm not always right, and when it comes to Mythic-grade drones, I think you're probably the leading authority on the subject."

Sal wasn't really sure what to say, but thankfully Fabi saved him with a follow-up question.

"What does the Sovereign ability do?" she asked curiously, eyes locked onto the drawing again.

"It consumes cores to make the user stronger. But like, if it killed a leecher, and then consumed more leecher cores, it would continually evolve until it was the pinnacle level of leecher." Sal used the word he read from the description, and knew he wouldn't have been able to explain it if Fabi questioned him further on it.

"That's oddly terrifying." Fabi sighed as she folded her arms. "But fuck is it exciting… You know this is going to be a monster of a build, right? You're sure you don't want to work on it and take all the glory for when it revolutionizes warfare?"

Sal shook his head. "Can't we share that accolade instead?" He was joking, but he honestly just couldn't afford to spend time on it. "I've submitted all my classes for this semester, and I went with eleven of them. The bursaries have requirements that I'll need to prioritize… I've got the elixir machine to work on, and I've also got a lot of training to focus on, too. Oh, and I need to sort out the guild! There's far too much for me at the moment, so I can't just add these projects without fear of spiraling and ending up in Sergeant Head's office again."

"We'll have to hit up Baron's Material Exchange a little earlier than expected. At least I'll get to use my Hunter Bureau Gold Card." Fabi lifted the blueprint and waved it at Sal. "Because whatever ability Sovereign is, it's thirsty for the most expensive materials. And even then, there's an essence thing here that I can't even figure out."

"Ah, that's a part that I can help with. Don't worry about essence sources, because I can replicate them with Skill Master," Sal said, as though it were nothing. He smiled at Fabi and gestured at the blueprint. "So… is it a yes?"

Fabi groaned as she looked at the ceiling. "Of course it's a yes. You knew I'd break because it's a drone, didn't you?"

"A little." Sal laughed. "I actually thought you'd laugh me out of the room because it's a little more ambitious than the usual stuff."

"It's perfect," Fabi corrected him. "Honestly, I'm just worried I'll screw it up."

"Then we'll fix it up," Sal suggested. "There's no need to worry about it. I have the funds to throw at this thing until it works, or until a point that we realize it's a doomed project. Hell, it could end up being perfectly constructed and then we realize that Sovereign doesn't even work the way we thought it would."

Fabi laughed as she nodded. "Okay, I like those kind of stakes. Let's have fun with it, do our best, and if we screw up… we'll know better for next time. But I have to admit, I'm curious. What's the end goal of this thing? Jackal makes you stronger, but this thing won't do that."

Sal nodded as though it were obvious. "But *it* will get stronger, which is the most important thing. If it can support itself out there and kill demons, then it makes everything a little safer."

Fabi paused as she looked at Sal strangely. "Did you enroll in Ethical Crafting? Because if you didn't pick it, I think you should. Stuff like this is pretty much the dream of that module."

"I'll be starting the class next week. I've been getting messages nonstop from Joanne and Quest, all the reading materials in advance of classes starting." Sal shrugged. "I've got no idea how well I'll do, but I had that first Essence Programming class. I'm not a natural in the slightest."

"Give it time. We can't all be a natural like Upgrade," Fabi shot back, chuckling. "When it finally starts to click, you'll be able to experiment with it, and you'll start having fun."

"Or, I can just ensure that both you and Upgrade have drones. Then I can steal all your good modules," Sal countered, smiling.

Fabi paused. "You know, now that I look at this blueprint… I don't think it's feasible at all. I think you're going to have to figure it all out yourself." A wide smile accompanied the thinly veiled threat. "Besides, it sounds like your drone doesn't even need my fancy modules. It can grow by itself."

"Okay, fine… I'll work hard at it." Sal mock-groaned before smiling. "But yeah, how do you want to do this… do you want me to pay you in advance for the materials and labor or do you want to price it first?"

"Give me a few days and I'll get back to you." Fabi handed the visor back to Sal. "Ideally, if you could get me a blueprint for that visor, that would speed things up. I love my eye-patch, but it's nowhere near strong enough to handle this sort of blueprint."

"Sent." Sal lifted his tablet to show her. "You'll need some scarlet screen to make it. I've detailed the current state of it, but I also sent over the original Scarlet Moon Visor blueprint if you want to evolve it yourself."

Fabi nodded as she looked at the file on her tablet. "My eye-patch could probably manage the Rare-grade build, and then I could probably just evolve it with the amount of Invention essence I've got access to." She grinned as a plan started to come together in her mind. "Thanks for that. I'll pester Doc Ameye to send the materials a little faster."

Sal was delighted to have Fabi working on the projects. One of the things he learned from Arbiter's Judgment was that he could get excellent results from just commissioning capable people. If he was able to get Fabi working on the mask and the drone, then he'd be unobstructed to work on the other things that needed to be done. The guild was likely going to take up a lot of his time, and the classes, too. Little things like this would be a great help.

"I really appreciate it. Thank you so much." Sal let out an audible sigh of relief. "If you need me for anything, just let me know."

Fabi nodded as she gestured at the door. "Go on, then. Get out of here. I'll make sure you have the mask first."

Sal paused as he looked at her strangely. "Why would you work on the mask first?"

"Argento Auction House gave me a bursary this semester." Fabi smiled as she looked at Sal. "Something along the lines of keeping their reckless son safe. I might as well keep that promise and make you some good Healing equipment."

"I'll leave it in your capable hands, then." Sal laughed as he left the workshop.

CHAPTER 29: NEGOTIATION

"Fabrication?" Blathnaid repeated the word as though it were unfamiliar to her. Strands of brown hair fell in front of her gaze as she stared at the unfurled blueprint in confusion.

Sal nodded as he pointed at the components list to the side of the parchment. "It's a build with a little less finesse than usual. There's a lot of big machinery required for it, and I'd end up spending half my time building vats and enclosures if I did it myself."

Blathnaid glanced up at him as she pulled her hair back into a ponytail. "And you just need me to build the big stuff?" She flicked to the next blueprint, frowning. "There's a lot of them, but most look feasible if I can manage my essence draw." Biting her lip, she glanced at the drawings as she continued to sift through the stack.

"I could get the coat from Rochelle, if it sped up the process. Just to give you as much essence as possible," Sal suggested, guessing that Rochelle would be fine with it if it was just for a few days.

"No need." Blathnaid smiled as she pulled back the sleeve of her jacket, revealing a pearlescent armguard strapped to her forearm. "I made a battery pack for myself, and it's constantly refining essence that I can use." She tapped at the pages in front of her. "I'm just wondering if I can get them all done today."

Sal blinked in surprise. "That's Epic grade… when did you make that?"

Blathnaid shrugged. "Over the break. I've been doing some dungeon runs with Darren, and it helped me get a healthy reserve of materials. Essence reserves were my weakness, so I wanted to find a way to cover it. It's not the perfect solution, but it helps for projects like this." She smiled warmly as she twisted her arm, appraising the construct.

"That looks fantastic…" Sal was about to ask for the blueprint, but then realized that he didn't need it with Capacitor. It had more essence in reserve than he'd conceivably need. Changing tactics, Sal asked what modules she decided on. "Are you taking Ethical Crafting? I know you're in Essence Programming."

Blathnaid nodded. "Yeah, and I'm moving into the Advanced Crafting class with Upgrade. She thinks I'm ready for it, and I'm just happy to see the progress. There weren't really any master classes that were open for me, but I'm hoping to have some unlocked next semester." She glanced at Sal before smirking. "Guess you had about twenty master classes?"

"Five, but I've only picked three for now." Sal chuckled. "One of them is from Quest. It's a System master class. I've got no idea what to expect with it."

"That does sound pretty ominous. Maybe he wants to retire and make you his successor?" Blathnaid ventured innocently, but it caused Sal to choke momentarily.

"No way." Sal shook his head vehemently. "Can you imagine? Me being a headmaster? I'd make Crafting the top subject and kick out all the Offense and Defense people. Give them to Chatfield or something, and hope for the best." He laughed at the very notion, but Blathnaid wasn't laughing.

"That sounds pretty damn cool, though. Maybe your guild will become a Crafter haven in the future. I wouldn't mind being a part of that. If you're the headmaster, would I be the new Forge or Upgrade?" She laughed with a small shake of her head. "But this is cool… I'm taking it that these are the results of the epiphany you had in the canteen?" She raised one of the parchments to illustrate her point.

"Yeah, the elixir machine," Sal agreed as he glanced at all the stacks. "It's the culmination of a lot of assumptions, but I think that it will work out. I realized that commissioning the pain-in-the-ass stuff would make things move a lot quicker."

"I'm flattered." Blathnaid grinned as she dropped the parchment and crossed her arms. "So, is this the part where we negotiate? Upgrade warned me that I need to be pushy when I do this."

Sal smiled as he nodded. "Of course. What do you think the work is worth?"

"What are you prepared to pay?" Blathnaid countered immediately, although she already looked flustered. It was clear that she felt bad in asking.

"Well played." Sal couldn't help but praise the new resolve. "I think that my budget for the job done would be two thousand Q-Cred. If everything is done perfectly, and to the specifications in the blueprints, I'll add another two hundred. If they're better than my specifications, or a higher grade, I'll pay an additional three hundred. Total of two thousand and five hundred if you finish on time, and with higher specifications."

Blathnaid bit her lip as she looked between Sal and the drawings. "That's too much Q-Cred…"

"What was that?" Sal asked loudly. He even went so far as to crane his ear in her direction. "I couldn't hear you just now."

Blathnaid sighed as she nodded. "Okay… I get it. It's still too much, though." She fidgeted slightly before putting her hands on her hips and looking at him sternly. "I don't want sympathy projects from you."

"What about this is sympathy?" Sal smiled at her. "Right now, my time is more valuable to me than Q-Cred, so I need to outsource projects that can be done faster by other people. Do I really need a Mythic-grade compression chamber?" Sal gestured at one of the drawings, laughing. "No, I don't think anybody needs that level of over-engineering. Your ability can have this done in minutes, while I'd take closer to an hour."

That approach seemed to mollify Blathnaid, who still looked a little unsure about the pricing. She tilted her head to the left before nodding quietly. It was as though she had just come to a decision. "Right, but I'll buy the materials out of the funds."

"Nope, they've already been factored into the build," Sal countered with a bright smile. "Thank you for agreeing to this. I'm glad I could count on your help."

Blathnaid's eyes widened as she shook her head. "No! I didn't agree to that."

Sal ignored her as he gestured at the drawings. "I'm really glad you can see that there are things in there like runes and stuff, areas you'll likely need to out-source to Jack. Hopefully, you're okay with being the contractor on this job and happy to take a cut out of the overall fund to pay him and whoever else needs to pitch in?"

Blathnaid's indecision vanished as she realized what was being asked of her. "Oh." She quickly flicked through the drawings until she saw a series of runes on one of the pages. "Ahhh!" A wide smile appeared as she nodded in understanding. "I like this plan."

"I'm relieved to hear that." Sal smiled as he looked at it. "Now, if any of the costs end up running over… just let me know. Don't undervalue your time, and ensure that you're giving the other Crafters rates that are fair. Don't get caught short, or give away your share to sweeten it for them. Got it?"

"Understood." Blathnaid laughed as she let out a sigh of relief. "Man, I hate this negotiating stuff. And I know you're going super easy on me, too."

"You'll get used to it… and you'll even come to enjoy it. When you've got a good team of people who can do the stuff you can't get around to, I'm sure you'll be fighting for their cut. You'll want them to get a good deal. That makes things so much easier." Sal gestured to the other benches in the workshop. "This build is going to be done in the new workshop. So, any finished components can be put there."

"And these numbers are the sequence you want them done?" Blathnaid pointed to the numbered corners on each blueprint.

"Yeah, if you could work on the enclosure first, that would be best. I have all the materials you'll need, and I can store them up in the Savior workshop if you want to do the construction there?" Sal knew he could simply store the finished components in Arsenal and then take them to the build site in the upgraded workshop space.

"Sounds good to me. Want me to get started on it now? I don't have any projects at the moment," Blathnaid asked hopefully.

"Yes, you can round up Jack and whoever else you need, and I'll meet you up there." Sal gestured to the other corner of the workshop. "I just need to talk to a few other people before I can get started on it earnestly."

"See you there." Blathnaid smiled as she excitedly picked up the stack of drawings, clutching them to her chest almost protectively. "And thanks for thinking of Jack with this. He's going to be so excited."

"Ha. I'm thinking of dragging Anthony up, too. There's an essence programming component to it, and although Fabi is hopeful I'll pick it up, I've got a feeling that he'd be a much better sponge for what she's teaching." Sal laughed.

"Leave it to me." Blathnaid smiled. "He'll just get nervous if you ask him directly, but he'll come when he knows Jack is going. Do you think Fabi will teach him?" She sounded a little unsure at the end.

"One way to find out." Sal gave her a shrug. "Anyways, I'll see you up there in around thirty minutes. Sound good?"

"Yeah." Blathnaid struggled to lift a half-full coffee cup. "We need Alex's coffees in the dorms, by the way. The machine up there sucks."

"Working on it." Sal laughed as he made his way toward Alex's coffee corner.

He was hopeful that Anthony would come along to the Savior dorms so he could introduce him to Fabi. If Sal's instincts were right about Anthony's affinity for essence programming, then he'd have another useful person he could outsource work to. Getting Blathnaid onboard was a no-brainer; he needed someone who could transform the raw materials into usable components for the build. Assembly as a Mythcrafter would be far easier than creating everything from scratch.

By having Jack on runes and Anthony with essence programming, it would give Sal a good team of people who could cover his weaknesses and make Crafting projects that much easier. Being able to fund it all with the proceeds from the simulation orb was a definite help, even though he was sure they would have done it for free. Sal was particularly happy that Blathnaid was learning her value. Upgrade had definitely taken steps to make sure Blathnaid wasn't getting cheated, but Sal still had work to do to ensure she wasn't being too soft in the deals she made.

As Sal made his way through the workshop, Alex's coffee setup came into view. The Alchemist's expression soured almost instantly, and he brought up a finger to wag from side to side.

"Ah, ah…if you're looking for an extension for our deadline, it's not going to happen!" Alex insisted as he put on a fake smile. "I did my own bit of investigating, and it looks like you're not on the roster for the Material Exchange. Looks like your little ploy of getting Lawrence Baron's interest didn't work out after all."

Sal sighed as he came to a stop in front of Alex's workstation. "Can you make me a coffee, first?"

Alex frowned as he looked at Sal in surprise. "What? No snappy comeback, or an excuse that everything is going swimmingly? Expected a little more bite from you, Mr. Argento."

Sal just shook his head and pointed at the coffee cups. "Everything is moving perfectly, but I wanted to have a chat with you. Let's say that you had an abundance of ingredients…what then? What is it that you want them for?"

Alex didn't answer immediately, but he did pull a cup from the stack. He looked thoughtful as he stared at Sal. "You're trying to change the deal? What's the angle? I'm still out of my ingredients, and I've not seen anything to assure me that you're actually doing something with them."

"Right now, I could give you those ingredients and reimburse you for their value five times over, so don't worry about the cost, okay? I'm just asking you what the goal is. If you had a ready supply, what would happen?" Sal pushed further, hoping that the answer he suspected would be vocalized.

"Same as all Crafters, I imagine." Alex laughed as though it were obvious. "Materials and ingredients are the same bottleneck for both groups. Although it's possible to salvage materials after a shitty build, the ingredients are destroyed when you're making elixirs. It's a costly business, and I need to make shit that sells. I can't experiment when I need to ensure I'm covering costs, and the suppliers know that."

"Does this coffee cover your costs?" Sal accepted the fresh coffee from Alex. "You've got pretty much everyone addicted to the stuff by this point."

Alex shook his head as he tapped the large dispenser. "Not a chance. Making this stuff is close to breakeven for me. It gives me enough to buy a few extra pieces here and there, but the good stuff is perishable." He gave another fake smile. "So, why are you asking all the qualifying questions about Alchemy…

months after you agreed to the request? Can't help but feel like you're focusing on the wrong issues, here."

"You've got two options available." Sal placed a lid over the coffee cup. "We can keep our original agreement and I get you those supplier contracts. You'll still end up paying for the ingredients, and I guess you'll have leeway to afford more of them in time."

"That option," Alex answered immediately. "I'm not looking for some gizmo or gadget that's going to improve my process. I need ingredients to properly experiment."

Sal nodded, ignoring the comment. "The second option is that you work with me on a contractual basis. I'm going to create an elixir machine." Sal made eye contact with Alex as he spoke. "It will grow the ingredients, use Alchemize on them and later it will use Refine. I've already got proof of concept and I'm working on the build with a team."

Alex scoffed at the suggestion. "What? You think you're going to scare me with that? The plan is to make me obsolete by getting a machine to do my job?" He openly laughed in Sal's face, but it was clear that he was annoyed by the topic. "Many have tried before you, and many will try after you. It's as feasible as replacing Crafters. You understand that, right? You can't just push a few buttons and expect a masterpiece."

"I understand that you're skeptical, but the first phase of the project will cover your initial requirements. That aspect will be proof of concept." Sal didn't waver in his explanation. If Alex was going to be a part of the process, it would make everything work smoothly. He wanted to give him a chance to be a part of the solution, rather than being someone steamrolled by it. "It's going to be a Genesis machine, and it will create the ingredients we need for the next stages of the project."

Alex paused as he stared at Sal. "You're deadly serious, aren't you?" He tried to laugh, but the noise died in his throat. "So... okay, let me get this straight. You don't have my ingredients yet, and your plan was never to open up a supplier agreement? You wanted to make a machine that would do the job for you?"

"I can get those if this fails," Sal replied confidently. Lawrence Baron's Material Exchange would still be sufficient for Alex's needs, and probably even Maccles Materials. "But, if this succeeds, I'd rather you were a part of it. I'm envisioning an outcome that doesn't make you obsolete but rather that you become an integral part of the business. If you had an endless supply of ingredients, and the Refine ability was on hand... you'd have no limitations."

"So, it's a win-win situation? I give you the week and change, and you either get this machine operational... or you get me those supplies through the Argento Auction House?" Alex asked dubiously. "What's the catch?"

Sal offered him an almost helpless shrug. "I would prefer for this to involve you as much as possible. Even if I can create a machine that uses Alchemize, it'll be useless without the right recipes. Any recipes you add to the machine in the initial stages will be treated as yours, with you getting a twenty-percent cut of every sale."

"Twenty fucking percent? For my life's work? Are you fucking kidding me?" Alex practically screeched as he planted both hands on the table and stared at Sal as if he were insane. "If you're able to get this thing up and running, and that's a big fucking *if,* buddy, then you'll need my expertise more than you know."

Sal smiled inwardly. The conversation was now into percentage rights rather than whether or not Alex was onboard with the project. Alex had unwittingly just entered the negotiation. With an audible sigh, Sal bit his lip as he looked to the tabletop for a few seconds. "What number feels better to you? I've already taken the cost of the essence cores and materials into account, so we're making a loss on the first fifty percent. I'd need to be paying wages with thirty percent, which is why I suggested twenty."

All of it was a lie made up on the spot, but that was a part of the fun. Sure, there would be costs, but there was no way that Sal was going to let Alex have the advantage.

Alex looked past Sal to the private rooms on the other side of the workshop. "Before I answer… tell me for real. What did you make in that private room? That will tell me if I want to be in business with you."

It looked like he was just fishing for information rather than it being a part of the negotiation, but Sal was happy to play along. "It was a Legendary sniper rifle for the Reavers Guild. Another time it was for Upgrade making the Legendary coat that I commissioned."

Alex whistled as a crooked grin pulled at his lips. "So… this machine, it would be Legendary? And you'd need me to operate it for you?"

"Twenty-five percent of the list price. Any additional recipes you make above market standards would be thirty percent. I'll find a way to make it work," Sal suggested with a heavy sigh, as though despairing that it was breaking him to offer such a sum.

"I'm thinking I could get an even bigger number if I let you sweat it out a little," Alex teased as he leaned closer. "Twenty-five isn't really going to pay the bills, now, is it? How do I know you won't just renege on the agreement after you get what you want?"

"I could do this without you." Sal raised the coffee cup. "But I'd rather this wasn't an ultimatum." He took a sip and waited for Alex's response.

"Poorly, no doubt… but let's just say that I'm intrigued. I want to see this Genesis machine operational before I decide. And if it's not going to work, then you can say goodbye to all this percentage talk," Alex said as he assessed Sal. It was clear from how his eyes bore into Sal's that he was testing him.

"That's fair. If there's still percentages at that point, I'll let you know if the deal is still on the table," Sal agreed with a bright smile as he turned to find Anderson Royce in the crowd. "I've got someone else to talk to about this." When he made eye contact with Royce, he waved at him.

"Royce?" Alex's eyes widened as he looked at Sal. "You cheeky bastard… what are you planning?"

"See you later, Alex!" Sal started to walk away.

"WAIT!" Alex shouted at him as he reached across the table to catch Sal's elbow, almost causing him to drop the coffee. "What… I mean, what incentive can you give me for the twenty-five percent cut? Just to sweeten the deal? Hypothetically, I mean… you know, if this thing all works out."

Sal paused as he looked at Alex strangely. "For twenty-five? Nothing. If you went down to something like five percent, I'd give you a premises in Silver Sanctuary to work out of with the machine, alongside other staff. It'd be an upmarket retail kind of thing, with support from the Argento Auction House."

All color drained from Alex's face. "That option. I take that one… if you went to ten percent?" He caught himself by the end of the sentence.

Sal winced as he started to slowly shake his head.

"Eight," Alex said in a strained voice, trying to salvage the deal. "You give me the ingredients and a half-decent Refiner, and I'll give you elixirs that will blow your fucking socks off!"

Sal sighed as he placed the coffee cup back on the table and stretched his hand out. "Eight percent and the premises in Silver Sanctuary. We'll have to draft up some contracts, but I'm happy to shake on it."

Alex's predatory smile stretched wide as he clutched Sal's hand with both of his own. "I've got plenty of paper. Let's get this written down now."

CHAPTER 30: ASSEMBLE

"Okay, we've got Alex and Anders," Sal said excitedly as he approached Fabi in the Saviors workshop. "Looks like it's full steam ahead with the elixir machine."

Fabi cocked an eyebrow as she pointed at the loading area. "You're responsible for this? I was trying to tell her that there were loads of workspaces, but she's setting up in the loading dock."

Sal walked up beside her and looked down to where she gestured. Anthony, Jack, and Blathnaid were each looking at the set of blueprints he had designed. Realistically, neither Anthony nor Jack would have much to do until Blathnaid did her part of the deal.

"Yeah, I asked Blathnaid for her help with the components for the build. Jack is the one who Nemesis has her eye on. He's really good with runes," Sal explained as he pointed at them.

"And who's the guy with the beard? He kinda ducked away from me when I said hello." Fabi folded her arms, frowning. "Another Crafting genius who didn't make the Saviors?"

"That's Anthony. He's top of the class in Essence Programming. You could tell that Upgrade wanted to move him out of the foundational class after just two sentences." Sal laughed as he pointed at him. "I was hoping you could talk to him, since I think he'll likely pick up essence programming a thousand times faster than me."

Fabi glanced at Sal curiously. "Why are you outsourcing everything? The Sovereign drone and now the elixir machine? Are you trying to bankrupt yourself?"

Sal smiled as he offered a shrug. "Honestly, I have Jackal and I'm really happy with it. I want to go into dungeons and get stronger with the Subsume ability. Then there's the Silverson Arts, and the administration stuff that will come with the guild. When I have a Crafting project in front of me, I end up losing all perspective for everything else." He pointed at the group in the loading bay. "But with outsourcing, I can include my friends and give them an opportunity to be a part of the next big thing. If this elixir machine works like we think it will… then each of them will get a cut of the profits. How amazing would that be?"

"You're giving them a share? Do you think that's wise?" Fabi asked in disbelief. "I mean, like… friendships are one thing, but if this thing topples the market, you could be sharing millions with them. Are they really that reliable?"

Sal nodded. "Yeah, I think it's wise." He smiled as he continued to look down at his three friends discussing the blueprints with one another. "Alex and Royce are going to work on the elixir machine. I'll have a Growth and Alchemize specialist, which reduces the number of calculations needed to be done. Hopefully their expertise will speed up the output."

"And you're giving them a cut on the profits even if they end up being useless? Like, it doesn't exactly help the Arkwright if you put Upgrade on a wage to just stand beside it," Fabi insisted with a pained expression. She bit her lip and shook her head. "I don't mean to be a bitch here. I just want you to understand that you're likely throwing money away by giving people a cut."

Sal chuckled. "Well, the other part of it is the premises in Silver Sanctuary. Royce's name has a lot of pull with the community, so he can be the friendly face who can take orders and do the selling. Alex wouldn't be a slouch either." He glanced at Fabi. "It'll be out of my allowance of storefronts, and I wanted to talk to you about it to make sure you were okay with it."

Fabi sighed before offering a shrug. "It's up to you. I just don't want their losses affecting my books. If you think that it will work like the Arkwright, and that they'll bring value, I'll trust you. I'd rather see profitability before you start offering investment opportunities."

"Very fair," Sal answered with a nod. "As it stands, I've set aside twenty-five percent with Alex, and Anders accounting for sixteen percent. I've another eight or nine there to sway a talented Refiner. Sixty percent for my guild, and the last fifteen percent for the Crafting Department."

Fabi's eyes widened. "Wait, you're giving a cut to the Crafting Department? Was this a condition Quest made for the upgraded workshop?"

"Nope. I just think it would be good to reinvest in the place that invested in me." Sal grinned. "Because if this machine does end up revolutionizing the elixir market… then it would make the Crafting Department the most well-funded domain of Quest Academy, wouldn't it? I wonder what sort of effects that would have on the curriculum and the types of students it attracts?"

Fabi couldn't help but smile. "A very noble goal… What makes you think it won't be squandered by the Hunter Bureau pulling the strings in the background?"

"I'll deal with that if it happens. Right now, I just need to ensure the project goes smoothly. If the guild is earning a stable income, then it removes a lot of barriers. I'll be able to fund all the master classes for the members, and offset the cost of equipment by using the Arkwright. If the face mask concept works, too…"

"And the elixirs… the members will be able to use the elixirs we make." Sal smiled as he thought about it. "Imagine it… they have access to Kaizen and can blitz through their gates. When I get approval from Quest to work on weaves, then I'll be able to unknot their potential. Everyone in the guild will be a powerhouse, and they'll all have their own revenue streams through investments or the depot."

When Sal didn't get a response from Fabi, he stopped looking at the group in the loading area and turned to see her face. He was met with the most wonderful stare. "What? Did I say something stupid?"

Fabi just shook her head slowly. "I'm starting to appreciate all that overthinking you do." She laughed and a wide smile appeared. "You've clearly thought about this, and I would love to see it happen." Fabi continued to laugh as she bit her lip. "And you even managed to sway Alex?!"

"He drove a hard bargain," Sal admitted, smiling. "But it turns out one of the reasons he's saving up is to have his own outlet. That's why he's lurking around Quest Academy. You should have seen it, he practically bit my hand off to get a premises in Silver Sanctuary."

Fabi was about to answer when something caught her attention. She whipped her head around to stare out the window with a surprised expression. "Is Blathnaid using Figment?"

Sal followed her gaze to see Blathnaid holding a freshly crafted canister. "Ah, no… her ability is Construct. It's a much less powerful version of Figment, but has the same sort of execution, I think. Blathnaid needs to understand the design, and she can use Construct to make it a reality if she has the necessary materials."

"That's exactly the same as Figment!" Fabi laughed as she placed her hands on the window, as though it would get her closer to Blathnaid.

Sal shook his head. "No… Figment doesn't need the right materials. It can create them with essence and whatever is nearby. That's what makes it so powerful."

Fabi stared at Sal for a few moments. "That doesn't sound right. Isn't that a bit ridiculous?"

Sal pointed at his chest. "You know the way Mythcrafter is a bit ridiculous?"

"Yeah…" Fabi answered apprehensively, clearly unsure where this was going.

"Mythcrafter is about twenty grades lower than Figment. The active essence gates I have are around half of what you have." Sal laughed as he continued. "And then there's the mastery aspect, where you're pretty much top of every category. You're probably the most powerful Hero in terms of ability and raw essence statistics. I wouldn't be surprised if you could create an entire building if you put your mind to it. That's how capable Figment is."

"Oh," Fabi breathed as she turned to look at Blathnaid. "Would it be rude if I asked to help her out? If she uses Construct the way I should be using Figment, maybe I could learn a few things from her?"

"I don't see why not." Sal moved toward the door. "But, in exchange… is there any chance you could help Anthony out with some essence programming tutoring?"

"Absolutely," Fabi answered, like it was nothing. "I would have suggested it anyway, since there's pretty much nobody except Upgrade to bounce ideas off. I don't want to be annoying her when she's busy with mentoring." She thought about it for a few more seconds before snapping her fingers. "If you're still using the payment system idea, then I can walk Anthony through its construction. That will be a lot simpler than getting him working on a calculation matrix."

"Ten Q-Cred says you'll have him working on the matrix by the end of the week," Sal said confidently as he made his way down to the loading area. "I don't think it'll be too long before you acknowledge him."

"Bet." Fabi grinned as she followed him out to the stairs.

When Sal reached the loading area, he waved at Jack, who was a little surprised at his sudden appearance. Blathnaid was concentrating on a blueprint, while Anthony was still marveling at everything around him. It was his first time up in the Savior dorms and he looked like he was just taking it all in.

"Hey… this is Fabi Maccles. She's one of the third-years and would like to help us on this project." Sal introduced Fabi, not really expecting either Jack or Anthony to know who she was. He was wrong on one of those assumptions.

Anthony's eyes lit up at the mention of her name. "I bought your course on the Credit Store! I've been researching modularity, and loved your concepts around component switching." It was like all his nervousness had evaporated as he heaped on the praise. "Just thinking of how you could fundamentally change a load-out on the fly, it's practically a master class in itself."

Fabi paused as she looked at Anthony with a gentle smile. Without saying a word, she took out her tablet and tapped a few buttons.

Sal felt his own tablet vibrate, and he pulled it out to see a message.

Fabrizia Maccles has sent you 10 Q-Cred.

Looking at Anthony, Fabi's smile grew wider. "I need to talk to Blathnaid for a little bit… stuff relating to my ability… but I want to have a conversation with you about essence programming to see where you're at with it. I'm guessing you're Anthony McGuinn?"

Anthony blinked in surprise, looking at her tablet for second, as though wondering whether she had looked him up that fast. "Yeah, I'm A. McGuinn on the Crafting Corner."

"Cool." Fabi tapped her tablet a few more times. "I've just sent you the entire catalogue of my courses on the Credit Store and refunded the ones you've already paid. See how you fare with them, and come to me with any questions you have."

Anthony reacted as if he had just won the lottery, and he fumbled with his tablet that was vibrating constantly with all the notifications from the Credit Store. "I can't accept all of this for free!"

"Oh, it's not free." Fabi grinned ominously. "I'm only here for another semester, and I'm going to need help with some projects. You're going to need to catch up as fast as you possibly can. It'll be a miserable few months for you."

"Awesome," Anthony breathed as he looked up at Sal in excitement. "Thanks for introducing us!"

Sal just smiled as he turned to Blathnaid, who was still looking at one of the blueprints, frowning. "I'm going to set up some of the materials to help you get started. Where would you like them?"

Blathnaid gestured at the floor space around her. "I've been using some of the communal pieces, but I'm limited to what I can actually build with what's here. After I see what we're working with, I'll need to get the other materials from the Credit floor…"

Sal nodded in agreement. "Work through Vanessa for what you need, and tell her that it's all to go on my account. If you pay for anything yourself, I'll find out."

"Do we have to use the runes in the blueprints, by the way?" Jack asked, his hand raised.

Sal frowned at the question. "I was going to say yes…but as long as they work the way they're supposed to, I don't have any issues with what ones you use."

"How experimental can I go?" Jack pushed a little further, his smile growing wider.

Sal felt like this was either a great opportunity or inviting disaster; there was no middle ground. "You know what… go wild. Have fun with it, but if it fails, default back to what works. Try not to destroy the equipment that Blathnaid is making."

Blathnaid shot Jack a warning look, as if to say that there would be consequences.

"Since we're talking about room for error…" Fabi slid into the conversation. "Can I help out, Blathnaid? I'm not good at controlling my ability, but when I saw your Construct from up there," she gestured at the window above, "I thought it looked amazing, and guessed you'd be a good teacher for me."

If Fabi's words were a tactic, and not her earnest feelings, it would have worked wonders. Blathnaid pretty much crumbled at the praise and ended up giving the softest nod of all time.

"That's… okay with me." She glanced at Sal awkwardly. "I mean, if Sal's okay with it."

"Perfect." Sal lifted his left arm. "Now, I'll need a few hands to help me carry out the materials."

"From where?" Jack asked with spread arms, gesturing around the loading area.

Sal smiled as he opened Arsenal. The subspace door appeared in front of him and led to Jackal's collection of harvested materials as well as the produce created by the Arkwright.

"You know what?" Jack sighed as he looked into Arsenal. "I'm not even surprised."

CHAPTER 31: TEAMWORK

Sal was not prepared for how quickly things had started to move. In just the space of a few hours, the shipment from the Credit Store had arrived... and the entire Savior workshop was pandemonium. Fabi was holding hands with Blathnaid, and Anthony was touching the edge of Fabi's eye-patch. Although that would have looked a little peculiar, the outcome was frankly ridiculous.

Anthony's Supercharge ability was pushing Fabi's tracker beyond its limits, and Blathnaid was attempting to guide the Invention essence for Figment, much like Divinity had helped steer Sal's visions when he used her ability. It looked like it shouldn't work. It was the weirdest setup, and it looked like it was positively exhausting both Anthony and Blathnaid...

But the manufacturing speed was insane. Each component was being created in minutes, and Jack barely had time to stack the pieces before the next part was done. Sal had jumped in to assist, and it was hilarious that his Mythcrafter ability was put on hold so he could work as a porter.

A pane of shadow glass melted with Fabi's essence to become six distinctively defined vials. Sal knew that they had their own names, but he couldn't fathom how Fabi was managing to create six entirely unique pieces from one cut of material. What made it ten times more difficult was the fact that Jack substituted out of being a porter so he could start to etch runes into the vials. The grin on his face was the clearest indicator that he was acutely aware of how much work he had left for Sal to complete.

Thankfully, the additional Strength stats from the hybrid dungeon were there to help. Sal was able to comfortably carry the distillation chambers that were made from scuttler chitin. Was it necessary to make them from that material? No. It was overkill, but that's what he had at hand and it was easier to use it than not. Did he need to use an advanced form of obsidian, like shadow glass? No, but that was just another one of those trade-offs that contributed toward the end goal. Sal wasn't going to be precious with his materials, especially when he knew how quickly the Arkwright could replenish his stocks. The Material Exchange, Ameye Locomotive, and the Argento Auction House were also all going to be gifting him materials. He'd use all of them.

"You're doing amazing," Blathnaid encouraged Fabi, laughing. "Your control is skyrocketing!"

Fabi smiled as she tore through the components, one after another. The evil distortion of essence didn't appear this time, which had manifested as a purple, hazy cloud back in the Argento workshop. Figment was laser focused on the task at hand, with no excess essence escaping. That had been Blathnaid's contribution to the build, by guiding Fabi's essence as much as she could manage.

Anthony wasn't really struggling either, as all he had to do was keep Fabi's Epic-grade visor locked in a Legendary-grade state. Because it didn't have erratic bursts of essence like the Voracious Rapier's Arc Strike, he was able to keep the flow of essence consistent. Still, the expression on his face looked like he was concentrating on it as though his life depended on it.

Sal glanced at Jack between component retrievals and was pleasantly relieved to see that at least he looked normal. He sat on crossed legs with a vial in his hands, making small markings with a piece of chalk, as though creating a rough draft of what the runes would be. At their current rate of progress, Jack was likely going to be their bottleneck, and that was absolutely fine.

"That's the purification chamber," Blathnaid called out to Sal, pointing with her free hand at a separate area. "You should put it over there with the rest of the Refiner station components."

Sal grinned as he looked at the purification chamber in his hands. The shadow glass interior was crystallized to catch any impurities within the elixirs. When it was coupled with the resonator and the infuser, the elixirs would have the highest chance of coming out at a top grade. Sal loved that Blathnaid had already planned out separate areas for each of the three builds. By the look of it, the Refiner station, which was the final phase of the overall build, was going to have all its components finished first.

"Are you going to create a bottling station?" Jack asked Sal, as he looked up from his sketch. "Because the blueprints don't really look like you've thought of that."

Sal placed the purification chamber down carefully before turning to look at Jack in confusion. "Why would I need a bottling station? I'm pretty sure that it'll be a one-at-a-time sort of process."

Jack slowly shook his head. "You should check with Blathnaid and Fabi to make sure, but I think you'll need to consider that this thing might be mass-producing." He raised the vial in front of him. "Because I'll need to calibrate the activation speeds based on what the actual outputs are. Also, if you're working with elixirs that can expire, I can put preservation runes on the bottles. I'd need to know that in advance, though. Laser engravers would work best if we needed to do it at speed."

"We can probably create a protocol to slow everything down," Anthony answered with a smile, surprising both Sal and Jack. "I thought that this was going to be a build that prioritized perfection over pace, but now that I'm seeing how industrial it is...it looks like it'll be mass-producing. Filling one of those vats would probably equate to about two hundred elixirs. There's no way that the reduction process would shave off ninety percent of the concoction."

Sal frowned as he looked at the setup. He was so excited that the components were being built that he didn't really pay attention to the small details. Each piece was being manufactured at Rare grade at an absolute minimum, which made him excited, with some of the pieces dipping into Unique and Epic grade.

"Sal, we need these moved!" Blathnaid called out urgently, pulling him out of his reverie.

Sal moved to the latest vat that needed to be relocated. When he put his hands around it, he realized what Anthony and Jack were talking about. In his drawings, the component should have been the size of a small keg. The reality? His arms couldn't wrap around its circumference. It was at least three times the size he had listed in the blueprint. Sal glanced at all the other components and was both horrified and relieved to see that the difference was replicated across *everything*.

"Shit," Sal breathed as he moved the vat to the Genesis station section. The whole build was now going to be at least three times the size. Had this been a result of Fabi's interpretation of the blueprint, or was it because of Blathnaid?

"Did we fuck up?" Anthony asked as he paid attention to Sal. He sounded worried, as though he had been an accomplice somehow.

Because of Anthony's proximity to Fabi, she heard both his words and his worry. The current build wavered and shattered… causing shards of shadow glass to scatter across the floor. Blathnaid cried out in surprise as she jumped away from the glass, while Fabi just looked over at Sal in confusion.

"Did I make them wrong?" She sounded surprised and a little reproachful. When her eyes caught sight of the components, her face blanched. "Oh… fuck."

Blathnaid went to retrieve the blueprints and pointed at them. "We're doing it in sequence, though. There shouldn't have been any issues… I stacked all the materials to use in the order of each build." She sounded confused as to what was going on, not making the same connection as Fabi.

Sal put up his hands and tried to calm them down. "Look, don't worry. There's nothing wrong."

"Like fuck there's not." Fabi groaned as she put a hand to her brow, as though she were in deep contemplation. "They're massive! When I was using Figment, I was making them to spec… but how come they're three times the size? Are we running out of materials?"

Blathnaid looked at the pile and shook her head slowly. "No? We've actually got a little too much…"

Fabi blinked in surprise, dropping her hand to take a look. "Wait… that can't be possible. Even if you're substituting materials with essence, there's no way to do that for two-thirds of a build."

"Hey, can I say something?" Sal asked with a warm smile. "This is a good thing… I think. We just need to keep going at the same rate to ensure that everything is the same size. Is that okay with you guys?"

Fabi looked at Sal as if he were crazy. "Sal, this is going to turn into a factory at this rate. We'll need half of the workshop floor to accommodate this thing."

"More like a fifth, if my guess is right," Sal corrected her, but then momentarily panicked as he saw the expression on her face. "But… the main thing is that there is uniformity in the build so far. I'll just need to work on more components to bridge the gaps. We'll likely need a bottling station, as Jack suggested."

Fabi sighed as she shook her head. "No, I think this was a mistake. We should have let Blathnaid work on it with Construct… this wouldn't have happened. Since we still have the materials, it might be a bit more work, but you can probably refit the components to the right shape. I'll give her my essence to lessen the load a bit."

"I can't make Legendary grade, though," Blathnaid highlighted with a raised hand. "Isn't that an important aspect?"

Fabi snorted. "Neither can I."

Blathnaid looked at her strangely. "But you did… like, twice. Your eye-patch flashed yellow every time it happened. Anthony told me that's what it meant."

Anthony nodded in agreement. "I can feel the essence surge whenever an item is Legendary grade, but yeah, the eye-patch was flashing the same color."

"My visor doesn't do that," Sal noted with a hint of disappointment. It would have been nice if it happened while a build was cooling down, because he genuinely had no idea what way it would turn out until it was done.

"It can with essence programming," Fabi explained before looking at the shards of shadow glass on the ground. With a wave of her hand, she looked at the pitiful display. "Don't suppose it can work like thi—"

The entire pane reformed instantly, pulling the available shards into a congealed mass that melted into the original shape. That single action was accompanied with a slow flash of yellow from Fabi's eye-patch.

"Yeah…" Blathnaid started awkwardly. "I think Fabi should keep going with the build."

"Agreed." Both Anthony and Jack spoke at the same time, their eyes glued to the reformed shadow glass.

Sal exhaled slowly before he let out an involuntary chuckle. "Looks like you're getting used to Figment?"

Fabi was horrified by what had just happened. Her hand didn't move from where she had just waved it. "It can't be that easy…" she breathed as she looked at one of the finished components on the other side of the loading bay. It was the purification chamber. With the same hand, she whipped it in the direction of the purification chamber and it suddenly started to glow.

"Hey… that's already done." Sal tried to chide her gently, thinking she was somehow confused. He had already inspected it and it was a healthy Rare grade.

A flash of purple on Fabi's eye-patch was the cause of celebration for literally everyone except Fabi. Apparently, Epic grade wasn't enough. Another wave, and another… and another, until finally a triumphant grin appeared on her face.

It took the eye-patch a few moments to catch up with what Fabi seemingly and inherently understood. It gave off an almost reluctant yellow flash, signifying that the purification chamber was now at the Legendary grade.

Sal didn't believe it as he started a quick Appraisal. It had to be an error in the essence programming that was accidentally attributing a Legendary grade. His Appraisal came back with the same information that he had feared… It was not only a Legendary grade, but the options on it had also evolved. It was now a named component—Absolver. What did that even mean?

"What the actual…?" Sal breathed as he looked at Fabi in disbelief. "You did not just upgrade that?"

It was incomprehensible that she was able to just wave her hand and bring up the item's rarity. Countless thoughts ran through Sal's head… like if she was able to do this with leecher cores, would she create a blight core with a few snaps of her fingers? What sort of properties did they gain? Would all components end up becoming named if she continued like this?

Fabi's grin grew wider. "This is fucking awesome."

CHAPTER 32: FIGMENT

"I'm genuinely speechless." Sal pulled his right hand through his hair. He looked at the fully stacked loading bay, where countless oversized components were waiting for assembly. Even the things that he had guessed would take a few days, like the resonator and harmonizer… both of them were ready and waiting. If there was one thing that was a minor relief, it was that despite countless attempts, Fabi hadn't been able to achieve a Mythic-grade component. It wasn't that he wanted her to fail, or to create a gap between them… it was more that he was terrified of the repercussions if she was able to hand-wave something better than the blight core into existence.

"I like this version of you." Fabi grinned as she sat beside him with a satisfied sigh. "This ability is absolutely amazing… like, I can just feel what needs to happen. I think it's because I had Anthony and Blathnaid helping me out."

Sal chuckled as he shook his head. "Absolutely not. That was all you, and I think I need to take a cut out of the guild's share so I can pay you for all of this. Legendary-grade components are going to result in something spectacular or disastrous when it all comes together."

"Oooh, that's a very good point," Fabi teased as she pretended to think. "You know the way you said that you had twenty-five percent allocated for a Refiner, Alchemist, and Grower? Well, I'll take the one percent left over."

Sal looked at her wearily. "Come on, you know that's not fair. At this rate, all I've done is supply the materials and you barely even used them."

"You also made some fancy blueprints," Fabi corrected him. "Proof of concept is enough for most patents, so it's totally fair when you think about it."

"I'm not going to win this, am I?" Sal laughed as he continued to look around the room.

"It's reassuring that you're learning." Fabi grinned as she clapped him on the back. "But, you know… none of this would be possible without the weave you made for me. No matter how much I trained or worked on my weave, I'd never have been able to unlock this sort of power. You made this for me, and I think it's only fair that I help you out like this from time to time."

Sal snorted as he thought about it. "Man… I can't believe the Mythcrafter is going to be the junior partner in our business relationship." He laughed as he gestured at all the Legendary-grade materials and components. "Seriously, you've just blitzed past the Arkwright's capabilities in a single day."

"Don't worry, I'll keep you around as an Appraiser. I've got a feeling you're still a little faster than my tracker," Fabi teased as she got to her feet. "But when it comes to the assembly of this behemoth, I'd trust nobody else. You're the one who designed it, and you'll be the one to finish it. Me and the guys helping out in between is just a bonus."

Sal looked at her curiously. "Are you going to flood the Credit Store with Legendary Macclemark suits? I'm wondering how this is going to change the last semester for you."

Fabi shook her head. "You had me thinking about it earlier… when you said that you'd fund the Crafting Department. I liked that idea." She grinned as she thought about it. "What if I did the same? How do you think our juniors would do if all the materials they had were upgraded to Epic grade? Or, at the very least, Unique grade?"

"How much essence does it take?" Sal asked, not feeling the same level of excitement over the prospect. It wasn't that he didn't think it was a great idea. No, he was in full support of that. He just worried what the cost was on Fabi. There was no way this route didn't lead to dregs.

Fabi waved it off like it was nothing. "Roughly five to ten percent for a Legendary grade, if I get it the first time around. Up to twenty if it's stubborn. I think that I need to be at full essence capacity to try for Mythic grade—that might be the issue."

"It's a cheat ability." Sal stared at her, completely dumbfounded as to how much essence she had available. He knew it was likely going to be insane, but she was able to make up to twenty Legendary-grade components at full capacity? It was borderline unfair, and he was certainly one to talk about unfair abilities.

"Salvatore Argento is jealous of my ability?" Fabi asked in mock-astonishment. "And here I thought you'd be excited about that Sovereign drone concept."

"Oh." Sal's eyes widened. He had forgotten about that.

"Oh, indeed." Fabi grinned. "I want to try the hand-wave on items with an evolutionary rune. See if it takes less or more essence to bring them up to higher grades, and if the attributes are different. There's so much testing I want to do!"

"I guess you don't really need the blueprint for my visor. Your eye-patch is probably next on the list to get an upgrade?" Sal looked at the tracker covering her eye. "I have to say, I quite like the design. It's far less bulky than mine."

"Good to know." Fabi gave him a wink.

Well, it could have been a blink, with one of her eyes obscured by the patch, but Sal tried not to overthink that. "Hey, if you're thinking of changing my visor, don't bother. It's Legendary grade and ridiculously good at calculations." He chuckled at the thought.

Fabi shook her head. "Nope, leave it with me. Your face mask is designed for combat, which is all I need to know. If there's one domain I know I have more of an advantage on, it's combat."

"That's because you've not seen Jackal," Sal countered, grinning.

"Only because someone keeps dodging my requests to run a dungeon," Fabi shot straight back. "I'll see the little guy eventually. Maybe Jackal and Sovereign will become friends."

"Let's maybe not give the murder death-bot a brain." Sal laughed at the thought of it. "Last thing we want to do is accidentally create a man-made calamity."

Blathnaid walked into view with a half-eaten sandwich. "Break is over. Do you have any trash you want me to throw out?"

Fabi held up the crumpled remains of her sandwich packaging, which had been transformed into a miniature sculpted dragon. "You can throw this out, thanks."

Blathnaid took it from her carefully and gave Fabi a look of incredulity. "Can I keep this?"

Fabi paused in surprise. "It's just a little experiment. It's not that cool. I just made a mini version of the dragon that Chronos locked up."

"I love it." Blathnaid practically beamed as she cradled the little thing in her hands. She walked in the direction of the workspace she claimed, no doubt with the intention to adorn her desk with the new decoration.

"You could probably make those out of materials and make a killing on the Credit Store," Sal suggested, chuckling as he got to his feet and stretched his back.

"I'd rather that not be my legacy. I draw the line at cute little hover bots." She smiled as she replicated his action, albeit far more gracefully. "So, are we moving onto the assembly part, or do we have more pieces to work on?"

Sal thought about it as he looked around the room. "I can start moving everything to the workshop floor with Arsenal. We'll be assembling it in that area, and I should probably clear it with Upgrade where it should be placed."

"No need. I talked to her already and she said anywhere is fine that isn't the center of the room. I think her exact words was that it can be a spectacle, but not at the cost of workspace." Fabi impersonated Upgrade's voice, a little too accurately to the point that it was unnerving.

"Okay, then I guess I can do the infusions here." Sal thought about it. He had created the blueprints with Alchemize and Genesis in mind, so the build would have reflected those abilities. What remained was Refine, which he didn't have an individual for. He had the record of it on his tracker, but he wasn't sure how it would work with all the new Legendary-grade materials. The plan was for him to replicate it with Skill Master and then infuse the Absolver component with it. It was going to be the same as when he used Hannah's Barrier essence on the gauntlet.

"You can infuse? I thought you just built toward ability outcomes?" Fabi asked in confusion as she looked at him strangely.

"Well…I guess we'll find out." Sal offered an awkward shrug. "I'm not certain it will work, and it would be better if we had a Refiner on hand."

"Best ones I know dropped out to work in industry," Fabi replied sadly. "There wasn't really much for them at Quest Academy. I could hit them up to see if they'd like a gig, but I doubt they'd leave the security of a guild for something like this." She thought about it for a few seconds, glancing at Anthony, Jack, and Blathnaid. "And being honest, even though they were good, they're nowhere near the capabilities of the team you have here."

"Fun fact, this was my team for the tournament. All of them were the second-last pick out of the entire cohort, with me as their team captain," Sal proudly said as he gestured at his friends. "An entire team of Support classes won."

Fabi grinned. "I love that. Do you have the footage? I'd love to see it."

"Upgrade watched it at some point, so I think you'd have a better chance of asking her. Blathnaid threw a Controller over her shoulder and got a standing ovation. It was awesome."

"I need to see this!" Fabi laughed as she moved over to where Blathnaid stood, clearly set on asking for all the details.

Sal was left to his own devices, and he thought a little more about what needed to be done with Refine. He hadn't contributed to the build so far, and he was ridiculously lucky with Fabi discovering how to use Figment. Legendary-grade components were going to make things so much easier when it came to assembly, but it would likely take a chunk of essence to get it all over the line. Capacitor might finally get tested, which was a fun thought.

Making his way over to the Absolver, formerly known as the purification chamber, he used his tracker to call up the weave for Refine. Although it was easy for him to bring it up to the best version possible, and possibly unlock a higher grade of it, Sal wanted to ensure that it was safe for his body. If he was going to be the medium that activated it, he didn't want to accidentally hurt himself in the process.

Salvatore Argento Profile
Refine: Grade 8
Synchronization Level: 100%

"Okay…ninety-five percent should be fine." Sal decided on the number arbitrarily as he pushed the boundaries of the weave: a few fundamental changes to the spacing between threads, the inclusion of the Ravel method and a few pieces of unknotting.

Salvatore Argento Profile
Refine: Grade 17
Synchronization Level: 82%

No more Ravel method. Sal undid it and kept the unknotted segments. He waited patiently for the numbers to update on his tracker. It was far different from the simulation orb, because it was watching him use his own Skill Master weave and assessing him based on his profile.

Salvatore Argento Profile
Refine: Grade 15
Synchronization Level: 97%

"Perfect," Sal breathed as he activated the weave. It was a strange sensation as his fingers started to glow on his right hand. Everything around him seemingly turned to greyscale, with all color vanishing from view. It was a surreal moment and caused Sal to momentarily panic. He tried to find some semblance of color and wondered how the Refine ability was manifesting. When he turned back toward the group, he could see fragments of lustrous purple on the ground. It was some of the residue from when the shadow glass had shattered. Was Refine suggesting that he could interact with it?

Assuming that it was correct, Sal ignored the shards on the ground and moved his attention back to the Absolver. It took a lot of effort and trial and error, but Sal managed to Refine a portion of his essence into the palm of his hand. It was like a series of web-like strands being pulled from every pore in his skin, and accumulating into a clump of grey essence on his palm. Sal concentrated until the ball was the size of a large rock, then he tried purifying the mess of essence, making sure it was the best it could possibly be. It was similar to the exercises he did with Barry when training the Illusion ability.

After about five minutes of concentration, the grey clump had turned into a smooth ball that rotated gently an inch from his palm. Sal let out a steady breath as he gently pushed the ball into the Absolver. He hoped it would work like the Barrier gauntlets.

The moment his palm made contact with the smooth surface of the Absolver, Sal let out a sigh of relief. He could see the same webbing burst across the Absolver, and it shot around like circuitry, almost like an electrical current was darting around the vessel, looking for an exit. Countless streams of webs created a tight net throughout, until finally it settled, seemingly locked into position.

Sal waited a few seconds before he finally let go of the Refine weave. Color washed back into focus, and a pulsating white light emanated from the Absolver. His tracker was faster than his eyes, and he was rewarded with a new name of the Legendary-grade component.

Refined Absolver

"Let's hope that's enough." Sal shook his hand and turned back to the group.

"Are we going to talk about that wild purple light?" Jack pointed at Sal. "Or is this just one of the things we pretend is normal?"

Blathnaid laughed as she sorted through the blueprints, double-checking that all the components were finished up.

Jack wasn't letting it go, though. "Seriously, he just pushed a ball of light into the chimney thing. Are we not even going to acknowledge that?"

Sal chuckled as he gestured at the nearby tower that was visible through the window of the penthouse workshop. "Who wants to help me carry all this over there?"

CHAPTER 33: PHASES

The journey to Quest Academy's main workshop wasn't nearly as much of an ordeal as the guys had expected. Sal pretty much just needed their help in stacking everything into Arsenal, which was thankfully able to accommodate everything, including all the spare materials that hadn't been used. It wasn't exactly quantifiable at a glance, but it was clear that Fabi had saved him thousands of Q-Cred by not using what he had set aside for the build. Hell, there was even a whole stockpile of stuff purchased from the Credit floor that hadn't been used.

When they got to the upstairs floor that was dedicated to the upgraded workshop, Sal was met with a much more modern setting than he had expected. Previously, it had looked like a construction site with dusty floors and machines wrapped up in protective cloth. Now, it had a series of modern workbenches on a polished marble floor. The glass panels on the workstations showed that they were design-oriented rather than simple workspace surfaces. The private rooms had glass walls, with all but one frosted-over to obscure the contents. Smaller workbenches were available in pods surrounded by foam walls, suited for those who needed peace and quiet to work.

Then there were the multitools suspended from the ceiling, all stacked in one station, but capable of being pulled to an area of the workshop floor. They could be placed over any of the workbenches, and seemed to just hover gently in their station. No cables limited their positioning, and Sal wondered whether they'd float endlessly into the sky if the ceiling weren't there to stop them.

"This is amazing." Jack looked around the room with a sense of awe. "Look at the etching room!" He pointed at an area that had an entire wall made of soft plaster. Words were formed in the putty, but made no sense. Likely a remnant of whoever had been playing around with it most recently. Underneath the incomprehensible letters were a series of runes drawn in hastily, as if to show the purpose of the soft wall.

Sal wondered how they suspended a soft substance like that on a vertical surface, but it wasn't enough to occupy his mind for long. There was a clearing along one of the walls, that stood opposite the frosted glass rooms. The whole place was open plan, just like the main workshop below, but Sal guessed they could create a few partitions that would section off the different groups. If his guild was going to be working on this floor while he was at Quest Academy, then there would be certain things that couldn't be seen by other students. Specifically, anything he made at the Mythic grade, or anything relating to the simulation orb.

"This place looks perfect. What do you think?" Fabi gestured at the long, empty space he had just glanced at.

Sal nodded. "Let's get everything out and set up in their respective stations." He opened Arsenal, which resulted in a groan from both Blathnaid and Jack. Anthony seemed to be the only one who retained a bit of wonderment for the subspace.

They didn't exactly make quick work of it, and there was a lot of cursing and calling out about which piece belonged where. Jack had taken some of the vials to the etching room to continue his work on them, and that meant they'd be limited in working on the Alchemy station until he was done. It didn't matter, though, because Sal still had two other phases to work through, namely the Genesis station and the Refiner station.

When everything was in its place, Sal placed his hands on his hips and looked at the setup. The space was going to be a little tight, but he assumed it would work. He had originally hoped to have Barry with them so he could throw up an illusion as a proof of concept… but things had progressed a little beyond that stage. There was no real turning back now.

"Where do we start?" Fabi asked happily as she looked at the entire setup. "This is going to be epic."

"Personally, I'd hope for Legendary." Sal chuckled as he looked at it. "Anything less, and I've done a disservice to the components you made." He thought about it for a few seconds. "I was going to take on the assembly, if you guys wanted to call it a night. It's getting pretty late."

"Nope, I'm here until it's done," Blathnaid proclaimed before the others could even open their mouths. "If I can help with the construction of it, I'd be delighted to. I can follow the blueprints."

"I'm with Blathnaid on this one," Fabi agreed. "It would be such a waste if I didn't get to see you work your magic at the final stage."

"If I'm allowed, I'd like to stay, too," Anthony suggested, looking warily over his shoulder to see whether Jack had already left, and whether he was the odd one out.

Jack hadn't left; he poked his head out of the etching room. "I'm here for the long haul. I've got a lot of shit to do…and this room is unbelievable. They've got all sorts of tools I can use! We're definitely leaning into experimental runes for this one."

Sal smiled as he shook his head. "Well, it's finally my turn to do something, but I'm grateful for all the help. I don't think I've had this much fun on a project in a long time." He looked around at each of them. "Thanks for helping me out with this."

"We're still getting paid, right?" Jack asked Blathnaid with a goofy grin and a cocked eyebrow.

Blathnaid laughed as she waved him off. "Are we starting with the Genesis station? We won't be able to complete it until we get dungeon soil."

"Ah," Sal muttered as he thought about it. Because he thought it would take much longer, he had assumed he'd have time to get dungeon soil before they attempted the build. Genesis would help the plants grow, but he still needed essence-infused soil that had the right collection of nutrients.

"Easy," Fabi stated as she shrugged it off. "I'll get my car and go get some. Who wants to come with me?" She looked around at the group with a raised eyebrow. "Blathnaid knows the blueprints inside out, and Jack is working on the runes." Her eyes landed on Anthony and her face broke into a wide smile. "Looks like it's just us going on the dungeon run. You can keep me company and we can talk essence programming."

Anthony looked horrified by the prospect, but at the mention of talking about essence programming, it appeared his mindset did a complete one-eighty. With a voice that wavered on breaking, Anthony agreed to it. "Let's…do it."

"Perfect. We'll be back in an hour or so," Fabi declared as she fished her keys out of her jean pocket. "Don't start the fun stuff without us."

"No promises." Blathnaid grinned as she placed a hand on the Refined Absolver.

"Ah, do you want us to register the dungeon as the guild? He's a member, right?" Fabi asked as she hiked her thumb at Anthony.

Anthony shook his head and tried to explain that it wasn't necessary, but Sal stopped him with a laugh.

"Anthony, do you want to join the guild?" It was a simple question, and he was probably going to ask him down the line. He wasn't exactly certain about the head count requirements, but there was a good chance he was already over the limit. If he had to shuffle things around and bring in Sakura and O'Brien at a slightly later date, then that would work, too.

"I would like to," Anthony answered quietly before adding a nod. "Is it okay if I bring the Voracious Rapier to the dungeon? I don't want to die."

"Go for it. Fabi will make sure you get out in one piece." Sal laughed as he gave him a thumbs-up gesture. "Although, I think she's in for a surprise when she sees what you can do with that sword."

Fabi's face brightened. "Oooh, a dark horse! Love it! Let's get going. See you guys later. If there's anything else you need, just send me a message."

"Do you think they'd have soil from a dungeon on the Credit floor?" Anthony asked hopefully, as though trying to avoid an evening of dungeon running with Fabi.

"Nope. Let's go." Fabi laughed as she led him out of the workshop into the stairwell.

Blathnaid smiled as she watched them leave. "A part of me feels bad that we just let that happen, but the other part of me is happy that Anthony is going to run more dungeons."

"Fabi took out a scuttler without having access to her weave," Sal said with an involuntary shudder. "Anthony is incredibly safe in her hands."

Blathnaid blinked for a moment before laughing awkwardly. "Yeah, very happy it's Anthony and not me." She turned her attention back to the components. "So… can we start?"

"Absolutely," Sal replied, grinning. "Let's skip the Genesis station for now and go to the Alchemy station."

Jack poked his head out again. "Actually, could you work on the Refiner instead? I'm going to need a bit more time with the vials for the Alchemy station."

With a sigh, Sal nodded. "Refiner it is."

One of the key benefits of getting into a flow state was that you lost all sense of time and perspective. That's what Sal felt when he finished screwing the Refined Absolver into the mounted frame. Having the components at hand was a godsend, and he simply had to go through the motions with the Perfect weave active. It was a massive jigsaw puzzle just waiting to be assembled. The fact that there were well over fifty parts wasn't an issue; it would have been thousands if he had crafted the components by hand.

He was so lost in the process that he nearly jumped out of his skin when Fabi came into view to support the frame on the opposing side. Blinking in surprise, he looked over his shoulder to see Anthony offer a friendly wave.

"Did you guys not get into a dungeon?" Sal asked breathlessly, willing his heart rate to return to normal. Perfect tried its best, but hadn't really succeeded.

"We did three." Fabi grinned as she nodded in Anthony's direction. "I let him clear one by himself, because he was an absolute force to be reckoned with. You should let him keep that sword, by the way."

"It's Salvatore's," Anthony insisted, but Fabi ignored him with a wave of her hand.

"So, you've been a busy bee while we were away… This is looking amazing," Fabi said excitedly as she stepped back from the build.

Sal couldn't help but agree. He had initially visualized it as an almost archaic setup, with a stone-like furnace, plant vines bearing fruits hanging between the stations, and some old-school mortars and pestles. It didn't make any sense why he had assumed it would look that way, but it felt like a nice aesthetic.

The reality couldn't have been farther from that image. His new Refiner station was an ivory-white chimney with a set of copper-colored pipes leading into it from every conceivable angle. There were segments that were completely transparent along the funnel to show the elixir concoctions within, and that transparent glass was curved around the cylinder. Sal knew that it would show appraisal-standard information on the contents. It was ridiculously modern and practical.

Even the vats that had tubing to pull the mixture from the Alchemy station were reinforced, and they were gargantuan. If Sal was still in denial about the elixir machine being heavy-duty, this was the fact he couldn't ignore. Each one of those vats would be capable of holding at least two hundred elixirs. If it was Kaizen, he estimated it at… actually, he didn't want to do that math. It was a ridiculous amount and clearly overkill.

"And Blathnaid set up the enclosure!" Fabi's eyes lit up as she turned to the other side of the build.

Sal glanced over in confusion. He had gone into a kind of autopilot and assumed that Blathnaid would just stand back to watch. However, judging by the gorgeous glass booth that seamlessly pressed against the corner of the room, she hadn't been standing around. He had to go over and have a closer look, but he already knew that it was excellent craftsmanship.

Just like he had constructed the small core plates for the Mythical blight jackal, Fabi had refined the cores into panes of glass for the enclosure which Blathnaid was now fitting. It would host the plants and ingredients they wanted to grow, and would radiate a constant stream of essence through them. The greenhouse aspect was far bigger than he had envisioned, but this was great. It also looked like she had evenly placed the dungeon soil on the metallic base plate.

"So, who wants to tag out? I can't watch this build without contributing." Fabi laughed as she looked between them.

Sal and Blathnaid looked at each other, neither wanting to stop. Thankfully, Jack came to the rescue, holding two vials in his hands.

"How about you start on the Alchemy station? I'm finished with the runes, but need someone to power them up." He smiled as he held up the dull, but highly elaborate etchings.

"These the experimental ones?" Sal asked dubiously as he looked at the glassware, wondering whether it was going to end in an explosion of glass.

Fabi was delighted as she raised her hand. "I've got plenty of essence to spare. I'll work on the Alchemy station while you guys finish your areas. Sound good?"

"If it's not overstepping?" Blathnaid asked Sal as she gestured at the half-complete Genesis station.

Sal shook his head. "No, this is perfect. Just let me do the essence flooding at the end to create the build." He couldn't help but laugh as he looked out the wall of windows. "This is absolutely insane, isn't it? We've literally done all of this in less than twenty-four hours."

"That's the power of the dream team, I guess?" Blathnaid laughed as she rolled up her sleeves and checked on the essence armguard.

"Oh, and if you need that recharged, let me know," Fabi pointed out as she glanced at the armguard. "I don't want you running out of juice mid-build."

Blathnaid let out a sigh of relief. "Okay, there goes the only anxiety I had. Thank you."

Jack made two return trips with each of the vials, setting them down carefully near Fabi.

Anthony sat on the ground in a sort of shell-shocked state, as though he were coming to terms with the fact that he just cleared three dungeons with Fabi.

Sal, Blathnaid, and Fabi launched right back into the build with enough tenacity that you'd have expected they were racing one another. Sal's approach was deliberate, calm and methodical. Blathnaid was very similar, albeit even more cautious.

Fabi was just a force of nature that came with experience and a knowledge that she could fix any problem her speed inadvertently created. It didn't take long for her station to catch up with the others, and there were more than a few purple and yellow flashes to indicate that she was playfully cheating when things went wrong.

Maybe it was because of the figurative speed-demon in the center of the build, but Fabi's performance lit a fire under both Blathnaid and Sal, who ended up getting faster with the sense of competition. Sal caught glimpses of their work and was constantly amazed at the productivity.

Eventually, after a few hours of cursing and laughing, the entire elixir machine was assembled. Each of them stood back to drink in the appearance of the most ambitious Crafting project they had ever worked on. Sal knew that because they pretty much repeated the sentiment throughout the build.

"You're up, Mr. Argento," Fabi breathed as she sat on the ground, grinning. "I'm dying to see how this thing turns out."

Sal stared at it with an enormous sense of pride. It didn't even look like it needed Mythcrafter essence to work. It was probably perfectly functional as it was, but that would be depriving the team of a show.

With a grin, he stepped forward and placed his palms on the Alchemy station. His tracker was on; his blueprints were loaded. Perfect was active. He summoned the Mythical blight jackal to his left arm, because he was absolutely going to need Capacitor for this one.

"Oooooh." Blathnaid practically cooed at the sight of the glossy black arm.

"It gets better," Fabi said without a shred of doubt. "He's got a drone in there."

Sal ignored them and chuckled as he poured his essence into the elixir machine. It was a steady flood that swept through each of the vials, the furnace, the vats, the compressor, harmonizer, resonator… through the tubing and pipework to the glasshouse enclosure, and the other way to the Refined Absolver. There were well over a dozen named components in this build, and Sal's essence coursed through each and every one of them. It took a solid twenty minutes of pouring his essence into the construct before Capacitor kicked in and started to donate some reserves to the cause.

An hour later, Sal stood in the exact same spot as the entirety of the elixir machine started to glow. There had been so few errors that needed to be addressed; as painful as it was to admit, his own work had the most rough spots. Blathnaid had come second, with Fabi not having a single issue. One of the strangest phenomena throughout the process were the vials that drank a stupid amount of essence from Capacitor. One of the five existing reserves was depleted on just the vials with Jack's runes.

He checked, then checked again… and then checked for a third and final time. When he was certain that he had covered everything, he poured even more essence in, until the elixir machine had reached its capacity. This was definitely a more arduous task than waving a hand and wishing for Legendary grade. Sal wouldn't have had it any other way. If there was one thing this project had taught him, it was the amount of fun there could be had with group Crafting projects.

When it was finally complete, Sal stepped back, his hands raised in the air. He reminded himself that he had to stop doing that.

"And we're done," Sal breathed as he turned around, half expecting them to have left at some point during the boring process.

Anthony, Jack, and Blathnaid were seated on stools they had dragged over. Upgrade was seated on the ground beside Fabi, a wide grin on her face. "Well done, Maestro."

Sal was about to ask why she was there, but stopped when Fabi's eye-patch flashed yellow.

CHAPTER 34: CONCERNS

"What the hell? That's too fast." Sal spoke as he turned around to look at the glowing machine. It was still doing the cooldown as he had expected, but Fabi was already able to determine the grade? It didn't make sense.

"What's wrong?" Upgrade got to her feet. "Did you make a mistake?" She stood beside him as though ready to assist if something were to happen.

He slowly shook his head as he tried to use Appraisal on the machine. His eyes told him that it wasn't done yet, and so many of the glowing fragments contradicted each other in terms of power levels. Some of the yellow glows had started flickering purple, which Sal assumed was normal. If the whole thing was to come out at Epic grade, then he wouldn't have any issues with it. Hell, if it worked like it was designed, he wouldn't care about grades at all. Sal tore his eyes away from the colors as his eyes started to sting.

"There was another yellow flash." Blathnaid pointed at Fabi's eye-patch. "Does that mean it's going to be Legendary grade?"

Sal bit his lip as he thought about it. "Appraisal is saying it's not ready yet, so I can't really figure out what's going on." He glanced at Fabi... well, more specifically, at the eye-patch. "I thought it could only do those calculations when Anthony was using Supercharge? How come it's reacting now?"

Fabi seemed to finally understand what was happening as she pointed at her eye-patch. "Oh, it's flashing yellow? Let me have a look…"

Sal waited for her conclusion, along with everyone else. A lot of the mirth and excitement had wavered somewhat with the current air of apprehension.

"Oh…" Fabi started with an awkward laugh. "I programmed the eye-patch to display a flash whenever it recognized a particular power level. Even though it doesn't have the capability to recognize anything above Epic grade, it's defaulting to the yellow flash as a signifier that it's higher than Epic grade."

"Okay… but can you just wave your hand and upgrade it into something that can give us a more stable reading?" Sal asked hopefully, not sure it would work.

Upgrade scoffed, as though the request were ridiculous. "Sal, please tell me that you've learned something from the Crafting classes. Abilities can't work like that."

"Are you sure?" Blathnaid asked with a nervous laugh. "You didn't see what Fabi was doing earlier."

Upgrade cocked an eyebrow. "What am I missing?" She looked at Fabi for an explanation, but the third-year just offered her a guilty shrug.

"I kinda learned how to use Figment," she admitted sheepishly. "And it's pretty cool."

Sal grinned at Upgrade. "She literally waves at things and they increase in grade level. She was turning Rare grades into Uniques and Epics."

"And Legendaries," Blathnaid corrected with a raised hand and a laugh.

Upgrade frowned as she looked at Fabi. "Like Overcharge? You're putting it into a temporal state of higher quality?"

"I think they're permanent." Fabi gestured at the glowing elixir machine behind Sal and Upgrade.

Upgrade turned slowly to look at where she pointed. With a sharp intake of breath, she bit her bottom lip, clearly trying to bite back whatever first came to mind. Eventually, she exhaled slowly and seemingly framed her response. "You're saying that you've taken an experimental process... and put it directly into a build?"

"Sal used Appraisal on them and verified that they were the new grades," Fabi insisted, but she sounded a little worried.

Upgrade shook her head as she folded her arms. "As wonderful as it is seeing you with your ability, Fabi, I need you to be a little more cautious going forward. You should be testing the limits of what works and what doesn't. Don't pick up this guy's habits of rushing to the finish line." She hiked her thumb in Sal's direction. "You're methodical and should keep that trait. Flooding things with essence could end up having adverse effects."

"Like what?" Blathnaid asked out of concern. Probably because her ability was a close match to Fabi's.

Upgrade's gaze softened as she looked at Blathnaid. "There's nothing wrong with how you use your Construct ability, Blathnaid. I'm just trying to caution Fabrizia away from complacency. If you try to short-cut your way to reaching higher grades by flooding components with essence, rather than material combinations, you'll end up with a range of instabilities."

Fabi frowned as she folded her arms, mirroring Upgrade. "Why do you think they're unstable? Sal told me that it was how my ability works. Isn't the Evolve version of your ability the same sort of principle? It's an equivalent exchange of essence for a higher grade of quality."

Sal wasn't sure how he felt about his name being used as a counterpoint. It was a shame that the tension in the air had completely dissolved all excitement. Upgrade's normally jovial tone had been replaced with her rarely used lecturing one. No matter how gentle the words were, it felt like they were being rebuked.

Upgrade put her right palm over her eyes and groaned. "I'm sorry I'm the one who's ruining the mood, here. I just need to be the Crafting lecturer for a few minutes, okay? Then we can go back to the excitement for the elixir machine." She pulled her hand away from her face and gave Fabi a grimace as though asking permission to continue.

Fabi gave her a curt nod, her expression unreadable. Well, unreadable to most. Sal was wearing his visor and could tell she was annoyed.

Upgrade's grimace was forced into a smile as she gestured at the elixir machine. "You've all worked very hard on this, and that is commendable... but you've skipped a few steps."

Fabi opened her mouth to argue, but Upgrade silenced her with a raised hand.

"Elixirs are for consumption, and they have to be rigorously tested to see if they're safe. This isn't the same as making a coffee machine. You're infusing essence into liquids, making things like Kaizen or Sleeping Tiger... elixirs that can twist the very nature of your perception and essence flow," Upgrade insisted, as if it were common sense. "I was going to wait until after things cooled down and you had done your celebrating, but I'll tell you now. This thing won't be allowed to operate until it's been vetted by the Hunter Bureau, or at the very least, by a recognized Alchemy body."

Upgrade looked at Sal. "An external Appraiser will be tasked with ensuring that the machine does what it says it will do."

Sal closed his eyes and took a breath. "And if the Appraiser can't handle something at a high level?"

"Then it won't be cleared for use." Upgrade grimaced. "Each and every component will be scrutinized, and if corners were cut in the making of this… then you're going to have to take it apart and rebuild it. They're very protective of this domain, so they won't give you an easy time."

"They?" Sal repeated in confusion. "Who would want this to fail?"

Upgrade looked at Sal curiously. "The Alchemy guilds that you'd be putting out of business. At the very least, you're going to need a licensed Alchemist to vouch for the machine, and getting them on board isn't going to be an easy task. Just try talking to Alex and you'll see what I mean."

"Oh." Sal tried not to smile. "Would Alex count as a licensed Alchemist? Like, if he gave the all clear, would that suffice?"

"Stop scheming for a second, Sal. This is serious," Upgrade insisted as she gave him a stern look. "You've clearly invested a lot of materials and time into this project, and I absolutely hate that I need to be the villain right now. Had I known you'd start production on this thing, I'd have cautioned against it for these very reasons. You won't be able to secure any ingredients when the guilds catch wind of this, which will destroy your supplier agreements. Maccles Materials would get blacklisted from suppliers if he sided with you."

Sal put up a hand and gave Upgrade a serious look. "Okay… just to be clear on this. If we get an Appraiser—"

"It can't be you." Upgrade was firm. "You don't have enough reputation as an Appraiser that the guilds would accept it, without mentioning how it's a massive conflict of interest. Not all of them are as lenient as the Reavers."

"Okay, we get an Appraiser that isn't me." Sal waited to see whether there was any objection. When there wasn't, he continued. "So, that's my dad."

Upgrade sighed as she gave him a nod. "Yes, okay… if the Argento Auction House approved it, then it would be enough. But you'd still need to overcome the Alchemist and supplier issues. If you're thinking that Lawrence Baron and Maurice can handle this, you're underestimating the obscene wealth of the elixir magnates."

"We already have Alex on board," Sal said with his hands raised in case it led to another mini-tirade. "And we've designed this to avoid the need for suppliers. The Genesis station is built to create our own supplies. It uses dungeon soil and—"

"Shit," Fabi muttered. It was an excellent warning, but came just a little too late.

"Dungeon soil?!" Upgrade practically screeched as she whipped around to look at the glowing mass, as though she'd be able to determine which aspect was using the cursed materials. "You're infusing essence into dungeon soil? Do you want leechers in Quest Academy? Because that seems like the perfect recipe for leechers."

"The blueprint said it was necessary," Sal explained quickly. "It wasn't an experiment—it was calculated… I promise!"

Upgrade looked directly upward at the ceiling. "I sometimes think that you two were sent to test me." She took a steadying breath before bringing her gaze back down to the machine. "Experimental essence infusions and dungeon soil… I don't even know if I should laugh or cry." Turning to look at Sal and Fabi, she shook her head in a daze. "Seriously, am I this shit at teaching? What part of this process made you think that this was a good idea?"

Sal shifted uncomfortably. "Is this one of those questions where you don't want the answer?"

"I'd very much like the answer." Upgrade laughed humorlessly. "And context, if it exists. Right now, it looks like you had an idea and ran with it… based off the success of a different automation machine." She didn't say the Arkwright out loud, but that was definitely what she meant.

"I designed the blueprint with Mythcrafter and Cypher," Sal responded. "I made the Genesis weave with the simulation orb, and built toward it with the materials that were listed in the blueprint. Alex's Alchemize ability is in the middle station, and the third one has a Refine infusion. We followed the steps that Mythcrafter said would work, and I used Perfect throughout."

Upgrade opened her mouth to respond, but then closed it again. Her brow furrowed in concentration as she went through everything. She seemed to be deep in thought before she looked up in confusion. "Wait, did you say that you got Alex on board?"

"Yeah, he's going to be a minority shareholder in this business," Sal offered with an awkward smile. "We've got Anderson Royce for the Genesis station. It's an evolved form of his Growth weave, so I'm hopeful he'll be able to navigate it."

Upgrade let out a sigh as she crossed her legs and sat on the ground. "Salvatore, if this works… Quest Academy will be in the line of fire from every Alchemy guild. Why did you build this here?"

"Fifteen percent of the profits are for the Crafting Department at Quest Academy." Sal grinned. "Sixty percent goes to our guild, which will be set up here while I'm enrolled. Eight for Anderson, eight for Alex, eight for a Refine specialist, and the last percent for Fabi."

Upgrade stared at Sal for what felt like forever. She blinked a few times before finally shaking her head. "I don't even know what to say. This whole concept goes against every fundamental I teach in my class. You're creating your ingredients in-house, processing them and refining them… all in a supply-chain environment."

"Wouldn't you consider it Ethical Crafting?" Fabi ventured with a sly grin. "Technically, he enrolled before we started this project."

Upgrade's gaze narrowed on Fabi. "We're still going to be having a talk about essence equivalency and your ability, so tread lightly." Her leveled stare only took a few seconds to cool off, and her trademark smile reappeared. "But it's a good point."

She glanced at Sal. "Depends on your pricing model, but this could be considered an Ethical Crafting project. If it reduces the danger of sourcing materials, and makes elixirs more accessible to buyers… then it would tick a lot of the boxes. The fact that you're reinvesting profits into the Crafting Department would also make it very sustainable."

"I'd still like to do the class, though," Sal explained as he looked at Upgrade carefully. "I wasn't trying to make this to get easy grades or anything. I just wanted something that would give me more Q-Cred to work with."

"What would you need more Q-Cred for?" Upgrade scoffed as she looked at him. "You're the wealthiest first-year we've ever had."

"To pay for everyone's master classes." Sal shrugged. "For the people who join the guild, I mean. I don't think I could pay for everyone's." He laughed at the notion.

Upgrade's smile became warm. "If this thing works and manages to turn a single Q-Cred of profit, that warrants full marks in Ethical Crafting. The class is designed to instill a compassionate quality that seemingly comes naturally to you. I was worried when I saw the other projects you've worked on, but this, if it works, could be something special. You'd only be taking the jobs of vultures that are squeezing the market dry, not fellow Crafters."

"Are we not in trouble anymore?" Jack ventured awkwardly, his hand raised as he looked around the room to check the vibe.

Upgrade shook her head. "Professor mode is finished; you can all go back to excitement." She sighed as she gave Sal a guilty smile. "Is it okay if I sit here for the verdict with you guys? I want to see what it looks like when it's done."

Sal laughed as he sat down beside her and Fabi. "I wouldn't have it any other way. Besides, when this thing finishes cooling down, there's a mountain of essence programming that needs to be done." He smiled sweetly at Upgrade, his intentions clear.

Upgrade returned the smile. "Guess you'll need to pick up the pace in the foundation class, huh?"

"You know, I'm starting to think even *ten* percent is a little too generous for the Crafting Department," Sal said with feigned regret while playfully lowering their stake. "I wouldn't want to invest in a place that doesn't foster collaboration."

Upgrade laughed as she glanced back at Blathnaid. "At least tell me you got a good deal out of him for the labor?"

Blathnaid gave Upgrade a small nod. "He went easy on me, though."

"Of course he did." Upgrade smiled warmly as she continued to stare at the glowing form of the elixir machine. With a small nudge to Sal's side with her elbow, Upgrade turned to him slightly, her eyes not leaving the elixir machine. Her voice was low enough that only he and Fabi could hear. "Aren't you going to ask me about Strategist's Dominion?"

CHAPTER 35: OVERLOAD

"Honestly, I thought you'd have been working on something else," Sal responded with a light chuckle. He had given her all the materials she'd need to create a gauntlet of her own with a drone component, but she was talking to him about the failed Mythmark suit? Strategist's Dominion was the clusterfuck of essence signatures that resulted in the most inefficient piece of equipment he had made to date. Well, excluding the shirt that tried to kill him.

Upgrade shook her head. "Nope, I wanted to… but I had a look at that suit of yours and could see how expertly crafted it was. It's been a nightmare trying to get it back to a good state, but it's a fun challenge. More fun than I've had in years, if I'm honest."

"I really appreciate you taking the time to do it, but there's no pressure if you can't get it to work. I sacrificed the revolver to make that thing, and even the uniform you made for me. I genuinely thought it was going to be something special, but it ended up becoming a mess." Sal wondered whether Upgrade would be annoyed or disappointed with him for getting rid of his previous equipment.

Upgrade surprised him by shrugging it off. "You're better off without that uniform. We've established quite a while ago that you're able to make better equipment than that, so don't get all sentimental about it." She grinned at him. "And I actually needed your input before I can continue on the Strategist's Dominion. How wild can I go with the redesign?"

"Redesign?" Sal repeated the word in confusion. "Isn't it just a flaw with the essence programming?"

"Wait… you actually wanted to be walking around in that gimp suit?" Upgrade asked in disbelief. "It's skintight, Sal. Practically indecent if you were to ever walk around in public."

Shaking his head and laughing, Sal tried to explain. "No, I mean… it's been built, so I thought that it was limited to the shape. If you made a cut anywhere, wouldn't that destroy the circuitry within and make it useless?"

"Only if you've got no idea what you're doing," Upgrade countered, grinning. "I'll take it that you're onboard with the redesign. I've got a few fun concepts in mind, but it'll need some finessing. Just promise me that you won't make any new equipment above the waist, because I'll be devastated if you end up making this creation redundant."

"I'm already working on equipment for the head, just so you know." Fabi leaned into their conversation. "It's a face mask thing. His dad wants it done, so I said I'd help work on it."

Upgrade nodded as she thought about it. "Might just be easier to work together on that one, then. You okay being co-pilot with me on the Mythmark?"

Fabi frowned, but not at Upgrade. Her gaze was leveled at Sal. "You're not seriously calling it a Mythmark, are you? Come up with your own name." Her smile showed that she was joking, thankfully, because the tone would have been terrifying.

"Are you sure that you guys aren't doing too much on this project? It did fail, and we can try again with different materials and go from there?" Sal offered, wanting to alleviate some of the pressure they were putting themselves under.

"No chance." Upgrade shook her head. "Besides, you already said that you sacrificed your revolver. The essence signature of it is loaded into the Myth-mark—which is a super cool name, by the way—and if I can preserve that, I absolutely will. The sniper rifle is awesome, too."

"Oh, you saw those?" Sal asked in surprise. "I didn't think you'd be able to activate it with the amount of essence it consumes."

Upgrade looked at him for a few seconds. "You wore it, didn't you? Instead of testing it on an essence bench?"

Sal stared at her for a few seconds before a recent memory surfaced. "Wait! You showed us that video of you using the Ravage ability… with the red lightning. That wasn't done on a test bench."

Upgrade's smile became guilty. "Okay, fine… I went to try it out because it looked cool. I could get off about four or five shots before I was completely drained, but I've found a few fixes for that. All I needed from you today was permission to start cutting it up and changing it. So, forget about it for now and the next time you see it, I think you'll be pleasantly surprised."

"Not ominous at all…" Sal muttered before chuckling. "I really do appreciate all the help you're giving me, and for not killing us about this whole thing." Sal gestured at the elixir machine that was still thrumming with golden light.

Upgrade looked at the machine for a few seconds before shaking her head slightly. "It's my fault for assuming the worst. I'm trying my best to keep up with you two, and now that Fabi is apparently waving things into Legendary grade, I can't help but feel like I'm failing as an educator. I know it's not real, and it's probably my own inadequacies flaring up, but I want you guys to do things the right way, rather than rushing to the finish line."

"I get where you're coming from. We had a few hiccups here and there, but I think that we did this with everything you've taught us so far. Blathnaid took on that entire station, by the way, while Fabi worked on the middle. I did the Refiner at the end," Sal said with a proud smile, glancing over at Blathnaid when he mentioned her.

Upgrade's smile returned as she nodded. "Gotta say, this is a pretty cool legacy if it works. Funding for the Crafting Department will definitely open some doors and make us far less reliant on the Hunter Bureau. If we can get out from under their thumb, it won't matter what fixes Chatfield proposes, because we can counter them if we're self-sufficient."

"Ha, well, we'll have to see what sort of job it can do when it's up and running," Sal agreed. "But I was serious about the essence programming. There's a whole load of stuff that needs to be put in place. There's a calculation matrix for the different recipes that Fabi's going to be working on with Anthony, and then the payment system, and the essence loader… all sorts of little things that will need to be fine-tuned before it can even be turned on."

Upgrade's smile grew wider. "That actually sounds like a lot of fun. Are you going to accept essence as a method of payment? Like, they pop in a core or two, pick their ingredients, and watch it go through the process?"

"Something like that, but I'll have to see what Alex thinks when he sees it. This thing is manual and not automatic like the Arkwright. It's going to need a lot of finesse and expertise to get going."

"I've never heard the word finesse and Alex in the same sentence." Upgrade laughed as she glanced at the elixir machine. "Did the color change just now?"

Sal followed her gaze and stared at the light. It seemed a little brighter, but otherwise wasn't any different from before. Between Fabi's eye-patch and Upgrade's comment just now, Sal felt like he was a step behind them with the skillset he grew up with. He intently looked at the build with his father's weave and tried to figure out what was going on with it…

His eyes started to water, and Sal had to blink a few times to clear his vision. It was annoying, but he could feel the progress as the colors started to shift and warp in front of his eyes. Rather than a sea of blues, purples, and yellows, it was now a swath of purples, yellows, and a singular red. Sal's mouth went dry as he watched in real time as another piece turned from yellow into red. Maybe it was because of the sheer scale of the project, but he could see each component clearly as they transitioned in color. It didn't take a genius to figure out that red likely represented Mythic grade. He could actually see the progress of the components moving between grades!

How many components needed to turn red for the whole thing to be classified as Mythic? At this point, with so much yellow, he guessed the machine would likely become Legendary grade. So many questions went through his mind as he got to his feet and cautiously moved closer to the elixir machine. He had already flooded it with essence, and he instinctively knew that no harm would come from him placing his hands on the device.

When he did so, he realized two things in quick succession. First, the machine was close to fully cooling down… something in the essence told him that the timer was reaching the final point. Better than that, he could literally see the changes. Was this an aspect of Mythcrafter he hadn't been using until now?

The second thing he realized was that he could channel more essence into it. Something had changed throughout the process, where all his fine-tuned essence was being depleted or siphoned off by particular components. Was it the suction from the Mythic-grade components? Had that thrown the rest into an imbalance? Either way, it didn't matter… all he had to do was continue feeding it with more essence. The real question was whether he'd have enough.

"Sal, what's going on? Is everything okay?" Fabi asked cautiously as she got up from the floor and moved over to where he stood.

"It wants more essence, and I'm wondering if it's wise to give it some." Sal looked through the components. None of them looked particularly flawed, so the essence siphoned hadn't compromised them. If he left it as it was, it would complete somewhere around high Epic grade and Legendary grade. If he was right.

"Then give it more," Upgrade stated, like it was a no-brainer. "If you have the reserves, go for it."

"I said it wants more essence, not that it needs it… If I was to give it, there's a good chance this would go to the highest level possible. Highest I can manage."

Sal turned to give Upgrade a meaningful stare. "Wouldn't that cause issues for the guild and Quest Academy?"

Upgrade looked at him as if he were insane. "If you have a chance of making a Mythic grade, you fucking take it. We'll handle everything that gets thrown at us later; just throw everything you've got into it and we'll figure out the details later!"

Fabi frowned as she looked at Sal. "But both Blathnaid and I worked on it. How can it possibly be able to go to the Mythic grade?"

"Sal fills in the gaps with his essence. I worked on the sniper rifle for the Reavers Guild, and it went from Rare Epic to Legendary grade, with capacity to evolve into Mythic," Upgrade explained as she stepped to the other side of Sal. "I'm serious. Don't squander this opportunity. Ignore everything I said about caution before and just give it your best shot, okay?"

Sal placed both hands on the edge of the Alchemize bench and looked at Upgrade. "You're not very consistent when it comes to lectures. Making this a Mythic grade, in plain sight of everyone who comes up here, is going to make it very obvious that there's a Mythcrafter."

Upgrade snorted as she pointed at Blathnaid. "Half of them think it's her. Some of the faculty who were *told* it was you have since turned a corner and think it's Blathnaid."

"What?" Blathnaid asked in a strained voice. Her face was like she'd just seen a ghost.

"Doesn't matter." Upgrade waved Blathnaid away. "Nothing to worry about; you're doing great." She focused back on Sal. "Come on, this could be an amazing thing for Quest Academy. Think about it. Everything you said to Quest about getting these upgrades and all this space? Making your first project here as a Mythic grade would be amazing. Quest Academy is like a fortress, so you wouldn't need to worry about the guilds or the Hunter Bureau coming in and trying to steal it."

"Hey, could you let me concentrate?" Sal laughed as he shooed her away with a jut of his chin. "I was already convinced when you started cursing. Just leave it with me, and I'll try to get it over the line."

Fabi appeared on the other side of Sal, although not too close that she'd disrupt him. "Do you need more essence?"

Sal shook his head as he looked at the glossy black arm of the Mythical blight jackal. Capacitor would likely get him over the line, but it was good to know Fabi was there on standby if he needed more. "I think I should be good. Thank you, though."

Upgrade took a few steps back, matching Fabi's retreat, her eyes not leaving Sal. "Since when have you been able to tell what's happening in the middle of a cooldown? You've never been able to do this before."

Sal shrugged as he started to channel his essence into the build. "I'm thinking it might be an effect of opening a hundred and eighty gates. It might be activating more aspects of Mythcrafter I couldn't use before."

Upgrade went quiet, or Sal simply didn't hear her response. All his focus was on the build, and pumping as much essence as he could into it. It was remarkable how many gaps had appeared throughout, with the Refiner being the least hungry of the three. The Alchemy station and Genesis station were so close to completion that they looked starved for essence. It was the little things; like the spaces between the pane-shaped essence cores. Little cracks here and there. Reinforcement required for the valves and tubing. Coating the pipes with another few layers of essence. There was no big thing that required his attention, just a series of little things that weren't as optimal as they could be.

Perfect was more than happy to evenly distribute the essence, and Capacitor was going strong. His refined essence was like water going into a sponge that had partly dried out. Rather than all the builds before, where he had to rely on instinct and the lack of essence being drawn, this time, he could literally see the colors changing from yellow to red. When small improvements were required on red components, the shade deepened into a more violent red, similar to the lightning color of the Vendetta Macclemark.

Sal kept going until the sea of yellow gradually started to turn red. It was a slow and steady process, with layers of essence preventing the build from finishing. Each wave was like adding time to the invisible clock, and each new burst of essence resulted in a flicker of red, rewarding his efforts.

"You really don't do anything in half measures." Fabi placed a hand on his back.

Sal didn't have the energy to flinch from the sudden contact. A reassuring surge of essence flowed through his aching joints, and it was cold and refreshing. It was like when Luke had poured that mist into him to calm his body after absorbing the Strength stats from the scuttler. Perfect took that essence and sent it straight to his head for some reason. It felt nice, albeit a bit erratic.

Had he been so in the zone that he didn't realize Capacitor was nearly empty? Sal blinked a few times to see his progress and was more than a little shocked to see no hint of yellow in front of him. There were a few hues that were closer to orange than red, but Sal didn't care. He had managed to bring it to the best point he could muster.

"Not as efficient as waving a hand, though," Sal tried to say, but his words came out slurred. Surely, he hadn't gone far enough to warrant the dregs? There was plenty of essence remaining, so why was he struggling? He blinked a few times and pulled his hands away from the build, looking at them in confusion, only to see four hands moving in a rippling effect.

That was weird.

Words of alarm sounded out from around him but Sal couldn't understand why they were panicking. The whole thing had worked. He just needed a bit of time to get his bearings, and everything would be fine. The elixir machine was going to be a Mythic grade!

When his body collapsed, Sal was barely conscious of the arms wrapping around him. He tried to look around to see what was happening, and was surprised to see that everything looked red around him. How was the ceiling going to become Mythic grade?

Fabi's panicked face appeared in front of him; her hand cupped the side of his face as her mouth moved. He couldn't hear a word she said, but saw a veil of red covering her, too. That was when he realized that he wasn't seeing Mythical essence.

He was seeing blood.

Sal would have laughed at the ridiculousness of it all, but darkness claimed him before he could so much as say a word.

CHAPTER 36: APOLOGY

"Hey, kiddo."

Sal wanted to open his eyes, but couldn't. There was an alien sort of thickness that was pressed against his face, and he couldn't understand what it was.

"Dad?" Sal tried, his voice coming through as a croak. Thankfully there was no slurring this time, but it wasn't enough to drive away the panic at not being able to open his eyes.

"Calm down, you've got nothing to worry about," Petro said in a soothing voice.

Sal's right palm was being gripped by his father, and a wave of relief washed through him.

"I was called in because I heard you had a bit of an incident. How are you feeling?"

"I can't open my eyes." Sal was trying to keep his composure, but it was difficult. There was no way that he went blind from something like this. He had still been able to see somewhat through the blood; it wasn't like he had lost all his vision. If his eyeballs had randomly popped, then he'd still have held out hope for a Healer with a Regenerate ability or something. But there was something about not being able to see that was making him frantic.

"Yeah, they've wrapped a set of bandages pretty damn tight around your head. I said it wasn't necessary, but they were taking every precaution they could think of." Petro continued with a dry chuckle. "Also, you don't need to be on guard. It's just the two of us here."

Sal swallowed, but it was no use; his throat was incredibly dry. "Am I going blind?"

"Not yet," Petro answered slowly. "You've been unconscious for a few days, and although that would normally be a cause for concern, the Healers said you just needed the rest."

"That's not reassuring." Sal tried to chuckle, but it came out as a wheeze. He tried lifting his left hand to his face, but found that it was bound to his side. Moving his fingers was fine, but he couldn't lift it at all.

"They bound that arm because they couldn't remove the black sleeve," Petro explained, clearly having seen the movement attempt. "I think they were worried it might activate, so they put a few restraints down to be safe."

Sal could hear the tone in his father's voice. "I'm really sorry this happened, Dad."

"Don't be sorry, Salvatore. This is my fault, if anything. I should have trained you with All Sight during the break, so that you wouldn't have tried to use it while you were Crafting. All the symptoms, including your eyes bleeding… it's the same as All Sight. Upgrade mentioned that you were seeing the colors of grades. It didn't take long for me to piece together what happened." Petro let out a heavy sigh, and his chair squeaked as he turned in it.

"Quest reached out to inform us, and thankfully I was the one who got the call. Your mother doesn't need to know about this right now, because she'd rip off that burrito thing you made for her and wrap you in it like a cocoon." Petro chuckled as he gave Sal's hand a reassuring squeeze. "The Healers believe that you'll make a full recovery, but they made it very clear that this was the most serious case of eyestrain they had seen in a very long time. Your body isn't strong enough to use All Sight. It might never be if we don't do something about it."

"When can I take the bandages off?" Sal asked wearily. He wanted to touch his face, but one arm was restrained, and the other was gripping his father's hand.

"My best guess would be in a few days. They're coming in every few hours to do additional Healing, and they don't want you seeing blueprints or appraisal sheets everywhere you look," Petro remarked, as though it were a funny concept. "They didn't take too kindly to my suggestion of sunglasses."

Sal felt like shit. He couldn't believe that his actions had resulted in his father being summoned to Quest Academy. He had missed the scavenger run with Barry and Divinity, and likely a good few classes, already. If it was going to be a few more days before he could properly see, then he was likely to miss even more.

"So… are you in a good headspace to talk, or do you need to rest a little more?" Petro asked cautiously, as though worried for Sal's current state. "I'll be hanging around Quest Academy to do some paperwork, so I can check in on you later if that's better?"

"I'm good… ish," Sal managed, smiling weakly. His throat felt better after a few sentences, and his head started to clear. There was no pain, just discomfort. Whatever the Healers had done had worked wonders.

"Good enough for me." Petro let go of Sal's hand and patted it a few times. "As great as it is coming here to see you, and as much as I'd wish it was under different circumstances… Quest had me doing some Appraisal work on that little project of yours."

"Did it turn out okay?" Sal asked, no longer sure how much of what he saw was real or not. If the red mist had been blood, then he was likely confusing everything to do with the Mythic grade. Hell, he would have been happy if the thing was functional.

"It's Mythic grade, Salvatore." Petro chuckled. "Upgrade explained to me that you cautioned against the risks of making something so flashy, and I'm proud of you for that foresight, but I agree with Upgrade on this one. It was only going to be a matter of time before it became common knowledge, and there was no better machine to create than this one. It validates your guild and will showcase the value you bring to everyone who works with you."

"Whoa…" Sal breathed as he let out an involuntary chuckle. It had actually been real. He expected a much better feeling from having contributed to the second-ever Mythic grade in existence, but… there was nothing. No excitement or anticipation. All that existed within him was a hollow feeling, coupled with the anxiety that he had unconsciously hurt himself. If he wasn't able to tell when his own eyes were bleeding, then he seriously had problems.

Petro seemed to sense the discomfort in Sal. "I'm going to need a few days here to sort out the Appraisal. You really went and made a mountain of work for me, but I won't complain… It's one of the most intricate things I've ever seen, and I'm genuinely enjoying it more because I know you've built it."

Sal smiled weakly. "I'm really sorry I didn't take care of myself better. I promised I would." There it was. The crux of Sal's emotions. The guilt he was feeling for having disappointed his father.

He had been warned about making a Healing apparatus and he had outsourced it to Fabi. His parents had generously handed out bursaries to all his friends, and even to him. How did Sal repay them? He went and did the two things they warned him against: putting a target on his back as a Mythcrafter, and injuring himself in the process.

"Hey, stop making yourself feel bad," Petro insisted as he continued to tap Sal's hand with his own. "Seriously, both your mother and I couldn't be prouder of the journey you've started. You've surrounded yourself with a wonderful group of people, made great friends and allies. That's not even beginning to talk about what you've made possible with your effort and skills. This chapter that you're in right now… it's not the full story, Salvatore. It's an ordeal and a lesson to take better care of yourself. What sort of hypocrite would I be if I told you to avoid danger, when I've started training you to face it?"

"You know what I meant," Sal protested as he tried to sit up, but his father's hand pressed against his chest, forcing him back into the bed.

"I know exactly what you meant…so I've come here with a solution for you," Petro explained, chuckling. "I don't know that you'll like it, but I think it's a sight better than the plan we had in place before."

"The plan about me getting stronger?" Sal offered, wondering which of the thousand plans they made he was referencing.

"When I said that you should make a Healing device, I was thinking of this the wrong way. Rather than having you react to the issue… why can't we just solve the problem?"

Petro asked the question in such a way that Sal felt it was wise to stay quiet.

"You've got Jackal now. You can literally get stronger when you use him in the field. Rather than hiding behind him with Healing equipment… why don't you focus on building up your health and endurance, with Jackal doing all the hard work?" Petro asked almost excitedly, as though it were the greatest epiphany he'd ever had.

"You didn't clear this with Mom, did you?" Sal asked dryly, imagining how his mother would react to Petro's master plan.

Petro coughed a little guiltily, and Sal was able to imagine the smile on his face. The bandages really made him aware of how much he relied on sight.

"I'm just suggesting that we solve the issue at the base, rather than trying to deal with how it manifests. If you become more resilient, build up your natural endurance and health profile… then there's a strong chance that your body will naturally adapt to the pressures All Sight and Mythcrafter will put on it."

His father sounded excited by the prospect, but Sal wasn't so sure. "We've only seen my Strength stat go up when I was in the dungeons, though. There's nothing to say that it will work on the other attributes. Even if it did, it requires Jackal to take down stronger opponents than that scuttler or those hulkers. I think it's a safer method if I just find a crafted solution to the problem."

"Ah, I didn't really factor that part in." Petro sighed. "Your mother probably would have pointed that out immediately had I brought it up." He chuckled at the mention of it. "But, I still think that there's a lot to be said for you training your body toward a better condition. We can't have another one of these scenarios, because if you went blind, I'd never forgive myself. I can't tell you to just give up Crafting because it's something you're clearly gifted at."

"I learned a flying jump kick with the Silverson Arts," Sal offered, as though it might change the subject to different matters.

Petro paused at that, a little longer than Sal's liking.

"Is everything okay?" Sal ventured again, unsure what expression his father was making.

"The manual I gave you shouldn't have any of the forms for the Dragon Kick. You should only have learned the first eight stances and their adaptive forms," Petro said in a confused tone. "I'm genuinely stumped here. Because I wrote the damn thing, and I'm pretty sure there's no way you could have interpreted an advanced move like the Dragon Kick from what was written."

"But there are thirty-six stances," Sal corrected him, remembering the details that were listed on the visor. "There's all sorts…like offensive, defensive, adaptive, and so on."

"There are…" Petro agreed. "But they're not in that manual, Sal. What in the world have you been learning?"

"I uploaded the manual to my visor and created a learning program for the Silverson Arts. It's been guiding me through the process, and I've achieved just under ten percent of the course. I need to do a move perfectly twenty times before it lets me progress," Sal explained, a little quicker than he normally would have, because he sensed there was disapproval incoming. "It's analyzed all the text and was giving me pointers on how to progress, like making combination attacks."

"Walk me through them," Petro said in a firm tone. It was like he didn't believe Sal, but wasn't going to outright say it.

Sal first tried to explain with the naming convention for the different moves, but he was quickly interrupted by his father and instructed to explain the movements of his body. Sal complied and started to describe his training in the sparring room. He was corrected a few times about areas of proximity, but Petro listened for the most part.

After Sal recounted the set of moves he practiced in sequence in his dorm room, his father finally stopped him with a pat to his hand.

"Okay, Salvatore. I believe you. It sounds like you've certainly been busy." Petro chuckled as he gripped Sal's wrist. "You've been putting in some serious training, and I'm genuinely glad that you've invested the time."

"But…" Sal knew there was one coming. "I didn't do it right, did I?"

Petro hesitated before continuing. "What you've described to me takes a lot of context from later editions of the Silverson Arts. I promised you that I'd give you more materials when you mastered the basics… but it looks like your visor has adapted the fundamentals and evolved them into a completely separate form. I don't know that you could call this new hybrid the Silverson Arts, but it's definitely rooted in it."

Sal hated the feeling of disappointment that welled up inside him. He had tried to make an efficient method, and once again had screwed up. It was yet another blow to his confidence that he had trained his body to react to the wrong martial style. Would he be able to overwrite that muscle memory now that he was so far into it?

"Whoa now, don't go tensing up. From everything you've said to me, this could be an adaptive style." Petro was back to his reassuring tone of voice, and Sal could actually hear the smile. "You might have ended up refining the Silverson Arts for a new era. Demons have evolved in the time since I wrote those manuals, so maybe your arts are more suited to the current threats? If you're feeling more confident in your abilities because of them, then I give you my full approval to continue working toward a hundred percent proficiency. I'll even spar with you to test it out from time to time."

Sal smiled weakly at his father's reassurance, but it didn't help him feel like any less of an idiot. He should have known the moment it had started recalculating the sequences. There was no way the manual had over two and a half thousand combinations, so why did he so readily accept it when the visor told him?

"Now, I've got to get back to that Appraisal since I'm holding up your programming friends," Petro claimed as he tapped Sal's hand twice. "You continue resting up, and I'll hopefully get to have a look at your eyes before I head back to Silver Sanctuary. We've still got a good bit to catch up on, including the paperwork for your guild. That new elixir machine might have just thrown you out of the Trainee Guild category."

"What?" Sal asked, not trusting his hearing.

"Yeah…there's a few things we need to talk about, but that can wait." Petro chuckled as his chair squeaked. "Besides, there's a long line of people waiting to see you and make sure you're okay. I'll fill your mother in on everything, so don't worry about that, either."

"Thanks, Dad," Sal said earnestly. Knowing his father wasn't annoyed at him was a massive weight off his shoulders, but it still didn't remove the annoyance at himself that lingered.

CHAPTER 37: RECOVERY

Despite Sal's confidence with his negotiation skills, he was no match for the Healers in the infirmary. None of his attempts to get the bandages removed were successful, and he was forced to remain blind for the procession of visitors who wanted to check on him.

"How are you feeling, Sal?" Divinity patted his hand with her own, as if to tell him that she was next to him. "It's just me here. Barry doesn't like the infirmary and said he'd only visit if you were dying." She chuckled, but it was clear that she disapproved of Barry's choice.

Sal forced a smile before letting out a sigh. "I've been better. I kinda feel like an idiot… like, I really thought that I was past this whole collapsing and fainting stuff. Did I skip too many steps and get punished for it, or was it something else? That's all I can think about right now." Despite the forced smile, he couldn't keep the bitterness from his voice.

Having had some time to think about the conversation with his father, Sal concluded that he wasn't taking care of himself. The stretches and the martial arts training were good, but he knew about the ocular injuries for a long time and did nothing about it. Outsourcing that project to Fabi wasn't very responsible, especially when he had access to Mythcrafter and an entire database of weaves with the simulation orb. Where had the self-preservation instincts gone? He couldn't blame the effects of the Moonsilver Monocle this time around. All blame fell on his own shoulders.

Divinity's hand left his own, but he could hear her sitting down on the stool his father had vacated. It was disconcerting not knowing what his surroundings looked like. He didn't even know whether there were other people in the room with them. Would he be able to talk freely?

"Well, if you'd like to share some blame around… I'm pretty sure I should be top of the list," Divinity began softly. "I've tried to avoid looking into your future too closely, because I don't want it impacting our friendship. I could have seen this happening, but was too complacent."

Sal snorted as he shook his head, regretting the movement almost immediately as the tightness of the bandages caused a shooting pain down his neck. With a grimace, he had to settle for a crooked smile. "It's not your responsibility to keep me safe, so please don't go thinking that this is your fault in any way. Hell, I'm the one who's been telling you to stop meddling. What sort of hypocrite would I be for blaming you, when you've done everything I've asked?"

Divinity didn't say anything for a few moments. The quiet in the room became almost deafening, until she finally let out an exasperated sigh. "Barry should be here! He'd say something to cheer you up, I just know it."

Sal's smile was genuine this time. "I don't need cheering up, Divinity. I need a plan to improve my eyes. If this is going to happen as my ability gets stronger, then I'll probably go blind."

"That won't happen." Divinity was uncharacteristically firm as she gripped Sal's hand again. "I'm serious… This whole event has one hell of a silver lining. There's a whole new future because of your injury."

A chunk of tension left Sal's body as he unconsciously relaxed against the pillows. "Really? Let me guess, I go straight to the simulation orb and make an unbelievable Healing ability?" He wanted to chuckle at how the answer was staring him right in the face the whole time, and he hadn't taken it.

Another pause from Divinity told Sal he was right. But when it went on for a little longer, he suddenly became unsure. To cover all bases, he went with the other idea that was playing in the back of his head. "Do I replicate Sergeant Head's weave? I'm pretty sure it's a Body Manipulation one, and those are pretty much impossible right now, but I could probably figure it out with enough time and motivation." He pulled his hand free from Divinity and gestured at his bandages. "You can consider me very motivated."

Divinity waited a few more seconds before speaking. "Sorry, I needed to double-check… but I'm afraid neither of those are registering as a part of the main futures."

"What?" Sal's tone was hollow. He was so sure that one of those approaches would work, or cause a revolutionary change like the Perfect weave. "Are you sure?"

"I thought you'd know about it," Divinity replied in a confused tone. "You commissioned it. Or did that not happen yet?"

Sal realized this back-and-forth would go on for some time if he didn't intervene. "Could you just tell me what you're talking about? I don't care if it's something that needs to happen. If I need to commission something, I'll do that and follow that future perfectly. I need to keep my eyes safe." He was a little anxious that the future where his eyes were protected wasn't in his own control. If he wasn't the one to make the solution, then there was a far higher chance of it not happening.

Divinity didn't hesitate this time as she explained. "You asked Fabi to make you a mask, right? It was supposed to be a piece of Healing equipment. That's the thing that will stop you from going blind."

Sal relaxed again with a relieved sigh. "Okay, there's nothing to worry about then. I asked her to do that before the accident. I'm very happy to hear that it works out, though." He felt almost giddy that the answer to his problem was already being made.

"Really? That's great!" Divinity exclaimed in excitement. "I know it won't be ready for another week or so, but it'll have a dramatic effect on the future."

"More than the elixir machine?" Sal laughed. "I was half expecting to wake up to a thousand messages from you about that. Didn't think I'd be in an infirmary, though."

"Ah, that's going to take a lot longer before it makes an impact… but it'll be worth it," Divinity agreed quickly. There was a musical lilt to her voice that told Sal she was smiling. "The coffees taste like crap for the first month, by the way. Just to manage your expectations."

Sal experimented with a shrug and was happy when it didn't hurt him. "We've got Alex on board for the project, though, so we should still have a ready supply of the good stuff."

"I'm glad you're in better spirits. Guess we didn't need Barry after all." Divinity laughed as she touched Sal's shoulder. "I'm really relieved that you're okay. I was worried when I heard, and even though I know you'll make a full recovery, it's still scary."

"Thanks, Divinity. I really appreciate having you around, both as a friend and as someone who can tell me everything will be okay." Sal smiled after he spoke, thinking about the whole situation a little more. "Besides, Barry would have absolutely put the fear of death in me. He'd be talking about my will or something. I much prefer the reassurance that I'm not going blind."

Divinity paused for a few seconds before responding. "Just so you know… you're going to be in here for a while. I think it's because of your abilities. Quest has the best Healers coming in from the guilds to ensure you're fixed up perfectly. So, it'll be a couple of weeks at most, I'd say. I think you could probably get the time reduced by jumping through hoops with Quest and the Healers, though."

"What?" Sal asked in confusion. "But all the previous visits were just a few days? You saw Doctor Bob fix up my eyes in just a few minutes. How can it take weeks?"

"I don't know why they're doing it, Sal." Divinity sounded exasperated by the notion, too. "But it's for the best, because they don't know about the commission you made with Fabi. They're going to try to find a solution for your eyes with the Healers. Quest let me come in first after your dad because I'd be able to reassure you that everything would be okay, but he'll be in next and can explain properly."

"But…what about classes?" Sal had a pang of dread, already fearing the worst. "If I'm stuck in here, I'll miss even more of them."

Divinity sighed. "I don't know… there are too many variables. I'll keep you in the loop if one of the futures becomes more likely than the others. But for now, I think you just need to wait it out. Quest won't budge on this, as he wants you protected at all costs."

"That's somewhat reassuring, I guess," Sal muttered. "Still, it's kinda frustrating. There's so much that needs to be done, and sitting here isn't going to help me keep my rank in the Saviors."

Divinity burst out laughing, which was so out of the blue that Sal literally jumped in shock. The pain that shot through his spine and into the back of his neck was considerable.

"Sorry!" Divinity was still laughing, but she tried to be compassionate as she pressed a hand against his shoulder. "It was just really funny."

"You think so?" Sal asked bitterly as he massaged his neck with his free hand. The left was still bound to the bed, despite his earlier attempts to pull at the bindings with his right.

Divinity might have nodded or smiled, but Sal had no idea. He could only rely on her voice for context, which followed a few seconds later.

"It might take awhile for the elixir machine to get operational, but it's still a Mythic grade." Her implication was very clear this time. "You've essentially given the Crafting Department a ridiculously good revenue stream… so there's no chance you're losing your spot as a Savior. I'm not certain yet, but Jack and Anthony might actually get promoted because they were working on it."

Sal froze. Anthony and Jack could be Saviors? "You're serious?"

"Yeah… and that's before we consider all the effects of the elixirs you make." Divinity laughed. "You were right, by the way."

"About what?" Sal was nervous and excited all at once. He wanted to know which of his catastrophe predictions, or stupidly optimistic guesses, was correct.

"You've got close to thirty messages from me, that you'll get to read when your bandages are removed." Divinity laughed as she patted him again on the shoulder. "The elixir machine is an incredible achievement, but is only slightly overshadowed by the Myth Mask."

Sal would have stared at her if he could. "Myth Mask? Is that what Fabi's commission is called?" His mind was going a mile a minute, trying to figure out why she called it the Myth Mask. Was it a play on words because he had called Strategist's Dominion the Mythmark? Or had Fabi discovered a way to bring it up to the Mythic grade?

"I guess? I don't really know all the details." Divinity sounded a lot less sure of herself this time. "All I know is that it eventually becomes mass-produced and people love it."

"Do you know what grade it is?" Sal asked, curious for every shred of information she had available. "Like, if it's mass-produced, I doubt it's a very high grade. Well, unless Fabi was just waving them into existence with Figment."

Divinity sighed. "I'm sorry, Sal. I don't know all the details of it. I know that yours is like a Legendary grade, I'm pretty sure of that, but the other ones use evolutionary runes. It has something to do with a white leecher core, but that's all I really know about it. Fabi will be able to explain the details, but maybe don't ask her for a while in case it screws the future up."

Sal paused for a few seconds as he thought about it. A white leecher core? Was that the one that Fabi was talking about when they went into the leecher dungeon? It was something to do with the Purify ability, but there was no way a low-tier core would be suitable for a high-grade piece of equipment.

Creating a blight core equivalent with the Purify ability sounded borderline impossible. After all the leechers he killed with his father, Sal would consider himself generous in saying they picked up two or three white cores. Fabi would need hundreds or close to a thousand to produce something at the level of the blight core, assuming the Arkwright could even handle that kind of research without Cypher.

"Besides," Divinity continued awkwardly, "you'll probably not see her for a bit. She's been tearing through dungeons like crazy."

CHAPTER 38: OCULAR

When Sal next awoke, he was delighted to find he could open his eyes without any issue. There were no bandages bound around his head, and it took him quite a bit to acclimatize to the surrounding light. Blinking rapidly, Sal tried to focus on the bedsheets in front of him as he sat up in the bed. He had a long visit with Divinity, and rather than moving straight to the next visitor, the Healers had recommended he get some rest.

Sal wasn't sure whether it was a result of their treatment, but both his mind and body were in a constant state of exhaustion. Had they done something to boost his recovery? Maybe the exhaustion was just a side effect?

When his eyes finally adjusted to the light, he looked around the infirmary to see whether there was anyone else there. He half expected there to be rows of unoccupied beds, but the reality was far different. It was a dedicated room just for him. An entire glass board of charts and reports showcased his vitals. None of it looked to be particularly confidential, and there were a series of numbers in the readings that he couldn't interpret without the visor.

Sal thought the room would feel a lot colder and clinical, but the golden curtains and bedsheets led him to believe that he was in a private ward. It was much different from when he had been checked out after the excursion. Was it because his father was visiting him that they put him in a nice location? Or was this a perk of being in the Savior class?

"Ah, you're awake." Doctor Bob appeared with an easygoing smile, a tablet in his hands. "A little less sleep than we would have liked, but you seem to be recovering well."

Sal frowned. He had met Doctor Bob at the Doom Society meetings, but why would they have called him in for treatment? Was the extent of his injury so serious that he needed special treatment?

"Heart rate is rising," Bob remarked as he gestured at the screen, laughing. "Which tells me that you get anxious talking to doctors, or you're distressed by something."

Sal followed his gesture and could see that one of the numerical readings had turned into an orange color among a sea of greens. "Ah, sorry about that."

"It's normal, so don't worry about it." He spoke as he pulled a stool over to the side of Sal's bed. "So, now that you're awake…we can have a proper chat about what's going on with your eyes."

Sal gripped the sheets with both hands as he prepared himself. His father's words had been reassuring, and Divinity's certainty that he'd be fine was a massive relief. Yet, when he looked at Doctor Bob, he couldn't help but feel like both of them had been wrong. "Am I going to be okay?"

"Yes." Bob waved his tablet, smiling. "You've only received temporary or quick treatments for your eyes in the past. Rochelle de Verdon has been doing some good work, but she's far too inexperienced to handle something at this level." His smile faded slightly, and his mouth angled into more of a natural frown. Sal guessed that it was the default expression he made, taking the smile out for special occasions. "Our staff did your check-up a few months ago, but you haven't been in to see us since then. That's going to need to change if we want to stay on top of the degradation."

"Degradation?" Sal repeated the word as though it were alien to him. "Isn't there a treatment for me to improve my eyes? Like, exercises or something that could build up their condition?"

Doctor Bob glanced up from his tablet, eyebrow raised. "Ocular treatment is nuanced, and although it would be wonderful if we could just pump you full of essence and hope for the best, that's not how it works. Strengthening your eyes isn't like building muscle. They're far more fragile and so many things can go wrong when trying to improve their condition." He put up a hand and seemingly forced the smile back onto his face. "But we have specialists who will be able to give you a recovery plan. You're someone Quest wants to protect at all costs, so we're able to allocate more resources to your development than we would for others."

Sal wasn't sure whether he was supposed to feel grateful for that. He debated telling Doctor Bob about the Perfect weave. If he activated it, maybe more solutions would be possible? Taking a breath, Sal tried to steady his heart rate before continuing. Ever since he saw the number on the chart, he had become fixated on bringing the number down. "I have a weave I can activate. It's called Perfect, and it had dramatic effects on a Healing elixir."

Doctor Bob put the tablet down on the bedside locker before folding his arms and giving Sal his full attention. "I've heard about it. I'd need to do some tests with you under observation to see what sort of effects we're dealing with. Last thing we want is to give you medicine that evolves into a lethal concoction."

"Can it do that?" Sal's efforts in reducing his heart rate had been dashed, dramatically. It was now in the red numbers.

"We don't know." Bob shrugged. "You can probably appreciate the sort of policy we have at Quest Academy. We take in injured kids and fix them up as fast as possible so they don't miss classes. For us to truly get an understanding of that Perfect ability, we'd need to dedicate a chunk of time to testing it… time that we can't necessarily afford."

Sal stared at the wall chart for a few seconds, thinking through everything. "Okay. Can I ask what your Healing ability is? If you could teach me how to heal my own eyes, then I wouldn't need to come in constantly for check-ups and tests."

"Ha." Doctor Bob snorted with a shake of his head. "You're not the first Replicator to try that approach, and I doubt you'll be the last. Although there is merit, there's far too much nuance for a non-Healer to appreciate. Diagnosis is a very tricky thing, and there are so many natural inefficiencies that Healing essence will try to fix." He looked at Sal's expression and let out a sigh.

"Just to make myself clear, don't try that," Doctor Bob stated. "If you flood your eyes with essence, it could lead up to a buildup of tissue around the lens, which would cause cataracts. Too much regenerative tissue could lead to tumorous growth. Retinal scarring could happen, too. There are so many things that can go wrong, like if the Healing essence fixes the neural input, correcting the connection to your eyes, it would result in you losing your eyesight permanently."

"Oh…" Sal breathed as he looked at his own hands, trying to quietly determine whether his eyesight had degraded from what he remembered. It was an incredibly sobering moment, because he firmly believed that a burst of Healing essence was all he needed to fix his eyes. Was Rochelle doing more harm than good when she treated him? How many times had he availed of her Healing?

"Now, before you start conjuring up catastrophic scenarios… we'll talk about your treatment plan," Bob continued as he picked up his tablet. "We're lucky enough to have specialists who were able to bring your eyes back to an acceptable condition. Unfortunately, there is some lingering damage that we can't treat just yet. We'll need to monitor you while you're using your ability to understand which parts of the eyes are being affected."

Sal didn't know what to think. When he had spoken to Divinity, he genuinely thought that everything was going to be smooth sailing and that his eyes would be fixed when he got the mask from Fabi. Now that he was listening to Doctor Bob, he couldn't help but feel like there was an entirely new mountain to climb. The circlet he had made for his father had been calibrated and calculated for him, which had assured Sal that the degradation could be reversed. Was Doctor Bob wrong, and Cypher was right? Or was he severely underestimating how complex everything was?

No, his Crafting wasn't wrong. He had done the impossible more than a few times. Cypher hadn't been wrong yet, and had managed to help him through the process of realigning his gates. Just that little burst of conviction was enough to calm Sal's heart as he thought about everything logically. Yes, there were problems with his eyes, and he had a Healing specialist to work with… but that didn't mean he was guaranteed to have the best answers. Deferring to Doctor Bob on this would have been a lot easier if he hadn't crafted that solution for his father.

"Additionally, we've asked Coach to stop by so we can understand what aspects of your ability are causing the most amounts of strain," Doctor Bob continued. "I was informed by Quest that you selected Coach's master class, so I guess you can consider this the start of it."

"When will that be happening?" Sal was eager to meet Coach and understand his ability, because everything he had heard from people seemed to contradict what he knew. Quest had said he was great at techniques and building the Mastery stat. Divinity had said he helped Gallant evolve his ability, and now Doctor Bob was telling him that Coach could identify the strain incurred by using weaves? It sounded like a complex combination, and he wondered how it would classify as a Skill master class.

"He's going to be arriving later in the week, so you'll have more time to recuperate. Thankfully, your abilities aren't combat-oriented, so you won't need to go to a dungeon with him. We should be able to get all the results we need from you working on Crafting and using your Skill Master weave," Bob explained as he got to his feet. "If we can find some safe parameters for you to gain more control over your abilities, then the treatment plan will be far more straightforward."

"What exactly can Coach do? Like, what's his ability?" Sal asked eventually, knowing that he'd end up wondering the whole night if he didn't get an answer.

Doctor Bob smiled as he looked at Sal. "If I were a Replicator, I'd take his in an instant." He chuckled as he thought about it. "I don't know the name, but I know what it does. He's able to look at a person when they're using an ability, and he can create a ridiculously accurate strategy for them to improve themselves. Be it an increase in ability weave grades, or developing a martial skill, he can tell instinctively what needs to happen for them to reach their next stage."

Sal's mouth dropped open. "That sounds ridiculously good, though. What's the catch? There has to be a catch." Sal needed there to be a catch, because the description of that ability had made it skyrocket up his priority list. If he were to get Coach's ability as a Skill Implant, then he'd be near unstoppable as a guildmaster. He could improve weaves with Skill Master and instinctively know what work the person needed to put in to get them to adapt to the improvements? It sounded incredible.

"The catch?" Doctor Bob pocketed the tablet in his lab coat. "Well, it depends on your temperament. Instinctively knowing that there is no way for a person to grow stronger can be a tough burden. Coach can see the limits of everyone he looks at, and it can be a crushing reality when you need to break that to a person. Couple that with the few people who regret their abilities evolving, or even the detractors who believe Coach is breaking more people than he's fixing... it's a tough role to occupy."

"I think it sounds incredible," Sal breathed as he smiled at Doctor Bob. Maybe being stuck in the ward wasn't the worst situation. If Coach was going to be coming to him, then he wouldn't be falling behind in at least one of the classes. It was a little ridiculous, though. He was admitted for ruining his eyes with abilities he couldn't handle, and now he was excited to replicate an ability he hadn't even seen yet.

"I agree." Doctor Bob smiled as he started to walked toward the door. "You can play with your tablet for up to an hour, but don't strain your eyes for longer than that. I'll know if you do."

"Thanks, Doctor," Sal responded as he lay back on the bed, staring at the ceiling. All he could think about was Coach's ability. If it worked half as well as Doctor Bob described, it was going to be amazing. He'd be able to fix it up, too. Maybe there were even higher grades of it, or evolutions.

Sal continued to think about all the possible permutations until he drifted off to sleep again.

CHAPTER 39: GUILT

"Come on, this is ridiculous," Sal complained as he dropped the artifact onto the bedsheets in front of him. He stared at Quest, who was seated opposite him in the private infirmary. "Just how long do I need to be trapped here? We could do these exercises around classes. It's not like I'm a danger to myself."

Quest smiled gently as he tilted his head to one side. "Really? You're telling me that you wouldn't run off to Craft a solution for your eyes? Your father told me about the regenerative circlet you made for him. And although I'll always commend you for stepping outside the box with your Crafting, this is far too serious for us to take unnecessary risks."

Sal gritted his teeth as he leaned back into the wall of pillows that were propped behind him. He stared at the ceiling and wondered how he had gotten himself into this situation. It had been close to a full week since he had been admitted into the infirmary. His eyes seemed fine and healthy, but they wouldn't let him use his tracker to find out. It was stored in his dorm, along with everything else that could keep him sane. He wasn't allowed to train or use any weaves, unless a specialist was around to monitor him.

"At least tell me that Coach is coming soon?" Sal asked wearily. It was the silver lining that he was waiting for, and with every passing day, he got the same answer.

"His schedule is a little unpredictable, but he's assured us that he'll arrive when he's next available." Quest's tone was apologetic yet factual. A slight pause hung in the air before he continued. "So, would you like to take another look at the artifact before we call in the specialist?"

Sal tilted his head so he could see the headmaster. "Appraising a Rare-grade artifact that you've picked up from somewhere isn't going to hurt my eyes. I've been doing them for years, long before I came to Quest Academy." With an almost impatient exhalation, Sal propped himself up into a seated position. "Now, if you just get them to take me to the elixir machine, they'll see me doing a high-level Appraisal. That will give them all the answers they'll need. Hell, I could just make some stuff in the workshop and they could watch the whole time."

Quest's smile didn't so much as flicker. It was almost like he was humoring Sal. With a gentle nod, and his own sigh of impatience, he spread his hands wide. "I'd love nothing more than to do that, but it's the opinion of the specialists that we take things slowly. They want to work up toward the higher levels, and you've done an excellent job with the Common and Uncommon grades. Once you've finished with the Rare grades, I'm sure we'll see some good data that will help you going forward."

Sal just stared at him. "I did seventy-three Appraisals in a single evening for the Reavers Guild. Your specialists have me doing a maximum of three, which I had to beg for. Half of the time, I feel like a prisoner. The other half, I feel like a child. Please tell me that you're frustrated by all of this? I can't possibly keep my grades up when I'm missing classes."

Before Quest could say anything, Sal continued with a pleading expression. "Okay, okay… what about the simulation orb? That doesn't take any essence and I'm not using my eyes. It's literally just instinct! I could be working on so many different weaves, and helping students. You can literally monitor me the whole time."

Quest gave Sal a sad shake of his head. "I know this is frustrating, and I do share that sentiment, but you need to appreciate the situation from our side. You're the first documented Mythcrafter, and your Skill Master ability is truly one of a kind. You've already showcased that you're capable of redefining whatever landscape you tread on." He held up a hand to stop Sal from interrupting. "But those abilities are hurting you. Serious injuries that would destroy those abilities. You have unfortunately curated a reputation as a workaholic, so nobody believes you'll take it easy if we discharge you from the infirmary. While you're here, we can take care of you and help you as much as we can."

"I'm at serious risk of gouging my own eyes out if you just keep me here," Sal stated flatly as he raised his fingers to his face. "With everything that happened at the gala, I half expected you to say that this was some sort of plan to keep me safe, or that you were locking me away from the elixir magnates or something." He laughed humorlessly. All it took was a week of solitary confinement for him to go stir-crazy. "But, even if you're doing all of this to help me, it's far too slow. I have master classes and advanced modules that I need to attend."

Quest waved his right hand like it was nothing. "You don't need to worry about the master classes. All your lecturers have been informed of the treatment plan, and you'll likely be dismayed to find out that they think it's a great idea. Even Jez, which was a pleasant surprise." He laughed as though it were a preposterous thought. "Captain Chatfield has also said that you can catch up with relative ease when you get back. A lot of his curriculum is geared around results rather than class participation, which wasn't too much of a surprise."

Sal wasn't sure how he should feel about it. He thought he'd be able to convince Quest by using the angle of wanting to study and not fall behind in classes, but that hadn't worked at all.

"And as for the Crafting courses, well… Upgrade saw the condition you were in, and she'll likely put you right back in this bed if she sees you walking around the place." Quest chuckled as he straightened his back. "I know this isn't the news you wanted, and I know that you'd prefer to be out there working on the next world-breaking project. You deserve a lot more fanfare for what you've done, and you'll get it… but only after we ensure you're healthy and not a danger to yourself."

"Is my dad done with the Appraisal yet?" Sal switched topics, seeing as there was no chance of making Quest budge. Divinity had made it sound like Sal would be able to talk them out of keeping him in the infirmary, but she didn't mention anything about it being this difficult. It felt like he'd graduate from the infirmary. Okay, that was a little much, but he felt sorry for himself, so he was content at acting the catastrophist.

"Mr. Argento is showcasing a ridiculous work ethic, and has been detailing it constantly. He's certainly earning his day rate." Quest smiled. "I'm sure you'll be very pleased with the results. The initial readings look promising."

Sal snorted as he shook his head. "You shouldn't have given him a day rate. If you paid him for the job getting done, you'd have had a fully completed Appraisal a few days ago."

"Ah, well…we thought with his son being hospitalized on our watch, it was the least we could do." Quest offered a guilty shrug. "It's also a good excuse for him to hang around and visit you."

"Are you sure he's not just scared of facing my mother?" Sal laughed as he thought back to the last conversation with his parents a few days ago. His dad had relented on the first day and told his mother about the collapse. She had been worried, but was relieved that Sal was being taken care of. There had been an hour-long call just to make doubly sure that he was okay. Sal wondered whether the overprotective care he was receiving at the academy was through his mother's meddling. That was definitely a possibility.

"I can't imagine many would feel safe if they were in your mother's bad books." Quest chuckled as he got to his feet. "Now, as much as I'd love to continue our chat, we're keeping the specialist waiting. I'll send him in. But, before that, I'll ask you to please just give this your best effort. I know it's mundane and exasperating for you to work at this speed, but we believe this method is your best chance at recovery."

"It's hard being annoyed at you when I know you're just trying to help me." Sal groaned as he picked up the artifact on the bedsheets in front of him. "And how do I know you're not just making me catalogue a load of Credit floor backlog? This could all be an elaborate plan to get free Appraisals." He waved the Rare-grade carving in front of him for emphasis.

Quest paused as he looked at Sal, his eyebrow raised. "Salvatore, you literally just made a Mythic-grade elixir machine… with revenue projections that rival our academic budget. In what world would I abuse your talents and have you doing Appraisals, of all things?"

Sal laughed properly for the first time in a few days. "Okay, good point." With a sigh, Sal watched as Quest moved to leave the infirmary. It was only when the headmaster reached the door that Sal thought of another question. "By the way, have you told Fabi to keep her distance or something? She and Upgrade have been messaging me, but said they can't come over."

Quest stopped walking and turned around with a sad smile. "I'm afraid not. My best guess would be that they're still processing what happened. If I was overseeing a student who collapsed in front of me, I'd be distraught. Even if it was in pursuit of greatness, the guilt would win any internal battle." He adjusted his glasses that were hanging close to the tip of his nose. "Give them some time, and they'll surely come to visit you. Knowing Upgrade, she's likely Crafting a protective bubble for you to live in. I dread to think what would happen if Fabrizia joined her on that pursuit."

"I appreciate that, thank you." Sal gave a halfhearted wave to Quest. He watched as the headmaster closed the door behind him. It would only be a few minutes before the specialist came in to make him do stupid Appraisal exercises, so Sal decided he'd send a few messages while he waited.

Salvatore: Hey Fabi, just had another meeting with Quest. All is good, just need to do more pointless Appraisals while they're watching me. Nothing to worry about.

Salvatore: Hypothetically, if I offered a bribe, would you bring me my visor?

Salvatore: No update on Coach coming to see me. I'll let you know when I have an update.

Clicking Send, Sal navigated to Divinity next. He was smiling as he typed out the message.

Salvatore: Okay, you know the way you said I'd need to negotiate to get out of the infirmary? You didn't mention that it would be impossible. I genuinely think that this is my new dorm. They've probably given mine to someone else.

Lastly, Sal went to message Upgrade. He didn't know whether Quest's words were even close to the mark, but he decided that the best method would be to approach it head-on.

Salvatore: When are you coming to visit me? I need someone here who doesn't look at me like my eyes will explode at any moment. Can't wait to see what you've done with Strategist's Dominion!

Salvatore: Oh, and on the off chance you're feeling bad about what happened, don't. It's better this happened now in a safe environment rather than if I was alone or something. I'll be fixed up in no time and we can get working on your Mythic drone arm. Just need to find something to do that will keep my brain occupied in the meantime.

To Sal's surprise, a message came back instantly.

Upgrade: Hey! Just running some equipment tests in a dungeon. Strategist's Dominion is in better shape, but I'm still not happy with it. I want it to blow your socks off when you see it.

Upgrade: And yeah, I do feel bad. As I should. I pushed you to go beyond your limits because I was excited to see a Mythic grade. It was a shit thing to do, and I'll apologize properly to you in person.

Upgrade: Fabi is here with me, and we're working hard on your commission. It won't make up for the shit situation, but we're hopeful you'll like it.

Sal was glad that he had asked Quest. If Upgrade had been avoiding him for this reason, he hoped that she'd now be more willing to visit. Even though he was curious about Strategist's Dominion, he was more bored by the fact that he only had Healers to talk to.

Salvatore: As long as you don't treat me like I'm super fragile when I'm back, then we're good. I don't blame anyone for what happened. I just need to learn my limits.

Upgrade: Don't worry, nobody will think you're fragile when you're wearing this gear. When we're done, this thing will blow the Arbiter's Judgment out of the water!

Salvatore: Can't wait! Healer is here so I gotta go.

Upgrade: Want me to drop off some Essence Programming materials so you can study?

Salvatore: No thanks.

CHAPTER 40: DISCHARGE

"Is there a problem?" Quest asked in a concerned voice as he entered the private ward. Beside him was Doctor Bob, a stern expression on his face.

"I didn't think you'd believe me if I told you, so I needed you to see this." Doctor Bob gestured at the room, as though the problem were clearly visible.

Sal smiled innocently from his cross-legged position on the bed. He hadn't even bothered to hide the evidence, because it was a statement. If they were going to keep him in that ward to monitor his use of Mythcrafter, then that's exactly what he was going to show them. To make it a little easier, he looked at the machine in question, just to help Quest find it faster.

"You brought him materials," Quest said before he exhaled slowly, looking at the collection of new equipment stacked around the room. "I believe I was very clear on the limits we set for his treatment." He looked at Doctor Bob meaningfully, but seemed surprised to see his colleague in full agreement, with his arms crossed.

"Yes, but we didn't bring him those materials. He pulled them out of thin air, claiming he found them under his bed." Doctor Bob stared at Sal the entire time. "The specialists managed to get their data, but I needed to bring you here to see this."

Quest groaned as he gave Sal a warning look, before following Doctor Bob to the strange machine that rested against the wall. "What… is this?" he asked in confusion, looking at Doctor Bob for some context.

"Ask him. He's the one who made it," Doctor Bob responded with a tight smile. "He's been Appraising every piece of medical equipment we have, which we thought would be good tests for him. But it looks like he was deconstructing them with Mythcrafter at the same time."

Quest's mouth opened, but no sound came out. He slid his right hand over the polished obsidian glass enclosure before lifting it gently, causing the curved screen to lock into position, revealing what looked like a mechanical armchair. "Salvatore… what am I looking at?"

Sal shrugged, as though he had no idea. "Depends. When is Coach coming?"

Quest groaned again as he looked at the ceiling. His back was turned to Sal, but it was clear that all vitality was seeping out of the headmaster as he fought back whatever his instinctive reaction was going to be. "I've told you that his schedule is unpredictable, Salvatore. You were supposed to run through the tests with the specialists, and stay away from projects that might hurt you." He turned and gave Sal a pained look. His arm jutted out to point at the armchair thing. "What part of this seemed like a good idea to you?"

Sal shook his head slowly. "I did everything they asked of me. They wanted me to do a few Appraisals, and I did. They wanted me to do some basic Crafting, and I did." He pointed at the machine in front of him. "That's just a collection of components that I made with Mythcrafter. I designed it to combine the medical devices I Appraised, and it came out pretty good. There was no secret Crafting when nobody was looking. I did everything while the Healers were monitoring me."

Quest looked at Doctor Bob for confirmation, and his jaw dropped when he got a reluctant nod of affirmation. With the mother of all grimaces, Quest sat on the edge of Sal's bed. An involuntary chuckle escaped his lips as he shook his head in wonder. "And he didn't injure himself further by doing this?"

Doctor Bob shook his head. "No, he stayed within all the limits we set for him. It's an Epic grade, according to him, but we'll need verification from another Appraiser to be sure."

"With evolutionary runes," Sal pointed out, smiling widely. "You'll need a few cores to power it up. I couldn't find any of those under the bed, unfortunately."

Quest nodded as though he was at his wit's end. There was an erratic nature to his movements as he waved at Bob. "Then I guess we'll need to get some cores, won't we?" He glanced at Sal and gave a strained laugh. "Why are you like this? Is this a statement or something? You could have just quietly rested and let our people find a solution for you."

"It just looked inefficient the way it was," Sal offered awkwardly. "If this manages to help people, then it's a win for everyone, isn't it?"

Quest stared at Sal for a few moments. "You might not be aware of this, Salvatore, but medical devices will fall under the same regulations as your elixir machine. If you've built something that's designed to operate on people or their essence, then you're going to be met with a ridiculous amount of red tape. Even if it's spectacular, it'll be a long time before it's approved for use."

Sal shrugged, as though it were no big deal. "Good thing it does neither of those things, then. Isn't it?" He chuckled as he pointed at the machine against the wall. "It's a diagnostics tool. It has only two abilities. Cypher, which is the same as my visor, and Scan. That was a new one for me, but I was able to infuse it from Cecile's weave."

"Cecile?" Quest repeated in confusion.

"One of our Healers," Doctor Bob answered for him. "She specializes in diagnostics with the Scan ability. I had no idea that he was capable of infusing abilities with Mythcrafter." It was remarkable how he could express surprise in his words, yet maintain the most stoic tone of all time.

"There you have it." Sal smiled. "Cypher is pretty much the pinnacle of computational abilities, and combined with Scan, it should allow for perfect diagnosis. I used Cypher for my dad's regenerative circlet, and for my own essence gate calibration. That's how I managed to get my essence fortification."

"Right," Quest breathed as he looked at Sal for a few seconds. "You did manage to do that." He nodded as though collecting his thoughts, and it only took a moment before he glanced over at the scanning machine. "And it's at no risk of harming anyone? It just reads the information of whoever sits in it?"

"Yep." Sal nodded as he shifted to stretch out his right leg. His feet were starting to go numb. "Who knows, maybe someday we can add Coach's weave to it and get a diagnosis for upgrading weaves?"

Quest just shook his head in wonder. "And that's why you're so eager to meet him? You're trying to make a scanner that will show progression for whoever sits in it?"

"Well, not exactly…" Sal began with an awkward laugh. "It wasn't anything as grand as that, but I wanted to see what his ability was like. If it's a good one, and I can work with the weave enough to make a suitable version for myself, I'd likely try to take it as my Skill Implant."

Quest turned his attention to the scanner and looked to be in something of a trance. It took him a few moments before he started speaking. "Hypothetically, Salvatore," he turned back to look at Sal, his brow furrowed, "would you be able to incorporate System with Coach's ability? Let's say with Cypher, too."

"It already gives readings on the obsidian glass," Sal answered, confused. "I mean, like Interface. It'll show all the information. Is that what you're trying to achieve with System?"

"No." Quest shook his head and got to his feet. "Forget I mentioned that. It was just a thought." He sighed as he looked around the room. "How many more tests does he need to go through before you can discharge him?"

Doctor Bob raised an eyebrow as he looked first at Quest, before shifting his gaze to Sal. "Well, if this thing is actually an Epic grade…"

"It is." Quest stated it as if it were obvious. "Salvatore is an excellent Appraiser, so I have zero doubts of his claims."

"Well, then. We'd need to see him work on a Legendary-grade piece to monitor the type of damage it might be doing to his eyes. All the tests up until now have shown his capability at handling Crafting up to the Epic grade. We can't really proceed with Skill Master tests until we have Coach here."

Quest nodded. "Then we can discharge him and let him get back to classes?" He gestured at the scanner. "We'll get the cores he needs to power this thing up, and I'd ask you to work with Cecilia to determine whether it's as good as Sal thinks it is."

"Cecile." Both Sal and Doctor Bob corrected Quest at the same time.

"Yes, of course. Sorry about that." Quest smiled with a curt nod in Sal's direction. "It looks like you've managed to secure your freedom… but I'd ask you to refrain from any Legendary-grade builds until we can assemble a medical team to observe you. Understood?"

"Understood!" Sal exclaimed happily as he whipped both legs off the bed and got to his feet. "This has been the worst three weeks of my life." He laughed as he glanced at Doctor Bob. "No offense intended, Doctor."

"None taken," Doctor Bob replied, his gaze drifting over to the scanner. "Should I presume we will end up getting billed for this? I'd rather not have to deal with budget discrepancies."

Sal shook his head. "If you don't want it, I can take it back to the workshop." He shrugged, like it wasn't really that much of an issue. "But if it's valuable here and helps people, I'd be happy renting it to you."

"Renting?" Doctor Bob laughed as he looked at Quest in disbelief. "Dare I ask what sort of rate?"

"Nothing extortionate." Sal smiled as he stretched his back. "Just priority treatment for members of my guild. If you're able to help them out in any way, then it more than makes up for the building and material costs… from what I had on me."

It was the first time he had seen Doctor Bob speechless, and it was absolutely worth the wait. His fake smiles were gone, and his gruff stoicism evaporated, too. All that was left was genuine incredulity. "You're serious? We couldn't possibly just take this from you. If it's Epic grade, as you said, and it's able to help Cecile with diagnosis, then we could absolutely find some room in the budget."

"Deadly serious." Sal smiled. "And hey, it might earn me a few points in my Ethical Crafting class. Who knows?"

Quest gestured at the door, and Doctor Bob took the hint immediately. The Healer left with a smile of wonderment on his face, tinged with confusion as to what just happened. When he was gone, Quest turned to look at Sal and smiled.

"Well done with this." He bit his lip. "I'm constantly surprised with your Crafting, and this is no exception. I don't think my heart can take all these surprises, but they're at least welcome ones."

Sal grinned as he pointed at the scanner. "I lied about not having any cores— I could fit them and we could check your heart if you want?"

Quest barked a laugh as he shook his head. "No… no, Salvatore. I'm sure I'll be fine."

"What were you talking about earlier, by the way?" Sal asked out of genuine curiosity. "About combining Coach's ability with Cypher and System. What are you hoping to do?"

Quest looked a little surprised by the question and seemed close to waving it off like a flight of fancy. Sal interjected before he could dismiss it.

"I'm serious. I'll promise not to try making it if you think it's too difficult, but I'd like to hear what it was." Sal spoke quickly and tried to assuage any of Quest's potential fears of him overworking himself. He desperately wanted to know what sort of commission someone like Quest would want. Combining those skills didn't make much sense, and Sal realized that he didn't know much about the System ability. Hopefully, he'd get more context from the System master class.

Quest looked at Sal carefully before a rueful smile tugged at his lips. "When you mentioned the scanner's ability to diagnose, it made me consider one of the key issues with the Quest System. I mentioned it to you before. It was a progression system that offered numerical values and introduced concepts like leveling. Although it worked great for the guilds, it became an almost obsessive compulsion with Heroes only accepting work that would increase their numbers. I personally deemed it a failure when I realized it was helping people achieve growth, but at the cost of their critical reasoning."

Quest looked at the scanner again thoughtfully. "If you were able to combine Coach's ability, with the Quest System, and Cypher…I think we'd be able to make something quite interesting. Imagine it, being able to see how many prowlers you need to kill before your ability grows stronger? How many Epic grades you need to construct before Mythcrafter evolves? What exercises you need to perform to achieve a higher Strength statistic? The possibilities are endless." His voice was filled with wonder at the prospect, and a guilty laugh escaped him as he shook his head wistfully.

"Although it could work, I don't know how it could be executed… and even if it were possible, it would still have all the pitfalls that the Quest System had.

Would guilds be motivated to reclaim territories or help refugees if it didn't help their personal progression?" His laugh this time was hollow, as though he already knew the answer.

Sal seriously thought about it. It did sound pretty incredible, and it was eerily close to what he was doing with the Silverson Arts and his visor. It was giving him a progression track to work toward, and it really helped his motivation levels in seeing what he needed to do to attain mastery. Still, Quest's concerns were very real. He wondered whether there was a solution to it, but nothing really jumped out at him. All he could think of were the aspects that would appeal to him.

"Well, when I did those scavenger runs, I was given Challenge crests for reaching certain grades. Having the reputation gains that unlock perks was pretty cool. Maybe you could add things like that to the Quest System, with perks for people. I don't know what sort of perks you could put in place for helping refugees, but I'm sure there's something. Worst-case scenario, just offer monetary rewards." Sal laughed as he brainstormed aloud, not sure he was really adding anything helpful to the conversation. When he looked at Quest, he was surprised to see the headmaster staring at him intently.

"I expected you to tell me that the build wouldn't be possible," Quest started slowly. "But I think there's definitely some merit to your suggestions. This is quite hypothetical. I'm sure there are more than a few glaring oversights that I'm missing." He laughed as he gave Sal a dismissive wave. "Let's just leave it at that for now. We need to ensure you're at no risk of injuring yourself, and plotting a new project like this isn't going to help at all."

Sal thought about it a little more. "What about your master class? Would that be a good time for us to brainstorm the project?"

"Absolutely not." Quest was firm as he shook his head. "The System master class is an opportunity for you to work with me on a project of your own choosing. I wanted to offer it to you so you could customize your own system, not so you could entertain my personal ambitions."

Sal laughed, nodding. "Excellent. Then I'll choose that project. It sounds like a lot of fun."

The sentence had caused a stalemate, with Quest staring at Sal in disbelief for a few moments of silence.

Eventually, Quest broke with a hollow chuckle, glancing over at the scanner mournfully. "I might take you up on the offer of checking my heart. I'm convinced that you're bad for my health."

CHAPTER 41: RECAP

"The Savior returns!" Barry called out triumphantly as Sal entered the canteen of the Savior dorms. He wore a wide grin as he beckoned Sal over to the nearest chair. "How come you're here and not in the workshop? I'd have guessed you'd be there the moment you got discharged."

Sal laughed, almost humorlessly. "I'm a different man now, Barry. Staying in that ward really helped me think through a lot of things. I think I'm going to stop Crafting... it's clearly bad for my health."

"Yeah, nobody is going to believe that. Great delivery, though, you get some points for the shit acting." Barry chuckled as he leaned his face against his palm. "So, come on... tell me everything. What did you get up to for the last few weeks? Anything exciting?"

Sal took a seat and faced Barry, offering a slight shake of the head. "I just did a few bits and pieces, behaving myself. Took it all very seriously."

Barry's grin grew wider. "Come on, are you giving me a hard time because I didn't visit? We would have both felt uncomfortable if I went there to check on you. Besides, that's not how our friendship works. I can't give you shit when you're close to dying, but I can make up for it now. You've missed a lot. But I want to know what you've been doing, because there's no chance you just sat in that ward like a good little boy for weeks."

Sal leaned back in his chair. "Was my acting really that shit?"

"The worst. Now spill." Barry laughed as he waved his free hand to get Sal talking.

"Okay... so where do we start. Eh, they only let me have my tablet for an hour at a time to start. Since everything was about my eyes, they were super careful about me looking at things that might irritate them," Sal began to explain, but Barry waved at him like he was wrong.

"No, no... not the practical stuff. Like, what did you do to keep yourself sane? I would have stormed out of there after a couple of days, but you lasted weeks. So, the only conclusion I could come up with is that you found something interesting to keep yourself there. That's what I'm trying to figure out," Barry countered, his gaze narrowing as he studied Sal's face, as though looking for some form of deception.

Sal's face broke into a wide smile. "You're asking if I spent the last three weeks working on your illusion training?"

Barry's eyes lit up in excitement. "I knew it! You did, didn't you?"

Sal folded his arms. "It wasn't easy, as I'm pretty out of practice... but yeah, it was good for keeping my mind active. I tried using it for fighting training, but my memory wasn't good enough to recall actual encounters. I switched to brainstorming builds for Crafting and that did the trick."

"For Crafting?" Barry asked in confusion. "But you can't use Mythcrafter when you're in an illusion. How would that be a benefit?"

Sal tapped against the side of his temple. "Because I've got countless Appraisals that I can draw on, and I guided myself through their deconstruction and construction. It didn't have the capability or finesse of Mythcrafter, but I learned a lot from it. When I'd wake up, I'd use my free hour to browse the Crafting Corner forums to ask and answer questions. Afternoons, I'd do some stretches and light exercise that didn't strain my eyes… just going through the motions I learned from my dad."

"That sounds… tame, actually," Barry said in a disappointed tone. "I half expected you to do something dramatic."

Sal shrugged as he spread his hands out wide. "What can I say, I'm a boring person. I also got through about eighty different courses from the Credit Store. Pretty much all of Fabi's catalogue has been listened to about four times over, and I discovered a few other great Crafters with uploaded courses. Picked up a few basic Alchemy ones, which will hopefully be useful."

"Eighty?" Barry repeated the word as though he wasn't hearing correctly. "Isn't that a little excessive?"

"I didn't have my visor to pick up the information, so I had to listen carefully. I was only able to make notes for a couple of hours a day, and I listened to the courses, so it was a strange sort of routine. It worked, though, and I could feel myself coming to grips with a lot of the course materials. Most of it is Crafting related, though, so there's a lot to catch up on in the other subjects." Sal grimaced, just thinking about how behind he was with the other courses.

"Not as far behind as you'd think." Barry chuckled as he sat up straight and folded his arms, before hunching over to lean on them. "Chatfield's Advanced War Zone is an absolute shit-show. I thought he'd be some incredible instructor, but his methods are ridiculous."

"Oh, please tell me." Sal laughed as he leaned in closer. "I'm guessing it's dangerous?"

"Exact opposite." Barry laughed. "He won't let us go near a dungeon or a tower. Everything is drills, formations, tactics, and stamina training. We spent the first week learning how to run away from a fight, can you even believe it?"

"And the second week?" Sal asked, delighted that he had bumped into Barry. It was great spending time with him, and although Sal had been a bit confused as to why he never visited like the others, there was no awkwardness. They just picked up where they left off. It was oddly reassuring.

"Second week, it was mock battle scenarios. He had Sinclair there to simulate battles, with Chatfield stepping into the role of Controller and issuing instructions. It was all about the response times. And you'd have loved seeing Erika being bossed around by him. It was priceless." Barry thought about it for a second, the smug grin on his face not budging an inch. "There were a few injuries, but nothing serious. A few people tried to steal the show with flashy theatrics, and Chatfield came down on them like a ton of bricks. Really pushed the whole teamwork thing, and wouldn't allow anyone to shine too brightly. It was actually kinda awesome. I liked that week."

"Really? Not being allowed to shine… sounds like the worst environment for you?" Sal chuckled. "No offense. I mean, you just strike me as the type that would love to steal the show."

"None taken." Barry grinned. "It was an odd week, but it was a lot of fun. Really humbled a lot of Saviors who thought they were the shit from ranking above the others. Brought more than a few egos back down to earth, and the teams started doing amazing after that."

"Ah, so teams have already been selected. Just tell me that I'm not going to be lumped into Erika's team or I'll admit myself back into the ward until the semester is over," Sal muttered with a groan.

Barry raised a single finger. "That's the thing, the teams were completely random. He picked them out before each exercise and had everyone else making notes on what went well, and what went shit. Kinda similar to Rust's exercise, but this was waaaay better. Chatfield told us what to look out for and stuff, and you could clearly see how all his matchups were terrible." Barry laughed as he thought about it. "Like, *actually* terrible. I've done so many simulations, Sal. He literally picked the worst compositions on purpose to make a point. It was glorious."

"And at what point did it become a shit-show?" Sal was eager to learn everything he missed. If the first two weeks had been about running away and formations, then he wasn't actually as far behind as he thought.

"Extraction games." Barry stated it like it explained everything. But for good measure, he broke it down. "He created all these scenarios for us to do out in the Reclaimed Zones. We had to secure an asset, similar to the tower's second floor. Sometimes it was a puzzle with another step, or it was someone who needed to be evacuated out of the war zone. Chatfield would walk alongside the group and explain what was happening around them, all simulated scenarios. Surprise attacks, terrain difficulties, missing supplies… there was so much!"

Sal stared at Barry for a moment. "You said it was a shit-show, but it sounds like you're really enjoying it?"

Barry blinked and tilted his head to the side. "Oh, everyone hates it. I love it. There's so many variables and it's playing mind games with Chatfield. He accepts unorthodox solutions if they have merit, and he encourages adaptive mindsets. It's literally the perfect landscape for me… but a nightmare for the more rigid types that see everything as black and white."

"Like Erika?" Sal guessed with a chuckle.

"No, actually. Divinity was having a nightmare out there. She'd predict the future, and Chatfield would change the conditions to ensure she couldn't win. He was clearly trying to teach her to stop relying on the future, and all it managed to do was infuriate her." Barry laughed as he wiped a single tear from his right eye. "Mica and Hannah were two of the most impressive ones out there, though. You should absolutely lock Hannah down as your Defense. She adapted ridiculously fast to the scenarios. Scarily fast, even."

Sal was happy to hear that Hannah was adapting to the class with the others. He didn't know she had taken the Advanced War Zone module, but it wasn't really a surprise considering she was in the Saviors class. Hearing that Divinity was having issues was a shame, but he guessed that Chatfield had a plan… or he was just being a prick. It was genuinely hard to tell with that man.

"And what about the most recent week? More scenario training?" Sal was curious because Divinity had sounded confident about being able to blitz through the module to unlock Strategic Warfare as a class.

Barry's smile evaporated. "Yeah, that's kinda where it all turned into a shit-show, if I'm honest. All the tempo and content we were getting went out the window." He folded his arms and looked to the side. "Have you heard of the Delvers Guild? They're working with Chatfield to help out the Savior training, and giving their *professional* take on how we should take on dungeons."

Sal's stomach clenched. Surely this was a joke. There was no way Robert would have signed off on this. It was obvious to literally everyone at the gala that the Delvers were being closely monitored, with Robert making the Hunter Bureau's stance very clear during the obituaries. The Delvers Guild couldn't be trusted, and Shade was a piece of shit.

"That's a joke, right?" Sal asked as seriously as he could muster. "Shade has a long and complicated history with the Argento Auction House, but the short version is that he's very possibly a Villain." Sal stared at Barry, as though trying to find out whether this was one of his mind games.

Barry grimaced as he shook his head slightly, finally turning to look at Sal. "Divinity already made a complaint to Chatfield, but he politely told her to back off. She thinks that they're using us as a sting operation to uncover that Shade is… eh, shady." He frowned at the poor choice of words, before laughing it off. "They're pretty decent at tactics, though. I don't like them, but I'm learning quite a bit from them. Lock is their vice-captain, and he's pretty smooth. He's shamelessly scouting some of the Saviors, and it's so obvious that Chatfield had to step in."

"So, let me get this straight. Shade isn't there, right?" Sal asked carefully. He didn't have the monitor to tell him that his heart rate was elevated. He didn't need it, as he could hear it thundering through his eardrums. "It's just that guy Lock and a few of the others?"

Barry shifted uncomfortably. "Well, for the rest of the Saviors… yes?" He averted his gaze and his voice pitched up a few notches. "But as a reward for ranking so highly, Shade has elected to teach the top five Saviors." Barry scrunched up his face to force a smile. "I'm sure it'll be fine?"

Sal just stared at him. It didn't take long for Barry to break into an awkward laugh.

"Yeah… he came in saying that it was the perfect arrangement. Salvatore the Support, Spectre the Offense, Derek the Defense, Thorsten the Healer, and Divinity the Controller… the top five make the perfect team, in his words," Barry said in that same high-pitched tone, as though disbelieving that it would be fine at all. "Spoiler alert, that composition isn't that good. Rochelle is a way better Healer for your team."

"Thanks, Barry." Sal groaned as he placed his face in his hands. "Why the hell is Shade involving himself with all of this? Is he trying to shank me in a dungeon or something?"

"Okay… here's a wild thought," Barry interjected, grinning. "What if he's actually there to teach you?"

"You don't believe that for a second, do you?" Sal laughed humorlessly.

"Nah, you're definitely getting kidnapped," Barry admitted, shrugging. "But other than that whole thing, how are your eyes doing?"

CHAPTER 42: MYTHIC

Sal had hoped to walk into the upgraded workshop feeling like a new man. He had gone straight from the infirmary to his dorm to take a long, hot shower. He Restored each of his uniforms to perfect condition and had stopped by the canteen to pick up a subpar coffee for the trip. Meeting Barry had started out like a nice bonus to the beginning of his day, but it effectively ruined it in just a few minutes of conversation.

His stomach was in turmoil, with pangs of anxiety coursing through him. Was Shade trying to redeem himself by working with Quest Academy, or was there something more nefarious at play? Being a Mythcrafter had certainly dialed up his fears when it came to the threats of kidnapping by the other powers, but the rational part of his brain just couldn't accept it.

Sal was surrounded by powerful and capable people who wanted him to succeed. If he was going to be abducted, it would have to be a power on the level of Bastion or the Hunter Bureau. Shade and the Delvers Guild didn't deserve the amount of anxiety that was afforded to them, and Sal knew that. It was just a battle to push those thoughts aside, and focus. He was about to see his second-ever Mythic grade, and he wanted to savor it. Both it and the Mythical blight jackal had been completed while he was unconscious, so Sal guessed that his third time would be the lucky one where he actually saw it happening.

"Sal!" Blathnaid blurted out in surprise as she dropped a half-formed jacket. She bounded over to wrap her arms around him in the gentlest bear hug imaginable. "Are you okay? How are you feeling? When did you get out?"

Sal laughed as Blathnaid awkwardly unwrapped herself from him, backing off and looking at him with concerned eyes. "I'm fine, thanks for asking… and thank you for all the reputation points on the Crafting Corner. I know it was you boosting my posts."

Blathnaid's headshake of denial was the least convincing thing Sal had ever seen. She fumbled around before pointing off to the side of the room. "Have you seen her yet?"

"Who?" Sal asked in confusion. "Upgrade or Fabi?"

Blathnaid's face broke into a wide smile. "No, silly… *Her*. Your fancy new elixir machine. She's gorgeous!" Her brow furrowed when Sal started to laugh. "Just wait until you see her, and you'll absolutely agree with me. I'm sure of it."

"I'm not sure how I managed to make it feminine, but I'll take it as a compliment, I guess?" Sal followed behind Blathnaid, looking around at the workshop. The few weeks they had with the place had transformed it into a vibrant hub of activity. Practically all the desks were stacked with personal items and mid-process pieces of equipment. There were a few weapons and parts of armor. Sal was almost certain he saw one of the power gauntlets he had made for the tournament.

One of the areas had been claimed by essence programmers. Sal was absolutely certain of it, as one of the previously frosted panes of glass was currently transparent… showing a series of screens within, covered in dense lines of code.

Sal was still turning his head when the elixir machine came into view. To say it caught him by surprise was an understatement. He had come to terms with the fact that Mythcrafter took design liberties when it was doing the cooldown transformation, but this was ridiculous.

The Genesis station had previously been a blocky cube of essence-plated glass, but the transformation had given it some glass-blowing treatment, swelling it outward into a curved bubble with no discernible edges. What had previously been an assortment of essence plates was now a smooth crystalline surface that revealed everything within. The only clue of the plates having existed was an ethereal web-like mesh that faintly rippled through the glass in a steady rhythm.

Sal walked over to it in almost a daze, not believing his eyes as he saw in real time, a dark-blue sapling growing rapidly… before suddenly bursting like popcorn to reveal a gorgeous blood-red flower. The process wasn't done; Sal watched the flower gradually mutate into a bouquet, with some of the arrangement looking completely different.

"Amazing, isn't it?" Blathnaid laughed as she watched Sal's reaction. "Anders was saying that there are different strains within the plants, so there can be countless permutations even if you use the same parameters. He explained it like humans—we're all the same, but different." She shrugged, as though the explanation didn't matter. "I've spent hours just watching all the flowers it creates. There's a glowing yellow one that is *stunning*."

Sal just nodded as he tried to take it all in. The Genesis station worked, and if Anders was already giving insights about the produce, it meant he knew how to use it! That was a definite win, and Sal was inwardly relieved. There were obviously going to be teething issues, but this was an excellent start. If they could only produce the materials, then Alchemize and Refine wouldn't even matter. They could earn money just from this, alone.

"Alex isn't here right now, but I can kinda show you how the Alchemize machine works if you want?" Blathnaid offered as she tugged at Sal's sleeve. "He was giving me a tutorial on it, but I'm still not very good at it."

That broke Sal out of his reverie. "Wait, what? Alex was teaching you?" It didn't sound right at all. Alex was far more likely to guard his secrets so he'd be indispensable. Was he actually volunteering his expertise?

"Yeah, he's been running little workshops because he needs help with the production. There are so many steps, but he's an amazing teacher." Blathnaid beamed as she pointed at the Alchemy station.

Sal had been intentionally trying to look at them one at a time. It was a conscious effort to take it slow so he could appreciate each of them. Like a reward in portions. Being cooped up in the infirmary for three weeks had him anticipating this moment for so long, and he didn't want to rush it.

That said, Blathnaid's enthusiasm was positively infectious. She practically bounced from station to station in excitement, wanting to show everything off, and he couldn't help but get caught up in it.

He traced his gaze along the clear tubing that led from the Genesis station and was very happy to see it partly loaded with an assortment of flower heads without their stems. It was almost surreal, watching a few red and blue flower heads loading into the tube as he stood there. He could even see one of the rare glowing yellow flowers that Blathnaid had mentioned.

"Oh, and your dad is so nice, by the way. He brings coffees and pastries every morning and everyone loves him." Blathnaid laughed as she came to a stop beside the Alchemy station. "He was saying that some of my designs could go into an auction if I was interested. I was actually speechless. You're just like him."

"He's great, but don't feed his ego." Sal chuckled as he looked around. Using his father's monocle would be much less risky than using his own eyes for Appraisal. "I thought he'd be here?"

Blathnaid checked the time on her tablet. "Nope. He'll be here soon, though. He's like clockwork… always on time. You'll see everyone arriving when he comes in, too. The place is more fun when he's around."

Sal's curiosity eventually won out over his restraint as he moved his attention to the Alchemy station. It had absolutely been worth the wait. It was an ivory and bronze palace. The furnace had a thick copper plate fused into the front of it, looking almost like a vault door. A series of valves and tubes came out uniformly, leading into separate vats and containers. Each of them shared the color scheme of white and bronze, and all of them had live-feeds of information reflected on a crystalline screen that showed the contents within. It was absolutely gorgeous, no matter what way you looked at it.

"Want to see the magic happen?" Blathnaid held her finger in front of the furnace's screen. It was located above the vault-like door. "We need to wait for Alex to do the extraction parts, since there's usually some pulp and stuff he doesn't let near the Refiner, but we're allowed to do the combination blast!"

"Combination blast?" Sal frowned. None of the tutorials he had listened to on the Credit Store had mentioned a combination blast.

Blathnaid tapped the screen and quickly pointed to the tubing that connected the Genesis station to the Alchemy station. "Watch those!"

Sal followed her gesture. "Oh!" He yelped as the entire tube of colorful flowers were sucked into the first vat. He knew they were in there because he could see the petals swirling through the screen. Yellow, blue, green, red, purple…he lost count as he watched them. It was fascinating to behold and he had no idea what to expect next.

A few seconds of nothing happening started to dull Sal's excitement…until he saw a single yellow petal fluttering around in one of the other screens. "Wait, is it separating them?"

Blathnaid nodded, grinning. "Yeah, it's separating them out first. There's a whole science to the ratios of when you're combining the different ingredients. The combination blast is when you use the furnace to create essence fire. It pulls out all the useful stats and sends the rest to the extraction chamber. Watch the screens and you'll see." She pointed at the various feeds. "I love how random it all is. You never know what batch is going to be really special."

"Random doesn't sound good." Sal wondered how Alex felt about the machine. If it wasn't giving predictable results, then it might have been a very big and very expensive experiment. Was he teaching others how to use it because it wasn't really working?

"Alex loves it," Blathnaid stated, as though it might put Sal's mind at ease. Her concern was apparent, and it was at war with her excitement. The result was a strangely positive conviction where she sounded almost threatening. "Your dad said the Appraisal is amazing. Anders won't go to sleep because he's playing with new strains, and Anthony is obsessed with the calculation matrix… There is literally nothing that could make this better."

Sal laughed and was about to switch topics, but Blathnaid stopped him and pointed at him accusingly.

"Say you're proud of it. It's amazing. I want to hear you say it." Her lips twitched as she suppressed a smile.

"Are you proud of it? You and Fabi helped me make it, after all," Sal countered, grinning. "And before you insist on an answer… yes, I'm very happy with it. I just don't understand how it all works, or what it's even doing."

Blathnaid frowned for a few seconds. "Ahhh, you're not allowed to use your eyes. I completely forgot."

Sal was about to tell her that it was okay, and that he'd wait for his father to arrive, but before he got a chance, Blathnaid had set off to one of the private meeting rooms.

"Just give me a second!" she called out before disappearing into the room, laughing.

Sal smiled as he looked at the petal collections swirling in their respective vats. Each of the colors had been separated, and were happily bobbing and flowing around with whatever unknown gases existed within. Sal was transfixed with just watching the process. More flowers were being shot through the tube from the Genesis station, and the collection of petals grew denser.

"Here you go." Blathnaid panted as she handed over a document to Sal. "We have to keep it secure in the other room, but it's fine if you look at it… obviously."

Sal's brow furrowed in confusion until he saw his father's familiar handwriting. He managed to read a few lines of the document before his heart started to race.

"Awesome, isn't it?" Blathnaid laughed as she watched Sal intently.

Name	Sal's School Project
Origin	Crafted
Age	New
Grade	Mythic
Materials	Refined Mythcrafter Essence | Refined Figment Essence | Refined Construct Essence | Refiner Essence | Shadow Glass | Abyssal Steel | Storm Steel | Starlight Steel | Bloodstone | Veilstone | Tempest Steel Alloy | Copper…

Attributes	**Transmute**: Grants a very high chance for the successful combination, alteration, or evolution of target organic matter. Essence cost is calculated by the difference between the starting quality and final state. Experimental organic strains will cost significantly more essence to produce. **Propagate**: Allows continuous growth and regeneration of organic matter. Requires a consistent supply of essence and a suitable environment. If conditions are met, Propagate has a chance to create hybrid strains of the target organic matter. **Invigorate**: Refuse organic matter is recycled back into the essence enclosure. Essence dissipation from refuse organic matter will gradually recharge the enclosure and enrich the soil. **Splice**: Allows for the selection and prioritization of traits in organic matter. Preferred traits can be designated as dominant or recessive, ensuring they are reflected in all future iterations of the produced organic matter. **Absolver**: Allows for absolute purification and optimization of target matter. When purifying or optimizing, produce will be destroyed in the process of recording optimal and sub-optimal properties. Recorded properties can be enhanced or removed from subsequent iterations without destroying the target matter.
Abilities	Transmute | Propagate | Invigorate | Splice | Absolver
Runes	Advanced Preservation Rune | Advanced Catalyst Rune | Advanced Amplification Rune
Power Source	Genesis Station (Invigorate)
Evolution	No
Quality	Perfect
Condition	100%
Value	*I'll never let him sell it! - P. Argento*

"Well, he definitely named it." Sal laughed as he looked at the heading of the document. It was clearly a placeholder title, but Sal was half tempted to keep it.

Blathnaid giggled as she stood beside him to look at the document. "So, the combination blast is a result of Transmute, I think. Alex explains it a lot better, but a lot of it is just trial and error to start. We've been using a lot of the produced ingredients to discover new strains, and Alex can't monitor it overnight, so we've been doing it in sort of loose shifts."

Sal blinked in confusion. "What…? For the last few weeks?"

Blathnaid nodded enthusiastically. "Yeah, when we started this week's experiment, the flowers were like a third of the size and just had purple petals. Everything you saw so far were just variants of a single ingredient." She practically beamed. "Between the hybrids and the preferred strains, we've got about a dozen new viable ingredients that Alex has never seen before. He's been doing his own experiments in his station before he trials the essence in the elixir machine. Said he doesn't want to waste the essence."

"Whoa…" Sal said in wonder as he looked at the descriptions again for the abilities. It was wild to think that the machine was actually capable of creating new plant life. At first glance, it seemed like the Genesis machine had completely monopolized the build, with three separate abilities relating to how they were grown, fertilized, and customized. But he was glad to see that Transmute and Absolver were there. Cypher would probably have more insights for him, but he didn't want to risk any eye injuries when he was finally out of the infirmary. Appraising a Mythic grade was likely asking for trouble.

Sal glanced up from the page to look at the Absolver, the cylinder that Fabi had waved into a Legendary-grade component. It matched the color scheme of the rest, with ivory and bronze, but the sheer length of the cylinder was imposing compared to the rest. It didn't look to be active, and Sal guessed it was because Alex wasn't there.

Sal had a thousand questions that the Appraisal wasn't answering for him. Where were the intakes? Like, where would the liquids go to make the elixirs? How were they able to enter the enclosure to take a few plants out of it? What sort of settings were required and how would the essence programming be installed? It had been a few weeks since it had been up and running, but was there anything to show for it? He guessed his father would have a lot of the answers.

"So, how long until he arrives?" Sal chuckled, enjoying the last line of the Appraisal form as he searched for answers to some of his questions.

Blathnaid looked at her tablet. "Within the next two minutes. He's always here fifteen minutes before he says he'll arrive."

Sal smiled as he looked in the direction of the doorway. "Great. I need to borrow his monocle."

CHAPTER 43: MEETINGS

"There's the beautiful bastard, himself," Alex declared as he came through the door with a series of boxes tucked under his left arm. In his right hand was a vat-like flask that looked heavy based on how he angled his torso to support the weight.

"Man of the hour!" Alex boasted as he put the flask down on the ground and placed the boxes on a nearby table. "No, man of the century! I always said you'd do great things… and boy, did you not disappoint me!" He walked toward Sal with both of his arms outstretched, looking like he was going to go for an embrace. The only issue was the twenty feet of space between them, making it a very drawn-out process, with Alex's delighted smile looking all the more terrifying as he got closer.

"How long has he been like this?" Sal asked Blathnaid cautiously.

"Three weeks." Blathnaid laughed as she stepped off to the side so she wouldn't be apprehended by the overjoyed Alchemist. "I won't complain, we get the special coffee for free now."

"For life. My concoctions will be free for life for my true Saviors!" Alex declared much louder as he stretched his arms even wider.

Sal sighed as he let it happen. "I take it that you're a fan of the machine, Alex?" The last words were barely out of his mouth before the shorter man embraced him, tried to lift him, thought better of it, and then disengaged, laughing.

"I fucking love it. Words can't describe my feelings, but there's a lot of expletives and a lot of merriment jumbled up in there." He sighed wistfully as he looked at the elixir machine, his hands on his hips. "She's an absolute beauty."

Sal looked over to the doorway, where his father was holding it open for the others to come through. Anthony, Jack, and Anders were the three stragglers who appeared. Sal had hoped to see Fabi or Upgrade, but it looked like they weren't in. Glancing in Blathnaid's direction, he asked whether she knew where they were. Alex was the one to answer him, his victorious pose not wavering in the slightest.

"Upgrade's playing in the dungeons with Fabi. They've been at it nonstop for weeks now, with both of them only coming back for classes. Haven't seen either of them around the workshop in ages." He shrugged, as though it were no big deal. "Fabi's been guiding your friend over there with the calculation matrix, and it's the only thing holding us back at the moment."

Anthony smiled at Petro and moved off in the direction of the essence programming room. When he passed Sal, he paused, grinning. "It's good to see you back. Sorry I missed your reaction to the machine. It's awesome, isn't it?"

"Yeah, I'm still coming to terms with it. Can't understand half of it." Sal laughed as he offered his own shrug. "Hoping to get more of an insight from our Appraiser, and maybe even our Alchemist."

"Well, it won't be long before the matrix is done. Every new strain that gets introduced wrecks the whole thing, so it's a fun challenge." Anthony chuckled as he excused himself into the private room, closing the door after him. Well, he almost got it closed before Alex stopped him with a repeated snap of his fingers.

Anthony stopped, not in confusion, but rather with a resigned expression on his face. The context came seconds later.

Alex clapped loudly. "All right team, we've got some good news and some bad news."

Sal looked at him strangely, wondering what sort of weird hierarchy happened in his absence. Was Alex acting like the project leader for the elixir machine? It was doubtful, but it was fun to watch.

"Good news is that Petro brought pastries and that flask is full of the good coffee." Alex looked around at everyone. "The bad news is that we've got a lot of work to do today. I've been experimenting with Plant-Test Nine, and it's a volatile little bastard. We're going to be switching out Plant-Test Fourteen today, and going to work on some Transmuting. You know what that means?"

Sal was completely lost.

"Lots of explosions." Blathnaid filled him in, grinning. "Not like… actual explosions, but it creates an atmosphere. You'll see."

Sal wasn't sure whether it was a threat or a promise, but judging by the amused expressions on everyone's faces, it wasn't actually bad news.

Alex shot Sal a grin. "I'd love to give you the guided tour and walk you through everything, but would you be okay with holding off until later this evening or tomorrow? Lots of work to get done, and I need Royce before he fucks off for his beauty sleep."

"I need to study…" Anders complained from beside Petro. "I've been missing classes because of this, and I need to catch up."

"Quitter's attitude, Royce. You're not going to get far like that." Alex glared at him before clapping his hands again. "So, can we get a move on? You've all got five minutes to stuff your faces and energize yourselves. Then we'll be working on Plant-Test Nine. Who knows, by the end of it, we might even get to work with the Absolver?"

"Then we'll leave you guys to it," Petro announced as he gestured at Sal. "I wanted to catch up with Sal anyway, so this is good timing."

Sal smiled as he handed the appraisal document back to Blathnaid. "I'll be back later for the guided tour with Alex. Please don't blow up the elixir machine while I'm gone."

"She's in safe hands," Blathnaid declared with a mock salute.

Sal shook his head as he moved over to his father, pausing only to say hello to Anders properly. Jack had vanished into the engraving room with two or three pastries and a cup of coffee. He had been impressively quick, likely a learned habit from evading Alex's tasks.

Petro gave Sal a look up and down. "You're looking healthy. Was there any funny business in the infirmary, or did they actually discharge you?" He had two cups of Alex's coffee in hand, and jutted his chin in the direction of the private meeting rooms.

"A little bit of both." Sal laughed as he slid open the door of the meeting room and let his father go in first. It looked like a conversational booth, with a table and plush couches on either side. It was surprisingly comfortable and Sal bounced on the cushion a few times to test it out. "This is really nice."

Petro nodded in agreement. "Apparently Upgrade has a flair for interior design. I've been wanting to get her thoughts for the layout of the guild headquarters, but she's a hard woman to get a hold of."

Sal smiled as he took a swig of the coffee. There was no mountain of fatigue to wash away, so Sal was instead greeted by a warm and fuzzy feeling that emanated out from his stomach. "Ahh, I missed this."

"It's quite addictive." Petro chuckled as he placed his cup off to one side. "So, I know you're just out of the infirmary, but I wanted to ask you how you were feeling."

"Good," Sal answered straightaway. "Rested and feeling good. They've assessed me all the way up to Epic grade with no issues. Crafting and Appraisal are both fine. It felt like they were teasing me about meeting Coach, though. It was three whole weeks and he was a no-show."

Petro nodded. "And what about everything else?"

"Guessing you heard about Shade?" Sal asked with a humorless chuckle. "He's going to be taking me into a dungeon to train for one of my class modules."

"It was brought to my attention," Petro muttered darkly. "Vanessa Blake. She's down as one of your guild advisors, and she reached out to introduce herself. Seems like a smart girl."

"She worked on the Credit floor. She's the one who brokered my services to the Reavers Guild." Sal grimaced as he tilted his head to check that the door was definitely closed. "She's also the first person who warned me about the Delvers Guild. She had a contract with them but it went south."

Petro nodded slowly. "And she's trustworthy? I don't think it's wise to align with someone who worked for Shade, even if they've ended on a sour note."

"As far as I can tell, yes. She's helped me out a few times and kept my identity as a Mythcrafter a secret," Sal explained without emotions. His father wasn't asking for his feelings right now; he was looking for the facts. "She told me the reason that the contract with the Delvers fell through, and it was because she wouldn't date one of the officers. They sold her contract to the Credit floor and she's been working there for the last few years to pay it off."

"Is she asking you for money?" Petro asked calmly.

"No, she's already paid her dues, but she is driven by money. She saw an opportunity with my abilities and was pushing for a guild," Sal explained as he thought about it. "She flirted a lot at first, but then shut that approach down when she wanted to do business."

"She sounds like she has some principles. I somewhat approve." Petro chuckled as he looked at Sal curiously. "And does she bring value to the guild?"

"Yes. She's a very good negotiator. I watched her take on Villa, and she was in her element." Sal explained what had happened with the Legendary sniper rifle, and by the end, his father was smiling.

"Okay…she already had points in my book for warning me about Shade, but the bait and switch with Villa is very good." He nodded finally. "No objections from me about her being an advisor. You know I already approve of Upgrade."

Sal took a sip of his coffee as he thought about his next words. "What do you think we should do about Shade? I've been telling myself there's nothing to be worried about… but it's pretty disconcerting that he's suddenly appearing in Quest Academy."

Petro picked up his own cup, but didn't take a drink as he thought about the question. "I would exercise caution, and keep your wits about you. I don't think he'll do anything, but I imagine there will be some goading or teasing. He might aim to discredit or embarrass you in some way, but I don't think he'd actually attack."

Petro finally took a drink before he placed the cup back down on the table. "You have Jackal now, which is not something he'd be ready for. Find an opportunity to show how savage your drone is and he'll second-guess himself; if there were any malicious thoughts to begin with." He offered a helpless sort of shrug and smiled weakly. "Worst-case scenario, he tries something stupid and you kill him. Just give me a call and I'll help bury the body."

"Thanks, Dad, that's very reassuring," Sal deadpanned before chuckling and picking up his cup. "So, now that I'm out of the infirmary, I've got a lot to catch up on. Anything on fire that I need to take care of with the Arkwright?"

"Nope. Everything is going perfectly with that, but I do need to borrow you this afternoon." He smiled warmly. "It's just a little administrative thing that we need to take care of before I finish up and head back home."

"What is it?" Sal was curious, trying to think of what it could be, when it suddenly dawned on him. "Oh, are we making the guild official?"

Petro's smile grew wider. "Yep, just waiting on confirmation from Upgrade and we'll be good to go. Jez and Quest will be there, as well as Vanessa. I'll be there as your guardian and to make sure you're not getting screwed over."

"Perfect." Sal grinned as he picked up his cup. "Okay, the day may have started shit, but this is good. The Mythic isn't imploding, and I'm going to be a guildmaster."

Petro chuckled as he started to stand up. "Did you like the name I put on the Appraisal? I was actually very proud of that one."

CHAPTER 44: PAGES

"So, are you ready for this?" Petro looped an arm over Sal's shoulder, squeezing him into his side as they entered the meeting room. "A few signatures and you'll be leaving here as a guildmaster. Not bad for a few months at the academy, don't you think?"

Sal smiled as he tilted his head to the left. "Come on, it's not that big of a deal. We're just doing the formalities. I don't think it's going to change all that much." He paused for a second, looking at the excited expression on his father's face. "But, yeah… I'm looking forward to finding out how we can climb the ranks."

"There he is." Petro laughed as he squeezed Sal's shoulder again. "I felt the exact same way when we were starting the auction house. You're entering a landscape with so many competitors and you need to build up your reputation, brick by brick. This isn't the Argento Auction House; this is your guild and it's going to be all you, with us helping in any way we can in the background."

"I appreciate it, really. I do." Sal smiled as they disengaged from the half bear hug to sit down, side by side, in the meeting room. There were a few other chairs, and it seemed they were the first people to arrive. Of course they were early; his father was with him and the man treated tardiness like a cardinal sin.

Petro smiled as he tapped his knees and looked around the room curiously. "I'm saying that this is your baby, Salvatore. You're getting a head start that most people couldn't even dream of, you've got the most capability out of all your peers, and you've surrounded yourself with incredible people. This moment right now will likely go down in history, so you should enjoy it!"

"Unless they tell me that we're going to be stuck at Tier 10 for the next couple of years. That would be enough to deflate the excitement." Sal laughed as he shrugged it off. "I know you said we'll probably go up a rank because of the elixir machine, but I'm preparing myself for the worst."

"You get that from your mother." Petro chuckled as he shook his head in disbelief. He looked at Sal strangely. "Seriously, you should trust me. You've put down a solid foundation already, and even if they decide that your contributions only start now, they can't deny the capability of the elixir machine. It's going to be generating revenue soon, and you'll probably be wealthier than guilds in Tier 5 by the end of the year."

"Probably shouldn't mention the Arkwright to them, then?" Sal grinned with a mock shrug of reluctance.

"Probably not," Petro agreed, laughing. "They don't need to know everything you're doing. Just give them enough to be impressed, and then blow them out of the water later with some serious production output."

Sal was about to respond when the door of the meeting room opened to reveal a few familiar faces. Upgrade and Vanessa walked into the room, and Sal could sense the tension between them. He wondered whether it was his first time seeing the two of them together.

"Vanessa Blake? I'm Salvatore's father, Petro." He was on his feet and offering his hand to her. Petro turned his attention to Upgrade. "And great to see you, too, Upgrade. I hope you're taking breaks from all those dungeon runs?"

Vanessa took the offered hand and gave the most disarming smile known to man. She was clearly in business mode.

Upgrade smiled as she took a seat beside Sal, ensuring that Vanessa had to sit beside his father. "Hah, I'm just here to see history being made." She gave Sal a playful nudge with her elbow. "I hope the Appraisal work hasn't impacted the auction house?" She looked at Petro with genuine concern.

"Nothing to worry about. We're just building up some reserves for the next one. It takes time to source the best showpieces, so the distraction was quite welcome." Petro waved it away like it was nothing.

Vanessa took her seat and leaned in closer to the group. "So, how are we feeling about pushing for Tier 8?"

Upgrade couldn't stop the snort of derision from escaping, and ended up staring at Vanessa as though she were an idiot. "Can you please take this seriously? He'll get all sorts of advantages if we start off at Tier 10. There's no pressure on him to rush his way up to the top."

Sal cleared his throat and gave them all a meaningful look, turning his head to ensure everyone knew he wanted to talk. "The main goal is to ensure we have head count. I've got a lot of people I've invited into the guild, and if there's a limit on who we can have… I'd push for a higher tier so we can have more people."

"If the majority of them are going to be Supports, then you can push for the Crafting designation. You'll be assessed on outputs rather than dungeon clearances, but it's going to be a very uphill battle. A lot of the time, it's calculated on volume and effect, rather than single pieces with high grades," Vanessa explained, as though it were common sense. Her tone was especially aimed at Upgrade, who shifted uncomfortably. "Since you have Upgrade as one of the advisors, it should be no issue with getting the Crafting designation."

"As opposed to what other ones?" Sal asked. "If we picked Crafting, would that make us ineligible to run dungeons or towers? I don't want to limit members like Sakura and O'Brien."

"Well, it seems you've all started without me." Jez barked a laugh as he walked into the room with a folio tucked under his arm. Behind him was Quest, who looked at his tablet in confusion.

"We're early, though?" Quest glanced up from his tablet, clearly wondering whether he had gotten the time wrong. "Or are we just excited to make this official? I can't say I blame you all."

Jez gestured to the remaining chairs, indicating that Quest should take one of them. He placed his folio on the desk and flipped it open, looking at a few documents with barely disguised disdain. "Okay, let's run through the boring stuff really quick. I'll skim it, so we can get to the good stuff. Any objections?"

When nobody said a word, Jez grinned. "Perfect, my kind of people." He traced a finger along the document. "In my capacity as the Guild Mastery lecturer, I'm acting as the representative of the United Guilds Association for the creation of the unnamed guild being set up by Salvatore Argento."

Jez squinted at the page and just shook his head with a sigh. "It goes on to say a load of crap about fairness and assessment, but we can skip all of that, because you've already gotten approval from the Hunter Bureau, Quest Academy, and your legal guardian." Jez waved his free hand in a circular motion, illustrating his own impatience with the verbose legalese.

"You've elected Vanessa Blake as an advisor." His eyebrows raised at that, but there was no other reaction. Well, it looked like there wasn't, but Jez paused for a little too long. When he looked up, his gaze landed on Vanessa. "Are you still registered as a Hero?"

"Yes," Vanessa said. "I'll be operating as a Hero and advisor for the guild."

Jez smiled as he picked up a pen and struck out a segment of the document. "You've elected Diva as an advisor. An excellent choice. As she is an active Hero and Controller, you'll be allowed to participate in dungeons, towers, and portals if she is acting as your Controller."

Sal's mouth went dry. "Wait, portals?"

Jez nodded, as if it were obvious. "Yes, but only if Diva is your Controller." He continued to stare at Sal, as though asking whether there were any more objections. His finger still pointed at an area of the document, to ensure he didn't lose his place.

"Sorry, please go on," Sal apologized as he laughed nervously. How was nobody else reacting to this? Just by having Vanessa as a Controller, they'd be able to take on portals? It sounded insane. Sure, she was a Body Manipulator, but there was no way that would be enough to keep a team safe on a portal run.

"Okay… where were we?" Jez glanced at the document, tapping his finger rapidly. "You've elected Upgrade as an advisor. As an active Hero and Support, you'll be able to take on Hunter Bureau and United Guilds Association contracts or commissions, as long as Upgrade signs off on them."

He waved his hand again, as though skipping through the other details. "Petro Argento will be acting as your guardian and as a sponsor for the unnamed guild. There's a whole section in here about collusion, but the key thing is to not get caught taking money from your parents. You'll have to submit your financials to the United Guilds Association to ensure that everything is aboveboard, but it's relatively straightforward. They're fair as long as you don't blatantly cheat."

Sal stifled the laugh that wanted to escape his lips. Jez was telling him to not get caught. Quest was literally sitting right there, his employer, but he looked like he didn't give a shit.

Quest, to Sal's surprise, nodded along, as though this were normal. When he made eye contact with the headmaster, he received a conspiratorial wink.

"You've already made agreements with the Hunter Bureau for accommodations in Silver Sanctuary that will act as your headquarters." Jez frowned as he looked through the document again. "And you've got a headquarters at Quest Academy?" Understanding dawned as he nodded with a roguish smile. "Ah, you're planning ahead for graduation. That's a smart move. We'll put the workshop headquarters as a temporary base, and list Silver Sanctuary as permanent residence. We need it for the license."

Sal sat and listened for the next five minutes as Jez swept through all the different factors that were being considered. There was far more paperwork involved than Sal had anticipated. It started to feel real. The excitement that hadn't been there before now bubbled up to the surface.

When Jez finally finished the contracts, he picked up a chunk of paper and dumped it to one side of his desk. An exasperated sigh of relief was followed by a hearty chuckle. "Thank you for making that quick and painless… Will we start with the fun stuff, now?"

"Please," Vanessa breathed as she craned her neck toward the ceiling. "I'm going to be pushing for Tier 7, by the way, just so you know."

"Glad to see the Credit floor didn't kill your sense of humor." Jez grinned as he shook his head, turning his attention to Sal. "So, I'll explain my role here fairly quickly, just so we're all on the same page. I've been granted the authority to designate the rank of your guild based on everything you've accomplished to date. I will be giving you guidance based on best practice, of how we want to see guilds progressing through the ranks."

"What are my options?" Sal asked out of genuine curiosity. "And is it only my accomplishments, or will you consider the people I've invited into my guild?"

"Just you." Jez was adamant. "If we allowed retrospective accomplishments, then there's nothing stopping you from taking in a swath of third-years and artificially boosting your guild's ranking. It wouldn't be fair. That said, as the guildmaster, your individual accomplishments can't be scrutinized in the same way."

Quest made a slight noise of dissent, but Jez shot him down with a stern look. "I know there has been leniency on first-years, but I don't like it." He glanced at Sal and offered context. "In the past, we've had Trainee Guilds taking in first-years to build up numbers, and their accomplishments had carried over."

"Speaking of numbers, what is the head count afforded to a Trainee Guild? How many members can I have?" Sal wanted to know whether he was going to need to cut people from the roster.

Jez glanced at Upgrade and Vanessa. "You've got two advisors, so each of them would give you an additional head count of five. If they sign off on the members, then it would give you a total capacity of fifteen. The guilds try to incentivize the advisory role, so that's why it comes with advanced permissions and head count. Their fees will be subsidized by the United Guilds Association, just to alleviate your costs."

Sal nodded cautiously. He didn't want to show Jez his relief, considering they were still in a negotiation. It felt strangely ironic that of all the people it could have been, he had to negotiate against the Administration lecturer. "Okay, so with my individual accomplishments… how do you quantify them?"

Jez grinned as he flicked through the documents. "Well, the obsidian hulker definitely helped." He chuckled as though recalling a memory, before landing on the page he was looking for. "For a Trainee Guild, we have a set list of requirements depending on the designation. You can either have a Generalist or Specialist designation…"

Sal waited patiently for more context, but his mind and heart raced. The excitement was at full throttle now.

"Guilds are organizations. Tiers represent capability as well as reputation. There are multiple departments within each organization, and they all need to work together to succeed. You'll learn more about it in the Guild Mastery class, but the basics are simple. A Generalist designation would offer a freeform approach, where you're not limited by the operational rules set out by the United Guilds Association." Jez sounded like he was pushing for this particular designation.

"You'll still be called on during a time of emergency, and you'll still need to climb the ranks to warrant funding and support from the United Guilds Association. Generalist guilds are like private companies, usually with a very narrow focus."

"I would have thought the narrow focus would come with Specialist guilds?" Sal said, not really connecting the logic. Vanessa nodded, as though she were in agreement with Jez.

"Specialist guilds… are made up of specialists." Jez spoke slowly, as though it was the most profound statement possible. "For example, a Generalist guild would never be approved for an Assassination contract. However, Anna Sakura has that specialism, with all the Challenge crests to prove it. If you were a Specialist guild and you had her on your roster, you could create an Assassination strike team and take those missions. There is a lot more risk, but a lot more reward."

Upgrade snorted audibly. "Your first example is Assassination? He's a Mythcrafter, and an Appraisal specialist. He could create a project team that takes on Crafting projects."

Jez folded his arms as he stared at Upgrade. "He has Sakura listed for his guild. The rewards would be far more lucrative by creating a team around her. No offense intended to the Crafting Department, but there's far more money on the table if you build a team around Sakura."

Quest bit his lip. "You haven't been to the workshop in a while, I take it?"

Jez frowned at Quest. "What am I missing?"

"I created a Mythic-grade elixir machine," Sal stated calmly. "It's still ramping up, but it will be generating revenue in the coming weeks. Sixty percent of the profits are set aside for the guild."

Jez's jaw dropped as he looked at Quest, dumbfounded. "You're verifying that? What sort of revenue are you estimating?"

Quest gave him a mock-grimace. "You should also put down that he's put in a diagnostic scanner in the infirmary. It's Epic grade, and Bob is raving about it. I'm pretty sure there's a social-impact score for the Trainee Guilds." He pointed at the document in front of Jez. "Page fifty-three."

Vanessa smiled sweetly. "Would the sniper rifle count, since it was Sal who made that? It's going to evolve into Mythic at some point, and the Reavers would happily verify it for the United Guilds Association."

Jez looked a little lost as he turned from face to face, his composure ebbing away by the second.

Petro raised a hand. "Come on, let's be nice." He smiled warmly at Jez. "Is now a bad time to mention that Salvatore has agreed to a mutual assistance compact with General Lucion Drake of the Dragoons?"

"That's in the Alliances section," Quest added with an almost apologetic smile. "Page seventy-six."

CHAPTER 45: SPECIALISM

Jez grumbled good-naturedly as he scribbled on the documents with a heaving sigh of exasperation. "Okay… we've got all the merits accounted for. Are there any other surprises I should be made aware of before we do the tally?" He phrased it almost like a threat as he looked around at everyone, daring them to say something.

"That's everything for now." Sal nodded, smiling. "I don't think the commission work with Chatfield would really count. I made a few evolutionary sets of equipment for him. Well, the blueprints for them at least."

Jez gritted his teeth as he shook his head. "It absolutely counts. He's an extension of the Hunter Bureau, so it would be classified as a specialist contract." He chuckled darkly as his pen strokes became more aggressive. "It would be different if you had a token like your arrangement with the Reavers Guild."

Vanessa drummed her manicured nails against the armrest of her seat as she watched Jez carefully. "So, how are your calculations looking?" Her tone wasn't curious. It was more like she wanted to check that their numbers matched.

Jez glanced up for a second before double-checking his notes. "Still a few considerations to make, but we're pretty close to the finish line." He tapped his pen against the page. "Things we can rule out from the outset are his academic record. That won't be impacting the case, as he has no specialist modules completed. The tower trial, while impressive, shouldn't be considered as an aptitude marker for a guildmaster. It might have been different if he was the Controller, but he was Support."

"But the uniforms he made for his team would fall into the Crafting specialism," Upgrade insisted in protest. "That had a direct impact on their success rate. Also, you can't forget the growth-oriented fort he made during the excursion exercise. There are consistent records of Sal over-performing in the Crafting specialism throughout his time at Quest Academy."

"Not to mention all the work he's been doing with Grant on the Skill Weaves," Quest added, smiling. "He's the reason that Fabrizia Maccles has access to her ability."

Jez slapped his hand down on the table and glared at them. "Just stop for a second, okay? This isn't a campaigning exercise. I'm trying to find a fair and equitable tier for this guild, and you lot aren't helping his case as much as you think you are."

Quest raised an eyebrow at Jez, before chuckling to himself. "Or you could just be done with it and give him Tier 8? We all know that's the best outcome here since Tier 7 is a steeper requirement. He has created a Mythic grade, has an external headquarters, an existing alliance, and a track record of delivering on special contracts. All of those factors point at Tier 8."

Quest looked around the room at the other faces. "I don't think anyone here would be willing to argue for a tier higher than that. Eclipse started her guild here and went straight to Tier 8, so there's already an established precedent. You wouldn't be accused of giving him preferential treatment. Anyone who had issues can take a look at the elixir machine and see for themselves."

Jez's temper reined all the way in as he sat in his chair with a thoughtful expression. "And you'll follow due process to get to Tier 7? No bullshit exceptions or extenuating circumstances?" He was looking at Salvatore this time. "Guilds aren't vanity projects. They're organizations that protect our people, fight the demons, and reclaim what was taken from us. If you're serious about being a guildmaster, you need to resolve yourself and rise through the ranks like everyone else."

"I'll follow the rules," Sal answered resolutely. "And I'd like the guild to be registered as a Specialist guild. I'll make sure that I have enough Q-Cred to put everyone through master classes and advanced modules."

Jez nodded quietly. "Going through the ranks as a Specialist guild will be a lot more grueling than a Generalist guild, especially if you're going to be doing it through Crafting. The vast majority of contracts you'll get for Crafting, at least initially, will be volume-based." He paused as he leaned on his elbows, his gaze weighing Sal up. "Are you sure you'd like to register as a Specialist guild? It will likely drag you into a lot of combat-oriented situations. Especially if you've got decent fighters like Sakura in your ranks."

"I'm positive." Sal was telling the truth. There was no way he was going to limit the members of his guild by playing it safe. "What are the requirements for reaching Tier 7?"

Jez's face broke into a wide grin. "Excellent question."

Sal could see his father smiling out of the corner of his eye. Vanessa was still staring at Jez like a cat watching a mouse. Upgrade looked positively bored, and Quest listened intently.

"Trainee Guilds at Tier 10 are usually afforded a six-month viability period. We monitor the organization, interview the advisors, and offer assistance where we can. If it is not deemed to be a healthy or productive organization, we move to dissolve it, offering a partial refund of the invested Q-Cred." Jez spoke factually, with a lot of the gruffness having left his voice.

"If they were deemed to be viable in that time, and they had the potential to grow, we approve the Tier 10 to advance to Tier 9. Regardless whether the organization is a Generalist or Specialist guild, we require that they have completed a checklist of recommended dungeons with their advisors. In the humanitarian-focused entities, we look at how many outings they've completed with the likes of Harmony and take the recommendations of those established guilds into account. With Crafting, we look at the build quality, production method, and if the end customer was satisfied. The simple way of looking at it is, are you doing your job as a guild?"

Jez sighed as he waved his hand, as though gesturing that there were a mountain of considerations. "We look at your balance sheet to see if you're profitable. We look at the investment into your people, and their individual performances. We look at your reputation within your sphere. Are you trusted to do good work? What results are guaranteed if you're selected for a contract?"

Sal smiled politely but shook his head. "Sorry, I meant what are the actual requirements? Is there a Q-Cred threshold I need to hit? Do I need to have a certain head count of specialists? Are there grades of contract that I need to fulfill?"

Petro chuckled as he leaned back in his chair. He propped his elbow on the armrest and placed two fingers against his temple as he watched Jez's reaction.

"Any number I pluck out of thin air will be arbitrary at best," Jez countered as he offered a shrug. "You coming in with a Tier 8 straight out of the gate will likely result in a tougher ask for Tier 7. Although you have merits that are transferable, you still need to complete the checklist from the previous tiers before you can progress. We ask that a guild has a thousand Q-Cred in net profit before considering moving from Trainee status to Tier 9. Reward Q-Cred isn't counted. It needs to be generated from guild activities."

He looked at Sal, smiling. "And I know that's not a hard sum for you to achieve, but here's the kicker. It's multiplied by your head count for the later tiers. If you've got capacity for fifteen people, then that's going to be fifteen thousand Q-Cred to move to the next stage. Your personal contributions can only make up twenty-five percent of that sum. The other seventy-five needs to be carried out by your guild members, with none exceeding ten percent of the total sum."

"And where does that Q-Cred go?" Sal's mood soured at the implication that it would be confiscated. He wasn't worried about earning Q-Cred, even if he was limited to just a quarter of the total sum. All the people he had selected would be capable of earning their way.

"It's reinvested into your guild." Jez laughed. "This isn't some sort of racket. You just need to show us that you have profitability and that you've assembled a good team. You delegate teams to run dungeons, you take on contracts, do your outings, achieve goals... and you'll gradually move up through the tiers."

"Goals?" Sal repeated the last condition back to him.

Jez shrugged. "Within Crafting, for example, achieving certain quality grades would constitute as goals. In combat, it would be taking down certain types of demon. Before you start planning on hitting Tier 7, I should warn you that you'll need to take down a commander as a guild before that's possible. Obviously with advisors present."

"Oh," Sal breathed as he recalculated his own expectations. Maybe there was nothing wrong with staying as a Tier 8 guild. He laughed nervously to himself. Sakura had already dispatched one, so he knew that she could probably do it again... but she had been backed up by dozens of capable Heroes.

"Just one?" Vanessa smirked as she continued to drum her fingers. "What do you want us to achieve for Tier 6?"

Jez gave her a meaningful look. "Please just do this the right way." He sighed with a slight shake of the head before looking at Sal. "You'll be given a checklist as a part of your course materials for the Guild Mastery module. I'll be outlining strategies that you can use to accelerate your growth, but in a sustainable manner. Racing to the finish line will only get people killed, and nobody wants that."

A moment of silence followed after Sal nodded. It was like a weight was hanging in the air, and Jez looked around at everyone before his face broke into a wide smile.

"Then, I guess that concludes it. We just need a signature and a name for your new guild," he declared as he pulled a piece of paper out of his folio, spinning it around and presenting it to the opposite side of the desk. "We have our witness, sponsor, advisors, and United Guilds Association representative... so all that remains is your best artwork." Jez smiled as he held out a pen for Sal to take.

Getting to his feet, Sal moved over to the desk and took the pen from Jez. He frowned as he looked back at his father. "Are you going to give me crap for not reading it? I don't want to ruin the moment."

"It's very standard, with nothing predatory," Quest stated with a knowing smile. "The only cause for concern is when you hit Tier 6, because you can be summoned onto the battlefront for joint operations if you have the necessary teams. Right now, the only thing worth noting is that you'll be required to provide regular financial reporting, and subject to a fine if you're late."

Sal smiled as he nodded at his dad. "That'll be outsourced, more than likely."

Petro got to his feet and clapped his hand on Sal's shoulder, looking down at the contract and scanning it quickly.

"Wise choice." Quest chuckled. "Being a part of the United Guilds Association will come with some benefits, too, but I'm sure that Jez will fill you in on them at a later date."

Sal looked at Vanessa and Upgrade. "Anything else before I sign?" He could hear the pages ruffling as his father went through it at ridiculous speed.

Vanessa just smiled as she shook her head, before glancing over at Upgrade. "Who would have expected this team-up?"

Upgrade ignored her as she gave Sal a reassuring smile. "Go for it. Just don't pick a shit name for the guild."

Sal laughed as he picked up the pen, looking at his father with a wide smile. "So... anything to worry about?"

Petro shook his head as he put down the last page. "We're good to go. It's all over to you." Rather than going back to his seat, he stood off to one side with a tablet in his hands, likely sending a picture to Sophia.

Sal leaned down and signed the page. "We can always change the name in the future, right?"

"It's not uncommon." Jez chuckled as he waited. "But some of them tend to stick."

Name	Salvatore Argento
Title	Guildmaster
Guild	Mythic Guild
Tier	8
Type	Specialist

CHAPTER 46: ELIXIR

They had left the meeting room after Quest. He went back to his office after congratulating them both. Vanessa went straight to the Credit floor to hand in her notice. Sal had tried talking her out of it, but she insisted she had some personal training to do to get ready. Upgrade had given him a hug, and went back to meet Fabi for another series of dungeon runs. Jez stayed in the room to correct all the forms he had filled out incorrectly.

"I'm going to go out on a limb and say that you're not in the mood to celebrate?" Petro asked as they rounded the corner toward the workshop. "I'm off the clock and I'm pretty sure they have a bar around here somewhere."

Sal smiled as he shook his head. "As much as I'd love to, I can't help but think about the elixir machine. I want to see it in action and get a better understanding of how it works. There's also a load of stuff that I've missed in the last few weeks, and I don't want to add a hangover to my list of stuff tomorrow."

"That was definitely a test, and you passed." Petro grinned. "Who would go to a bar in the middle of the week, celebrating something as trivial as you becoming a guildmaster? No, no… we'll head to the workshop and see your machine in action. Sounds like a bit of fun."

"When do you have to leave, by the way?" Sal asked, not really sure he wanted the answer. It was great having his dad around, and the infirmary visits had been a nice bonus over the last few weeks.

Petro waved his palm from side to side. "I'll probably head back tomorrow evening. Just a few last-minute administrative tasks to finish up, and then I'll be off to tell your mother everything. She loved the picture of you signing the contract, by the way." His smile was proud as he opened the door of the workshop for Sal.

"Glad she liked it." Sal stepped through the entrance. "Would you be up for some sparring tomorrow? Maybe at some point in the afternoon? I want to see how far I've deviated from the manuals."

Petro nodded. "Sounds good to me, but I told you that you shouldn't worry about it too much. I just wanted you to have a method of protecting yourself, and now you have it in an abundance." He smiled before tilting his head a little to the right. "But I'd be lying if I said I wasn't excited to see how you adapt the armor."

Sal paused at that. "Wait… what?"

Petro gave him a sideways glance. "I saw those plans on the Arkwright… What did you call it, the Auctioneer set? Jackal was a part of the arm from that set, as far as I could tell."

He was completely wrong, but Sal could see where the misunderstanding came from; the whole fiasco in the prowler dungeon with his father and the Silverson gauntlet being reforged with a dead prowler for materials. Sal had saved the Silverson set as the Auctioneer set, but it was blueprints so his father must have thought he was trying to make them.

"Well, in any case, the first care package we've sent you has a few ingots of silver for you to play with," Petro continued, chuckling. "My selfish request would be for you to make good boots, because we're roughly the same size feet.

I'd obviously sacrifice myself and test them out for you." He gave Sal a conspiratorial wink. "Unless they shoot lasers or something ridiculous."

It was a compounded misunderstanding, but it wasn't actually that bad. Upgrade had forbidden him from making anything above the waist, but he was completely free to make leg-based equipment. Sal smiled as he gave his dad a slight nod. "What sort of specifications would you like in them, then? These boots, I mean."

"Jumping is an absolute must," Petro declared as he gestured at his own two feet. "But I think the most important aspect is style. Go with a classic wingtip design, two-tone, maybe a touch of felt and strong laces."

Sal laughed as he stared at his father in disbelief. "You want to take wingtip shoes into a dungeon? They're better suited for a gala!"

Petro waved him away. "Seriously, though… there's nothing wrong with looking stylish on the battlefield. Far too many Heroes are out there with oversized armor and swords. They're begging to be noticed and lauded. But that's a sham. You've already made something sleek and elegant that is very discreet." Petro gestured at Sal's left arm. "So, why not keep that sort of aesthetic?"

"I can't for the life of me decide if you're criticizing my fashion sense, or giving me advice for equipment," Sal said in mock disbelief. "At least talk about the factors I can actually understand. You want jumping? How high? Are we talking about buildings, or are you looking to hop over hulkers?"

Petro smiled as he continued toward the upgraded workshop. "Ignore me when it comes to Crafting. I used up all the good advice by pointing you toward the Arkwright concept. Everything else I'll suggest will be doomed for failure." He paused, giving Sal a funny look. "Besides, I realized who I was talking to. I'd have a better chance of getting you something fancy if I convinced Blathnaid to take the commission."

"Hey, I don't want the Mythic Guild's first contract being for dress shoes!" Sal warned him with a pointed finger and a laugh.

They chatted in a back-and-forth manner, playfully teasing each other as they made their way up to the upgraded workshop. The normal workshop was pretty standard, with a lot of people hunched over their desks and not really paying any heed. There weren't any familiar faces around, so Sal didn't stop to introduce his father to anyone.

When they finally entered the temporary headquarters of the Mythic Guild, it was chaos. Alex's shouts were heard over a repeated series of thunderous cracks. Sal would have been worried that something was going wrong if he didn't hear the joy in Alex's tone.

"You're falling behind, Royce!" Alex shouted with a maniacal laugh in the distance.

"Shut up, I'm concentrating!" Anders fired right back at him.

When Sal moved over to the elixir machine, he could see a cloud of steam hanging a few feet below the ceiling like an ominous smog. Hues of pink, blue, and yellow flashed through the steam in erratic intervals. A swirling vortex of green light pulsated from within the essence enclosure, with Anders letting out a cry of relief as it got sucked through the transparent pipework, shooting straight into the furnace.

"You're up!" Anders declared with a laugh as he took his glowing hands away from the surface of the enclosure to tap at a command console with practiced efficiency. "Next batch in fourteen seconds."

Alex's right palm was against the copper-colored vault door while his left frantically tapped at the visible screen on the body of the furnace. "Make it twelve or I'll switch you out with Blathnaid. Precision is everything!"

Sal watched in bewilderment as each vat filled to the brim with multicolored flower petals. The furnace rippled against the frame as the thunderous cracks started up again. Each one came accompanied with a fresh plume of colored steam that billowed into the ceiling.

Petro chuckled as he raised a finger to his lips, the universal sign to not interrupt them while they were working. He pointed at an empty space along the walkway that led to the elixir machine.

As though he knew it would happen, Jack and Anthony appeared side by side, holding a large keg between them. They shuffled over to where Alex was deep in concentration. Wordlessly, both of them started to hook up the keg with a series of tubes, adjusting the valves and slapping the side of it for some reason.

Alex looked directly up at the plume of smoke and held his left hand at the ready, controlling some sort of setting on the screen. An unknown change must have occurred, or a quiet count came to an end, because with no visual cues, Alex tapped the screen and snapped his fingers before stepping back with a wide grin. "That's the third best, yet." He glanced over at Anders and gave a slight head tilt. "Could have been even better without the two-second loss…"

"Incoming!" Anders shouted as another jet of green light shot through the tubing. "Just fucking work on it and stop giving me shit. That one was twelve point four."

Alex laughed as he placed his hands back on the furnace. "See? The goading works wonders. You're getting moderately better even though you're stressed. This is fun—you can admit it!"

Sal just looked at his dad in bewilderment. Both Jack and Anthony had gone to collect the next keg, and Blathnaid was nowhere in sight.

Petro gestured at the steam above. "He's able to determine the success of the elixirs based on the steam it emits. It's a very interesting approach, and clearly one he's come up with from experience."

"I'm not sure what I'm even looking at." Sal tried to take it all in. "It doesn't look like he's making coffee. The smell is completely wrong."

"Of course he's not making coffee." Petro chuckled. "He wants to make money because of the profit share, which means he's going to drag poor Anderson to the gates of hell to get there. I'm sure the perfection he's chasing is going to be worth the effort."

Sal nodded slowly, his mind going a million miles an hour. "Should they be struggling this much, though? If it's a Mythic grade, I thought it would be a lot more straightforward… or at least a little more hands-off?"

Petro nodded in Anthony's direction. "While Fabrizia and Upgrade are out in the dungeons, he's stepped into the role of programmer. Alex assures me that this whole thing can be automated in the future, but for now, it needs to be done manually to get the best results."

"Any idea what they're working on?" Sal tried to come up with the answer himself. Something that would go for a lot of Q-Cred would be the main goal, but he didn't really know much about elixir prices. Probably a health or essence one? Kaizen or Kakushin would probably be a safe one to make, but Alex was already able to make those with his own setup. What would he use the Mythic-grade equipment for?

"Something to keep you on your feet would be my best guess," Petro answered with a proud smile. "Upgrade and Fabrizia may have had a few words with Alex about his priorities. From the looks of it, he's taking them quite seriously."

Sal didn't know how he should feel. It was reassuring that they were concerned about him, but there was no way Quest or Doctor Bob would approve of him taking an unknown elixir to improve his condition. Whatever the first batch was likely to be, it would be scrutinized by the elixir magnates until it was deemed safe for use. According to Quest, there would be a field of red tape they'd need to wade through before getting approval to use it.

"Ah, we have guests!" Alex announced as he looked over his shoulder to where Sal and Petro stood. "You here to see the magic happen, or do you just want to see the end product?"

Anders pulled his hands away from the enclosure with an aggravated sigh. "Eleven nine. Knock yourself out!"

Alex grinned as he gave the furnace his full attention. "You both have some great timing. You're going to see a masterpiece!"

"What are you making?" Sal knew he only had a few seconds before Alex restarted the cycle.

"I've got no fucking idea." Alex laughed as a thunderous crack rocketed up the furnace, causing a plume of pearlescent white steam to float straight upward, ignoring the clouds drooping around it. "But it's the best one yet!" His grin couldn't get any wider as he watched the steam intently.

CHAPTER 47: MASTERY

"So, we need to let it percolate?" Sal watched the glowing white mixture accumulate into a rune-inscribed vial at the edge of the furnace. "I think we were wrong about the amount of output this thing would do." Sal pointed at the tiny stream that was coming through gradually.

Alex snorted as he pointed at the Refiner station. "The bulk is all heading over there. What you're looking at is just a small extract that can be used as a recipe for future concoctions." He tapped the side of the rune with a proud smile. "Plant-Test 9. Looks a lot prettier in this form, doesn't it?"

Sal wasn't sure whether it was rhetorical or whether he was expected to answer. He just nodded politely as he turned his attention from the milky white liquid to Alex. "You said you've got no idea what it is but, can I ask what you were trying for?"

Alex shrugged. "I'm not a Healer by any stretch, so I'm not the best person to consult when it comes to health elixirs." He smiled as he pointed at Sal. "But your problem was a lot more straightforward to solve."

"It was?" Sal would have guessed the inverse. Health elixirs sounded a lot easier than whatever Sal's issue was. He wasn't going to hold out hope that Alex, of all people, would find a solution for him.

Alex smiled as he spread his hands wide. "It was obvious… you came to me with the issue last semester. Your Mastery issue is why you've been struggling to use your eyes? That was the problem, wasn't it? This whole thing was set up because of Mastery, and that's a potion I know a lot about."

He pointed at the furnace's chimney. "We just needed one that could be turned into a vapor without losing its properties. Upgrade was very specific about the requirements, and I think we managed to crack it." Alex smiled as he tapped the vial. "It also gets us around the whole ingestion thing… which is a bullshit loophole, but we're thinking it could be sidestepped by integrating the elixir into a piece of equipment."

Sal stared at Alex as if he had two heads. "Wait, so the plan is to make a mask that boosts innate mastery? All the quotes you gave me before had a tiny duration, though?"

Alex frowned as he gestured very slowly at the Mythic-grade elixir machine. If that wasn't obvious enough, he stepped back to point at the Refiner. "Everything you've made here will dramatically improve the base stats of the Mastery elixir. I've been pushing for the term Myth-Master, but Upgrade vetoed it immediately. I swear, that woman has no dramatic flair."

Petro smiled as he grasped Sal's shoulder. "What do you think? Sounds pretty exciting, doesn't it?"

Sal's mind was a whirlwind of questions. He had presumed that the mask was going to be unrelated to the elixir machine. Sure, his initial idea had included it, but he didn't think that everyone would work together on making it a reality. If the answer to their problems was being made by the elixir machine, why were Upgrade and Fabi clearing dungeons relentlessly?

A few moments of thinking through the implications had resulted in Sal standing awkwardly among his father and friends. He realized he hadn't answered them. With a guilty laugh, he just shrugged. "I'm trying not to get my hopes up, but it sounds like a pretty good outcome. I don't know that artificially improving the mastery of my weave will matter when it's injuring me, though."

Alex nodded in agreement. "There's a type of dregs for overdosing on elixirs. I warned them about that, but they had already factored that into the build design. But really, all that matters is that I did my part. Plant-Test 9 worked far better than I imagined it would. It has good balance."

Sal glanced at the Genesis station, where Anders tapped at the terminal, as though filling out a report of some kind. "What do you mean exactly by Plant-Test 9?" His question was to Alex as he continued to watch Anders.

"Well, you've likely already seen the Appraisal stuff for it…" Alex shrugged, as if it were obvious. "We loaded up a few ingredients into the Genesis station, and it started creating hybrids. Rather than moving straight into the next stage, I pushed the ingredients through the first stage repeatedly. Worked Royce to the bone to get the optimal splice. I knew the traits I needed and what was nice to have, so we didn't need to rely on any programming for that part."

"You're making it sound easy," Anders complained without turning around. "Tell him how many attempts it took to make Plant-Test 9. Otherwise, he'll think it was just the ninth one."

Alex laughed as he glanced at Anders. "Complaining about the workload doesn't increase your profits, mate." He shook his head, smiling good-humoredly. "But yeah, it was a… *trial* to get to that particular splice. We ended up burning through hundreds of unique samples, but it was worth it. Each of the plant-tests have dozens of tests done with them, adapting strains and picking new traits."

Sal just stared at him, not really understanding the significance of what was being explained to him.

Alex frowned before letting out a sigh. "Okay… I'm not a teacher, but I'll try to explain it in a way you'll understand." He adopted an almost singsong voice, like he was talking to a child. "The ingredients I use on a day-to-day basis are kinda like Uncommon grade. They each have an ability of sorts, but they also have a negative ability. If the quality of the Uncommon grade ingredient is bad, then it has more negative abilities that need to be purified out later in the process. Are you following?"

Sal nodded, hating Alex's educational voice with a passion. What made it worse was that Alex's explanation was far more insightful than his previous one. Sal smiled politely as he listened.

"Better ingredients mean less negatives. Higher grades mean more abilities." He waved his hand, gesturing at all three stations. "This beauty minimizes the negatives, and allows us to pick some of the positives. If I was using Uncommon before, at questionable quality, then this is producing, wait… no, it's actually *creating* from scratch… Rare and Epic-grade ingredients, all at perfect quality."

Anders turned around from his terminal with a tired smile as he waved at Sal half-heartedly. "Better context is that we started with low-grade ingredients, and the abilities of this machine are turning them into better ones. We're picking the traits we want the new ones to have, and then experimenting with combinations to make even better ingredients. All the plant-test flowers are numbered after how many iterations they've gone through."

Sal's eyes widened. Hadn't they said they were switching away from fourteen to prioritize nine? Each of those had that many iterations or evolutions? It was only a few weeks that he was away… surely the progress was far too advanced for that amount of time?

"Ah, Royce… I think that did the trick. Look at how horrified he is." Alex chuckled as he pointed at Sal's dumbstruck face. "This is very much a labor of love, and despite all of his complaints, he's getting a massive kick out of all this." He gestured at Anderson Royce almost dismissively.

Petro smiled as he looked at the slowly filling vial of milky liquid. "What estimates do you have for its potency? I've never sold consumables, so I'd have a tough time of Appraising it for fair-market value."

Alex hesitated before answering. He glanced at Sal for a few seconds, before looking back at Petro. "Before I answer, you're on our side… right? You want to make money with this thing?"

Sal wanted to laugh at how preposterous that question was. Alex was asking an Auctioneer whether he wanted to make money, and whether he was going to be supporting his own son.

Petro nodded. "Yes, so you don't need to lie about the production cost. I know that's the usual tactic of padding out the price."

Alex let out a sigh of relief as he moved over to the vial. "First, you can thank our little rune artist. This preservation on these things is the best I've ever seen." He hiked his thumb over his shoulder to where Jack sat on a keg, listening to Anthony.

Jack was oblivious to the only compliment he was likely ever to get from Alex. He seemed to be engaged with whatever Anthony was talking about.

Alex glanced between Sal and Petro. "I can't be sure yet, because we'll need to put it through the Refiner before we have some results… but the efficacy of this thing will be reduced because it's being inhaled as a vapor."

"Ah," Sal muttered, realizing that his plan had accidentally screwed up the elixir. He wondered whether there was a way to just make it as a consumable so it could benefit more people. If it was only useable through a mask that Fabi was making, then it would—

Sal's eyes widened as he came to the realization of why the mask was seemingly so popular in the future. It was the only way to use the Mastery elixir. He had thought that it would have some incredible ability after Divinity said it was the greatest invention, but this was completely outside of his expectations. If they were the only supplier of both the masks and the elixir…

Alex wasn't oblivious to Sal's sudden epiphany. With a wide grin, he nodded in agreement. "Yeah, this is a massive deal…"

"Could you spell it out for me, please? Preferably in your normal voice." Petro chuckled as he gestured at the milky substance, as though it would bring Alex back to the original question.

Alex smiled sheepishly as he put up both hands defensively. "Now, I know we Alchemists have a tough time keeping our excitement in check, but I want you to believe me when I say this thing is pretty spectacular. It can be improved from this point as we get our automation set up, but right now, it's the best I can come up with on our timeline."

"Timeline?" Sal repeated, and before Alex could answer him, Petro interrupted with a hand.

"What can it do, Alex?" Petro repeated, this time a little more firmly. It was clear his patience was running thin with how scatterbrained Alex was.

Alex, for all his bluster, had the grace to look apologetic. "Sorry, just a little all over the place with the excitement is all." His eyes narrowed as he looked off into space for a moment, his lips moving as though he were doing some invisible calculation. After a few seconds of uncertainty, he nodded quietly. "As a vapor, we're looking at close to a full hour of effect, with four administrations being the maximum dosage every two days. I'll need to check the math on that a few more times to ensure I'm right, but it's definitely on the side of caution."

Petro blinked in surprise. "So, two hours a day? That's a lot better than I was expecting. What's the uplift in Mastery?"

Alex frowned in confusion. "What do you mean?"

Petro stared back, equally confused. It was like he wasn't sure how else to ask the same question.

Sal tried to bridge the gap. "As in, how much percentage points of Mastery can it add to the person?" He looked at his father to verify that they were asking the same thing, and got an affirmative nod.

"Ha!" Alex barked as he looked between them, like they were simple. "It's Mastery! It's not called the elixir of being slightly better at using your ability!" He laughed, as though it were obvious. "It brings you up to a hundred percent. That's what we've been aiming for the whole time, isn't it?"

Sal's jaw dropped and he could see Anders smiling from the Genesis station. He looked at the milky liquid in a whole new light. "Four hours in two days…of having a full Mastery stat. What's the catch? Do you lose essence permanently or something?"

Alex shrugged. "As with all elixirs, sustained usage will lead to less efficacy. The stat will always go to a hundred percent, but the duration will weaken over time. I'm confident that we can make this even better, though."

"How could you possibly make it better?" Petro asked with a laugh of disbelief. "It's perfect as it is!"

Alex frowned as he pointed at the Refiner. "We haven't Refined it yet." Tapping his finger against the rune-inscribed vial, Alex looked thoughtful. "We'll likely have to destroy this batch to lock in the traits for future elixirs, though. Now that we have the vapor build perfected, we just need to work on the potency. It's an excellent result to start, and I'm sure we'll get those numbers up soon."

Anders nodded in agreement. "Want to burn it now so we can get on with the next iteration?" He had his sleeves rolled up and looked slightly more energized than before. "I think I can get it down to ten seconds if I push at it."

Alex's eyes lit up. "That's what I'm talking about, Royce! Fucking, yes!" He pumped both of his arms downward with a laugh as he glanced at the elixir machine, before almost reluctantly looking back at both Sal and Petro. It was clear that babysitting onlookers was keeping him from working.

"This is wonderful. You clearly know what you're doing, so I think we should leave you both to it." Petro looked over at Sal. "I think we'll only get in the way with silly questions for now."

Sal felt as though he couldn't breathe. Were they seriously going to destroy it? Maybe it was just a joke to mess with him. Had Upgrade put Alex up to it, because of Sal's habit of wanting simulated weaves deleted when they weren't perfect?

Petro's hand gripped at his shoulder. "We're only going to get in their way at this point."

"I'd still like to stay and watch, though. If that's okay?" Sal looked between Alex and Anders. Neither of them looked disgruntled by the suggestion, and his father was more than happy to hang around to see the process again.

With a shrill whistle, Alex got the attention of both Anthony and Jack. "Break time's over, gentlemen."

CHAPTER 48: REACTION

Sal stood there for close to an hour, watching the frenetic pace of the two men as they worked. The chaotic shouting started to make sense after a while, and Sal was able to piece together what was happening. When he had taken the Alchemy courses on the Credit Store, he had assumed he'd have a base understanding of what was going on… but Alex and Anderson were playing a completely different game.

What made Sal's heart race was the almost electric enjoyment both men were taking from the work. It wasn't like Crafting with long moments of tedium and precision. Rather, it was like watching them both fighting against the machine, optimizing their timing… with percussive explosions signifying their successes and failures. It was a thousand times more dramatic than a green light flashing from above. Couple that with the multicolored steam clouds, and you had a process that was a genuine joy to behold.

Petro slid a stool behind Sal, with another in hand for himself. He sat down contentedly and crossed his arms. "Is this what you're like when you Craft?"

"No, not even close," Sal answered, without a shred of doubt. "If there was a time limit, then maybe… but this is like a science. It's so strange seeing Alex being all confident." He glanced at his dad. "You don't look as surprised as I am. Did you watch them before?"

Petro nodded. "Yeah, but there was more cursing than actual progress. It's great to see the evolution of their process. Anderson Royce in particular. I had thought he'd quit after just a few days. Alex was holding Anders to his own standard, and it looks like Mr. Royce has stepped up considerably."

"I didn't think he'd actually be using his power," Sal admitted as he gestured at the enclosure with his open palm. "The Genesis station uses an evolution of his skill. We were supposed to have a terminal for Anderson to utilize it… Growth shouldn't be able to work like that."

Petro smiled as he snapped his fingers. "I think we've just figured out where Alex's frustrations were coming from. I was trying to understand the timing issue, but it looks like your friend is taking between ten and fourteen seconds to imitate the effects of that higher-form ability." A laugh escaped his lips as he shook his head in disbelief. "I can't even fathom how you'd go about doing something like that… Do you think he's just using that time to activate the machine, or that he's actually trying to augment the creation process?"

Sal's brow furrowed as he watched Anderson work. "You're saying that it would be like me helping the Arkwright by fueling essence into the equipment as it's being constructed?"

Petro shrugged. "It's the only method I can think of, and it's not like we're going to get an answer any time soon. What's happening with the Refiner? It's starting to glow."

Sal tilted his head to get a better look at the Refiner that was partly obscured by his father's body. True to his words, the Absolver had started to warm up. Ripples of light looped around the base of the cylinder, coiling like a spring. It was difficult to observe from the distance, but Sal could see the milky white liquid splashing within the Absolver. He wasn't sure he should highlight it to Alex. It might have been planned, and he didn't want to break the Alchemist out of his flow.

To both Sal and Petro's surprise, it was Anthony who stood in front of the Refiner, with no less confidence than Alex and Anderson. He loaded up a sequence using the terminal and, for good measure, tapped the interface on the cylinder itself.

"I thought he'd use his ability, but it looks like he's just running a program or something?" Sal muttered as he watched Anthony carefully. "It feels weird that I built the thing and I haven't got a clue what's going on. That's weird, right?"

Petro shrugged, chuckling. "I couldn't tell you. There's a whole swath of knowledge required for this. I think it's for the best that you don't understand it."

"Why is that?" Sal asked in confusion. "I want to help them as much as possible. If this can be half as successful as we expect it to be, I can't just rely on others to be available when we need to work."

Petro shook his head, smiling. "Then train others to fill in for them. You can't be tied to this project. There's a whole realm of expertise that won't apply to you in the future, and as a guildmaster, you're going to need to get comfortable with delegation."

With a broad gesture around the room, Petro looked at Sal. "This is your headquarters while you're at Quest Academy. You heard from Jez that you can only account for twenty-five percent of the earnings threshold, so it makes sense to let your members find their feet until they can thrive like you." He let out a satisfied sigh. "And just look at this. Rather than feeling inadequate that you don't understand what's going on, feel proud. You built this, and gave each of these people an opportunity to prove themselves in an entirely new way. They'll be excited to explain it to you."

Sal realized that his father was right. It wasn't a feeling of inadequacy that coursed through him. It felt like far too many things had happened in his absence, and Sal was worried about being left behind. Yes, he helped build the machine, but watching everyone working so happily on it… made him worry that he was missing out, somehow.

"I know we said that we'd do the sparring tomorrow, but how would you feel about doing it now?" Sal asked suddenly. If he wanted to feel competent, it wasn't going to be in this room.

He was happy for Anderson, Alex, and Anthony… but he was itching to use the time he had with his father to actually accomplish something. Being trapped in that infirmary had made him feel helpless, and now that he was watching others excelling, he wanted to catch up.

"Are you asking for the right reasons?" Petro asked quietly, his eyebrow raised. "Because if you're angry or frustrated, sparring isn't the right outlet."

Sal shook his head. "No, I'm not angry. I'm probably closer to being inspired. They're working so hard on a solution for my injuries… and I'm just sitting here, watching them. I want to help and be useful, but I think I'd just get in the way, and it's frustrating." With a heavy sigh, Sal looked at his dad. "I don't want to get left behind, if that makes sense?"

Petro smiled as he got to his feet, straightening his jacket. "Perfect. Lead the way… I'm not sure about the bar, but I'm positive they have a training area somewhere around here."

"Just one second." Sal took out his tablet. "Is it okay if I ask Divinity to join us?"

Petro nodded. "Absolutely. I'm curious how much better she's gotten with Style."

"Would you like the good news, or the bad news?" Petro wiped at his brow and took a deep breath. He looked positively elated, but that was the least of Sal's worries.

Sal clutched at his chest, trying to maintain his balance on one knee as he panted for breath. It wasn't like he had regressed during his time at the infirmary. All the new techniques he had learned with the adaptive Silverson Arts had seemingly made him a more competent combatant. The problem was the reaction it caused in his father.

The sparring had started out normally, with just a few exercises and stretches to get them loosened up. When he started to use the basic combinations, he could see the surprise in his father's eyes. That was when his dad tried to get an attack through, at a speed that should have been unavoidable… likely just a test to show the differences between their skills. Maybe it was going to lead into a lesson?

What was the problem? Sal's body reacted perfectly to the attack and launched a counter in a flash. Disbelief colored his face as his left hand gripped his dad's forearm; he could barely form a single word as he pulled his father in to deliver an uppercut with his right fist. Next thing Sal knew, he was being thrown through the air.

The ensuing spar had turned into a flurry of perfectly executed counters and blocks, with his dad actually pressing with his attacks. Sal got to see him fully concentrating on the battle… which was terrifying in itself, because Sal was only a single error away from getting seriously injured. When he finally launched the jump kick, his father was completely dumbfounded.

Right until he intercepted it with two strikes, one to Sal's right thigh with his elbow, and the second to Sal's chest. It resulted in Sal on one knee, panting to catch his breath.

"The good news is that you're definitely learning the Silverson Arts." Petro grinned as he paced around with his hands on his hips. "A truly terrifying repertoire you've designed for yourself… I had to go all out for a second there."

Sal could only manage a croak. "Did you have to hit the chest? I… would have stopped after you got my leg."

Petro waved it off like it was nothing. "Be honest with me… were you using something like Absolute Counter? I won't be annoyed if you were."

Sal shook his head, which elicited a whistle from his dad.

"Well, then… I think you should absolutely keep up with whatever training that thing is giving you. I'll send you all the other manuals. Just feed it to that thing and see what it comes up with." Petro was almost giddy as he crouched down to look at Sal. "You were absolutely amazing just now. You should have seen yourself." He looked behind Sal, grinning. "What did you think?"

Sal had to turn to see Divinity sitting at the edge of the sparring area. She looked aghast at what had just happened, and Sal couldn't tell whether it was from seeing his dad kick the shit out of him, or whether it was surprise at his progress. Either way, he was happy for the quiet support. Waving his hand in Divinity's direction, he stumbled to his feet, groaning. "You're up… Your turn."

With that, he started to move toward where Divinity sat. Until his father's hand clasped his shoulder, locking him in place. "Sal, I didn't get to the bad news part…"

Sal grimaced as he looked at his father, almost pleadingly. "It's not another spar, is it?"

"No, no… don't worry. You're safe for now." He chuckled as he helped Sal over to the edge of the sparring area. "Divinity, if you'd be so kind as to warm up?"

Divinity nodded slowly, clearly still processing what she had just seen. She glanced at Sal again to make sure he was okay, and upon receiving a smile, went off to get herself ready for the spar.

"So, what's the bad news?" Sal managed as he slumped to the ground, this time feeling very sorry for himself. It was the curse of competence, where he had been dispatched ruthlessly for getting a lucky shot in.

Petro sat down beside him, still grinning. "The bad news is that we need you to get faster and stronger. Those techniques are the real deal, but the limitation is your body. If any of those kicks landed with the right amount of force, the result would have been a lot different."

"As if." Sal chuckled, before regretting it instantly. The ache in his chest made him feel like he'd need to stop by the infirmary to check for internal bruising.

"I'm deadly serious," Petro insisted as he pointed at the training ground. "You had four very impressive moves out of twenty-eight. Your distancing and breathing need some work, but your follow-through is a lot better than I expected. I was genuinely caught off guard a few times, and although some of that is attributable to complacency on my part, it was still a very praiseworthy effort."

"Okay, speed and strength. Got it." Sal nodded as he gave his dad a weak thumbs-up.

Petro smiled as he nudged Sal gently. "I really enjoyed that. If you're feeling up to it tomorrow, we should do this again. I want to see what other moves you've learned."

"That was pretty much it," Sal lied, grimacing. "I think I prefer the easygoing lessons where you don't attack me."

"Nice try." Petro chuckled as he got to his feet. "But I'm genuinely relieved to see how far you've progressed. I was worried when you started talking about the adaptive style, but this has worked out brilliantly."

"Are you going to go easy on Divinity?" Sal asked with an awkward laugh, looking past his father to where Divinity was doing stretches with such focus, you'd swear she was in front of a judging panel.

"That depends." Petro smiled as he waved at Divinity. "What do you say; want to take it easy, or do you want to go all out like Sal?"

Sal couldn't help but be surprised as he watched Divinity get into a serious battle stance, her eyes completely white. She didn't look like she was backing down, even after seeing what his dad was capable of.

Petro laughed as he clapped his hands together. "There's nothing a teacher loves more than a student willing to learn." He assumed a stance that was eerily close to Sal's.

Surely, he wasn't going to imitate all twenty-eight moves that he just fought against?

Sal watched in disbelief as his father not only imitated his moves, but did it with far better execution and timing than Sal believed possible. If Sal had been under any illusion that he was catching up to his dad, the fight with Divinity was conclusive evidence that he wasn't even close.

Rather than internally grumbling about it, Sal intently watched the spar. He was being shown this for a reason, and he was going to learn as much as he could from it.

CHAPTER 49: HERMES

"Are you sure you don't want an ice pack or something? We could go to the infirmary to get you checked out if it's really bad?" Divinity asked in a concerned tone as they got out of the elevator. She managed it a lot more gracefully than Sal, who still clutched at his ribs, grimacing.

"I'll be fine. Thank you for asking, though," Sal managed to grunt, with a half-chuckle peppered in for good measure. "I thought he would have stopped after that first round."

Divinity's smile was bright as she shook her head. "I didn't know either, but it was a lot of fun! I love training with your dad. I wish he was a Combat lecturer here… because, don't get me wrong, Rust is pretty good, but your dad knows so much more about individual combat styles!"

Sal stood upright, despite his body's protests. He was tender after the repeated blows to his sides. The evening had been an education on blocking and defense, and Sal's was sorely lacking. All the moves he had learned with the Silverson Arts had been for attacking, which had left him wide open. If he was feeling up to it, he'd start focusing on the defensive maneuvers in the morning.

"Are you going to work on Crafting when you get back to your dorm?" Divinity followed up, as though trying to keep the conversation going. She was looking at him strangely.

Sal shook his head. "Nah, I think I'm going to have an early night… and I know I always say that, but this time I'm serious."

"Are you sure about that?" Divinity asked sweetly. "Because I've got a feeling you're going to be exhausted tomorrow."

Sal paused in the hallway. "Is this your instinct talking, or is it a vision?" He wasn't annoyed. They hadn't spoken about the Shade thing yet, and this was probably a good enough segue into that conversation.

Divinity's smile grew wider. "If you actually intend to get some sleep, you should close your eyes when you get into your dorm. I could cover them for you and try guiding you past the problem?"

All thoughts of Shade seeped away as confusion took over. He couldn't help but smile as he thought about it aloud. "Wait… so there's something in my dorm that will stop me from sleeping? But if I don't see it, I'll be able to rest?"

"Exactly." Divinity laughed as she offered him a slight shrug, her tone still playful. "It's nothing dangerous, and I haven't actually looked into the different permutations. All I can say is that there's something there that will make you exhausted tomorrow, and you'll skip your classes."

Sal folded his arms as he tried to think of what it could be. "I'll admit, this is an intriguing use of your power. I'm dying to know what it is… Do you want to come over and see?"

Divinity shook her head. "As fun as I think that would be, I want to get back to my own dorm for a shower. Your dad really didn't hold back on us."

"Suit yourself… But before I go, I don't suppose you've got any insights about Shade?" Sal asked warily, not even sure what he wanted to ask her. Did he want to know whether he'd get kidnapped, or whether there was a larger threat at play?

Surely she already knew that Shade was a scumbag, so an open-ended question would probably suffice.

Divinity frowned at the mention of Shade's name. "Ugh, yeah… it's a bit of a nightmare, but nothing you need to worry about. Everything will reach its natural conclusion."

Sal blinked in surprise. "Really? It's not some big threat like murder or abduction?" Had he really been overthinking everything?

"I didn't say that." Divinity sighed as she gave him a half-smile. "I said everything will happen the way it should. You've already set up your guild, so that changed things for the better. I don't want to ruin the outcome, but I think you'll be pleasantly surprised with how things go."

She raised her hand as though to stop him asking a follow-up question. "It was already brought up at the Doom Society meeting, and the best course of action is what's happening now. I've looked up dozens of futures and permutations, and can tell you that you're fine in all of them." A gentle smile graced her face. "I would have come to you immediately if I thought there was a problem. I promise."

"I trust you." Sal smiled, his heart already feeling more at ease. "So, I'm guessing that I don't set Jackal on Shade?"

Divinity laughed as she moved off toward her dorm. "I didn't say that," she called back over her shoulder, as she gave him a wave.

He returned it before continuing in the direction of his own room. As he approached the door, he steeled himself. If there was going to be a massive distraction waiting for him, he'd push past it. He was stronger than his curiosities. Now that he knew of Divinity's vision, he'd be able to successfully avoid it.

As the door slid open in front of him, Sal caught sight of three massive crates stacked up in the hallway entrance to the dorm. His unbreakable willpower had already started to waver. Seeing the placards on each crate wasn't helping either. Worse than that, there was a flat rectangular stack that hung precariously off the top of the three crates.

Surely there would be no problem with leaning it against the wall. He wouldn't even need to look at it. That was the first of many excuses he told himself as he reached out to pluck it from the top of the crates. There was an engraved title on the packaging. Sal tried to avert his gaze from it, but it was too late.

The Invention: Blueprint Challenges, 1-5

"Okay, just looking at the descriptions should be fine…" Sal rationalized as he placed the blueprint stack against the wall. The transparent film that obscured the half-completed blueprints were facing the wall so he wouldn't be tempted to have a closer look.

With hands clasped behind his back, Sal glanced at the three crates. His gaze darted between the placards… and his willpower self-destructed at the sight of the first one.

Ameye Locomotive: Specialist Package No. 1

Argento Auction House: Care Package No. 1

Material Exchange: Care Package No. 1

A small note was attached to the side of the care package. Sal guessed it was going to be a note from his parents, but it was instead from the Credit floor.

A penalty has been applied to your account for failing to collect these packages within a two-week period. Please visit the Credit floor to balance your accounts. Thank you.

Sal chuckled as he crumpled up the note and took a step away from the crates. "Not tonight." He practically whispered the words to the collection of materials and blueprints. There was so much he wanted to catch up on, and weaves he wanted to experiment on. Adding in blueprint challenges and Crafting challenges from Doc Ameye, he'd end up being very busy.

"Shower and bed," Sal said aloud, as though it would spare the feelings of the material trove. "I'll wake up early and have a look." He nodded to himself, doing a pretty poor job of lying to himself.

And yet, he followed through on his promise. Sal went straight to the bathroom, had his shower and got into bed. His body ached from the sparring with his father, but he was proud of himself. There had been a slight fear that he had somehow regressed while he was in the infirmary... but judging from the bouts with his dad, Sal was far more capable than he had been a few weeks ago.

Drifting off to sleep had been easy. He was battered and bruised and the exhaustion from the day had really taken its toll. Maybe it was the excitement of the crates, or the anxiety from having so much he needed to catch up on... Whatever it was, Sal awoke wide-awake, with the absolute certainty that there would be no more sleep. It had been four hours of somewhat fitful rest, and Sal was happy enough with that.

He gingerly got dressed and moved back out toward the hallway, pausing only to equip his visor. The reassuring screen over his right eye was something he had missed quite a bit. Not having it in the infirmary had been a form of torture, and he was happy to have it back.

Sal went over to the crates and stopped himself from just opening up everything. He was going to do this in stages so he didn't miss anything. The care package from his parents was likely going to be materials from the Arkwright, with a few additional ingots of silver for good measure. That one would be opened last. First, he was going to take a look at the blueprint challenges that were sent over by the Invention Guild. There were Q-Cred prizes for completing the challenges, and Sal was genuinely curious as to what they expected from students.

He picked up the flat-pack sleeve of blueprint parchments and moved over to the couch in the living area. Sitting back and crossing his legs, he pulled a strip of soft metal material to break the seal, revealing the sheets of paper within. Sliding out the first, Sal looked at it and wondered what the challenge was supposed to be.

His tracker was clearly more awake than he was because it instantly started to interpret the blueprint. In just a few seconds, he knew that the challenge was broken down into categories: material substitutions, feasibility score, design improvements... the list went on. There were countless themes to the challenge, and Sal couldn't help but be impressed with his visor figuring it all out, until he saw the exact same list written in the bottom right-hand corner of the blueprint.

Sal stared at it for a few seconds before he let out a humorless chuckle. Sifting through the blueprints, Sal realized that all five of the challenges related to the same build. Each of them focused on different mechanisms of a barrier generator.

It looked to be an incredibly involved process, and Sal was sure that there were hidden traps within the build. Was the Invention Guild asking him to show his value by correcting the blueprints, or were they looking for a new type of solution?

Either way, it was going to earn him Q-Cred if he managed to complete them. It felt nice that the challenges were on an ethical build. He had expected some form of advanced weaponry design, so improving barriers was a welcome surprise. Sal continued to inspect the blueprints, already seeing some areas that he instinctively felt could be improved. It was a sign of his individual growth that he hadn't even activated Mythcrafter yet.

Placing the blueprints down on the coffee table, Sal glanced back in the direction of the chests that were practically calling to him. With a smile, he hopped up from the couch and made his way over to the chest that Doc Ameye had sent him. There was no hesitation as he unclasped the metal buckles and lifted the lid. A pneumatic hiss added to the suspense as the lid lifted with the support of two rods. Just for dramatic flair, a set of lights blinked into existence on the interior lid, bathing the contents in a warm golden light.

Sal just stared at the craftsmanship. It was a storage crate, and it had no right to be so flashy and sophisticated. He looked at the topmost layer of the crate and was surprised to see a series of blueprints that were engraved into sheets of metal. There were more than ten of them, all stacked neatly on top of one another. When Sal pulled them all out, he was worried that there wouldn't be enough space for materials.

It took a few minutes, but Sal laid out each of the components as per the instructions on the first engraved blueprint. There was a white blanket that he laid out on the ground, made with some form of micro-fiber material. He wasn't sure whether Doc Ameye was treating him like a child, or he was just this precise, but the blanket had a series of visible segments that highlighted the material placement. There was a small circle for a series of yellow crystals, and a few poles that were stacked within a rectangular segment. All told, there were close to twenty sections for the materials, and Sal could only marvel at how they had all fit into the singular chest.

His visor was still working on the blueprint, which told Sal that it was something complex. It didn't feel like a challenge, so much as it felt like an assembly operation. When everything was laid out on the floor, Sal took a seat on the couch, the first engraved blueprint in his hands. It was an exciting moment because he had no idea what he was looking at. It wasn't a weapon, or a piece of armor. It looked like it would come together to make a platform. The crystals were the surprising thing, because they looked identical to the ones he had used for the engraver in the Arkwright. Yet, the use-case this time was likely very different.

Some of the materials had already been fashioned into components and were lying on the blanket. Sal guessed that Doc Ameye didn't want him screwing them up, or he was impatient for Sal to get this thing built.

After a few minutes of deliberation, the visor finally parsed what was being asked of it.

Hermes Dock Blueprint has been successfully added.

- o Hermes Dock allows for instantaneous receipt of materials across long distances.
- o Hermes Dock cannot send materials. It can only receive from a linked outlet.

Sal was reminded of the words Doc Ameye had said to him back at the auction house. The limiting factor of the Arkwright was that it couldn't transport materials. It looked like the Hermes Dock was the first step in solving that problem.

He couldn't help but laugh as he looked at the blueprint in front of him. Doc Ameye was likely frustrated with the logistics of sending Sal crates, so the first project was a new supply-chain solution?

Sal placed his tablet on the coffee table and moved over to the components and materials. He had a few hours before class, so there wasn't really any issue with getting started on it. If he was being honest with himself, there was a surge of excitement and anticipation. He was creating a supply route from Ameye Locomotives… and he had no idea what the next batch of materials would be.

CHAPTER 50: EVOLUTION

After two hours of straight Crafting, Sal was delighted with the progress on the Hermes Dock. There was no room for interpretation or embellishments. This was a puzzle with only one solution, and Sal was guided through the entire process, with Mythcrafter not having a single suggestion for improvements. It was a testament to Doc Ameye's capability as a Crafter, and it genuinely raised Sal's bar for what a good Crafter looked like.

Because it was Epic grade in quality, Sal didn't need to worry about his eyes getting overloaded. He matched his essence output with Perfect, shaped it with the guidance of Judgment and Cypher on his visor, and simply followed the instructions clearly laid out. It was the most straightforward build he had ever worked on, and it felt like cheating. He fused the crystals into the sockets on each of the poles. He threaded an essence-infused cable—it was very similar to the simulation orb's weaves—through each of the pre-cut holes on the poles. It created a mesh-like fence that intertwined into the shape of a pentagram.

Next had been the enclosures that connected each of the poles; each of the plates had perfectly lined grooves to house the essence-infused cable. Everything fitting together was so satisfying, and Sal found himself marveling at each of the small details. Was there a need for all the plating to be in chrome? No, there wasn't. Everything was a stylistic choice, and it made the build look incredible. Sal felt like he didn't deserve the satisfaction he was getting from the assembly.

When he fixed the last of the enclosures, the yellow crystals started to thrum. A faint golden glow lit up the small rivets in the poles, which was followed by each of the cables activating with the same golden light. Sal let out an appreciative sigh as he placed the transparent sheet of glass over the pentagon. He wasn't even surprised when it clicked and locked into place. The glowing thread started to pulsate and occupy more space within the enclosure, until the transparent glass was obscured by a golden cloud of warm light in the shape of a five-pointed star.

Sal continued to push his essence through the build, and it turned out to be another lesson in precision. There wasn't a single mistake that needed to be smoothed out. His essence was only acting like glue that fused everything together. There was no need to inject more essence to push up the grade; everything was made to perfection already. It was ridiculous that something like this was possible.

When he was finally finished, Sal took a step back and looked at the Hermes Dock. It looked like an ultra-modern coffee table with a glass countertop, a golden star glowing from within. Each of the poles were angled slightly away from the star, narrowing the base and giving the top a wider surface area. It didn't look to be mechanical at all, but Sal knew that there were several machines lined in the base plate. They had already been assembled, and all he had needed to do was orient the poles in the right sockets. Same with the crystals.

The cooldown didn't take longer than five minutes, and the shape didn't change dramatically, either. All it accomplished was a smoothing out of the edges, making the construct a singular entity rather than a collection of pieces.

Sal wasn't exactly sure what to expect now that he was done. Did he need to reach out to Doc Ameye to tell him that it was finished? It was still early in the morning, so he guessed it would be best to wait until later in the day.

In that exact moment of uncertainty, the gold star erupted like a beacon, shooting a beam of star-shaped light at the ceiling of Sal's dorm. A thunderous crack echoed throughout the dorm, and Sal's attention snapped upward, praying that it hadn't created a hole into the area above. His fears weren't realized, as the crackling noise happened again and again in quick succession…

Sal panicked as he looked at the Hermes Dock for some sort of solution. He had made it to perfection, and the visor told him that everything was fine. The noise was a bit ridiculous, though. He was likely going to wake up every Savior at this rate.

And then it was over. The light vanished, revealing four new poles perched on the base of the dock. Sal wasn't sure what had just happened. Did Doc Ameye send those poles to him? What was he supposed to do with them?

The visor was much faster than he was in figuring it out.

Hermes Rod x 4
- Tether
- Synergy

Sal blinked as he read the words in disbelief. He wanted to be sure as he moved over to pick up one of the rods. The moment his hand gripped the nearest one, the base detached to create an independent stand. Was he supposed to set them up around the Hermes Dock? Sal tested it out by placing them in a small square around the dock. His reward? An angry flash of red that was reminiscent of the simulation orb.

Sal gradually extended the size of the square, each of the corners moving farther out until they practically dominated the room. It took a lot of iteration until he found the sweet spot, rewarded with a golden flash…and a much more aggressive cacophony of thunder than before. Sal cursed himself for not thinking ahead. He had been so caught up in his excitement that he forgot about the deafening activation sound.

There was nothing he could do to stop it while it was in process, so Sal just hoped that it didn't cause any issues. He was tempted to go out to the corridor to see how bad the sound was from out there, but realized that opening the doors would make it worse. So, instead, he just stood there and hoped it would finish up whatever it was doing soon.

A painful two minutes of ear-splitting cracks resulted in an entire suite of materials being sent over. The first was a leather-like blanket that settled onto the floor. It had a cutout for the Hermes Dock, and it fit almost perfectly into the large square he had created with the rods. Sal wanted to tighten the rods to the blanket, but didn't want to interrupt what it was doing. Just like the micro-fiber blanket, this leather-like one had detailed sections for materials. Yet, Sal didn't need to do anything this time. Each crack had resulted in the sections being neatly filled with materials. Some were crystals, others were ingots; there was cabling and an entire wall of fabric that was secured in bolts.

To Sal's great surprise, his visor picked up a trove of scarlet screen and lords crystal among the piles. Just seeing that the rare material was on his living room floor was a massive surge of excitement. Moonsilver being in there too was enough to make Sal giddy. He had all the materials he needed if he ever wanted to remake the revolver.

If Sal thought there was nothing he could be more excited for, he would have been wrong. When the first commander core appeared on the mat, Sal felt as though he had won the lottery. When he counted five of them, he realized that there was likely a massive catch with all of this. There was no way that Doc Ameye was giving him all of this for free… the man definitely wanted something from him. The only question that remained was what that ask might be.

Seeing the collection growing by the second, Sal started to wonder just how wealthy Doc Ameye truly was. He knew that the Arkwright was capable of producing a veritable treasure trove of materials, but there was a limit. Commander cores weren't something that he could simply synthesize toward. Scarlet screen was exceedingly expensive, too. Yet, there were countless materials spawning into his living room that he had never seen before. His visor catalogued everything with record speed, and Sal got dizzy from just looking at it.

Eventually, the thunderstorm of light came to an end. The Hermes Dock was completely obscured by the stacks of ingots and racks of fabrics. Sal wondered whether it would have been smarter for him to create this in the workshop where he had more space… but it was too late for that. Well, he'd be able to relocate the dock if he actually needed to, but it looked like he was going to be doing his Crafting in the living room… or he'd be storing everything in Arsenal until he needed it.

He glanced over at the remaining two crates. One from Lawrence Baron and the other from the Argento Auction House. He could just take out everything and add them to the pile to see what he was working with. Sal started to move in that direction when he stopped, frowning.

"No," Sal breathed as he shook his head. "We're going to do this right." He opened Arsenal and looked at the meticulous setup of Doc Ameye's material transport. It had highlighted to him just how haphazard his own storage solutions had been up until now. Rather than just dumping everything into Arsenal, he wanted to create an actual floor plan. There were plenty of materials in Arsenal that he could use. It wasn't like he didn't have enough space in there.

The other limitation that Sal had been aware of was how naked he felt without his visor. Being in that infirmary for weeks would have been a lot more bearable if he had stocked Arsenal better. There were so many incredible things he could have made to make his life easier, but he had left them lying around the place in different workshops and storage areas. Arsenal needed to be kitted out properly if he was going to use it as it was intended. He was sure he could set Jackal to depositing materials in certain storage units, rather than just dumping it wherever.

Placing his hands on his hips, Sal thought about what he could do with the space in Arsenal. He thought about the storage they had in Maccles Materials, which had been excellent but cramped. Lining the walls with shelving and storage would be best. Separate bins for the different cores he got from dungeon runs, then a few fabric racks where he could store the various hides and skins of the demons. It felt like such a waste to use the good materials for something like shelves. He wasn't going to make a rack out of abyssal steel. It would end up being the most expensive rack in history.

Sal frowned as he stepped out of Arsenal, looking around for some inspiration. His eyes landed on the decorative bookshelf that lined the wall of his living room. It felt wrong to gut his own dorm for Arsenal, but a part of him was warming to the idea, especially considering he could always replace them later when he got access to some wood. He could end up replenishing his stocks with just a few dungeon runs.

"What if we made the units with prowler bone?" Sal asked aloud, chuckling. It would probably look menacing… but also completely unnecessary. He didn't need to overcomplicate everything. Surely there would be something suitable on the Credit floor. Wood or basic metal would do the job perfectly. Besides, he had a fine to pay.

Even if he didn't have the wood or bone to build the units, there was still plenty of space in Arsenal to hold the new materials from Doc Ameye. Sal started with the largest stuff first, and it was actually a good workout, taking the various metal ingots through to Arsenal. The trick was to physically place a material in a location and then tell his visor that the area around it was designated for that material type. Once it was done, he could then use Arsenal like Pocket and simply touch the stack of materials, sending it to the designated spot. It didn't stack them like he hoped, though.

It was only when Sal got frustrated with one of the hellfire titanium ingots and dropped it to the side, that he paused in confusion. Because it didn't fall. It was suspended in midair, where he had let go of it. Sal tentatively put his fingers around the edge of the ingot and immediately felt the weight of it as gravity seemed to resume around it. As an experiment, Sal set it in an empty space at eye level, and was both shocked and elated to see that it stood perfectly in place. There was no need for units! He could stack them wherever he wanted.

Sal was practically giddy at the new revelation and deactivated and reactivated Arsenal to check that the floating ingot didn't move. It hadn't budged from its location, and that was all that Sal needed to prove its usefulness.

Which then resulted in another hour of painstaking effort, organizing each and every material into a designated location. Judgment helped him optimize the spaces, and Sal was loving it. Knowing that he could literally summon every ingredient or material to his hand made this extra organization worth it. His supply of obsidian was almost completely depleted, but Sal didn't mind. He had scarlet screen and shadow glass, and a whole range of other great visor materials. There were fabrics that he never heard of that looked incredible. Some were scaly and reflective, while others looked feathered or stitched.

He was proud of himself for not breaking out of his trance by the opening of the other two chests. Sal was a man on a mission, and he put them into neat storage in Arsenal. It started to look like a menagerie of different colors and styles, and it looked ridiculously impressive. He had a whole section mapped out for each type of core that was farmed in dungeons. There were a series of empty sections that he was reserving for stronger demons in the future, with the commander core section making up the final area.

When he lifted the first commander core and entered Arsenal, a different prompt appeared on his visor. Sal stared at it for a few seconds, making sure he was interpreting it properly. And when the reality of the situation finally registered in his brain, a wide grin pulled at his lips. He brought in another two of the commander cores, hoping that the text would change.

Jackal has access to the required materials for the first stage of Evolution.

Stage 1: Commander Core (3/3), Plague Crest (2/2), Venomstone (8/8)

Would you like to proceed?

"Absolutely," Sal agreed with a laugh as he willed Jackal to start its evolution. It was saying that it was just the first stage, so Sal didn't hold out hope for anything truly spectacular. His instincts told him that it might improve the battery life because it was using the commander cores. Plague crest was something he got from Lawrence Baron, and the venomstone was from the Arkwright, sent in the chest from his father.

Sal waited for his arm to start to glow, but there were no special effects. All he got was a counter on his visor with a percentage, estimating the completion time for the evolution. His visor truly was the best when it came to managing expectations. Without it, Sal would have been pacing around the room for hours, wondering when it would happen.

8 hours 4 minutes 12 seconds.

Checking his tablet, Sal still had a little bit of time before his first set of classes. He glanced at the timer again and smiled. "We'll do a dungeon after class." He looked at his shoulder, where Jackal was hibernating. "And we'll see if there's any serious improvements. Sound good?"

There was no answer as Sal closed the Arsenal and made his way to the bathroom. He wanted another shower before he met with Jez for his first-ever Guild Mastery class.

CHAPTER 51: EXPECTATION

"Go on then, take a seat," Jez muttered as he gestured at the single chair and desk opposite his own. "We've got a lot to get through, and you'll likely need to take notes."

It wasn't a large classroom like Sal had expected, and instead was a small meeting room like he had with Sergeant Head. Jez was seated with a stack of notes in front of him, each adorned with countless scribbles along the edges highlighting his frustration or boredom. Sal took his seat and was a little unnerved at how he was the only person in the room.

Jez waited for him to get settled before he smiled. "Congratulations, Mr. Argento. Becoming a guildmaster is no easy feat, and to start off as a Tier 8 is an excellent vote of confidence from everyone concerned. I had a little visit from Villa, with claims that she's also one of your advisors." He chuckled, as though the thought were ridiculous. "I've got no idea how you managed such an eclectic lineup, but all you're missing are two powerhouses from the Defense and Healer classes."

"Would having more advisors be a good thing?" Sal flipped open the leather folio in front of him and picked up the provided pen. "I know they increase our head count, but would it become unmanageable if there are too many assessments from them?"

Jez's smile widened as he nodded. "Excellent thought, but a little flawed." He wagged his finger as he spoke, but it didn't feel like a lecture…more like a conversation. "As I explained during the registration of the guild, you'll have advisors who will be there to assess your capabilities as a Specialist guild. With Upgrade and Diva, you'll be assessed on your Supports and Controllers for special contracts. Bringing in the likes of Villa will open more opportunities, but would also raise the expectations of your Offensive capability. Anna Sakura won't be able to take on every contract, so you can't simply rely on her."

Sal nodded in understanding. "What would be your suggestion? I'd be leaning toward taking Villa's assistance as an advisor. I want my guild to have a strong Offensive capability. You said yourself that, at later tiers, we'll be required to step up in times of emergency." Sal was being serious. If he wanted to attract the best Heroes to his guild, then he needed to have something for everyone. If Villa was able to guide Sakura and help train her, then it would be an amazing win. He just needed to ensure there were no downsides to bringing Villa into the operation.

"Well, you've already accepted her into your guild with that bursary. I believe it was one of the conditions." Jez chuckled as he waved his hand over the document. "But I'd be suggesting you take her onboard. As an Offense class, myself, I can't stress how important it is to have someone like that in a time of crisis. Villa is an exceptional talent, and you would have bankrupted yourself a hundred times over if you tried to recruit her through the normal channels."

"And does she give us more head count?" Sal asked hopefully as he made a few notes. "You gave us five additional head count for Upgrade and Diva."

Jez nodded. "Normally, yes; but we haven't seen any benefit to the head count you've been established with. My advice would be to work with the people you have and build toward a higher head count after meeting a few metrics." He lifted a sheet from in front of him and raised it for Sal to see. "These are the dungeons that we ask our Trainee Guilds to complete. I know you've done a few here and there, but you'll need to dispatch a minimum of two hundred leechers and fifty prowlers. Demonic head counts are averaged, so a completed dungeon will give you a set number unless you produce proof of more kills."

Jez pointed at the top of the list. "You'll also need to have a registered uniform for your guild members, but this is only really scrutinized for Specialist Combat contracts and battle-readiness during times of crisis. For a Trainee Guild, we ask that you have Common-grade equipment with at least one defensive ability. You can request these uniforms through the United Guilds Association, or you can create them yourself."

"And if our uniforms were Epic grade?" Sal paused his notetaking. "You already know that I'll be Crafting the uniforms in-house. They'll likely have evolutionary runes, too. With at least the capability of reaching Legendary grade."

With a nod, Jez's finger traced three-quarters of the way down the page. "That would be sufficient for Tier 2. Higher if the uniforms can actually get to Legendary. It's only one aspect of the requirement list, but would be an extraordinary feat. At those levels, we would ask for abilities to reflect the specialist teams: Controller, Support, and Offensive abilities." He smiled as he pointed at Sal. "Just know that we assess on the current state, rather than what it could eventually become. That rifle you made for the Reavers would be counted as Legendary grade."

A sudden thought occurred to Sal. "Wait, did the Legendary grade give the Reavers a better chance of getting to Tier 1?"

Jez grinned. "Correct. It's an Offense-class weapon, so it gave them a great boost. They're now able to take on more difficult specialist contracts that required a Legendary-grade weapon. When they finish a few more of them, they'll be granted the highest tier status."

Sal tried not to get ahead of himself. Knowing that he'd be able to easily make uniforms for his team was great… but it didn't guarantee him a place in the higher tiers. He looked down at his notes for a few seconds before asking his next question.

"Epic-grade uniforms aside, what are the rest of the requirements for the Mythic Guild to be considered a real Tier 8? And, follow-up question, what do we need to achieve to become a Tier 7?" He didn't want to get to the higher tiers on a technicality. If he could make the Mythic Guild a powerhouse, then it would make other guilds second-guess themselves if they tried to mess with him and his friends.

Jez placed the page back on his desk before folding his arms and leaning back in the chair. "You have a few avenues available to you." One of his hands peeked out from under an elbow, a single finger raised. "First, you do everything by the book. You could blitz through all the requirements from the earlier tiers, and it would give you a lot more credibility as an organization. Your individual capability is extraordinary, but it is your guild that is being assessed. The world will look at you and your advisors, and people will naturally assume that you're being artificially boosted through the rankings."

A second finger appeared beside the first. "Second option is that you start performing at Tier 8. You take on contracts and complete them, both efficiently and effectively. That would highlight that you're deserving of the current tier. The risk is that you're not yet equipped or trained for those contracts. It would require quite a bit of preparation and would rely heavily on your senior members and advisors."

Jez's third finger arrived with a grin. "Third option is that you do both, concurrently. Keep everyone in the Mythic Guild busy. Have the specialists working on contracts, and the generalists working on clearing the basic dungeons. The Q-Cred will start pouring in, and you'll gain a lot of credibility and respect within the United Guilds Association."

Sal nodded as he continued to make notes. "I'm leaning toward the third option. But I'm curious; how much should I care about the credibility aspect? If we're doing everything right, shouldn't it come naturally, or will other guilds want us to fail because we started at Quest Academy?"

Jez blinked in surprise. "Credibility and reputation are the pillars of the United Guilds Association. If they can't trust you to complete contracts, they won't issue them to you. A strong track record will give you preferential treatment, which is vital for growth and climbing through the tiers. If you look at the likes of Paradox, they could lay claim to any newly secured territory and the United Guilds Association would honor it. They could claim delving rights to any portal they wanted, and they'd leave with over ninety percent of the spoils."

He laughed as though it were obvious, but not in a mocking manner. Jez was emphatic in his reasoning, his tone passionate. "That sort of authority can only be earned by building a successful brand. Competition is rife, and that's what the association is encouraging. All the other Tier 1 guilds will be trying to dethrone the likes of Paradox by performing to the highest level. Contributions to war efforts, securing hostile territory, clearing towers and portals, saving civilians… it all adds up and counts toward your reputation and standing within the Association."

Sal's hand glided across the page, Perfect helping him take immaculate notes without a single mistake. It was all making sense, and Sal underlined the importance of building a successful brand and reputation. He wanted to know more about the contracts that would be open to them, and wondered whether the Mythic Guild would be able to make a strong name for itself on the back of Crafting projects. From what he had learned so far, they rewarded a volume-based approach rather than a single creation. Maybe the mass-production of the Myth Mask would shift those odds?

"You said that we'd need to kill a commander class to get to Tier 7?" Sal looked up from his notes. "What other thresholds need to be reached, in terms of killing demons?"

Jez tilted his head to one side. "If you're thinking that Sakura will be able to take on a commander by herself, you should reconsider. Commander class demons are capable of utilizing abilities, just like us. Not knowing what you're going up against is a death sentence unless you have a trained team of Heroes to support you. For all their bloodthirst, even Villa would advise against such a course of action until you were ready."

A moment of silence washed over the room before Jez let out a sigh and threw a folio into the air. "Here is the list of dungeons and more specifically, the list of demons you should work on taking out. Don't be intimidated by the numbers. You'll be working toward those figures over your time at Quest Academy."

Sal watched as the thrown folio opened in midair with its pages fluttering. It glided in a natural arc before sliding onto his desk from the left, landing perfectly center in front of him. A ridiculously impressive feat that had nothing to do with Jez's power. He had seen the lightning-style powers he had used during the raid in the first semester.

"As your Guild Mastery lecturer, I'll be offering you guidance and advice on how to move through the tiers." He gestured at the page in front of Sal. "But I won't know how to make a plan for you until you get started on that list. When I know what we're working with, I'll be able to adjust accordingly."

Looking down at the open pages, Sal noted the key aspects he and the guild needed to work on. Jez hadn't been lying about the chasm of expectation between a Trainee Guild and Tier 7. Rather than listing them out by tier requirement, all of them had been combined into totals.

- Leechers Killed: 1,000
- Prowlers Killed: 400
- Voiders Killed: 100
- Hulkers Killed: 20
- Commanders Killed: 1

There was also a list of forty separate dungeons that needed to be completed. Sal scanned through them and didn't recognize any of the names. Most of them were located in areas of the city he hadn't visited before. A detail that Sal quite liked was the recommended head count and team composition suggestion. There were even notes for what sort of equipment should be worn and highlighted information on known variants and evolved demons.

"This is incredible." Sal moved to the next page, which detailed effective strategies for the listed dungeons. "It almost feels like cheating." He laughed awkwardly as he continued to flip through the dossier.

"Well, we don't want people dying." Jez chuckled. "You'll have your own preparations to do and insights you can add to that dossier over time. We treat them as shared resources, where we build on our knowledge base and distribute it to our members. The Tier 1's are the guilds that go into these situations almost blind. At the lowest tiers, you'll have an insane amount of context and resources to help guide you. It becomes vaguer as you climb the ranks, but your experience will always keep you sharp. That's why we insist that guilds don't skip through the tiers. You should be learning as much as you can."

Sal made a few notes as he nodded. "Got it. Do you have any homework for me before our next meeting?"

Jez barked a laugh as he shook his head. "You can get started on your uniforms, I guess? You won't be approved to enter any of those dungeons without the right equipment. If you end up doing one of those crazy all-nighters in the workshop to get your equipment made… then, I'd urge you to take on a low-level leecher dungeon with your teams. Learn how to work together in a low-stakes environment. We want incremental gains, Salvatore. This isn't a race to the finish line. Is that understood?"

"Understood," Sal agreed as he dotted the last period of his notes, smiling. "I will warn you in advance, though. We have some serious heavy hitters on the team."

Jez grinned before he waved in the direction of the door. "This class will be quite flexible. Since you're catching up to others in terms of course content, we can't bring you into the third-year class until you catch up. We'll meet every two weeks to assess your progress, but can meet more regularly if you need it. You have a lot of work ahead of you."

"Thank you." Sal smiled as he closed his folio and got to his feet. "I'll let you know if I've got any questions."

"Please do." Jez snapped his own folio shut, returning the smile. "Because if people come for my head when you die in a dungeon, I need a record that I tried to stop you."

CHAPTER 52: SECRETS

Rather than head back to the dorms for the break between classes, Sal went to the main canteen with his new folio so he could learn more about the dungeons he'd be expected to clear. He was going to be doing a dungeon run later, so he figured that there would be no harm in taking on one of the entries on the list.

"You hate the food in the Savior canteen, too?" Blathnaid laughed as she sat across from Sal with a tray of food in her hands. "Oh, what are you reading?"

Sal smiled as he placed a finger on the spot he had just been reading. "Hey, yeah… I just thought I'd come here to do a bit of reading before the next class. It's like a codex of sorts for all the dungeons the guild needs to do, with all sorts of information."

"Oooh, are we doing a guild run, soon?" Blathnaid asked excitedly as she leaned forward to get a better look. "I'm super curious what sort of teams we'll have. Do I need to sign a contract or something?"

Sal nodded as he lifted out his tablet. "It's actually a lot more straightforward than that. Vanessa worked on the contracts with my dad. I can send it across to you, but there's still a few things we need to work out before we get official signatures."

Blathnaid waved her hand like it was no big deal. "I trust you guys, so don't worry about it. If Upgrade signs it, I know it'll be a good deal." She practically beamed as she looked between the folio and Sal's face. "Have you gone to see her yet?"

Sal frowned. "I actually got the impression she was avoiding me. I haven't seen her properly since I got out of the infirmary, except for the Guild signing thing. Everything has been hectic since, and she was doing dungeons with Fabi nonstop."

"That's… not what's happening." Blathnaid laughed awkwardly as she shook her head slowly. "Upgrade felt bad about your accident. I know it's not my place to speak for her, but I know she was angry. I thought the dungeon stuff was just stress relief, but she was apparently looking for a very specific material."

"Was it something for the mask I asked her to make?" Sal asked, pretty sure he knew what was going on.

"The mask?" Blathnaid repeated slowly, clearly confused. "No, this was for the beret. The mask has been done for a few weeks now."

"Beret?" Sal repeated in the exact same fashion. "Wait… what are they making a beret for?" He suddenly felt very unsure of himself. Weren't they looking for the white leecher core that had a purifying ability? What was this about a beret?

Blathnaid's eyes widened. "Wait, they didn't tell you *anything*?"

Sal laughed as he placed both palms on the table. "Okay, I hate to do this… but I'm pulling rank as guildmaster. Can you please tell me what's going on? I have no idea what's happening."

Blathnaid pointed at his tablet on the table. "But I didn't sign officially, so I guess I don't have to tell you?" She offered a slight shrug, before a guilty smile won out after a few seconds. "A few hints shouldn't hurt, though?"

With an exasperated sigh, Sal's head slumped forward. "Okay, I'll settle for hints. Can you at least vaguely tell me what's going on?"

Blathnaid folded her arms, her eyes practically sparkling with excitement. "Okay, okay, but you have to act really surprised when you see it all, okay? Promise that, and I'll give you a few clues."

"I promise." Sal laughed as he rotated his hand, urging her to get on with it.

"Okay, you knew about the material they were trying to get in the dungeon? It's a special leecher core," Blathnaid said in a hushed whisper, as though she had just revealed the mother lode of gossip. "It might drop once in a few hundred kills, so really super rare."

Sal's smile tightened. He already knew that part, but he wasn't going to ruin Blathnaid's fun. Instead, he just listened quietly, nodding her along.

"The normal form of that core wasn't good enough, so Fabi asked your parents if she could use the Arkwright. They were in on this, too. Just so you know." Blathnaid laughed at the surprised expression on Sal's face.

"The thing is…they needed a lot of those special cores. So, it took them awhile to get enough. Apparently, the machine was able to make a super special core. That's what they used for the set!"

"Set?" Sal repeated the word back to her. "I just asked for a mask, though. Why are they going to so much trouble to make a set?" He was trying to figure out what Upgrade and Fabi were thinking. Even if they felt bad about what happened to him, which wasn't their fault, it didn't make sense for them to go to so much trouble on his behalf.

Blathnaid put up both of her palms defensively. "Don't shoot the messenger!" She laughed as she picked up her fork and poked at her salad. "You gave Upgrade a project to work on, and it sort of inspired the set. The initial beret was my design, because the cowl thing they had would have looked ridiculous on you. It's gone through a few different iterations since then, but I think you'll like it. The mask works sort of like a collar that can be activated to cover your nose and mouth. It requires the rest of the set to activate, though." Her gaze darted toward his left arm, before she lowered it to regard her salad.

Sal let out a sigh as he looked at Blathnaid, exasperated. "So, you're saying that the Strategist's Dominion that Upgrade worked on… is now a jacket? And there's a beret to go along with the new collar mask?"

Blathnaid paused for a second in confusion. "And an eye-patch. Fabi said you liked hers, so she made you one… and the jacket isn't a jacket." With that said, Blathnaid happily ate her food, glancing up at Sal between bites, as though waiting for his verdict.

"When you say it's not a jacket… does it still cling to the body?" Sal was trying to figure out how the bodysuit could have possibly been converted to something other than the skintight material. Did it mean she got rid of all the essence signatures when she was altering it?

Blathnaid shook her head. "No? Well, yes… but it's stylistic, if that makes sense? The right arm is designed to match your left arm. Initially, we couldn't settle on a color palette because we didn't know what the guild's color scheme would be." She thought about it for a few seconds, before blinking, as though suddenly realizing the other part of the question. "Oh, and don't worry…it can totally do the things it could do before. The bullet changing summon thing, and the lightning."

Sal couldn't believe what he was hearing. He had been curious about Upgrade's work on the Mythmark, and the result wasn't just a new bodysuit, but something else entirely? If it could still summon the weapons, and could even use Ravage... that would be incredible. He was a little confused by Blathnaid's understanding of his *bullet changing summon thing*. Not to mention whatever the jacket/non-jacket was.

"I'll admit, I'm kinda speechless." Sal laughed as he sat back in his chair, the folio in front of him forgotten. "I didn't need an eye-patch, or a beret... so this is a little beyond expectations. I'm really curious about the shirt now."

Blathnaid continued eating, a smile dancing on her lips.

Sal folded his arms as he looked off to one side. "And the mask... I really want to Appraise it. I can't figure out why Alex wanted to make the Mastery elixir for it. I thought it would be a Healing one, instead."

"Oh," Blathnaid interjected with a guilty laugh, before she put a hand up to cover her mouth. "Sorry, still eating..." When she pulled her hand away after finishing, she smiled excitedly. "That's why the set is important. It's not a conventional set where everything works together, but rather... a combination of beneficial things? Ha, being vague is kinda tough. I don't know the logic with the Mastery elixir thing, but Upgrade was the one who created the blueprints that needed it."

Sal could only shake his head with a bemused expression. "Would it spoil the surprise if I went to have a look at it? Do you think Upgrade and Fabi are ready for me to see it?"

Blathnaid nodded slowly. "Yeah, they've been working on the neck brace... so it's mostly just finishing touches at this point. I'd still check in with them, though." She paused as she looked at him almost sheepishly. "You don't look very excited. Are you disappointed?"

Sal shook his head, smiling gently. "Not at all. I just hate the idea that they've been killing themselves working on all this stuff that I might not need." He offered a helpless sort of shrug. "I really do appreciate the work and time they've put into it, but I think my visor is perfect as it is. If I end up not needing it, then it'll mean they've worked themselves to the bone for close to a month for nothing."

"Ahh." Blathnaid seemed to finally understand, but she continued to smile. "If that's all you're worried about, then we're going to be fine."

"I'm sensing that you're not taking this seriously," Sal said in surprise. "Should I take it that you're just really confident that I'll like the beret and... neck brace?"

Blathnaid nodded enthusiastically as she paired up her knife and fork on the half-empty plate. "Yeah, I'm really confident. Even if it *was* useless—and it's not—you'd want to wear it all because of how it looks. That, I can guarantee."

Sal folded his arms and raised an eyebrow. "Come on then, tell me what I'm missing." He was enjoying this side of Blathnaid. It was a fun part of her personality, and he liked seeing her confident in her own capabilities.

"Well… for a start, the color scheme. Your dad gave Fabi and Upgrade a few ingots of silver, which was a massive deal, apparently. Upgrade freaked the fuck out when she saw them. We paired it with the black tone of the uniforms and that suit you gave Upgrade to fix. Then, we used the purple for Supports." Blathnaid was practically giddy as she described it, using her hands to indicate where the different colors appeared on her own torso. "If you decide you'd prefer a different color, we can definitely work on changing it, but it looks ridiculously good and should even work on your left arm."

"I want to see this." Sal closed the folio in front of him. "You said that it's in the Savior workshop?"

Blathnaid hesitated for a second, before she finally rooted through her pocket for her tablet. "Yes, but at least let me warn Upgrade and Fabi. We've got a little group set up for the project, so I can message them both now." She turned the tablet quickly to give Sal a glance. "And your dad is in it, too. He's been so helpful with a lot of the practical stuff."

Sal just stared at her, not really comprehending what he was hearing. "He didn't say anything to me about this…"

"*Because it was a surprise?*" Blathnaid laughed awkwardly. "Seriously, though. We all thought you'd go straight to the workshop when you got out. Your dad sent us a message last night that he finished sparring with you and that you'd probably turn up in the workshop. Hell, Divinity pinged me to say that you were definitely going to be Crafting."

The fact that Divinity knew he was going to Craft was somewhat entertaining. He did feel bad that he kept them waiting, but only a little. They could have just called him to tell him to go to the workshop and he would have met them there. He fought the urge to apologize, and thankfully, Blathnaid interjected before he could.

"I was going to message you to come to us, or just knock on your door… but Fabi insisted we let you get rest if that's what you needed," Blathnaid explained, sighing. "But the main thing is that we want to be there when you see it."

Sal was still standing with the folio. "Don't suppose now is a good time?"

Blathnaid stared at him in confusion. "We have class in like, twenty minutes. Ethical Crafting?"

The tablet on the table vibrated, causing Blathnaid to break eye contact and check her messages. She stared at it for a few seconds before a giddy laugh escaped her lips. "Guess class is being postponed?"

Sal plucked his own tablet from his pocket as he felt a vibration. He opened the message to see an important notice.

Quest Academy Administration

- o   Ethical Crafting Class is postponed until next week.
- o   Reading materials will be sent out later this afternoon.

"Oh, that's strange timing." Sal laughed as he showed Blathnaid his tablet. It vibrated again in his hand, and when he turned it around to look at the screen, he saw a new message from Upgrade.

Upgrade: I canceled your next class. Come up to the workshop in the Savior dorms!

Blathnaid grinned as she picked up her tray. "I'm not even surprised… She's been dying to show you for weeks."

CHAPTER 53: SURPRISE

Sal wasn't sure what to expect when he got up to the workshop. Blathnaid had been practically bouncing in excitement, peppering him with questions throughout the short journey. She was eager for him to guess the attributes of the new armor, and no matter how outlandish he had been with his responses, she was confident that the reality was far superior. The problem Sal faced was that Blathnaid wasn't Barry. She didn't unnecessarily hype things up, and she wasn't the type to lie. It was pretty difficult for him to manage his own expectations after just a few minutes of listening to her.

"Also, if you don't like the design… don't worry. I've got a few different approaches lined up for the next iteration." Blathnaid smiled as she walked alongside him. "We wanted your version to look the best out of all of them, for obvious reasons."

Sal looked at her strangely. He wasn't sure what she meant by iterations. The set was adapted from the Strategist's Dominion outfit, so there would only be one chance at fixing it up. Why was she so convinced that there would be iterations? Clearly the question was written all over his face, because Blathnaid's smile faltered ever so slightly. Rather than having her think he was annoyed, Sal smiled as he gestured for her to continue. "Sorry, I was just wondering what you meant by iterations. I only gave Upgrade one suit to work on."

Realization dawned on Blathnaid's face before the bright smile returned with a vengeance. "Oh, we've been looking at the designs as a potential uniform for the guild. Obviously we wouldn't go ahead with anything without your say-so, but we just thought it could be a fun project while you were in the infirmary." She gestured at herself. "Besides, we pretty much have everyone's measurements. It was a fun challenge to tweak the designs to suit individual members, though. I learned so much about material composition for creating specific ability types."

Sal scratched at the back of his head and let out an awkward chuckle. "Wow… between this and the elixir machine, you've all been really busy while I was away." He brought his hand down with a resigned sigh. "But, it's not a bad thing. I'm grateful for all the help, and you're the one I'd trust most when it comes to uniform design."

Blathnaid waved her hand like it was nothing. "Come on, if you hadn't been locked away for so long, you would have revolutionized something else at Quest Academy. We have a running joke in the workshop about how you'd solve all the problems in the world. My personal favorite is one where you make the Darwin Cruises into airships."

"Airships?" Sal repeated the word slowly, not really sure how he should respond. "Lifting an entire cruise ship out of the water… so it could fly?"

"Yeah… that was Jack's idea. Yes, it's ridiculous, but we all really enjoyed it. It's been a week, but Alex is still giving him shit about it." Blathnaid practically cackled. It was an uncharacteristic level of wicked mirth, and it strangely suited her. She glanced at Sal before smiling warmly. "But we were just playing around when making those jokes. All of us know how crazy skilled you are, and with enough time and materials, there's very little you wouldn't be able to accomplish."

Sal tilted his head slightly to the side, his tone one of disbelief. "Ahhh, I'm not so sure about airships, though. That seems a little outside my comfort zone."

"Oh no, you have to tell Jack that it's possible. With a completely serious face. Please, just do it when I'm there to witness it!" Blathnaid laughed as she came to a stop outside the workshop room. "And we're here! Any last-minute guesses?"

Sal spread his hands wide and offered a good-natured shrug. "No matter what I say, you're going to tell me that the super-secret equipment is way better."

"Because it is," Blathnaid said sweetly as she opened the door, stepping through to the workshop with a dramatic flourish of her hands.

Sal couldn't help but marvel at how assured she was in relation to the new uniform. Even the Legendary coat that she made with Upgrade didn't get this sort of treatment. When he followed her into the workshop, he was greeted with a strange sight. It wasn't the equipment, which he guessed would be in one of the frosted cubicles. It was the loading area that opened out in front of him. What had previously been a mixture of containers and a half-finished drone dock… was now an industrial-grade factory! It looked like a brand-new setup, with equipment that would put even the Arkwright to shame.

Sure, he didn't know what any of it could do yet, but from just a first glance, he could tell that it was impressive. The cubicle that he had requested for himself, that had access to the landing bay…was almost completely walled off. An enormous metal frame had been embedded into the exterior glass, in a strangely door-like fashion. Even without an Appraisal, Sal could tell that Fabi had taken his idea for a drone door and made it a reality.

He continued to look around in astonishment. The heavy machinery didn't resemble anything familiar at first, but it was only when he walked into the loading bay and looked up that he saw the enormous mechanical arms poised at the ready. They were so menacing in appearance that Sal stopped in his tracks and his heart raced. Multitools on automated arms, each of them attached to floor mounted weights… that were connected by cables to the drone dock. It was so big that Sal was certain it could build a car-sized drone.

"Oh, did I forget to tell you about all this?" Blathnaid asked with a knowing smile. "See? I did manage to leave some things a surprise!"

"This is incredible…" Sal practically whispered as he tried to look at everything. There were so many consoles giving off readings, and there didn't look to be much space left for any materials. "Where do you get deliveries?" He practically laughed as he gestured at the lack of floor space around them.

Blathnaid pointed at the newly fashioned metal window. "That's where the deliveries come through."

Sal frowned as he followed her gesture. "So, that's not for a drone?"

Blathnaid laughed as she turned to the original loading bay. "No… the drones need the big door for the flight tests."

"Drones," Sal repeated slowly, looking at her to detect whether she was joking. "Plural?"

"Yep, they're pretty ungainly… but they're getting a lot better. They're not docked, so they must be out doing flight tests?" Blathnaid guessed aloud before she pointed to one of the cubicles above. "Upgrade is powering them up with a super rare set of cores. Not that you'd know anything about that?" She gave him a mischievous look, as though asking him to confirm her suspicions.

Sal was immediately reminded of the void seeker core that he had gifted to her for the drone arm. Had she somehow found a way to harness its power as a battery? A small part of him was disappointed that she had used it for something other than the design he made for her… but a larger part of him was annoyed at himself for getting injured in the first place. If he had been around, he would have managed to build that Mythic with her. It was just like her to use something for others rather than herself.

Still, even if that was the case, he'd be able to make another void seeker with the Arkwright. Material synthesis only required a few buckets of voider cores, so it wouldn't be a huge hassle. He was going to be doing a dungeon later, so maybe Jackal would be able to secure some for him.

"Are you spacing out?" Blathnaid laughed. "Sorry, I didn't mean to give you a hard time about the plates. I know it was you because it's the same ones from the Genesis station."

"Oh, she just used the plates?" Sal let out a sigh of relief. "I was worried she used the super-secret thing I made for her."

The look of desperate curiosity on Blathnaid's face was a just reward. It was a fun way to pay her back for all the guessing games.

She eventually smiled guiltily before shaking her head with a light laugh. "All right then, keep your secrets."

Sal laughed as he gestured at the cubicles above them. "So, which one of these has the new equipment?" He pointed at one at random, as though it might be correct.

Blathnaid shook her head as she practically skipped over to the nearest stairwell. "Nope. This way, please." She gestured with her arm for him to follow as she took the stairs two at a time.

He followed her, still looking over the railing to see the massive drone dock from a higher angle. He found himself wondering whether it was limited to just drones, because it genuinely looked like it could build a new car. Was Fabi running through dungeons to get materials just to build this thing? Was it for the Sovereign drone? He had a thousand questions and not enough answers. Even if the uniform wasn't to his tastes, he was excited to find out more about their drone progress.

When Blathnaid opened the door, she barely got out of the way in time as Upgrade launched herself at Sal, wrapping him in a bear hug that knocked the air out of his lungs. He could barely wheeze a hello.

Upgrade pulled herself off him and gripped his shoulders tight. "First of all, I've missed you." She smiled dangerously at him. "Secondly—but more importantly—if your eyes start bleeding during a build… stop the damn build!"

"Noted." Sal half chuckled, half wheezed as he placed his hands over Upgrade's. "I appreciate the concern, but it was as much a surprise to me as it was to all of you. I don't want to go near that infirmary again, I promise."

It looked like it took Upgrade a few seconds to register the words, before she chuckled and let go of his shoulders. "Sorry for the dramatic attack. I just needed to distract you real quick."

"Distract me?" Sal questioned her as he looked over her shoulder to see Fabi adjusting the beret on the mannequin that had been hastily dressed. "Oh…"

"That's why." Upgrade laughed as she stepped to the side to give him a proper look at the new build. "Fabi refused to spear tackle you, so I had to do the honors."

"Feeling better?" Fabi asked with a concerned smile as she stepped away from the mannequin.

Sal barely heard them as he numbly took a step closer to the equipment. Blathnaid's description hadn't done it justice at all. He could barely find the words to describe it himself. Thankfully, he was surrounded by the people who made it.

"The epaulettes are my favorite part," Fabi said in response to Sal's lack of reaction. She moved to point at the gunmetal-silver plates on each shoulder that rose into a decoratively flared high collar. Her fingers lifted the plates to show where it attached to the black and silver layered chest-piece. "It might look restrictive, but we've ensured that all the articulation points throughout the build have mechanical segmentation."

Upgrade snorted. "It's a fancy way of saying you'll be able to move perfectly while wearing it. Your dad was a great help in testing the fit."

Sal was so transfixed that all he could manage was a nod. The chest-piece was fashioned like an inverted triangle, with broad shoulders that tapered into a narrow waist. The pectorals and abdominal shape were aesthetically pronounced, but not enough to look unnatural. Each set of muscle groups looked to be layered on, with purple fabric as the base, black metal for the plates, and silver for the accents. The metallic design looked almost cybernetic, with a high-polished texture.

"We went with a royal purple because you're in the Support class, and it goes well with your eyes when you're Mythcrafting," Upgrade added as she walked into view and gestured at the color scheme. "Black and purple worked well together, and we used the silver accents sparingly. Blathnaid went ahead and designed it like a general's coat, and the style really worked out nicely." She gestured at the striking metal epaulettes that covered the shoulders.

It definitely gave a militaristic vibe, especially with the layer of purple and black fabric that hung off the back of the left shoulder. Sal assumed it was only visible because there was no left arm on this new set. The metal shoulder plates just hovered over empty air on that side.

Sal had to force himself to look at Upgrade and not the new uniform. "What part of this is the Mythmark?"

"All of it." Upgrade grinned broadly. "You'll see when you give it an Appraisal. You're able to handle Legendary grade, right?" A touch of concern carried into her voice as she looked at Blathnaid for the answer. Like she didn't trust Sal to be truthful.

Whistling to himself absentmindedly, Sal had thought it would be a faint noise of surprise… but he forgot about the effects of Perfect, and the practice he had with whistling in the dungeon with his father. The result was an ear-piercing assault that had everyone covering their ears.

Sal winced instantly. "Sorry…"

Upgrade laughed as she continued to hold her hands near her ears, as though worried there might be another whistle. "Your Mythmark was flawed, but there was no way I was letting Ravage and Assimilate go to waste. I don't want to even tell you how long it took to make it work with this build." Her voice was much louder, probably as a punishment for his audible warfare on her ears. "As it stands, you can now shoot purple lightning from your hands… even though you probably won't want to."

Sal stared at her until she brought her hands down from her ears. It didn't look like she was going to elaborate, so he played along. "Why wouldn't I want to shoot lightning from my hands?"

"*Purple lightning*," Fabi corrected almost reproachfully. "It took a *lot* of work to make the color array play nice."

Upgrade pointed at the right arm of the new build. Well, the only arm. "Ask me about this." Her smile seemed to grow wider.

"What does the arm do?" Sal laughed as he shook his head. "Other than shoot *purple* lightning… which sounds amazing, by the way."

"Thank you." Fabi sighed from her perch on a worktable.

"First, you're going to need this." Upgrade smiled as she handed him a ridiculously detailed eye-patch.

The stretchy material at the back was the exact same fabric he used for the Mythmark, but the front was something he had never seen before. In a sea of glossy black metal, there was a single *M* lasered in a purple finish into the face of the eye-patch. Looking at it closely, Sal could see the tiny runes that had been meticulously etched into the metal, all filled in the same purple coloring. He didn't recognize any of them, but they looked ridiculously stylish. Sal cradled it in his hands as he turned it over to check the back of it, wondering how his right eye would manage to see through solid metal.

"Before you start looking at me, that was very much designed by Jack and Upgrade," Fabi highlighted with a smile, causing Sal to look over at her in surprise. "I helped a bit with the essence programming." She shrugged before gesturing at the armor. "My contributions are mostly the stuff you can't see."

Blathnaid snorted at that, before bringing her hand up to her mouth in surprise. When Sal looked in her direction, she let out an awkward giggle. "Sorry, but Fabi did just as much as Upgrade… and that's saying something."

Sal smiled as he brought the eye-patch over his head carefully, stretching it out at the back and sliding the metal plate in front of his right eye socket. "I love it already."

"Ooooh, you look like a Villain!" Upgrade clapped excitedly. "Slicked black hair and an eye-patch. Nobody is going to believe he's a Support." She chuckled as she lifted the beret away from the mannequin.

When Sal reached out to take it from her, she shook her head. "Sorry, but this isn't for you. Fabi put the wrong one on the doll."

Fabi shrugged, like it was no big deal. "We've gone through too many iterations. They all look the same to me at this point."

Sal was a little confused. First of all, he was able to see clearly through the eye-patch… like, crystal clear. With just a little effort, he knew he could hyperfocus on something in the distance. Yet, in that very moment, he was looking at the Legendary-grade beret that Upgrade was packing into a box. His eye-patch was certain that it was a lower-tier Legendary grade. Was Upgrade sure that was the wrong one?

Upgrade rifled through the box until she found what she was looking for. When she turned around, she held a peaked officer's cap… sporting a glossy black visor and made with a lustrous velvet material. There was a tasteful silver trim around the edges, and it looked positively regal. Upgrade laughed at Sal's stupefied expression as she reached up to place it on his head. "Can't have the guildmaster wearing a beret. Those are for the other members of the Mythic Guild."

Sal was about to answer her when the cap landed on his head, and a wave of pleasant energy pulsated through his body. It melted away the remaining fatigue from the sparring session with his dad, and it brought a sense of alertness that put Alex's coffee to shame. If Sal was to try to describe it, it was like he had the Calm effect active, while drinking restorative coffee… during a Healing session from Doctor Bob. All of that happened in a split second, leaving him both speechless and refreshed.

Upgrade smiled warmly at him. "I hope you don't mind, but we needed to borrow the Arkwright for a bit."

CHAPTER 54: CAPE

Sal could only stare at the suit in front of him. His mind was clearer than he could remember for a very long time. There was no emotional imbalance like when he was using the Moonsilver Monocle for the Calm effect. Rather, it was like he had woken up from a wonderful sleep, and was ready to seize the day. The peculiar aspect of it all was that he never realized how tired he was, until he wasn't.

Yet, as amazing as the restorative effects were with his peaked cap, he couldn't help but be astounded with what was in front of him. The eye-patch took all the heavy lifting out of the Appraisal, so all he had to do was look at it for a few seconds before the information flowed in front of his eye. What was a little unnerving was how the essence programming in the eye-patch manifested. Sal didn't know enough about essence programming to understand what he was seeing, but it was clearly loaded into the piece of gear, probably by Fabi or Upgrade.

Name	Tempest Marshal (Guildmaster Variant)
Origin	Crafted (Rework)
Age	New
Grade	Legendary (Upper)
Materials	Refined Upgrade Essence | Refined Figment Essence | Refined Construct Essence | Hastium | Storm Steel | Venomstone | Broodweave | Veilstone | Tempest Steel Alloy | Onyx Catalyzer | Obelisk Core | Eternal Core…

Attributes	Automate: Integrated functionality of Tempest Marshal Set will be activated either by will or automatically when conditions are met.
	
	• Tempest Marshal (Inactive)
	   o **Stratagem Function:** Requires Jackal Drone
	   o **Assimilate Function:** Requires Capacitor + Overdrive
	   o **Tempest Function**: Requires Assimilate Function
	   o **Manifest Function:** Requires Capacitor + Overdrive
	
	Overdrive: Drastically increases the output potential of inherent and equipped abilities. Overdrive will place a great

	strain on the user and equipment if they are incapable of handling the output. Regenerate: Passively converts all available internal essence for healing purposes. Depending on how much essence is available, fatal wounds can be treated. • Fatigue Mode: Minor Internal Healing • Training Mode: Internal + External Healing • Combat Mode: Major Internal + External Healing • Calamity Mode: Regeneration
Abilities	Automate | Overdrive | Regenerate | Ravage (Inherited) | Assimilate (Inherited)
Runes	Advanced Calibration Rune | Advanced Reinforcement Rune | Advanced Supercharge Rune | Advanced Overcharge Rune | Advanced Catalyst Rune
Power Source	Requires Capacitor
Evolution	No
Quality	Perfect
Condition	100%
Value	Unknown

"You know, usually at the end of the Appraisal, I'm the guy with all the answers." Sal laughed awkwardly as he continued to stare at the armor in front of him. "But I have no idea what I'm looking at. There are so many locked functions and prerequisites, and I don't normally see any of that in an Appraisal."

Fabi let out a sigh of relief. "Thank fuck it works." Her shoulders sagged as she looked at the ceiling in silent victory.

"What she means to say…" Upgrade interjected, chuckling. "Is that we specifically wanted you to *see* the essence programming… which was an endeavor, to put it lightly." A warm smile appeared as she moved over to stand beside Sal. "Just point at the things you don't understand and the three of us will do our best to explain it."

Sal was about to shrug and tell her to explain all of it, but decided against it after seeing the excitement on her face. "Okay… I recognize Automate from the Mythmark outfit I gave you. I can see Assimilate in there too, but as a function.

Overdrive looks like it's designed to kill me and destroy my gear. I thought that maybe it was a plan to equip gear with evolutionary runes to trap the overflow of essence, but there's no evolutionary rune on it?"

Fabi perked up at those words. "Oh shit."

Sal gave her a confused look. "What's wrong?"

Fabi looked at him with a wry smile. "Well, it's just... that's a really good idea. We didn't even think of that."

"Then, if that wasn't the reason, why do you have Overdrive as part of the build? Don't get me wrong, it sounds amazing... well, if I didn't have a very recent history of overloading myself." Sal laughed as he looked over at Upgrade to see her reaction, and to his surprise, she looked very happy with herself.

She tilted her head slightly to the left. "Don't suppose you had a chance to visit Alex to see what he's been working on?" Her smile was suddenly quite meaningful, where she nodded along to see whether Sal would connect the dots.

It didn't take him long. Upgrade had insisted that Alex work on a Mastery elixir... which would likely negate the effects of Overdrive. Well, as far as he could tell from reading the description. It would be far too convenient if it all just worked. "I'm not sure this is something we should be testing out..." He tried to approach the topic tactfully, and hoped he didn't sound ungrateful.

"No need. We've already tested it out." Upgrade shrugged off his concerns. "We've been running dungeons nonstop to refine this set. Each and every function works exactly as we intended."

Sal pointed at the missing left arm of the armor. "But you don't have Capacitor, and it needs that. I assumed you were going to have me test it?"

Fabi raised her hand. "I acted as the Capacitor in this instance. We tested it with my internal reserves to calculate how quickly it saps essence from the wearer. The Capacitor reference on the essence programming is tailored for you. It will never work without a healthy supply of essence in your batteries. Pretty much everything is designed with you in mind. Next objection?"

Sal couldn't help but grin. "Not an objection, but... Tempest Protocol. What's that?"

"Tempest Function," Fabi corrected, not breaking eye contact with him. "It's what happens when you combine purple lightning with Overdrive. Throw in the Assimilate Function for good measure and you're killing everything while boosting your innate stats. It's by far the coolest part of that outfit, which is how it got the name Tempest Marshal."

"And the Stratagem Function?" Sal turned his body to face her, giving Fabi his full attention. "Requires Jackal...but for what? It's perfectly capable of learning by itself."

Fabi pointed directly at Sal. "It's not for Jackal. It's for you." She gestured at her right eye with a smile. "That eye-patch will be able to transmit a lot more information between the two of you. When Jackal learns its countermeasures, you'll be given a breakdown of what it learned. Rather than trying to improve Jackal, we thought it would be better to improve how Jackal works with you. Jackal is never going to learn how Heroes work, so Stratagem is an excellent way to bridge that gap."

"Okay, that sounds pretty cool." Sal laughed as he thought about his next question. He was wearing the peaked cap and the eye-patch, so he hadn't had a chance to Appraise them yet. Which was why it was confusing him to see the Regenerate ability on the main armor, and not the hat. There was no Synergy ability tying their capability together, so how was it working?

"You're wondering what Manifest is, aren't you?" Upgrade asked as she lifted the right arm of the outfit again. "I'm more than happy to actually explain this time…"

Sal glanced over at her, tearing his attention away from Fabi for a split second. "I'll be back with some very well-thought out-questions," he said in a mock-stern voice at Fabi, who just continued to smile at him like she was ready for whatever he could come up with. His attention fully on Upgrade, he gestured for her to continue with the show. "Sorry for getting distracted with the Appraisal… What is Manifest?"

Upgrade lifted the arm up and pulled two fingers outward, in a somewhat-Hannah fashion. "You can't summon your guns anymore. That functionality was unfortunately lost as we prioritized the others." She paused dramatically, as though waiting for some form of outburst from Sal. When he merely shrugged it off, she laughed and continued. "Okay…tough crowd; you're supposed to be all crestfallen and stuff." She waved her free hand in a circle. "And then, I'd tell you that Manifest works in a far more efficient manner than Dominion. There was so much essence waste by giving the guns a physical form, which is why Manifest simply gives you the aspect of each weapon. You can pretty much aim with your hand and shoot. How cool is that?"

Sal couldn't believe it. He was going to be stealing Hannah's signature pose. "How will that work for a sniper rifle? I doubt I'd have great aim just waving my arms around."

Upgrade quietly pointed over in Fabi's direction.

Sal laughed as he turned to look at his senior. "Let me guess… the eye-patch?"

"Bingo." Fabi smiled, with a good-natured shrug. "It'll give you the trajectory and target locking you need to hit things that the revolver can't reach. It's only really accurate to about two to three hundred yards, even if you were seated and super still when aiming. It still packs a massive punch, so I think it's a pretty decent compromise."

With a heavy sigh, Sal pointed at the eye-patch. "Come on, give me some of the downsides."

"No dramatic computational abilities outside of combat." Her response was immediate. "Trajectory will work in a predictive sort of manner, but you won't be getting anywhere near the detail you'd have with Cypher and Judgment. We built it to be perfect for combat and working with a drone, not to replace your current visor." Fabi slid off the table and stretched her arms over her head. "Other downsides are that you don't have as many abilities in the set like you would have with other Legendary grades. We took up a lot of the capacity with the automations."

Upgrade scoffed at that last part. "Come on, that's not a downside. This thing is perfection."

Fabi waved her away, smiling. "He won't know that until he tries it on and takes it for a test drive."

Sal put his hands on his hips. "Funny you should mention that… I was going to go to a dungeon later today. Just wanted to get back into the swing of things before Shade tries to murder me in the Strategic Warfare module."

"Jokes aside," Upgrade said seriously, "there's not a lot of things that will be able to murder you when you're wearing this."

"And don't forget about the Regenerate ability," Blathnaid piped up from the back of the cubicle, as though reminding the others that she was still there. When everyone turned to look at her, she started to go a little red. "Hey, I was just waiting until we were talking more about the design stuff. He hasn't even seen the back of it with the cape."

"The what?" Sal repeated as he looked at Fabi to see whether she had greenlit that particular design choice.

Fabi smiled. "It's more like a sash, and it's a very stylish one-shoulder kind of thing." She waved her hand like it was no big deal. "But even though we're leaving the legs part up to you, we're all very much adamant that it needs to fit the aesthetic. If you can't agree to it, then you'll just have to give us a few more weeks to make them ourselves."

Sal laughed as he gave each of them an exasperated look. "Hey, I literally only asked for a mask that would keep me alive… and I still haven't seen it. Is the hat healing me? How am I even supposed to take the elixir?"

"Oh, don't worry. It's in there, but will only come out when it's activated. That collar isn't just for show," Upgrade tried to reassure him as she smoothed out the metal plates. "Besides, we can show you in the dungeon. You're not opposed to having us tag along?"

Fabi gave Upgrade a stern look. "Don't phrase it like a question. He's taking us there so we can see Jackal. It's been close to a month since he offered to show me."

Upgrade laughed as Fabi seemingly fought to suppress a groan. The latter turned to Sal with an agitated expression. "I mean, if you're healthy enough to go. I don't want to be forcing you to do it, and I can wait a little longer to see Jackal."

"I'm feeling great." Sal flicked at the peaked hat that rested on his head. "Pretty sure this thing has given me a whole new lease on life."

Fabi snorted at that. "It better be…" She bit her lip, a smile half forming. "Do you know how many leechers you need to kill to guarantee they drop the purify stone?"

"Average is roughly around two hundred," Upgrade added in a deadpan voice. "Fabi's luck isn't average. It was closer to four hundred each time."

"And your bastard of a machine kept eating them and telling us that it needed more." Fabi laughed humorlessly. "But we were able to make the eternal core. Which is in both your hat and your main armor. You're very welcome."

Upgrade put a hand up to get their attention. "I'd like to point out that I was the one who programmed the restrictions on Regenerate so it doesn't give him the dregs any time he so much as farts."

"Is it that essence-hungry?" Sal asked with a nervous laugh. He wasn't exactly sure how he felt about the wording of the Regenerate ability. All his essence being used to continuously heal would be a nightmare.

"As I said… not anymore," Upgrade answered. "But Fabi did go through the dregs a few dozen times as we calibrated it… which was less fun for everyone involved."

An awkward silence overtook the room, which was thankfully interrupted by Blathnaid, who had her arm raised like she was in class.

"Can we please talk about the cape? He hasn't said anything about the shirt or fastenings! Did you even show him the Challenge crests embedded into the epaulettes?" She sounded practically unhinged as she emphatically pointed at the design from afar. "I want to show him all the other designs so he doesn't go and make something horrible for his legs."

Sal's jaw dropped as he looked at her with a surprised laugh. "Seriously? Have you no faith in me to make nice things?"

"Zero," Blathnaid answered without a shred of hesitation.

It would have only been a little insulting, had Fabi and Upgrade not responded at the exact same time with their own choice words of immediate dissent.

"None."

"Fuck no."

Rather than answering, Sal withdrew his tablet and summoned the Mythical blight jackal to his left arm. "Not even this?" He laughed as he waved the arm around and looked at them in mock indignation.

Upgrade gave him a sad smile as she squeezed his shoulder. "I'm sorry, Sal, but the exception does not make the rule."

Fabi clapped her hands together, drawing everyone's attention to her. "So, dungeon?"

Sal grinned as he nodded in agreement. "Dungeon."

CHAPTER 55: PREPARATION

"Don't get me wrong, I'm grateful for the invite," Barry started off, grimacing. "But don't you think this is a little overkill?"

It wasn't clear whether he was referring to the amount of people they had brought along for the dungeon, or the actual dungeon itself. Either would have made complete sense, considering he was joined by Blathnaid, Divinity, Jack, Anthony…as well as Upgrade and Fabi. They had a lot of combat potential, which could have been classified as overkill. Which was why Fabi balanced things out by selecting a higher-tier dungeon she was extremely confident with.

"I think it's perfect," Divinity responded excitedly, her eyes not leaving Sal's new ensemble of equipment. "And trust me, it's better to go into a tough dungeon if we want to see Jackal at his best."

"Jackal?" Barry repeated slowly as he glanced over at Jack with a comical expression. "Coming up with Hero names can be hard, but not *that* hard. I'd have gone with something classier…like Rune-Boy."

Jack stared at Barry with the most unimpressed face imaginable. "It's not my Hero name."

"Rune-Man?" Barry suggested with a grin. "You could always go with Ruin, and constantly correct people on the spelling."

Sal ignored them as he reached over his left shoulder to adjust the cape-like sash that whipped around in the breeze. Blathnaid had designed it for aesthetics, but in practice, it was an interference as it coiled around his arm or flew up in a strange direction. The epaulettes weren't pronounced enough to cover the glowing green orb that represented Jackal, and the green light seemed more pronounced against his dark outfit. Upgrade assured him that the form would shift once he activated Tempest Marshal.

Barry's bickering with Jack continued, and Sal had managed to zone most of it out… until he heard a new nickname being thrown his way.

"Purple Pirate?" Sal repeated as he turned to look at Barry in disbelief. "Come on…"

"You're wearing an eye-patch. You're pretty much asking for the name. I don't make the rules." Barry shrugged helplessly, as though it pained him to mock them relentlessly.

Fabi appeared beside Barry with an unreadable expression, pointing at her own eye-patch. "So what nickname are you thinking for me, then?"

It was clear from her tone that Barry needed to be careful with his answer. So, he took the opportunity to gesture at the dungeon administrator who had just returned to his desk. "Oh, look at that for timing. Guess we can go inside now?"

Fabi chuckled while walking over to the desk with Upgrade, shaking her head. Since they had been running dungeons nonstop, they had earned quite a bit of respect from the surrounding dungeon administrators. Upgrade had been the one to suggest they take the lead on it, with her acting as advisor for the Mythic Guild. Her logic was that there would be less questions surrounding Anthony and Jack's suitability for the dungeon.

Sal twisted his hips for the dozenth time, trying to find some form of limitation to his movements. No matter what he did, the Tempest Marshal moved fluidly, like it was made of loose-fitting cloth. It was positively bewildering how they had managed to create it. He ran his hands over the carved abdominal section of the fitted shirt, still in denial how it felt like solid steel from the outside, but like cloth on the inside.

Sal wasn't very vain, but even he had to admit that the tailoring was very complimentary to his physique. The epaulettes, with their metal plates and high collar, managed to emphasize his shoulder width while simultaneously giving him a regal aesthetic. Hell, it even improved his posture. He brought his right hand into view, enjoying the details of the purple and silver accents on the glossy black metal. It was twinned almost to perfection to the Mythical blight jackal.

"I'm glad you like it," Blathnaid whispered from beside him with a wide smile. "But I can't wait for you to see the purple lightning!"

Sal returned the smile. "Is there an area of effect for it? Like, is there any danger to people around me if I use it?" He experimentally flexed the arm, wiggling his fingers in the glossy black, glove-like metal.

Blathnaid shook her head. "No, there shouldn't be. They spent the whole time you were away working out all the kinks in the programming. All sorts of perimeter stuff and protections, so don't worry about using it. We'll be able to protect you while you come to grips with it."

Sal glanced at Blathnaid and saw that she was serious. He knew she hadn't seen Jackal's combat capability, but it was something else entirely to see her as a protective force. Whatever had happened in the last few weeks had been incredible for her personal development, and Sal was delighted to see it. It felt like forever ago that she threw Victoria over her shoulder during the cohort tournament. "Don't suppose you know how to work these connections?" He turned to show her his left shoulder of the Mythic blight jackal.

"Nope, that will have to be Upgrade. She doesn't want you playing with it out in the open, so she'll only connect Capacitor to the Tempest Marshal when we're going into the dungeon," Blathnaid answered before smiling brightly. "It'll be worth the wait, though."

Sal nodded in understanding. "Fair enough. By the way, I thought I'd hate the cape thing... but it's actually really stylish." It was true; despite the fluttering around, it did look quite good.

"I went with a three-quarter length so it wouldn't trail on the ground. I thought it added a nice bit of character to the build, and it really catches the eye," Blathnaid agreed as she brought a hand up to cradle the black and purple fabric. "We'll be able to put the Mythic Guild insignia or logo onto this when you design it. Having a banner is important, because it's pretty much free advertising."

"What about something like this?" Barry suggested as he whipped a hand up with a curl of his fingers. An illusion burst to life in front of all of them, using a silver and black color scheme. It rotated in the air so they could see it from different angles.

Sal couldn't help but marvel at how quickly he had both formulated the concept and brought it to life. Having used the Illusion ability himself, Sal knew how tricky it was to manage. The simple act of conjuring a custom image was a testament to Barry's control over his weave. That was where the praise ended, though.

"Is that a hulker?" Blathnaid squinted at the image to get a better look. "Swan-diving?"

"Body-slamming Sal," Barry finished the thought for her with a wide grin. "Personally, I think it's an excellent representation of the guild."

Sal was about to bite back when he caught sight of Upgrade waving them over. Divinity was already at her side, which was clearly a sign of her cheating. He followed Jack and Anthony over to the edge of the dungeon entrance, laughing and shaking his head at Barry's illusion.

"Everything is squared with the administration team. Sal, they just need your card. I think only Jack needs to get one made?" Upgrade said first to Sal, before turning to look at Jack with a raised eyebrow. "It's a token like your Q-Card that will allow you entry into dungeons. I'm guessing you don't have one?"

Jack plucked a white card from his pocket and presented it to Upgrade. "Nemesis made me get one."

He sounded haunted by the memory, and Sal was instantly curious as to what happened in his master class with her. Was that how there were so many advanced runes on the Tempest Marshal?

"Perfect." Upgrade plucked the card from him and looked at Anthony. "You're already on their database from your runs with Fabi." She jutted her thumb over her shoulder. "Divinity gave hers, and we took the liberty of putting Barry through…mostly to spare the administrator from having to deal with him personally." With a wide grin, she then gestured at Blathnaid. "And our rising star has the most dungeon runs clocked in the Mythic Guild."

Sal tilted his head. "You're already competing? We haven't even signed contracts!" He gave Blathnaid a wink to show he was only joking with her, and she smiled happily in return.

Fabi clapped her hands together, a serious expression on her face. "This is an evolved dungeon. We're going to be facing off against leechers, prowlers, voiders, and hulkers. The evolved elite is more often than not a hulker variant, so we need to exercise caution. Our primary goal here is safety, and our secondary goal is to test Salvatore's new outfit. Each of you will need to listen to Upgrade. She has absolute authority as the advisor of the Mythic Guild, with myself as secondary. Salvatore will take that mantle in the coming weeks, but we're prioritizing experience over rank in this instance. Any objections or concerns?"

Barry shook his head. Everyone else followed suit as they waited for Fabi's next words.

"Good. Then we're going to prepare ourselves just outside the entrance. If you need assistance with your equipment, let us know. Both Upgrade and I will be operating as team leaders. When you hear us speaking, listen to what is being said. Don't wander away from the group, and do not pursue your opponent. We're going to maintain our formation and rotate each person so they'll have a chance at combat." Fabi looked at each of them. "Do not collect materials or equipment until we've cleared the entire dungeon. You'll just make yourself a target."

She finally smiled, losing the disciplinarian tone. "There is no room for pride in a dungeon. If you feel incapable of taking on an opponent, let us know and we'll switch you out. This is an opportunity for you to learn and grow stronger, not a platform to prove your bravery. We want each of you to come out of this with a sense of accomplishment, no matter how big or small. Improve yourself while maintaining safety and formation. Practice makes perfect."

Barry chuckled at that last part. "Pretty sure it was Sal that made Perfect."

The glare that Fabi directed at Barry was enough to quiet him in a second. When there were no signs of any additional quips, Fabi continued. "That's it for the briefing. If you've got any questions, now is the time to ask."

Sal gestured at his left arm. "Can you help me connect Capacitor?" He looked between Upgrade and Fabi, and the former smiled and was over to him in an instant.

"Just give me a few seconds…" Upgrade muttered as she pulled what looked like an adhesive layer from the underside of the epaulette, and carefully aligned it with the edge of the Mythical blight jackal. It took a little finessing, but she managed to match them up perfectly, with small streaks of electrical circuitry shooting up and down the connection point. Upgrade reached under Sal's armpit and repeated the same process, adjusting the connection.

Sal wasn't sure what to expect when it was done, but he got the greatest surprise when the glowing green orb suddenly flashed into a vibrant purple color. The light emitting from it was different from the Arkwright's dungeon fragment, which had looked quite villainous. This was more of a dark lavender.

Upgrade grinned triumphantly before lowering her voice to a whisper. "And now we don't need to worry about people misunderstanding what powers this thing." She winked at Sal before releasing his arm. "And we've finally got a cohesive color scheme!"

Sal was about to answer when the eye-patch suddenly populated with a series of new information. He had already synced it with Nexus back in the workshop, and was eternally grateful that it shared all the recorded information from his visor. It wouldn't be able to replicate the capabilities of Cypher or Judgment, but it meant he had access to all the same databases of intel.

Tempest Marshal (Active)
- Overdrive has been activated
- Capacitor has been activated
- Automate has been activated
- Regenerate has been activated

Stratagem Function has been calibrated.
- Stratagem can be used indefinitely
- Jackal Evolution: 3hrs 38mins 21secs

Assimilate Function has been calibrated.
- Assimilate can be used 72 times
- Passive Recharge every 4 minutes
- Active Recharge every 22 seconds

Tempest Function has been calibrated.
- Tempest can be used 23 times
- Passive Recharge every 15 minutes
- Active Recharge every 1 minute 11 seconds

Manifest Function has been calibrated.

- **Scarlet Strategist Set**
    - Revolver Aspect can be used 440 times. (Estimate)
    - Sniper Aspect can be used 200 times. (Estimate)

Regenerate

- Fatigue Mode has been activated
- Minor Internal Injuries will be treated constantly

"So, how are we looking on the calibration?" Upgrade glanced back at Fabi. "We estimated that you'd get to use the Tempest Function around fifteen times."

"Twenty-three." Sal read through the information with a wide smile, surprising both Fabi and Upgrade. "Eh, by the way… how long do you think this dungeon will take?"

Upgrade frowned as she thought about the question. "That's not really a good metric to aim for. We'll be taking it slowly to rotate people, so between two and three hours at the minimum. Do you have somewhere else to be?"

Sal shook his head as he pointed at the now purple light of Jackal. "He's hibernating at the moment and won't be ready for another three and a half hours." Sal wondered whether Jackal was no longer an "it" in his own mind. His mother would likely be proud.

Upgrade stared at Sal for a few seconds. "I was wrong about the time limit. This thing will take at least five to six hours. If you blitz through it, then we're doing another one."

"Agreed," Fabi stated with her arms folded. "I want to see him."

Barry just looked at the Crafters around him in confusion. "I feel like I'm missing a key piece of context here." His gaze landed on Sal, followed by a raised eyebrow. "What is Jackal?"

Sal shrugged with a placating smile. "Guess you'll find out in a few hours."

CHAPTER 56: LIGHTNING

Sal followed Fabi down the stairs into the underground dungeon. He was third in the line of people, with Upgrade ahead of him. They insisted on securing the perimeter, because even though there usually weren't any demons around the entrance, they wanted to take as much precaution as possible. Sal guessed it was because of Jack and Anthony, as neither of them were particularly well-equipped. When he had asked Blathnaid about issuing out the Tempest Marshal iterations to the others in the guild, she had simply laughed it off. Apparently, they just had a collection of pieces that were calibrated around Sal.

"Excited for our first dungeon together?" Barry asked from behind him. It wasn't aimed at him, though, which became clear when Divinity answered him.

"Yes, but you should focus. It's going to get a little chaotic." She didn't sound particularly worried, but it was worth heeding. "Try not to make too much noise. Fabi and Upgrade are concentrating."

Barry sighed audibly as he followed the retinue quietly. The sound of his feet scuffing against the ground indicated that he was feeling restless.

Sal wondered whether it was nervousness at facing off against higher-grade demons. The leechers and prowlers from the tower were one thing, but this was going to include voiders and hulkers. It was a little funny how relaxed he felt. He wasn't sure whether it was because of the training with his dad, or whether it was the knowledge that he had Jackal. Probably not the Jackal part, considering it was out of commission for a few hours. A smile crept onto his face as he continued down the stairs to join Fabi and Upgrade at the base.

Glancing up at him, Fabi smiled. "You ready for your big debut?"

Sal nodded as his eye-patch started to pick out targets. More than a dozen leechers bobbed around the ceiling of the cave-like structure. Mossy stalactites pierced down from above, with the characteristic bioluminescence that Sal associated with the first dungeon he ever entered. What he hadn't expected was a small lake at the base of the dungeon. The murky surface looked more like an enormous puddle, but the eye-patch highlighted a series of enemy signatures residing more than ten feet below the surface. They were too big to be leechers, too.

"Excellent, then let's get you primed for Overdrive. I thought the water-logged surface would be a good test for the purple lightning." Fabi moved behind Sal and adjusted the epaulettes, and more specifically, the raised collar around his neck. "Don't worry, I only need to do this the first time so it can learn the right shape of your jaw."

Sal frowned at that part. "I'm not sure I understand."

Fabi didn't answer immediately as she continued to fiddle with the collar, until she stood in front of him with a satisfied smile. "It's the mask you commissioned. It won't have any of Alex's elixirs, but it should still come in handy." She checked her hands that were on either side of his neck. "Activate the Overdrive Function for the Tempest Marshal."

Sal did as she requested and his left arm vibrated as though it had just powered up. A slight ripple of foreign energy pulsated through his shoulder and into his chest, before rising through his collar. The result was a gradual transformation of the collar clasping around his throat and crawling up his jaw, only stopping when it had encased his mouth and nose.

"Testing… test," Sal said aloud, wondering whether he'd be able to speak with the contraption over his mouth. To his great surprise, he wasn't impeded at all. Opening his mouth wide, he found that there was nothing restricting his movements. His confusion was only compounded when he reached a hand up to touch the stretchy fabric, and felt like he had just struck metal.

"Perfect." Fabi beamed as she stepped around him to look at it from every angle. "It'll be a lot faster in the future, but I'm very happy with that. If it's uncomfortable, let me know immediately and we can calibrate it a little better back at the workshop."

Sal just nodded lamely as he continued to poke and prod the area around his mouth. He really wanted to see what it looked like. Maybe he'd be able to look in the surface of the water after getting rid of the demons lurking within?

"Whoa… I take it back," Barry said in surprise as he joined them at the base of the stairs. "You're not a pirate anymore. Purple Ninja?" He looked at Divinity as though he was going to get her support for the new nickname. Not only didn't he get the validation, he received a smack to the shoulder, which seemed to hurt Divinity's hand more than it hurt Barry.

He winced slightly as he revealed the Vengeful Vambraces that had been obscured by an illusion. "My bad."

Divinity glowered at him before turning her attention to Sal, a bright smile on her face. "It looks amazing! You really do look like a Villain, though. The eyepatch and the mask really complete the look."

Blathnaid folded her arms. "Since when did fashionable become synonymous with villainy?"

"Children," Upgrade said in a stern voice as she glanced over her shoulder. "If you wouldn't mind focusing on the fact that you're all standing in a dungeon, that would be wonderful." Her smile was tight as she gestured at the three cave entrances on the other side of the lake. "This whole environment is perfect for ambushes. Please be mindful of your surroundings."

Barry nodded as he took a few steps to stand away from the rest of the group. Not far enough to endanger himself, but far enough that he wouldn't be a distraction to others. "Would you like me to cloak our presence with illusions? I can't do much about scents, but I can alter visual and audible perception to an extent." He had slipped into a professional mode that took both Upgrade and Fabi by surprise. "If you'd prefer me to prevent them from clumping up, I can take care of it."

Fabi smiled as she nodded. "Good to know. I'll call on you for whatever I need, but your primary focus should be on conserving your essence until we start fighting. Are you able to manifest light, or are you only able to bend it?"

Barry blinked in surprise, seemingly looking at Fabi in an entirely new light. "I can do both, but bending is easier."

"No need to worry, you'll have plenty of light to work with." Fabi chuckled as she gestured at Sal. "We're about to have ourselves a lightshow. Whenever you're ready, Sal."

Sal nodded as he moved closer to the lake, flexing his fingers as he assumed a fighting stance. He wasn't exactly sure what to expect from the Tempest Marshal, especially with all the essence programmed functions. He wasn't going to activate the Tempest Function just yet, but instead use the Assimilation Function. It required Overdrive and Capacitor, both of which were currently active. With a click of his fingers in anticipation, Sal was pleasantly surprised to see a spark of electricity emanate from between his fingertips. In the dark gloom of the cavern, it looked quite impressive as a warm-up. The crackling noise was a little less welcome, as it seemingly alerted a couple of the nearby leechers overhead.

Stretching his arm out, Sal pointed at the ceiling and mimicked Hannah's signature finger-gun pose. His eye-patch had identified six leechers that he could target, and he guessed he'd need to use six separate attacks to get them all. Aiming at the first one, Sal activated the Assimilation Function.

The once-dark cavern was suddenly illuminated in a brilliant purple, accompanied by a thundering crack like a rock being split in half. Sal's eye-patch wasn't fazed by the light and kept a lock on each leecher as the bolt of lightning roared upward like a crackling storm of devastation. The bobbing leecher didn't stand a chance as it was instantly obliterated. Before its charred ashes could drop from the ceiling, the lightning lanced to the next target. Each corpse was being used as a launchpad for subsequent annihilation. Sal thought it looked beautiful.

Insufficient Essence Draw (5)

    ○   Recharge will not be impacted

Sal watched as the error report populated with a higher number as each leecher died. He had pretty much forgotten in the current excitement that Assimilate was designed to siphon off the essence and stats of his targets. It wouldn't have made any sense if the leechers had sufficient essence to power up his attacks. He'd likely need to take on something more deadly.

"Looks like you've got their attention," Fabi called out to him, laughing. "Voiders and prowlers give stats, so don't worry."

That sounded wrong. Sal had used Jackal in a dungeon and he didn't get anything from the defeated prowlers or voiders. Was it a difference between Assimilation and Subsume? Either way, it didn't really matter. Sal watched the far-right cave entrance with a confident smile. His eye-patch highlighted a veritable horde of demons rushing in their direction, clearly summoned by the sounds of lightning. He had a few seconds before they appeared, so he turned to look at Upgrade.

"Would you like me to give the others a chance? There's a group of them approaching from the third cave." He didn't want to take the spotlight for the full dungeon, even if he was incredibly curious about the rest of the Tempest Marshal's capabilities. If they were going to be doing this for a few hours, there was no need to rush to the finish line.

Upgrade shook her head as she pointed at the cave. "Just be mindful of the demons lurking in the water. They'll likely go for an ambush while you're fighting. We're going to use this as an opportunity to see how calibrated you are with the suit. If there are any touch-ups for fixes we'll need to do. So, feel free to go all out. You can even activate the Tempest Function if you want."

Anthony and Jack stared at the cave entrance he had just mentioned. They stood behind Blathnaid and Divinity, who looked ready for combat. Fabi stood with her arms crossed, looking at the cave expectantly. Barry was off to the side, crouched down and looking quite pensive.

"Cool. I'll test it out a few more times. Was the initial attack supposed to lance out to the other targets like that?" Sal gestured at the ceiling, as though there could possibly be any confusion about what just happened.

Fabi nodded as Upgrade answered. "Yeah, that's completely intentional. You've got company coming, so, I'll be quick. Your eye-patch targets each opponent sequentially, and the Assimilation Function attacks will take that opportunity if it's possible. If the distance is too large, it won't activate, but it's good when they're in range. It won't work for Manifest, or for the Tempest Function. That one doesn't need anything like targeting."

Sal turned just in time to see a hulker lumbering forward at speed. The water separating them didn't seem to register with the hulker, who plunged directly into the lake, sinking to the bottom with a dramatic wave that threatened to soak Sal. A pack of prowlers paused at the opposite bank before turning to run along the pathway that led to their group.

Rather than waiting for them to get any closer, Sal snapped his hand in their direction and let out another burst of lightning. It was incredibly satisfying to watch the beam get reflected on the surface of the water before it smashed into the lead prowler. The corpse was thrown a few feet, with the momentum of its charge causing it to slide against the cave floor. Before it even came to a stop, the lightning lanced toward its next target, punching another hole through the demon. Sounds of crackling and sizzling was all that separated the kills, with none of the prowlers granted an opportunity to so much as growl.

Each of the targets on the eye-patch were visible, and Sal re-routed the attacks for maximum efficiency. The sequence was incredible, and he loved watching the erratic lightning doing its job. Everything looked to be going to plan when a new target registered in Sal's peripheral vision. Without thinking, Sal remapped the sequence and found that it didn't have the range to take out the new target. Cutting his losses, Sal let the Assimilation Function cease before whipping his right hand around to point at the new target, sending out another blast of lightning.

His hand moved faster than his head, and when Sal turned to look at what had happened, he saw something extraordinary. A voider was halfway through a constructed portal when the lightning hit. Having no mapped sequence, the lightning had simply punched through the voider and carried through the portal. The extraordinary aspect was the second target he managed to kill within the depths of the cave. Likely another demon that was too close to the portal.

Laughing to himself, Sal brought his hand back to take care of the prowlers that had survived the first barrage. If he had a bit more time, he would have attempted to use the Manifest Function... but the prowlers were too close to his friends. The result was another bolt of lightning that pierced and ricocheted between the demons, killing everything in quick succession.

Sufficient Essence Draw (11)

    o   Passive Recharge has been reduced by 2 minutes 12 seconds.

Regenerate

o   Training mode has been activated.

That was underwhelming, but Sal didn't mind. It would only become a hindrance when he ran out of charges and needed to wait for Capacitor to recoup essence. He was curious why the Healing ability had moved from the fatigue mode up to the training one. The answer appeared in front of his right eye in just a few seconds.

Assimilation Function Report (11)
- o   Mobility has increased by 0.11
- o   Speed has increased by 0.20
- o   No Technique Improvement
- o   No Ability Grade Improvement
- o   No Essence Reserve Improvement

Sal's laugh was vocalized this time as he sent another rocket of lightning into the group of demons at the cave entrance. Regenerate was mitigating the effects of new stats being applied to his body. He hadn't even noticed it! All his consideration for his friends getting a chance to fight had been put on hold. He had a method to increase his base stats without having to kill hulkers and scuttlers. Jackal wasn't even needed for this.

It was a great feeling, and Sal was genuinely enjoying himself. He couldn't wait to find out what other secrets Tempest Marshal had hidden.

CHAPTER 57: RESOLVE

Sal sat on a rock as he caught his breath. It wasn't from exertion, but rather from the adrenaline coursing through him. Having Perfect active hadn't improved the stats he got from Assimilate, so rather than expending any essence with it, he deactivated it. The result was a borderline euphoric sense of accomplishment. Sure, it had only been a few fights with voiders, leechers, and prowlers, but he felt incredible. Assimilate Function had skyrocketed up to a must-have for anything he made in the future. It was ranged, strategic, and gifted him stats…not to mention that it was able to kill mobs of demons with relative ease. Sal couldn't help but wonder how different the dungeon with his father would have been if he could have just sent bolts of lightning down those caves. A hell of a lot easier, but definitely not ideal for learning.

He wasn't going to throw in the towel on studying the Silverson Arts. Instead, he was already formulating how he could use the Assimilation Function with his fighting style. If there was a way to program the lightning to activate when he threw a punch, then it could be something truly extraordinary. Sal was even thinking about how he might be able to incorporate a similar function to his kicks. The more he fought in dungeons, the stronger his body would become.

Sal blinked as he watched Divinity's body blur through a series of light and fast attacks. She was up against a prowler and rather than dispatching it quickly, she aimed for a critical hit. To anyone else, it might look like she was struggling… but Sal could tell that she was trying to train a fatal attack. Luckily, Upgrade could see the same thing and stopped Blathnaid from trying to help her.

It slowed their pace down, but it was worth it. Barry was training his control by holding back three prowlers from advancing on Divinity. His essence constructs, enabled by the Vengeful Vambraces, constantly shifted in shape to prevent the demons from breaking through. He was lucky that there was a lake, otherwise the prowlers would have a wide area to avoid his blockades.

Blathnaid, on the other hand, after being told to wait for Divinity to take care of the prowlers, had settled into staring at the dead demons. It was clear she was itching to harvest them, and Sal for one was grateful that they had her on the team. He was still jealous of how effective and efficient she was at carving up that prowler in Professor Syme's class.

Divinity's bare hand was held in an open-palm position, and Sal saw the exact moment she went for the killing move. Her elbow drew back as she feinted to one side, throwing the prowler off-balance. Before it could rebound into an attack with its open maw, Divinity's fingers plunged directly into its eye socket. Her other hand came up to gouge out the other eye, gripping the prowler's skull with her hands and keeping its jaws away from her torso. There was no finesse to the move, but there was definitely a raw intensity. Only then did Divinity throw her entire bodyweight behind the attack, leaping over the prowler and twisting its neck with a loud snap.

"Incredible work!" Fabi shouted encouragement. "Do you want to switch out, or take on another?"

Divinity brought both of her hands up and threw them in the direction of the ground, causing some of the excess green blood to slap against the dirt. "I'll take another one, please."

"You heard her, Barry," Fabi said as she gave Divinity a nod of approval. "Were you using your ability for that fight?"

"No," Divinity answered with a shuddering breath as she got back into position. "I want to train without it."

Barry gave Fabi a tentative look as he held up his hands, as though asking whether she was sure about it. Fabi gave him a nod, which resulted in a single prowler bursting through the newly created gap in the blockade. It barely managed to bound into range before Divinity's foot caught the side of its head. Her entire bodyweight was behind the kick, but it looked like it wasn't enough to do lasting damage. She was relentless with kick after kick, not using her hands at all. It took a while, but eventually, she was rewarded with the same opportunity to gouge out the eyes. The prowler had learned to avoid her kicks, and didn't see the hands coming until it was too late.

"Savage," Barry breathed as he watched Divinity once again throwing the excess prowler blood from her hands.

Divinity looked over at them, sweat lining her brow and a resolute expression on her face. "Another, please."

Sal continued to watch her fight another three prowlers, each being killed with the same severity. Divinity had managed to bring the somewhat jovial vibe all the way back down to a pensive and somber one. Her attacks had become sluggish as her stamina depleted, but they didn't lose their lethality. If anything, she had stopped caring about lulling her opponent into a false sense of security. Instead, she just overwhelmed the prowlers with a relentless series of jabs and kicks.

It was the first time Sal had seen her going all out with an intent to kill. All their sparring had been just that: a friendly back-and-forth. Even when they had trained in the sparring room in the Savior dorms, it had been relaxed. This was a whole new side of Divinity that Sal was witnessing, and it was worthy of respect.

When she eventually tapped out, she half staggered over to their group with a tired smile. Her hands were clenching and unclenching as though trying to reduce discomfort. Blathnaid noticed the movement and plucked a cloth from her breast pocket to give to Divinity.

"Wipe your hands and it won't itch as much." She smiled as Divinity gratefully accepted it. Blathnaid looked concerned, but rather than saying anything, she just nodded and stepped back to give her some space.

Upgrade gestured for Barry to take his turn against the demons. It could have been argued that he was already working against them with his essence constructs and illusions, but there was still a combat focus to the dungeon. He had already highlighted that he wanted to get some practice in, and Upgrade was seemingly happy to give him a turn. She was probably curious as to how his abilities worked.

Rather than watching Barry's turn, Divinity instead moved over to where Sal was. Her shoulders slumped as she wiped at her hands with the cloth. "That could have gone better." She sounded frustrated as her lips formed a thin line.

"Hey, take a seat." Sal got to his feet and offered her the flat-ish rock that he had been sitting on. He half expected her to refuse, but he was glad when she plopped down with an aggravated groan.

Finishing the hand cleaning, Divinity looked up at the cavern roof, before letting out a tired sigh. "That was so rough." She chuckled humorlessly. "Do I need to get lightning abilities to keep up with you guys?"

"I don't know," Sal answered honestly. "I'm guessing Psyker's Dominion isn't much help when you're not using your ability." He knew that there weren't any Offense-style abilities in the piece of equipment, and it wasn't like Divinity let any of the prowlers close enough to activate the protective barrier. "Why aren't you using it?"

Divinity smiled wearily as she stretched her arms. "I just wanted to prove to myself that I could if I wanted to." She brought her arms down and gave him a shrug. "When I took out the first one, I wanted to see if I could do it again…and again."

"You were pretty amazing, though," Sal admitted as he gestured at the demon corpses. "Like, just taking them out with your bare hands is incredible. I thought you were training with the bow? You know, back when we were picking weapons for the excursion."

Divinity waved her hand, like she was dismissing the thought. "That was just me fighting against a vision. The bow was never my weapon of choice." She looked up at him with a tired smile. "I'm trying to build up my understanding of Style Arts so I can use it more effectively. This was a part of that training."

Sal nodded as he carefully looked at her. He couldn't understand what she was frustrated about. His visor would have been helpful in this situation, but he was using the eye-patch and it gave him no insights on how she was feeling. With a reassuring smile that likely wasn't conveyed through the mask, he tried to reassure her. "You never need to worry about keeping up, by the way. There will always be a place for you at the Mythic Guild. You're a great Controller, and I'd trust you completely if you were on my team."

Divinity laughed as she raised an eyebrow. "Sorry, but you've only had one other Controller. I don't think that it's much of a compliment when Erika is my competition." She leaned back on the rock to rest against the wall. "But I appreciate the sentiment. It's hard not to get frustrated with the slow progress when I'm surrounded by savants."

"I wouldn't go that far. It's just a lot of great equipment," Sal chided her gently. He didn't like seeing her like this and wanted to make her feel better, but couldn't think of the right way to go about it. She was usually so composed, with all the answers for the future, so hearing her talk about her own perceived inadequacies was difficult to navigate. "What equipment would you want?"

"No." Divinity was firm as she looked at him seriously. "I don't want you working on something for me. I'm just venting and not looking for solutions." She smiled as she shook her head. "Forget I said anything. Everything is good."

Sal raised a hand to his head and took off the cap. He turned it around and placed it on Divinity's head. "This should at least help you recover a bit. If you're feeling up for another few rounds, this will help you get there a bit faster." The cap looked a little comical on her, as his head was quite a bit bigger than hers.

"You look better without it, by the way." Divinity smiled sheepishly as she adjusted the cap. "Thanks, Sal."

With another smile she likely couldn't see, Sal gave her a thumbs-up and a chuckle. "Don't worry about it." He turned halfway so he could see what was going on with the demons, and more specifically, to see how Barry was doing. "Think he's taking it seriously?"

Divinity snorted at the notion. "Absolutely not. It would take a lot more than this for him to push himself," she muttered with a slight shake of her head, her eyes locked onto Barry, who was duplicated three times around the dungeon floor. Each illusion moved in a counterclockwise rotation, floating slightly above the ground and moving out of the way of the attacking prowlers.

Sal frowned as he watched the display. It didn't look like anything special compared to what Barry would normally do. As if to test his theory, he decided to call out. "Hey, can you wrap it up so the others can have a turn?"

In a flash, all four prowlers died on the spot. It was like each of them had their brain explode at the exact same time: four corpses fell to the ground in a synchronized thump. The illusions all disappeared, to reveal Barry standing a few feet away from them, leaning against the wall. He gave Sal a wry smile. "No problem."

Divinity let out a groan as she shook her head again in exasperation. "What part of that was training?"

Barry shrugged as he gestured at the dead prowlers. "I needed to see how they turn in a tight rotation. It lets me tailor illusions in a more realistic way."

Divinity just stared at him, her expression softening. "Sorry... I just—"

"I get it." Barry defused the tension with a chuckle. "We've all got different things we're working on, and some look flashier than others. I would have been scared shitless if I had to get up close like you did."

Sal blinked in surprise at the sudden bout of compassion from Barry. It was a rare aspect that usually warranted a double take.

Divinity smiled as she clutched the cloth that Blathnaid had given her. "Thanks, Barry." In what was probably an effort to change the topic of conversation, Divinity nodded in the direction of Blathnaid, who had stepped up to the arena of corpses. "How do you think she'll do?" She glanced at Barry and then Sal, as though to include both of them in the question.

"I've never really seen her fight, other than the tournament and the highlight reel," Sal answered first, as he folded his arms.

Barry walked over to them with a slight shake of the head. "Nah, I think she'll be good. Her scores in the simulation machine are ranked really high against other Supports."

Upgrade turned to look at their group with a knowing smile. "She'll be *very* good."

Blathnaid started to bounce on her feet, side to side, like she was psyching herself up for the fight to come.

"Whenever you're ready, Sal." Upgrade looked at him meaningfully as she brought her hands up to her ears. Divinity, Barry and the others all followed suit.

Without bringing his fingers near his lips, Sal let out a piercing whistle that echoed throughout the entire cavern. The surrounding walls bounced the sound through each of the cave entrances, and it only took a single whistle to get the attention of the next demonic wave. It wasn't an efficient strategy, but they had managed to camp at the entrance to the dungeon. That alone had been enough to relax the likes of Anthony and Jack, who clearly didn't want to go exploring.

Blathnaid's bouncing became more spread out as she went from foot to foot, covering a wider space. She had been pretty good with the hand-to-hand combat training, but Sal had guessed that she would take up a ranged type of attack to keep herself safe. The sight of the knuckle-dusters on her hands was a definite surprise.

"Wait…she's going to fight with her hands?" Sal asked Upgrade incredulously, as though he hadn't already witnessed Divinity doing the exact same thing. He got ahead of Divinity's protests before they were even uttered, looking at her in disbelief. "You've been training in martial arts for years, but Blathnaid hasn't."

"She's a fast learner," Upgrade stated with that same smile. "And she's a damn good Crafter."

A hulker materialized at the entrance of the cave, making Sal's heart sink. He stepped forward, his right arm rising in anticipation.

"No need." Upgrade shook her head. "Let Blathnaid do her thing."

Sal stared at Upgrade in horror, not understanding how she could be so calm and composed in a situation like this. He had faced a hulker before, and it had pretty much shattered his ribs… despite him having Epic-grade equipment.

Blathnaid's body was a blur of movement as she launched herself forward in the direction of the hulker. Her right arm drew back in a dramatic fashion as she imitated the same haymaker punch he had used in the tower.

Had he accidentally inspired her to do something ridiculous? He wanted to trust Upgrade, but she was the one who had taken him to a dungeon when he was scared shitless of demons. Had she indoctrinated Blathnaid in the same way?

"Holy shit," Barry whispered as he moved off the wall to get a better look.

Divinity's jaw dropped as the hulker's arm shattered into more than a dozen pieces.

Blathnaid's left foot bounced against the ground as she repositioned herself to the hulker's blind spot, keeping distance, before launching another vicious punch. Her knuckle-duster barely grazed the lumbering hulker, but it was enough to carve out a chunk of its side. The next attack left a fist-sized gash in the rubble-like mass of demon. All the while, Blathnaid's expression was that of resolve and composure. She didn't hesitate or look emotional as she moved; each of her attacks was well-placed and seemingly designed to dismantle the hulker's offensive capabilities.

The final blow obliterated the head of the hulker, and without missing a beat, Blathnaid was back to bouncing from foot to foot. Her attention was on the prowlers and voiders that had come into view.

"How many dungeons did you take her on?" Barry asked incredulously as he stared at Blathnaid's back.

"Enough," Fabi answered this time. "She's fun to teach."

CHAPTER 58: SUSPENSE

"Just give it a few more minutes," Sal answered for what was probably the hundredth time. He understood the collective excitement, but he couldn't rush the process.

They had managed to clear more than a dozen waves of demons that had been coerced into approaching the entrance. Whenever too many approached, Barry had stepped up to limit their advance. Divinity was tied with Blathnaid for most bouts of fighting. Jack had spent his turn preparing a series of runes on the dungeon floor to ensnare any demons that stood on them. It was a good example of how runes could be deployed in battle, but the preparation time was a definite drawback. When a prowler had been unlucky enough to step on the rune... the ensnaring hadn't exactly trapped it, so much as crushed its body, flattening it into a mess of fur and paste.

Anthony was content to watch them all do their thing. He hadn't brought the Voracious Rapier with him, and seemed reluctant when it came to fighting. Sal couldn't blame him, and respected that he wasn't combat-oriented. Hell, Sal wasn't particularly combat-oriented, so he could never judge him for it. It was enough for Anthony to just watch and learn. Both Fabi and Upgrade highlighted what was happening to give Anthony a better grasp of what he was seeing. It was loud enough that everyone else could understand the tactics at play.

Sal glanced at the countdown timer. He knew that Divinity's eyes were locked on him. She was just as bad as Fabi and Upgrade at this point.

Stratagem Function has been calibrated.
- Stratagem can be used indefinitely
- Jackal Evolution: 2 minutes 18 seconds

Rather than take the opportunity to fight more with the Tempest Marshal, Sal had remained at the back with Divinity or Barry whenever the other was fighting. It was a good opportunity to see how they fought and developed their approach to combat. Yes, he was curious about the other functions and wanted to test them out, but Jackal would be an excellent finale to this first dungeon. If it could perform at the same level as it did in the dungeon with his parents and Luke, then the Supports and Controllers were in for a spectacle.

"You said a few minutes more than five minutes ago," Fabi muttered as she looked over at Sal in a sulk. "You could have just told us how many minutes were left."

Upgrade nodded in agreement. "Is this some Auctioneer showmanship? Or do you want to keep us on edge?" She smiled as she glanced over at him. "How long is left?"

Sal didn't answer immediately and watched the timer tick downward. "Are you sure you don't want to get another bout of fighting in? Once Jackal comes out, there won't be anything left to do."

Blathnaid crossed her arms. "Come on, it's a drone. It can't be *that* good... I've seen the ones Fabi made and they're pretty impressive, but I wouldn't trust them in a dungeon." She seemed to realize what she had just said and momentarily panicked and sent an apologetic glance in Fabi's direction, who shrugged like she agreed with the assessment.

"Suit yourselves." Sal chuckled as the counter hit zero. There was no dramatic flourish or evolutionary light. All that occurred was the timer disappearing from the Stratagem Function description.

Stratagem Function has been calibrated.
- Stratagem can be used indefinitely
- Jackal has been successfully paired

Stretching out his left arm, Sal summoned Jackal. Each tentacle unwrapped from his arm as the head of the drone materialized from the side of his shoulder. The first dramatic moment was when the purple lighting flickered to reveal the sickly green hue of the blight core. The new source of light bobbed above them as it quietly waited in standby mode, each abyssal steel tentacle floating in midair like it was submerged underwater.

"Fuck me," Barry whispered as he took a tentative step backward. He looked over at Sal, his eyes wide. "It lives in your arm!"

Sal nodded. "Yep. Do you want to take a look at it…or do you want to see it in action?"

"Both," Fabi complained with a laugh. "But I think a demonstration would be nice. Do you want to whistle to get the next wave up here? How many should Barry hold off?"

"None," Sal responded. "And there's no need for a whistle." He looked at Jackal fondly, ensuring that Stratagem was active for the next part. The evolution hadn't significantly changed Jackal's appearance, but Sal was able to see flecks of the same sickly green at the tips of each tentacle. It wasn't apparent whether that was a result of the plague crest or from the venomstone it absorbed.

"Don't suppose you're all patient enough for me to check the stats?" Sal asked, already knowing the answer.

"Don't you dare," Upgrade practically growled as she pointed at him accusingly, a smile fighting against the scowl. "You'll have all the time in the world to play around with the settings later. For now, we want to see what it can do."

Fabi hesitated at that. "But if there's any error reports, he should probably check it out?" She bit her lip, as though torn between wanting to see Jackal in action and making sure the evolution went to plan.

There was no plan. The evolution kind of just happened. Sal looked through the details and was relieved to see all the information he needed with just a glance.

Jackal Evolution Report
- Efficacy of Subsume has been increased.
- Efficacy of Growth Mode has been increased.
- Efficacy of Learning Mode has been increased.
- Efficacy of Harvesting Mode has been increased.
- Subsumed Ability Capacity has increased from 3 to 4.

- Subsumed Ability Grade Cap has increased from 3 to 8.

"Oh, wow," Sal muttered as he instructed Jackal to enter Harvesting mode, making sure that it adhered to the Nexus settings for Arsenal. He didn't want his new organizational structure to be undone by prowler parts being thrown in every direction.

"You checked it, didn't you?" Upgrade said almost accusingly as she stared at him. "Anything you feel like sharing with the class?"

Her tone was jovial, so he wasn't worried that she was actually annoyed.

Sal pointed at the corpses on the ground. "Keep a close eye on them. Jackal is entering Harvesting mode."

As he spoke, Jackal angled its body and lazily approached the corpses, as if it were scanning the area for suitable targets to loot from. Just as it reached the area with the corpses, it stopped abruptly.

"Something wrong?" Fabi asked in confusion, before taking a step back in surprise.

The black protective layer snapped into place around the blight core as Jackal wound its tentacles tight and shot directly into the lake at unbelievable speed. It was so fast that Sal didn't even have time to ask the question about Jackal working underwater. Surely it wouldn't be a suicidal protocol? It would be a nightmare to try fishing it out if that was the case.

"That was…surprisingly underwhelming," Barry said after a few seconds. "Did it not see the corpses?"

Upgrade's jaw had long-since dropped as she gaped at Sal in disbelief. "It recognized that there are hulkers in the water?"

That question reformed everyone's opinion in a flash, with Divinity looking positively excited.

"Sorry, I need to get ready for the next part," Sal apologized as he braced himself for what he knew was coming. "Stats are incoming. Hulkers tend to give me a Strength boost."

Barry stared at Sal in confusion. "Like, temporarily?"

When nobody answered, he looked around at them, absolutely horrified. His attention turned to Sal. "Is this a joke?"

Jackal had clearly found a target, which was indicated by the vanishing light from the eye-patch. It was one of the deepest sections of the lake, where the hulkers had seemingly got caught in the sludge.

Sal braced himself as a notification popped up in front of his eye.

Regenerate
- Combat Mode has been activated
- Major External and Internal Healing

The once-painful surge that rocketed through Sal in the last dungeon had been reduced to a comically subtle tickle. It wasn't anywhere near the kick he had been anticipating from Subsume. No abilities were added to his profile, which was to be expected, but Sal knew that there would be a little boost to his Strength when he next got the update.

Another light flashed, followed by another. Were they leechers, or had two more hulkers found their way into the body of water? Sal didn't really care, as they were dead now. A feed of ingredients popped up, and Sal remembered that Jackal was in Harvest Mode. It felt ridiculous that the little drone was able to take down hulkers in the pursuit of materials. He got three cores for his trouble, which was a testament to the proficiency of Jackal extracting them so flawlessly. It didn't look like there was much else of value, but he got a few chunks of something called quartz. It sounded mystical, so Sal was excited to check it out later.

With a dramatic burst of water, Jackal broke through the face of the lake, twirling its tentacles to dislodge the excess water. The black enclosure snapped open to reveal the green light of the blight core, and it happily bobbed over the collection of prowler and voider corpses. With practiced strokes, each tentacle cut away the hides, sending them directly to Arsenal. A collection of cores, bones, claws, and fangs were added, too. It was great seeing the live feed of materials being added, alongside a running total of what was contained in Arsenal.

"Where are the materials going?" Barry stepped into view beside Sal. He looked positively ruffled, glancing at Sal warily. "I don't understand what's happening here."

Upgrade appeared on the other side of Sal. "It's a lot faster than I anticipated… and taking out submerged demons is remarkable in itself." She let out an almost explosive sigh. "It's transporting all those materials to Arsenal, isn't it?"

Sal nodded, smiling proudly. "Yeah, it's learned how to extract everything without damaging it."

"I'm sure that took a while." Upgrade chuckled as she just shook her head in wonder. "So, any chance of us seeing it in action? It feels a little cheap that it did all the work out of view."

Sal had intended to just send Jackal throughout the dungeon to hunt down targets, but it seemed like a poor choice now. They wanted to see a show, and he was happy to oblige. It wouldn't put any of them in danger if he summoned more demons with his whistling skills. If Jackal wasn't enough to take care of them, he still had the Tempest Function to try out. Coming to his decision, he nodded and gestured for Upgrade to cover her ears.

Barry seemed to catch the memo, and that was enough for the others to mimic the action.

The shrill burst of noise went on for far longer than before, with Sal aiming it at each of the three cave entrances. It started the invisible clock in his mind. Would Jackal finish harvesting before the next group appeared, and would the little drone be able to handle a large group of them?

"Sal, there should still be around a hundred or so demons in this cave. You might want to step back into the perimeter," Fabi warned him as she got ready for a fight. She looked a little flustered at the sudden change in plans, but was ready for whatever was required.

Sal didn't answer as he pointed at the left-most cave entrance. "We have a few more incoming. You should all step back… I haven't seen Jackal's crowd control yet. It's mostly just been single targets."

Only Barry heeded Fabi's advice as he stepped back to join Divinity, Anthony, Jack, and Blathnaid. Fabi took his space, with Upgrade on the other side of Sal. It looked like they were ready for whatever happened next.

As soon as the first hulker appeared, the black enclosure snapped into place, and the rotary blade of death was unleashed upon them. There was no finesse or style to it, but rather a barbaric cleaving as Jackal took off both arms of the approaching hulker. Its rock-like head hit the ground before it could complete a single step into Jackal's domain. The two hulkers that had flanked it were no better off, with one losing a leg and the other having its core pulled out by two interlocked tentacles.

Sal couldn't help but be surprised at the savagery. He had witnessed Jackal attacking hulkers like a jackhammer, chipping away at their defenses while looking for an opportunity to take them down. The Jackal he was looking at now could punch a hole through a hulker to find what it was looking for. It was like a loss of strategy in favor of the results. Sal wasn't sure how he should feel about it… until he saw the list of materials populating with Jackal's new finds.

It was only when a streak of green blood decorated the area around the cave entrance that Sal noticed the prowlers had arrived. Glancing behind him, Sal smiled at the group, who all gaped at Jackal, their eyes wide. "So, what do you guys think? Pretty cool, huh?"

Sal's smile vanished as he got an alert from the drone. It looked like it was from Stratagem, and Sal gave his permission instantly. He barely turned his head in time to investigate the truth of the report before Jackal shot through the cavern like a bullet, blasting past Sal's head with tentacles rapidly twirling to build up speed. At the last moment, before it reached Divinity, it unfurled its blades to attack a section of the wall, barely two feet above her head.

Divinity darted to the left to avoid it, but it was clear that if Jackal had been aiming for her, it would have killed her instantly. That same realization seemed to be on Divinity's face as she looked at Jackal in horror. Each of the blades tore clumps out of the wall, until a voider's head dropped into view, and a disguised cavern became visible in the dull light. There would be no materials to salvage from the corpse that had been slashed to oblivion by abyssal steel.

Protection Protocol Successful
    o   Protect Divinity Khan

"Sal, what the hell just happened?" Fabi warily stood by in case Jackal did something to endanger the other students. She looked at him frantically, urging an answer so she wouldn't have to take Jackal down.

Sal put his hands up, smiling awkwardly. "The Protection Protocol was the first thing I instructed Jackal to do after I built it. It's designed to protect my friends, so I greenlit the kill command when it popped up from Jackal through the Stratagem Function."

Fabi stared at him for a few seconds before turning to look at the carnage on the other side of the cavern. "So, when you turned around to look at us… that was all the time it needed?" She looked like she was calculating something in her head, and judging by the frown and bitten lip, she was struggling with the conclusion.

Upgrade had her right hand holding back her hair as she stared at Jackal with barely disguised disbelief. "This is unbelievable… We've done this dungeon countless times and never once saw that cavern."

"We've never hugged the entrance, either," Fabi argued as she gestured at their group. "We should have set up a defensive perimeter."

Upgrade shook her head as she stared at Jackal. "Sal, I better be on that protection list."

CHAPTER 59: TOXIC

While the rest of the group followed behind, away from the protection of the dungeon stairway, Sal made his way through the first cave, with Jackal leading the charge. Once Fabi and Upgrade had seen the capability of the drone, they didn't voice any arguments about navigating through the dungeon. Fabi had made a few suggestions throughout the trip, keeping all the students between her and Upgrade. She highlighted what they needed to look out for, namely the telltale signs of voider ambushes.

Her voice trailed away every so often, usually when the fighting resumed. All of them were seemingly transfixed with what was happening in the tunnel. Sure, Jackal was a terrifying force of nature, but nothing had prepared them for the Silverson Arts.

Sal leapt into the air, twisting dramatically to drive the back of his heel into a floating leecher, which exploded on impact. Even without the silver boots, Sal was strong enough to do serious damage to his opponents. His kicks wouldn't be as effective against prowlers or voiders, but his punches were practically unstoppable. Bludgeoning the demons to death was quite cathartic, but Sal knew it could be improved. He had Perfect enabled while he fought, as he was trying to refine the timing of activating the Assimilate Function at the time of a punch. It was still a hypothesis, but Sal was sure he could find a way to activate it in the split second before impact, which would hopefully give him the effects of Assimilation to drastically increase the damage output.

He was relentless as he leapt, kicked, punched, and tore the demons apart. Jackal was ahead, sending the demons toward him with a few minor injuries. Voiders would appear with a single arm; prowlers would be limping, while the leechers were left untouched. There was no way that Jackal could touch a leecher without killing it.

Just knowing that the Tempest Marshal was recharging while he fought was exciting. Strategist's Dominion had many limitations when it came to essence and output, but they didn't exist with the Tempest Marshal. He could freely use its abilities without needing to worry about the cost.

Sal was still curious about using Manifest, but he guessed that could wait for the next dungeon. What was taking priority was the timing for the punches. It was somewhat frustrating that Perfect wasn't picking up on his intent, and it kept activating the Assimilate Function a little too late or a little too early.

"Do you need to switch out, Sal?" Upgrade asked from behind him. "You've been doing a lot of fighting, and we should be coming up to the boss pretty soon."

Sal shook his head as he looked at his right arm. "Nope, I'm all good for now. Did someone else want to take a turn?" He looked around to gauge their reaction, and was surprised to see them all staring at him like he was insane.

"What?" he asked awkwardly, looking down at himself. "Am I covered in blood again?"

Upgrade shook her head with an amused smile. "I think I speak for everyone when I say… *what the fuck, Sal?*" She gestured at the cave around them. "You've been kicking the absolute shit out of anything that came near you. When the hell did you learn all of that?"

Sal grinned as he offered a slight shrug. "My dad taught me a few things during the break." He glanced back to see another leecher bobbing in his direction, a little higher than the others. It was a good opportunity to test the flying jump kick. "Like this."

He launched himself upward with his right leg at full extension, his left angled inward for support. His toes connected with the bulbous head of the leecher, before the momentum of his body carried him through it… resulting in an eruption of sickly, rotten vegetation covering his shin. Sal landed with a flick of his leg, sending the excess remnants at the wall with a sickening splat.

Barry was lost for words. His mouth was wide open as he just stared at Sal in disbelief.

Blathnaid was a little faster with finding her voice. "You made Jackal *and* learned all these martial arts… from your dad?" Her eyes practically sparkled as though inspired by the insane work ethic. "All during the break?"

"And don't forget he made the Arkwright," Fabi added with a knowing smile. "He was a very busy man."

Upgrade nodded in the direction of the cave. "I haven't seen Jackal in a while. Is he still fighting?"

Sal checked with Stratagem, which gave him a clear report of where Jackal was at all times and what it was doing. "He's sending all of the hiding demons into the boss room… well, the ones he's not killing."

Upgrade looked at Fabi. "What do you think?"

Fabi shook her head. "I say if he's feeling confident, we should let him at it. I can take on the boss if he's not up for it."

Sal raised a hand to interrupt. "I was going to attempt the Tempest Function in the boss room when they're all gathered." He flexed his fingers of his right hand. "I'm just trying to combine my punches with the Assimilation Function, to see if I can activate it at the point of impact, but I won't try that with the boss hulker. Going to play it safe with the lightning storm."

Fabi tilted her head to the side. "Why?"

Sal shrugged. "To give it more impact and destructive power. Right now, it's just my own strength and the armor over my hands."

"Try Manifest. If you use the aspect of your revolver, that should work a lot better," Fabi suggested as she glanced at Upgrade, to see whether she agreed.

Upgrade gave a nod. "It should work. And the timing would be a lot easier, as it's literally imitating a trigger sensation."

Sal clenched his fingers into a fist as he nodded. "Guess we'll give it a shot."

"Terrible pun," Barry muttered as he dropped the illusion around his armor. He also had essence-based knives at the ready. "Do we just follow you and watch, or do you want us to help?"

Upgrade shook her head. "All of you should keep training your awareness… and hang back a bit. Anything could happen while we're in here, as you all saw with the voider that tried to ambush us earlier. We're going to progress after Sal into the boss room and then we can determine the best course of action. If he requires assistance, then we can jump in to help him. This is a test of the Tempest

Marshal more than anything else, but we will be able to give more people a shot in the next dungeon."

Glancing in Divinity's direction, Upgrade looked cautious. "Would it be okay for me to ask you to use your power? Just to see if there are any unforeseen variables we might be missing?"

Divinity smiled as she shook her head. "After the ambush, I made sure to check. Everything is fine and will happen as it needs to."

"You'll get used to the vagueness in time." Barry grinned at Upgrade. "Well, somewhat."

Divinity scowled at him, her eyes narrowed. "Hey, if I just blurt out the future every time people ask, then they'll never benefit from learning it the hard way. You can't just cheat your way to capability overnight."

"You sure about that?" Barry nodded in Sal's direction. "Pretty sure he couldn't kick like that in the tower."

Fabi cleared her throat and gave them both a meaningful look. "We're in a dungeon. Please keep your focus and refrain from agitating each other."

Divinity nodded while Barry just shrugged. He stared at Sal, a wry grin tugging at the corner of his mouth. "Come on then, show us what else you can do. Any more secrets you've been holding back?"

Sal smiled as he shook his head. "Nope, the killer drone and martial arts are the highlights. Nothing else to report." He turned and gave his full attention to the dark cavern in front of him. Jackal was already en route with the next batch of demons, and he was curious how Manifest was going to work.

Testing the activation didn't do anything obvious. There was no ethereal form of a gun in his hand, nor was there a solid materialization. It looked as though it hadn't activated, but Sal could feel the change throughout his arm, like it was somehow primed and ready. He had gone with the Revolver Aspect, and it was ready to fire. Rather than testing it with Hannah's signature pose, he instead clenched his fist. Hopefully, the activation wouldn't blow up his hand.

With a half-nervous, half-excited chuckle, Sal started to bounce on his heels in an imitation of Blathnaid's earlier fighting style. He hoped that the next demon would be a prowler, because it would be an excellent test for the punch.

"Oh fuck!" Fabi shouted as she bolted forward to stand in front of the others. "Barry, get illusions around Anthony and Jack so they don't get targeted! Blathnaid, secure the rear and ensure no voiders get through!"

Sal chuckled as he got into a battle stance, staring at the boss hulker charging toward him through the tunnel. Its enormous form was laced with tentacles and vines, looking like it had been hibernating for decades in a decaying forest. He could tell from just a glance that this variant was created from the hulker absorbing a variety of leechers. It likely meant there was a Siphon or Poison ability at play. His mask would be able to keep his breathing normal, and he was far more of a Siphon threat than the hulker. There was a split second as Sal watched the hulker approach, where he questioned why he wasn't nervous. He had fought an obsidian hulker, and he assumed there would be some underlying trauma... or a blocker in his mind that would make him fearful.

Yet, as he clenched his fist and stared down his opponent, he felt… at ease? Confident, even.

Sal stopped his bouncing as he launched himself forward in the direction of the hulker. There were two aspects of Tempest Marshal he wanted to test. His left arm came up to intercept the fist of the rock-like golem. Decaying and fragmented stone smashed against the Mythical armor, and cracked. It was still a heavy enough attack that Sal's arm bounced backward, and a throbbing sensation rocketed through his arm… which reduced to a dull tingle after just a second. With the failed attack and more than a fifth of the hulker's arm disintegrating from the impact, it tried to retreat, showcasing enough intelligence for self-preservation. Unfortunately, it couldn't get out of the range of Sal's right fist that had the Scarlet Strategist's Revolver primed and ready. The punch was vicious as it swung into the exposed side of the hulker, and Sal activated a gunshot at the point of impact.

Blowing a hole straight through the hulker.

Well, not exactly through, but enough to make a serious impact. Sal stepped backward and watched as the hulker stumbled into the side of the cave wall, exposing the shattered wound the size of Sal's head. It had clearly done a chunk of damage, and Sal wasn't going to let up. He pressed forward again, making a special effort to maintain the right striking distance while leaving space to evade or dodge. Most of his techniques with the Silverson Arts were related to kicking, but he had trained a few sequences that relied on striking. Just the knowledge that his left arm was capable of blocking attacks without injuring him, and that the right had the destructive power to tear chunks out of the hulker… he felt confident.

The boss hulker furiously waved its right arm around, as though warding Sal off from approaching. Toxic gas spewed from a set of embedded pores on it, clearly designed to take Sal out or paralyze him. Sal didn't put his entire faith into the Regenerate ability or the mask, so he held his breath and advanced on his target. They were in an enclosed space, and he didn't want to risk the others taking any damage from the hulker's special attacks. Sal continued to duke it out with a rapid set of punches, each one accompanied with a revolver shot every time they landed. The sounds of gunfire echoed throughout the tunnel, signaling their battle to every remaining demon in the dungeon.

Even though Jackal was taking care of the ones in the boss room, there were clearly far too many of them for the drone to take on at once. Which led to a sizable force rushing toward their battle. The first sign was the distress from the prowlers, hearing them roar after every loud shot sang out.

Sal wasn't going to let them outnumber him and make a choke hold in the tunnel. After jumping back to maintain distance from the boss hulker, Sal switched from Manifest to the Assimilation Function. He aimed his two fingers down the tunnel and let off a continuous charge of purple lightning. It went on for a few seconds before the hulker recovered and swung at Sal again.

A few notifications popped up, and Sal ignored them, knowing that they were simply reports of confirmed kills and the new stats that came with them. A glance to his left showed that Barry had erected an essence barrier of sorts with the Vengeful Vambraces. There was no way he'd be able to prevent all the toxins from getting through, so Sal hoped they had evacuated when they had the opportunity.

"Don't worry, they're fine. Do you need help?" Upgrade's voice came from behind him.

Sal shook his head. "I'm good; just wanted to make sure. Will you be okay with the poison?"

"I've got a mask," Upgrade responded as she darted into view, standing in front of Barry's barrier and primed to fight at a moment's notice. Her hands had transformed into mechanical claws, with each finger resembling a nasty-looking knife. The bottom half of her face was obscured with what looked like a scarf, and her eyes were locked onto the hulker. "Let me know if it's too much for you."

Sal nodded as he launched forward again, his right fist blowing a hole into the armpit of the hulker's shoulder. It wasn't enough to remove the arm completely, but it was a good start. The toxins continued to spew out, albeit with less force than before. Sal sidestepped to flank the flailing hulker and managed to get another great shot in at the same shoulder. This time, it was more than enough to do the job, and the toxins stopped as the decaying rock crumbled upon hitting the ground.

With a scream that was like glass shattering, the hulker whirled around erratically to swing at them with its remaining arm. It had clearly marked Sal as the key threat, and went into a state of overdrive to get rid of him. Wild and furious swings within the enclosed space were quite deadly, but Sal was more than able to avoid them with a few well-timed ducks and jumps. Although he was confident that the Mythical armor could successfully block an attack, it was easier to just avoid them.

When the last swing came, Sal ducked and watched as the hulker overextended itself, struggling to regain its footing to launch a consecutive attack. Sal didn't need a better invitation than that to start a veritable barrage of punches, all focused on the same spot. There was no benefit to using lightning on the creature, as the explosive shots were capable of doing the job. After the eighth explosive punch, the boss hulker fell backward to slump against the wall. Its left leg twitched as though it were trying to use it as a weapon, as both arms were either shattered or reduced to a stump. Sal would have felt sorry for it, if it hadn't been screeching bloody murder at him in that glass-shattering wail.

With it close to death, Sal turned his attention to the tunnel where the remaining demons were screaming. He couldn't see them without the assistance of his eye-patch, but he could tell that they were being annihilated by Jackal. Sal sent another burst of purple lightning down the dark passage, just for good measure.

When he turned to look at the dying hulker, he switched back to Manifest and primed his arm for one last shot.

Upgrade seemingly understood his intent. "Use Assimilation so you can get some stats from it," she suggested as she adjusted the cloth around her mouth. "No point in letting it go to waste."

Sal nodded as he gestured for her to step back. "Good point. But I don't want you to get caught up in the blast." He glanced at her and smiled, knowing she wouldn't see it through the mask. "Thanks for sticking around, by the way."

Upgrade moved backward a few paces until she was at the edge of the barrier, which had changed in color. It looked like Barry had been replaced by Jack when it came to their defenses. Upgrade nodded that she was far enough back. "You know I wouldn't ever let anything happen to you in a dungeon, right?"

"I know." Sal chuckled. "We've come a long way, haven't we?"

His sentiment was further compounded by the explosion of lightning that burned through the remainder of the hulker's defenses. The crackling bolt of electricity found every available wound, seeping into it and charring the remaining vines. Every crack visible on the boss hulker was illuminated by the purple lightning, until it finally reached critical mass… and exploded in a shower of decayed rubble and yellow steam.

Sal held his left arm in front of his face to defend himself, and was glad he did so when he felt more than three vibrations. Two hit his chest, and one hit the protective arm. Thankfully, none of them actually hurt him, with Regenerate quickly nullifying any pain before it could flare up.

Glancing over at Upgrade, he was relieved to see that she was okay. There were still some sounds of screeching down the tunnel, and Sal gave Jackal the command to finish them all off.

"So, time for the next one?" Sal asked as he dusted off some of the hulker residue from his left arm.

CHAPTER 60: TEMPEST

"Okay, so do we just stand back and let him do his thing?" Barry asked as they descended into the second dungeon of the day. "Or are we going to do the rotations again?" He looked at Upgrade for clarity on what was happening.

Fabi shook her head, answering before Upgrade got a chance to. "We've seen him use Manifest and the Assimilation Function. Overdrive and Capacitor are working exactly as we intended, and Regenerate successfully activated whenever he blocked attacks." She gestured at Sal's eye-patch. "Stratagem linked with Jackal perfectly, so all we really need to see now is the Tempest Function in action."

Upgrade smiled as she nodded in agreement. "Which is why we picked this dungeon in particular. It should give us all a nice view of everything that's happening, and there won't be any voiders to worry about. This is more of a wind-down, and we can absolutely take you to another dungeon if you want after he tries the Tempest Function."

"You think it'll be finished in one go? What's so special about this dungeon that it can be cleared so fast?" Barry asked as they reached the base of the stairs. He took a tentative step forward while taking special note of his surroundings, looking for a clue as to why this dungeon was different. It didn't take him long to find an answer.

Sal, on the other hand, couldn't stop smiling. "Gotta say, this looks like an absolute nightmare to run."

Upgrade gestured at the crater in front of them. There was a winding path that went downward, nestled tightly against the edge of the crater in a loosely circular pattern. Countless nooks and crevices were visible along the path, as perfect murder holes for demons lying in wait.

Barry bit his lip with uncertainty. "How is this perfect, though? We need to walk down a narrow path, while being open to attacks from everything hiding in the walls? If Sal tries a flying jump kick, he'll fall into that abyss." He peered over the edge of the crater to the murkiness below. "And I'm pretty sure Regenerate can't bring him back from the dead."

Fabi nodded, grinning. "Yep, which is why this place offers much higher rewards, because nobody likes clearing it. Well, except the Heroes who can fly… and the ones with large area attacks. They love it."

"Is there a boss in this dungeon?" Blathnaid peered over the edge, getting far closer than both Anthony or Jack. "It's probably at the bottom?"

"Yep," Fabi countered as she pointed at the crevices in the wall. "It's a scuttler. Which would normally be a reason to avoid this place at all costs, but it will have great difficulty in getting up here."

Barry's eyes widened. "Great difficulty? It would be a hell of a lot more reassuring if you said it was impossible! I get that Sal is super strong and capable now, but there are useless people here, too." He glanced at Anthony. "No offense."

"Offense taken," Anthony muttered, even though he was nodding in agreement with what Barry was saying.

Jack grinned. "Guess I got promoted out of the useless category?"

Barry ignored him as he continued to look at Fabi desperately. "How were we allowed in here in the first place? A scuttler is way beyond our capabilities, especially if it can make its way up here."

Fabi sighed as she glanced at Upgrade for help.

Upgrade smiled warmly. "Hunting a scuttler is very straightforward. They're heavily armored, hulking creatures with far too many legs. If it tries to scale those pathways, it'll fall. If it tries to follow the path, then it will be a very predictable target."

"I hate this," Divinity breathed as she took another step away from the ledge, her eyes white. "There are spiders here, too."

"Okay, yes… there are." Upgrade laughed. "But they're not really worth worrying about. They've covered the lower layers in webbing that is sharp as a razor and strong as steel. There's a good chance that the scuttler won't be able to get up through those webs without seriously injuring itself."

Barry shook his head as he moved back to join Divinity. "None of this is reassuring."

Fabi shrugged and spread her hands. "Hey, this is where we originally tested the Tempest Function. We thought it would be a quick and fun dungeon to show you."

"Quick and fun?" Barry repeated the words slowly, staring at Fabi and Upgrade as if they were insane. "Are you guys actually psychotic Offense types, by any chance? I'm not getting a single Support class vibe from either of you."

"We could always make some gear from the corpses if that helped?" Blathnaid teased with a straight face. "What do you say, a little spider hat? Wouldn't take long."

Divinity visibly paled as she shook her head, no words coming out. Barry, on the other hand, looked around him in confusion, specifically at the walls.

"What are you doing?" Sal frowned. He wasn't feeling anywhere near the amount of anxiety his friends were having. Jackal had taken on a scuttler on its first-ever trial run, so there was a very good chance it could solo the dungeon boss by itself.

Barry waved him away as he continued looking around. "Just checking that there's nothing trying to kill Divinity. With her luck, there's a spider directly above her head."

Divinity immediately darted away, somehow managing to give Barry a glare before checking the ceiling for signs of any spiders. There were none.

Sal smiled as he glanced at the crater again. "So, are you suggesting I activate the Tempest Function while going down?"

Fabi shook her head. "Nope. Just aim downward and fire."

"That simple?" Sal questioned as he looked at his right arm. "I thought there'd be a bit more technique or finesse involved."

Upgrade shrugged. "All of the technique and finesse went into the design, not the execution. So, come on, give it a shot."

Sal chuckled as he aimed at the center of the abyss. It wasn't really a tough target as the crater narrowed at the center. If he had to guess, he would have assumed it would take a few hours of walking to get to the bottom. That was without even taking the fighting into consideration. He activated the Tempest Function, getting it primed before firing. A part of him expected the same sensation as Manifest or the Assimilation Function, where neither had any telltale signs of being active.

He was wrong.

Lightning sparked through his right arm, sputtering and crackling, while forcing his arm to vibrate chaotically. Holding his aim became a lot more challenging as his left arm heated up through the effects of Capacitor and Overdrive. Purple lightning shot through his own torso, creating a current between both arms and humming as it suspended like an erratic wire in front of him.

"Awesome," Anthony breathed in wonder.

Sal's eye-patch locked onto the unseen target within the abyss, and Sal finally let the Tempest Function trigger. All the wires of purple lightning that had floated around his chest were sucked into his glowing right arm, before getting violently expelled through his open palm. The resulting form was… unimpressive to say the least.

A purple ball of volatile electricity floated away from his hand, at a painfully slow speed. It was roughly the size of his head and it seemed to be descending through the darkness, its only tether being a single strand of crackling light that was attached to Sal's right arm. To everyone watching, it looked like the most dramatic and overhyped fishing performance… with Sal launching a ball-shaped lure into the murky pit.

Barry's laugh was both immediate and explosive, managing to defuse any tension in the group. Even Divinity's fear had been put on hold as she moved closer to the edge to see the sinking ball of light.

Sal glanced at Fabi, his eyebrow raised. "I fucked it up, didn't I?"

To his surprise, Fabi shook her head, smiling. "Nope… the fun stuff starts now."

Sal frowned as he looked back at the orb, which had descended around fifty feet into the hole. In terms of pathways, it was close to the third floor. There was nothing remarkable about the bobbing ball of light. Was it going to do something when it hit an opponent? Did Sal have to angle it toward something? There were more questions in his head than answers.

"That should be low enough." Upgrade grinned as she peered over the edge. "Anyone who wants to see some fried scuttler, this is your chance." She beckoned for them to come closer to take a look.

Jack lay down on the ground and peered over the edge, with Anthony following suit. Clearly neither of them trusted themselves enough to not fall into the crater. Divinity seemed to fight against all her natural instincts and came to stand beside Blathnaid—well, a half step back from her. Barry was the last one who moved beside Upgrade, as though determining that she'd be best equipped to save him if anything went wrong.

Sal was just as confused as they were. He didn't feel particularly confident in the Tempest Function. In terms of battle capability, it was ridiculously slow, and very demanding on essence. He couldn't really think of a use-case for something like this… unless he had a lot of preparation time.

"Ye of little faith," Fabi muttered as the first lance of lightning speared out from the floating ball. It curved in the air, crackling loudly, before smashing into an unseen section of the wall. A demonic roar sounded out as quickly as it died.

More bolts of lightning shot out from the ball to strike in different directions. Each of them was ridiculously fast, and all happened within the space of a second. Sal only saw two, but the eye-patch counted eight. There was no indication of it stopping, with a barrage of light-based attacks happening on repeat. A cacophony of screams was drowned out by the thundering bolts of lightning, each crackling aggressively like an unrelenting storm. Sal couldn't even hear himself think as the bangs continued, one after another.

He couldn't feel any excess draw on Capacitor, which meant that the Tempest Function was using all the essence it required in that purple ball. It was a wild thing to experience, where he was essentially just holding a line to this murderous disco ball of death. The shots of lightning didn't look to be slowing down as the ball descended farther into the depths. Each and every demon that took up residence in the dungeon was vulnerable to the attacks, as the walls themselves seemingly weren't capable of stopping the barrage. Chunks of demons and rock fell into the webbed pit, with Sal able to see some of them getting diced as they went through the invisible razor-blade webs.

The best part of it, besides the fact that he had nothing to do other than watch, was the updates coming through his eye-patch.

Tempest Function Report (132)
- o   Strength has increased by 1.32
- o   Mobility has increased by 2.83
- o   Speed has increased by 2.29
- o   Endurance has increased by 2.41
- o   No Technique Improvement
- o   Skill Master has improved by 0.6
- o   Mythcrafter has improved by 0.2
- o   No Essence Reserve Improvement

Regenerate was doing its job perfectly, and Sal hadn't noticed any discomfort from the addition of new stats. There was a vague tingling sensation in his body, but he really had to focus on it to even know it was there. The Tempest Function had apparently included all the kills from the previous dungeon, as it used the Assimilation Function, too. Just in a very different way.

Sal's eyes widened when he saw the numbers that had been earned from just the two dungeons. There was no way that it would be like that in the future, though. Diminishing returns was a real thing, and it would get progressively harder to build his stats in the future. Just to test out his theory, he called out to Fabi over the sound of the lightning machine gun.

"When do the stats start slowing down?" Sal shouted.

Fabi's laugh was beautiful and infectious, when Sal was able to hear it. With the current lightning concert in the dungeon, it looked like she was enjoying a particularly good yawn. Thankfully, she had the sense to shout back.

"They slowed down for me after hitting twenty! But there are new stats that come from stronger demons, like Endurance."

Sal smiled as he checked his eye-patch to see the Endurance stat. It was his first time seeing it, and it definitely wasn't one that had appeared on his self-analysis in the past. "What does it do?"

Upgrade was beside him now, Barry choosing to remain where he was, his eyes fixed on the mayhem happening below.

"Endurance is like physical resistance. How much punishment your body can take," Upgrade said loudly so he could hear, somehow finding the perfect timing to speak between demonic screams.

Sal was about to answer when Upgrade held up a hand. Each of her fingers counted down, and when the last one came down, the ball of lightning dissipated, giving the demons a very welcome reprieve from instant death.

She smiled broadly at him. "We've capped it at thirty seconds so you have plenty of uses. Between the Tempest Function and Regenerate, you can probably appreciate why Fabi had the dregs so regularly."

Sal smiled as he looked over in Fabi's direction. "Thank you so much for all the help with this. It's genuinely amazing. I love it."

"If you learn EssPro properly, you'll be able to do stuff like this, too," Fabi said a little reproachfully, as though trying to get him to see the beauty in the topic. "There are so many functions you can make that will transform how abilities operate."

Upgrade nodded in the direction of the crater. "We're in a dungeon, so we should focus on that for now. Sal, you've got a few options. Want to send down Jackal to root out the boss, or do you want to send another Tempest down their way?"

Sal went through the same motions to create another ball of purple light, which bobbed down just as slowly as the previous one. It took longer for it to reach a point where it could start killing demons, as the previous iteration had taken out a massive chunk of the dungeon's forces. One new development was the webbing getting electrified with a purplish fire… and a whole host of variant spiders were killed from just that alone. Each of them popped from the surge of electricity.

Eventually, the ball came to a stop at the base of the abyss. It fired bolts of lightning at a single target, relentlessly, and in the space of three seconds, with over twenty-five attacks, the last enemy in the crater was defeated.

The silence at the top of the crater was almost deafening. Nobody was sure how to process what had just happened, with many of them looking at the burning webbing in a transfixed daze.

As per usual, it was Barry who broke the silence. He looked at Sal, his face white. "How is this even possible? I'm genuinely trying to get my head around it… but it's not making any sense. You were getting stats, implanted into your body, just by standing there?"

Sal nodded slowly. "If we can get enough cores for the Arkwright, then we'll be able to hopefully make more equipment with Capacitor. With that, we'll be able to replicate this design for the other members in the guild." He glanced at Upgrade to see whether there were any objections.

Upgrade shook her head, smiling. "And don't forget about the stupid number of demonic cores required to get the Assimilate ability… without even thinking about what Regenerate requires."

Barry's frown deepened. "Guessing you need to kill a really strong demon to get the right ones?" He looked at Sal with the most genuine expression of dismay. "Or are they just really expensive?"

Sal's smile tightened. He wasn't sure he had it in him to tell Barry that the stat-stealing ability came from killing leechers. All the materials he'd need to make something with Assimilate were in Arsenal at that very moment.

"Far too strong for your current abilities," Fabi agreed with an amused expression aimed at Barry.

CHAPTER 61: PLAN

While Upgrade and Fabi discussed the results with the dungeon administrator, Sal stood off to one side with the report from his eye-patch. Running two high-level dungeons had been ridiculously lucrative for him, and not just from a materials perspective.

Tempest + Assimilation Function Report (216)
- o   Strength has increased by 1.67
- o   Mobility has increased by 3.36
- o   Speed has increased by 2.85
- o   Endurance has increased by 2.70
- o   No Technique Improvement
- o   Skill Master has improved by 0.7
- o   Mythcrafter has improved by 0.3
- o   No Essence Reserve Improvement

Seeing the cumulative gains from the dungeons was quite sobering. Sal knew that it was a great method for bringing up his base stats, but he had severely underestimated just how dramatic an improvement that would be. Sure, Fabi had said that there was a ceiling around the twenty-point range, and he was quite curious which stat she managed to maximize.

He navigated to the totals section of his stats, just to see how things were looking. His only real benchmark for physical stats was Darren Lenihan, who was able to jump through the ceiling of a three-story building. He managed that with a Strength score in the mid-teens.

Salvatore Argento Stats:
- o   Strength: 7.3
- o   Mobility: 12.5
- o   Speed: 10.1
- o   Endurance: 2.7
- o   Fitness: 9.8

Sal stared at the numbers in a sort of daze. It looked like he had sorely underestimated the amount of Mobility and Speed he had gained in just two dungeons. He was under no illusion that the training with his father, coupled with the Silverson Arts training in his own time wasn't helping... but it was nowhere near the explosive stat gain a dungeon offered him.

"You doing okay, Sal?" Divinity asked with a warm smile as she moved into his field of view. She still wore his peaked hat.

Name	Tempest Warden (Guildmaster Variant)
Origin	Crafted
Age	New
Grade	Legendary (Upper)
Materials	Refined Upgrade Essence | Refined Figment Essence | Refined Construct Essence | Eternal Core | Storm Steel | Moonsilver | Lux Crystal | Tempest Steel Alloy | Onyx Catalyzer | Obelisk Core | ...

Attributes	Automate: Integrated functionality of Tempest Marshal Set will be activated either by will or automatically when conditions are met.
	• Tempest Warden (Active)
	   o **Composure Function:** Requires Warded + Nullify
	   o **Recovery Function:** Requires Regenerate
	   o **Regenerate Function**: Requires Tempest Marshal
	Warded: Protects user from all Influence and Psionic attacks.
	Nullify: Protects user from all Energy Manipulation attacks.
	Regenerate: Passively converts all available internal essence for healing purposes. Depending on how much essence is available, fatal wounds can be treated.
	• **Recovery Function:**
	   o Fatigue Mode: Minor Internal Healing
	   o Training Mode: Internal + External Healing
	• **Regenerate Function:**
	   o Combat Mode: Major Internal + External Healing
	   o Calamity Mode: Regeneration

Abilities	Automate | Warded | Nullify | Regenerate
Runes	Advanced Calibration Rune | Advanced Reinforcement Rune | Advanced Warding Rune | Advanced Attuning Rune
Power Source	External Essence

Evolution	No
Quality	Perfect
Condition	100%
Value	Unknown

"Everything is good, don't worry," Sal answered Divinity as he did a quick Appraisal with the eye-patch. It confirmed a few things for him, but also left him with some questions for Fabi and Upgrade.

"Well, I thought I'd give this back. It was a great help." Divinity took off the peaked cap and handed it to Sal. "Thank you for giving it to me for a while."

"You're welcome." Sal placed the cap on his head, feeling the recovery starting to kick in. There weren't any injuries, so he assumed it was just working off some of the fatigue he had accumulated in the dungeon. Maybe it was because it was limited to his head rather than his body, but it looked like they had designed the set to have specialist areas that they treated.

Divinity paused for a few seconds as she glanced back to the rest of the group. She looked like she was about to say something, but hesitated.

"No need to hold back," Sal said with a knowing smile. There was no way that the future hadn't changed now that she saw the combat potential of the Tempest Marshal. "I promise you're not going to upset me."

Divinity's smile turned guilty as she let out a reluctant sigh. "Honestly, I don't even know where to start…" She gestured at Sal's chest. "That's not the equipment I saw in my vision." She brought her gaze up to meet his. "There are so many things changing, and I don't know how to process all of it."

Sal reached out and placed a hand on her shoulder. "I was sure that you were going to tell me something about Blathnaid's future. Did you see her in there?"

Divinity's eyes widened. "I know! Like, when the hell did she learn to fight like that?" A guilty laugh escaped her lips as she glanced over at Blathnaid with the others. "It was amazing seeing her like that. When you think of the people who were left over for the cohort battle, did you ever imagine something like this?"

"Hey, that was my question!" Sal feigned annoyance before chuckling. "Seriously, though? I would never have imagined they'd become powerhouses. Barry was always a dark horse, but seeing how Jack and Anthony are excelling in their own domains… it's amazing. And we had nothing to do with it, which is the best part."

Divinity raised an eyebrow at Sal. "What do you mean you had nothing to do with it?"

Sal shrugged as he gestured at them. "I didn't do anything to their weaves, nor did I make any equipment for them." He winced slightly as he turned his hand to point at Anthony, specifically. "You could argue that giving him the Voracious Rapier was a big help, but that's not really a factor in his growth."

Divinity shook her head slowly from side to side. "Yeah… we clearly see things very differently." A smile crept onto her face before she pursed her lips. "So, now that you're healthy, what's the next big plan?"

Sal frowned as he thought about it. "Doc Ameye sent me a lot of cool materials to work with, and I want to make more of the Tempest Marshal armor set for my legs and feet. I still have a lot of classes to catch up on since I was in the infirmary for so long. I don't think I'll be able to fast-track through the Advanced War Zone module like we planned."

Divinity bit her lower lip. "That really depends. We still need to go through that shit-show with Shade, but after that, you'll likely get fast-tracked."

"Don't suppose you'd break your cardinal rule of not telling me facts? It would really help if I knew what to expect," Sal asked as gently as he could manage. He felt like he was likelier to get an answer if he was serious with her, rather than jovial.

Divinity hesitated before she shook her head. "Everything seems to be changing around me, so what's the point in holding back?" She let out a frustrated sigh before laughing humorlessly. "Shade is going to give us an example of what the Tier 1 guilds do on a daily basis. His guild will bring us to a teleportation gate that leads into the heart of a Red Zone. It's a big show of force to scare us."

"What could he possibly gain from that?" Sal asked out of genuine curiosity. "I mean, him trying to scare us makes sense… but I can't understand why Quest Academy would approve it."

Divinity rolled her eyes. "It's a power play. He's trying to show everyone what the Reclamation guilds need to do on a daily basis. It's not him trying to scare them away from fighting, but rather a way for him to make the Delvers Guild look like a good career choice."

"He's using it as a stage for recruitment?" Sal asked in disbelief. "So, there's no big plot for him abducting me or something like that?"

Divinity shook her head. "Nope. He's going to mess with you, though. There's a whole big song and dance about how great their cloaking and stealth abilities are. Apparently, they can adjust their power levels to keep a large group of us safe in the Red Zone so we can observe the demons there."

Sal remained quiet as he tried to figure out what Shade was planning.

"So, Shade will ask everyone what their equipment is, the grades and what they can do." Divinity stared at Sal with a tight smile. "He's convinced you've got something special that helped you get to the top rank, and this is his method of getting you to admit it."

"And if I don't?" Sal muttered in annoyance, crossing his arms. "What's he going to do?"

Divinity smiled as she offered a good-natured shrug. "There are countless possibilities. One of the recurring ones is that he tries to blame you for lying about your equipment, and will use that as a basis to extort compensation damages from Quest Academy and the Argento Auction House. He's trying to paint the Delvers Guild in a sympathetic light, by helping the next generation of Heroes."

"You're joking," Sal said in disbelief. There was no way Shade was going with that angle, after all the shit he had pulled and countless deaths in his guild. "Nobody would believe it for a second."

Divinity nodded in agreement. "Yeah, it's ridiculous... which is why I told you there's nothing to worry about. The Hunter Bureau is on high alert and Captain Chatfield has been briefed on everything. There are a few other variables at play, like if any fighting breaks out... but you don't need to worry about that either. It will get taken care of pretty quickly."

"How would they feel entitled to compensation?" Sal asked in confusion. "I'm trying to think how Shade would make a case for it, and I'm not coming up with anything."

"Destruction of gear," Divinity replied with a tired smile. "When the cloaking and stealth fails during their protective exercise, they'll make a show of fighting off a few demons... which will lead to some contrived injuries and 'priceless' gear being destroyed. They'll demand that the Argento Auction House outfits them with equivalent or better artifacts."

"Just when you think you can't hate someone more." Sal chuckled humorlessly. "So, there's no abduction threat or actual danger? It's just them trying to pull a fast one on my family and Quest Academy?"

Divinity nodded. "Yeah, it's a pretty shitty situation, and I've already highlighted it in the last Doom Society meeting. Quest wasn't happy with the answer they got back from the Doom Council, which was to the effect of business as usual."

"I kinda feel hollow after hearing all of this," Sal admitted as he crossed his arms. "I mean, I'm grateful that you told me... but it's incredibly frustrating." His brow furrowed as he thought through the details. "What happens if I tell Shade that my equipment is all Legendary and Mythic grade?"

Divinity's jaw dropped. "That's a terrible idea... don't do that." She genuinely looked panicked as she stared at Sal in disbelief. "Seriously, that's a surefire way to force an abduction attempt. If Shade catches wind that your equipment can boost internal abilities and stats, then he'll do whatever he finds necessary to take it from you."

A smile appeared on Sal's face. "Whatever necessary? That sounds like a good method to spur the Hunter Bureau into action, wouldn't you think? If they start attacking, wouldn't there be a good chance that the Delvers would be destroyed?"

All color drained from Divinity's face. "Sal... you could get seriously hurt if you go down this route. It's better to just go with the safer outcome. There's no way his demands will actually go anywhere, and there's no need for you to put yourself in danger!"

"You've got nothing to worry about." Sal chuckled as he thought about all the possible outcomes from Divinity's words. "I wouldn't put myself in danger like that."

Divinity's eyes narrowed as she stared at him. "If you're thinking that this is the best method to get rid of them, you need to remember that they're a Tier 1 guild. Even with Jackal and the Tempest Marshal, you're not going to be able to take on an entire organization. All we need to do is work with the facts, and let the Hunter Bureau do their job."

"So, it's fine if Shade forces my hand, and not the other way around?" Sal asked in a genuinely perplexed tone as he stared back at Divinity. "He's going to be putting the other students in danger just to extort my family. You think we should just wait for it to happen and trust the Hunter Bureau? They haven't done anything to the Delvers so far, and we heard at the gala how their members have the highest mortality rates."

"I don't like this train of thought, Sal." Divinity sounded almost pleading as she stared at him intently. "Please don't force the worst outcome with Shade. It could genuinely lead to your death!"

Sal nodded as he turned his attention to the others. "Just thinking aloud." Blathnaid and Anthony were busy stacking a trove of materials onto the desk in front of the dungeon attendant, balancing the spoils that Jackal hadn't deposited into Arsenal.

"I shouldn't have said anything." Divinity cursed herself as she grabbed Sal's elbow. "Seriously, Sal… please don't go down this path. You could defer the Advanced War Zone class until the next semester and everything will smooth over. There are plenty of other ways for you to navigate this. You could just refuse to go on that exercise, and it'll only result in a small drop in your Savior ranking."

Sal shook his head slowly. "He's threatened me and my family, already. Now, he's trying to extort them." He chuckled humorlessly. "Don't worry, Divinity. I won't do anything stupid. By the way, how long do we have until we have the outing with Shade?"

"You promise?" Divinity pulled his elbow so he would look at her. "Because it doesn't sound like you're thinking straight."

Sal met her gaze and gave her a slight nod. "I promise." He forced a smile. "So, how long?"

"A week," Divinity responded slowly. "This week is recovery from the last exercise, but it was definitely so the Hunter Bureau could perform their investigation into Shade and the Delvers."

A week was more than enough time. Sal was already planning his next steps. His father wanted him to become a powerhouse that nobody could mess with, and this was what he was talking about. Shade thought he was able to push him around, and Sal wasn't going to take that one sitting down.

Divinity's eyes turned white as she stared at Sal, as though not trusting his reassurance. It only took a few seconds before she saw what she was looking for.

"You promised!" she complained, frowning, before a smile eventually broke through, followed by a surprised laugh.

"That I wouldn't do something stupid," Sal corrected her. "You said nothing about coming up with a smarter plan."

Divinity's eyes widened as she looked at some form of new future, her smile faltering. "There's no way this will end without any casualties…"

Sal wore a resolved expression, his mind working at full speed to make a solid plan for the outing with Shade. "That's the point."

CHAPTER 62: REPUTATION

"We're not sparring?" Petro asked in confusion as he sat down in the center of the training area. With a pat on the polished concrete beside him, he gestured for Sal to sit down. "What's going on?"

Sal sat with a strained smile. "A few things happened earlier. You already know about the Tempest Marshal set. They told me that you helped test it out."

Petro grinned as he offered a playful shrug. "Ah, I hope you're not going to treat that as a lie. It was all in good fun." His smile faltered as he caught Sal's expression. "What's wrong? Did something happen?"

"The outing with Shade. I got more context from Divinity, and it's not great," Sal said before going on to explain everything that had happened during the dungeon and the new information he got from her visions. It took a while and Petro didn't interrupt him throughout.

When Sal got to the end, he looked at his dad with an awkward smile. "So, what do you think?"

"First thing I want to know is what plan you had that managed to shock Divinity," Petro answered in a reluctant tone. "I hope you didn't choose to do something you'll later regret."

"Like killing him?" Sal suggested with a laugh. "I won't lie, that did cross my mind… but his actions so far don't exactly warrant that sort of response. I'd rather see him discredited, and his guild destroyed. I think it would be a far more just punishment than simply ending his life."

Petro raised an eyebrow. "Okay, and how do you plan on doing that? I won't deny that I'm hesitant to let you go through with this. It sounds dangerous, and I'd rather solve these issues behind closed doors than on a stage in front of your classmates and teachers."

Sal took a steadying breath as he started to explain his thoughts. "Since we're going into a combat area, and I'm a guildmaster… wouldn't it make sense to bring my advisors?"

Petro's surprised face quickly morphed into a wide smile. "Let me guess… Villa?"

"And Vanessa." Sal smiled. "I was thinking we could ask Luke and the Dragoons, but wasn't sure what you'd think of that."

"They're unaffiliated with Quest Academy, and their relationship with the Hunter Bureau is awful at best. It would be wise to leave them out of this until it's a genuine emergency," Petro explained with a slight shake of his head. "I'm not trying to minimize the risk or danger that Shade presents, but it's not at a level where we'd need to enlist Luke."

Sal frowned, suddenly a lot less sure of the outcome. "And do you think that Villa and Vanessa would be enough to keep me safe and keep Shade in check?"

Petro grinned as he placed a hand on his chest. "I think you're forgetting about another advisor."

"Upgrade?" Sal guessed playfully, laughing at his father's feigned look of disappointment.

With a wave of his hand. "Between the four of us, you're guaranteed to be safe. The problem it presents is how overkill it will appear to everyone else," Petro explained. "I know you likely don't care about the optics, but it will be hard to control the narrative when all of your peers see you flanked by so many power-houses."

"What if you were waiting in the Red Zone, instead?" Sal laughed at the stupidity of the idea. "Sorry, it was the first thing that came to my head."

Petro paused as he thought about it. "It's not the worst idea, actually. We could play it as an exercise with the third-years you enlisted. O'Brien and Sakura?"

"If I explain things to Fabi properly, she'll probably go with them," Sal reasoned as he looked at his dad. "Is this insane? Should I just avoid doing the module?"

Petro shook his head. "Shade is relentless. If it's not this, it will be something else. If he's dead set on cornering you, or taking your equipment, then he's clearly prepared to deal with whatever fallout comes with it. What's urging me along this path, or plan, is the fact that Divinity was convinced he'd try abduction if you revealed that you had the Subsume or Assimilation abilities. We can't let that slide."

Sal bit his lip as he thought about it. He didn't want to endanger his allies by sending them into a Red Zone. Because Shade was trying to make a point, there was a very good chance that the location he visited would end up being extremely dangerous. Even though they were scum, they were still a Tier 1 guild, and that wasn't something to be taken lightly. "I'm suddenly a lot less sure of my plan."

"What in particular?" Petro laughed as he raised an eyebrow. "If you get all sentimental and say it's because I'm in danger, I'll just have to remind you that I'm ridiculously badass. Besides, as a parent, there's no way I'd let you go through this shitstorm by yourself. Shade's animosity stems from my actions back at the auction house, and there's no reason for you to take the blame."

"I did antagonize him a good bit," Sal admitted, sighing.

"Which he deserved," Petro answered as he pointed at Sal's chest. "And you should never apologize for standing for what you believe in. It's a horrible injustice that he's been allowed to swing his dick around and demand that everyone else adapt. This will be a lesson for him in humility, and a reminder that he's just as accountable as everyone else."

With that said, Petro got to his feet and dusted himself off.

Sal gave him a curious look. "Are we done talking about it?"

"You're frustrated as hell, and we've got a much better outlet for working that out." Petro grinned as he got into stance. "Besides, I'm curious to know if those new stats of yours will be any use with the Silverson Arts."

Sal smiled as he got to his feet and readied himself. The Tempest Marshal set was carefully stored in Arsenal, so he was just facing his father in the standard Quest Academy uniform. "Is there anything I'm overlooking?"

Petro launched forward with a high kick that swept toward the left side of Sal's head. It was blocked perfectly, which brought a smile to Petro's face. "Probably… but most people deal with troublesome scenarios without knowing the future. You're far more prepared than you've got any right to be."

Sal darted to the right to put himself in a more favorable position. His body glided along the polished concrete, so much so that he overshot the mark and left himself three feet away from his intended position.

"Interesting," Petro remarked as he closed the distance with a jab at Sal's chest. "Looks like your timing is a little off?"

Sal frowned as he brought his hand up to block his father's attack, surprising himself once again at the speed in which he managed to get there. "It's faster and more fluid, if that makes sense?"

"Well, yeah… you did say that it increased Speed and Mobility, so I was curious." Petro sent four more attacks, all at varied speeds, toward different parts of Sal's body: two punches and two kicks.

None of them managed to get through and Sal stared in shock at his own hands. "This is crazy… It's taking an insane amount of control to just stop my arms where I want them."

"Less daydreaming, more adapting," Petro instructed in a firmer tone as he started their spar properly, with a few gradual attacks at a low speed, that built momentum over time. Each new attack came with a little more speed and power.

Sal weaved his entire body through the attacks, ducking and dodging as he fought to control his ridiculously agile movements. The sensitivity of his movements was taking a lot longer to adapt to, to the point that even Perfect struggled to grasp the timing. It defaulted to the perfect form of his attacks, while his body instead tried to use the fullest range of motion possible.

"Good, you're getting there," Petro remarked as his attacks gained a lot more speed and force. His distance to Sal kept closing, and his kicks became less telegraphed.

Sal's limbs moved like a blur as he embraced instincts to stop the flurry of incoming attacks. One stellar moment throughout their bout was when Sal unceremoniously slapped away his father's palm and went for a kick to the head. It felt right, and his brain knew it could work, but it was a movement never attempted by his body. Sal's head was ridiculously close to the ground as he leaned back, sending his right leg up to explosively kick at his father's upper chest.

The attack failed when Petro blocked it—although with a surprised expression. Sal cartwheeled backward to maintain distance, and landed in stance with an equally stupefied face.

"What just happened?" Sal looked at his hands in disbelief. "That's not a part of the Silverson Arts."

Petro stared at him for a few seconds before a wide smile appeared. "It's an unorthodox evasion, and a little flashy for my tastes… but it worked. That's all that matters." He chuckled as he gestured at Sal's hands. "You're far faster than our last spar, and your reaction speed is getting ridiculous. With more training, you'll be formidable on the battlefield."

"I'm still not feeling very reassured by the whole Shade situation," Sal admitted as he got back into stance. "I don't want to put anyone in danger, even though I want to see him punished."

Petro shrugged, like it was no big deal. "Want me to just go and quietly murder him?"

Sal stared at his father in disbelief, which made blocking the flying jump kick extremely difficult. Yet, somehow, he managed to bring his arms up defensively to turn his father's body in midair. The additional strength really helped in throwing his father, but the surprise didn't stop there.

Petro landed on one hand and cartwheeled backward in a perfect replication of Sal's earlier move. He glanced at himself, grinning. "Might need to add that to the next edition of the Silverson Arts. It's quite good."

"Murder him?" Sal whispered harshly, his eyes wide. "He's a Tier 1 guildmaster!"

Petro chuckled as he spread his hands. "Come on, I needed to lighten the mood a little. Also, it was a good opportunity for a surprise attack. You did great, by the way."

Sal groaned as he looked at his father in disbelief. "I don't know how you manage to see the funny side of everything. I'm genuinely worried about all of this, and trying to come up with a plan that minimizes injuries."

"Don't bother, Sal." Petro dismissed his concerns. "You've come up with a great strategy, and now we just need to see it through. Anything else will just overcomplicate it. We can get your senior members out into a Red Zone, and we can even take out a few of the requirements for getting your guild to the next tier. There are bound to be a few commanders in that Red Zone."

"Even more reason that you shouldn't be there," Sal insisted. "An evolved prowler is one thing, but a commander is an entirely different entity."

Petro sighed as he put his hands on his hips. "Is your concern emotional, or is it factual?"

"Factual," Sal answered seriously. "You're an incredible fighter, but I don't believe that you're equipped to handle a commander class."

"Then make me the right equipment," Petro answered seriously. "Send the blueprints to the Arkwright, and I'll be *equipped* to handle a commander class."

Sal just stared at him, mouth agape. "No, that's not what I meant!"

"Facetiousness aside, you should try to have a little more faith in me. I may be a touch out of practice, but I'm not as helpless as you imagine me to be." Petro spoke slowly. "If we're going to take this guild business seriously, I'm going to be stepping into combat more regularly. It's a good opportunity to establish some trust with your advisors, and elevate our standing in the Hunter and Hero communities."

"Everyone already knows and trusts the Argento Auction House," Sal said in a strained voice. He didn't want his father risking his life just to prove that he could still fight. There was far more value in having him working in an administrative capacity.

Petro's smile grew wide. "But there are guilds that think we can be extorted, Salvatore. It's not good business to let things like that slide."

Sal could only stare at his father. Apparently, he wasn't alone in being pissed off with Shade's machinations. "I guess I was being emotional."

"You get that from your mother." Petro grinned as he moved back into a combat stance. "I'm going to have quite the task of convincing her to stay out of this."

CHAPTER 63: PURPOSE

Unknown Contact: Hello, Little Argento. It's your favorite advisor.

Unknown Contact: Petro told me that we have a Delvers problem.

Unknown Contact: I like solving problems.

Sal stared at the words on his tablet. There was no doubt in his mind who it was. He tapped at the screen, before inputting the new name on the keyboard.

You have saved Unknown Contact as Villa.

It had only been a couple of hours since his father had taken the trip back to Silver Sanctuary. Sal had taken the time to sit in his dormitory, wearing the full Tempest Marshal set. Why was he ready for battle? Well, it was for the Regenerative Function. There was no way he was going to leave the sparring pain to heal naturally. What he had hoped would be a peaceful evening had suddenly taken a terrifying direction.

Salvatore: Vanessa?

He couldn't resist. The moment he sent the message, he regretted it. There were people who could take a joke, and he was certain Villa wasn't one of them.

Villa: Cute.

Villa: I should have remembered you have a problem with identities.

Sal's smile turned into a grimace. He had hoped there would be no animosity around him lying about Myth being a different person. It looked like Villa's memory hadn't exactly moved on.

Salvatore: Thank you for the generous bursary, Villa.

He took his hands away from the tablet and waited for a response. It was wild how she managed to make him worried with just a few short words by message. When she had unleashed her aura during the Appraisal in the Credit floor, Sal had realized she wasn't someone to be taken lightly.

Villa: You're welcome.

Villa: I'll keep Petro safe on our little excursion.

Sal paused as he looked at the message. Had his father explained how worried he was? Or was this Villa's own instinct? Either way, it was possibly the best thing she could have said to him. A relieved sigh flowed out of him as he smiled and picked up the tablet again.

Salvatore: Thank you. I'm delighted to have you as an advisor.

There were no other messages for a while. Sal kept glancing at his tablet to see whether he had missed anything. He didn't necessarily want to keep a conversation going with her, but he was equally worried of not responding to her, either.

To distract himself from the tablet, Sal moved across to the living room that had been dominated by the Hermes Dock. There was an eclectic mix of new materials that had been sent by Doc Ameye. Sal placed his tablet on the table and opened Arsenal to start picking up the materials and sending them into the right compartments.

At least, that was his intention. He took one step inside Arsenal and saw a chaotic mess of webbing, spider limbs, and scuttler chitin. With a tired sigh, he realized that there weren't enough areas earmarked for newly discovered materials. As for the scuttler chitin, that was just a case of overflow…which led to the horrible crumpled mess of materials on the floor.

Sal was tempted to call out Jackal to scold it, but there was zero point. It was likely an essence programming solution rather than issuing instructions to the drone. There was so much space in Arsenal, and it could easily house all the materials in his living room, a few times over.

With an agonized groan, Sal got into the tedious work of reorganizing Arsenal with all the new materials. It took him close to two hours to get it all neat and tidy. It then took another hour to ensure that Jackal had twenty new bays to deposit newly sourced materials.

It wasn't like he had done the task in a mindless daze. Sal had been thinking through the trousers and boots he wanted to make for the Tempest Marshal set. He had questions surrounding his own eyes, that he'd need Doctor Bob to answer. It was too limiting for him to be stuck at the Epic-grade level of quality, which he knew was a ridiculously privileged thing to even consider.

It was just another thing he needed to add to his growing list of problems. Skill Master was locked down by Quest until he could prove his proficiency with it. Coach's master class was somewhere on the horizon, and then there were so many modules he had likely fallen behind on. Ethical Crafting had been canceled so they could go dungeon diving, which was another module he probably should check in on.

With a pained sigh, Sal exited the newly organized Arsenal… just in time to see more materials being warped in through Doc Ameye's Hermes Dock. The accompanying thunder with every addition wasn't even a shock anymore. Sal just stared at it numbly, waiting for it to end. It wasn't late enough in the evening to wake the other students, but it was still annoying. What the hell did Doc Ameye want him to build that would require all of this?

Sal continued to stare at the materials that kept warping in from Ameye Locomotive. Yes, he was happy that there were new materials. But with everything mulling in the back of his mind, it started to feel oppressive. If he wasn't apathetic, he'd be angry. There was no excitement or curiosity to Craft, especially with the dread that it might cause irreparable damage to his eyes.

He stood there in his living room as the materials continued to appear. The fatigue in his body had been cleared away by the Regenerate Function. Sleep felt like it was not in the cards, so that wasn't going to be his escape. Sal glanced at his tablet for a few seconds, wondering whether there was any follow-up message from Villa. There was.

Villa: Send me the list of dungeons you need to complete for Tier 7.

Sal navigated to the file that had been sent to him from Jez. He forwarded it in a message to Villa. With it open in front of him, Sal scrolled through the list. He did that for a few seconds, looking at all the names carefully.

Reaching up to his face, Sal pulled off the eye-patch and moved to his bedroom, where his visor rested on the bedside table. Equipping it, he blinked a few times as it powered up. The screen was still on the Tempest Marshal set that he had synced up with Nexus. Navigating away from that, he focused his attention on the tablet.

"I want you to calculate a route between all of these dungeons," Sal said to the visor as he willed it to follow his instructions. Judgment and Cypher would be the best combination for creating a game plan. "Sort by easiest to hardest."

It only took a few seconds for the request to be completed. Sal looked at them and was delighted to see that the visor had even given a series of estimates.

1st. Haven Vanguard, Exchequer Street, Dungeon A-14
- o   Estimated Travel: 34 minutes
- o   Estimated Clearance: 2 hours 13 minutes
- o   Estimated Values: 34 Leechers, 15 Prowlers, 4 Voiders
- o   Captain Variant: Voider - 80%, Prowler - 20%

2nd. Haven Vanguard, Exchequer Street, Dungeon B-07
- o   Estimated Travel: 35 minutes
- o   Estimated Clearance: 3 hours 18 minutes
- o   Estimated Values: 42 Prowlers, 16 Voiders
- o   Captain Variant: Voider - 95%, Prowler - 5%

Sal was a little confused at the clearance times. He went in to have a look and saw the issue. His visor wasn't factoring Jackal or the Tempest Marshal into its calculations. It instead used the average time for completion based on the Hunter Bureau records. Likely from the data that Cooper had gifted him during his first dungeon run.

What was a pleasant surprise was that the first dungeon they had cleared earlier in the day was the eleventh dungeon on the list. It meant that his guild only needed to take on another thirty-nine to make up the numbers. Sal wondered how much the time estimates would change when he used his new equipment.

He went through the list before letting out a frustrated sigh. They would be good practice grounds for everyone, not just him. Sure, he could go with Jackal and blitz through a chunk of them, but that would only make him stronger. He needed the Mythic Guild to be able to stand on its own two feet. The antsy feeling coursing through him, coupled with the growing frustrations, needed an outlet.

Sal sat on the bed and took off the visor, sighing. Placing it back on the bedside table, he sent his Tempest Marshal set to Arsenal, as well as the Mythical blight jackal. Running into a series of dungeons wasn't going to do much for his mood. It would probably be more of a risk to him if he was going there without a clear head.

He had a full week before he had to meet Shade. What was the best use of his time before then? Having a team of advisors and the senior members squad was already being set up. There was nothing for him to do on that front, outside of making some gear blueprints for his father. He needed the all clear from Doctor Bob before he worked on anything above Epic grade. Hell, he wondered whether he could just sit in that scanning machine he built to see how his eyes were doing.

"Oh." The smile vanished from Sal's face as he got to his feet. The scanner had been Epic grade. It had Cypher, and it had the Diagnostic ability. A surge of excitement washed through him, pushing all the doubts and worries to one side.

"This could work," he said to himself with a chuckle as he picked up the visor and moved back to the living room.

"This could really work." He grinned as he summoned the door to Arsenal in the center of his living room. "We just need to keep it to Epic grade." Sal spoke to himself, as though it would somehow make it a fact.

He grasped at a set of markers, but didn't go near the small whiteboard in the hallway. Instead, he moved straight to the wall of glass windows. Blueprints wouldn't be too hard considering he had already built the machine once. A few upgrades for his needs wouldn't go amiss, either… It wasn't like he was starved of materials like last time.

With Perfect active, Sal started to draw out the blueprint he could see clearly in his mind. There had been cut corners with the first build because he had to use what he had. This was going to be far more adventurous, while still—loosely— adhering to the Epic-grade restriction. It was just the planning phase, so he could go a little wild.

His tablet vibrated, which broke him out of his flow state. Sal frowned as he dug through his pocket to withdraw the glowing screen. Glancing at it, he half expected to see a message from Villa, but was surprised to see a very different name.

Quest: Salvatore, Coach will be arriving at 6:00 tomorrow. I know it's an early start, but this will just be a meet and greet before he sets a time for your master class.

Sal checked the time in confusion. It was seven hours from now? Talk about short notice. He put the marker down for a second and typed with both hands.

Salvatore: Sounds perfect. I'll go to your office?

It took close to five minutes for Quest to reply, which felt like an eternity for Sal, who was eager to get back to his blueprint.

Quest: He'll meet you in the Savior workshop.

Sal glanced at the doorway that was only a few feet from him. It led directly into the Savior workshop, so it wasn't much of a commute.

Salvatore: I'll meet him there. Thanks for arranging it.

Quest: Good luck and let me know how it goes.

A smile appeared on Sal's face as he continued his blueprint. He was going to find out what Coach's ability was in just a few hours. With that weave, he'd be able to find out more about the limitations of his own abilities. Subsume allowed him to progress the grades of both Mythcrafter and Skill Master, but he was sure that Coach's weave had far more insights on how he could achieve it without relying on Jackal.

Taking a step back from the start of his blueprint, Sal's smile faltered. A realization gripped him as he stared at the drawing.

"A method for diagnosing problems?" Sal muttered aloud in confusion. He had built the machine to identify injuries, with Cypher providing methods on how to solve them.

Sal's gaze fell back to his tablet, locking onto Coach's name. Everything seemed to click into place in his mind, with the final piece of the puzzle arriving to meet him in just a few hours.

Moving around to the couch and collapsing into it with a laugh, Sal looked through the doorway of Arsenal at the trove of rare and exotic materials. All the cloudiness and indecision evaporated as a plan came together in his mind. If they thought Arkwright or the elixir machine were a big deal, they weren't prepared for what came next.

Sal grinned as he started to ideate on a scanner with Coach's ability.

CHAPTER 64: COACH

"Salvatore Argento?" An impossibly tall man craned his neck down to see through the tunnel that led toward Fabi's drone dock. The deep voice carried through the artificial tunnel, and it sounded imposing as hell.

When Coach appeared into view, Sal could see that he was close to six and a half feet tall. Yet, there was nothing gangly about the man. If anything, he looked just as imposing as Thunder did at the gala. Sal wondered whether they were related.

"That's me. You must be Coach?" Sal moved forward at a brisk pace to offer his hand.

"Yes. Thanks for arriving early. I've got another appointment in an hour, so I can't dawdle around here for too long." Coach took Sal's hand in a vise-like grip. It wasn't strong enough to be considered a test, but was still tighter than ninety percent of the handshakes Sal had experienced.

"Do you mind if I wear my visor?" Sal held up the Legendary-grade Scarlet Strategist. "I recently had an eye injury and I don't want to strain them if I'll be doing tests."

Coach waved the question away. "By all means. I heard about that; nasty business altogether. Hopefully we can make a good diagnosis to stop you hurting yourself in the future."

Sal smiled as he equipped the visor and inspected Coach's weave. He made special note to save it. There was no time to do a full analysis, but he was happy to just have the weave. There would likely be a good opportunity in the next hour to get a full read on his ability. One of the exciting aspects of what he had seen was the number of knots in Coach's weave. It wasn't working at full capacity, which was great because Sal could easily fix it up with the simulation orb. If he was invaluable with the weave as it was, then there was no telling how incredible it would be at full capacity.

"So, Quest didn't really tell me much about your ability. Would you mind telling me what it is we're going to do for the master class?" Sal followed Coach, in the direction of the drone dock.

"Well, as the Hero moniker implies, it's an ability that allows me to Coach individuals," Coach responded with a deep chuckle. "All the limitations that you currently have, I'll be able to see them with my ability. I can break them down into manageable chunks, and we can build out a progression path to get you a few extra grades." He looked at Sal with a crooked smile. "Grant told me how good you are with the simulation orb, so I know I don't need to tell you all about the ability grades."

"It's been a lot of fun researching weaves. I've learned a lot from it," Sal responded honestly. "Specifically, the evolutionary paths. I didn't realize so many of the common weaves we see in students are just a part of a wider family of abilities."

Coach paused as he looked at Sal in confusion. "Expand on that for me."

Sal shrugged. "Assemble, Innovate, Fabricate, and Customize." He picked the ones that were in memory from Fabi's weave. "I was able to see how they're all reliant on each other to build the next one in sequence."

Coach whistled as he leaned against one of the machines, folding his arms. "You genuinely figured that out with the simulation orb? Was it a pattern recognition sort of thing?"

Sal shook his head. "No, it's just a part of my ability. I can diagnose imperfections in weaves and how they can be corrected. There are usually a lot of knots that form naturally over time, and it causes degradation in the weaves. I've seen it with my own father, where his Appraisal ability became less effective over time."

"Well, we'll certainly keep that little fact to ourselves." Coach chuckled. "Can't have people doubting the capabilities of the Argento Auction House." He looked off to the side as though he were deep in thought, a curious expression on his face. After a few moments of silence, he shook his head wistfully. "I'm sorry, I'm just trying to get my head around the fact that you saw those correlations without any sort of guidance. It's a step removed from what I was expecting."

"What were you expecting?" Sal asked, genuinely curious as to what Coach was talking about.

Coach gestured at himself. "I'd be a hypocrite if I was to say that instinct doesn't play a factor. There are ability manifestations that just let you… know things. Like, I could look at your ability and tell you the blockers in an instant. But they wouldn't have a defined form, like these knots that you're talking about." He hesitated as though trying to find the best example. "It's like a muscle. I can look at how developed or underdeveloped it is, and I can immediately tell you the exercise you need to perform to train it up properly."

"Even when you've never met me or seen my ability weave before?" Sal asked in confusion. "You just inherently know what fixes the problem?"

"I don't like to think of them as problems," Coach corrected, smiling. "More like inefficiencies. It's the old adage… ah, what was it? If you judge a fish by its ability to climb a tree, it'll forever think it's stupid? I'm able to look at that fish and tell you that it needs to train in the water. I see my ability as a means to help people find the best environment for them to thrive."

"So, what do we need to do to get started?" Sal asked, eager to find out what would help him develop Mythcrafter and Skill Master. "Quest probably told you already, but I'm a Replicator who created a new ability weave for myself."

"Yeah, it came up." Coach smiled as he continued to lean against the drone dock. "But we've got a few things to cover before we get into that."

"Such as?" Sal wasn't sure whether he missed something. Was Coach going to make him promise not to replicate his weave? He wasn't sure if Quest told Coach about his ability to adjust weaves, so maybe Coach was going to ask him to do some unknotting?

"I'm interested in your insights regarding Gallant." Coach unfurled his arms, gripping the base of the machine to readjust his seated position. "As someone who has worked with him on a team, you've likely seen the problematic Soul Forge. Why do you believe it's possible that the ability is able to outgrow the body it was born into?"

"But he was born with Hype," Sal answered. "His body was likely acclimatized to Hype, but unable to handle an evolution of the weave into Soul Forge."

Coach's smile widened. "Excellent! I don't need to catch you up. Go on, tease out the question a little more. If the ability is capable of evolving, then shouldn't the vessel be equipped to handle it?"

"I don't think it was an issue of the vessel being unfit for the weave," Sal answered as he thought about it. "His Mastery stat was ridiculously low, which told me that he didn't have control over the ability."

"Mastery? How would you differentiate that from Control?" Coach pressed again, his blue eyes locked onto Sal. His haggard appearance made him look tired, but he was ridiculously alert for a six in the morning start.

Sal, on the other hand, wasn't exactly prepared for this without a heavy dose of coffee. It was supposed to be a meet and greet, not an interrogation. Still, he had to think it through, as he wasn't exactly sure of the question.

"Mastery, I believe, is the activation and execution of an ability." Sal spoke aloud as he went through his thought process. "A hundred percent in Mastery would allow you to execute the ability in whatever way you imagined… without any sort of negative effects?"

Coach's smile grew wider. "And Control?"

"I always thought that was just for essence, which I see as separate from Mastery," Sal answered truthfully. "I could be wrong, though. Professor Lombardi had us doing Control exercises on our first day in his class, and it was all essence-based, like tethering our own essence to an external core."

Coach nodded, the smile not leaving his face. "A very good answer. You are correct on Mastery, but there are many more factors to Control. We can cover some of those in the master class, but that's not why our meeting has been arranged. I've heard that you've managed to unlock essence fortification?"

"Is that why we've been introduced?" Sal asked skeptically. "Because I'm pretty sure we were being introduced so you could help me increase my ability grades… you know, to prevent further injury to my eyes."

Coach sighed as he shook his head in disappointment, the smile finally being retired. "I had hoped you'd be a little more engaged with the academic side of things, but I assume you're just here for treatment rather than a cure. If that's what you're looking for, then we can get it over and done with now." He offered his hand to Sal. "Take it, and I'll tell you how to increase the grades of both of your abilities."

Sal's jaw tightened as he looked at the offered hand dubiously. "I'm not saying I don't want to learn. I'm trying to explain that my eyes bled because my body can't keep up with my ability."

"Well, as emphatic as that lie was… it doesn't change the fact that it's a lie." Coach chuckled as he withdrew his hand. "I could tell the moment you walked in here that your body is more than capable of handling your weaves."

"Just by looking at me?" Sal looked at Coach's hand. "Is your ability a Body Manipulation type? Where you can look through my body when we shook hands?"

Coach cocked an eyebrow in surprise. "Oh, that's a new one." He smiled before shaking his head. "But no, as I said… instinct, and all that. I can tell with just a glance at a person's weave. Probably in the way you can see knots, I can see everything else that's wrong with it."

"I wasn't lying, by the way." Sal stared at Coach. "You can wear this tracker, and it'll tell you I'm not lying."

"That's a neat trick." Coach smiled before shaking his head again. "But even if you believe it, it doesn't change the facts. I can tell just from looking at you, that you have capacity for another five grades of Skill Master, and probably another seven grades for Mythcrafter."

Sal's jaw unclenched and dropped all at once. His visor was telling him that Coach was telling the truth. Or, at the very least, that he believed what he was saying. This was still the man who broke Gallant, so his conviction wasn't as profound or reassuring as he believed. Sal stared at the ground, not sure how to process this. Should he believe Coach, and risk getting injured further?

Coach sighed as he gestured at Sal's eyes. "I'm not a Healer, nor will I pretend to understand the intricacies of the body... but they're completely fine. I can understand abilities, and how they're executed. You use your eyes for Mythcrafter, right? There's no blockages or inefficiencies that I can see. Was the injury before you unlocked the Endurance stat?"

Sal's eyes snapped up to Coach's face. "How did you know about the Endurance stat?"

"I'm a Coach," he responded lamely. "I see what needs to be fixed. You have a slight imbalance between your Strength and Mobility, but that's fine. It would be far worse if it was an imbalance between Speed and Mobility. That would lead to some very nasty sprains, or bones breaking. Strength and Endurance are the most egregious... but you're a Support class, so it's not like you're going to be taking that many hits. I'm more surprised you have it, if I'm honest. Kudos on all the resistance training to get it built up."

Sal made the decision there and then to trust him. Coach just gave him incredible insights with a single glance.

"Are you able to see my Spirit stat?" Sal asked out of curiosity. "I had a dungeon attendant tell me that my Spirit stat dropped in a dungeon, and I can't see it with any of the trackers I've made so far."

Coach snorted as he waved his hand. "That's a useless stat, so don't pay attention to it. It's kinda like a before and after snapshot, that some of our passionate dungeon attendants use to calculate psychological impact for the dungeons. It's just another metric they use to score the dungeons and assess their difficulty. You could replenish your Spirit with a good cup of coffee, or a good sleep."

"Oh," Sal answered, feeling a little hollow.

"How long did you agonize over that one?" Coach laughed as he asked, his blue eyes practically sparkling.

"A few months," Sal admitted with a groan.

"Well, just to let you know how useless it is, your Spirit stat dropped by zero point zero four when I broke that news to you. See what I mean? It's a mood number, so it's not the best metric to use." Coach tilted his head to the side. "Unless your ability manifests based on your mood... in which case, it's vital to keep it in the high numbers."

"Like Gallant?" Sal guessed.

"Like Gallant," Coach confirmed with a tight smile.

CHAPTER 65: CONDITION

"So, what way do you want to do this?" Sal asked awkwardly as he gestured around the room. "Do I have to go to a dungeon or something with you?"

Coach waved a hand to dismiss the question. "Nope. It would be ridiculous if a Replication or Invention ability would progress based on killing demons. Gallant was a special case where he needed to accomplish greater feats, as each success boosted his Hype ability. It wasn't about killing many foes, but rather about surpassing his limits."

He pointed at Sal's chest, smiling. "Most people in the lower stages of their progression can progress through repetition alone. When you get to the middle stages, you'll need to take on more challenging projects; either in terms of duration or complexity. It'll be a tough one for us to determine the most effective method for you with just talking, so we'll likely need to create an environment for you to push yourself."

Sal frowned as he thought about it. "Our meeting today is only for an hour, though? I'm guessing you need to go and do something else?"

Coach nodded. "Time is money, which I'm sure you can appreciate. But we'll have plenty of time to talk in the future about this. My schedule should be opening up next month."

It was frustrating. Sal was so intrigued about Coach and his ability, but the time he had with the man was incredibly limited. If he wanted to keep Coach there, he needed to figure out a surefire method to catch his interest. By all accounts, the man was successful and likely had everything he needed. Sal wasn't going to be able to just bribe him. Unless it was something Coach couldn't get anywhere else…

"I've started a project earlier this morning that would require me to use both Mythcrafter and Skill Master. Would you like to watch me work to see how my weaves react?" Sal asked calmly, making sure to keep the desperation out of his voice.

Coach faltered as he looked at Sal. "A project that uses both? That doesn't sound… likely. Are you trying to rebuild the simulation orb?" He sounded genuinely confused, but also curious.

"No, it's something far better." Sal realized he'd need to lay down more groundwork to really reel him in. "After creating the Mythic-grade elixir machine in the workshop, I realized that there were far better methods for helping the students." Sal watched his reaction carefully, and there was no surprise at the mention of the elixir machine. Coach already knew about it.

"Go on." Coach crossed his arms again, the beginnings of a smile appearing. "You're setting the bar pretty high. I'd need to see you really working on both of your weaves. Building an Epic grade or Legendary grade might give me some insights, but it would likely need to be something at the Mythic grade for me to really know what we're dealing with."

"It'll be Mythic grade," Sal lied. He had no idea whether he'd be able to design something to that grade intentionally, but he was more than happy to try now that he knew his eyes were fine. "But I'll need your help to make it work properly."

Coach's eyes lit up in surprise as he gestured at himself. "You need my help? For a Crafting project?"

Sal nodded, delighted that he had caught his interest. "Yes. You probably already know how the elixir machine was built around the abilities of Anders and Alex. It can work without them, but their ability really brings out the top potential in the machine."

Coach nodded along, not voicing any complaints. He looked intrigued and still more than a little confused.

"Well, the build that I would be making would be an ability scanner." Sal started to describe the idea he had earlier in the morning to replicate the scanner he made for Doctor Bob. "It would use your weave, integrated through Mythcrafter, to create a platform that can give a basic level of coaching to whoever uses it. I'd be more than happy to give you a cut on whatever profit it ends up generating."

Coach's hands came up. "Wait…slow down." He laughed almost humorlessly. "You're saying that you'd implant my ability into this machine of yours? You didn't even know what it was twenty minutes ago!" He looked at Sal in disbelief, before a thought suddenly dawned on him. His jaw loosened as he looked at Sal, almost accusingly. "You've already memorized my weave, haven't you?"

Sal nodded. "But I wouldn't use it without your consent. I prefer to do business fairly. Anders and Alex get a fair percentage of all profits from the elixir machine. Quest Academy's Crafting Department gets a sizable chunk, too. I'm not trying to screw people over when I'm making equipment."

Coach bit his lip as he checked his watch. "How long would it take you to make a Mythic grade?"

"Eight to ten hours." Sal lied again, not exactly sure how long it took him to do the Mythical blight jackal. "But it really depends on how complex your weave is. If it's a difficult one, it could take a good bit longer than that." Sal added that last part to give himself more breathing room. Who wouldn't want to be told that their weave was complex?

Coach winced at the mention of the duration as he looked at his watch, clearly thinking of the appointments he had for the rest of the day. "So, we're probably talking closer to a full day? And we don't even know if you'll be able to manage a Mythic grade…" He let out a frustrated sigh before staring at Sal.

"Let's be very clear here. You're looking to showcase your abilities to me, so I can give you a proper report on how you can increase your ability grades." He gestured at himself. "I'm here to see where your baseline is for the Skill master class. If I was to humor this request, I'd be disappointing quite a number of people who have paid good money for my services."

Sal raised his hand as though requesting to speak.

Coach gestured at him to continue.

"Well, if you were to go along with my plan and the machine worked… wouldn't you be able to profit from the same people, and free up your time?" Sal asked the question like it was an obvious conclusion. "You could just send them to the machine to get their results."

"With the assumption that it could even work. As you've said, it'll only be a basic representation of my ability," Coach countered, almost dismissively.

Sal snorted as he shook his head. "No, that was just thrown in to make you feel better. I can implant your ability without the knots, but I thought it might make you feel uncomfortable."

Sal realized he was playing with fire, but he also had an idea that he wanted to try out. If Coach was anything like himself, there was a good chance that he wasn't able to interact with his own weave. Sal couldn't use the simulation orb to improve Skill Master, so maybe Coach couldn't use his ability to figure out how to improve his own grade.

Sal spread his hands meaningfully, and kept his tone earnest. "If we go with the improved weave, then you'll probably be able to get insights for how you can increase your own grade."

Coach's eyes widened. "You're fucking with me, aren't you?"

"No," Sal responded firmly. "Skill Master is a core component of Mythcrafter. I'm able to implant replicated weaves into the items I Craft. I've already done it a few times. If there's a better version of your weave, I can make it, and then I can replicate it and put it into this new scanner."

"And you'd do this for free?" Coach asked suspiciously. "You're not going to ask me to fund this little project of yours?"

Sal shook his head slowly. "I have more than enough materials to do this justice. I just need time and your consent to use your weave."

"And if it works, I'd get a cut?" The smile returned to Coach's face. "I'm trying to find your angle here, Mr. Argento. I was led to believe you were a good businessman, but I'm not seeing the angle."

Sal shrugged. "If it helps people, and I'm able to make some Q-Cred from people using it, then it's worth it, isn't it?"

"An altruist." Coach chuckled as he bit his lip. "I'm not sure how long you'll survive when you go up against Doc Ameye."

"He's the one who's sent me all the materials." Sal smiled as he gestured toward the door that led to his dorm. "So, are you interested, or do you want to wait until your schedule is free?"

Coach put his hands on his hips as he stood up straight. He was looking at Sal strangely, as though weighing his options.

"I will point out, though," Sal started as he motioned to the door. "The moment I go through that door, and you don't follow me, your cut disappears. Let's call it an opportunity cost, since I'll have to figure out my own limitations without your help."

Coach smiled warmly as he gestured at the door. "I'm relieved to see there's a shark in there. I'd hate to enter a contract with someone naive to the world." He pulled out his tablet and sighed. "But, I have some conditions. I'll be ordering the food—your canteen here is an absolute joke." He tapped at the screen a couple of times. "And when I get an angry call from my secretary, you'll need to take it."

"Fine by me," Sal agreed as he swiped his Q-Card against the glossy black door. "Are you freeing up the full day?"

"Three hours." Coach pocketed his tablet. "You have that long to convince me that you know what you're doing."

Sal nodded as Coach walked into his dorm room. He smiled as he saw the entire glass wall of windows covered in marker. There were close to a dozen blueprints all drawn to perfection on the glass, each one leading in sequence to the next one on the right. All the minutiae of the scanner design for the infirmary were on full display, with multiple segments dedicated to material selection. Sal wasn't limited to obsidian glass for this build, so there were plenty of the exotic materials being factored into the potential project.

Turning around to look at his guest, Sal was happy to see Coach looking dumbfounded at the sight of it all. Knowing that he needed to use the time he had available, Sal went a step further by summoning the Mythical blight jackal onto his arm. For dramatic effect, he snapped his fingers and summoned the door to Arsenal.

Coach's eyes widened at the sudden appearance of a doorway opening up in the center of the room. "What in the world is that?" He asked the question as he took a tentative step forward to investigate.

Sal was wise to how the Hermes Dock worked. Doc Ameye had an entire supply line that would feed new materials into Sal's living room whenever an available space opened up. With that in mind, Sal picked up a stack of materials from the pile, drawing Coach's attention to it as he moved the plates of hellfire titanium into Arsenal. He was barely a step into it before the crack of thunder echoed throughout the dorm.

Coach stared in disbelief at the new stack of metal rods that appeared out of nowhere, transported into Sal's dorm. He tore his eyes away from it to look at Sal in surprise. "Are you seriously a first-year?"

Sal smiled as he dusted himself off and closed Arsenal. "I'll tell you in three hours and one minute."

Coach burst out laughing as he took out his tablet and held it up. "You win this round, Mr. Argento. But I will admit that I do know a few things about Crafting. There are no certainties when it comes to the higher grades. You sound confident and you put on a good show, but I don't personally believe that a Mythic grade is possible with these sorts of parameters."

"Why do you think that?" Sal raised his eyebrow. "I'll need to adjust the blueprint to fit the new weave, but I've got all the materials we could ever need. Is it the time limit?"

Coach shook his head, the smile not leaving his face. "You made the first-ever Mythic grade with Fabrizia Maccles, who has the highest-grade weave that Grant has ever witnessed. I was wondering if you'd factor her assistance into your plan for this."

Sal stared at him for a few seconds. "And who do you think made her weave?"

Coach gaped at Sal before tapping his tablet a few more times. "Okay, Mr. Argento…the ball is in your court. You have the rest of the day to show me you're not full of shit."

"Same goes for you." Sal smiled as he tapped his own chest. "Try not to get distracted by the process and make sure you get a good look at my weaves in action."

CHAPTER 66: SHOWCASE

"I think Grant would actually kill himself if he saw this." Coach chuckled as he leaned against the stairway banister, his eyes locked onto the glowing cables of the simulation orb.

Sal smiled as he continued to work with Coach's weave. "I got a lot faster with practice." He had already replicated Coach's weave with the cables and was now going through the routine checks to take out the obvious knots. Despite the fact that he was being careful and taking his time, it apparently looked fast to Coach.

"It's bewildering, though," Coach said in confusion as he gestured at Sal's chest. "Your Skill Master weave isn't reacting to this at all. I thought that this would be the best method to increase your grades, but it looks like it's doing nothing for you."

"I probably have to replicate it with my own thread." Sal shrugged as he continued to pluck out the knots. There was no impressive design like the Predator or Sovereign ability, but it was still a very complex collection of lines. The best example Sal could come up with was a star, but rather than a five-pointed one, it had fifteen points, all going out in different directions. Most of the corrections were small improvements, and Sal genuinely wondered how much of an impact he was going to be able to make with it.

"Does the green light mean success?" Coach asked as the room was bathed in light. "If not, I'd question if Grant was color-blind." He chuckled at his own joke.

Sal smiled as he continued working on the weave. There were only a few more knots to undo, and then he could concentrate on optimizing the weave.

"Why are you still working on it? You already got a green light," Coach asked in confusion as he gestured at the ceiling where the light had flashed.

"Because it's not as good as it could be. Success for Grant is an improvement over what already exists," Sal explained as he finished the last of the knots. "Why settle for an improvement, when you can get it to its ultimate state?"

Coach didn't say anything to that as Sal moved onto the Ravel method. There were a few points of the star shape that looked like it could support the method, and he instinctively knew that it would benefit from it. Because Coach was standing over him, Sal put on the visor so he could downplay his capability with the weave. It was confirming all his instincts, which was a nice little massage to Sal's ego.

After ten minutes of silence, Sal stepped back from the weave with a smile on his face. "Okay, this version is great. We'll use this one for the machine."

"But you don't know if it's a success yet." Coach pointed at the ceiling in confusion. "Don't you need to wait for the green light?"

Sal glanced at the ceiling, frowning. "That? No, it takes too long. We'll already be halfway through the blueprint by the time it registers the new ability." He smiled as he looked at Coach. "Okay, it's not that bad. Because the database didn't have a record of your ability on it, there's going to be a delay before it properly registers."

"You're that confident?" Coach tilted his head to the right. "And not just playing the role of savant because I'm here?"

"Skill Savant is Grant's ability, not mine." Sal smiled as he made his way to the stairs. "We're on the clock, so I don't have time to wait around for the lights."

"Are you not going to take a picture of the weave?" Coach asked finally as he followed Sal down the stairs. "Most Replicators need a reference to work off of."

Sal laughed as he glanced over his shoulder at Coach. "I could tell you that it's saved in my tracker, if that made you feel better about it?"

Coach just shook his head as they made their way down to the living room again. "So, what's next? We have the weave, which was a bit of a dud from a coaching perspective. Are you going to try to Replicate it now?"

Sal nodded. "I won't activate it, though. One of the downsides of making a weave without knots is that my synchronicity with it is usually very low. I'll keep it replicated in my body to use it as a reference for the blueprint. If it doesn't generate a method to make it with materials we have available, then I'll work on infusing it instead."

"So you have a fail-safe? That's oddly reassuring." Coach smiled as he sat on the couch and rubbed his hands together. "Don't worry, I have a clear view of you. Feel free to start whenever you're ready."

Sal didn't need another invitation as he started to recreate Coach's weave with Skill Master. He hadn't managed to get the description of the weave from the simulation orb as it was still calculating. Coach's guess from earlier wasn't a bad one. It wouldn't be the worst idea to create an improved simulation orb. If he was able to combine Skill Master with Cypher and Judgment, there was a good chance he could automate the weave research.

The multiple-pointed star took a little longer than usual to recreate, but Sal was able to manage it with relative ease. He didn't need a reference image to do it justice because his instincts recalled it perfectly.

"Oh… that's working." Coach sat forward on the couch. "Skill Master is responding well to whatever you're doing. It's slow, but it's definitely ticking upward."

Sal couldn't help but be confused. "But I've not activated it? I'm just designing the weave in my subconscious with the thread from Skill Master."

"And it's working," Coach stated, as if it were obvious. "You've gotten about three-quarters of a percentage point toward the next grade with what you've done. It's nothing to go crazy about, as it's far slower than what I'd normally want to see. I'm thinking that the complexity of the weave is what's causing the increase."

Sal smiled inwardly. "Are there any negatives with activating your weave? I could probably try it for a few seconds to see if that creates a higher percentage?"

"Absolutely not," Coach answered immediately. "I don't want you testing something new. If you've got a weave that you're more comfortable with that you've tried before, I can look at that, but I won't allow you to take any risks."

Sal nodded in understanding, strangely reassured that Coach didn't want him to put himself in danger. Ever since he had worked on the Refine ability for the elixir machine, he felt like he could afford to be a little more daring with his Replication ability. Coach's cautionary tone was a good grounding for that desire.

"Okay, I'll get working on the blueprint. Give me a few minutes." Sal opened his eyes and looked at the windows in front of him. Mythcrafter came alive and pulled at the different designs to create an entirely new blueprint. Sal coaxed it into accepting Coach's ability as a basis of the machine, and it surprisingly didn't shatter.

Cypher, on the other hand, did not play nice with Coach's ability. That was okay, though. It would have been a little too lucky if everything worked out from the beginning. This part would create a bit more of a challenge.

"You're gradually improving Mythcrafter with whatever you're doing," Coach added from the couch in a hopeful voice. "It's not much, but it all adds up."

Sal ignored him as he continued to brainstorm the problems with Cypher. Through some weird logic, Sal decided to see whether he could create a bridge by using another ability. If the two abilities he wanted weren't going to happily co-exist, maybe he could find something that would provide a more stable foundation. The logic part was that another strong ability would likely push the grade closer to Mythic. Making attributes through material composition rather than infusing would also likely utilize the ultra-rare stock he got from Doc Ameye.

The question was, which ability would work best with the two he needed? Sal glanced back in Coach's direction. "In an ideal world, what functionality would you like this machine to have?"

Coach shrugged. "Well, the greatest challenge the machine will face is context. I need to be sitting here looking at you actually using your ability to tell you how to improve. A machine isn't likely to understand the nuances involved. Hell, even if it was going to tell someone they need to kill a few prowlers… how will it calculate it?"

"System," Sal muttered to himself as he added it into the build. "And Nexus?" He asked the question, not to Coach, but to the room itself. It was tough trying to pretend like he had all the answers, especially when he had essentially lied to Coach about his confidence in completing this project.

Nexus combined with System would give them an absolute trove of information from dungeons, towers, and portals. He'd just need to sync it with his own tracker, or get access from Quest and Grant. If they could populate this machine with the insights from the simulation orb, as well as the information gathered by all the trackers going into dungeons, then they'd likely be able to build a pretty good predictor.

Sal smiled as he thought about it. The project that Quest had spoken to him about was the Quest System. If it was able to provide the students with an action plan of what they needed to do, that was backed up by Coach's ability, then they'd have a streamlined method for estimating progression and weave growth.

As amazing as Mythcrafter was, it was painfully stupid sometimes. Starting with Cypher and adding Coach's ability broke the blueprint. Starting with Nexus and adding System… did not break the blueprint, even when Coach's ability was added next. It only shattered when Cypher was included at the end. Sal played around with the abilities in the blueprint and refused to make separate stations like he had done with the elixir machine. This was going to be a single entity. And judging from the images flying in front of his eyes, there were so many design inspirations from all his previous builds and everything he had seen with the tracker.

One design was a massage-style chair beside a massive interactive terminal. The next was a clone of the machine he made in the infirmary, but with better materials. Next was just an enormous terminal that was half the size of the Arkwright. It didn't really look feasible as a build in the time constraint he had set out with Coach. He dismissed all of them and just focused on finding a method to include all four abilities. The winning formula was, apparently, Coach, Nexus, System, and then Cypher. He needed to keep Coach's ability as far from Cypher as possible, even though they were in the same machine.

"This is truly riveting," Coach deadpanned. "I'm not sure if you're aware, but you've just been staring at the window for the last thirty minutes. You missed the green light, by the way."

Sal blinked as he turned around, grinning. "Thirty minutes? That was a lot faster than I expected. We're making good time."

"What was faster?" Coach pointed at the window. "Weren't you just reading the designs?"

Sal tapped the side of his head. "Blueprint for the machine is finished. We have all the materials we need, and there's no requirement for an infusion, which is great news."

Coach got to his feet. "So, I take it we're going to move back into the workshop?"

Sal shook his head. "No need. I've got everything I need right here." He looked around the room. "We might just need to move the couch out of the way, but other than that, I think we've got plenty of space."

"Are you one of those Crafters who go into the zone and lose all sense of perspective and time?" Coach asked warily as he took out his tablet, glancing at the screen.

"Yeah, I kinda just lock into a flow state." Sal chuckled as he offered a friendly shrug. "You can make yourself at home, though, if that's any help?"

Coach smiled as he shook his head. "No, it's perfect. It's better to see your abilities operating at a constant rate. I'll be able to get a better understanding the longer I see you in a flow state."

"Oh, and before I forget. Can you check Skill Master for a second?" Sal gestured at his chest.

Coach nodded as he waited for something to happen.

Sal activated Perfect, summoning the phantom weave and holding onto it subconsciously. "Just wondering if that had any noticeable effect?"

Coach stared at Sal in disbelief. "You activated a weave, didn't you?"

Sal nodded, delighted that Coach was able to see something at least. A few seconds of silence followed as Coach watched Sal carefully. Eventually he shook his head and let out a pained sigh.

"You got a nice boost of close to a full percentage point when it activated, but nothing for keeping it running," Coach eventually admitted as he looked up at Sal. "I'm really sorry about this, Salvatore. It looks like both of your abilities are conspiring against you. Their growth rates are some of the slowest I've seen in quite some time."

Sal waved his right palm back and forth. "You've only seen them activating—you haven't really seen them in progress. The weave I have active only really shows its value when I start doing Crafting, and the same with Mythcrafter."

Coach smiled as he sat back down on the couch and gestured at the window. "Then by all means, continue. I look forward to a good show."

Sal grinned as he sent the blueprint from his tracker to the Arkwright through Nexus. He didn't want the machine at the Argento Auction House to start working on it. Instead, it was a test, with failure being the best possible outcome.

Sal sent the command to start production, and was overjoyed at the automated response from the Arkwright that fed through to his visor.

Mythcrafter Crafting Algorithm is unable to complete this request
     o   Mythic-Grade Blueprints cannot be simulated

With a relieved sigh, Sal deleted the request and turned to Coach. "Want to make a bet on if it'll be Mythic grade?"

CHAPTER 67: REFIT

"I don't know what to tell you, Sal." Coach chuckled as he lounged on the couch with a half-filled plate of sushi. His chopsticks gestured at the trolley with a series of straps covering it from every conceivable angle. "It kinda feels like you're making all of this up as you go along."

Sal pulled a hand through his hair as he turned to look at what Coach gestured at. His gaze landed on the destroyed Skill Registration machine that stood out like a sore thumb at the edge of the entranceway, blocking the exit. When you added the wealth of materials that had been donated by Doc Ameye in the living room, there was no real space left. Grimacing ever so slightly, Sal offered a helpless shrug. "I'm just following the instructions the ability is giving me. How are we looking on that front, by the way?"

Coach frowned as he moved the chopsticks in midair to point at Sal's chest. "It's quite interesting, but all the ideation and focus you're giving it… it's not really boosting your ability all that much. My best guess is that you're only gaining progress when you're actually Crafting. When will that start, by the way?" He smiled as he looked at the haphazard placement of countless materials, all stacked in a sequence that clearly appeared unplanned. "You certainly have a… process."

Sal nodded, half to himself and half for Coach's benefit. "It'll all start making sense soon enough."

"Well, just so you don't think I'm slacking off, I can give you a basic report." Coach chuckled as he placed the sushi plate to one side, resting the chopsticks on it before sitting up and dusting off a few pieces of rice. "If we were to assume that the vast majority of your time is spent in this stage, then I can tell you that it will take between eight and ten months of weekly Crafting to get to the next grade of Mythcrafter."

Sal whirled around to look at him in surprise. "Just from planning out a build?"

"Is that what this is?" Coach laughed as he pointed at the surrounding chaos. "And yes, that's my professional opinion. I'd need to see more of your work on weaves, but I think that you could probably increase Skill Master by replicating, but not activating, around eighty-seven weaves."

Sal stared at him in disbelief. "Around… eighty-seven? That sounds pretty precise to me."

"It's just a hypothesis." Coach shrugged. "Some weaves are going to be more demanding than others. I'd need to see you do more of them at higher and lower complexities to really understand the growth aspects. Your ability is still in its infancy, so there's a lot of potential for improvement." He smiled quizzically before finally letting out an exasperated sigh. "Come on, are you going to tell me why you lugged that thing in here? You don't expect me to pretend that I don't know what that is."

"The Skill Registration machine?" Sal gestured at it in surprise. "I destroyed it on my first day at Quest Academy. Both Quest and Upgrade told me that I'll need to repair it at some point…and I have the commander core to do it."

Coach frowned as he looked between the machine and Sal. "Why do I feel like you've got no intention of repairing it while I'm here?"

"Good instincts." Sal laughed as he pointed at the blueprints on the window. "I got to thinking, and realized that the Skill Registration machine is the lower-tier version of what we're trying to create here. Rather than repairing it, I thought I could just factor it into this build."

"You can do that? Do you not need to take it apart to understand how it works?" Coach was confused as he looked at it dubiously. "And do you not think it's a little disingenuous if you were to abuse their trust like that? You could end up destroying it beyond repair."

Sal shook his head. This was one aspect he had zero doubts on. "If it's a monetary value, I can pay it. I have the funds. And if it's a workload problem… then I'll be able to make something far better with enough time and planning." He was resolute as he met Coach's gaze. "I don't want to sound arrogant, but I'm very confident with my skills. As an Appraiser, I can literally look at it and see how every part works and comes together. I don't have the essence programming instincts yet, but I'll get there eventually."

"And this confidence comes from creating a single Mythic grade?" Coach challenged him.

"That you know about." Sal shot back with a tight smile. "What sort of Auctioneer would I be if I led with my best item?"

Coach's jaw dropped as he looked at Sal in confusion. "You're joking, right? You've made another Mythic?"

Sal spread his hands wide as he gave a theatrical bow. "And you get to see the third attempt. I'm two for two, so there's a good chance this will all blow up in our faces." He smiled as he checked the time on his tablet. "I'm going to be getting into a bit of a flow state, so I won't be the best conversationalist. Just warning you in advance."

"I've got some calls to make, so it should be fine." Coach gestured toward the stairs leading up to the simulation orb. "If I can manage to get through this sea of scrap, I'll do them out of earshot."

Sal rotated his shoulders as he geared himself up to start. "Then let's get started." He spoke with a smile as he looked at the collection of materials with Mythcrafter active. Adding the Skill Registration machine had been a stroke of genius that he hadn't even considered. Sure, it added a few hours of delay, without knowing whether it would work until he saw it, but it was a good investment of time. When Greg and one of the delivery guys arrived from the Credit floor, Sal had to deal with the polite but firm statement that they weren't bellboys. Tipping them had changed that attitude dramatically, and it was definitely worth it. The Skill Registration machine slotted into the build almost seamlessly. He learned that the shattered core that had offered him an endless pool of essence was in fact a repurposed commander core. He had a few of them in reserve from Doc Ameye's supplies, and he was more than capable of just repairing the machine with Mythcrafter and that single core.

The sound of metal plates clattering to the ground told Sal that Coach was nowhere near as dexterous as he had claimed. He didn't bother turning around to watch the towering man's exit from the living room. It probably would have been a lot smarter to do this in the workshop, which was only a few paces away, but Sal had everything he needed in the room. And, if he was honest with himself, he didn't want this machine to be in an open area. If it could do what he wanted, then he'd be able to test it out in private. If it failed, then there would only be one person who would see…and he had already told Coach that it might not work.

The other, more sensible part of him knew that Fabi and Upgrade would have thoughts about his build, and he didn't want to delay the process any more than necessary. He only had a week before he needed to deal with Shade, and if they were to intervene on this project, there was no chance that he'd get it built in time.

Sal imbued his hands with Mythcrafter essence as he started pulling at the cover plates for the Skill Registration machine. He liked how it had the arm slot, but it wasn't perfect. That wasn't his own instinct, but rather an insight from Mythcrafter. The blueprint that he was going for was like a cocoon sort of seat. Sal guessed it was closer to a skill-pod than anything else. His plans of creating a massive screen had been dashed the moment he factored in the Skill Registration machine. It changed everything for the better and created a sleek form factor that would reduce space by a considerable amount. He still wanted the screens, but guessed that the cocoon would enhance the privacy element. If the person in the pod was getting all the information, then that would work just as good.

When he got to the innards of the machine, he finally appreciated how much damage his Skill Imprint had done on it. It was pretty much a crater of destruction, with an almost perfect sphere of devastation that had incinerated everything in its path. Sal groaned inwardly as he moved backward and glanced at the floor around him for the materials he needed. Mythcrafter would smooth things out, but he still needed certain components to fix it up properly. Because he was on a stricter timeline, there wouldn't be much finesse happening, and he was grateful for Coach leaving for a bit. He could show his technical prowess later. This was something he was just going to brute-force with essence.

Sal smiled as he placed three plates of scarlet screen in the center of the destroyed console with five ingots of moonsilver. There was some hellfire titanium in there for good measure, and starlight steel as an extra, which wasn't really required, but his visor told him that the composition was complementary to the other elements. If it made it work a little better, or made the materials play nice with each other, it would be worth it. Even though he had been gifted all the materials, Sal was keenly aware of how flippant he was being with them. The cost of everything in that living room would have been enough to buy his own auction house. That thought was very poignant as he placed the commander core among the materials…but Sal tried not to think of that as he started to melt them down.

It was a slow process, despite the brute-force method. He took things slowly as Perfect guided the essence flow through his fingertips. The different hues of red melding with white-silver was oddly satisfying, and Sal had to fight to keep focus on the task at hand. Starlight steel added a glossy sparkle to the effect and almost seemed to pull the other materials into the fissures caused by the blast damage. As he stood there as a glorified battery, he was able to appreciate the slow reconstruction of the different mechanisms. There wasn't really anything to compare it to as he hadn't seen the interior of a repaired machine, but it looked very impressive.

Mythcrafter told him that there was no need for the cover panel, so he discounted it from his design. The scarlet screen resurfaced from the sparkly silver goop and started to balloon upward. It was a wild experience, because he was channeling his essence throughout the build, and he knew that there were countless corrections happening under the surface of the balloon. He tried to approach the build in the same way that Doc Ameye had designed the Hermes Dock: no room for error, less scrappy, and perfect in scope.

Obviously, he failed. Adding a Skill Registration machine to a build will do that.

Sal didn't care, though, because although the pursuit of perfection was an admirable goal, he was more interested in getting everything working. He was the only Mythcrafter out there, so he guessed he could set the precedent on how a Mythcrafter should build things. It was a shitty excuse for the chaotic Crafting process, but it was enough to make Sal smile. He wanted to eventually get to the level of precision that Doc Ameye showed him, but that was a future goal.

The scarlet screen continued to bubble up until it filled the edges of the original paneling. If Sal was to try to describe it, it was like a red-tinted window into the inner workings of the machine. Well, at least it would be when the moonsilver, hellfire titanium, and starlight steel finished cooking. Each of them was still forming new mechanisms, melding into existing components and creating new pathways around the commander core that rested in the center. Perfect continued to work its magic by ensuring everything aligned to specification.

Taking a step back from it, Sal appreciated the first part of the project. It was the new and improved battery for the actual build, with the functionality of being able to assess the abilities of whoever interacted with it. Sal checked the arm slot for the machine and started to plan the next segment that would plug into that space.

"Time to make our chair," he muttered as he looked around the room, his gaze landing on the couch... causing Mythcrafter to start reworking it to the current plan. "Quest is going to kill me." Sal laughed as he moved to pull it apart.

CHAPTER 68: EGG

"You can disregard the eight to ten months suggestion, by the way." Coach appeared in front of Sal, expertly stepping around the remnants of the couch and planting himself in plain view. "Actually, utilizing Mythcrafter has what I can only describe as explosive acceleration. There's like a buffer in place that is over-clocking your weave, and I can't for the life of me figure out what it is."

Sal smiled as he pointed at his visor. "There's an ability called Calibrated, and it gives me a ten percent increase to my abilities when I have it active."

"Fuck me..." Coach breathed as he crouched down to get a better look at the visor. "How is that even possible? I've never heard of an augmentation for core abilities, outside of the typical ones like Supercharge." He shook his head in an almost dazed wonder. "And I'm going to go out on a limb and guess that you made it yourself?"

Sal nodded as he continued to stuff the padding of the cushions into the newly fashioned seat he made with a few bolts of stormweave fabric. The storm-like effect was very similar to the obsidian; it almost seemed like a waste that someone would be sitting on it. "Yeah, that was me. I did have a bit of help from Prestige at the excursion." He paused as he tilted his head to one side, as though deep in thought. "And at the gala, actually. It never actually evolved by itself."

"Evolved," Coach said slowly. "You've made equipment with evolutionary runes?" His tone was one of disbelief, but the cadence said that he wanted to be absolutely sure he wasn't getting anything wrong.

"Yep, made a few of them. You probably heard about the sniper rifle at the Reavers Guild." Sal grinned as he hiked a thumb at himself. "That was my first project, with help from the other Crafters in the workshop. Reworked an evolutionary rune from an ethos blade."

"Why didn't you mention any of this in the workshop?" Coach breathed as he stood back up to his full impressive height, looking around the room as though it might reveal even more answers. "If you're able to make evolutionary runes and you can create that Calibrated ability, why do you even need this? You could make a complete set that raises your abilities to a hundred percent. It would push you into the higher grades with minimal effort."

Sal shrugged. "I never really thought about it that way. I'd rather strengthen my own abilities rather than relying on equipment." He glanced at Coach, grinning. "Don't get me wrong, I love having good equipment, but I don't want to get complacent. You can probably appreciate that there are a number of people who would want to monopolize my abilities. I don't want to make it easy for them."

Coach snorted as he shook his head. "I practically wrote the playbook on how not to get abducted. You've got no idea how stressful it was knowing that I had the power to map out a person's potential. The failure surrounding Gallant did wonders for my safety, as the Hunter Bureau stopped treating me as a sure bet. It reduced the bookings, but I finally felt like I could breathe easy."

"Do you suggest that I fuck up a few big projects to keep them at bay?" Sal laughed as he focused on the task at hand. It wasn't really a Mythcrafter part of the process, but rather a monotonous lesson in upholstery. "My father suggested that I just become ridiculously strong and capable so they'll think twice about abducting me."

"You could do that," Coach agreed. "I mean, screwing up a few projects… except this one. I really want to see this one work out." He smiled as he shook his head almost in wonder. "I've never actually seen a project work this way. Usually, my clients are nervous wrecks who overcomplicate everything and can't show me a realistic use of their abilities. This is quite refreshing."

Sal smiled. "I'm surprised you're not bored. You've been here close to eight hours, and I know I'm not the best company when I'm in the flow state."

"Very engaged, actually." Coach waved the suggestion away like it was nothing. "If this project actually works, then it could make my life a lot easier. I'd be lying if I said I wasn't intrigued." He paused for a few seconds as though running through his own thoughts. "I was blown away by the elixir machine. I didn't tell you that before, because I wasn't sure about how involved you were. But seeing all of this, I can tell that you're very likely the architect behind the whole thing. There hasn't been any doubt in any of your actions, and you've not had a single fluctuation in your essence flow. Everything is intentional, even if it doesn't look like it."

"Appreciate it." Sal smiled as he put down the finished cushion. "But buttering me up isn't going to increase your stake in the project. You'll get a cut, but I'll need a lot more than compliments to increase your share."

A wild grin appeared on Coach as he crossed his arms. "You're a fun one, I'll give you that." He laughed before biting his lip. "So, what are we talking about? You need me to help train up the machine until it knows everything I do?"

Sal shook his head. "Nothing as intensive as that. I just need the credibility and endorsement from you. If you can tell people that this thing is the real deal, then we'll have a solid reason for hiking up the price."

"Not a man for charity? There are a lot of broken students who would benefit from this," Coach said carefully as he watched Sal's face intently for a reaction.

"Well, for a Skill Implant, they're talking about charging close to fifty thousand Q-Cred," Sal stated as he looked at Coach seriously. "While I'm not opposed to pro bono work, I'd rather hike up the prices for the people who can afford it. If this machine works as we intend it to, then we'll be able to map out exactly what students need to do to progress with their abilities."

"After an assessment," Coach corrected him. "Just looking at an ability isn't enough to go to that level. Especially for people with manifestation style abilities."

Sal sighed as he looked at the machine, frowning. "It'll have all the answers that we need, but we just need to figure out the right questions."

Coach pointed at Sal's face. "Why don't you make more of those trackers? You could have them record themselves when they're using their abilities, and then upload the data to the machine."

Sal tilted his head to one side. "That would cost… a lot." He didn't want to dismiss the idea completely, but there was so much more work involved in it. Sure, he could outsource a lot of the painful work to the Arkwright, but it would still require a lot more hands-on work than he had intended. Sal wanted the students to walk up to the machine, pay for the service, get the answers they needed, and leave. That was the whole process in his mind.

"It's a compelling reason to hike up the price. You'd be renting the equipment to people, create scarcity of availability. You'd need to find a way to lock down the visors so that nobody could create counterfeits." Coach continued to brainstorm as he glanced at the designs on the windows. "I'm making this far more complicated, aren't I?"

Sal shook his head. "No, you're fine. I just need to think it through... I kind of thought that it would be enough to give them the answers of their weaves, but your ability doesn't work that way."

Coach nodded and left a few seconds of silence before he proposed a new solution. "Or, I could interpret all that information for you. I'm the leading expert on the Coach ability."

"What about the Awakener ability?" Sal countered, smiling. "Because that's the weave we're using this time around."

Coach faltered for a second as he looked up in the direction of the simulation orb. "Wait, you're not using my ability?"

"I am, just the evolved version." Sal laughed as he gestured at Coach's chest. "Just like you can see my potential, I can see the evolution of your ability... and what the weave would need to look like to get to that level. You should check in with Grant to see what your synchro rate is with Awakener, because it might be a suitable imprint for you." His half-lie was blended with a truth, and it was absolutely worth it when Sal saw Coach's reaction.

Coach was absolutely flummoxed as he stared at Sal in disbelief. "No." He shook his head, his voice getting deeper. "No... I watched you! I saw how long you spent up there, and I know you were going slow for my benefit. That wasn't enough time to fix a weave, let alone create an evolutionary version of it." He looked like he was close to breaking down.

Sal shrugged, his hands spread out. "I'm very good at what I do. You should check with Grant if you don't believe me." He was relieved that he had checked the simulation orb when Coach went to retrieve the sushi. It played into his minor theatrics of instinctively being all-knowing. A part of him felt bad for messing with Coach, but it was his only form of entertainment during the build.

Coach hesitated before he reached into his pocket. He was surprisingly graceful as he weaved through the stacks of materials in the direction of the stairs. "We're not done talking about this." He laughed, but it was humorless, as though he wasn't ready to be hopeful. "I'll apologize if I'm wrong, but... your ego is putting mine to shame. That's saying something!"

With the momentary reprieve from Coach, Sal was able to get back into the zone. He had all the cushions upholstered to specification, and he was quite happy with it. It didn't have the flair that Blathnaid would undoubtedly add to it, but he could Refine it with Mythcrafter to make it more presentable. That was a problem for later, because he had the cocoon to work on. It required an eye-watering amount of scarlet screen, and Sal was desperate to find a substitute, despite knowing from both the visor and Mythcrafter that there wasn't one. After this project, he'd be left with barely a handful of the material, which was depressing.

Sal sighed as he fitted the cushions to the frame of the chair, struggling a little with the mechanism to lock it into a reclined position. His additional strength was helpful as he picked up the entire chair, with its metal bracket, and slotted it into the dock that was cutting into the carpeted floor. He had to shove the chair forward so it would click into place, but it was a euphoric sound when the mechanism found purchase. A sigh of relief escaped Sal as he glanced over the side of the reclined chair, to see the collection of circuitry that was waiting to be connected through the sleeve of the former Skill Registration machine.

"Later," Sal whispered to himself as he got to his feet and looked at the scarlet screen stack. It was time to make the curved casing that would descend over the chair, locking the inhabitant in the most expensive red egg known to man. He tilted his head at that internal analogy, before snorting at himself. "I need to install a coffee machine up here. I'm starting to get loopy."

"Talking to me?" Coach called out from upstairs. His head poked over the balcony of the mezzanine to check on Sal, his tablet still pressed against the side of his face.

"No," Sal responded with a dismissive wave before lying down on the ground to have a better view of the connections between the chair and Skill Registration machine. "Just talking to myself."

Even though he said he'd do it later, there was no point in skipping ahead to the fun parts of the build. Everything needed to be done, so he figured he might as well get it over with so he could enjoy himself with the red casing. That enthusiasm and resolve lasted all of a minute until he was cursing with the flickering view of the different cables, contradicting what Mythcrafter was telling him.

Sal sighed as he got to work untangling the cables. It was going to be a long evening.

CHAPTER 69: STUNT

"Is it supposed to glow like that?" Coach asked from the other side of the room. He had taken more than a few cautionary steps backward when the Mythcrafter essence caused the structure to glow. "Kinda looks like it's about to blow. You should get back here just in case."

Sal laughed as he shook his head. "This is kind of like the cooking process. I put it together, but I need to blend the components with refined Mythcrafter essence. Think of it like filling in all the cracks to ensure that it's seamless."

It had been a long and arduous build, but Sal was happy with the result. The matching red glass on both the terminal screen and the chair casing made it look incredibly polished. He hadn't anticipated that the hellfire titanium would take to the runes so well, with the glossy black frame shimmering to reveal blood-red etchings on a constant rhythm, like a heartbeat. Stormweave bolts had been an incredible decision, as it looked like a thunderstorm was brewing within the fabric. It didn't look particularly inviting, and actually looked dangerous to sit on... but Sal didn't care about that. From a purely aesthetic standpoint, it looked great.

His only real hope was that the transformation wasn't too dramatic. The Mythical blight jackal had morphed from a janky and overweight mess into a sleek sleeve for his arm. Sal didn't know whether his chair casing would compress to the point that it could only accommodate short people. It wasn't exactly catastrophizing, but if the casing ended up making a tight humanoid-shaped coffin, there wouldn't be anyone willing to get into it.

"You seem confident," Coach suggested as he got a little closer to the glowing structure. "Do you really think it's going to work?"

Sal nodded. "Yeah, I actually have a way of checking... but the last time I did it, I got hospitalized."

Coach frowned as he came into view beside Sal. "Is it a weave?"

"Yeah, it's All Sight. Have you come across it before?" Sal asked curiously as he gestured at his eyes. "It's my father's ability, and it almost blinded me when I used it during the build for the elixir machine."

Coach bit his lip as he looked at the machine and then back at Sal. "Can you load it up and not activate it?"

"Yeah," Sal answered as he quickly formed his father's weave.

Coach's jaw dropped and his eyes widened, looking at Sal in disbelief. "Do not activate that!" He waved his hands and got closer to Sal. "Get rid of it!"

Sal frowned as he dismissed the weave in confusion. "That's what I use for Appraisal. I've been using it for years."

"When you get your Endurance stat up to eighteen, then we can talk about a plan for gradually training you with that ability. For now, please trust my professional opinion." Coach was uncharacteristically serious and firm, his eyes locked on Sal's. "It's no wonder you nearly went blind. That weave is ridiculous." He shook his head and let out a humorless laugh. "It's perfect in every way, but you're the problem."

Sal just stared at him, as though the silence would bring more context. Thankfully, Coach had more to say.

"Not the problem. I mean… your physiology is nowhere near ready for it to activate. I can't believe you've managed to get this far, if I'm honest." Coach exhaled audibly as he continued to shake his head. "Mythcrafter is a high-proficiency ability, and you're gradually improving every time you activate it. It's a slow but steady improvement over time, and I have no qualms with you using it."

He pointed at Sal's chest. "Skill Master is an inherent ability that is tailored for you, but it wasn't designed to be paired with All Sight. You've seemingly managed to bypass the limitations of the ability by visualizing the weaves through your father's ability, which explains why Skill Master has such a slow progression rate. All Sight is pulling it down."

"That's… not good." Sal frowned as he thought about it. "Being able to see weaves and gates is an aspect of All Sight, rather than Skill Master itself. I kinda knew that but didn't really think about it as a problem. I thought it was just a blend of my parents' abilities." He stopped himself from continuing. There was no need to highlight his mother's actual weave to Coach. Even if he already heard about it, there was no way that Sal was going to be the one to confirm it for him.

Coach seemingly dismissed the statement as he paced around Sal, tripping up slightly over the rogue materials strewn across the floor. "It's not good at all. I can't ask you to not use All Sight for Skill Master, but it's definitely a factor into why you're not progressing as rapidly as you should. It also throws a monkey wrench into my theories about the weave itself. You're not using All Sight when you're working on the simulation orb, which should be giving your Skill Master ability an opportunity to thrive. When you're inwardly customizing new weaves, that's when we see the most improvement." He grimaced as he placed his hands on his hips. "I don't like this. There are too many questions and not enough answers."

Sal smiled hopefully as he gestured at the glowing mass. "Well, guess we'll get to test out the machine. It might have the answer we need?"

Coach stared at him for a few seconds, appearing as though he was going to dismiss the thought. He seemingly bit back whatever retort he had and nodded slowly. "Yeah… let's see how the machine works out." Then, as though his conscience got the better of him: "But, in the event that the machine doesn't work out, I'd like to use our master class time to really delve into your imbalances."

"Or, I could raise my Endurance stat to eighteen, like you said? That would fix the problem, or give me a good baseline?" Sal shrugged. He wasn't in the mood to catastrophize and there was nothing really worrying about what Coach was saying. If the simple action of Appraisal was sabotaging him, or All Sight for that matter, it didn't really matter. He was building up his internal stats, and there was a silver lining that he could eventually build toward a body that wouldn't be at risk of internal injury.

"Salvatore, I don't want to sound facetious… but building Endurance isn't that easy. You need to dedicate close to a decade of strenuous effort and discipline to get there, and even then, your physiology might have a ceiling that prohibits you from reaching that number. You're, what… twenty? And your stat is less than three. That's not a good sign." Coach tried to sound reasonable, and his tone was gentle.

Sal nodded in agreement. "Hypothetically, if I can reach those numbers… will that fix the problems? Or does it need to be a higher number?"

Coach inhaled slowly as he looked up at the ceiling. "Yes. Higher numbers would be better, but you'd need to ensure that there's no imbalance with your other stats. Since your Strength stat is relatively high, I'd be confident that you'll have no issues in the initial stages. Healthy Mobility and Speed are excellent, too." He smiled wearily and offered a shrug. "It's great to see you driven like this, but a lifestyle cooped up in a workshop isn't going to lend itself well to the training required to build up the stats you'll need."

After a few seconds, Coach pointed up in the direction of the simulation orb. "I can't talk to the intricacies of synchronization rates, but I can talk about adaptability. Abilities manifest in different ways, with two people having the same weave, but their output can be radically different. Just like you've learned to use your eyes for Skill Master, Grant has only learned how to harness Skill Savant through touch. I use neither as I rely on my senses, which is why I instinctively understand what's happening rather than seeing it or touching it. Do you understand?"

"I think so?" Sal answered, curious to hear more about how abilities manifest. He had been categorizing them by grade and evolutionary capability. Seeing how they were actually activated was a very interesting concept. "Do you think there's a reason they manifest differently in people?"

Coach nodded as he pulled his hand away from the direction of the simulation orb and pointed at Sal instead. "You've never given your Skill Master ability the opportunity to manifest an output. By utilizing All Sight, you've essentially isolated it. On one hand, that might make it ridiculously potent as you naturally develop over time, but it could also stunt your future potential. All of this is just conjecture and I can't be certain, but my best guess is that All Sight has deprived you of a method to activate your ability properly. I wouldn't be surprised if there was more to Skill Master than just replicating weaves."

Sal was impressed. Coach had literally pieced together that there was more to his ability than just Replication. Given enough time, it was likely he'd understand that Sal could unknot the weaves of others. As great as their rapport had become over the course of the day, Sal wasn't going to trust him with the context he was missing. He had managed to learn a lot from Coach, and there was definite value in spending more time with him. Even if just to find out information like how much of a stat he would need to avoid injuring himself.

"Could you humor me for a second? Don't panic." Sal activated Appraisal and looked at the fridge on the other side of the room.

Coach looked confused before the color drained from his face. "Don't activate it!"

Sal casually Appraised the fridge, noting that it was Common grade, with little to no essence capability. He wasn't doing it to antagonize Coach, but rather to uncover a sneaking suspicion that was at the back of his mind. His father had taught him how to Appraise, not how to use All Sight. There weren't any injuries throughout his childhood, so there had to be more to the story than what Coach had seen.

"Oh," Coach said finally as he looked at Sal in confusion. "How did you do that?"

Sal let go of the weave and looked at Coach, grinning. "That's the question. What did I just do?"

"You only activated a segment of it. It was like an invisible limiter of about five percent of the actual ability." He frowned at Sal. "I've seen people with high levels of Control, but this is a little ridiculous. How can you impose a limiter like that?"

"My father taught me," Sal answered. "Taught me how to use the weave for Appraisal, and not All Sight."

Coach nodded and exhaled slowly. "Then your father is likely the best chance Gallant has of activating his ability." He looked at Sal seriously. "You're full of surprises, Salvatore Argento. I'm genuinely appreciative that Lombardi fast-tracked you to a master class with me."

"And to think, you could have had this conversation a few months ago." Sal smiled brightly as he spread his arms with a laugh. "Glad you could fit me into your schedule."

"I deserve that." Coach chuckled before snapping his attention toward the flash that burst out from the machine beside him. He stumbled backward in a hasty retreat, only to trip and fall on his ass with a pained groan.

Sal grimaced as he offered Coach a hand. "I didn't know it would do that… This is my first time seeing a Mythic grade after a cooldown."

Coach stared at him in barely concealed confusion. "But you said you've successfully done it twice?"

Sal shrugged as Coach clasped his hand. "Yeah… I slept through the first one, and my eyes were bleeding for the second." He laughed as he pulled Coach to his feet. "But you know what they say, third time's the charm."

"You're definitely full of surprises." Coach chuckled as he dusted himself off with a wince. "So, what do we do now?" He was about to say something else when he caught sight of the newly crafted machine. "Oh."

Sal grinned as he watched Coach's reaction. He lifted the visor in his hand and offered it to Coach. "Want to do the honors, or would you like me to show you how we Appraise at the Argento Auction House?"

"I wouldn't even know what to look for," Coach breathed as he tentatively reached out a hand to touch the glossy red screen, before pulling it back in alarm as a series of text appeared on it. "How in the world?" He looked at Sal in bewilderment.

Sal equipped his visor and accepted the synchronization request for Nexus. He used the opportunity to give the machine its name.

Athena has successfully synchronized.

"Can't let Doc Ameye have all the good names." Sal chuckled proudly as he started the Appraisal.

CHAPTER 70: ATHENA

Sal was not prepared for the Appraisal. It wasn't the scary experience of having his eyes bleeding, but it was an onslaught of information trying to format itself constantly. The best example he could recall was when he first activated Analysis and was hit by information on everything. With Appraisal, he felt a lot more comfortable, but the overlapping data kept correcting itself, like it was folding on itself and creating a new description. Sal had to focus intently on the wording and block out Coach's voice from beside him.

Realization dawned on Sal when he saw the familiar names of abilities flickering into existence, only to be overruled by new context. System appeared a few times, only to be warped into Cypher…and eventually, Protocol? That instance was scary enough, to think that Doc Ameye's train was actually just an ability name. Protocol wasn't finished, though, as it overlapped again to become an ability called Codex? Or was it Prime? There were too many things happening all at once, and Sal tried to keep up with the logic as the Appraisal struggled to identify the end-state of the registered abilities.

All the white noise evaporated from Sal's mind as he saw Skill Master appear. He held his breath, wondering whether he was going to see an evolutionary step for his own inherent ability. Sal had an almost desperate curiosity to know what came after Skill Master considering he couldn't get the simulation orb to tell him. It was a little funny that he was more interested in that one outcome than the machine actually working.

"Skill Paragon." Sal read the words aloud as they appeared on the screen. He wanted to hyper-focus on it for a description, but before he could even train his right eye on it, it was gone…or rather, replaced? A singular word appeared, the result of a combination of Awakener and Skill Paragon. "Fuck," Sal breathed as he looked at it carefully.

"What is it?" Coach grasped Sal's shoulder. "Did something screw up, or is this good cursing? I don't know you well enough to identify good cursing."

Revelation.

That was the name of the new ability that combined Skill Master and Coach, or rather, their evolved forms of Skill Paragon and Awakener. Was it the pinnacle, or just the Mythic variant of their abilities? The fact that it was there was the clearest sign that he had been successful in creating a Mythic grade. Yet, all he could do was watch as the information continued to fold on itself, highlighting the improvements to each of the basic stats. Despite the problematic combination of abilities, and his attempt to bridge them together, it looked like they all had an incredible cohesion in the later stages of evolution. Nexus and Cypher worked together to create something called Codex.

It was Codex and Protocol that joined hands to become Prime. Sal was taking it all in when the Appraisal information finally calmed down. Apparently, Cypher and Judgment needed extra time to sort through the new logic. It was the first time Sal had seen his visor struggle with a calculation, and the fact that he had stood there for a few minutes just watching it shit itself was oddly cathartic.

"You're worrying me, Sal," Coach said in a strained voice. "You're just staring into space and mumbling. Are you okay?"

Sal just nodded numbly as he went through the Appraisal that formed in front of his eye. "Yeah, I'm more than okay… but there is something a little scary with all of this." He wanted to be doubly sure before he even vocalized his thoughts, but something made him uncomfortable and he needed to lock that down first. "Just give me a few minutes."

Navigating through his visor, and utilizing Nexus, Sal limited the permissions of the entity known as Prime. The garbled information that had been nigh-impossible to parse… all had the same sentence after them. He couldn't be sure, but if this was the evolved form of Protocol, then he was dealing with a very intelligent machine that had taken the liberty of helping his visor identify the attributes. It went against everything he thought he knew about the Adaptive Behaviors that Fabi told him about. Maybe it was the exhaustion that had him on edge, but Sal fully expected that Prime would forcibly reject the permissions limitation.

Permissions have been successfully updated for Prime.

Permissions have been successfully updated for Codex.

Permissions have been successfully updated for Nexus.

It might have been overly cautious, but Sal didn't want a hyper-intelligent machine roaming through all his creations. Specifically, he didn't want it to get anywhere near Jackal. His fears of a murder drone uprising were fantastical and ridiculous, but he wasn't going to take any unnecessary risk.

Breathing a sigh of relief, Sal smiled and glanced at Coach. "You ready for the good news?"

"I think so?" Coach responded after a few seconds of hesitation. "It looks the part, but you really looked spooked for a second there."

Sal nodded. "Yeah, just wanted to ensure there wasn't a robot uprising. You've heard of Protocol, Doc Ameye's train?"

"Of course." Coach glanced at the machine warily. "Why do you bring that up?"

Sal pointed at the red casing. "Well, I guess you could call Prime the older brother of Protocol. It's the evolved form of the Protocol ability, and it already hijacked my visor to correct my Appraisal."

All color drained from Coach's face. "That's… absolutely terrifying."

"Yeah, I thought so, too." Sal laughed as he took off the visor. "But all the permissions are fixed now. I'll need to have a chat with Doc Ameye, and probably Upgrade and Fabi. Just to make sure I'm playing this safe."

Coach nodded slowly. "Does this usually happen? You know, where you want one particular outcome, and a super powerful, but incorrect ability comes out of it?"

Sal looked at him in confusion. "Oh, no… this time it was intentional. It needed a brain to process all the information. Here, have a look."

The Appraisal was preloaded onto the visor, but Sal already knew what it said.

Name	Athena
Origin	Crafted
Age	New
Grade	Mythic
Materials	Refined Mythcrafter Essence | Refined Skill Master Essence | Refined Perfect Essence | Scarlet Screen | Commander Core | Moonsilver | Stormweave | Starlight Steel | Tempest Steel Alloy | Lords Crystal | Switcher Sinew…
Attributes	Codex: A continuously evolving repository of catalogued information. Codex constantly updates and recalculates gathered data to provide the best insights possible. Enriched data sets will be shared with Prime. • Context Provided by Prime. Prime: Evolving Intelligence model with integrated learning capability. Specializes in instantaneous data processing and interpretation. Requires enormous amounts of data for best results. Behaviors are customizable. • Context Provided by Prime. Revelation: Grants understanding of limiting factors that are preventing user from reaching their full potential. A detailed action plan will be provided through calculations granted by Codex and Prime. • Context Provided by Prime. Ascension: Allows user to create a corrective treatment plan to repair broken ability weaves. Can be used to create stable foundation for ability evolution. Requirements from Revelation need to be met before Ascension can be activated. • Context Provided by Prime.
Abilities	Codex | Prime | Revelation | Ascension
Runes	Advanced Calibration Rune | Advanced Attune Rune | Advanced Essence Replenishment Rune
Power Source	Commander Core | External Essence

Evolution	No
Quality	Perfect
Condition	100%
Value	Unknown

The scary part was how this was possible without a dungeon heart, or even a fragment piece like they had used for the Arkwright. Sal had been sure that it was a rule after Doc Ameye told him about adding a "will" to a machine. The only argument he could think of were the countless individuals who had calculation-type abilities. They didn't need to be powered by a dungeon heart. Hell, the simulation orb was knocking out calculations with just Deduction, so why couldn't Prime operate without a fragment?

"Revelation…and Ascension?" Coach breathed heavily as he stumbled backward, falling into the decimated remains of the couch. Sal had taken far more than a tenth, and it looked pretty damn rough for it. Coach looked at Sal with wide eyes. "How is this even possible? This is far beyond anything I can do… or even what you can do!" His mind was clearly firing on all cylinders as he looked at Sal in horror. "This thing will bankrupt me!"

"Or make you very rich." Sal laughed as he offered a shrug. "We're just seeing the report for it, so the reality could be very different. I'll need to run some tests with it, and like I said, I should probably tell Upgrade and Fabi about it."

Coach nodded numbly as he continued to stare at the machine. "If this Codex ability can take all the gathered information from a tracker and feeds it to Prime, it'll be able to make a plan with Revelation. Am I understanding that correctly?"

Sal wobbled his hand, as if to say that he was half right. "I can't give you a real answer for that just yet. I have a lot of stuff on my visor that I want to keep away from Prime, but there is a lot of battle data that I can sync up with it. I've got an eye-patch that I only used in the dungeons, so that might be a good starting point to see how Prime processes it."

"Could you give it access to the simulation orb?" Coach asked out of curiosity. "You couldn't ask for more than an entire database of registered weaves. It would definitely train it for the actual purpose of the machine."

Sal blinked in surprise. "That's a good idea… but I'll have to check with Upgrade first."

"You seem to defer to her quite a bit." Coach laughed in disbelief. "Yet, you're the one knocking out Mythic grades."

Sal chuckled as he sat down on the ruined couch. "I've learned that asking for forgiveness works a lot better with Upgrade than asking for permission. She's likely going to kill me for attempting a Mythic after what happened last time." His laugh turned into a smile before he shrugged. "I know that I have a lot of capability, and I'm trying my best with Crafting, but Upgrade is excellent at pointing me in the right direction when I feel aimless."

Coach shook his head as he pointed at the machine. "Nobody will ever be pissed off at you for making this."

He paused for a second before holding up a finger. "Except, maybe Robert. I doubt he'll be too pleased. But, when is he ever?" He chuckled at his own joke, choosing to stare at the machine again. "It truly is remarkable, and I'm desperate to know if it works as intended. This Appraisal is pretty damn exciting; I can't believe how calm you're being about all this!"

Sal frowned as he tore his attention away from Athena to look at Coach. "Why would Robert be annoyed?"

Coach took off the visor and handed it back to Sal in confusion. "Because you've essentially just created a tool that could give Bastion ability weaves?" He smiled, as though it were obvious. "Even if they return to the surface and get essence sickness, the fledgling mutation in their system would be enough for Athena to give them a route to power."

Sal's heart froze at those words. "Oh… fuck."

"Oh fuck, indeed." Coach laughed as he slapped his knee. "But do not let that minor threat dampen the mood. We could argue that the Skill Implant machine is far more dangerous in Bastion hands than Athena. Besides, you've pretty much paved the way for every struggling Hero to reach their full potential. What are you planning to do with it? I know we had a small chat about you wanting to charge good money, but this could demand a fortune from the guilds alone."

Sal grimaced as he thought about his answer. "I was kinda hoping this would be a selling point for people joining my guild."

"You're a guildmaster?" Coach asked in surprise.

"Yeah. You probably think it's a waste?" Sal laughed as he gestured at Athena. "Keeping this as a private revenue generator?"

"Fuck no." Coach laughed, looking like he was genuinely entertained by the response. "Need any more advisors? What are you, ninth tier? I could bump you up to fifth with a single phone call."

Sal was about to answer when Coach held up a hand to interrupt him.

"Sorry, that was me being facetious." He chuckled as he looked at Athena. "I don't think there's much value in me advising you, and I'd probably be able to swing eighth tier at best." He grinned as he looked over at Sal. "Let me know if you'd like to hire me on a full-time basis. I'll even drop my rates."

Sal smiled, but he couldn't shake the thought that he might have given the Bastion a new method of gaining power. They were an invisible threat that had already infiltrated Quest Academy in his first semester. If Coach's words were to be believed, then Sal had done the exact opposite of what his father had asked of him. If his own fears were valid, then he likely needed to keep this a secret. He needed to talk to his dad to get some rational advice. For all of Coach's excitement, he wasn't coming across as rational.

"If this is a genuine threat, and it would piss off Robert, then do you think we should just keep it under wraps? We're the only two who knows it exists," Sal asked awkwardly, still unsure of how to proceed. It could help a lot of people, just like the Arkwright. He kept that a secret because he knew the damage it could cause. A small part of Sal had hoped that Athena would deflect people's attention from his real abilities with Skill Master. If Athena could do something similar, they could just fight over it instead of him.

"Under wraps?" Coach scoffed as he looked at Sal with an expression of incredulity. "Absolutely not. If you're worried about getting abducted in the middle of the night, then just use it as much as you can before it happens."

Sal laughed humorlessly. "Having a perfect Mythcrafter or Skill Master weave isn't exactly going to make me less of a target."

Coach snorted dismissively. "Who said I was talking about you? Put each and every one of your guild members into that thing so they're a force to be reckoned with."

Sal faltered as he looked at Coach in surprise.

Coach nodded slowly. "Build up your own little legion of Heroes. If you fix someone who's broken, they'll never forget it." He smiled warmly. "I can tell you that from personal experience. If the war broke through the barriers, there are hundreds of people who would step up to keep me safe. That's not something you can buy, but you can absolutely earn it."

Sal ruminated over everything. The mention of Bastion and Robert had certainly soured his mood, but the idea of using the machine to build up his own private army was a novel concept. He couldn't for the life of him imagine the likes of Dave Delgado or Kane Brigadir becoming certifiable badasses. The image of Harold Gunn appeared in his mind, and Sal couldn't stop the laugh that escaped his lips.

"That's the spirit." Coach clapped his hands together. "So, is now a bad time to talk about my stake in Athena?"

CHAPTER 71: CONTEXT

"You think he's lying, too?" Upgrade asked Fabi as she leaned against the doorframe to Sal's room. They were in the private Savior workshop, and talking to each other like he wasn't standing right beside him.

Fabi nodded in agreement. "Absolutely. I saw Coach skipping in the hallways yesterday." She smirked at Sal. "It was terrifying."

Upgrade grinned as she tilted her head and gave Sal a knowing look. "All it took for Alex to start dancing was a Mythic grade. What did it take for Coach?"

Sal sighed as he put his hands on his hips. "And here I thought you both enjoyed surprises and suspense? If you don't want to go in and see the destroyed couch, that's completely up to you." He started to move toward the door, but Upgrade's hand shot up to block his way.

"Ah, ah, come on. We're just psyching ourselves up for whatever surprise you have cooked up for us in there." She smiled before looking over at Fabi. "Do you think it has anything to do with the thunder noises we've been getting complaints about?"

Sal bit his lip. He hadn't realized there were complaints. It made sense, but it wasn't ideal.

Fabi shook her head as she placed a hand on Sal's shoulder. "Don't worry, we know you wouldn't have been stupid enough to work on a big Crafting project without supervision… especially after getting hospitalized." She smiled sweetly at him. "Because, if you collapsed when nobody was around to help you, we'd be upset."

"Very upset," Upgrade added, the smile on her face becoming menacing. "So, with that little disclaimer out of the way, how about you show us this couch?"

Sal laughed as he waved his hand dismissively. "Actually, now that I think about it, it's more of a Blathnaid issue. I shouldn't be taking time out of your day like this. Forget I said anything." He moved toward the frame and placed his back to the door, smiling apologetically at the two of them. "Sorry for wasting your time like this. Obviously, I wouldn't be stupid enough to Craft something dangerous without supervision."

"You had a day," Fabi stated slowly as she glanced at Upgrade nervously. "So… Legendary grade?"

Upgrade's gaze was locked on Sal. It felt like she was staring directly into his soul. "He wouldn't bother building up suspense for a Legendary, and the fact that it was just a day would make a Mythic grade all that more impressive. In his head, at least."

"Open the door, Sal," Fabi instructed, groaning. "You've built your stage, so if it ends up just being a wrecked couch, you can have the last laugh."

Upgrade laughed, her gaze not budging from Sal's face. "Open the door, Sal. You're screwed either way."

Sal's conflicted expression melted away with a laugh as he tapped his Q-Card against the mechanism, opening the door behind him. He could see both Upgrade and Fabi shift their stances to see into the room behind him, but he intentionally blocked their view. "Ready for the ground rules?"

"You're playing with fire, Salvatore." Upgrade laughed in disbelief. "Seriously, if you actually went ahead and Crafted a Mythic grade without us being there to monitor you, I'll be very disappointed."

"You don't look disappointed," Sal teased as he swirled his finger in a circle in the direction of her face. "You look curious. I'll settle for that."

Fabi crossed her arms and let out an exasperated sigh. "Ground rules, go." She glanced at Upgrade. "Just play the game so we can figure out what's in there. It might be the legs for the Tempest Marshal!"

Upgrade's eyes widened as she looked at Fabi in shock. "Oh…that's a good call." She gave Sal her full attention, all frustration seemingly gone. "What are the ground rules?"

Sal didn't care that they confused it with leg armor. He was pretty sure they'd see the immense value of Athena, but he needed to swear them to secrecy first. They already had so many of his secrets under wraps, this was just one more. If he wanted to use it, he needed to be sure that Prime was something that could be trusted and utilized. For that reason, he hadn't paired Athena with any of the databases he had access to. If he got the all clear from Fabi and Upgrade, then he'd give Prime limited access. They seemed to be a lot more knowledgeable about that sort of thing.

"I need both of you to swear to secrecy." Sal looked at both of them seriously, letting his smile fade. "This thing is more of a risk than Jackal, and the capability of Skill Master."

All color drained from Upgrade's face as she pushed Sal directly into the room, her palms on his chest. He was so surprised by her behavior that he didn't resist. With the entrance no longer barred, Upgrade walked past him and moved into his dorm. Fabi followed her, twisting her body so she didn't bump into Sal. She shot him a look of confusion and concern as she passed.

Sal sighed. He probably could have played that better. The playful attitude had seemingly been destroyed with just a single sentence. He tapped the mechanism to close the door before following the women into his living room. A part of him had wanted to see their reactions, but he guessed that it was a small price to pay for worrying them. When he rounded the corner, he smiled inwardly. Their reactions were still on full display.

"Well, it's not legs," Fabi observed with confusion as she glanced at Sal curiously.

Upgrade's jaw was slack as she traced a finger along the blood-red casing of scarlet screen. Her gaze darted from point to point, as though trying to take everything in. Just when it looked like she was about to say something, her eyes locked onto the Skill Registration machine. "What the fuck?"

"What?" Fabi looked at Upgrade in confusion. "Is something wrong?"

Upgrade pointed at the machine. "You were just supposed to *fix* it!" She lifted both of her hands to her head and pulled at her hair as she laughed nervously. "What have you done?"

"A better question would be about the whole thing," Fabi suggested with a wince. "I can't figure any of this out. It kinda looks like a fancy machine for assisted suicide."

Sal was about to answer Upgrade when he heard Fabi's comment. It was enough to make him falter. "Wait… what?"

Upgrade looked aghast at the suggestion, but stared at Fabi, not at Sal.

Fabi pointed at the encased seat. "I don't know, it just looks like it's designed to get rid of bodies or something? Does it recharge cores from melting them down in that pod?"

Upgrade was speechless as she stared between the two Crafters she was supposedly mentoring.

"That's not… even remotely close." Sal laughed awkwardly. "I've named it Athena. It's a device that combines abilities from Coach, Quest, and me."

"Strategy and Wisdom?" Fabi asked the question, still smiling at Upgrade's look of revulsion. "Or did you just try to find a name that Doc Ameye hasn't used yet?"

Upgrade raised a hand to interrupt Fabi. "Sorry, you lost question privileges for that last guess." She suppressed a shudder before looking at Sal warily. "A Skill Registration machine is a good match-up for Skill Master, and I know that Coach's ability is insanely sought-after. Why did you bother with Quest's System ability?"

Sal moved to the edge of the coffee table, stacked with materials. He had done his best to clear the room by storing as much as possible in Arsenal, but there were still remnants of the build littered around the area. Reaching down, he picked up his visor and offered it to Upgrade. "When you see Prime, you'll understand why I need your help."

Upgrade took the visor from him and pulled her hair back on one side, securing it to her face. "Is Prime a result of System?" She sounded like she was in business mode, or crisis management. They both sounded the same.

"Prime is the evolved form of Protocol." Sal offered a helpless shrug. That single statement was enough to change the atmosphere from one of dubious uncertainty to excitement.

"Fuck off," Fabi breathed as she stared at him, a wide smile appearing on her face. "You made something better than Protocol?" Her hands were already up and reaching for the tracker, as though begging Upgrade to hurry up and give it to her.

Upgrade's arms came up defensively as she stepped away from Fabi to keep her distance. She was torn between looking at the Appraisal and Sal. Her curiosity eventually won out and her gaze locked onto Athena.

Fabi, realizing she wasn't getting the tracker, turned her attention to Sal. All caution had evaporated, only to be replaced by a burning desire to know more. "Is this because I told you about the limitations with Jackal's learning modules? Making something like Protocol is insane! It's the greatest limiting factor for the drones, and you've just made it!"

Sal sighed with an awkward smile. "We're going to need to talk to Divinity to find out if you're a calamity in waiting." He chuckled at the surprised expression on Fabi's face. "I mean, I'm pretty sure we're going to have a drone uprising, with you at the center of it. Prime was able to override my tracker when I was doing the Appraisal. I limited the permissions for it, but it wanted to connect to every-thing. I'd be worried of it going rogue... especially if it's smarter than Doc Ameye's train."

"It's an ability, though." Fabi laughed as though Sal were missing something incredibly obvious. "It's designed to be harnessed. It's like a tool to be used in pursuit of something greater, not something that's capable of desire or motive. You can teach it to behave in certain ways, but it will never go rogue."

"She's right, Sal." Upgrade continued to read through the Appraisal with a deep frown of concentration. "There's no such thing as original thought when it comes to calculation-style abilities. No matter how convincing the outputs look, they're calculations from a data set. Prime looks like it's just the highest form of processing and interpretation."

"So, it's not going to try to kill us all if I give it access to everything?" Sal asked with an awkward laugh. He didn't feel like he was being unreasonable with his fears.

Fabi just stared at him in bewilderment. "How can you not know these things... and make this?" She gestured with both hands at Athena. "I think I need Mythcrafter as my Skill Implant." She shook her head with a melodic laugh. "Like, how are you able to make stuff like this through instinct?"

"Mythcrafter is special for him because of Skill Master. You wouldn't get the same results as Sal," Upgrade corrected her as she continued to pace around Athena. "You'd still be better than Doc Ameye, though. That would make it worth it."

Fabi bit her lip as she watched Upgrade move around. "I'm trying to distract myself, but could you just tell me what you're seeing? Sal is too busy catastro-phizing the apocalypse to tell me more about Athena." She winked at him to show she was joking, before locking her gaze back on Upgrade. "Literally, just give me the description of Prime. I'm going crazy over here."

Upgrade smiled as she shook her head. "Prime isn't the most impressive thing here, not by a long shot. You're going to love Codex, too."

Fabi's chin raised as she looked at the ceiling with a groan of exasperation. "Why are you tormenting me?" She seemingly asked the room rather than Up-grade. When her chin lowered, she looked at Sal desperately. "You know what that is, don't you? Can you just explain it?"

Sal tilted his head, enjoying this immensely. He instead looked over at Up-grade. "I thought she'd be more curious about Revelation?"

Upgrade shook her head. "It's an incredible ability... but Ascension looks phenomenal, too. I don't know how you managed this without a dungeon frag-ment. It's more impressive than the Arkwright, but I can see your concerns on how it'll actually be used. It's going to need a lot of data."

Fabi looked as if she were on the verge of hyperventilating. She removed her-self from the conversation and sat down on the couch. Or...at least she would have, if the cushions hadn't been plundered for their padding. Fabi lurched to one side and tumbled to the floor, her eyes wide.

"Told you that the couch was destroyed," Sal offered meekly, not liking the expression on Fabi's face. Even without the tracker to read emotions, he felt like his lifespan had just been cut short.

Upgrade appeared in front of Fabi and offered her the tracker, smiling excitedly. "Before you kill him, you might want to take a look at this. We've got a lot of work to do."

"Is Prime safe?" Sal asked in a hopeful voice. "Like, do you think we can test it?"

Upgrade smiled warmly at him. "I know why you made this, Salvatore. It was a stretch for us to consider the elixir machine a product of Ethical Crafting... but this?" She looked at Athena, her expression softening before a proud smile graced her lips. "This is by far the best thing you've ever made, and a beautiful use of the Mythcrafter ability."

Fabi took the tracker from Upgrade, getting to her feet unassisted. "Okay, you guys can stop now. I'm going to put this on and it's not going to have a single trace of essence." She pulled her hair to one side and clipped the tracker over one eye. "You really got me, though. Never thought you'd work together on a prank." She sounded annoyed, right up until she started reading. Her entire visage morphed as her lips parted in surprise. "Oh..."

"Welcome to the context club." Upgrade smiled as she patted Fabi on the shoulder. "Sal's just made a machine that can help everyone, just like how he helped you with your weave."

CHAPTER 72: ROMAN

Quest sat on the broken couch, not even bothering to keep himself righted. His whole torso leaned off at an angle as he stared at Athena in a fugue state. The tracker looked comical on his face, with his spectacles resting lopsided on top of the screen. He hadn't said anything for a few minutes as he went through the Appraisal information.

Sal looked at Fabi, who smiled contentedly. She had refused to do a quick repair of the couch because she wanted someone else to fall. Even if that person ended up being Quest. When he sat composedly on the ruined furniture, she had been a little disappointed, but looked to be enjoying the comical setup. Ever since she had gone through Athena's Appraisal, she had been a little different with Sal. She didn't make as much eye contact, and seemed to be lost in thought more often than not.

Sal was just happy to see that she was enjoying herself. There hadn't been any follow-up conversations about the drone army, so he guessed she was processing something else in her mind. Maybe the Skill Implant of Mythcrafter? Sal didn't know.

Upgrade was perched on the elevated corner of the couch, watching Quest intently. She had provided a few pieces of context throughout when he had questions. Her insights were far more tuned in than Sal's, and she seemingly understood more about Codex and Prime as abilities than he did. Most of his concerns were related to the security of Prime, and what would be prudent to share with it. They had discussed a few different databases that Sal hadn't even heard of, but if it helped Athena get up to speed faster, then he was all for it.

"I have no words for this," Quest said finally as he took off the tracker, almost reluctantly. "I have spent decades dreaming of a solution like this… and I never could have anticipated that it would materialize in a far more ambitious form." He bit his lip before glancing over at Sal. "I cannot praise you enough for this. Any platitude I throw your way would only be arbitrary. You already know the impact this will have."

"Remind him," Upgrade suggested with a knowing smile. "His first reaction on making this was anxiety, because Bastion could target him."

Quest's eyebrows rose, causing his spectacles to fall back into place on his nose. "Excuse my language, but fuck Bastion!" He aggressively pointed at Athena. "You've single-handedly created a solution for countless students and Heroes who have been overlooked by society. I tasked you with an extraordinarily difficult task… to right the injustices that the Support classes face. It was meant to inspire you, but you've ended up inspiring me!"

He laughed, his expression one of stupefied joy. "The elixir machine was an excellent method for building the wealth of the Crafting Department, but this is several steps beyond that achievement." He chuckled as he looked at the machine. "Athena is a remarkably apt name." He sat there, seemingly content with just looking at Athena.

Sal couldn't share in the joy that they were all feeling, nor could he feel worthy of the praise. This had been a project of curiosity, rather than a noble goal. Sure, he had thought it would help people, but his first instincts were how he could monetize it. That was what made him feel dirty, because he was surrounded by people who saw him as a Savior, far beyond the rankings in Quest Academy. He had tried to soften the reverence by explaining it to Upgrade, but she had shot him down immediately. It was time to try to burst the bubble for Quest. He couldn't just stand there and accept misplaced praise. That wasn't how he was raised.

"I need to explain something," Sal began after a momentary pause. "When I started planning out this project—"

Upgrade snorted. "If you're going to try to tell him that you're a heartless bastard who made this for profit, don't bother. He won't care."

Sal twisted around to look at Upgrade in surprise, and was further confounded when he heard Quest's laughter.

"Upgrade is correct. I couldn't care less what your motivations were," Quest explained as he slapped his knees with almost childlike excitement. "You made Athena with intent. This wasn't a project designed to kill people. You could have made more evolving weaponry and sold your soul like Doc Ameye, but you didn't. If your motive was profit, then you've succeeded. Humanity profits from this, and no matter what number you price the service at, we'll find a way to make it work." He smiled warmly at Sal. "If you're feeling guilty about misplaced praise, I'm confident that your pricing strategy won't be prohibitive."

"We don't even know if it works," Sal muttered, not sure how to deal with the positive atmosphere surrounding him. "And I won't rip people off… I was already thinking that people below a certain grade of ability could use it for free. You know, to get them started."

Quest stared at Sal for a few seconds before his smile deepened. "I think that's a very noble goal. But you're a guildmaster now—you're not running a charity. Assuming everything works as the Appraisal suggests, the academy will subsidize the usage of Athena for those students. We're going to have more funds from our Crafting Department, so it shouldn't be too expensive."

"Get that in writing," Upgrade said in a teasing voice, a wide smile on her face.

Sal nodded as he looked between Quest and Upgrade. It was nice to see that they had so much faith in him, and he wasn't an idiot. He knew that Athena was a ridiculously powerful machine, and it had the potential to help so many people. Prime was the only reason that Sal hadn't sat in it and fired it up. He needed confirmation from the essence programming experts that it was safe to do so, or that the permissions were locked tight.

"So, what are the next steps before we run some tests with it?" Sal glanced at Upgrade.

She smiled as she pointed over at Fabi. "If she's willing to help me, we can put in some clear directives for Prime. That shouldn't take more than a few hours. We just need to be very, very clear on what it is allowed to do and what is a waste of resources." Her hand moved toward Quest. "And then we'll need permission to get Quest's System access. If we can get Grant's database, the Hunter Bureau database… and the Scavenger Network… we can cover all bases."

Quest smiled as he nodded along. "There are a few other databases that are off record. You might have already seen the simulation data in the war room. We can give that to Athena, too." He laughed as he thought about it. "Imagine it, we could have a student sit in that very chair, and have an entire plan customized to their personal growth… be it sparring, taking down demons, or simply meditation. We could tailor our lesson plans for each individual, and greatly enhance their chances of success."

Fabi uncrossed her arms as she looked at them. "And dungeons. If you get the Strategic Warfare database that the Hunter Bureau uses, then you would have access to all the raid information and dungeon guides. It could create a shopping list of sorts for students, telling them where they need to go to increase their stats."

Sal frowned. "I'm pretty sure that Revelation is able to do that part."

"My System will be more than capable of that," Quest explained as he smiled at Fabi. "When I created the Quest System for the guilds, it was fundamentally flawed. There was no guaranteed progression from following the steps, and there were far too many generalizations. This would solve all those issues, and provide a wealth of more useful information."

"No offense, but I know if people saw an updated version of the Quest System, they'd flinch," Upgrade said softly as she looked at Quest. "It ruined so many guilds that adopted it."

"Time for a rebrand, I guess?" Quest chuckled. "If you can get Coach to put his name behind it, then you'll be infinitely more successful. I'd rather we made an entity that didn't highlight Athena's existence. If we could frame it that Athena is simply a tool for the new system, then we can hand-wave the process and keep people's attention on the results rather than how we got there."

Upgrade's face brightened. "Oh, that's not a bad idea. Coach has been out of the public eye for a while now… so we could say he's been working on this? Maybe you've been helping him."

"Is this really necessary?" Sal laughed as he looked between them. "I mean, I've never even seen the Quest System, so I don't really have that much context. I just remember you telling me that Heroes got addicted to seeing the numbers going up."

Quest smiled. "It's quite outdated at this point, but it was a simplistic method of attributing scores and statistics to actions. It made some very broad assumptions, like calculations on how a Strength stat would work with a Speed stat. Couple that with leveling up mechanics, which were essentially just a points tally for defeating certain types of demon, or clearing dungeons."

"It would be a good way to keep Athena a secret from people," Upgrade suggested to Sal. "I know it might not feel good taking a back seat on this, but it would keep you out of the public eye as the money rolls in."

Sal thought about it for a few seconds, trying to figure out how they had gone in this direction. "Okay, just so I'm clear. You're suggesting that we market this new system as the solution, rather than Athena?"

"Correct," Upgrade agreed. "The less people who know about Athena's capability, the better."

"And… how are we planning on delivering the new system to people? Like, I had assumed they'd just read the information from Athena." Sal turned from Upgrade to Quest, not sure who was more qualified to answer him. He wasn't opposed to the idea if it meant there was no target on his back. If it helped people and didn't endanger him, then it was a net positive. "Coach had suggested producing trackers that could be connected through Prime, for real-time data. Would that work?"

Fabi nodded, but still glanced at Upgrade to double-check with her. "That sounds like something I could help with. Mass-production of the same design would be possible with Figment, if I had the materials ready."

Quest sighed contentedly. "That's a good method. I've been using System with my tracker for years, so I've got a bit of experience with this. I don't understand the technical aspect, but I would imagine that you would only require the trackers to pair up with Prime. They wouldn't need anything else. That should reduce the cost, I'd imagine?"

Upgrade glanced at Sal and laughed. "I think we're close to frying his brain with all this."

Sal grimaced as he shook his head. "No, it's just feeling like a wild overcomplication. I don't have an answer, but I don't understand enough about this to know if it will work." He sighed as he gestured at Athena. "I'll feel a lot better when I know that this can work the way it was designed. It would be great having multiple methods of accumulating data, but I don't know how I feel with having so many people connected with Prime."

Fabi frowned as she tilted her head to one side. "It would only be one-way, though. They'd only get the reports that are sent to them. They'll never get to interact with Prime. We can solve that with just an hour or so of essence programming. I haven't looked at your terminal, so I've got no idea what way the code looks."

"It's gorgeous." Upgrade smiled as she answered Fabi. "That directive would only take us a few minutes."

Quest looked at Sal, his face a mask of concentration. "What if we pared everything back? Let's treat this as a trial run. We make…what, three or four trackers that use the new System. We bring in some of the people who already know about your gifts, who we know we can trust, and we see how it works for them?"

"Well, obviously we'll do a controlled test before rolling it out." Upgrade laughed as she looked at Quest in disbelief. She glanced at Sal, and realization dawned. "Oh… you thought we were going to just give this to a thousand students and hope for the best?"

Sal bit his lip. That's exactly what he was thinking. "No…"

"Since we're diving headfirst into this, what should we call it?" Fabi asked out of curiosity. "Also, are we able to move Athena somewhere else to run tests? Sal probably needs a bit of privacy."

"I'd prefer if we kept it here," Sal answered. "I'll be running dungeons for the next few days anyway."

"Why on earth would you do that?" Quest asked in disbelief before catching himself. "I mean, with your contributions… and the amount of materials you have, there shouldn't be any need for you to run dungeons. You don't have a deadline for the guild rankings, either."

"Personal training," Sal answered vaguely, smiling. "I need to improve a few things, and ensure I'm ready for when Shade tries abducting me."

Quest's face drained of color, creating a blank canvas that was then splashed with a violent red. "Can I ask why you believe you would be abducted? To my knowledge, those visions were edge-cases that required a series of unlikely events, like you being highly antagonistic toward him. I was assured that the possibility wasn't even a fifth of a percentage point." He clenched his fist as he looked at Sal seriously. "I can cancel the entire class, or get them kicked out of participating."

Sal shrugged and offered him a smile. "No need to worry. I've got it under control." He had a roster of people who would be at the location for when Shade was there. If there was any hostility, he'd be ready. It was interesting to hear Quest's version, showing the odds to be so low. Why would Divinity have warned him if the odds were so low? Were the Heroes with Foresight wrong? Was it Scry? There were too many questions, but the only answer Sal needed was in his own preparation. He had work to do.

Silence washed over the room, and it was an awkward one. Sal felt a little guilty about it, but it was Fabi who came to the rescue.

"You never answered my other question. What would you name the system?" she asked hopefully, in a lighthearted tone that was clearly designed to dissolve the sudden tension.

Sal listened as Upgrade threw out a few ideas, her contribution to change the topic away from Shade. None of them were particularly gripping, and Sal thought of his own suggestion. The idea that Coach had, of creating a personal army of people who would protect him if everything else went to shit. That single thought kept popping up in Sal's mind.

"We'll call it Legion," Sal stated as he came to his decision. Sure, it didn't lend itself to the fact that they'd be trialing it out with a handful of people...but it could grow over time.

Upgrade laughed. "You had to pick another Greek name?"

"It's Roman," Quest muttered under his breath. "Phalanx doesn't really roll off the tongue, I guess."

"What?" Upgrade asked, clearly bewildered. "Flanks?"

CHAPTER 73: DISTRACTION

Sal felt like an out-of-place visitor in his own dorm. He already knew that there would be a lot of activity happening with Fabi and Upgrade working on Athena, but he didn't expect them to bring in a massive terminal to work on the essence programming. Most of the natural lighting in the room was cut off as the enormous collection of screens were installed in front of his windows. Each of them booted up at various times, all showing off different modules being loaded up.

Upgrade had helped Sal load the stacks of materials into Arsenal so they'd have more space to move around. Hermes had thankfully stopped sending over new materials, and Sal couldn't believe that he was relieved to have less rare materials appearing in his room. While they worked on that, Fabi had shipped over most of the stuff they'd need from the workshop, and now they were talking to each other about how they were going to go about the essence programming. It started with the basics, where it looked like they were trying to include him in the logic, but after a certain point, it became an impenetrable conversation where Sal couldn't follow even a tenth of what was being said.

If he had to choose between understanding and having Athena fully operational, he'd choose the latter every time. The only thing that niggled at the back of his head was how the project had gotten away from him. Stepping back from the elixir machine was one thing, because he had built it with other people in mind. Anders and Alex were integral to its successful operation... but Athena? That was something he had made for Coach and himself to use.

Sal was very grateful that Upgrade and Fabi were able to lend their expertise to the essence programming side, especially because Prime wasn't a known quantity. He wasn't exactly sure how he felt about the Legion System, though. It felt like they had just latched onto their first idea, and then brainstormed it out. Even for Sal, who was used to moving fast on projects, it felt a little excessive. Most of the plan was half-baked at best, but it seemed everyone else was on board with it.

Maybe it was because he hadn't seen the Quest System that was given to the guilds. Further context from Quest had been insightful, but it didn't really answer all his questions. One of the apparent reasons for its failure was the points system they utilized as rewards. The United Guilds Association backed the project and gave preferential funding bonuses for the guilds that ranked high on the Quest System. It apparently led to abuse, with multiple guilds min-maxing their results and shirking their actual duties to reach higher scores.

If taking down a scuttler gave a guild five points, and a leecher only gave one, then they weren't incentivized to work on the lower-yield objectives. Apparently, shifting the guild mentality toward competition rather than duty really messed things up. Upgrade had been critical of it, but admitted that it was a good idea with horrible execution. Quest wholeheartedly agreed with her.

"Anything I can help with?" Sal perched on the side of the broken couch that had been placed on the edge of his kitchenette area.

Fabi glanced in his direction with an expression of surprise. It was obvious she had forgotten he was there. She looked at Upgrade before starting to slowly shake her head. "I think we have everything we need to get working on this?"

Upgrade nodded in agreement. "I'd love to include you in all of this, but it's closer to the advanced module for Essence Programming. There are some shortcuts we'll use that I never want you learning, because they'll only end up creating bad habits."

"If you say so," Sal answered with a smile as he looked out the sliver of window that was still visible. It was still early in the afternoon and it looked like a nice day outside. He wondered whether he should go out and relax, or maybe hang out with Barry and Divinity.

Upgrade seemed to sense his mood as she gave him a thoughtful smile. "You know, I'm pretty sure that Quest is going to lock down your calendar the moment he gets back to his office. If there's anything you want to do while you still have freedom, now would be the time to do it."

"You really think he's going to try to stop me from running dungeons?" Sal laughed as he looked at her in disbelief. "Come on, isn't that why we're here?"

Fabi pointed at Athena with a grimace. "First the elixir machine and now Athena? I don't think he's going to let you leave this building without a written permit. You saw how surprised he was that you were in the Advanced War Zone module."

Sal could only shake his head in amazement. "You'd think it was the first he was hearing about Shade and his plan. I was genuinely surprised at how little he knew about the whole thing."

Upgrade frowned as she glanced in Sal's direction. "You'll know better than anyone that the Doom Council has a lot more resources than we do. If Quest went to them with a genuine concern and they overruled it, then there was good reason. They knew that the Psionic commander was screwing with Divinity, so put a little more faith in them."

"Who do you think is on the Doom Council, by the way?" Fabi asked Upgrade curiously; she looked over at Sal to include him. "Any thoughts?"

"Robert Locke, probably." Sal shrugged. "I'd imagine they'd have someone insanely wealthy in there, so I wouldn't be surprised if Doc Ameye was on their team."

"Unlikely. He doesn't play well with others or authority." Upgrade laughed with a shake of her head. "Robert is a good guess, though. I'd imagine they've got a few of the top ten Rankers in there, too. That said, I wouldn't be surprised if they didn't actually exist. Just someone behind a curtain claiming to be a collective of powerful minds, telling everyone what to do."

Fabi sighed as she put her hands on her hips, looking at some of the readings on the terminal. "Did the Crafting process just spit this out naturally? It feels unfair."

Upgrade glanced at the terminal before chuckling. "Come on, you can't be surprised that a top-tier calculation ability has a nice framework. I've written a few papers on how Epic grades tend to come out cleaner than Rare grades, but I'd love to update it with Legendary and Mythic grades. There's definitely a correlation because the internals get incrementally more optimized."

Shaking her head quietly, Fabi continued to read through the results. "Prime really is gorgeous, though. I've never seen cleaner code in my life."

With a satisfied sigh, Upgrade nodded. "And Salvatore made it. How wild is that?" She laughed as she shot him a wink, showing she was joking. "We'll get the directives in place, work on locking down the security, and then we should be safe to run some tests."

"Any suggestions on who we start with?" Fabi finally tore her attention away from the terminal to look at Sal. "We'd ideally need someone with room for development who we can trust. Anthony or Jack?"

Sal shook his head as he pointed at Upgrade. "Nope, we're going with Upgrade for this one."

Upgrade blinked in surprise as she pointed at herself. "Me?"

Sal nodded with an encouraging smile. "Since you don't have the foundations for the earlier iteration of your weave, I think it would be perfect to test the diagnosis capability. You also have room to move up to Evolve, so it'll be interesting to see if it can suggest an improvement method." He glanced at Fabi and shook his head slightly. "Anthony's ability is already pretty strong, but Jack is a good suggestion. I'd rather we kept this between ourselves for now, and Upgrade is the perfect person to test it."

Upgrade hesitated for a moment before nodding. "No shortcuts, then." She laughed awkwardly before giving Fabi a guilty glance. "I'm sure they'd work perfectly, but the self-preservation is kicking in."

Fabi grinned at Sal. "This makes me a thousand times happier. Do you think Athena will make Upgrade a Ranker? I'd love to see Doc Ameye's face when she starts making Legendary grades with a wave of her hand."

"Stop." Upgrade laughed. "We need to manage expectations, even though that would be pretty fucking awesome."

Sal smiled as he watched them work, feeling a little out of his comfort zone. They knew what they were doing, but he was just sitting around and watching them. "Should I start making some blueprints for visors? You know, for the Legion thing?"

Upgrade shook her head. "Nah, that'll be the last step. We need to see the extent of Prime's abilities, so there's going to be some rigorous testing before we give it access to the various databases. Even if it's a supercomputer, the data sets are chunky and will need time to process. We've got some time while Quest pulls his administrative strings to get access."

"You could fix up your couch?" Fabi suggested as she pointed at the deconstruction with a shrug.

Upgrade smiled before shaking her head. "Seriously, you're underestimating Quest." She turned away from the terminal to look at Sal. "If you want to run some dungeons, now is the time to do it. I saw that look in his eye... Your schedule is going to be stacked by the end of the day. Every class you've missed because of the infirmary, he'll throw all of them at you."

"A little excessive, don't you think?" Sal laughed as he pulled out his tablet, just to make sure there wasn't any notifications from Quest. "I thought making a few Mythic grades would increase his trust in my capabilities and let me spread my wings a bit?"

"Nope." Upgrade chuckled. "The only way you're getting into a dungeon is with Chatfield on an approved module. You'll barely have time to eat or sleep."

Sal just stared at her for a few seconds, not really sure how she was so certain. Surely it wasn't going to be that bad? He had missed a few classes here and there. Okay, he'd missed *a lot* of them, but the modules were electives that he just had to pass throughout the rest of his time at Quest Academy. There was time for him to focus on them in the future; he could wait for the next intake. That was the weak logic he had convinced himself with.

"Then…I should maybe go to a few dungeons today?" Sal asked slowly.

"If you want to play with your armor and raise your stats, yes," Upgrade answered, fully convinced it was the right course of action. "Fabi agrees with me."

Fabi snorted dismissively before eventually nodding. "Well, yeah; you should probably get used to the Tempest Marshal a little more before you go back to the War Zone class. If it's going to be your main gear, you should get a feeling for how it works. Just don't go into too high a dungeon; work your way up."

Sal nodded as he thought about it. "There is a list of dungeons I need to do for the guild. I could cross some of them off."

"Sounds like a good plan." Upgrade smiled. "Build up your stats, get more familiar with the gear, and earn some Q-Cred. It's a win-win-win."

"And it gets me out of your way," Sal added, grinning.

Upgrade gave him a guilty shrug. "I didn't say that, but it would speed things up a touch."

Fabi gave him a thoughtful look for a few seconds. "You should go to the Haven Borough. Exchequer Street has a great assortment of dungeons at varying levels. You'd be able to switch between the difficulty levels if something is too easy."

"And the attendants are super lax about Heroes going in solo," Upgrade added as she pointed at Fabi. "Good call. It'd be a decent hunting ground, and I'm sure a few of them are on your list. Everyone loves those dungeons."

Sal got to his feet. "Then I guess I should leave you both to it?"

"We'll be turning off our tablets, so make sure to knock when you come back. Otherwise, Fabi might accidentally kill you," Upgrade said with a sweet smile. "Or turn you into a material. I've got no idea how her powers work."

Fabi glanced at him as he started to make his way toward the door. "Oh, and just so you know…voiders increase Mobility. Prowlers increase Speed. Hulkers boost Strength. And I'm pretty sure Endurance gets added at random with stronger opponents—I was only getting it with killing scuttlers."

"Anything else?" Sal asked, genuinely curious for more insights.

Fabi shook her head with a guilty smile. "Not right now, because I don't think you'll really be taking on thumpers or switchers any time soon. They boost Evasion, by the way."

Sal just stared at her for a few seconds. "The Tempest Marshal can kill high-level demons?"

"Oh yeah," Upgrade agreed, grinning. "Little Miss Maccles butchered a couple of commander classes with your suit; and she didn't even have Capacitor to activate half of the fun stuff."

Sal just shook his head in a daze. "Not going to lie, that's pretty damn awesome." He chuckled as he moved to the door, still trying to figure out how it was possible.

Fabi smiled as she gave him a playful thumbs-up. "Have fun!"

CHAPTER 74: ADVENT

Sal sighed as he looked at his tablet. His plans of running dungeons had nearly been put on hold by the influx of messages that pinged relentlessly on the screen. It didn't take a genius to figure out what had happened. Quest clearly didn't like the idea of him running dungeons after their conversation the other evening, so he had pulled some strings. What sort of strings? Well, it looked like every lecturer was suddenly keenly aware that he had classes to catch up on. Reading through the most recent entries, Sal couldn't help but grimace.

<u>Automated Module Messages</u>
- Crafting Master Class with Forge
  - Mondays and Tuesdays, 9 a.m. to 1 p.m.
  - Saturdays, 3 p.m. to 7 p.m.
  - Lecturer Notes: Orders came from up top, sorry for eating your weekend.
- Demonic Behavior & Analysis with Harlan Geist
  - Wednesdays and Fridays, 9 a.m. to 1 p.m.
  - Saturdays Catch-Up, 7 p.m. to 10 p.m.
  - Lecturer Notes: Feels a little excessive, but I look forward to having you in class.
- Skills Master Class with Coach
  - Saturdays, 6 a.m. to 2 p.m.
  - Lecturer Notes: They told me we need to do eight hours a week. This is the best I can do.
- System Master Class with Quest
  - Sundays, 11 a.m. to 2 p.m.
  - Wednesdays, 4 p.m. to 7 p.m.
- Dungeon Delving with Chatfield
  - Weekdays from 7 p.m. to 10 p.m.
  - Lecturer Notes: We've got a lot of catching up to do. I can use this time to speed you up on your War Zone module.
- Advanced War Zone with Chatfield
  - Mondays and Tuesdays from 3 p.m. to 7 p.m.
  - Fridays from 2 p.m. to 6 p.m.
  - Lecturer Notes: We've got a lot of catching up to do. This is more important than Dungeon Delving, so we'll prioritize our time accordingly.
- Guild Mastery with Jez
  - Thursdays, 8 a.m. to 11 a.m.
  - Lecturer Notes: I told Quest we had a loose schedule, but he wanted me to put this in place. See you on Thursdays.
- Essence Programming with Upgrade
  - Thursdays, 2 p.m. to 5 p.m.
  - Sundays, 2 p.m. to 5 p.m.

- Lecturer Notes: Managed to get you out of compulsory Ethical Crafting and Advanced Crafting, but couldn't stop Quest from locking you into EssPro.

Sal exhaled slowly as he closed the notifications, not wanting to let his annoyance get the better of him. He was a student and he had picked all those classes, so he knew he didn't have the luxury to point fingers at Quest. It was only natural that he would need to do extra classes with the lecturers to catch up on what he missed over the last month. It just didn't feel right that he only had a few hours to himself throughout the week. Upgrade had thankfully gone easy on him, not requiring him to be in two of her classes. He'd still need to do six hours of Essence Programming a week, though.

Looking up from his tablet, Sal pocketed it and looked to see whether the line to the dungeon had diminished. Considering it was already a Tuesday, he guessed that the classes would take effect the next day. Chatfield was offering daily dungeon runs as part of the Dungeon Delving module, and although Sal would have been happy to get a few credits for attending, he had no desire to hide his capabilities. What he needed right now was the Endurance stat. Going into a dungeon with a class of people would just slow him down and paint him as a show-off if he used the Tempest Marshal set. Hell, he'd probably cause mass hysteria if he let Jackal roam around.

He took a few paces forward before stopping. The line had given the impression that it was getting smaller, but it looked as if people were leaving out of frustration farther ahead. Sal didn't mind the waiting. He needed to go into this dungeon in particular, as it was one of the ones on his guild list. From the dossier that Jez had given him, Sal knew that there was likely going to be some voiders, prowlers, and maybe a hulker. Even though Jackal was more than capable of soloing those demons, Sal couldn't justify entering by himself to the dungeon attendants. It would look like he was just trying to kill himself if he tried to get into a scuttler dungeon. Hopefully the recent track record of successful clearances would give him some credibility.

"Mate, are you going in by yourself?" a nasally tone asked from behind Sal.

He immediately dreaded being asked whether he wanted to team up with a group of strangers. Turning around to look at the guy, Sal had to glance down to see a squat man with a series of knives strapped to his chest. Wavy black hair was slicked back by some form of product, and the expression he wore was one of annoyance.

"I am, yes," Sal answered, doubly sure that he didn't want to team up with this man.

With a derisive snort, the guy shook his head and started to walk away, disregarding Sal completely. He gestured to one of his companions, another guy with a shield, and Sal was able to overhear his parting words. "It'll take forever if he's running it solo…we'll just go somewhere else."

Sal smiled awkwardly at the Hunters who took the guys' place in the line, but they didn't look like they were in the mood to chat. He was happy enough to leave it at that, and turned back to face the dungeon. A vibration in his pocket signaled yet another module update, and Sal didn't have the heart to even check it. He knew it would depress him and take away one of the small chunks of time he still had left to himself. It was probably going to be the Administration module with Jez. Sal hadn't seen that on his new schedule, and knew it was only a matter of time before they added it.

The group in front of him all reached into their pockets to take out their tablets and phones. Sal frowned as a series of bleeps and ringtones fired off, all around him. He turned to look at the group behind him, who were all reading their tablets with concerned expressions. Sal reached into his own pocket, convinced that he wasn't going to find any context for what was happening around him.

He was wrong.

Hunter Bureau Alert: Location-Based Evacuation Notice!
- o Barrier Breach at Haven Vanguard, Exchequer Street. Airlock has been compromised.
- o Quest Academy Students and Non-Combatants are asked to evacuate immediately.
- o United Guilds Association Members are asked to make themselves available for assistance.

Sal's heart froze as another message came in straight afterward. He had never come across anything like this before. What were the guilds doing? Hadn't someone with Foresight warned them about this? It was a built-up area with a lot of dungeon activity, and the Hunter Bureau home turf. How were they letting this happen on their own doorstep?

United Guilds Association Alert: Assistance Request
- o Mythic Guild has been tasked to Support the Evacuation efforts.
- o Members in Vicinity: 1, Salvatore Argento

"Four barriers would need to break for them to get this far," someone farther ahead in the line said in confusion as they pointed at the skyline to the immediate left.

Sal followed the gesture with his eyes, not exactly sure what he was looking for.

What should have been a transparent barrier with a blue sheen was now an angry red wall that loomed in the distance. The Red Zone had gotten closer.

Sal didn't know what the process or procedures were for an event like this. He could follow the people evacuating, but the message from the United Guilds Association stuck in his mind. They needed assistance, and if they were taking a single member of a Tier 8 guild, then maybe it wasn't as bad as he thought?

"All dungeon activity is halted until the breach has been dealt with. If you haven't received a notification to participate, please make your way to the evacuation site. Additional trains will be sent by the Hunter Bureau to transport you out of here," the dungeon attendant called out as he slung a backpack over his shoulder. "Active-duty Hunters and Heroes, please follow me to the barrier!"

With that said, he started to move down the center of the street. Close to fifty people followed him, each of them looking around warily, on high alert.

Sal was caught in the middle of the crowd, with more than three-quarters of them moving toward the evacuation zone. If they were capable of taking on a dungeon, why were they leaving? There weren't that many students in the line; he had already checked. Sal felt conflicted, as he knew he should probably go with them, but it felt wrong to him.

"You should get out of here, kid," an older man said with an encouraging smile. "There are plenty of fights to come, so don't worry about this one." He gave Sal a thumbs-up as he followed the Hunters, an enormous glowing sword strapped to his back.

Sal opened his mouth to answer, but the sound of cannon fire drowned out everything. His attention snapped toward the Red Zone barrier, where all the surrounding buildings were launching suppression fire. Enormous turrets thundered in sequence, all of them aimed at the base of the barrier.

His tablet vibrated again, and Sal numbly raised it into view at arm's length. It was from Quest Academy, but had nothing to do with his modules.

Quest Academy Emergency Alert
- o All Students located in the Haven Borough are to evacuate immediately.
- o Partnered Guilds are en route to assist with containment and evacuation.
- o Captain Chatfield has created a rendezvous point on Exchequer Street for immediate extraction. If you're in the area, make yourself known to him as soon as possible.

Another message came through, this one aimed at the guilds. It was pretty chilling that Sal was receiving real-world notifications because of his status as guildmaster.

United Guilds Association: Urgent Quest Academy Notice
- o The following first-year students are unaccounted for within the Haven Borough. If you find anyone on this list, please bring them to the nearest extraction point.
- o Descriptions are attached below as well as their last known location.
  - ▪ Adam Beswick
  - ▪ Chris Spectre
  - ▪ Derek Norman
  - ▪ Jack Brophy
  - ▪ Michaela Egan
  - ▪ Seth McDuffee
  - ▪ Salvatore Argento
  - ▪ Tabitha Geier
  - ▪ Yasmin Darya

Nine first-years were currently in the Haven Borough. Gallant—aka Jack Brophy—was one of them, as well as Mica and her boyfriend, Seth. Sal recognized Derek as one of the top Saviors, and Chris Spectre as the guy he met on his first day back. He'd at least be able to recognize them if he saw them, but he had no context for the others.

Sal was conflicted about what he should do. On one hand, he was told to evacuate as a first-year student. On the other, he was asked to assist in the evacuation as a guild. Looking up, he watched as the older man with the massive sword moved with the rest of the crowd, seemingly encouraging everyone around him as he psyched them up for the battle to come.

After just a few seconds of quiet deliberation, Sal found himself alone at the dungeon. Both groups had made their choice, with the smaller segment choosing to fight. Just looking toward the train station was enough to sicken him. How were they supposed to win a war when seventy-five percent of people chose not to fight?

"It's just evacuation," Sal breathed to himself. "We're just offering Support." He said the words as he started to move after the man with the massive sword. "This is what it means to run a guild."

As though sensing the hesitation in Sal, the man with the sword looked back in his direction, his face a mask of confusion. It felt like Sal was being tested and weighed in that momentary glance. Was he going to walk away with everyone else, or was he going to follow a different path? He already knew what everyone at Quest Academy would say. They'd try to stop him from putting himself in danger.

Self-preservation was the smart play, but it conflicted with the resolve that had been fostered at Quest Academy. What was the point of incredible equipment if he just retreated with everyone else? What sort of guildmaster would run off to hide when tasked with helping? As Sal ran through all those thoughts, he was left with a single question. One that mattered more than anything else.

What would his parents do in this situation?

He already knew the answer as a guilty smile appeared on his face. Adrenaline started pumping, and Sal activated Perfect for what was to come. He pulled off his shirt, which only made the swordsman look more confused. There was a method to the madness, though. It must have looked comical to start stripping during a demonic invasion, but modesty was a small price to pay for effectiveness.

Raising his arms into the maestro pose, his entire torso morphed to accommodate the Tempest Marshal set. The Mythic blight jackal snapped onto his bare left arm, and the ethereal green glow switched to a villainous purple hue. His eyepatch appeared perfectly, but his peaked cap needed a minor adjustment.

The final moment of clarity was more than welcome. Sal had spent far too long agonizing over the actions of people like Shade and Bastion. But they weren't the real enemy, the demons were. There was no more hesitation as he moved to join the Hunters.

A wide grin appeared on the swordsman's face as he gestured with his arm for Sal to hurry up and join them. "Come on, you're going to miss all the fun!"

CHAPTER 75: TRENCH

Exchequer Street had been one of the most densely populated dungeon areas in all of Haven. Dozens of guilds established their headquarters in the area, which should have made it a veritable fortress, or at the very least, protected.

Sal looked at the carnage all around him. Fire and ash filled the air; not from chance explosions, but rather from a group of Hunters who seemingly had a personal grudge against architecture. Everything that Sal had been taught by Lars in the gauntlet had either been forgotten or dismissed by the Hunters around him. If there was a single leecher in a building, that building apparently needed to be taken down.

Glass and rubble rained onto the streets from the skyscrapers overhead, with Heroes throwing up protective barriers to stop it from injuring anyone. Smoke pooled around the invisible walls, reducing visibility. That would have been bad enough, but when you combined it with the roar of turrets and the shouts of disorganized guilds, it was a shit-show.

Sal had barely arrived before he was given several conflicting instructions. One was to look for survivors in the surrounding buildings; the other was to clear wreckage for the guild transports to land safely. He was at the back of the fighting, but it was essentially a long runway of street that led directly to the Red Barrier. Some of the demons had slipped through the air lock and were wreaking havoc. Blue barriers had been erected in a staggered sequence to protect as much territory as possible, but the demons' advance was both brutal and efficient.

His eye-patch had taken the liberty of identifying the targets in the distance, and Sal felt genuine anxiety at the nine commander class demons leading the charge. None of them looked the same, and their stats were wildly inconsistent. The most terrifying was a war spider that draped between two skyscrapers, watching everything play out below. Every time a Hunter tried to take it out, another commander class would intercept the attack.

Sal genuinely wondered why Robert or Prestige wasn't there to deal with them. They both had incredible strength, and what better time for them to use it?

"Come on! What are you standing around for? We need this area cleared for the resupply!" an angry Hero shouted at Sal as he gestured wildly at the massive pile of rubble that had been a shop front just a few hours ago. "Start over there!"

Another voice piped up from behind him. "There's no fucking resupply. Eclipse Guild is incoming and we need to bring the casualties for her to treat. Landing on a few rocks won't kill them!"

"Where the fuck is the Hunter Bureau?!" Villa shouted as she slid into view with daggers in hand. She looked around wildly, as though Robert might reveal himself through the smoke. When her gaze landed on Sal, her eyes widened.

"Hey," Sal said with an awkward smile. "Long time no see."

All color drained from her face as she shouted into her earpiece. "Blink, I have an immediate extraction request. Salvatore fucking Argento is standing beside me!"

A deafening shot roared between the row of skyscrapers and smashed directly into the war spider's head. It wasn't enough to kill it in one go, but the damage was visible. The next shot caused it to sway dangerously on the thick webbing. The third had it scrambling for purchase with a guttural shriek, followed by a harrowing clacking noise.

Sal turned to look at the direction of the shots leaving a trail through the sky. The eye-patch struggled to quantify how far away the shooter was, but Sal instinctively knew who it was.

"Keep it up, Watcher." Villa spoke into her earpiece. "Blink, where the fuck are you? I need him out of here right now!"

"I need to stay." Sal spoke loudly, but not in an aggressive tone. "I don't want to stop my attack prematurely. The ambushes aren't stopping."

Villa stared at him in confusion. "The what?" She looked through the barriers of smoke, where an erratic burst of purple light continued to flare up.

Sal snapped his attention to movement within the smoke; his fingers extended at the perfect moment to launch a burst of purple lightning into the gloom. He concentrated on what the eye-patch was showing him, and watched as the lightning attack bounced from target to target. It wasn't just prowlers and voiders this time. Each enemy looked like it was on par with a dungeon boss, and it was testing the limits of the Tempest Marshal set.

"Can someone tell them to stop smothering us!"

A Hunter appeared from behind them and clapped his hands together with a resounding crack. The effect was instantaneous as the smoke billowed directly upward in a vortex, restoring visibility for all the Hunters and Heroes on the back lines. Two things became apparent very quickly. The first was that the demons had attempted to flank them and launch a surprise attack.

The second was that a ball of pure lightning was killing each and every one of them before they got a chance. Remnants of Sal's Assimilation Function attack were still bouncing between targets, leaving a trail of corpses in its wake. As a bonus for all the backline workers, they got to witness Jackal in all its glory, bursting through a building and piercing through the center mass of a hulker.

Villa whirled on the Heroes, her expression thunderous. "What sort of defensive perimeter allows hulkers to sneak up on us?!"

"We're volunteers," a man bit back. "The guilds haven't done shit to help, so don't get snippy with us! If you can do it better, then please, feel free!"

Villa cursed as she dismissed one of her daggers and raised a hand to her right ear. "Trench, I need you back here on the defensive perimeter. Put up a blockade to stop them from ambushing us." She glanced at the assortment of Heroes and Hunters. "Thirty-eight people. Semi-circle formation."

Sal kept watch for any new threats that might appear, but the eye-patch didn't pick up any demons targeting them. The ball of lightning was close to dying out, so Sal was happy to have a momentary reprieve. All the commanders were much farther ahead, so he guessed he'd have time to recover some essence.

"Offense should be up front with the rest of them, rather than here." The man who had cut back at Villa was looking at Sal this time. His arms were crossed, and he looked as if he had a bone to pick with anything that moved.

"Me?" Sal frowned. "I'm a Support."

The man scoffed as he shook his head, glancing at the remnants of the lightning attack. "Coward, you mean?" He walked off, muttering angrily to himself before shouting instructions at a group of people lifting the rubble.

"Charming," Sal muttered as the ground in front of them tore itself open to create an enormous blockade that encircled them. He took a tentative step backward at the sudden appearance, but his eye-patch didn't sense a threat.

"Good work, Trench. Blink, cancel the extraction request," Villa shouted as she continued to hold her earpiece in place. Looking around at the buildings behind them, she tapped her finger against her earlobe. "Watcher, keep an eye on our location. I'll take care of Salvatore—"

Another deafening shot rocketed between the skyscrapers, but because of the blockade, Sal couldn't see whether it hit. The only clue was the screech and clatter of the war spider far in the distance. It being heard over the sounds of chaos was impressive enough in itself.

"I'm fucking talking, Watcher!" Villa shouted. "Keep us in your sights." She dropped her hand from her ear and looked royally pissed-off. Everyone around her earned a glare, with the single exception of Sal.

When her cold gaze landed on him, she tilted her head slightly to the side. "That mechanical leecher yours?"

"Yeah, it's called Jackal," Sal answered with a nod.

"I want one," Villa stated as she resummoned a dagger into her free hand. "But we're going to need to keep you alive if you're going to fulfill that commission for me." She looked around at the blockade. "This whole thing is a fiasco. How much do you know?"

"Next to nothing," Sal answered instantly. "I got a notification to assist as a guildmaster, so I wanted to help."

Villa nodded slowly. "You shouldn't have gotten that." She sighed in exasperation but her ire thankfully wasn't aimed at him. "Well, this isn't the only attack happening right now. There's a whole thing happening at the Shard, and the entire Hunter Bureau is trying to prevent the demons from killing Chronos." She gave him a meaningful look. "It's a coordinated attack, and they're trying to get a dragon on their team."

Sal stared at her, his mind going completely blank as he realized the severity of the situation. "This… is a distraction? There are nine commander classes in front of us!"

"I counted thirteen." Villa smiled as she offered a shrug. "We need to hold the line in all the territories while we wait for the Reclamation guilds to come back and regroup. Haven isn't being hit as bad as the other places. The Shard and Pinnacle areas are the worst off."

"Is Sanctuary safe?" Sal's heart raced, despite Perfect's best attempts at keeping it steady.

Villa nodded. "Yeah, no need to worry about your family. We've got people coming in from far and wide to help us deal with this, and we'll have more cohesive instructions soon. Volunteers and locals aren't exactly equipped to handle large-scale attacks." She glanced backward, as though deep in thought. "Looks like the evacuation systems didn't shit the bed, so that's something."

"Does this happen often?" Sal asked, unsure whether he was overreacting. He had been sheltered from this sort of reality, so he didn't know whether this was an ongoing thing.

"At least once a year, but rarely with this level of complexity," Villa answered curtly as she dismissed a dagger and lifted her right hand to her ear. "Give me a second."

Sal watched as her expression darkened; clearly, she heard something she didn't like.

"We're not leaving here. Tell him he can fuck right off with a retreat order," Villa hissed, touching her ear. "Better yet, get him off his fucking throne and throw him into the fight!"

"Robert?" Sal ventured a guess, realizing that speaking when Villa was infuriated wasn't his smartest move.

"Fierce, leader of the Reavers Guild," Villa spat as she dropped her hand and let out a shuddering breath, as though it took everything in her power not to go insane. "Robert's a prick, but he's the type who would save everyone and gloat endlessly about it." She looked like she was about to continue when a dagger snapped back into her hand and she crouched in wait. "Get ready."

Sal assumed a battle pose from the Silverson Arts, wondering why the eye-patch hadn't given him any sort of warning. He sent an instruction to get Jackal closer, rather than having it roam across the battlefield. If it ended up getting taken out by a commander, his survivability would plummet.

Villa launched her hand forward, sending one of the daggers directly through the blockade, resulting in a bloodcurdling scream that sounded distinctly human. The despair and fear in the voice made Sal's chest tight. He couldn't see through the small fissure in the rock, but he knew that it was a killing blow. Had Villa just attacked one of their comrades?

"I fucking hate switchers." Villa groaned as she recalled the dagger to her hand with a look of revulsion. "Whatever you do, don't look at them when they're dying. That shit will haunt you for life."

Even though Sal was going through an emotional rollercoaster, Jackal was apparently having the time of its life. An endless stream of notifications came through the eye-patch, of all the loot that Jackal was plucking from dead demons. Villa's words were further confirmed when Sal saw switcher materials being added to Arsenal.

Villa's eyes narrowed as she looked at the wall thoughtfully. A curious smile that seemed woefully out of place graced her lips as she stared at something Sal couldn't see. "I really want that drone."

Sal guessed she'd want it even more if she knew how many stat improvements were being sent his way. He thought it would take a serious number of dungeons to get his Endurance stat up, but it turned out he just needed to wait for a demonic invasion.

"Get behind me." Villa spoke in an uncharacteristically cold voice. "As far back as you can, and bring everyone here with you."

Sal's eye-patch highlighted a humanoid commander class that broke away from the battle ahead and charged at their wall at full speed. Even the blue barriers that had been erected were shattering, one by one, as it moved through them like they were made of glass.

"Everyone, get back!" Sal shouted at the top of his lungs, but he couldn't elevate his voice enough to get their attention. With a sharp intake of breath, Sal let out the most powerful whistle he could muster.

Over thirty people faltered as they looked in his direction in a mixture of shock and confusion. He used hand signals to indicate immediate danger and started to run to a safer location. Thankfully, enough people followed him in time to avoid the blockade being destroyed.

Villa grinned as she gave him an appreciative nod, her daggers raised and ready. She practically danced away from the rubble, while simultaneously launching a surprise attack at the enormous humanoid commander.

Sal ignored the thanks from the surrounding Hunters and Heroes, and instead focused his attention on the demon that broke through their lines. It looked completely different from all the enemies he had seen so far. Smoldering metal was fused to its body like a protective armor, with lava-like fissures between the plates. There was no face, just a flat surface that seemingly sensed its surroundings. Most terrifying were the legs, which had essence-based augments surrounding them. With just a single glance, Sal knew that a kick from this demon would be instant death.

If that wasn't enough, the commander assumed a combat stance, with yellow flames bursting from its back like wings. His eye-patch confirmed that it had an acceleration-style ability, and the threat profile was the highest recorded entry Sal had ever witnessed. He stood there in a daze, trying to determine a weak point, but it seemed Villa's instincts were faster than all his equipment combined.

Which was probably why she went for its neck.

CHAPTER 76: REGROUP

Sal didn't need his visor to know that the fight was one-sided. The problem was that Villa wasn't winning… and it wasn't even close. Her entire fighting style was a horrible match-up against the commander class, who surpassed her in both speed and strength. Factoring in the destructive power of its legs, Villa was fighting a losing battle. Her only moments of reprieve came from Watcher's suppression fire that forced the commander backward.

Neither of her daggers were able to pierce through the metal-like plating, and all her slashes were far too shallow. One thing she did manage to do effectively was scare the shit out of every Hunter and Hero in the area, so that they actively started to retreat. This was the area for Supports, and nobody looked like they were in a position to help. A new trench of rock separated Villa and the commander for a few seconds, but it was blasted aside with a single kick. Trench was useless, and if Blink extracted Villa, it would spell disaster for everyone evacuating.

If there truly were thirteen commanders in total, then there was no chance of the Hunters on the frontlines looping back to offer assistance. Sal had to assume that the Defense classes were already broken through for the commander to reach them. There were no illusions in his mind that he was in danger, but the reality of what that meant struggled to register in his mind. He knew he needed to get out of there, but he couldn't leave Villa to die.

Villa, for all her faults, was relentless in attacking. She had managed to avoid any fatal injuries, but it was clear that she'd also lose in a war of attrition.

Sal saw the final attack coming before Villa, and he sent the command without a second thought. Villa was so focused on the deathly kicks that she was blindsided by the punch that was leveled at her face. Time seemed to move in slow motion as the fatal punch descended, but it wasn't a dilation of time… it was Jackal, with its abyssal tentacles wrapped around the wrist of the commander to slow the attack.

Villa danced backward in surprise, repositioning herself and catching her breath while the commander tried to fight off Jackal. Both of her hands shook from the exertion of holding it off that long. She wouldn't last much longer.

Self-preservation went straight out the window as Sal activated the Assimilate Function with Tempest Marshal. Overdrive and Capacitor heated up his left arm as he directed his right hand at the neck of the commander. A bolt of purple lightning smashed high into its chest with enough force for it to ignore Jackal completely. His aim was slightly off, but the effect was dramatic enough for him not to care.

The essence augments that covered the commander's legs were suddenly redistributed as protective layers over its chest. Both of its arms came up in a cross to protect against the blast, but the damage had already pierced through in a shower of sparks. Chunks of molten metal fell to the ground as the commander lost some of its armor.

Sal wasn't sure how he felt about the demon's blood being molten lava. Had Villa managed to spill blood, it likely would have killed her on the spot. If they were going to prevail, they needed to fight at range. That was excellent foresight from Sal, which he probably should have relayed to Jackal.

Abyssal steel plunged into the open wound, causing Jackal's tentacles to take on a scary black-red glow. Sal had no idea whether the abyssal steel was able to withstand the surge of heat, and he was sorely tempted to recall Jackal. The only problem was that he needed the offensive power of the drone to have any chance of winning.

Redoubling his efforts with the Assimilate Function, Sal aimed the lightning at the areas of the commander that weren't protected by the augmented essence plates. It resulted in a continuous stream of sparks, lighting the commander up like a Christmas tree. Another shot from Watcher obliterated a chunk of the face-shell, revealing a sickly mess of sinew and lava.

In an instant, the gap was filled by one of Villa's daggers. Sal glanced over at her and saw her holding a hand to her ear. In her other hand, there were three kunai-style blades gripped between her fingers. *Had she really created that plan with Watcher on the fly?*

Sal brought his attention back to the commander, cursing himself internally for getting distracted. His essence reserves were still healthy enough to keep going, but he'd need to recuperate after this fight. There was no way he'd be able to use the Tempest Function more than a couple of times. It sounded arrogant in his own head that he was planning for whatever came after the fight. There was no guarantee that he'd survive this encounter.

Maybe his complacency was communicated telepathically to the demon, because it abruptly stopped fighting against Jackal's attacks, and instead launched itself at a blistering speed in Sal's direction.

"Fuck!" Sal shouted as he made the split-second decision to move toward the commander. Despite his warnings, so many of the Heroes and Hunters had remained at the scene to watch everything unfold. If he retreated into the crowd, then there would be far more casualties. By closing the distance, they'd have more time to evacuate. It sounded quite noble, but Sal justified his actions because he only had a half second to think and forward seemed better than backward.

The intensity of the lightning slowed the commander's approach, but it seemed hell-bent on killing him. Apparently, sacrificing chunks of its torso was a worthy trade.

"Get out of there!" Villa screamed at him as she tried to catch its attention with countless blades flung at its back. None of those attacks gained purchase, and Watcher's next shot completely missed the mark by grazing its left shoulder.

Sal recognized the commander's stance and instinctively moved into a counterattack. He knew his Strength wasn't extraordinary, but he did have a potential trick up his sleeve. If a Legendary-grade sniper rifle was effective from long range, how good would it be at short range?

His right fist smashed into the incoming punch from the commander, and Sal activated the Legendary version of the Scarlet Strategist Sniper Rifle. The bullet effect was to pierce through a target, and through the Manifest ability, Sal's counterattack was significant. It felt like he just punched a boulder... with the only sign of success being the explosion of molten blood splashing in an almost perfect circle around the impact zone.

Jackal's tentacles whirled around in a deadly blade as it swept behind Sal to launch its own counterattack against the demon. Sal instructed it to focus on aggravating the injuries while he tried to employ everything the Silverson Arts had taught him. Kicking was out of the question, but he was confident enough with just his fists.

A terrifyingly fast kick attempted to crush his entire torso, and Sal was forced to defend with crossed arms. He already knew what it felt like to have both arms shatter, so he was very relieved to just feel a devastating amount of pain wash through him.

Regenerate: Combat Mode has been activated.

By the time the commander launched a punch at his face, the pain had been reduced to a dull ache. Rather than blocking again and wasting valuable essence on healing, Sal met the attack again with his fist. He learned something interesting in that split second. The commander could clearly see, despite not having eyes. How did he know? Because it hesitated when the sniper punch resurfaced.

That hesitation gave Sal more momentum and power behind his attack, and the resulting explosion of molten lava reduced the commander's right fist to a charred stump of metal and bone. The crack in its head armor allowed a shriek of rage to spread across the battlefield like a blanket.

Abyssal steel wrapped around both of the commander's shoulders, pulling it backward and off-balance. It was the perfect opportunity, and Sal took it with both hands. He reached up to pull Villa's dagger out of its face with his left hand, while his right sent a concentrated blast of purple lightning directly into its brain. If it really was a metal shell, the lightning managed to turn it into a bomb.

Sal darted backward, keeping the lightning trained on the commander's head as it exploded in a guttural roar of agony and frustration. The essence augments flickered before vanishing, and the commander's body slumped back slowly to fall on the ground with a wet slap. Molten blood sizzed on the ground as it pooled out of its body.

It should have been a moment of celebration, but Jackal once again ruined the atmosphere by cutting its body up for parts.

Sal watched it work in a grim satisfaction, taking a seat for the surge of pain that was about to hit.

"You're no longer Little Argento." Villa smiled as she took a knee and focused on getting her breath back. "We'll have to find a better nickname for you." Her gaze moved from the hole in the defensive trench to an area in the sky. It was accompanied with a derisive snort. "The cavalry arrives after the work is done…classic."

Sal followed her gaze and saw a number of transport ships descending from the sky. He didn't recognize all the logos, so he looked at her for help.

She pointed at the yellow one. "Paradox. Useful but slow." Her finger moved to the next one. "Delvers. Scumbags." The third one got a smile. "Eclipse. She's a good egg. Healers who know their way around a battlefield are worth their weight in silver."

Sal knew he should have felt something when hearing about the Delvers descending to their location, but he couldn't for the life of him care. Everything about Divinity's vision seemed so ridiculous and trivial at this point. He was going to be abducted? Well, maybe if Shade was immune to lightning and abyssal steel. He laughed at the thought in his head. It wasn't complacency, but rather just a tired realization that he was very much on track to having full independence and autonomy. He just took out a commander, and the sense of accomplishment was extraordinary.

As the transports landed, the guilds descended onto the battlefield and were immediately swamped by the Hunters and Heroes wanting an evacuation from the area. Apparently, they hadn't sign up to be attacked by a commander class demon. Sal would have listened to what they were saying, but Assimilation had other plans.

The stats from the commander permeated through his body at that very moment, causing him to wince as his chest tightened and his breathing picked up. Perfect and Regenerate managed to soften the blow, but it was the strongest opponent he had ever defeated. If he had to judge the sensation, it was at least five times more dramatic from when he absorbed the stats from the scuttler.

Villa got to her feet and moved toward the guildmasters of Paradox, Delvers, and Eclipse, who were waiting for a debrief on what happened. That was something that Sal absolutely wanted to listen in on, but all his attention was focused on not passing out. He navigated to the numbers and specifically parsed for just the commander result.

Assimilate Function Report (1)
- o   Strength has increased by 1.23
- o   Mobility has increased by 1.91
- o   Speed has increased by 3.87
- o   Endurance has increased by 1.56
- o   Skill Master has improved by 0.7
- o   Mythcrafter has improved by 0.7

A hand touched Sal's back, but it didn't feel like a threat. He still had to stop Jackal from reacting, so he sent a quick command to back down. It looked quite comical to see the drone pausing in its feast of components to bob threateningly in the air. Glancing up, he saw the familiar face of Eclipse, looking very confused.

"You're not injured." It was a statement rather than a question. "Rather, you're healing at an alarming rate." A befuddled smile graced her face as she took away her hand and stepped around Sal to face him. "I was just told that your equipment is purely combat-oriented."

Sal smiled as he gave her a nod. "It's Legendary grade, and has a whole range of functions designed to keep me alive and everything else dead."

Eclipse laughed as she nodded in understanding. "Sounds pretty incredible. Great work, by the way. I arrived fearing the worst, but I'm delighted to see you're in one piece."

"And thank you for arriving," Sal breathed as he got to his feet, grimacing. It would take a short while for Regenerate to soothe the aching from Assimilation.

"Better late than never," Eclipse quipped as she glanced at the group of people getting into their transports. "We've saved you a seat for the evacuation, so don't worry about the crowding. There's plenty of space."

Sal smiled as he shook his head. "I just need a bit of time to meditate and then I'll be good to continue fighting."

Eclipse's eyes widened before she laughed. "You are very different from what I expected."

"What did you expect?" Sal wiped the dried ash from his sleeves.

Eclipse shrugged. "An Appraiser? I saw you rush to help that Fabrizia girl at the gala, but I didn't think that same mindset would apply to fighting a commander." She laughed as she looked at the remains of the commander. "I thought Quest Academy lost its way a few years ago, but you're a pretty compelling endorsement for what they're teaching there."

"Not bad for a Support class, right?" Sal grinned as he glanced over at Villa. She was talking to Shade with her arms crossed. Shade, on the other hand, stared at Sal with wide eyes.

"Hey, wait until you see how I heal," Eclipse said in playful reproach, gesturing at the battlefield in the distance. "Suck the life right out of them to keep our side nice and healthy. It's a spectacle for sure."

"I've got a friend with the Transference ability. It's a pretty terrifying ability, for sure," Sal agreed as he pointed at Villa. "I should check in with Villa to see what the plan is."

Eclipse didn't answer immediately as she stared at him. "You could tell my ability with just a single glance. You really are a Replicator, aren't you?"

"Sure am," Sal answered with a polite nod before heading over to Villa.

She seemingly sensed his approach because she turned to face him with a bright smile. "How do you feel about killing a big-ass spider?"

CHAPTER 77: BACKUP

Sal managed to get quite a few surprises in quick succession. The first was how the guildmasters had no objections to him remaining at the site of the battle. He had expected Quest to threaten them or something, but nobody seemed to want to piss off Villa. She had seen Sal in action and was acting as an advisor for his guild. It was such a weak excuse that it was almost laughable, but it was enough for the others.

Shade, of all people, who Sal expected to be a prick throughout, genuinely seemed impressed by the fact that Sal took out a commander class demon. He kept asking for details, despite Villa repeating the same sentence over and over again.

"He stuck his hand into its brain, and it exploded." Villa spoke in a deadpan tone, no longer bothering to add a fake smile with the words.

Shade didn't look convinced. "Your sniper on the roof, though. I'm sure he softened it up."

"And who do you think made the rifle he used?" Villa snapped back, clearly tired of Shade's incessant line of questioning. She pointed directly at Sal. "He did, after a night of Appraising an entire catalogue of portal artifacts we threw at him."

Eclipse bit her lip to stop from laughing, while the guildmaster of Paradox, Enigma, stared directly upward, as though praying for something to take him away from their conversation. It was Sal's first time meeting Enigma, and he gave off Prestige vibes. Likely because his weapon of choice was a cane, and he looked distinguished. Actually, no—it was the condescending persona.

"Is there a reason the Delvers Guild decided to answer the summons?" Enigma drawled as he looked at Shade, his eyebrow raised. "You know there will be fighting, right?"

Shade scoffed as he waved the comment away. "Robert specifically asked for my assistance, so how could I refuse an old friend." His smile was as fake as his words. "Besides, what guild has more experience than the Delvers when it comes to uncharted territory?"

"We're in Haven, not some otherworldly plane." Villa spoke slowly, with the most withering glare she could muster. "Who are we waiting for?" She looked at Chatfield, as though willing him to speak up or face the consequences.

They had commandeered one of the untouched guild offices that had survived the first wave of attack. With the additional forces coming in, they were able to put up better defenses, which earned them the luxury of planning their next move. Sal had happily tagged along with Villa, and was surprised to find that Chatfield had already made his way to their location, a gaggle of first-years in tow.

"We're waiting on approval from Quest," Chatfield muttered after tapping his earpiece, clearly unimpressed with the recent turn of events. His ire was aimed at a collection of people, namely a few students from Quest Academy.

Mica grinned as she sidled up next to Sal, dragging her boyfriend Seth with her to make them look like a team. That was one of the big surprises that Sal had to deal with. Mica and Seth were happily tearing through the demons, but because they were unaffiliated with a guild, they were being sent back to Quest Academy by Chatfield.

"What's our guild called, by the way?" Mica whispered to Sal with a conspiratorial grin.

"Mythic Guild," Sal whispered back, trying not to laugh at the absurdity of it all. He had accidentally recruited one of the top prospects in all of Quest Academy, because she wanted to kill demons during an invasion. Seth had been apparently dragged along for the ride, and the accolades that came with her achievements.

Sal thought he looked positively drained, but he couldn't blame him. It was a harrowing experience, and Sal was relieved to see that not everyone was naturally disposed to war.

Mica caught Sal's expression and smiled. "Don't mind him. His clones are out fighting at the moment so he needs to concentrate."

Sal blinked in surprise. "Wait, what?"

A tired smile tugged at Seth's lips. "Got 'em." He looked over at Mica and shot her a wink. "Voider," he mouthed to give her the context.

Chatfield adjusted his earpiece and looked off to the right. He was nodding along, while his eyes looked devoid of life. "He was given the mandate by the United Guilds Association," Chatfield corrected whoever he was speaking to. "If he wasn't a student of Quest Academy, he would be eligible to participate. There are no special protections that come from him being a student. If he wishes to be here, that's up to him."

Chatfield winced at whatever was said on the other end of the line. His eyes narrowed, and he looked at the ceiling, squinting. Eventually, he reached a hand up to his ear. "Glad we're on the same page. The students not affiliated with Salvatore's guild are already en route back to the academy. I'll ensure the participants in the battle come back alive and unharmed." His hand got closer to his ear, before retreating, as if he was anticipating when Quest would end the call. Finally, he nodded. "Got it."

When he plucked out his earpiece, he let out the mother of all relieved sighs. "We're golden on the student front. Villa, you're the only advisor for his guild here, so you're in charge of making sure he stays alive until backup arrives." He pointed at Sal meaningfully. "I'll make sure his *official members* are safe." His glare was very much aimed at Mica and Seth, neither of whom seemed to care.

"Are we able to start the briefing now?" Villa leaned against the wall, her arms folded. "I'll keep him safe, but he's perfectly capable of looking after himself."

It was the highest praise imaginable, and Sal was more than happy to receive it. He was nowhere near Mica's kill count when it came to commander class demons, but it was a great start.

Chatfield nodded. "Yeah, we're in a bit of a tight spot when it comes to resources. The front lines are exhausted and although Eclipse's members are keeping people upright, they need reinforcing." He sighed as he tapped his tablet's screen to power it up. "Reports show that there were thirteen commander class variants that breached Haven. Our Hunters with Foresight believe that we're dealing with a Psionic commander. I've prepared some countermeasures with my ability, so everyone should be Warded from its influence. Keep those hairclips equipped at all times."

It reminded Sal of the first commander he ever came across. It had skewed all of Divinity's visions, showing her fake versions of future events. If they were up against another one, it would explain why nobody saw this coming. But for such a large-scale attack from so many angles, how could they possibly fool that many Hunters?

"It's probably the spider." Chatfield sighed as he looked at Villa. "Good instincts."

Villa nodded. "It positioned itself to command the other demons. Watcher did some damage, but it has a reinforced chitin that seemingly regenerates within seconds."

Sal wondered whether that was a trait of the material or a part of its ability. If he could make self-repairing armor, that would be pretty cool. He caught himself within that small thought and instantly rebuked himself with a guilty smile. If he was seriously thinking of a commander class as a material experiment, he had lost all sense of perspective.

Chatfield folded his arms as he got to his feet and moved to the window to look at the devastation unfolding in the distance. "Evacuation efforts were a little slower than I would have liked, but we've ensured that there are no civilians left in the area." He pointed at the rooftops on the horizon. "I can't see any more shuttles taking off, so that's a good sign."

Villa rolled her eyes as she let out an exasperated sigh. "You don't need to justify the destruction. We know that taking them out will result in collateral damage." She pointed at Eclipse, Enigma, and Shade. "Healers, Controllers, and Backstabbers. Everything you need for a big fight."

Shade opened his mouth to refute the comment, but Chatfield turned and gestured for him to stay quiet. He frowned as he glanced at Villa, before shaking his head. "Our Defenders can keep them at bay for another few hours. Our orders are to hold them here until backup can arrive. The Reavers are great with Offense, but you're not here in your full capacity. I didn't see Fierce make his way here."

"What did you expect from a Tier 2 guild?" Shade managed to get his snarky comment in this time, his smug grin aimed at Villa. "He's probably trying to clear a few dungeons while we're saving innocent lives."

Enigma let out a groan as he tapped his cane impatiently on the floor. "Can we please get a move on. I don't understand the need for us to be in here while the fighting is happening out there. You've validated that the students are safe, and that our civilians are evacuated. We know that the spider needs to die. What else is on your agenda?"

Chatfield leaned over the table and tapped an interface, pulling up a series of photos as three-dimensional images that he pushed across the table length, so they were all visible at once. One of them looked familiar to Sal. It was the commander class he had killed earlier.

Tapping the interface, the familiar image was soaked in a red light to denote that the subject had been dealt with. Chatfield pointed at the nearest picture, rotating it around for everyone to see. It revealed the war spider up close, and it was far more terrifying than Sal had imagined. If it was a regenerative chitin, Sal absolutely wanted it. Not only did it sound incredible as a resource, it looked amazing: bright-white plating with lava-like joints, and blood-red eyes. Okay, no, it looked terrifying, but Sal wanted that white metal.

Chatfield pointed at the other commanders and was about to speak when one of the portraits suddenly washed red. He paused as he looked at it in confusion. "Okay, that's one less to worry about." He smiled in relief. "We've still got a few Offense-based Heroes here. A few lucky shots are to be within expectations."

Bringing everyone's attention back to the war spider was made more difficult by the next portrait taking on a red hue… followed by another. Three commanders killed in quick succession wasn't a fluke.

Chatfield tapped the interface and froze for a second before reaching to his ear, not finding the earpiece in place. He had taken it out after his call with Quest, and it seemed he was missing a lot of context because of it. Without wasting more time, he secured the device into his ear and looked around to stare outside the window. "Is it another guild bringing backup?" A slow pause crept around the room as Chatfield tilted his head. "What? Can you at least identify them?"

Sal wasn't exactly sure what was happening, but from the surprised expressions on the guildmasters' faces, and Villa's, whatever was happening was quite impressive. He was sure that Prestige or Robert could have just snapped their fingers to kill all of them… so there had to be something else that was happening that was earning their respect.

"Just one person?" Chatfield repeated with a laugh. "So, one of the Rankers was in the area?" He looked around in excitement and gave everyone a thumbs-up.

Villa's head suddenly snapped up as though she had just sensed something. She darted to the window and pointed in the direction of the Red Zone. "I'd recognize that essence signature anywhere! Fuck me, this is the best day ever!" She laughed in what could only be described as maniacal excitement, her blood-red fingernails tapping excitedly against the glass, somehow sounding scarier than the clattering of the war spider.

Chatfield's jaw dropped as he watched something unfold outside.

Sal was about to move forward for more context when another portrait suddenly darkened in red. Each of the creatures looked to be ridiculously strong, and yet, someone was taking them out in quick succession.

"What the fuck was she doing hiding all these years?" Villa laughed as she pressed her hands against the glass, a look of pure excitement and hunger coloring her features. Villa tore her eyes away from the screen to glance back at Shade, grinning widely. "You're so fucked."

Sal felt a pang of dread. Had his mother come out of hiding to start fighting? He had to admit, almost ashamedly, that he didn't think his mother was capable of taking out a commander class. She did tick all the boxes though, considering Villa knew her, and it was no secret that his family hated Shade.

Chatfield was in complete denial as he pressed his hands against the glass. "Why the fuck was someone like her working on the Credit floor?"

Realization dawned on Sal as he moved toward the glass to see outside. He glanced back to see the same realization mirrored on Shade's very pale face. With an almost guilty laugh, Sal looked outside to see Vanessa Blake purposefully walking toward their rendezvous point, dragging the decapitated corpse of a commander class. He looked at her destination and was surprised to see a pile of four more dead commanders.

Vanessa was covered in blood as she glanced up in their direction, a wicked smile on her lips. She threw the enormous body of the demon like it was a toy, at least thirty feet in a straight line so it landed with the others. Standing upright, she gave Chatfield a mock salute before turning back toward the Red Zone and getting into a crouched position.

"Who the hell is that?" Mica breathed in a whisper, excitement all over her face as she watched Vanessa burst forward at inhuman speed in the direction of the battlefield.

Chatfield groaned inwardly as he let his forehead rest against the glass. "If you're going to pretend to be a part of Salvatore's guild, you should at least know its members."

Sal pointed in the direction that Vanessa sped off in. "That's Diva. She handles most of our administrative tasks."

CHAPTER 78: ENIGMA

Sal walked with the others to the battlefield. Chatfield wanted to pick up the pace, but Enigma had insisted they take it slowly. Apparently, there was no need to rush. It gave Jackal plenty of opportunity to take apart the commanders that Vanessa had deposited outside the guild building. If Enigma or Eclipse noticed the little drone, they didn't mention it. Shade had left with his people the moment it became clear that Vanessa was on a rampage. His excuses had been paper-thin, but Chatfield was more than happy to be rid of him.

Ahead of Sal, he could see Chatfield with Mica and Seth, the latter playing with his new Concept hairclip. Eclipse and Enigma had remained around Sal. Their people were off to the sides, investigating buildings and clearing through the rubble. Villa informed him she was going to keep an eye on Shade, but that she'd be close by.

"If you selected the Reavers out of desperation, there was no need." Enigma spoke candidly as he kept pace beside Sal on their route toward the battlefield. "Paradox are always keen on investing in the next generation of Heroes, and if your Mythic Guild needs additional guidance, we'd be willing to sit at the table and discuss it."

Sal smiled as he looked at Enigma. It was frankly ridiculous that one of the heavyweight guilds was actually interested in supporting his. He hadn't exactly given Enigma much to go on. All the man had was a few reports that he took out a commander class, and that he had Vanessa in his ranks. Had he watched Sal at the Hunter Bureau gala? There were too many questions, and Sal kept defaulting back to his identity as a Mythcrafter. If that was the reason, then it would make a lot more sense. Greed was always the greatest motivator.

"I really appreciate the kind offer, but I don't think now is the right time to discuss it. I'd be more than happy to have a conversation in the future, but I have no intention of trading the Reavers. Villa gave me my first break when I arrived at Quest Academy," Sal explained as he watched his surroundings with his eye-patch.

Enigma sniffed at that, and Sal could have sworn that his cane struck the ground a little harder than before. He was definitely a Prestige-type of guildmaster. "Perhaps we'll have a more detailed discussion at a later date." His tone sounded frustrated, as though there was little to no chance of a future conversation.

Eclipse appeared on the other side of Sal, a warm smile on her face. "Tell me more about this friend of yours with the Transference ability."

Sal was a little taken aback, and wasn't sure what angle she was going with. "What would you like to know?"

Eclipse glanced at Enigma, as though silently requesting he make himself scarce. Either he didn't take the hint, or he flat-out ignored it. Enigma was seemingly content to listen to their conversation, despite having his own offer rejected.

"Well, I know how much of a pain in the ass it is to progress, so I've got a lot of methods that can help accelerate the development of the ability. Little tips and tricks I'd be happy to share with your friend," Eclipse answered in an encouraging tone. It sounded like she genuinely wanted to help.

"In exchange for…?" Sal asked the question with his own smile. Nothing was free, and although he had a good impression of Eclipse, he was sure there was an angle.

"In exchange for knowing that I've helped a Healer progress with this bitch of a power." Eclipse laughed as she offered a slight shrug. "In more practical terms, if there was ever a joint operation with our guilds, I'd prefer to know that you had at least one well-trained person in your ranks."

Sal frowned as he thought about it. "You want to train her up so she's reliable? Then, yes… I'd obviously have to talk to her to see if she was okay with it, but I'd be happy to give her that opportunity."

Enigma cleared his throat audibly. "That was the offer I was making, too." He looked at Sal as though disappointed that he hadn't somehow connected the dots already.

"You would like to help train one of my guild members?" Sal asked to clarify, not sure how to interact with this man without seemingly offending him. "One of the Controllers?"

"Your most strategic," Enigma answered flatly. "None of this wild streak stuff." He gestured at the carnage around them that was left in Vanessa's wake. "Body Manipulators are the most physically gifted among us, and yet they never use their minds. If you give me someone who can understand tactics, then I will give you back a general."

Sal smiled as he looked between them. "I understand the benefits, but I can't understand the timing. We're only a Tier 8, so we shouldn't be getting interest like this from the Tier 1's."

"There's a very good chance that your guild will fail." Eclipse shrugged, earning her a glare from Enigma. "So, it makes sense for us to build a relationship with you now… so that when it does dissolve, we can potentially get you and the person we've trained. It's just business."

Sal brightened at those words. "In that case, I wholeheartedly accept." He laughed as he looked at Enigma. "Barry Francis is the perfect person for what you've asked for." He turned his attention to Eclipse. "And Rochelle de Verdon is the Healer you're looking for."

Eclipse frowned as she looked at Sal carefully. "You have that much faith that you won't fail?" Her smile returned slowly, as though she was both intrigued and entertained by the confidence.

"I'm not sure if you've heard it, but it's the worst kept secret in Quest Academy," Sal started with a laugh. He realized after fighting the commander class, that if he wanted to live without fear, he needed to get in front of the secrets that were holding him back. "I'm able to make Mythic-grade equipment. All my guild members will eventually be equipped with the best gear in the world. I've got no doubts on being able to attract the best talent, and we've already established multiple revenue streams that will keep us active for a long time."

Eclipse's mouth opened, but no sound came out. She looked at Enigma for some assistance, but he seemed to be just as lost. Well, as lost as his dignified appearance would allow. His confusion manifested as a thousand-yard stare into the distance, likely trying to find some semblance of logic that would explain everything.

Sal smiled as he looked between them. "One of my friends with Foresight told me that there was a chance that Shade would try abducting me at some point. Then there was the whole Bastion infiltration at Quest Academy. I've spent my first semester living in a state of constant fear, but… between us, it was pretty exhausting."

"What's changed?" Enigma asked curiously. "To suddenly start telling your competitors?"

Sal gestured at the war zone around them. "I realized that this is the real war. Shouldn't I be fighting against the demons rather than the likes of Bastion or the guilds that just want my abilities? Secrets are just going to get harder to keep, and I'm honestly tired of them. I'd rather just use my Mythcrafter ability to help people, and it's nearly impossible to do so when I can't tell anyone about it."

Enigma's hold on his cane loosened as he nodded. "You're either a very good judge of character, or too loose-tongued for your own good."

"I'm going to guess the former." Eclipse laughed as she shook her head, still thinking through all the implications. "Do you need us to protect you?"

Sal shook his head. "I'd rather my guild could protect itself. If you're going to help train my people, then I'd want to be able to trust your reasons for doing so. There's going to be changes happening at Quest Academy in the next few months, and I need allies for my plans to succeed."

"Vagueness isn't helping your case." Enigma sounded miffed as he tapped his cane. "What are your plans, and what do you need from me? My initial goals were in securing you for your work on weave research. I've heard on good authority that you're gifted in that domain." He hesitated for a few seconds before letting out an exasperated sigh. "In the spirit of transparency…Paradox has been working on our own version of the Skill Imprinting technology, but we've hit a few walls."

Eclipse blinked in surprise, primarily aimed at Enigma. She let out a guilty laugh before speaking. "I have it on good authority that Salvatore made a diagnostics machine for the Quest Academy infirmary. I wanted him to make something like that for us since it would drastically cut down our workloads."

Sal was a little taken aback by how much both knew. He had never met either of them in person, yet both knew about completely different aspects of his work. It made him realize that there were likely many other guilds that knew about his work on the evolutionary sniper rifle, or about the elixir machine. He was relieved that he had trusted his instincts with the two of them.

"You may not need the weave research," Sal said quietly in Enigma's direction. "I've been working on something that could help people break through their bottlenecks in terms of ability progression and evolution. Coach has been assisting me with it, and it's currently in testing."

Enigma's jaw dropped as he stared at Sal, then at Eclipse, then back to Sal. "Would you show me this…machine? I have so many gifted Heroes who are so much more than their limitations." For the first time since meeting him, Sal saw a desperation in the guildmaster's eyes.

Sal smiled as he gestured at the destruction around them. "After we finish up here and I clear some of my workload, I'd be more than happy to talk about it. I want to manage expectations, because it could all go to shit."

That was apparently all that Enigma needed to hear as he gave a curt nod and a curious smile.

Sal guessed that they would drop the topic and reconvene later. He was incorrect. The first clue was the wreckage and rubble all levitating off the ground before melting into each other. In just a few seconds, there were close to a dozen spears that looked almost fluid in nature.

Members of the Eclipse Guild all threw themselves backward, out of the way, whereas those in Paradox seemingly understood what was going on. A few shouts and cheers rang out from their ranks as they looked at each other in excitement.

Glancing to his left, Sal saw that Enigma was no longer beside him. Looking around didn't reveal his location, but he did see Eclipse looking upward with a grin on her face.

"Can't believe you managed to get the guildmaster of Paradox worked up." She laughed excitedly. "You're in for quite the treat."

Sal looked up to see Enigma floating thirty feet above ground level. Close to a hundred spears whipped around him in a circle, each of them curving as if they were made of water. Both of his arms were outstretched as he flew forward. His long jacket billowed behind him almost theatrically as he rotated his wrist to point his cane at the Red Zone in the distance.

"What is his ability?" Sal asked in confusion. But before Eclipse could answer, the attack commenced. An armada of spears shot toward the barrier at a blistering speed, all of them disappearing in the blink of an eye. Visually, it was stunning. Audibly? It was terrifying. The noises made by the mishappen spears cutting through the air was like countless wails of despair.

"What the fuck is he doing?!" Chatfield bolted over to them in a panic, looking up into the sky. "He could hit our guys with that sort of attack!"

Eclipse shook her head. "Enigma doesn't miss." She pointed into the distance. "Ever."

Chatfield looked like he was about to respond when something caught his attention. He raised a hand to his ear and confusion crossed his face. "What?" he shouted into the earpiece. "What do you mean?"

Eclipse grinned at Sal. "It takes a lot out of him, so you must have really made him excited."

A familiar clattering noise echoed out to their far right, which caused Sal's heart to race. Enigma's attack had seemingly drawn the war spider out of hiding. Its first mistake was screaming, because that informed its worst nightmare where it was.

Sal's eyes widened as he watched Vanessa burst through a fifth-story window of a half-destroyed skyscraper, the remains of a scuttler head falling from her bloodied grasp as she landed on the ground with a thundering crack. Her enhanced body created a crater of broken concrete beneath her feet as she gracefully reached up with her blood-soaked hands to tie back her mane of blonde hair.

Glowing red irises were locked onto an unseen position in the distance, which Sal guessed was the location of the war spider. The wild smile on her face was oddly reminiscent of the bloodlust Gallant had in the tower. Sal couldn't help but worry that Vanessa had somehow lost control in the chaos.

Vanessa glanced in his direction and gave him a sly wink, putting his heart at ease almost instantly. She crouched down like a runner preparing for a start, but when she took off, the only indicator that she had ever been there were the chunks of concrete that shot backward from her position.

Chatfield tore his eyes away from Enigma, to the direction that Vanessa had just vanished into. "Wait! Fuck!" He turned back to look up at Enigma. "Why is he pushing himself like this?" He looked conflicted as he turned to Eclipse. "Enigma's apparently just taken out half of the invading force. There's no way he can keep this up."

Eclipse nodded as she rolled up her sleeves. "You go play with the spider, and I'll make sure he doesn't kill himself." She glanced over her shoulder in confusion. "Where are Shade and Villa? Did they already go for the spider?"

Chatfield shook his head and cursed under his breath. "Shade left, and Villa is supposedly monitoring him." His frustration was both visible and understandable as it meant he was stuck as chaperone for Sal and the other students.

Mica was practically hopping on the spot from where Chatfield had been walking with them. She looked excited to start fighting. Seth, sitting beside her, was a sobering comparison. He looked drained by every conceivable metric. Chatfield had apparently designated Seth as a flight risk, as his entire body was covered in essence-constructed armor.

When Sal made eye contact with Mica, she pointed after Vanessa. "Do you think she'll let me take its heart? I'm pretty sure this guy is the strongest commander I've come across."

"If we can catch up to her," Chatfield muttered as he gestured for them to follow him. "She doesn't know it's Psionic. If it's able to control her, there's a good chance we'll be facing Vanessa as an enemy." He looked at Sal meaningfully. "Be prepared for anything."

CHAPTER 79: APEX

When Chatfield had told him to be prepared for anything, Sal's mind went toward the possibility of Vanessa being injured or potentially turned against him. He had not been mentally prepared for the reality of an invasion.

That reality came in the form of fatalities, and the massacre of people who surrounded the white-armored war spider. Sal tried not to look at the dead bodies, but his eye-patch didn't discriminate and pushed through all the details, giving him a better idea of how they died. He was grateful that it ignored his feelings, because it potentially just saved Seth's life.

"Don't move!" Sal shouted at Seth, stalling him completely. "There's an invisible wire in front of you."

Mica practically snarled as she brought her hand down in the space in front of Seth, her skin not even compressing upon contact with the razor-like material. Instead, a selection of mortared bricks were forcibly dislodged from a nearby wall.

The war spider had seemingly burrowed into the ground floor of a guild building to create the ideal den. Perfectly preserved panes of glass were secured between the webs reaching up four floors, giving the spider a complete view of every direction around it. Depending on your vantage point, you'd be able to see the evacuation zones, the dungeons, the guild buildings, and the Red Zone. It was a demon-made command center and the wire-like webbing was the perfect defense.

Chatfield had expertly navigated ahead of them with an essence-construct shield raised in his hands. "I told you all to stay back!" He watched along with everyone else as the struggling form of the war spider was viciously yanked back down into the hole at a right angle. Its white-armored forelegs clawed and scraped at the entrance, not finding purchase on anything as it was pulled backward in violent bursts. Each jagged movement was enough to tear through the concrete like butter.

"You're playing with me, not them." Vanessa laughed from behind the massive war spider, and it was honestly terrifying to see how nonchalant she was being. It was a demonic creature that looked custom-designed to slaughter, and she was dragging it behind her like a petulant child.

How Vanessa got past the wiring was anyone's guess, but it looked like she couldn't be followed easily. One member of their group hadn't gotten that particular memo, and seemingly saw it as a challenge. Probably because the war spider had nearly killed her boyfriend.

Mica walked purposefully forward despite Chatfield's continued warnings. Segments of her clothing cut perfectly as it came into contact with the razor wire, but her skin was completely fine. It didn't take long before both of her sleeves were in tatters, as well as the thighs of her pants. Her hair didn't fare much better, with some of it getting sheared off as she cleared through the webbing. Other than her advance, the only constant was the sound of the webbing supports being forcibly pulled out. In less than a minute, the guaranteed death by razor wire was completely reversed, with Mica looking pissed-off rather than satisfied.

The clattering noise had been scary at a distance, but the sound of mandibles clicking at close range was absolutely terrifying. Sal's entire body fought against

Perfect, and maintaining calm was a real challenge. Something at the back of his head suddenly flared up, to the point of actual pain. With a pained wince, Sal pulled the searing-hot warding device from the back of his head. It was the basic one that was supposed to protect him from Erika, gifted by his parents during the break. Thankfully, the peaked hat was more than capable of fending off whatever was trying to hurt him.

Barely a second later, Sal saw Chatfield slump to the ground, his Concept devices exploding, with Mica and Seth's following suit. They were still conscious, but clearly trying to resist an onslaught of some unseen attack. He was the only one protected.

Everything clicked into place as Sal realized they were up against the war spider's Psionic attack. His hat was keeping him safe from harm, but the little device practically imploded in his hand from overload. With just a quick glance, Sal could see that Seth was the worst off, with Chatfield not much better than him. Chatfield was attempting to create another Concept device, but everything he tried shattered between his trembling fingers.

Mica, on the other hand, looked as if she were ready to murder someone. Thankfully, her ire was aimed at the tunnel and she just looked angered by the unsolicited passenger in her mind. Sal guessed that Body Manipulators and Mimicry types had a higher resistance to Psionic essence, which was good to know. That theory was confirmed just a few seconds later farther into the tunnel.

"Get out of my head, you little shit!" Vanessa's scream from the depths of the den echoed out, followed by a frantic scuttling sound.

"Jackal, go and assist Vanessa," Sal instructed with a wince as the Warded ability activated in his hat. The sensation was new, like the fabric was tightening around his head. He made sure that Jackal was only going to attack demons, as he didn't want it fighting with Vanessa. Through the next pang of discomfort, he watched as Jackal unfurled from his arm and shot forward into the tunnel, the flickering light disappearing as the protective casing snapped around the blight core.

Mica's eyes widened as she took a tentative step backward, her murderous gaze flickering to doubt as she looked at Sal in confusion. It wasn't the best introduction to Jackal, but he didn't have the luxury of warning everyone in advance.

"What the fuck?!" Vanessa's voice sounded out in a surprised tone. It was interesting that she didn't sound panicked, despite Jackal's somewhat menacing appearance.

Sal gritted his teeth as he called back to her. "It's my drone. It'll help!" He wasn't sure his words were strong enough to reach her, but he hoped that it would be fine. Turning to look at Chatfield and the others, Sal activated Mythcrafter and started to look for something that could give the Warded attribute. He didn't care about style or complexity, because only function mattered at this point.

The design came together in front of his eyes in seconds, and every time Mythcrafter tried to iterate, Sal denied it. A small hairclip would do the job perfectly and it didn't even need a core. Each of them would be able to use their own essence to keep it active.

When Arsenal opened, he knew exactly what he needed, so it didn't take long to locate. There was an absolute mess of materials that had been deposited into the space. Most interesting of all was what looked like a series of blood-red eyes. Sal glanced out the door of Arsenal to the tunnel. Surely Jackal hadn't stolen one of its eyes? Weren't they still fighting?

Another eye materialized in front of him, followed by a massive leg that was still twitching. White-plated, with lava-like joints. It was definitely from the war spider. It just didn't make any sense why the materials were coming through when it was still alive…

Mythcrafter flashed and reorganized itself the moment Sal picked up one of the eyes. Apparently—and honestly, unsurprisingly—the new material was perfect for subduing Psionic attacks. Sal picked up a shard of obsidian and placed it to the side of the eyeball, fueling his essence into it. It was going to be an unrefined, brute-force method to get the job done, and Sal only hoped it would be quick. If he could get it onto Mica or Chatfield fast enough, they'd be able to help Vanessa.

Sal walked back out of Arsenal. He saw from the corner of his eye that another leg had been added to the subspace.

"Stop fucking regenerating!" Vanessa's scream of anger from the tunnel carried all the way out to where he stood.

Sal's eyes widened as he looked at the materials with a newfound context. The war spider was regenerating its eyes and limbs after Vanessa ripped them off. It was far beyond what Sal thought was possible. If it had the ability to command other demons with Psionics, then how did it have an ability like Regeneration?

Looking back at the blob of essence in his hands, Sal smoothed it out with his fingertips. It felt a little awkward because of his armor, but his will and intent carried into the essence. If anything, Overdrive was on the sidelines, begging to overclock Mythcrafter. Sal had zero intention of running that experiment while he was in an active battlefield.

When the device was finally complete, Sal waved it in his hand as though that would cool it faster. It didn't, and all he could do was stand there patiently waiting as he heard the ongoing fight between Vanessa and the war spider. A small part of him had thought Vanessa would kill it instantly, as she had shown off a ridiculous capability earlier.

A movement out of the corner of Sal's eye drew his attention to Arsenal, where he saw a small white spider materialize. It was half the size of Jackal, with all its legs turned inward post-death. It was enough to stop his heart as he realized why Vanessa was struggling. There was more than one enemy in that den.

Sal threw the still-cooling device to Chatfield. "Put that on when it's ready!" he shouted as he closed Arsenal and focused his attention on the tunnel. With his right arm extended, he activated Overdrive and Capacitor in preparation. A part of him was worried that the Tempest Function would hit Vanessa, but it hadn't done anything like that when he had used it around the volunteers.

His eye-patch could determine roughly where Vanessa was in the war spider's burrow, so he specifically marked her as an ally. It was moments like this he missed the scarlet screen on his actual visor, as it would see through everything to help him pick out targets.

The disco ball of death burst out of his hand and moved through the tunnel. After a few seconds of it hanging in the gloom… doing nothing… Sal wondered whether he had made the wrong call and overreacted. He had presumed that the small spiders were hatchlings of some variety, and that they would end up swarming onto the battlefield. Judging by the Tempest Function not having a single target, Sal figured he'd just wasted a chunk of essence for no reason.

Just when Sal was about to dismiss the Tempest Function to conserve some essence, he felt a vibration through his arm. A streak of lightning burst out from the electric sphere, killing…something. Sal waited to see the report on his eye-patch, and wished it would just load quicker so he could know what to do next.

Tempest Function Report (1)
- o   White Arachne Hatchling has been killed
- o   Speed has increased by 0.06

Sal felt relieved that there was at least one small spider that came too close. He was under no illusion that the attack would have been enough for the war spider, but it was nice that it wasn't a complete waste.

That first flash seemed to open the floodgates, as Sal felt a continuous draw on his arm, with the Tempest Function finally going crazy and shooting laser-like bolts of lightning in every direction. His eye-patch overloaded with data of confirmed kills as more and more small spiders leapt to their deaths. Sal grimaced as he thought about how fucked Arsenal's layout would be when Jackal started to retrieve them.

"Thank you, Salvatore," Chatfield said with a relieved sigh from behind him.

Sal tore his attention away from the lightning long enough to see Chatfield wearing a black and red clip over his ear. The same design was replicated in a shimmering red light on both Mica and Seth, who were checking on each other.

Chatfield looked like he was about to ask what was happening, when his eyes widened and a shield appeared in his hands.

Sal looked back just in time to see a small white spider lunging at his face. The lightning pierced through its body just in time, and Sal had to quickly sidestep to avoid getting hit by its corpse. Almost the entire lip of the tunnel was covered in a moving mass of white limbs. Tempest Function was killing them at rapid speed, but there were far too many.

"Will that lightning hit me?" Mica asked in an uncharacteristically cold tone.

"No," Sal answered, not risking turning to look at her. He had to keep his focus on the Tempest Function, with a few Assimilation Functions being thrown in for good measure to keep the swarm of spiders back.

"Good. Then I'm going in to help." Mica burst forward with both hands lowered at her side.

Sal caught sight of her hands transforming into claws. As she moved into the tunnel, everything her fingertips touched… exploded. There was no hesitation as she vanished into the darkness, with the only signals of her fight being the shadowed versions of her flickering with every burst of lightning.

"Seth, don't run in like her!" Chatfield said through gritted teeth as he reached a hand to his earpiece. "Yes… it's Captain Chatfield. We had no intel that the war spider was able to hatch eggs. Where the hell is our support? We have casualties here—seven unconscious and losing blood, and eighteen dead. Vast majority are from the Delvers Guild, with some from Paradox. I've put them in stasis with Concept, but I'm unable to fight until backup arrives. Send backup as soon as you can. We've taken down the wires so you can approach."

Chatfield hesitated for a few seconds as he looked at the base of the tunnel. "We also have reason to believe that the commander took captives into its den. We have two combatants down there and will need an extraction team. Blink from the Reavers should be nearby. Get her on this channel."

Sal blinked in surprise as he glanced at the outfits of the surrounding victims. Why had the Delvers approached when they knew how dangerous it was? Were they trying to take the glory of dispatching the war spider? His eye-patch told him that their wounds weren't all from the wires, as many of them had been stabbed, likely with one of the war spider's legs.

Chatfield nodded silently as he came into view beside Sal. His hands came together to create a partial blockade at the entrance. It was designed in such a way that it allowed Sal's lightning to go through the gap, but prevented the small spiders from launching attacks at them.

"Looks like Enigma tired himself out, but he managed to take out four of the remaining commanders." Chatfield spoke to Sal like he was a peer. "Eclipse is on her way over here, so we should be able to save some of these people." His voice was controlled as he looked at Sal meaningfully. "We're on the home stretch, Salvatore. Keep up the good work, and we'll get both Michaela and Vanessa out of there safely."

A rumbling in the cave caused the ground beneath their feet to shake. The entire swarm of spiders seemingly sensed the same thing and started to move back into the cave, chasing after Mica.

"Vanessa must be going all out," Sal breathed in surprise as he looked around uncertainly.

"Nope." Seth smiled tiredly as he took a seat. He gestured at the entrance where the small spiders had vacated. "Those demons just got told to retreat. You start learning the signs after a while."

"I don't follow." Chatfield kept a wary eye on the tunnel entrance. "Why would they retreat?"

Seth grinned, his exhaustion fading away almost magically. "Because their mother is facing off against an apex predator. They're going to need all the help they can get."

CHAPTER 80: CONSEQUENCE

Seth hadn't been lying about Michaela's capability. Sal had been quite under-whelmed by her manifesting some claws and walking into the tunnel, but apparently, she had waited until she was next to the war spider before going all out. It had been a quick affair from that point, with Vanessa laughing as she emerged from the tunnel with her arm draped around Mica's shoulder.

Sal's body was in absolute bits, figuratively speaking. He hadn't anticipated any new stats from the war spider, but apparently Jackal contributed enough to activate Subsume. His eye-patch was absolutely useless, though, because it was still cycling through all the components being added to Arsenal.

"We're absolutely signing this one." Vanessa smiled brightly at Sal, which would have been reassuring if it wasn't for the luminous orange blood that covered her entire face and torso. Combined with the glowing red irises, Vanessa looked more like a demon than the commander opponent he had faced earlier.

Mica smiled at Vanessa as she nodded. "Can I have the heart as a signing bonus?"

Vanessa wagged her finger as she lifted her arm off Mica's shoulder. "Ah, ah, we'll only designate that after the contracts are complete. Can't have you skipping out of the guild the moment you get what you want. There will be endless clauses for us to keep you." She smiled sweetly at Michaela. "But, you'll get to fight shit far stronger than this if you stay with us. So, it's not really a bad deal."

Mica just shook her head in disbelief. "I really thought it was a Crafting guild. Like, how did he convince you to join?" She looked so confused, likely after see-ing Vanessa fighting at her best. Mica probably didn't mean to give Sal a dis-missive glance, but it was sent all the same.

"Money," both Sal and Vanessa answered at the same time.

Chatfield cleared his throat, bringing their attention back to him. "Can you please clarify that there are no more demons in there? We want to send people in to investigate." His gaze snapped to Vanessa's right hand, which was holding a foot. "Wait…"

Vanessa threw the foot forward, and as a result of physics, the rest of the body followed it. "Found this guy hiding in the shadows. He didn't indicate his presence and got caught up in the attack. My best guess would be a paralytic from the spi-der, but I'm not really a medic." She smiled sweetly as she looked down at the paralyzed form of Shade, who looked as if he had seen a ghost. "I had a nice little chat with him to keep his mind active. I heard that sort of stuff is important, to keep them awake."

Chatfield just looked between the guildmaster of the Delvers to Vanessa. "And…Villa?"

"Refused my offer of a princess carry, so she's in there sulking." Vanessa snorted as she offered a shrug. "Also paralyzed. That spider had more than a few tricks up its… legs?" She tilted her head to one side, laughing to herself as she moved over to check on Sal. "I want to hear all about that drone, by the way! He's in there having an absolute feast. Poor thing looked like he was struggling to eat everything."

Chatfield had absolutely no words as he stared at the tunnel with his hands on his hips. He looked at Vanessa for a few seconds, before shaking his head and making his way inside, probably to retrieve Villa.

Mica's expression darkened at the mention of Jackal. "I don't like that thing."

Sal raised an eyebrow as he looked at Vanessa for context. "What happened?" He winced as he sat up properly, his body still tender from the shock waves of multiple improvements happening throughout.

Vanessa chuckled as she playfully nudged Mica. "She wanted the killing blow, but your little friend took that privilege for himself." She glanced over her shoulder to see that Chatfield was out of sight. When she confirmed it, she gave Shade a swift kick to the side. He couldn't move his body, but his eyes were locked onto Vanessa.

Looking down at him, she smiled sweetly. "Sorry, thought there was a spider on you. Can't be too careful." When her attention returned to Sal, her smile became genuine. "Do we have a list of all the dead Delvers? Want to check for a few names."

Sal shook his head as he looked at Shade. "Is what you told Chatfield true? He wasn't trying some sneak attack on you or something?"

Vanessa shook her head. "Nah, he went in to see if there was anything worth looting while his team fought it out here." She grinned as she gestured at the tunnel. "Last thing he expected was me dragging it back in."

Mica moved off to sit with Seth with an uncharacteristically gentle smile. Sal made a note of the heart that had been added to Arsenal. He'd need to keep that part out of Crafting if it meant getting her on his team.

Glancing up at Vanessa, he smiled lightly. "Thank you for coming to help. I think this would have gone very differently without you."

"Gotta keep my employer safe. Pretty sure that's a guild rule somewhere." Vanessa laughed as she sat beside him, a little distance away so her blood-soaked body wouldn't rub off on him. "You've got nothing to worry about with Shade, by the way. We had a nice little chat about professional boundaries. The Delvers should be giving us a wide berth from this point onward."

"You believe him?" Sal scoffed as he glanced at the now twitching body of Shade. "He's a notorious liar at the best of times."

Vanessa shrugged as she looked at the guildmaster coldly. "Well, he did get to see firsthand what happens when I don't hold back." She pointed a manicured finger at Mica. "And he's witnessed the latest monster you've added to your ranks. His self-preservation will always outweigh his greed. It's not exactly justice, but it's the best we can hope for."

"And is Villa okay? Why was she in there with him?" Sal asked, not understanding the logistics of how everything had happened. If Shade arrived first and went in, did Villa follow him? Everything he knew about her would have put her fighting outside with the others.

Vanessa smiled as she shook her head slightly. She leaned in close to Sal, whispering in his ear so nobody else could hear. "The spider can't paralyze its victims." She leaned back and gave him a wink. "But Villa can."

Sal's jaw dropped as he stared at her, causing her to laugh in genuine amusement.

"Villa owed me one, so let's just keep it as our little secret. Okay?" She might have tried to look earnest, but the blood dripping off her face, combined with the glowing red irises, had the opposite effect. It felt like Sal was making a pact with a devil. Yet, Shade was alive, and nothing bad had really happened. A future showed him abducting Sal, and although that was only a possibility, it was damning enough for Sal to have zero sympathy for him.

"Deal," Sal said with absolute conviction. He owed Shade nothing, and was happy to keep that secret for Vanessa and Villa. "Just tell me that there was nothing you could do to save all the people out here." He looked at her seriously. The only deal-breaker for him would be if she got potentially innocent Heroes killed. The Paradox people specifically. They were likely just victims of circumstance.

Vanessa smiled as she shook her head. "I suppose I could have torn the wires down, but I went for a more acrobatic approach to the problem. They ran straight into them despite my warnings." She glanced at Sal, thoughtfully. "I won't grieve for them, if that was the question?" She gestured at a few of the corpses. "Paradox guys were dead before I even arrived. I think they were stationed in the area and killed by the spider earlier in the day."

"Sorry, I didn't mean to doubt you," Sal said with a relieved sigh as he placed his palms on his knees. Regenerate was doing wonders on his body, and he was already feeling quite acclimatized to the new stats.

"Pfft, never apologize for having a conscience." Vanessa laughed as she looked at him seriously. "You were very guildmaster-esque just now, just so you know." She smiled as she got to her feet. "I'll be honest, though." She looked around the area. "I half expected Upgrade to appear at some point. Did you guys have a falling-out?"

Sal shook his head. "Nope, she's just working on a project for me, and I doubt she even knows any of this is happening." His smile faded slightly. "Do you two not get along, by the way? You were quite tense with each other during the signing."

Vanessa waved it off like it was nothing. "Just a few disagreements over the years. She wasn't too pleased at how I took every opportunity away from her…and seemingly squandered them."

"Because of the Delvers?" Sal asked in a quiet voice, just trying to make sure that he understood what he was hearing.

"In part," Vanessa answered before dismissing the topic with a wave. "Anyways, we should be celebrating. Hardest part of getting to Tier 7 is taking out a commander, and you've just had one of your members take one out." She pointed over at Mica excitedly. "They'll disqualify my contributions, but they'll listen to me in an advisor capacity."

"He killed one, too." Villa, with a pained expression, walked out of the tunnel unassisted, holding her side. Chatfield followed her out, looking like he had no idea what to do with his hands. "Blew the commander's head right off, and it was an absolute bastard of a fighter."

Vanessa's jaw dropped before a wide smile blossomed. "Fuck off." She glanced at Sal excitedly. "You killed a fucking commander?! When were you going to tell me?"

Sal was grateful for the praise, especially from Vanessa. She genuinely looked excited and proud, and he was happy to go up in her estimation, even by a little. In a reversed perspective, she had skyrocketed in his opinion. The placards in the Savior dorm didn't do her justice at all. "I was kinda just focused on making sure none of you guys died. It slipped my mind."

Wincing, Villa straightened her back, and even with Chatfield in full view, she launched a swift kick at Shade's paralyzed body. Looking back at him, as though daring Chatfield to say something, she pointed at Shade. "You already have my report. Do I need to bring it to Robert to ensure something happens this time, or will you do your job?"

Chatfield's expression was resolute as he gave her a curt nod. "I'll be informing him after the battle in Pinnacle is resolved."

"Shard is safe?" Sal asked, suddenly remembering that there were multiple attacks were going on. He didn't remember which one had Chronos, but he was sure there would be a lot more panicking if the dragon had been freed.

"It was secured close to an hour ago." Chatfield placed his hands on his hips. He glanced at Vanessa for a second, before returning his gaze to the ground in front of him. "Thank you for the assistance today. We would have lost a lot of good people had you not been here."

Vanessa looked like a cat playing with a mouse. She leaned forward in her seat and rested her chin on her palm. "Not bad for a Tier 8 guild. We did pretty good for only having a few of our members here, didn't we?" Her smile grew wider. "I hope that'll be reflected to the United Guilds Association and the Hunter Bureau."

Chatfield nodded. "As I said, I'll be reporting to the president as soon as we wrap up everything here." He glanced over to where Eclipse leaned against a wall. "Were you able to save them?"

Eclipse looked absolutely furious as she stalked across the uneven rubble. "What kind of operation requires you to send this many people to their deaths?" She glared at Shade with balled-up fists, before regaining her composure and looking at Chatfield with a grimace, shaking her head slightly. "We were able to successfully treat five of the seven people you put in stasis. Had you not taken action, we'd potentially have only saved one." She forced a smile to her face. "Thank you."

"I'm sorry." Chatfield genuinely sounded remorseful as he pointed at the clip over his ear. "My Concept ability was interrupted by the Psionic attack, and—"

"What's done is done," Eclipse interrupted him in a firm tone. "Thank you for saving five of them. It's our understanding that these men were sent to their deaths by Shade." She raised her hand to gesture for one of her guild members to come closer. "Mort, tell them what you've found."

Mort was dressed in a white and blue uniform. His eyes looked devoid of happiness as he looked at Chatfield. "My ability allows me to speak with the recently deceased or those nearing death." He took a steadying breath before exhaling slowly. "The Delvers were instructed to lock down the area and distract the war spider. If they didn't, they'd be selected to participate in the next portal run."

Eclipse put her hand on Mort's shoulder. "Go on."

Mort glanced at Shade for a moment before closing his eyes and continuing. "Their portal runs are treated as survival of the fittest, with the rewards being shared among the survivors. The strongest members of Delvers pit the weakest against each other during the portal runs."

Vanessa tilted her head to one side. "Don't forget about the crippling loans they make you take from the guild." Her smile was sweet, but her tone was anything but.

Mort's eyes widened. "How do you know that?"

Eclipse turned to look at Vanessa. "You knew about this and let it continue?" She sounded positively disgusted, both at the situation and at Vanessa.

Chatfield's hand moved in the air, and a set of shimmering red restraints appeared. "As a captain within the Hunter Bureau, I'm placing Shade of the Delvers Guild under arrest." He spoke as though he was required to say it, but it looked as though it took everything in his power not to let his emotions seep through.

"He's got potential, but it won't mean shit tomorrow." Vanessa smiled as she watched Chatfield turn Shade onto his stomach and secure his arms together in the Concept-created restraints. She turned to look at Eclipse. "I was recruited into the Delvers after I graduated from Quest Academy." She shrugged. "Thought that all the scary stories were from people who just couldn't cut it. I was wrong."

Eclipse's harsh expression softened at those words, but her ire was still very much aimed at Shade. "Good riddance," was her only further comment.

Sal looked at Chatfield. "What's going to happen to him?"

Chatfield grunted as he pulled Shade's half-paralyzed form to his feet. The guildmaster was starting to slur words, but Chatfield ignored them as he started to walk him toward the street. "That'll be a decision for Robert and the United Guilds Association."

"So, nothing," Vanessa said loud enough for Chatfield to hear. "Nothing will be done."

CHAPTER 81: AFTERMATH

Sal genuinely expected that, after the fight, there would be some high fives, congratulatory remarks, and then an expedited trip back to Quest Academy. He was wrong on a few aspects, namely the fact that there was a mountain of follow-up work that needed to be done. As a Support, the requests kept flowing through, from removing rubble, to creating supply paths for the various guilds so that they could treat the frontline Heroes and Hunters.

Close to three hours went by, until Sal's voice was hoarse from explaining—at length—how he didn't know which buildings were safe to be returned to. All the evacuees had been granted access to the Haven Borough after the new barriers were reformed. The air lock being established was the trusted sign that they could return to their homes, or rather, to verify whether their homes still existed. Sal was given a stock phrase from one of the other Support workers, which, in essence, just told them to contact the Hunter Bureau with their address, and if it was on the database, they'd be given compensation as well as a timeline for when their property would be restored.

"Yes, please make your way to the emergency shelter location. Any of you who have accommodation facilities in a neighboring borough are encouraged to go there. We want to prioritize those who have nowhere else to stay tonight." Sal's voice cracked halfway through the rehearsed speech, and he was both troubled and surprised that there weren't any outraged remarks aimed at him. Most of the reactions he got were subdued nods of understanding.

He could see some of the residents on their knees, outside of destroyed buildings, just staring at them quietly. It was like a solemn moment of grieving. What really struck Sal as strange, was how, used to it they were. Nothing like this had ever happened in Silver Sanctuary, and Villa had said it was an annual occurrence. How many times had these people lost their homes and businesses?

"Those bastards are getting less and less subtle," one man muttered as he walked past Sal, talking to a woman who looked like she had participated in the frontline battle. "I'd half expect the demons were let through on purpose so your friends could buy up the rest of the borough."

The woman rolled her eyes as she shook her head in exasperation. "You couldn't go two minutes without blaming them, could you? They've been helping us rebuild for years…what could they possibly gain from destroying Haven?"

"Loyalty," the man answered curtly before letting out a heavy sigh. Gesturing at a ruined building in the distance, he grimaced. "And I'm getting more inclined to support the fuckers if it stops these damn raids. It's going to take months before the Restoration guilds will get this fixed…at a massive-ass premium."

"But it'll get fixed," she insisted, as though he missed the point. "You might even get some good contracts from the Bureau or the Association for the lost income. It's not all bad, and might end up for the better!" Her positivity seemingly aggravated him further as he kicked a massive chunk of rubble about ten feet away.

Sal couldn't follow their conversation as they walked out of earshot. He wasn't sure what to believe. Clearly the man wanted someone to blame for the invasion, and emotions would naturally be high after losing a business. Sal couldn't imagine how he'd feel if the Argento Auction House was destroyed by demons. Well, actually he could, and he'd be far more in line with the man's reaction than his friend's.

"Are you with the bureau?" Another person came up to Sal. "Was Hamilton Avenue hit?" It was an elderly man with a haggard, weary expression. It looked as if he had been dragged through the battle by the scuff of his neck, which told Sal that he had been clearing through the wreckage with the others.

"I'm a student at Quest Academy offering Support." Sal found that leading with that statement was best. Identifying as a guild was the worst introduction, as it invited victims into a tirade of how ineffective the association was. "The Hunter Bureau has created a database of the impacted areas, and you can see if you're entitled to compensation and emergency accommodations. I'm sorry that I don't have more information."

The elderly man just looked at Sal for a few seconds before nodding. "Thank you." He tried to smile, but there was far too much bitterness in his voice. With a frown overtaking his expression, he turned and moved off to find someone else to talk to.

Sal waited on the spot for another while, wondering whether there would be more people coming to speak with him. There were close to a hundred people from the United Guilds Association, all at varying ranks and with differing uniforms. The key difference was that Sal's outfit was covered in marks from battle, while the others looked pristine. Maybe that's why people thought he'd have more information than the others.

"You're still here?" a familiar voice announced with a good-natured chuckle.

Sal turned to see the man he had followed when the announcements happened. The massive sword on his back was smeared with blood of varying colors. An attempt to wipe it down had only made it worse, but he didn't seem to care as he approached, grinning widely. "I'm still here." Sal smiled. "Glad to see you're alive."

The clap on his shoulder should have been enough to make his knees buckle, but he stood firm and maintained the easygoing smile. The additional stats had clearly made him far sturdier than before.

"Purple and silver. Don't know those colors…are you with the Reavers?" He offered his hand to Sal. "Oswald. I'm a Hunter with the Bureau."

Sal accepted the handshake. "Salvatore. I'm the guildmaster of the Mythic Guild." It was the first time he had introduced himself as such, and he half expected ridicule from Oswald. Still, it felt good to say it out loud.

Oswald's jaw dropped as he looked at Sal strangely. "Holy shit. Are you serious?"

Sal wasn't following. Was he playing with him because they were a brand-new guild? Sal could read expressions pretty well, even without the visor. It didn't look like he was being made fun of. "Yeah, we're still Tier 8 and based out of Quest Academy for the moment, but we'll be going through the ranks eventually."

"Fucking right you will," Oswald declared as he wiped his hand over his bald head with a laugh. "Your guild took out like six commander classes! The whole front line was freaking the fuck out."

Sal stared at him for a few seconds, not registering the words he had just heard. "How did you know that? I didn't get any notifications or reports about the battle." He reached for his tablet, but Oswald just waved his hand dismissively, like it was a useless endeavor.

He pointed at his ear. "Hunter Network. We have shared communications, and we got reports from all the battles happening around Haven." Oswald's grin widened as he tapped Sal's shoulder with a relieved sigh. "So, does that mean you're the kid with lightning?"

Before Sal could even respond, Oswald lifted his hand from Sal's shoulder. "Wait, sorry…force of habit." He chuckled with a slight shake of his head. "Can't call you a kid when you've taken out a commander. It's nice to meet you, Guildmaster of the Mythic Guild."

"My friends call me Sal." Sal smiled, relieved that he had seemingly earned the stranger's respect.

"Then I endeavor to one day earn that right." Oswald laughed as he looked at the wreckage around him. "They're not seriously stationing you here like this after the fight, are they? You guys were top of the leaderboard."

"I'm a Support class." Sal shrugged as he gestured around them. "The United Guilds Association instructed me to do this, and I already wanted to help."

Oswald snorted at the ridiculousness of it. He glanced over at another Hunter who was covered head to toe in plate armor. A golden light hung like a crown over his head, and everyone who stood within its glow seemed energized. "Justice! Come here for a sec!"

The armored knight snapped his attention to Oswald and moved instantly. All the people who had been bathing in the glow of his crown looked devastated by his departure. In just a few seconds, he stood at attention in front of Oswald, as though waiting for a command.

Oswald looked at him and pointed at Sal. "This is the guildmaster of the Mythic Guild."

Justice's eyes widened, and Sal was able to see gold irises, similar to Erika's when she used her powers, but far less terrifying. Justice pointed at Sal silently, as though asking Oswald if he was being serious.

"And they have him doing canvassing." Oswald folded his arms with an incredulous expression. "Help me make sense of that."

"It makes no sense," Justice replied in a surprisingly gentle voice. His armor creaked as he shifted on the spot, as though he was unsure why he had been summoned. Glancing at Oswald for a moment, and then back at Sal, he continued speaking in an unsure tone. "He should be celebrating?"

"Bingo." Oswald smiled as he nudged Justice's chest plate. "You're learning fast." He winked at Sal before turning to Justice. "Now, what class do you think he is?"

"Offense," Justice answered immediately. He glanced at Sal's outfit before nodding in agreement of his own assessment. "Purple means Support, but he's not a Support."

"That's what I thought, too." Oswald smiled as he gave Sal an appraising look. "Some incredible armor you've got there. Looks perfect for the front lines. My eyes were never great at picking out grades, but it's definitely better than Rare."

"It's Legendary," Justice answered, as though it were a question. "Except the arm." He pointed at the Mythical blight jackal. There wasn't a shred of doubt in his voice.

Okay, maybe the golden eyes were a *little* terrifying.

Sal had already told himself that he wasn't going to keep secrets. He had named the Mythic Guild because of Mythcrafter, but it didn't mean he needed to recklessly divulge every detail to people. With that in mind, he used the lie he had been concocting. It would align with the facts that had already been established, and would potentially reduce people's expectations of him.

"The outfit is Legendary grade, and it was made by a team of people who are either in the Mythic Guild or helping out." Sal smiled as he looked at Justice. "I'm able to make evolutionary runes that can bring items up to the Mythic grade. You might have seen the sniper rifle at the Reavers Guild?"

Oswald's eyes widened as he let out a whistle. "Man, there's even less reason for you to be out here dealing with all the sad sacks." He shook his head. "Fierce wouldn't shut up about that damn gun. To think you were the one who made it."

Justice, on the other hand, stared at Sal in a mixture of awe and disbelief. "So, your arm is Mythic grade? It's supposed to be impossible. Stryker and Ameye have countless talks on how it's potentially feasible through evolutionary runes, but it's all just theory." His whole torso, which was significant, came closer to Sal as he leaned in to speak. "How can you be an Offense…and make Mythic-grade runes?"

"Easy, Justice." Oswald tapped him on the shoulder. "Salvatore has been very kind in answering our questions, and he's probably exhausted from all the fighting today. Let's not interrogate him. He's a Support class, not an Offense. I was surprised, too."

Justice looked like he wanted to argue, but backed down after a moment. "You've given me a lot to think about. Thank you."

Oswald nodded as Justice moved back over to the original group he had been showering with light. Sal noted that there were no effects when he had come over to them, so he wondered whether it was designed to heal people.

"He's a little direct, but he means well." Oswald chuckled as he gestured at Justice's retreating form. "He's a wonderful Vanguard in battle. Now that he knows your name, if he ever sees you in need, you'll be saved."

"That's reassuring." Sal laughed awkwardly, not sure what to make of the encounter. "It was nice to meet you. It's probably rude to ask what Hunter rank you are? I'm still learning the ropes, so feel free to not tell me."

"Top five hundred or so." Oswald shrugged, as though it were no big deal. "Probably up or down twenty based on my performance today. I'm more of a slugger, so dealing with volume isn't a good match-up. You put me in a drawn-out fight with a big bastard, and I'll jump a hundred places." He grinned in such a way that Sal knew it wasn't an idle statement.

"Should you have a Hero name, you know, like Justice?" Sal pointed at the armored knight who was bent at the hip to pick up some rubble.

Oswald shook his head. "Nah, I don't bother using it anymore. It wasn't a fancy one that inspires people. If people are going to remember me, I'd rather it be for my family and our legacy." He brought his hands together gently. "Speaking of which…you're at Quest Academy? Are you taking on new members for your guild?"

Sal was suddenly unsure where this was going, but he was happy to humor the man. "I think we're at capacity at the moment, but head count will increase as we move up the ranks."

Oswald smiled broadly. "I've got a second-year there. Shouldn't be too hard to find them—they'll be the only ones with the Oswald surname. If they're shit, don't recruit them…but I'd be a bad father if I didn't ask you to take a look."

"He's an Offensive slugger, I take it?" Sal laughed as he gestured broadly at Oswald. There was a very high chance that his kid had the same genetic ability, and if they were stronger than their father, then Sal would be very interested to see how the power manifested. Being honest, there were already a lot of members, but he didn't want to be rude.

"*She*…is a Support." Oswald's smile faded ever so slightly. "It's rare coming across a guild with a Support class as its master…so, you know, I thought I'd ask. You don't know me and don't owe me anything, but I just want to ensure the kid has a chance."

"I'll see what we can do," Sal promised him. "Is she a Crafter?"

Oswald shook his head sadly. "She has this Supercharge ability…thing?"

Sal was immediately reminded of Anthony. "Oh, she can boost the grades of items? It's a great ability. We have someone with that exact ability in the guild." He expected a smile or something from Oswald, but all he got was confusion as his response.

Oswald frowned as he shook his head slowly. "She can't do that. She can only boost people. Does she need to learn how to Craft? I'm sure she'd pick it up pretty quickly—she's a smart girl."

Sal just stared at him. It didn't sound like Amplify, especially if she was a Support. There was nothing to lose by meeting her. "I look forward to speaking with her."

"Good." Oswald smiled in relief. "Now, I think we should get you back to Quest Academy. You look like you're ready to collapse into bed. The Hunter Bureau can afford to send their own people here to clean up."

CHAPTER 82: VENT

Oswald managed to become one of Sal's all-time favorite people… not for the conversation, but for the fact that he got Sal sent back to Quest Academy. The notification had been sent through to his tablet, and he was finally relieved of service with an apology from the United Guilds Association for the mix-up in messaging.

His participation in the invasion hadn't been recorded by their tracker, so they had allocated him Support duties for the cleanup activities. The fact that the Hunter Bureau had been the ones to acknowledge his guild's contributions was wild. Vanessa had to sit through a series of debriefs with Chatfield and Villa. Mica and Seth had pretty much vanished onto the evacuation ships the moment they arrived, and Sal regretted not going with them. It was good for him to see how the aftermath was dealt with, but he was pretty exhausted from a full day of fighting and talking to despairing residents.

The amphitheater was packed with people when Sal walked there from the train stop. It felt odd that he was one of the only people on the service getting off at Quest Academy, and although he could have certainly afforded a taxi, he wanted time to decompress. His armor was still equipped because his shirt was lost somewhere in Haven. Had he been thinking clearly, he would have put his shirt in Arsenal so he could change back afterward, but the whole invasion thing had been playing on his mind.

Sal looked up at the holographic screens that were showcasing the destruction of Pinnacle and Shard. Without context, it looked like a propaganda video concocted to show how badass humanity were against the demons. The cheers of the crowd were deafening, and Sal was a little annoyed by their celebration as he walked around them toward the dormitories. It was an odd feeling, but he felt somehow disconnected from them. Weren't they training to be Heroes?

The irony wasn't lost on Sal, who didn't possess a shred of conviction for months and would have happily sat in that crowd just a few months ago, rejoicing over the security and safety that Quest Academy provided them. He wondered whether his friends were in the crowd, and what they were feeling as they watched the destruction.

Closing his eyes for a moment and taking a deep breath, Sal continued his journey toward the dorms. He was exhausted, that's all it was. There was no point in belittling the joy of others because he was in a bad mood. Dozens of faces kept appearing in his mind. All the people who had lost something during the invasion… the fact that they were just resigned to it, as though it was within their expectations. If that was the new normal, Sal hated it. They should have been angry with him. They should have been emotional.

"Welcome back, Mr. Argento." Quest spoke as he stood up from one of the benches on Sal's route.

"Oh, I didn't see you there," Sal responded with a slight smile as he put a hand to his chest. Perfect had been running all day, and it would take a lot more to actually surprise him.

"Have a seat." He gestured at the bench beside him. "I'd like to talk about what happened today."

"Can it wait until tomorrow?" Sal remained standing. "It's been a long day, and I'm emotionally drained. Every little thing is annoying me, and I don't want to take it out on you."

Quest shook his head. "Have a seat."

Sal sighed inwardly as he looked at the dormitory tower in the distance that was still within reach. All he had to do was shake off the headmaster and in less than ten minutes, he'd be in the shower, and ready for bed. It sounded positively euphoric, but he couldn't. Quest didn't look angry, so it probably wasn't going to be a lecture. His bed could wait a few more minutes.

Sitting down on the bench, Sal faced the amphitheater, wincing at the new-found cheers from the student body. "Can we at least go somewhere else?"

Quest looked at him quietly for a moment. "Captain Chatfield informed me that you were one of the first on the scene... and saw the deceased members of the Delvers Guild."

Sal blinked as he looked at Quest in confusion. "Is that what you wanted to talk about?"

Quest looked at Sal carefully. "You told me yesterday that you had a method to solve the problem with the Delvers Guild."

Sal's mouth dropped open as he stared at the headmaster. "You don't think I killed them, do you?"

Quest's eyes widened. "Of course not!" An awkward laugh escaped his lips as he stared at Sal. "Heavens, no... wow. No! That is *not* what I meant. I know you would never do something like that." He shook his head, still laughing at the ridiculousness of it.

When he calmed down, he tried again, this time planting his hands on his knees and smiling at Sal. "What I meant to say... was that I didn't want you solving this problem by yourself. I had the Delvers removed from the Advanced War Zone class, and was in the process of securing new instructors for the module. I guessed that keeping you busy would mitigate any opportunity of you going rogue."

Sal bit his lip. "Ah."

Quest nodded. "Yeah, and then you managed to solve your problem in less than twenty-four hours. Shade has been arrested, and both Eclipse and Enigma have offered their services for the Advanced War Zone class and individual master classes. Both Barry Francis and Rochelle de Verdon have been requested." He looked at Sal with an exasperated expression. "I was really proud of that schedule. I half expected you to storm into my office so we could reach a compromise. It was obnoxiously packed."

"I noticed," Sal muttered with a smile as he pulled out his tablet and ignored the countless messages, navigating to the schedule. "A little excessive, don't you think? I don't even get lunch breaks on some days."

Quest sighed as he spread his hands. "I tried to harness that monstrous work ethic toward your classes while I ensured there were no more fears regarding the Delvers Guild. I picked the wrong approach this time, and wanted to apologize for that."

Sal forced a smile to his face and started to stand up. "Apology accepted."

"I'm not done. We still need to talk about that evacuation order." Quest touched Sal's elbow. "You enlisted two students into your guild, for the sole reason of allowing them to engage in combat."

Sal sat down, sighing. "As guildmaster, isn't that my right?" He was done with the conversation and just wanted it to be over. Quest had been well-intentioned, but had placed unnecessary roadblocks in front of him. The schedule hadn't actually changed anything, as Sal was already in Haven when he got the updates.

Quest looked at Sal seriously. "Where has this reckless abandon come from? Are you not aware of how valuable your skills are? Athena has the potential to revolutionize how we interact with Skill Weaves. Your elixir machine will undoubtedly end up creating something extraordinary in the future, I've got no doubts about it." He looked genuinely confused as he continued. "There's no reason for you to be throwing yourself into danger like this. I understand the desire to have your guild progress through the rankings, but this... to face against a commander so early in your journey is incredibly irresponsible."

"Mica has already taken out four. Five if you count the war spider." Sal tried to answer neutrally, but he couldn't help the defensive tone that seeped through. "I don't think there's that big of a difference. I have a lot to catch up on, and my equipment is more than capable of protecting me."

"Michaela Egan is an Offense class who has been training her whole life," Quest corrected him with a meaningful look. "I can overlook you taking her into your guild, but Seth McDuffee is far more fragile. You already know that he's working closely with Professor Maxwell on Advanced Tactics. He shouldn't have been out there, and neither should you."

Another cheer from the crowd caused Sal to frown. "Would you prefer that I was sitting in the amphitheater right now, with the rest of them?" He pointed at them just so Quest had no doubts to what he was talking about. "I don't know what you want from me, Quest. If I was supposed to be a Support class who avoids Combat... then why did you throw me into a tournament and then the excursion? The tower was a nonnegotiable, and next is likely going to be a portal expedition. I built a guild and want to see it progress through the ranks. The battle today in Haven was an absolute shit-show and I know... *I know* that the Mythic Guild would handle it better. Hell, Vanessa pretty much took out half of the enemy leadership by herself. How good will she be when I make Mythic gear for her?"

Quest stared at Sal for a few moments, not saying a word. Sal was more than happy to take that time from him.

"People wouldn't evacuate, they didn't follow orders, and just pointed at each other, looking for someone to blame. The barriers broke way too easily... and there was so much chaos. None of those buildings were properly defended, and the Hunters just blew through everything without needing to. You couldn't see through the smoke, and a hulker managed to flank us; the slowest, biggest demon, *flanked* us." Sal was incensed as he thought about it all, his anger growing with every word.

"And the residents who were there, they just accepted it. They weren't angry with me, and they lined up to be told that they have to wait for compensation? No fight, no complaints, just acceptance and moving on. How often does this happen that people's hope is crushed? It's unfair, and I hated it. If Shade hadn't been such a greedy prick, his people wouldn't have died. Why has the Hunter Bureau been protecting him for this fucking long when he's a slimy son of a bitch? Does he literally need to murder someone in broad daylight to get punished?"

Sal pointed at the amphitheater. "And this! They're just sitting there, laughing and joking without knowing the fear and pain that is on the other side of that screen. Why aren't they grieving for those who were lost? Why aren't they at the devastated battlefield helping the survivors with the cleanup?" Sal's voice trembled. It had been hoarse from all the talking in the day, and now it had finally cracked, as his emotions came out in a jumble.

"I know that I wasn't the perfect student. That I was scared, and I get that. I'm getting better and I'll continue to get better." Sal looked at Quest as he took a shuddering breath. "I will get stronger and my guild will be unstoppable. In what world does it make sense that a first-year Support and his Credit floor advisor took out more than half of the thirteen commanders in Haven?"

Sal pointed at himself. "I know how many people would have died when that commander broke through the Support lines. Villa would be dead, too. If I wasn't there, Quest, they would all be dead. I refuse to apologize for being there, and I refuse to justify my actions because I'd do it all again. I'd be better, smarter, and more experienced."

Quest nodded. "How can I help?"

Sal opened his mouth, but no sound came out. He tried again, and managed to croak out a single word. "What?"

"How can I help you going forward?" Quest repeated with a smile. "My judgments have *clearly* been off, and it would be a crime to try to waver that conviction of yours. The best thing I can do is to facilitate you and help you on your journey to ensure it's as safe as possible. So, how can I help you?"

Sal's shoulders slumped as he offered a halfhearted shrug. "I… have no idea. There are so many broken things, and I've got no idea where to even begin."

"I'd start with the barriers." Quest smiled. "Prevent the invasions from happening in the first place. That can be a later conversation, though. You should probably get some rest." He got to his feet and took a few paces forward, looking at the amphitheater for a moment before turning back to Sal.

"Thank you for what you did today, Salvatore. My worries should never overshadow your accomplishments. Your recounting of today's events, no matter how colorful, pales in comparison to the call I had with Captain Chatfield a few hours ago."

Sal smiled weakly. "I doubt he was happy with how it all played out."

"An understatement if there ever was one." Quest returned the smile. "But he was very impressed with how you conducted yourself, and more than a little curious how you managed to get Vanessa Blake onto your side."

Quest put his hands on his hips as he looked at Sal curiously. "But I do want you to tell me something… did you see Upgrade at any point during your fight in Haven?" He raised his hands. "I don't want to alarm you, because we have no reason to believe she was there… but both she and Fabrizia are unaccounted for at the moment. They have been clearing quite a number of dungeons together recently, so it's not yet a cause for concern, but I just wanted to check with you."

Sal frowned as he thought about it… until realization dawned. "Oh."

"Oh?" Quest inquired with a raised eyebrow. "Do you know where they are? We've already tried the workshops and the usual roster of dungeons they frequent." It was clear that there was a touch of worry in his voice, but he was trying to keep his composure.

Sal nodded with a guilty laugh, remembering that both Fabrizia and Upgrade turned off their tablets so they could concentrate. "They're in my room, working on Athena."

CHAPTER 83: SUBSUME

"Oh! Just the man we wanted to see!" Upgrade laughed as she stumbled past Fabi, who lay down on the ground with both hands over her face.

"Is she okay?" Sal pointed at Fabi.

Upgrade snorted as she shook her head. "Prime corrected her code. She's still recovering her pride." She immediately switched topics as she looked past Sal, to where Quest stood. "We're ready for those databases. How many can you give us?"

Fabi brought her hands away from her face to glare at Upgrade. Her expression softened as she caught sight of Sal in the Tempest Marshal outfit. "Oh, did you get to a dungeon?"

"He did not." Quest answered for him as he looked at Upgrade. "You haven't been checking your tablet. I've been trying to get in contact with you all day."

Upgrade pointed at all the terminals displaying countless blocks of text. "We were working with Athena nonstop since we last saw you. You've no idea how amazing this thing is!"

Fabi nodded as she sat up. "It's far better than we thought, and Prime is genuinely unbelievable. I've got zero doubts that it's superior to Protocol."

Quest raised an eyebrow as a smile overtook his face. "And you think it's ready for the databases? You've made sure there are no security risks?"

"We've got all sorts of partitions in place." Upgrade grinned as she pointed at each screen in sequence. "Prime will have its own separate instance for the Arkwr—" She paused and corrected herself mid-sentence, as though unsure whether Quest knew about the Arkwright. "Sorry, for Sal's own devices. We didn't want Athena to be completely monopolized by the Legion project. This way, he won't get bogged down with the processing times when Athena is solving everyone else's problems."

"If there even will be processing times," Fabi muttered. "It's a monster of processing capability. I haven't seen a single loading screen, which is why I'm pretty excited to see it struggle with the databases. I've thrown in all the learning materials from the Credit Store that I accumulated in the last three years, and it didn't even flicker."

"What else did you put into it?" Quest folded his arms. "I can give it access to the Quest System if you think that would be beneficial. The records would be out of date, but there could still be some value in them."

Upgrade nodded slowly. "Yeah, it's tearing through things and ripping apart fallacies. It started correcting some of Fabi's courses. That was quite entertaining—so be warned… Prime will absolutely poke holes in your best work."

"I look forward to it." Quest grinned as he withdrew a Q-Card. "Do you have a reader set up, or are we doing things through the network?"

Sal looked at Quest with a tired smile. "Can I go and have a shower? Or do you need me here for this part?" He was interested in everything they were talking about, but his emotional battery was at an all-time low. They would eventually be told about the whole invasion thing, and Sal was a little surprised that Quest hadn't led with it. Maybe the headmaster knew that he didn't want to answer questions and just wanted rest. If that was the case, Sal was grateful.

Quest shook his head with a gentle smile and gestured toward the bedroom. "Go for it. I'll give them the rundown of everything that happened. Just rest up and don't worry about that schedule. It'll be far more manageable when you wake up."

Upgrade's gaze narrowed. "He managed to sweet-talk you into changing the schedule?" She looked at Quest in disbelief. "I absolutely need to hear this."

"Chat tomorrow." Sal's shoulders slumped in relief as he smiled at both Fabi and Upgrade. "Can't wait to hear about Athena. Good luck with the databases."

"What's going on?" Upgrade asked in genuine concern as she turned her attention from Sal back to Quest.

Sal wasn't going to get drawn into another conversation, though. He was in the safety of his own dorm, and on the way to the bedroom, he sent the Tempest Marshal and Mythical blight jackal to Arsenal. He couldn't have cared less if they saw him topless. He had been dreaming of getting out of it for hours.

By the time his room door was closed, he had managed to strip off everything else. His zombie-like shuffle to the bathroom was in a fugue state, and Sal was excited to just wash off all the fatigue of the day. He didn't want to talk to Upgrade and Fabi. If he snapped at them like he had with Quest, he'd have felt horrible. Their enthusiasm for Athena had annoyed him, and it made no sense. So, it was better for him to decompress and get some rest.

The shower was everything Sal had dreamed of. Waterjets at full heat took all the grime from his body, and gave instant relief to the remaining aches and pains. Regenerate was excellent for healing, but muscle fatigue still needed good old-fashioned sleep. He knew that he'd be unconscious the moment his head hit the pillow.

After his shower, Sal dried himself off and got dressed. The first thing he noticed was how tight the T-shirt was on his chest. There was actual stretching on the fabric, and Sal had to do a double take when he saw himself in the mirror. His shoulders had broadened… again? It wasn't a massive difference, but it did look like his frame had filled out more. Turning around, he saw a pocket of empty space between his shoulder blades. Just rotating his arms gave him an incredible appreciation of the new physique.

With a tired smile, Sal threw the towel into the laundry basket and made his way into the bedroom. He looked at his visor on the bedside table and decided there would be no harm in checking the new stats he had accrued throughout the day.

He sat on his bed, wincing slightly as he pulled his legs up onto the mattress. He propped himself up with every pillow within reach before putting on the visor. With a concentrated effort, he used it to summon the eye-patch from Arsenal. They were probably already synced, but he thought it would be better to use the one he had actually used in combat.

A familiar report was waiting for him in the statistic menu. He looked through it for a few seconds, quietly appreciating the impact a single commander class had on his stats.

Assimilate Function Report (1)
- o   Strength has increased by 1.23
- o   Mobility has increased by 1.91
- o   Speed has increased by 3.87
- o   Endurance has increased by 1.56
- o   Skill Master has improved by 0.7
- o   Mythcrafter has improved by 0.7

When he undid the filters, he was able to see a snapshot of where his stats were currently. He had expected an improvement, but he wasn't prepared for just how dramatic the jump had been.

Salvatore Argento Stats:
- o   Strength: 13.2
- o   Mobility: 19.8
- o   Speed: 17.2
- o   Awareness: 3.4
- o   Endurance: 11.7
- o   Fitness: 14.5

"Awareness?" Sal repeated the word that appeared below the Speed stat. Was it something that was unlocked because of his battle? If he had to guess, it would have been the split-second decision to charge at the commander. Was that Awareness? Or was it from noticing the razor wire and stopping Seth from advancing? Both of those times were judgments rather than physical reactions, though. How could it possibly quantify his ability to notice things?

Sal navigated to the Stratagem Function report. There was an unread notification, and Sal guessed that the Harvesting level had increased dramatically after the amount of loot Jackal ate.

Jackal has learned a new Ability:
- ■   Subsume Target: Arachne Titan [Elite] [Psionic] [Invention]
- ■   Subsumed Ability: Deathtrap [Rare] [Invention]
- ■   Subsumed Ability Grade: 8 [Rare]

It took quite a bit of time for Sal to register what he had just seen. Deathtrap would need to be verified in a dungeon, but Sal was pretty sure that it was the same ability that allowed the war spider, which was apparently an arachne titan, to make those razor wires. That said, it could have been an ability that let it burrow into things, but that didn't seem particularly interesting. Sal couldn't help but feel a little disappointed that the Subsume grade cap only went up to eight, as it looked like he might have gotten a better ability if Jackal's evolution was higher.

He could see an option for him to select "Forget," which would remove the Deathtrap ability for Jackal. Instead, Sal locked it in place. With four slots in total, there was no point in trying to optimize the abilities until he was at capacity. By that point, he'd have hopefully managed to get Jackal evolved to a higher state, and would have more room to pick and choose abilities.

Sal bit his lip as he read through the report again. He had taken out a commander in close combat, and that hadn't been enough to grant Jackal an ability through Subsume. The arachne titan must have been different. Was it because of the Invention tag that appeared beside the name? Was Sal only going to be able to Subsume abilities that fit Replication and Invention?

Navigating to the Assimilation results again, Sal went looking for the increases to his own ability grades. He wasn't sure whether there would be anything dramatic there waiting for him, but it was worth checking.

Tempest Function Report (492)
- o   Skill Master has increased to 14.7
- o   Mythcrafter has increased to 20.1

Sal stared at the number of killed demons. Unless it was counting the individual tiny spiders, there was no way it could be that many. Five hundred kills would have put his Speed stat at closer to thirty if it was the case. He navigated through the reports and was surprised to see that the drop-off that Fabi referenced seemed to happen as he approached the higher numbers. The point zero six stat for each small spider eventually dwindled to a point zero one by the end. Was it diminishing returns for repeated use? Or was it just that he got an initial larger boost because his starting values were so low?

He was happy to see that he was only a few fractions away from reaching the cap for Skill Master. There was still a long way to go for Mythcrafter, but that was fine. Endurance needed to be another seven points higher before he could safely use All Sight, so it was a definite improvement.

Reaching up to pull the eye-patch off his face, Sal dismissed it into Arsenal by using his visor for a second. He then dropped the visor back onto the bedside table and settled onto the bed, pulling the pillows out from under him and relaxing back with a heavy sigh. There were definite improvements, and… being honest, far more than he deserved. Just one invasion with the Subsume and Assimilation abilities had skyrocketed his stats up to an unbelievable level.

He didn't think he was ever going to be on par with Vanessa for raw combat potential, but he guessed that he would be closer in potential to Darren Lenihan. Sal wasn't going to experiment by jumping off buildings or anything like that, but he would need to test out the new stats one way or another.

As he closed his eyes, wishing for a good night of sleep, Sal started to think about what he could make with the arachne titan materials. White and gold were a great color scheme, and if they had Psionic and Invention properties, then it would be a very good match for Divinity, or even Fabi.

If it could regenerate like the arachne titan, then it would be great for Vanessa. Maybe even Rochelle? A smile tugged at his lips when he thought of Crafting something for Barry or Divinity… made from a giant demonic spider.

CHAPTER 84: PRIME

Sal awoke to the streams of sunlight crossing his face. Blinking rapidly, he pushed himself up to look around the room blearily. He could hear the sounds of conversation coming from the next room, and it was definitely a cause for confusion. Had they not left last night?

Getting out of bed, Sal dressed himself in the basic black uniform and smoothed back his hair. He went into the bathroom to brush his teeth, and he was pleasantly surprised to see that his tired mind hadn't been playing tricks on him. His body had definitely shifted and changed through all the stat improvements. Maybe that was why he was starving? It could have been the fact that he hadn't eaten in a day, or it could have been the stats. It was hard to know.

After a few twists and turns to admire the new shape, Sal smiled and exited the bathroom and made his way out to the living room, pausing only to retrieve his visor from the bedside table. He felt well rested and there weren't many aches or pains in his body. After all the exertion of yesterday, he half expected to be in crippling pain, but was pleasantly surprised.

When he opened the door to the voices, he was surprised to see Coach in the room with Quest, Upgrade, and Fabi. It was unexpected, as the man had a far worse schedule than even the one Quest made as Sal's new schedule.

"Salvatore!" Coach exclaimed, smiling widely. "I heard all about your exploits yesterday. A truly incredible achievement." The mirth seemed to drain away from his face as he stared at Sal's chest.

Sal understood what had happened. "Okay…I can explain."

Quest looked at Coach with a raised eyebrow, but clearly couldn't see what was upsetting the taller man.

Coach blinked as he lifted a hand to point at Sal. "It's been… less than two days." He looked up from Sal's chest to lock eyes with him. "What did you do to increase your Endurance that dramatically? It shouldn't be possible."

Upgrade's smile tightened, as she knew the answer, but wasn't sure what she could share. She looked at Sal as though asking for permission to fill in the gaps.

Rather than having her explain, Sal did it himself. "I discovered a venomstone. It's a Crafting component that can give the Assimilation ability, which allows me to siphon off the stats of demons. There were over four hundred confirmed kills with the ability yesterday, so it really elevated my scores."

"Assimilation," Quest repeated, rolling the word on his tongue. "Is it a temporary boost to your capabilities?"

"Permanent," Sal answered, thankful that the focus was on Assimilation rather than Subsume. They didn't really need to know about Jackal. And if they did ask, he could always say that the blight core evolved from a venomstone. Considering he was the only one who could make evolutionary weaves toward Mythic, it was a safe lie.

"Could that be incorporated into uniforms?" Quest asked, almost scared of the answer. "Or is it too valuable a resource for mainstream equipment? Where did the venomstone come from?"

Coach glanced back at him in disbelief. "Your first thought is to equip people with this sort of capability? It throws out every semblance of balance and progression. What are you teaching them if they can just skip to the finish line without putting in the work?"

Quest shook his head slowly. "He said it himself, he killed four hundred demons with that ability, which is plenty of work by my estimation." He spread his hands as though it wasn't an unreasonable ask. "If it was able to give the students a proper grounding, and was able to cover their shortcomings, then why wouldn't we explore it?" Quest's attention moved to Upgrade. "Was this something he achieved with your guidance?"

Upgrade pointed at Sal. "Salvatore was able to create it during the break with material synthesis. The project Doc Ameye helped him with was able to produce it after eating countless resources."

Sal smiled inwardly. The countless other resources were just standard leecher cores. She was telling the truth, but obscuring the accessibility so he'd be able to deny it if he wanted. With her being asked at point-blank by Quest, he was happy to see Upgrade covering for him. Sal knew there was no malice in anything Quest was asking, and it was genuinely a relief to hear his first questions being around student uniforms. It showed that he was firmly invested in actually helping. The only potential issue in that room was Coach.

"Did you see the improvements to the weaves?" Sal tapped at his chest. "Both Skill Master and Mythcrafter have moved up a few points through the Assimilation ability. It could help people improve their innate abilities as well as their base stats."

Coach hesitated as he looked at Sal carefully. "I'll admit, it's a ridiculous pace of growth; but it could be unstable. Your body hasn't had time to adapt to the improvements, and without a concurrent increase in Mastery, you'll potentially fall into the same condition as Gallant."

Sal sighed as he gestured at Athena. "Is it ready for us to test? We could get it to determine whether the additional stats are a problem, or not."

Upgrade's smile grew wide as she nodded enthusiastically. It was only when she moved closer to the terminals that the trove of empty coffee cups were revealed, confirming his earlier suspicion that they hadn't left the dorm. "We just got the weave database from Coach. He shares his research with Grant, so it was one of the last ones to get sent through. Chatfield got us approval for the Hunter Bureau database, and it was a lot beefier than the one Cooper uploaded onto your tracker. We've got the Scavenger Network in there, too. Vanessa sent that one over."

"And the Quest System," Quest said, almost defensively. "It was a framework I was very proud of." His smile was faint, and Fabi was the one to provide context.

"Prime ripped it apart in seconds and highlighted all of its shortcomings." Fabi grimaced. "But it did that with pretty much all the databases, showing the conflicting information and redundancies." Her attempt to make Quest feel better hadn't exactly been successful.

Upgrade brought her hands together in a clap to catch their attention. "Which is all to say, that yes… Athena is ready for her second maiden voyage."

"Second?" Sal looked at her. "Did you already test it?"

Upgrade's smile remained fixed. "I want you to see, firsthand, how ruthless this fucker of a machine is."

Sal glanced at Fabi for more context, but she shook her head slowly. He ventured a guess as to what happened. "Did it give Upgrade a report?"

"A report would be helpful." Upgrade scoffed. "This thing just tore me to shreds… figuratively. Giving it access to the Credit Store was probably a mistake, because now it thinks it understands Crafting." She paused for a second before snapping her fingers. "Ah, that's what I wanted to say. Give it access to the Arkwright. That's one of the ones we're missing. It's already been synced with the elixir machine; because we were the ones to set that up, we had permissions." She smiled at Sal before offering a guilty shrug. "Quest read the name Arkwright and started asking questions. We were still quite vague, though."

"Mystifyingly so," Quest confirmed in a deadpan tone.

Sal equipped his visor and immediately saw the request. He was surprised to see the prompt ready and waiting, as though it had been pushed to him by Athena. Despite how unnerving that was, he trusted Upgrade and Fabi to keep Prime under control, so he accepted the synchronization request.

One of the terminals lit up, drawing everyone's attention.

"Please show a loading screen," Fabi practically begged, as if to reassure herself that Prime was capable of struggling. "Just a little one."

A pause on the terminal screen was followed with a progression wheel that spun around slowly, catching a few times and remaining stuck before continuing.

"Thank you," Fabi breathed as she looked at Sal gratefully. "Looks like the Mythcrafter algorithm is still too much for Prime."

"Aaaand, it's done." Upgrade laughed, destroying Fabi's momentary relief. "Giving it access should be a great help."

"I don't see how," Sal answered. "Isn't it just more bloat? There's no Crafting involved in this machine, so I don't see how the Mythcrafter algorithm is supposed to help the people who sit in it."

Upgrade grinned as she lifted the red shell casing on Athena, revealing the seat within. "On the contrary, I think you're going to be very pleasantly surprised."

"Not ominous at all…" Sal muttered as he stepped up into the chair and sat down uncertainly. "What do I need to do?"

Upgrade reached up and unclipped his visor. "First of all, you won't be needing this." She smiled as she slid it into her pocket. "You're going to treat it like your Skill Registration."

"You're telling him to blow it up?" Quest raised his eyebrow.

"No, I'm telling him to let Athena see everything he's got," Upgrade corrected him before smiling at Sal. "Athena will pull it from you, like it's testing your limits without you needing to contribute."

"Then how is it like the Skill Registration?" Quest asked in confusion, looking at Fabi and Coach to see whether they were following.

Upgrade sighed as she stepped back and closed the lid over Sal's body. "I haven't slept in two days—give me a break."

Sal was surprised when all noise outside of Athena cut off when the lid shut down around him. The seat was comfortable, and he leaned his head back to test the headrest. If he hadn't just woken up, there would have been a strong chance of him falling asleep within the machine. The clear red sheen started to shimmer around him, and Sal guessed that it was the effects of Athena powering up. He had questions about how many commander cores it would take to power it consistently. They had a few extras since the invasion, but he didn't want it to suddenly cut off during a session.

A tingling sensation washed over Sal's body, and he couldn't help but feel like his internal essence was being lifted through his skin. It wasn't painful, just very surreal. Closing his eyes, he tried to focus internally on his own weaves, and was surprised to see each of his gates lighting up in his own subconscious... all in sequence, as though they were being counted. At the same time, his weaves were being assessed by a foreign essence, as though they were being checked for inefficiencies.

That was when the muscle contractions started. The rippling essence started to flex his muscles, twisting them in a way that was a few touches more than discomfort. It was like an electrical shock had gone through his body, resulting in involuntary spasms happening in a controlled sequence. Sal didn't know how to keep track of everything, as so many things happened around his body at once. When his eyes started to water, he knew, instinctively, that Athena was checking them for defects.

He hesitated and even held his breath, but that didn't last long as his lungs contracted and his breathing capability was assessed. It was absolutely bizarre how quick each of the checks were, and how non-invasive they were at the same time. There was no conceivable way that it was getting enough information from him with just those little moments.

Sal sat there for what felt like just a few minutes, and in that time, his skin had started to sweat, his muscles had been both spasmed and massaged... his joints had a layer of essence weaving through them, while his internal state was going through a gentle version of Vanessa's Configure ability. Nothing was sacred, and Sal felt the invading essence look at every aspect of him. When he tried to concentrate on his own weaves, he saw a flicker of what looked like a reference image. Had Prime just shown him what his weaves were supposed to look like?

A momentary reprieve followed, and Sal was grateful for it as he caught his breath. As far as he could determine, Athena was focused solely on Skill Master. It was the only area he could feel the foreign essence in his body. Looking within, Sal could see the essence swirling around his phantom thread that he used to make new weaves. Sal was a little unsure why it was there, and was about to inspect further when his weave suddenly started to move.

Sal could only watch in shock as his Skill Master weave was seemingly hijacked by Athena and was contorted and reshaped to create a new weave. The glow of activation was a flicker before the weave started to reshape again, with another flicker. Sal didn't know what the weaves meant, and he couldn't for the life of him understand how Athena was able to remotely activate them. Was it going through Grant and Coach's catalogue of weaves to see what his limits were? If that was the case, he might have accidentally created the best training method for increasing his Skill Master ability... well, assuming that something nasty didn't activate and kill him prematurely.

It was only on maybe the twentieth or thirtieth weave that Sal had a guess on what was happening. The simulation orb needed his input to test the feasibility of the weaves he was working on. Prime was apparently doing the same thing, but in reverse, utilizing Sal's Skill Master ability to test new weaves. Sal actually laughed as he realized how ridiculous it was. Was Athena creating a loop for him to endlessly bring up his Skill Master ability, while adding to the database?

After maybe the hundredth or so weave, Athena stopped replicating them. The complexities had massive range, and Sal didn't see a single familiar one. He actually felt like he had learned quite a bit from how those different weaves were structured. Another thing was how Athena created space within the phantom thread. There were small maneuvers that would grant a little extra thread by being smart, and Athena had highlighted those efficiencies.

Sal sat there for a few more seconds, waiting for the lid to open and for the results. That didn't happen as his eyes activated with the Mythcrafter ability. "No way…" Sal breathed as he watched the design in front of him show a Common-grade axe.

"You don't expect me to mentally build this?" Sal asked of the design that hung in the air. He smiled as he looked at it for a few seconds. "Okay then, let's see how fast we can blitz through this."

Sal started to play along with Athena, working on the designs in his eyes. "Let's see what you think of Mythcrafter," he goaded the machine that encased him.

CHAPTER 85: LEGION

Sal's face was white as he exited Athena, almost stumbling out as he turned around to stare at it in disbelief. "How is it able to do all of that?" He practically breathed the question as he looked frantically at Upgrade, who grinned from ear to ear.

"I'm delighted that you went through the same ordeal." She crossed her arms as she pointed at the terminals. "You were in there for close to two hours. I'm guessing it's because of your two separate weaves. I was in there for just under an hour."

Sal shook his head as he rubbed at his face. "Seriously, though. What was it doing? Is that the way it's supposed to work?" He glanced at Coach, suddenly unsure how he should try to explain everything. "It wasn't like an Analysis at all, it was like… a physical examination, and then a series of tests that had to be completed. It pretty much took over my Skill Master ability and started to create weaves by itself."

Upgrade nodded as she pointed at a different terminal. "You've now got your own suitability matrix for Skill Master."

"What?" Sal repeated as he turned to look at the terminal.

Replication Suitability Matrix: Salvatore Argento
- Psionic [Unsuitable] [Point of Failure: Weave 2, Factor 1, Grade 8]
- Mimicry [Unsuitable] [Point of Failure: Weave 1, Factor 1, Grade 5]
- Mobility [Partial Suitability] [Point of Failure: Weave 4, Factor 2, Grade 12]
- Influence [Unsuitable] [Point of Failure: Weave 2, Factor 1, Grade 7]
- Invention [Excellent Suitability] [Point of Failure: Weave 10, Factor 4, Grade 32]
- Replication [Excellent Suitability] [Point of Failure: Weave 8, Factor 3, Grade 26]
- Body Manipulation [Good Suitability] [Point of Failure: Weave 7, Factor 3, Grade 19]
- Energy Manipulation [Good Suitability] [Point of Failure: Weave 7, Factor 3, Grade 18]
- Body Transformation [Unsuitable] [Point of Failure: Weave 1, Factor 1, Grade 4]

"What does factor mean?" Sal looked through the list in confusion. "I know the weaves and grades, but I've never seen factor before."

Coach smiled as he offered a slight shrug. "I had the same question while it was populating all that information. The best guess I can offer is your work on weave evolutions. Factors may be the evolved form of a base ability. Evolve would be a Factor 4, by my understanding."

Sal blinked as he looked between Upgrade and Coach. "Did she tell you about the final form of her weave?"

Coach shook his head and pointed at Athena. "Nope, your machine did. I was reading her report when you came out of your room. I think there are far more interesting insights to learn from yours, though." He caught himself and glanced at Upgrade. "No offense intended."

"None taken. I want to see how Mythcrafter worked. Athena tore my ability to shreds, so I'm hoping she didn't go easy on him." Upgrade laughed as she looked at Sal excitedly. "So, come on, how was it?"

Sal wasn't intentionally ignoring her. He couldn't help but look at the terminal in a whole new light. If this chart was to be believed, then it meant he wasn't incompatible with every weave out there. Athena had run those simulations as a stress test for his body and weaves, with all the points of failure highlighted for safety. Just learning that he had an affinity for Body Manipulation and Energy Manipulation was wild. Sure, his mother was a Body Manipulator... but this was a very fun revelation.

Sal moved onto the next terminal to see what other information was being shown, but it was all over the place. "Is there a way for me to see all this on my visor?"

Upgrade nodded, a little deflated that she wasn't going to get gossip on how traumatizing Athena was to him as a Crafter. "Yeah, it should be already synchronized. But we can also compile a report from all this data. It's just so much that it'll take a bit to parse into something useful."

Sal accepted the offered visor from Upgrade and clipped it onto his face. He wasn't sure whether he'd get another prompt, or whether he'd have to navigate for the insights. Thankfully, it was already waiting for him.

Replication Suitability Matrix: Salvatore Argento
- o   Weave Suitability Complete
- o   Weave Categories Complete
- o   Weave Limitations Complete

That information was what he had just looked at, so Sal navigated to the next one on the list.

Essence Profile: Salvatore Argento
- o   Meditation Method Complete
- o   Customized Essence Profile Complete
- o   Essence Mapping Method Complete
- o   Essence Fortification Method Complete

Sal stared at those entries for a few seconds, not sure how it was even possible. His visor had created a remap of his essence gates, which greatly enhanced his abilities and scores... yet Athena was suggesting it wasn't optimal? Also, the essence fortification, which Lombardi had said was impossible... could be improved beyond twenty-five percent?

Sal went into the files and saw exactly what he had expected: it was the same as the one he had done on his visor, but with far more complexity and justifications. He couldn't make any sense of it, and rather than feeling excited, he was more intimidated. Those memories of hugging a toilet and vomiting for close to three days were too fresh in his mind for him to be excited. Sal did not want a repeat of that experience.

When he went to the meditation method, he was happy to see that the breathing technique that Barry showed him was the best method available. How Athena had managed to assess all of that within such a short timeframe was ridiculous.

Legion System Profile: Salvatore Argento
- o   Customized Legion System Profile Complete
- o   Skill Master Progression Framework has been added
- o   Mythcrafter Progression Framework has been added
- o   Scavenger Network Progression Framework has been added
- o   Hunter Bureau Ranker Progression Framework has been added
- o   Quest Academy Student Progression Framework has been added
- o   United Guilds Association Progression Framework has been added

Legion Conquest Profile: Salvatore Argento
- o   Customized Legion Conquest Profile Complete
- o   Demonic Bestiary has been added
- o   Demonic Territory has been added
- o   Demonic Bounty System has been created

"What am I even looking at here?" Sal laughed nervously as he read through all the headings. Each of them practically invited him to go into them for more context. "I thought we were testing the concept of the Legion System, rather than just rolling it out?"

Quest cleared his throat awkwardly. "Well, as Fabrizia said… it pretty much took the Quest System, and tore it apart." He gestured vaguely at the monitors that reflected what Sal was seeing in his tracker. "It took my framework and radically improved it. I never even considered separating personal and professional progression; so, for it to go a step further in creating another track to eradicate the demons? I'm sufficiently speechless."

Sal stared at him for a few seconds before looking at Upgrade. "Wait, so it just made all of this based on Quest's old guild System?"

Upgrade nodded happily. "You'll probably have the same setup as my report, but it'll have a whole section in there that's designed to bring up your main ability. For me, it pretty much gave me a schedule of homework I need to do."

"You… have to do homework?" Sal repeated the words in disbelief. "But you know everything when it comes to Crafting, and you've already made a Legendary grade. What does it think you need to learn?"

Upgrade smiled warmly, either from the praise, or from Sal saying something stupid, he was unsure. She shook her head a little. "It's telling me I need to learn how to do Assembly and Repair. Build up my weave from the ground up, rather than trying to push Upgrade to its limits. There are a lot of small exercises and methods it's suggesting for me to use trace amounts of essence in each session to build up the actual capability."

"To what end?" Sal tried to make sense of it all. "Is it going to get your Upgrade ability to turn into Evolve?"

"Apparently." Upgrade shrugged. "But first I need the earlier versions, and it's made a whole plan for me to get there."

"Whoa," Sal breathed as a smile tugged at his lips. "I guess we can call it a success?" He looked around to see whether the verdict was unanimous.

Fabi wore a grimace as she looked at the terminals. "I don't know how I feel about the leveling up thing. It kinda trivializes the danger. Rewarding people with a bounty system will likely backfire, too." She glanced over at Sal with a slight smile. "I mean, I think the stuff relating to abilities is incredible, but I'm not really sure about how it'll actually help people improve."

Quest nodded in agreement. "That was one of the key aspects that failed with the Quest System. There was no substance behind the requirements. We tried to incentivize the guilds by giving them additional funding for achieving high scores, but it eventually lost its luster."

Upgrade snorted as she moved over to tap one of the terminals, changing the contents on the screen as she navigated within Sal's profile to a segment of the Legion System. After a few more taps, she got what she was looking for and blew it up wide across all available screen space, so everyone could see.

Legion System Profile:
- o   Name: Salvatore Argento
  - ▪   Mythcrafter [Invention] [Factor 3, Grade 20]
  - ▪   Skill Master [Replication] [Factor 3, Grade 14]

Tapping on Mythcrafter, Upgrade stepped back so everyone would have a clear view. The smile on her face was evidence that she thought she had just made her point. Beautifully, at that.

Legion System: Mythcrafter Progression Track
Mythcrafter Progression Track
- ▪   [Factor 1: Epicraft] [Grade 18]
- ▪   [Factor 2: Legendcraft] [Grade 24]
- ▪   [Factor 3: Mythcraft] [Grade 30]
- ▪   [Factor 4: Divinecraft] [Grade 42]
- ▪   [Factor 5: Cosmicraft] [Grade 60]

Requirements for Next Factor
Crafting Only: [Select One]
- o   Create Mythic Grade [0/12]
- o   Create Legendary Grade [0/52]
- o   Create Epic Grade [0/261]
- o   Create Unique Grade [0/1,183]

      o   Create Rare Grade [0/3,047]
Assimilation Only: [Select One]
      o   Defeat Elite Commander [0/4]
      o   Defeat Unique Commander [0/7]
      o   Defeat Standard Commander [0/11]

Upgrade tapped on the "Create Legendary Grade" option, creating a drop-down menu. It had a requirement of fifty-two pieces that needed to be completed to ensure evolution to Divinecraft.

Sal was still trying to figure out why Divinity was wrong about the skill names. Was Athena wrong, or was the future changed that much? Celestial Craft wasn't anywhere on the list, and Cosmicraft had replaced it? It wasn't worth overthinking at the moment, and even if Sal wanted to, he wouldn't have been able to manage with the new content that was appearing.

Create Legendary Grade [0/52]
Planning Builder [Athena] [Arkwright]
      o   Build Calculation
      o   Ability Calculation
      o   Material Calculation
      o   Essence Calculation
Required Knowledge [Salvatore Argento]
      o   Essence Infusion
Additional Knowledge [Athena] [Arkwright]
      o   Material Fusion
      o   Material Synthesis
      o   Essence Programming

Sal was curious and navigated to the Ability Calculation section, wondering what he would find. When it opened in front of him, he was greeted by walls upon walls of text, all highlighting which material compositions would result in a specific ability being created. It was clear from the text that Prime had cross-referenced the information from the Arkwright against the database for the simulation orb. It was equally terrifying and impressive, just how much the machine had been able to piece together.

Upgrade grinned. "This is what makes it a game changer. You can pick your own speed, and Legion will adapt to you. We don't need to send someone into a dungeon to take out a commander or a scuttler. They can work in the safety of the workshop and gain the skills a little slower." She looked at Quest meaningfully. "You know better than anyone that the biggest frustration in students is the lack of progress. This will give them a path that will show them how to reach the next stages."

Coach was speechless as he looked at it. He had moved over to a terminal and was going through a series of reports that looked ridiculously dense to Sal. If the man was able to make sense of it, more power to him.

Quest smiled as he looked from the terminals to where Sal stood. "What do you think? Is this what you wanted to achieve with Athena?"

"I don't know," Sal answered truthfully. "It's an awful lot to take in, and I don't exactly know if it's what I expected. With abilities like Revelation and Ascension, I kinda expected it to do the heavy lifting. Like, we'd put someone in, and they'd come out with a perfect weave or something?"

Quest raised an eyebrow. "Salvatore, trust me when I say that it's far better this way. Giving people the information on how they can progress is the best gift possible. It means they'll need to put in the hard work if they want to see the results."

Upgrade nodded sagely before she pointed at Athena. "We're only really scratching the surface with this. There's so much more it has to offer, but we're just not asking it the right questions."

Fabi nodded in agreement. "The dungeon stuff is pretty incredible, too. It pretty much highlighted all the materials we can find in which dungeons, and even created a training plan around taking them down."

Sal stared at Athena while he listened to everyone talking about it. He couldn't help but feel a little excited for what was to come.

"So…is now a good time to ask you about yesterday?" Upgrade crossed her arms. "Quest told us all about you killing a commander."

"What?" Coach asked in disbelief, clearly not there for that conversation. He was unanimously ignored, so with a helpless shrug, he went back to looking at the graphs and reports on the terminal screen.

Sal grinned at Upgrade as he shook his head. "Nope, now's not a good time at all. I think it's a good time for us to have our first-ever guild meeting, though."

"What are you planning, Salvatore?" Quest asked in confusion as he looked between Athena and Sal. "Are you going to invite your members to use Athena?"

"Yeah, and I need to get all their sizes for the new uniforms as well as some signatures." Sal glanced at Upgrade. "We've got something we need to Craft, too. Don't go thinking that I've forgotten."

Upgrade smiled warmly at him. "I appreciate that."

CHAPTER 86: GUILD

"Don't you think this is an abuse of power?" Upgrade asked in utter disbelief as she looked at Quest. "You can't make a school announcement to summon them all here."

"I just did." Quest shrugged as he sat down on one of the stools in the upgraded workshop. "Besides, I'm very invested in the Mythic Guild succeeding. It was more efficient doing it this way than waiting for them to check their tablets during classes."

Sal turned his tablet around to show Upgrade. "Vanessa is on her way, and she's said that Villa might take a little longer to get here, but that she said she'd come."

Fabi held the door open for a very confused Blathnaid and Barry. Anders and Alex had graciously paused their work, and due to Quest sitting just a few feet away from him, Alex was surprisingly silent.

"Who are we waiting for?" Fabi asked as a blur of darkness shot past her, into the room. She blinked and shook her head, laughing. "Please tell me you weren't racing O'Brien."

Sakura skidded to a halt as she surveyed the room in confusion. "I thought it was an emergency. Why else would Quest request me?" Her dagger was suddenly sheathed as she smiled sheepishly, deactivating the stealth aspect of her outfit.

"Oh, it looks great on you!" Blathnaid announced as she moved over to Sakura for a better look. "How is the fit? Do you need any adjustments to it?"

O'Brien arrived next with a confused expression, but when he saw Fabi, a warm smile crossed his lips. "We're here for something fun, then?"

Fabi grinned as she gave him a nod and jutted her chin into the room. "Make yourself comfortable. We've got a few more to wait for."

Sal actually felt bad for Rochelle when he saw her standing at the door, looking uncertain. She hadn't been to the upgraded workshop before, and without the Legendary-grade coat, she was likely feeling a little out of her depth. He waved at her and gestured for her to come in.

Upgrade's eyes lit up when she saw her. "You're the one who wears the Arbiter's Judgment!"

Rochelle's eyes widened, but not in recognition. It probably sounded like an accusation, and she had no idea who she was speaking to. "I'm Rochelle." Sal wanted to ease her into the crowd, but there was seemingly no need.

"Excuse me? You're not just Rochelle... You're Rochelle de Verdon. The Battle-Healer!" Upgrade laughed as she went over to shake her hand. "I keep watching the video of you jumping out that window. That engineer screaming is just perfection."

Rochelle relaxed as she smiled over at Sal. The look of relief on her face spoke volumes. When Sal looked past her to where Barry stood, he felt a twinge of regret. He hadn't spent much time with him over the last while, and he guessed he was due a lecture on how friendship works.

Barry had his arms crossed as he leaned against a wall, his gaze flitting to the elixir machine and then back to the doorway. Sal guessed that there would be nothing that would really catch his attention in this crowd, as he had already met everyone.

At least, until Mica walked through with Seth behind her.

Barry's face was absolutely priceless, and there were no illusions to disguise it. His jaw dropped as he looked at Sal in disbelief. It was like every birthday had come together all at once, and he was over to them like a shot to verify that it was true.

"Where is Divinity?" Blathnaid came over to stand beside Sal. She looked in the direction of the doorway, as though expecting Divinity to walk through at any moment.

"She didn't want to join the guild, so we're going to be doing this one without her." Sal shrugged. "This is official guild stuff, but we'll all hang out soon."

Blathnaid snorted as she gave Sal a look. "Don't make promises you won't keep. You should try harder to convince her. You got me, after all."

Sal grinned. "You were a fearsome negotiator to go up against. I'll just have to try harder with Divinity."

Blathnaid nodded, seemingly appeased. "She's been a little frantic the last few days, like… really pushing herself. Do you know if something happened?"

Sal didn't. He guessed that it might have something to do with the invasion, but there wasn't really any way to tell. Looking around the room, Sal grimaced. There wouldn't be any harm in inviting her, considering she kinda knew everything…and would know everything that would happen.

Smiling, he took out his tablet and sent her a message.

Salvatore: Hey Divinity, we're just having our first guild meeting in the up-graded workshop. You're more than welcome to join us if you'd like. It doesn't feel right with you not being here. I'm not trying to pressure you into joining, just wanted to send an invite.

The response was instant, like Divinity had been waiting to send it.

Divinity: Really appreciate the invitation, but I shouldn't be there. I've got some module work I need to catch up on, anyway. Hope you guys have a great first meeting!

Sal turned the tablet around so Blathnaid could see the text. "What do you think?"

Blathnaid smiled and offered a shrug. "I think it's fine. You asked and she appreciated it, so all good in my book." When Jack walked in alongside Anthony, Blathnaid moved to go over to them, but paused to look back at Sal. "Maybe just send her a message to say that you want to hang out soon. I think she'll like you making a plan."

Salvatore: Would you like to hang out later today, or tomorrow? It's been a while since we've had a catch-up.

Divinity: I'd like that. Let's do it. :)

When Vanessa walked into the room, Barry took a step backward from Michaela. His eyes were wide as he looked at her, and Sal knew him long enough to know that it wasn't simply because she was gorgeous. That said, Sal wondered whether Barry would look at Vanessa the same way when she was covered in orange blood.

Barry walked around her, giving her a wide berth as he approached Sal. His voice was in a whisper as looked at Sal strangely. "Is that Diva? From the pictures up on the Savior floor?"

Sal nodded. "Yeah, that's her. What's got you so spooked?"

"Yeah, what has you so spooked?" Vanessa asked, her mouth inches behind Barry's ear.

Sal bit his lip as Barry whirled around in shock, stumbling back a few feet to put distance between them. Vanessa seemed to be having fun as she advanced on him.

"Barry Francis, right?" She smiled sweetly. "It's nice to finally meet you. Sal has told me *a lot* about you."

Barry regained his composure as he straightened and dusted himself off. He looked at Sal for a second before chuckling to himself. "You're fast." He looked at Vanessa, who was checking her nails.

"I am," she confirmed with a slight smile. "But you didn't answer my question." She gave him a level stare. "Full disclosure, though. I'll be handling your guild membership contract, so you might need to choose your words carefully."

Barry let out a sigh as he offered a shrug. "Sorry for the overreaction. I just didn't expect to see you here. I'm a big fan."

"A big fan?" Vanessa looked at him in confusion. "Were you at the battle yesterday?"

Barry shook his head. "Your stats in the simulation room. They're honestly… terrifying." He looked across the room to where Michaela chatted with Seth. "I already knew that Body Manipulators were strong, but I didn't think perfect scores were possible."

"Oooh, we've got ourselves a Tactician?" She smiled at Sal. "You've picked a good one." When her attention turned back to Barry, the playful veneer disappeared. "So, who should I be on a team with? And yes, this is a test."

Barry hesitated as he averted his gaze from Vanessa, thinking about the question. It only took him a few seconds, because it looked like he had the answer but didn't want to say it.

"Go on," Vanessa insisted.

"Nobody," Barry answered. "You actually lose points when there are others around you."

"Why?" Vanessa pushed, seemingly enjoying the line of questioning.

"Because you have to protect them?" Barry ventured, a little unsure of himself.

"Good insight," Villa responded from directly behind Barry. "But terrible spatial awareness. I thought you were supposed to be good at trickery? Is Vanessa making you *that* uncomfortable?"

Sal wasn't sure whether it was because of the Awareness stat, but he actually felt when Villa approached. He didn't say anything, because it was genuinely fun seeing Barry squirm.

Barry had jumped for the second time in quick succession. He looked like he was going to snap at Villa until he realized who it was. Rather than opening his mouth and saying something he'd regret, he turned to Sal. "You put *them* up to this?" He sounded both impressed and agitated.

Sal offered an innocent shrug. "Nope. They're our guild advisors, so maybe it's just some good-natured hazing?"

"Nope." Vanessa laughed as she placed a hand on Barry's shoulder. "I'm the Controller advisor, which means we're going to spend a lot of time together."

Villa smiled as she nodded. "And if you decide that being a Controller isn't for you, I'll be waiting to make you into a world-class Offense."

"I'll never be an Offense," Barry stated with absolute certainty, looking at Sal for help.

Sal glanced around the room and saw that everyone was there. Hannah had entered last, and offered him a friendly wave as she stood over to one side, not really mingling with anyone. Getting to his feet and clapping his hands for their attention, Sal smiled at Barry, as if to say he owed him one.

Vanessa shrugged as she looked at Barry with a sly smile. "Hope you have fun with Enigma."

"What?" Barry asked, clearly confused, but he was cut off when Sal started to speak.

"Thank you all for coming here at such short notice," Sal began as he tried to find a vantage point that would allow him to see everyone. Thankfully, they all started to congregate so he didn't even need to move that much.

"This is the first meeting of the Mythic Guild," Sal continued as he looked at each of their faces. "The reason for the name, as some of you already know, is because my ability is called Mythcrafter. I created it from a collection of ability weaves, and it caused the Skill Registration machine to explode." He gestured behind him to the elixir machine. "I've started building Mythic-grade items, but it takes a lot of time and resources to do so."

It wasn't supposed to be an inspiring speech or anything like that. He just wanted to give them the context of why they were operating the way they were, and what they should expect from being members of the guild.

"Some of you joined because you've seen what I can do, while others have joined because they're curious of what we can do in the future. Either way, thank you for being a part of this guild. We're already at Tier 8, and we'll be aiming to push through those ranks throughout this semester and the ones to come."

Sal looked at Fabi, Sakura, and O'Brien. "We have two third-years on our roster, and some mutual assistance from Fabi. To ensure that they have a guild worthy of them at the point of graduation, we're going to need to accelerate our plans. Which is why I wanted to get us started as soon as possible." Sal gestured at Vanessa and Villa. "In addition to Upgrade, we have Vanessa and Villa as our guild advisors. Vanessa will be sitting down with each of you to walk through your guild contracts. If you have any requirements of us for signing, please do let us know."

Moving onto the next topic, Sal smiled. He was looking forward to this part. "What will set us apart from other guilds is our equipment. The vast majority of us are Supports, and although we're a Specialist guild and we'll be creating special teams… at our core, we'll be a Support guild. What does that mean? Well, for starters… it would be a pretty shit guild, if I could make Mythic grade and didn't share them with our members."

The expressions were priceless. Blathnaid looked horrified at the prospect of getting a Mythic grade, while Barry didn't believe it for a second. Anthony clearly thought he wasn't supposed to be there, while Jack looked around in confusion. Sakura and O'Brien talked to each other, and their mirror was Michaela and Seth, who looked equally confused. Rochelle looked conflicted, probably thinking she'd have to give up the Legendary coat. Quest stood beside Upgrade with a wide smile on his face. He clearly approved of the decision.

"I've created a piece of equipment that many of you have seen already." Sal lifted his right hand up to his left shoulder. With a swift pull, Sal ripped off the entire sleeve of fabric and let it fall to the ground. "It's called the Mythical blight jackal." Raising his hands into the signature pose, the Mythical blight jackal snapped into place on his bare left arm.

Sal looked at all their reactions, and got Jackal to bob beside him for a bit as a prop. "Jackal, standby mode." As soon as he spoke the words, the abyssal steel tendrils detached from his arm and the glowing green orb dislodged from his shoulder, to reveal Jackal in all his glory.

"Fuck." O'Brien cursed with a tentative step backward.

Michaela's expression darkened, while Seth looked quite amused by the whole thing. Quest, on the other hand, had never seen Jackal and was pretty transfixed by the sight of it.

"This will be the standard issue for our officers. Each created to complement their abilities," Sal declared as he looked at Upgrade. "We'll start with the advisors, giving them their own Mythical arm. Everyone else will be given one with the evolutionary potential to reach Mythic grade over time. It will require hard work and strategy, but it will be worth it. The rest of the equipment will follow, with evolutionary traits."

"Awesome," Rochelle breathed as she stared at Jackal in wonder.

Sal smiled and let them all take in the sight of Jackal for a few seconds. "We're going to have access to the Mythic-grade elixir machine that is operated by Alex and Anders. I don't have a timeline for when we'll have useful concoctions, but I'm sure it won't be long."

"Three weeks." Alex muttered in a sulky voice with crossed arms. "Don't suppose I get a fancy arm for my troubles?"

"Are you a member of the guild?" Sal asked, eyebrow raised.

"Well...yeah?" Alex answered as he glanced over at Vanessa. "Just need to sign with the viper, and then it's official?"

"Then you'll get one," Sal said in a resolute tone. "This is the reward for being the first members of the guild. I know we've got a lot to learn, and we've got a lot of tiers to progress through, but I firmly believe we can make a massive difference."

Alex's arms went down in disbelief. He stared at Sal, his mouth opening, but no words coming out. It was a rare moment, that Sal would savor for years. Rewarding them for their help was within his capability, and it felt right to give them the same trust they gave him.

Sal suddenly stopped himself as he frowned at the group. "Actually, no. Reward is the wrong word. It's an *investment*. I've worked with Coach and Upgrade on creating a new device. It's still in testing, but it has the capability of bringing each of you to your fullest potential. Methods to open your gates, progress and evolve your abilities, and how you can grow stronger. Combine that with the best gear in the world, and we have everything we need to be the best guild out there."

"If you've got all this amazing stuff, why do you even need a guild?" Seth asked from the back of the crowd. "You said yourself that it's always going to be a Support guild, so it's not like you've got some grand vision of us ending the war."

O'Brien shot Seth a glare, which was promptly ignored. Michaela, on the other hand, gave O'Brien a look that made him turn his attention back to Sal.

Sal nodded. "That's a very good question." He smiled as he spread his hands. "I could give you a bullshit reason, like how I just want to help… but that would be a lie."

Sal laughed as he thought about it. "During the invasion yesterday, I saw the Hunter Bureau and the United Guilds Association, with all the Heroes and volunteers on the scene. It was an absolute shit-show. A chaotic mess, where nobody knew what to do… and when it was all over, the residents who came back to ruined houses, they thanked me."

Sal stared at Seth. "Thanked me. There was no anger that they had lost everything. They were so desensitized, so used to this happening, that they just accepted it."

Barry had a strange look on his face as he listened to Sal. Blathnaid looked frustrated, but equally, she looked like she understood those people. To Sal's surprise, Anthony looked livid. Had he been displaced, or was it something else that resonated with him?

Vanessa smiled as she cocked her head to one side. "Aren't you forgetting the most important part of yesterday?"

Sal smiled at her. "Yes, you're right. Our esteemed advisor took out the arachne titan commander class demon, with help from Michaela Egan." Sal gestured at Mica in the crowd.

"Not that, you idiot," Villa snapped with a heavy sigh. She took it upon herself to turn to look at the gathered people. "Your guildmaster stepped up when he was told to go back to Quest Academy."

Vanessa nodded from beside her. "And he killed an enemy commander, saving thirty volunteers."

"Including me," Villa said in a matter-of-fact tone. "I'd be dead if Salvatore hadn't taken out that commander."

Upgrade nearly choked as she looked between Villa and Sal, and then at Quest. He had clearly left out some aspects in his retelling.

The effect across the room was wild. Everyone had broken into discussion with the person beside them, either trying to refute the claim or express amazement. It was next to impossible to call Villa a liar, especially when she was a few feet away from you. Yet, the claim was so unbelievable that they had to express it.

Most of them had no frame of reference as to how this could have happened. They knew Sal, and his temperament, so it was that much more unbelievable. It was a peculiar thing, that the Mythic-grade equipment was no longer the topic of discussion in the room.

Sal cleared his throat, but sighed when he saw there was no bringing their attention back. He gave an apologetic glance to the advisors, all of whom covered their ears. Fabi tried to warn Sakura and O'Brien, but it was too late.

Sal whistled.

CHAPTER 87: CONTRACT

After much apologizing for rupturing their eardrums, Sal managed to get his impromptu meeting back on track. He walked them through what they should expect from the Mythic Guild, elaborating on how he envisaged the guild would operate going forward. A lot of it was to explain the back-end finances, to show that they were financially secure. He didn't outright tell them about the Arkwright, but he did allude to the contract agreement with the Dragoons. Combined with the earning potential from the Skill Weave research, and the elixir machine, he could see the visible relief on a few faces.

Vanessa was instrumental for the next part, and she was clearly primed and ready for the task. She told them how they would be building up specialist teams for dungeons and eventually towers and portals. Rather than scaring the first-year Supports, or putting pressure on the first-year Saviors, Vanessa assured them that everything would be gradual and that the most important aspect was their own personal growth. She went on to explain how the tier progression systems worked, and how they would need to contribute to the success of the guild. That seemed to surprise the likes of Jack and Anthony, but rather than intimidating them, they looked more engaged than ever.

Upgrade went next to explain how Athena worked in more detail. She did an excellent job of highlighting all the benefits of the reports, and even referenced her own progression indicators. The Legion System was still in its infancy, but by the end of her speech, every hand was in the air with follow-up questions.

"So, it will just look at us… and assign us a level? Then we just kill demons to make the level go up?" Sakura asked in confusion. "Is that not a little reductive? The moment you trivialize the demonic threat to a series of numbers, complacency will start to fester."

Upgrade nodded in agreement. "You are correct, but this is not the system that the guilds pushed on its members in the past." She was careful not to attribute that system to Quest, so as to not make him look bad in front of them. "The levels are just an easy-to-understand representation of your current state. It won't task you with taking out a level-ten commander or something like that. Rather, it will tell you that if you defeat three commanders, your weave will ascend to the next grade. These are calculations that are personalized to each of you, with the ultimate goal being your own development."

Sakura blinked in surprise before she nodded in understanding. "Okay, that sounds good."

"If I use that machine of yours, will it tell me that I need to mix a certain number of elixirs?" Alex laughed as though he were making a joke.

"That's exactly how it works," Sal answered seriously. "You'll be able to see how to bring your Alchemize ability to the next stage of growth, which we can map out for you." He looked toward the wider group. "I used it earlier today and found out that there are another two levels beyond Mythcrafter. The requirements would have me making a few thousand Rare grades, or twelve Mythic grades. There's a breakdown of what materials I should use, the essence costs, the abilities that give the most amounts of development, and even walkthroughs for areas I haven't learned yet. It has incorporated all the courses available on the Credit Store, and compiled it into a progression framework."

Anthony just stared blankly at Sal as his hand raised into the air. He was the only one who didn't just speak at Sal.

"Yes, Anthony?" Sal pointed at his friend, smiling.

Anthony looked confused as he momentarily glanced in Fabi's direction before finding his words. "What about people who don't have an output for their abilities? I don't actually create anything with Supercharge, and despite training for years with it, the only thing that increases is the duration." He hesitated before continuing. "Are there abilities that aren't worth investing in?"

"No." Sal was firm in his response, so there was no doubt left in any of their minds. "I want to make it very clear that the reason you're all here has nothing to do with your abilities. Don't forget, Anthony, we came out top in our cohort because we had better training and gear than everyone else. We'll do the same with the United Guilds Association."

Anthony smiled at that as he gave a nod. "Thanks, Sal."

"Come on, it kinda does have a little to do with abilities, though?" Seth remarked as he glanced at Sakura and O'Brien. "You've recruited Saviors into your ranks, which isn't something you'd manage with just ideals and dreams." He looked amused by the whole situation, but there was no malice in his tone. "Seriously, I know we're stragglers, which was just because of circumstances, but I can't get my head around the unwavering loyalty. We've all been here a few months, but this feels more like a cult than a guild."

Sal opened his mouth to respond, but to his surprise, Barry stepped forward.

"Seth McDuffee, also known as Factor." Barry threw up a perfect illusion of Seth in front of the group, which silently rotated on the spot. "Strengths: Michaela Egan." Barry paused for a second before shrugging. "That's it. On the weaknesses front? There are many…almost too many to count, but we've got some time. Seth's clones sap him of both essence and vitality. When he has all four of them acting independently, he becomes incredibly vulnerable. Signs to look for are lethargy, exhaustion, and him being uncharacteristically quiet for periods of time. Turns out that managing four other versions of yourself is quite taxing. Who would have guessed?"

Michaela started to move in on Barry, but Seth's hand shot out to stop her. He stared at Barry intently. "Continue."

Barry smiled as the illusion separated into five distinct versions of Seth, with the one in the center looking visibly distressed and frail. "Cohort battle results had him placed last, as everyone knew that targeting the main body would deactivate the clones. Excursion had better results, but poor teamwork held you back as you weren't designated as a Controller. You were there as a Support, despite Professor Maxwell putting you forward for the Tactics master class." Barry was ruthless and to the point as he continued looking at the real Seth. "The tower trial was initially a failure until you were boosted by your greatest strength, Michaela. Your own efforts got you to the second floor on the third attempt."

"If you have a point…make it." Seth's drawl was more pronounced as he stared at Barry. "I didn't come here to be mocked."

Barry waved a hand and the four clone illusions disappeared, leaving just Seth. A new figure appeared beside the illusion, causing Blathnaid to look at Barry in bewilderment.

"Blathnaid Clean, no Hero name yet… She's very unassuming. She had severe issues with activating her ability. She's now in the Savior class." Barry threw up another one. "Rochelle de Verdon, no Hero name… Seeing the trend here? She is pretty much crippled by how limiting her ability is. She's now in the Savior class."

"Put me up next," Fabi said to Barry, who complied with a smile. When her image joined the illusion, Fabi looked at Seth.

"I couldn't access my ability for my entire life." She smiled as she pointed over at Sal. "What Barry is trying to say is that we're all here because we've got a reason to be grateful to Sal."

Barry winced as he shook his head. "I had this whole dramatic thing planned where I revealed myself last. It was going to be super emotional and dramatic…" He laughed as he dismissed the illusions. "Fabi's sentiment is really nice, but it's not the angle I was going with, Seth. You have a problem. Sal fixes problems; he can't help it. If you hang around him long enough, he'll fix yours and you'll be able to stand on par with Michaela. I don't know how he'll do it, and neither does he, probably? But he'll make it happen."

Seth didn't look convinced, but rather than reasoning with Barry, he turned his attention to Sal. "That true? You can fix all my problems?" He smiled as he gestured vaguely at himself.

Sal shrugged. "I've got no idea. This is the most I've ever heard you talk."

Michaela smiled at that as she nudged Seth. "I guess he did stop you from getting cut up by that wire."

"True." Seth nodded. "And he didn't take Chris Spectre."

"You could have gotten Chris Spectre?" Barry asked Sal in a strained voice. "Why didn't you? His stats are great!"

"He's a prick," Sal answered simply before realizing that Quest stood only a few feet away. "Ah, I mean… he's not Mythic Guild material."

Quest chuckled as he shook his head and looked at the group. "So, are we done with the presentation? Is it time to sign the contracts? Because I'd love to get some pictures of the momentous occasion, if you'll allow me."

Sal looked at Vanessa and Villa, who nodded in agreement.

Upgrade was smiling as she sat on one of the desks. "Sounds good to me." She spoke as she looked around the room. "Is everyone happy to do contracts, or are there people getting cold feet?" Her gaze landed on Seth and Michaela.

Michaela looked at Vanessa and bit her lip, but her loyalty won out as she stood beside Seth. Apparently, there was no need for her to be conflicted, because Seth smiled broadly.

"You did help us with the luggage, I guess." Seth shrugged before letting out an exasperated sigh. "Those sleeves do sound pretty cool, too." He looked at Michaela. "What do you think?"

"I want that commander heart." Michaela looked between Vanessa and Sal. "If you're giving me that, then I'll sign and be a part of the guild."

Sal raised his left hand and summoned the commander heart from Arsenal. "Done."

Michaela took a step back in surprise. "How the hell did you do that?"

Upgrade rolled her eyes but couldn't help but laugh. "You're such a show-off."

Vanessa made quick work of the contracts. It was a one-at-a-time affair in one of the private meeting rooms, and every time a person came out, they had a wildly different reaction.

Rochelle appeared shell-shocked as she looked at Sal upon exiting the meeting room. "You never told me we get paid!" Her reaction was by far the crowd favorite, with a few people gently teasing her for it. She genuinely thought that the gear would be the payment, and didn't think she'd be getting a wage.

Sal was able to utilize Q-Cred for the payments, and although the figures wouldn't be much for the likes of Sakura and O'Brien, it was substantial for the likes of Rochelle, Anthony, and Jack. If he didn't make a single extra Q-Cred, he'd be able to fund the Mythic Guild salaries for about six months. If he sold the contents of Arsenal, with everything Doc Ameye, Lawrence Baron, and his father had sent, then he'd be able to pay their wages for about thirty years… with yearly wage increments. It was a reassuring thought, which was why he wasn't anxious about it.

If things ever got bad, all he needed to do was auction off a few Legendary-grade pieces and it would be fine.

"What are you thinking about so seriously?" Fabi leaned against the bench beside him.

Sal smiled as he gestured at everything around them. "Just all of this. I want the guild to become something special, and I don't think we could have a better group of people to start us off on the journey."

Fabi grinned at him. "Well, if my own business endeavors go to shit, I might hit you up for a membership someday."

Sal snorted as he looked at her in disbelief. "You? Failing? As if… You're going to turn that depot into the center of commerce. Robert will be begging you to relocate to Haven."

"Our depot, you mean," Fabi corrected, smirking as she nudged him playfully. "I'll make sure it's worthy of whatever heights you bring the Mythic Guild to. Should be easy enough, though. I've got two years and your parents helping me."

Sal looked at the meeting room where Sakura and Vanessa were talking contracts. "Do you think they'll actually sign? They have the weakest reason out of everyone here to join… and they'd be welcomed into pretty much any of the top guilds."

Fabi shook her head. "They'll join."

Sal wanted to ask why she was so certain of that, but decided to just trust in her. "I think Barry's had the longest negotiation. He still looks a little shell-shocked. What do you think happened in there?" He glanced over in Barry's direction; he was sitting down with Alex, nursing a restorative coffee.

"Hmm?" Fabi frowned as she glanced over at him. "Ah, I think Villa handled his contract."

Sal laughed. "Yeah, okay… that would explain it, then." He glanced at Barry, sympathizing with him. He couldn't be certain, but he guessed that Villa probably let some of her aura leak out on purpose. There was no way that Barry would be that shell-shocked over a few contract clauses.

Upgrade appeared beside them with a fatigued expression. "We're just waiting on Sakura, right? All the others are done?"

Sal nodded. "I think so. When are you thinking of getting them into Athena?"

"As soon as possible." She thought about it. "Actually, we should push it to tomorrow or the next day." A bright smile appeared on her face as though she had just thought of something great.

"Any reason?" Sal laughed as he looked at her. "Why do I feel like this is a trap?"

Upgrade grinned as she gestured at her arm. "We have some Crafting to do… after sleep. I haven't slept in days." She bit her lip as she thought about it. "But I guess I could pull through another night?"

"No, you need sleep. We'll Craft your new arm when you're up," Sal insisted with a chuckle.

"Can I watch?" Fabi asked Upgrade hopefully. "I'd like to see a Mythic being made without worrying that we've killed Sal."

CHAPTER 88: SCHOLARSHIP

"How did the first meeting of the Mythic Guild go?" Divinity blew at the edge of her steaming cup of tea. "I half expected you'd be out celebrating with them or something."

"I already made plans with you, didn't I?" Sal smiled as he adjusted the coffee cup in front of him. There were very few people in the main canteen, and Sal had selfishly requested they meet there. He had his fill of steak and vegetables—okay, he had two steaks. It had been a while since he had eaten, and he justified it to himself.

"I'm grateful." Divinity smiled as she looked at him, but Sal noticed that it didn't reach her eyes. "I'm guessing you want to know about the whole invasion thing and why I didn't warn you?"

Sal shook his head as he continued to rotate the coffee cup. "Nope, I don't, actually." He smiled at her before continuing. "I told you that I'd ask you about the future when I wanted to know something, and you promised me you'd tell me about the things I needed to know. I trust you, so there's no need for you to tell me anything."

Divinity faltered as she looked at Sal strangely. "You actually mean that? I thought you'd want to talk about Shade or something to do with Crafting or modules."

Sal nodded. "Yeah, I mean it. I sometimes think back to when we sat here and you told me about all the possible futures involving me. All of them seemed so ridiculous, like me walking into a portal and never coming back, or me becoming a hermit-like Crafter who didn't participate in classes." He laughed a little guiltily. "I'm kinda falling into the last stereotype, but I'm going to catch up soon. Quest's made me a custom schedule so I won't fall behind."

Divinity took a sip of her tea, and it looked like she had something on her mind. The conflicted expression was still there, as though she was mulling over how to bring it up. He didn't need the tracker to read her.

Rather than waiting for her to speak, Sal continued with what he wanted to talk to her about. "I've created a new machine that will work on abilities and internal stats. It's still in the early stages, but we're going to try to roll out a version that will help people progress and grow stronger."

A faint smile appeared on Divinity's face. "That sounds pretty great. I hope it works out for you."

Sal faltered at that. "Wait, you don't know about it?"

Divinity's smile faded as she offered him a guilty shrug. "That's a part of why I didn't warn you about the attack." She looked at him with a conflicted expression. "I didn't see it, Sal. I don't know if it's a psychological block or something… but I haven't been able to look into the future properly since you were in the infirmary."

Sal wanted to ask how she knew about Shade's abduction attempt if she hadn't been seeing the future, but he guessed that she was still able to use it, but just not at the same strength as before.

A bitter laugh escaped her lips as she stared at her teacup. "It's funny, isn't it? That I didn't see this coming… despite looking into countless futures, I seemed to miss all the signs pointing at my own issues." She straightened her back and put on a brave smile. "I had no idea you'd reach out today, so it was a nice surprise. Thank you, but sorry that I'm not better company. The whole thing still feels pretty raw."

"Was there something that led up to it?" Sal asked out of concern, but realized he might have overstepped because Divinity's lower lip started to tremble slightly.

Divinity nodded as she looked off to the side. "Yeah, there were a few signs." She let out a shuddering breath and refused to look at him. "I was complacent because the future version of myself had progressed at a scary rate. I figured that with hard work, I'd get there without cutting corners. But at some point, I started ignoring the signs that I hadn't caught up to that version of myself. Imagine it, I'm underperforming against myself!" She laughed humorlessly and shook her head in frustration. "I used to be content with just seeing and discarding possibilities, because I was tasked to look for calamities. Most of my early training was spent looking for world-ending events."

Sal didn't know what to say, so he listened.

"But then I saw an incredibly bright future." She smiled and gestured at him. "The one that you could have built, with the Argento Plaza. It created this impulse, almost like a neurotic obsession where I needed to preserve that single future at all costs. Maybe it was from a lifetime of seeing death and destruction, but I just couldn't let go of it."

"Could have built..." Sal repeated the words. "I'm guessing it's gone?"

"Oh yeah." Divinity laughed humorlessly. "Almost immediately after showing you. Fabi getting the Figment ability pretty much destroyed everything. No more Macclemark and Mythmark suits for the next generation of Heroes. That future was built on a family legacy where your parents existed as Auctioneers."

"I'm sorry." Sal watched her. It was clear that this was hurting her, and he didn't know how to comfort her. His apology was genuine, because he was sorry she was feeling like this. There was nothing he would change from his side. Any future where he only knew his parents as Auctioneers would have been a lie. He didn't want that life for himself.

"Don't be." Divinity smiled as she tapped her temple. "The problem is up here. In what world is it okay for me to wish your parents kept secrets, or that you clipped Fabi's wings? I made jokes when you were shaken by Upgrade's death in sixty years, where I should have been compassionate, like a sane human being." Tears rolled down her cheeks as she looked at him. "I just...I latched onto that future and held it tight, assuring myself that I could get us there."

Sal exhaled softly as he adjusted his coffee cup, just to have something to do with his hands. "And at what point did your ability start... you know." He frowned as he thought about it. "I honestly can't imagine what you've been going through, but it sounds horrible."

"That's the thing... I was actually relieved." Divinity cupped her hands over her face. "How fucking selfish can I be? I was blessed with an ability that can save lives, prevent calamities and guide people to a better future... and I'm sitting here crying because I'm relieved that it's not working? I'm going to lose everything because of this."

"You never asked for that power, and people put far too much weight on your shoulders," Sal insisted as he lowered his head to make eye contact with her through her fingers. "I don't think you should blame yourself for this, like, at all."

Divinity pulled her hands away from her face and gave him a flat look. "Who else is there to blame? You? Sure, you changed the future… but you're living your life. How could I ever blame you for that? I'm the one who's lived in countless futures while everything in the present falls to pieces."

"So, what are you planning to do?" Sal asked gently. "Are you going to try to fix your power, or are you going to try to live without it?"

Her eyes widened as she looked at him. "Are you serious? I'm here on a scholarship, Sal. I have to get it back, and get back to work as soon as possible." She hesitated before continuing. "Can you… see if there are any new knots? Something that can explain what's happened?"

"But you're a Savior," Sal said lamely as he gestured at her. "You've clearly proved your worth far beyond a scholarship, so just give it up and pay your own way. Hell, if it's money, I'll pay. I'm loaded at this point." He smiled and thought it would cheer her up, but she just shook her head.

Taking a deep breath, Divinity looked at Sal solemnly. "The scholarship that I got was from the Hunter Bureau." She offered a pitiful shrug before continuing. "My family were re-homed in Haven, given jobs in the bureau and… it's in a really nice place. They're so *happy* there." Tears continued to stream down her cheeks as her voice cracked. "They'll get to keep it if I graduate from Quest Academy, keep good grades, work with the Doom Society, and serve with the Hunter Bureau for two years."

"Oh." Sal leaned back in his chair in surprise. "That changes things."

Divinity nodded, trying to regain her composure. "The Hunter Bureau won't allow me to join any guilds while the scholarship is active. I've already missed a major event and got an official warning. Next time it happens, I'll lose everything and my family will be punished for it."

"I think I have the perfect present for you." Sal smiled gently as he sat up in his chair. "I don't know if it will help, but I'd love to try."

Divinity shook her head. "It doesn't help, but thank you. I appreciate the sentiment."

"Athena doesn't help?" Sal asked, just to clarify.

"Is that what you called them?" Divinity forced a smile. "It's a good choice— Athena being the Goddess of Strategy and Warcraft makes perfect sense."

Sal paused as he looked at her. "I think we're talking about very different things."

Divinity's laugh was real this time. "The Wings of War, that's what you called them… I saw that future months ago. You refitted a Valkyrie suit to make me a set of wings, because you felt guilty about the time I saw you use my ability." She sounded exasperated by having to explain it. "Sal, I'm genuinely so grateful that you went to all that trouble, but the wings aren't going to help me see the future.

"I feel like such a bitch throwing your generosity back in your face like this, and I'm sorry. If it's not a knot that's formed, and it's purely mental, I need to figure out a method to fix it. You could take my power and check for me." Her tone was desperate and her eyes wide. "Please, Sal. I would never ask you to use

Skill Master like this, but I don't have any other choice. I know how much of a hypocrite I'm being, asking you to use your power, when I gave you so much shit about it."

"I'm not ignoring your request." Sal got to his feet. "But Athena isn't the wings. I never finished those for you, because, as per usual, everything got in the way." He gestured toward the exit. "Follow me up to the dorms so I can show you Athena. I just need you to trust me on this."

Divinity closed her eyes and took a deep breath. "I trust you, Sal." Exhaling slowly, she looked up at him. "But, I'm not in a very good headspace right now. I came here to spend time with you, but ended up dumping everything onto your shoulders and feeling horrible for it. I should probably just walk it off, and we can catch up another time. I'm sorry… for all of this."

"Come on. It'll only take a few minutes, I promise," Sal encouraged her as he held out his hand.

Divinity's voice cracked again. "Can't you just check? Like, just a quick look? You know everything about weaves, so you'll know immediately if I'm broken."

"You're not broken, Divinity," Sal said firmly. "I'm not trying to distract you or take your mind off things. I'm repaying a debt that I never thought I'd get a chance to."

Divinity frowned as she looked at him for a few seconds. "You're not indebted to me." She reached out to take his hand, looking confused through the tears.

Sal smiled as he shook his head slowly. "On the contrary. Mythcrafter wouldn't exist without you. Which means Athena wouldn't exist without you. You've given me the ability that made so many things possible and changed my life."

"I just gave you advice—you're the one who put in the work," Divinity corrected him with an awkward laugh as she got to her feet. Wiping the tears on the back of her sleeve, she looked frustrated at herself. "Sorry for crying like this. I just—"

"Nope, no apologizing." Sal cut her off. "And when this all works out wonderfully, I want you to know that you made it possible, okay?"

Divinity shook her head in denial, but didn't argue the topic. They walked to the Savior dorms, making the worst small talk ever, with Sal not wanting to upset her with questions, and her not wanting to break down again.

"Feeling a little better?" Sal asked as they exited the elevator.

"Pretty horrible, if I'm honest." Divinity laughed bitterly. "When was the last time we actually hung out without there being a future we needed to prevent, or an argument, or a misunderstanding… It feels like we're doomed to just exist like this, and I hate it." She sniffed as she stared at the floor. "And I feel horrible thinking that if the ability never works again, it might not be such a bad thing. Sure, my family and I lose everything, and my ability to be a Hero vanishes…but, I'd finally be able to sleep."

Sal had to take a steadying breath as he continued guiding her toward his room. Seeing her like this was heartbreaking, but hearing how hurt and vulnerable she was, Sal wanted nothing more than to protect her and find a solution. Athena was that solution. Sal was sure of it.

When he got to the dorm, Sal swiped his Q-Card and led Divinity into the living room. When she saw Athena, there wasn't so much as a flicker of recognition.

"Is this Athena?" Divinity asked in confusion as she walked around it. "I don't actually know what I'm looking at."

Sal moved to the casing and lifted the lid to reveal the chair within. "Sit in there."

"What will it do?" Divinity asked in an uncertain voice.

"Like you said… you gave me advice, and I put in the hard work. Athena operates in the exact same way," Sal explained as he gestured at the terminals. "If you sit in there, Athena will create a custom plan for you, which will result in you having your own wings. Greater and more brilliant than the ones you saw me manifest." Sal smiled as he looked at her warmly. "Your ability could evolve to become something even greater, and Athena will show you the path on how to get there."

"Sounds too good to be true." Divinity smiled between sniffs as she looked at it warily. "What's the catch?"

Sal sighed as he shook his head. "It takes a bit of time to get through it all."

"Days or weeks?" Divinity asked anxiously.

"A few hours." Sal smiled as he gestured at the seat again. "Which means you could have your full report before you head to bed. All you have to do is trust me."

Divinity nodded as she stepped into the red cocoon and sat on the chair. "I trust you." Her smile seemed genuine this time as she looked around the interior. "You're not going to leave, are you?"

Her voice was uncharacteristically uncertain, which was just another stab in Sal's heart.

"You won't hear me, but I'll be out here," Sal explained in a calm voice. "The essence will be a little invasive, but don't resist and let it work through you. It'll help the results."

Divinity closed her eyes as she leaned her head back. "Even if this doesn't work, I appreciate you trying, Sal." She faltered for a moment. "And I'm sorry about all of this."

"When have you seen me fail?" Sal countered, grinning.

Divinity couldn't resist giggling at that. "In about a thousand futures."

"All going well, you'll be seeing a few thousand more in no time." Sal gripped the lid. "I'll be out here the whole time. You've got this," he said before gently closing Athena. Clipping on his visor, he issued the instructions for the machine to start.

It was his first time seeing the process happening from the outside. The scarlet screen lid started to glow until it resembled a heat lamp. The terminals were going through the different stages, and Sal guessed that it wouldn't take nearly as long because Divinity wasn't a Replicator. A lot of his testing came from weave research and playing around with Mythcrafter. Divinity just had a single weave, and it was likely a similar profile as Upgrade's. Her weave was ridiculously knotted to begin with, so Athena would have its work cut out for it.

Profile Match: Divinity Khan

"That was fast," Sal muttered as he looked at the terminals that started to populate in front of him. Moving over to the one that focused on her weave, Sal maximized it so he'd have a clearer view. It looked like Prime was focused on creating a Legion profile for Divinity, so it would be a bit of time before it got to the information he was looking for.

Seconds. That's how long it took. Sal just stared at Athena and suppressed a shudder. It was insanely fast, to the point that he worried that the information was wrong, or that it had skipped some steps in the analysis or something.

Legion System: Divination Progression Track
Divination Progression Track
- [Factor 1: Prediction] [Grade 12]
- [Factor 2: Foresight] [Grade 18]
- [Factor 3: Prophecy] [Grade 28]
- [Factor 4: Divination] [Grade 40]

Sal frowned as he looked at the results. Divinity was already at the pinnacle of her ability? He had seen her stats at the end of the tournament when wearing Quest's tracker. There was no way that Divinity's ability was between twenty-eight and forty in terms of grade. Was there no path for evolution because he hadn't discovered new weaves in that area? That couldn't be it, because he had never seen Cosmicraft, and Athena had highlighted it to him.

Sal continued to monitor the updates to see whether there were any interesting insights. Prime started to build out the progression frameworks for Divinity, and Sal couldn't read as fast as it was being generated. There was a wealth of information, and he ended up having to pick and choose what to read.

A workout plan was generated on one screen, while a custom meditation that differed from Sal's was generated on another. Style, of all things, was recognized as a trained martial art, and a new progression plan was created for that, too. Sal couldn't resist his curiosity and had to investigate that one. There was no way it could figure it out just from inspecting her body.

Sal was proved wrong. The invasive essence had identified the martial art that Divinity was learning. That would have been impressive by itself, if it wasn't for the training data that was pulled from the simulation room. Divinity's attack pattern had been analyzed from the points of impact on the fake demons, and that was then cross-referenced to identify the Style martial art.

"Fuck, you really are terrifying," Sal muttered as he looked at Athena with an expression of pure astonishment. Just as he was about to turn back to the terminals, he had another thought. With an almost guilty laugh, he glanced back at Athena and lowered his voice. "By the way…I built you, please never kill me." He decided to err on the side of caution by adding that last part.

Ascension Update: Divinity Khan
- Current: Divinity [Psionic] [Factor 4] [Grade 11]
- Proposed: Divinity [Psionic] [Factor 4] [Grade 17]
- Divinity Khan meets Ascension Requirements

Sal accepted the prompt that appeared on his visor. He'd need to look at the report and would be able to correct her weave when she got out of Athena. It was good to know that she was able to jump up so many grades in a safe manner. Sal had been anxious when she had experienced headaches the first time he had un-knotted her weave. Admittedly, it was the first time he had ever used his power in that way and had no idea what he was doing…but he was different now. He'd be able to bring her to the seventeenth grade with no issue.

Ascension Update: Divinity Khan
- o   Ascension Successful
- o   Current: Divination [Psionic] [Factor 4] [Grade 17]

"Oh." Sal read the message twice, just to make sure he wasn't imagining it. "That's not terrifying at all."

CHAPTER 89: PREDICTION

Sal was not prepared for the reports coming from Athena. It was his first time seeing the process as it unfolded, and with so many screens updating every few seconds, it really put into perspective how much data had been collated from his two-hour session with it. The focus today wasn't on him, though. It was on Divinity, and her issues.

He didn't know how he was going to break the news to her, but there was seemingly nothing preventing her weave from activating. Athena had activated it without issue, so did that mean that Divinity's block was mental? If that was the case, then there wasn't much he'd be able to do to help. Athena had access to countless databases, but it wouldn't have any sort of data on emotional states. Would they need to enlist Sergeant Head and his Resilience sessions?

Legion System: Divination Progression Track
Reconstructions Required to increase Divination Grade
- [Factor 1: Prediction] [Not Found] [Increases Grade 17 to 22]
- [Factor 2: Foresight] [Not Found] [Increases Grade 17 to 28]
- [Factor 3: Prophecy] [Not Found] [Increases Grade 17 to 40]

Sal stared at the words for a few seconds, trying to understand what he was seeing. If he was to accept it at face value, it validated what he had suspected with his own weave research. Layering in the early versions, which Athena was calling factors, as a foundation… actually increased the overall capability of the weave? So, Divinity's maximum capability with Divination would likely pause at seventeen if she didn't have the previous iterations?

Sal tapped on the screen and went through the more detailed information. There was a lot of recommendations, and thankfully, there was no request to just rebuild her weaves. It wouldn't have been good for his sanity if Athena was able to reconstruct weaves that didn't exist in a person. That would be no different from the Skill Implants. Just to be sure, he went into the reports to see what sort of recommendations Athena was making. It was one thing to just explain the problem, but he wanted to know what sort of solutions were being offered.

Legion System: Divination Reconstruction
- Optimal Solution: Manual Reconstruction
  - Add to Divination Weave: [Factor 1: Prediction] [Grade 12]
  - Weave Reconstruction Reference Design
  - Suitable Profile: Salvatore Argento
  - Estimated Duration: 43 minutes
- Optional Solution: Weave Reconstruction Training Program
  - Weave Rehabilitation: [Factor 1: Prediction] [Grade 1]
  - Suitable Profile: Divinity Khan
  - Estimated Duration: 5 months, 28 days, 4 hours
- Optional Solution: Athena Reconstruction
  - Additional Essence Power Source Required

- o Recommended Upgrade: Lord Core [Standard] - Lord Core [Ultimate]
    - Last Registered: Lord Core [Ultimate] Acquired by Robert Locke in Portal Raid, Case 22.
    - Last Registered: Lord Core [Elite] Acquired by Doc Ameye in Portal Raid, Case 43.
    - Last Registered: Lord Core [Standard] Acquired by Ryn Stryker in Portal Raid, Case 72.
- o Current Capacity: Commander Core [Elite] x 1
- o Required Capacity: Commander Core [Elite] x 5

"Just when I think I can't be surprised any more, you throw this at me," Sal breathed as he looked through the list while shaking his head in astonishment. In a way, it was nice to know he was still a step ahead of a machine in terms of capability. But in reality, it was only because he fitted it with a commander core instead of a lord core. Why? Because he hadn't heard of a lord core before. Was it any relation to lords crystal that he had wanted for his original visor?

Athena was suggesting that there were three options available. Either he do it himself and manually remap Divinity's weave to include the grade twelve version of Prediction, or he could let Athena create a training plan for Divinity to unlock it herself… in half a year. Or, he could get a lord core from one of the three people listed. One he had heard of from Coach, and two who would be highly unlikely to part with it. Doc Ameye was his closest bet, but there would be no way he'd hand over something so valuable, especially after already gifting materials worth millions.

Sal sighed as he looked at the list. Tapping at the screens that kept popping up, he put the upgrade of the power source on hold. He went into the weave structure map that had been drawn up to reflect Divinity's current weave. It looked a lot healthier than before, but he could see the additions Athena was suggesting marked in a different color. A series of small notes were attached at various points of the weave, warning him that he would need to leave them alone.

It was honestly so refreshing having context for the instinctive corrections he had been making for months. He really wanted to see what it thought of his Ravel method, to see whether that was actually a scientific thing, or something unnecessary that he had convinced himself was helpful. Sal read through the snippets of context with a smile, nodding along as he went.

Sal couldn't help but feel a swell of pride. This was his domain, and perhaps only Grant would be able to understand the terminology on the screen. Even if he could, he wouldn't be able to do anything with it. It was a great feeling, and Sal studied it for close to an hour. Why so long? Because he wanted to perfectly replicate it with Skill Master and figure out the best method of doing it fast without it being too invasive. Athena was positive that this was within Divinity's level of capability, so her body wouldn't reject it. Sal was going to attempt an implant of sorts, on an actual person who was dear to him. There was no way he was going to cut corners.

When he had it completely memorized and understood, inside and out, he selected the option to manually implement the weaves. He guessed that Divinity would need another session in Athena afterward, but it was better to give Athena a heads-up about his intentions, just in case it changed her progression plan.

To his surprise, Athena paused everything. Clearly the weave changes were more important than the rest of the tests. Sal could hear the click of the red lid, and he moved around to make sure Divinity was okay. When he reached down to lift it up, he was met with a warm golden light that started seeping through the grooves, bathing the living room in its glow. Sal pulled the lid up to see what was going on, and was rendered speechless by the disintegrating golden feathers that encased Divinity in a cocoon.

When more of them vanished into thin air, Sal made eye contact with Divinity, who looked positively serene. Her eyes weren't white, but rather… golden. There was no way that six stages of her ability were enough to give this much of an effect. In the time it took him to have that single thought, the gold hue flickered and reverted to white. Divinity seemed to awaken from whatever trance she was in, her breathing erratic from the shock.

"You okay?" Sal asked in an uncertain tone, not sure what had just happened. It clearly wasn't a full manifestation of the wings, but it was something. Whatever had happened in there, her powers were definitely activating.

Divinity's eyes switched erratically from their normal blue, to the familiar white of her using her ability. It was like it was flickering through activations at a ridiculous pace, and she was fighting to bring it back under control. "I… have it… It's… I can't," she breathed as she looked around her in confusion. "It was there. I could, I mean, when I'm in this, I can see!" A relieved smile appeared as she nodded to herself, as though trying to convince herself that this was a good enough solution. "I can use this to see the future, Sal. It literally pulled it straight out of me, and I could… wow, it's hard to explain, but I was able to see so much more than usual."

She switched her sentences so much that it was almost like babbling as she went from excited to anxious in a flash. "Could… could we go again? I don't think it's done. I could feel so much happening, and I don't think it finished." She looked at him a little desperately. "I feel like it's giving me my control back, which sounds ridiculous, I know." She laughed a little awkwardly as she looked at the lid above her head, smiling. "Athena is incredible… and I've got no idea what it's even doing."

Sal smiled as he stepped closer to her. "Athena suggested that I make a few corrections to your weave before we continue. I wanted to give you a choice, though. You can do it yourself, but it will take half a year by Athena's estimate, or I can do the work in less than an hour."

Divinity blinked in surprise as she stared at him. "You do it. I trust you, remember?"

"Is that just because you saw the wings?" Sal chuckled. It was completely understandable, though. Anyone would take a chance at having their power manifest at its strongest capability. It was still uncertain as to how much of an impact it would have, giving her Prediction, but it would hopefully create a path for her to fill in the gaps between Prediction and Divination.

"What wings?" Divinity asked in genuine bewilderment as she looked over her shoulder to the empty space behind her.

Sal shook his head. "You'll hopefully see them next time." He rolled up his sleeves and gestured for her to move her hands out of his way. "I'm going to work on your weave now, and it'll probably be boring, so just relax."

Divinity nodded. "Thank you so much for all of this." She laughed a little as she leaned back against the chair, resting her neck back and looking at the lid above her head. "I cried like five times in this thing and was so worried I was skewing all the results. It pulled the future straight out of me, and I was so relieved that I just broke down."

Sal activated Skill Master and started to look at Divinity's weave. It was a picture-perfect replica of what he had seen on the screen, which was both a relief and reassurance. He was ready to get started, and although Athena had estimated it would take him over forty minutes, Sal knew he could do it in half that time. It wasn't arrogance; it was preparation and expertise. Athena only knew his innate ability, not the practice and hard work he had put into refining it.

"Do I just stay quiet?" Divinity watched Sal's hands start to move in the air in front of her stomach. After a few seconds of silence, she nodded, giggling. "Okay, quiet it is."

Sal was in a flow state as he started to remap her weave. It was like he had a checklist of fifty things that needed to be done, and he blitzed through them, one after another. He hooked the weave to different gates to keep it active at all times, so it wouldn't feel like it had been cut off. It added a little complexity, but that was fine. The extra thread that had been freed up by Athena's proficiencies was enough to create the foundational weave, or Factor 1 as it was called. Prediction was shaped like a looping weave that looked somewhat like a dream catcher. Sal just needed it to line up with Divination, which was seemingly designed by a drugged-up child who loved circles. Everything was interconnected and able to rotate on an invisible axis.

Sal was conscious of those axes as they were the breaking point for the weave, according to Athena's report. He worked through each of them carefully, adding in Prediction while cleaning the weave in a way that felt like it would be safe. It was a little unusual, but he wasn't concerned because he knew that it was necessary. There was no conceivable way for him to layer Prediction into Divination without making adjustments outside of Athena's recommendations. Sal was confident as he made the changes and started to hook the weave to the correct gates. It was a slow process, but this was his first time working on an actual person to this level. Upgrade, Martin, and Gosia had simply required unknotting. This was a borderline implant.

"Oh fuck," Divinity breathed as her eyes started to flash in bursts of gold. If that had been the extent of it, Sal would have been able to continue. However, Divinity's sudden surge of capability resulted in two golden wings manifesting from within her, and flapping outward in a flare of defiance.

Sal fell backward onto his ass and looked up in surprise as Divinity stood in the center of Athena, her glowing golden wings unfurled in all their glory. It looked positively majestic, and Sal was actually speechless as he watched her levitate off the ground. Gold wings, eyes, and… veins? It was as if molten gold had etched its way across her visible skin, like she was being corrupted internally by some divine power.

"Whoa! This is… amazing!" Divinity laughed as she looked at herself in wonder. "This was the version of myself I was chasing. How did you manage to make this possible?" Even her tears were gold as they streaked down her face, or maybe it was just the lighting. It was hard to know with everything looking so otherworldly and holy.

Sal got to his feet and had to still look up at her. "Could you get down? We're not finished yet."

Divinity's gaze snapped toward him, her eyebrows raised in surprise. "How can it get better than *this*?" As the words left her mouth, the wings started to vanish, causing her to look at them in alarm as she half stumbled, half fell back into Athena. She looked confused as her eyes flickered back to their normal blue. Her mass of black hair was tangled after floating above her head, and she looked positively lost as she stared at her hands.

"Well, my best guess is that you'll be able to keep it activated for a little longer." Sal grinned as he gestured for her to take a seat. "So, let's get back to it."

CHAPTER 90: DIVINITY

Divinity couldn't stop smiling. It was the happiest that Sal had ever seen her, and it was positively infectious. All the fear, uncertainty, and doubt had seemingly vanished in just a few short minutes. Her attempts at staying quiet had disappeared as she chatted excitedly to him about everything she had experienced within Athena. Sal had to work a little slower as he listened to her and focused on the task at hand. There were still some finishing touches he needed to complete, and he had so many questions that only Athena would be able to answer for him. Divinity's experience was unreliable as she was only talking about how things felt, rather than what actually happened.

"You remember we had that analogy of a forest of trees? That we could look at the countless branches? This was… nothing like that. It was an interconnected web with hundreds of thousands of lines, all tethered to what looked like an ocean. The rising water level representing the passage of time, locking out possibilities as it got higher." Divinity was awed by the whole thing as she shook her head slowly back and forth. "You should have seen it, Sal. I need to hold your hand when I activate it again, so you can see everything."

"And did you have trouble activating it?" Sal asked, just to participate in the conversation. He wasn't convinced that a weave correction would suddenly remove her mental blocks. There was likely going to be a lot of hard work in Divinity's immediate future, and although she would be capable of doing it, he was worried that the current excitement would end up getting destroyed when she was faced with reality.

"A little," Divinity admitted as she brushed her hands through her hair, smoothing it back. "But it was a completely new sensation. I was able to grasp the power so much easier than before. It was like a feather touch to get it going, but to actually see into the future… it was a massive upshift."

Sal smiled as he glanced up at her from his crouched position. "That's Prediction being activated. It's the first of four stages with your ability. You're essentially going from first gear straight to fourth, when you've only ever started in fourth."

Divinity looked at him with wide eyes. "You gave me another ability?"

Sal nodded as he continued to work on the weave.

"When did you learn how to do a Skill Implant?" Divinity breathed in wonder. "Does this mean that you're going to make the second and third gears? Is that even possible?"

Glancing up at her, he shook his head. "Nope, that work will be on your shoulders, I'm afraid. Athena is going to create a training program for you to activate those aspects of your weave. You have the beginning and the end, and apparently training can help you fill in the gaps in between."

Divinity didn't say anything for a few seconds, but when she did, it started with a nervous laugh. "When you said that it would give me advice, I wasn't really expecting this sort of outcome."

Sal smiled as he finished up the rest of the weave, checking over it a few times in silence to ensure that it was perfect. The axes were the tricky part, because they were moving pieces within Divinity. Athena had shown him static corrections, where he had to think of them in motion. It was a very fun project, and Sal was still a little shell-shocked from seeing how Divination manifested at higher grades. Had Divinity only ever been activating a portion of her weave? It would explain why she hadn't been progressing with it as fast as she hoped.

"Are you done?" Divinity asked curiously as she sat up properly in the seat. "What happens now?" She sounded excited as she looked at him expectantly. "Should I try activating it?"

Sal chuckled, shaking his head slightly. "Nope, now we close the lid and see what Athena thinks of the changes. It'll update the instructions for your training."

"Awesome." Divinity practically bounced in the seat as she looked up at the lid excitedly. "Ready when you are."

Sal laughed as he brought his hand to the lid and looked at her carefully as he put a hand behind his back, unfurling three fingers. "I'm going to show you my hand in a few seconds. Can you activate just the feather-touch version of your ability? I've got no idea if this is how Prediction works, but it could be a good test."

Divinity nodded, frowning slightly. "Cool. Just give me a second." It was clear from her expression that she was anxious about being unable to activate it without the help of Athena. That fear was unfounded as her blue eyes started to glow. She tilted her head to one side. "This… is super weird."

"How so?" Sal asked, a little unsure of himself.

"It's… like I can see afterimages, with movements rather than words." Her gaze snapped to the left of him. "Three fingers!"

Sal brought his hand into view as he had planned, smiling broadly at her. "Guess Prediction works fine?"

Divinity trembled as she looked at her own hands in shock. It was like she was trying to rationalize what had just happened.

"You okay?" Sal asked in a gentle tone, not sure whether she was going to tailspin into panic again.

"More than okay," Divinity breathed as she looked around the room in antici-pation. "This… is so much better for fighting than my normal ability. I can use this so much faster, and it's not taxing at all!" A laugh escaped her lips as she looked at Sal almost reproachfully. "You're going to close the lid while I'm still talking! That's so mean."

Sal grinned as he offered her a shrug. "Was going to make a joke that you didn't see it coming, but I guess that's ruined now."

Divinity leaned back as she gestured for him to close it. "I just have one question, though."

"Yeah?" Sal hesitated with the lid. "What do you want to know?"

"Is this actually my power, or is it a temporary thing?" Divinity asked seriously, as if trying to understand whether she should manage her expectations. "Is Athena just giving me a boost to show me what's possible with hard work?"

Sal shook his head. "No, this is all yours. There will be a training program to make sure that you're progressing to full mastery of it. Athena already identified the optimal meditation and essence replenishment technique for you. There's a catalogue for learning Style, and checkpoints with time estimates… There're countless plans made for you, like for every contingency while you're getting stronger."

Divinity just stared at him, not really registering what he had said. "In what world does this repay a debt to me? You've pretty much indentured me with this." She laughed as her eyes widened. "This is an unfair amount of progress, and you're just giving it to me? I could give you predictions and visions for decades and it still wouldn't be enough to pay you back."

Sal frowned as he started to close the lid slowly. "Stop thinking so much. None of this would be possible without you, so don't underplay your contributions. If you hadn't become my friend, I'd be back in the Argento Auction House by now because I definitely wouldn't have lasted a single semester."

"*Lies*." Divinity smiled as the lid clicked into place, locking her in.

Sal went back to the terminal, chuckling. It seemed like the work had been a success, but he wanted Athena's verdict before he did any celebrating. Having all the reports open on the mass of screens was great, and Sal made a mental note to get his own screens. All of these were brought in by Fabi and Upgrade to work on the essence programming stuff.

One by one, the reports were recalculated with the new readings from Athena.

Legion System: Divination Progression Track
Reconstruction Completed
- [Factor 1: Prediction] [Grade 12]

Development Required
- [Factor 2: Foresight] [Not Found] [Progression Track Updated]
- [Factor 3: Prophecy] [Not Found] [Progression Track Updated]

Estimated Final Result
- [Factor 4: Divination] [Grade 36] - [Grade 40]

A relieved sigh escaped Sal as he looked at the results with a satisfied smile. He had suspected that his improvements to the weave would result in a higher Prediction grade, but he was delighted that Athena calculated his contributions perfectly. It meant he could trust that the machine was accurate. Looking through the drop-down menus, Sal could see that Divinity would need to develop Foresight and Prophecy by herself. It also had factored in an acclimatization plan for her to get used to Prediction, with basic steps and challenges for herself.

Sal couldn't have been happier with the results. Athena was making an entire plan for Divinity, and through Legion, she'd be able to mark her progress toward those goals. He moved through the reports, checking to see whether there was anything else of interest. A lot of the calculations were done behind the scenes, and there were plenty of things that weren't really that exciting. Calendar management and eating schedules were a little overboard in his opinion, and Sal assumed that the results for his own would tell him to eat vegetables and to sleep more.

"Ignorance is bliss," Sal muttered as he made a mental note to not check his own nutrition report. "Steak and coffee is a balanced diet," he lied to himself, laughing.

Legion System: Equipment Recommendation for Divinity Khan
Adaptive Armor [Researched]
- Material Synthesis Required
    - Switcher [Standard] - Core [Adaptive]
    - Arachne Titan [Elite] - Chitin [Adaptive]
    - Charger Commander [Standard] - Plate [Augment]
- Grants Ability:
    - Augment [Epic]
    - Reconstruct [Legendary]
    - Regenerative [Mythic]

Psionic Weapon [Researched]
- Optimal Material in Arsenal
    - Arachne Titan [Elite] - Reigning Eye [Psionic]
- Grants Ability:
    - Instruct [Rare] [Unique]
    - Designate [Epic]
    - Command [Legendary]
    - Dominate [Mythic]

Sal could barely contain his excitement as he went through the list with a goofy smile. He couldn't believe that Athena had collaborated with the Arkwright to such a scary degree. The fact that it was calculating the ability outcomes was insane, and made his life a thousand times easier. Was it because of the weave database, or was it information determined by MythOS? Either way, it was a godsend and he was very happy for it. The fact that it was telling him what Mythic abilities could be produced was fantastic, especially considering he would be able to create the most suitable items for his guild members.

Going through the information, Sal could see which materials were compatible with evolutionary runes, and which would need to be crafted at the flat grade. Dominate, for example, wouldn't be possible from an evolutionary piece of equipment. He'd have to make it at Mythic to get that ability. Dominate seemingly worked on demons, which was an excellent ability to have… especially if Divinity was able to make them fight each other. Command seemed like a buff of sorts, that would empower the people around her. It was dangerously close to Erika's ability, so Sal wanted to get Divinity's thoughts before he started drawing out any designs.

Taking a deep breath, Sal took a step back from the terminals and caught himself. There were a thousand things to do, and he couldn't afford to just run off to start Crafting for Divinity. She wasn't even in the guild, and he had promised a shit ton of equipment to people already. He'd help her as much as he could, but it was good to know that there was this sort of functionality in Athena.

"Was it supposed to just open?" Divinity asked in confusion from behind him. She had already exited Athena and stared at all the terminals that contained her results. It probably looked intimidating as hell, seeing so many data points about you, without the context to understand them.

Sal turned in surprise, looking at Divinity in confusion. He glanced back over his shoulder at the reports and was able to see that the overall assessment had been complete, with her profile saved and ready to be sent.

Sal accepted it with his visor, before realizing that there was no method for Divinity to get the results. He hadn't figured out the tracker part of the plan.

Divinity reached into her pocket with a smile. "Okay, that's ridiculously fast." She laughed as she produced her tablet and accepted the prompt on the screen. "Oh, it needs to update the system?" She frowned as she turned the screen to Sal, showing him the loading screen. "Is this normal?"

"I think so?" Sal laughed as he offered her a shrug. "I had intended on making trackers and stuff so people could see the information and get real-time feedback. Quest gave us a lot of access and databases, but it's still a little worrying how it pushed the stuff to your tablet that fast. You're a test subject, I guess?"

"I'm honored." Divinity grinned as she pocketed the tablet and moved forward at a ridiculous speed, wrapping her arms around Sal's waist. "I don't know if this all worked the way you hoped, but it's incredible." She laughed as she glanced up at him, her eyes flickering between blue, white, and gold. "Thank you, so much for… everything!"

"Hey, hey… you don't need to thank me." Sal laughed as he rubbed her shoulder reassuringly. "I broke so many of your futures that hopefully this will make up for some of it."

Divinity sighed as she disengaged from the hug, the smile still playing on her lips. "You're going to need to work on that." She gestured at Athena. "You can't make something like this and be shit at taking compliments."

"Come on." Sal put his hands up. "There's still so much work that needs to happen before everything is working perfectly, but this is a good first step."

Divinity grinned as she looked directly upward. "It's a good thing these places have high ceilings."

Before Sal could ask what she was talking about, Divinity manifested her golden wings… this time accompanied by a glowing crown that looked similar to the one Justice had during the invasion. The golden veins were back as well as Divinity levitated off the ground, a wide smile on her face.

"Whoa," Sal breathed as he looked at her. She looked like an actual angel as she hovered a few feet from the ground, bathing everything around her in the warmest light he had ever experienced.

Divinity smiled down at him. "Would you like to know the future I'm seeing right now?"

Sal grinned up at her as he placed his hand on the edge of Athena. "I'm pretty sure I've already got a good idea of what lies ahead."

"I wouldn't be so sure." Divinity laughed as she lifted her gaze to look into the distance, through the windows and out to the wider world. "It's going to be hard not getting attached to this one."

"You know I'm just going to change it." Sal chuckled as he offered her a guilty shrug. "So, probably best you just stop looking at it for now. It'll only end up disappointing you."

Divinity lowered herself to the ground as she dismissed her wings with a delighted laugh. "There were no hiccups or anything… I didn't have to fight for control or anything!" She did a little twirl as the remnants of the golden feathers melted into the air. "This is the *best*."

Sal wasn't sure how he felt about her immediately looking into the distant future after everything they had spoken about. Was she just going to repeat the same problematic cycle of getting obsessed and then disappointed? When he was thinking about the words to choose, Divinity surprised him.

"No need to warn me." Divinity grinned, predicting his reaction. "The future I looked at wasn't decades away." She gestured at Athena. "I just wanted to see what sort of impact she has."

"And?" Sal asked, not sure he wanted to know the answer. Okay, he did. He absolutely wanted to know what Athena's future would be like. "Do people try stealing it?" he guessed lamely.

"We're going to need to get some lord cores." Divinity laughed as she shook her head. "A *lot* of lord cores… and then you'll see Athena working at her best."

Sal snorted as he looked at the requirement list on one of the terminals. "And do you think I'll get one from Ryn Stryker, Doc Ameye, or Robert Locke?"

Divinity bit her lip as she looked at him. "You're not going to like the answer." Before he could even get a sigh out, she continued. "The Mythic Guild will need to go on a portal expedition… or deep into Red Zone territory. That's where the lords are, and you'll just need to have enough contributions to claim them as materials."

Sal blinked as he looked at her strangely. "Oh, that's actually… not so bad?" Obviously, they'd need a lot of training and preparation, but having fought in the invasion, Sal had a different perspective than usual. With the right equipment and team, he was sure that they could make a terrifying force. Vanessa and Mica were already phenomenal, but with Mythic gear, they'd be unstoppable. He started thinking of the impact Hannah or Rochelle would have, too.

Divinity laughed as she nudged him playfully. "You're funny, but I'm being serious. In the future, you'll feel a lot more comfortable with fighting and the team will be ready for that sort of conquest."

Sal nodded in agreement. "Killing a commander did open my eyes a bit to what's actually possible."

Divinity stared at him. "What?"

"A commander," Sal repeated with a grin, realizing he hadn't told her the news. "The Mythic Guild got seven confirmed commander kills during the invasion. I got one of them, where Vanessa took on the rest of them."

"How is that possible?" Divinity breathed as she looked at him for any signs of injury. "An actual commander? Like the one we saw on the video feed, with the lecturers taking care of it?"

Sal nodded, enjoying the fact that she knew none of this. "Yep, and Shade got arrested. It was a big day."

Divinity's mouth hung open in disbelief. "Why didn't you tell me?!"

Sal gestured vaguely at Athena and Divinity. "We had more important stuff to work on. Besides, it was just a commander, no big deal." He intentionally downplayed it for the reaction, and he got it.

Divinity cupped the sides of her face with her hands, looking at him in horror. "Who are you and what have you done to Salvatore Argento?"

"Who knows?" Sal smiled as he gestured at the door. "So, now that you've got your fancy Prediction ability... what do you say to some sparring? We can even make a bet."

Divinity's gaze narrowed on him, her playful smile reappearing. "What sort of bet?"

"Oh, you know... nothing drastic." Sal shrugged. "Just that if I win, you let me take care of your scholarship issue."

"What?" Divinity asked in surprise, clearly expecting something more jovial. "That's not something you can fix, Sal."

Sal shook his head. "The Mythic Guild needs you, Divinity... so, if I need to take on the president of the Hunter Bureau to make it happen, then so be it."

Divinity was lost for words for a few seconds before her smile returned. "Okay then, but only if you win... which isn't going to happen. If I win, you need to promise to not make me any more equipment. Deal?"

Sal laughed. "That's the spirit... But you probably should have looked into the future before agreeing."

"What?" Divinity asked in confusion as her eyes turned gold. "You're not going to have your equipment in a spar, so I don't see why—" Her words died off as she looked at the immediate future. "This doesn't make any sense. How can you become so fast with no equipment?"

Sal chuckled as he moved toward the sparring room. "Come on, I'll make it quick."

Divinity's irises snapped back to blue as she stared at him defiantly. "Oh, you're *so* on."

End of Book 5

<u>REVIEWS</u>!

So, how did I do? Did you enjoy reading Quest Academy? If so, it would be a massive help to me if you left a review for the story. With millions of books being published on Amazon, it's very hard to get any sort of traction and discoverability. If you share the book with people that you think might enjoy it, that would be incredible. I'd love for as many people as possible to have the chance to read the story, and for that, I need your help.

If the story does well enough, I'll be able to spend more time writing, which will cut down the time between releases... and fuel my coffee addiction.

If leaving reviews isn't something you can do, then I'd really appreciate you helping to share the story to people that might enjoy it. No matter what though, you've read my story and that's the most important thing to me.

Thank you!

QUEST ACADEMY BOOK 6

You're probably thinking to yourself, "Why is Brian here instead of the synopsis of Book 6?"

Well, if you're on my Patreon or Discord, you'd know that I'm currently about 75% of the way through the book right now, with the submission date being late December.

I'm doing my best to get it into shape, and when it's done, we'll have it up for pre-order on Amazon with the fancy new cover and... the elusive blurb.

Then the gauntlet of editing begins again. No thoughts or prayers necessary, just send coffee. :)

ARISE: ALPHA

By Jez Cajiao

When you steal a hundred grand from some very bad people, the best way to survive is to stay small and quiet…

Possibly it's not to save a pair of drowning girls, not go viral on social media, and certainly not to let the local police take your passport, trapping you on a small "party" island in the middle of the Mediterranean Sea.

But Steve isn't the average guy: he's ex-military, ex-enforcer, and ex-human. He's a one-man, nanite-fueled nightmare for those who cross the line, and he's decided that it's time to clean up his act. He's going to make up for the things he's done, and save "the little guys."

It's a nice fantasy, but even he has to admit, it's really just a justification, because he's a very bad man, with horrifying abilities, and he's only just learning what he's capable of. He needs a reason to not go to the dark. And if that's hunting down the creatures of the night and beating them to death with their own femurs?

Well, he's just the man for the job.

Stolen money. Greek Islands. Werewolves and Enforcers…what could possibly go wrong?
https://mybook.to/AriseAlpha

WANDERING WARRIOR: JUDGE

By Michael Head

A divine quest to deliver justice. One year to accomplish his mission. After nineteen planets, there's something different about this one.

James Holden has reached the maximum level there is for a human. That's perfect, since he's the only one of his kind: a wandering warrior, without control of his destination, tossed between universes by gods who've failed to tell him why. James is the lone Judge on a new world in need of someone to balance the scales. He isn't afraid to do so with extreme prejudice. As the Chief Justice, he has to right the wrongs the innocent can't fix themselves.

As James quickly discovers, the roots of corruption run deep. Guilds choose to protect themselves rather than the people. Monsters roam the wilderness unchecked. Judgment is usually a decision between right and wrong, but nothing is ever that simple. This time, being the strongest human won't be enough to punish the guilty. James might have to recruit some new blood, even if he prefers to work alone.

On his twentieth world, he is going to win, no matter the cost. James will have to find a way to break past the limits of the system if he's going to have a chance at making a difference.

https://mybook.to/WanderingWarrior

KNIGHTS OF ETERNITY: CALAMITY

By Rachel Ni Chuirc

When Zara awoke to find Valerius, leader of the legendary Gilded Knights, towering over her, she thought she'd gone mad.

She was the Fury, mistress of claw and flame—armies trembled at her name! Now she lay chained and broken, a prisoner in her own home. But that wasn't why she thought herself mad.

Only yesterday, she remembered a different life. She remembered her nephew in the local arcade, struggling to beat the villainous Zara the Fury in Knights of Eternity. She remembered her uncle and his big booming laugh.

...and she remembered the gun that changed everything.

https://mybook.to/KoE_Calamity

WELCOME TO THE DARK AGES

Morgan and Merlins excellent Adventures
Book One
By
Malory

When Merlin needs a hero to save the world, he gets... well, me.

Fan-bloody-tastic.

I was supposed to be dead. Instead, I wake up face-down in Dark Age mud, possessing some poor bastard's body, while the ghost of history's most famous wizard rambles on about being murdered, cosmic energy and the end of all reality.

Just one tiny problem: I know about as much about cultivation as a pig knows about particle physics.

Now I'm fumbling with mystical energy that feels like juggling nitroglycerin, trying not to get shanked by everyone and their grandmother, and dealing with Merlin's constant "helpful" commentary.

Something dark is rising in Arthurian Britain.

Something that made even Merlin scared. They say fate has a sense of humour. Turns out it's the kind that laughs while setting your hair on fire.

Welcome to the Dark Ages, where cultivation meets chaos, and the only thing sharper than a sword is my questionable wit.

Read Now!

THEFT OF DECKS

By Lars Machmüller

When the deck is stacked against you? Change the game!

In the frontier town of Isarn, Chase will never be more than the lowly Dark-born thief he is. Banned from training, banned from acquiring better cards, if the Lightborn had their way, he'd be banned from life itself.

He's not alone though, and the one thing he and his friends have is determination. Losing a hand to a brutal punishment only fueled his obsession to get access to his own amazing, reality-bending cards.

That is the path to power and a future for them all. Nobody cares where you came from when you're rich enough. For now, though, they're facing both established powers, churches and age-old prejudices. It's time to get to work, and if the Lightborn won't share and play nice?

Sometimes the only way to get dealt a better hand is to steal the whole damn deck!

Buy on Amazon

FACEBOOK AND SOCIAL MEDIA

If you want to reach out to talk about Quest Academy or just get to know me a little bit, you can find me on my swanky new author page on Facebook. There's a very high chance that you'll be one of the very first people to like it that wasn't involved in getting me published:

www.facebook.com/BrianJNordon

Alternatively, we've a new Facebook group to spread the word about cool LitRPG books, called LitRPG Legion. It's a fun space to share old and new books, and to discover great titles you might have missed along the way.

Only rules for joining are to spread the word about great new books, and not being a dick! As a bonus, if you join… you'll have access to dozens of author interviews conducted by me or Jez.

www.facebook.com/groups/litrpglegion

If you'd prefer to catch me over on Discord, here's a link:

https://discord.gg/GAN5RgNJGn

I created the Discord for my first ever series that I started over on Royal Road, called Wildcards: The Dread Captain. It's a fun story that I absolutely loved writing and will get back to after Quest Academy is established. I'm not the fastest at replying, but I do always reply!

PATREON!

Okay then, now for those of you that don't know about Patreon, its essentially a way to support your favorite authors, you can sign up for a day or a month or a year, and you get various benefits for it, ranging from my heartfelt thanks, to advance access to the books, to me sending them books, naming characters and more.

My Patreon was very focused on my time writing Wildcards, and I'll be incorporating new tiers in the future for advanced chapters of Quest Academy. I'm talking with Legion Publishers to find out what we could offer fans outside of more chapters, so it might be worth keeping an eye on. If not now, maybe in the future when there's more on offer!

All support is appreciated, but not compulsory. Honestly, a review or just recommending my story to others is more than I have any right to ask.

www.patreon.com/BrianJNordon

<u>RECOMMENDATIONS</u>

I'm not sure if they'll be your thing, but if you like reading my stories, then you might be interested in these books too. This is only from my own personal enjoyment though, so take my words with a pinch of salt.

Death, Loot & Vampires by Benjamin Kerei

Heretical Fishing by Haylock Jobson

Restarting The Apocalypse by Michael Chatfield

Portal to Nova Roma by J.R. Mathews

The Bad Guys by Eric Ugland

Shattered Dreams by Shawn Wilson

Iron Prince by Luke Chmilenko & Bryce O'Connor

Meet Your Maker by Seth McDuffee & Johnathan McClain

Wayspring Wanderer by Joedan Worley

I'm Not The Hero by Tommy Kerper / SourpatchHero

Player Manager by Ted Steel (Yes, it's Football/Soccer, which I hate, but trust me on this one)

LITRPG!

To learn more about LitRPG, talk to other authors including myself, and to just have an awesome time, please join the LitRPG Group

www.facebook.com/groups/LitRPGGroup

FACEBOOK

There's also a few really active Facebook groups I'd recommend you join, as you'll get to hear about great new books, new releases and interact with all your (new) favorite authors! (I may also be there, skulking at the back and enjoying the memes…)

www.facebook.com/groups/LitRPGsociety/

www.facebook.com/groups/LitRPG.books/

www.facebook.com/groups/LitRPGforum/

www.facebook.com/groups/gamelitsociety/

www.facebook.com/groups/litrpglegion